THE
GREAT RIFT

ALSO BY EDWARD W. ROBERTSON

THE CYCLE OF ARAWN

The White Tree
The Great Rift
The Black Star

THE CYCLE OF GALAND

The Red Sea
The Silver Thief

THE BREAKERS SERIES

Breakers
Melt Down
Knifepoint
Reapers
Cut Off
Captives
Relapse
Blackout

OTHER FICTION

The Cutting Room
Titans

THE
GREAT RIFT

THE CYCLE OF ARAWN, BOOK 2

EDWARD W. ROBERTSON

Copyright © 2012 Edward W. Robertson

All rights reserved.

Cover art by Miguel Coimbra

ISBN: 1494494256
ISBN-13: 978-1494494254

To Caitlin, for letting me get lost in other worlds.

Mallon, Gask, and other lands.

EDWARD W. ROBERTSON

1

They would know his treason in two hundred feet.

The wagon jolted over a snow-covered hole, shaking the swords in its belly. Down the path through the pines, six soldiers waited, laughter drifting on the icy air. Dante's blood ran as cold as the snows. The soldiers stood across the road astride their horses, red shirts glaring from their chests, straight swords hanging from their hips. Their mounts were lean and travel-worn and snorted gouts of steam that mingled with the mist. The wagon rattled again. One of the men pointed down the path. Dante swore. It was too late to turn back.

Blays leaned in to the driver. "Stop the cart."

"What are you doing?" Dante said.

"Stopping the cart."

"Should I stop the cart?" the driver said.

"Only if you don't want to get punched," Blays said.

The cart's wheels skidded in the snow-mucked dirt. Dante pitched forward, grabbing his wooden seat before he spilled into the road. Down the way, the riders stared.

"Well, that ought to throw them off our trail." Dante twisted in his seat to gaze at the muddy wagon. "What do we tell them? That we're taking these arms to Narashtovik?"

Blays rubbed his mouth. "Those swords are seven feet long. They weigh twelve pounds. What are we going to tell them, they're bound for the race of giants it *isn't* treasonous to arm?"

"Well, then think of something."

"I'm trying."

"Because treason, as it turns out, isn't one of those look-the-other-way crimes. Except for people who attend the execution of the traitors, because you really don't want blood splashing into your eyes or—"

"I know!" Blays said. The redshirted soldiers kneed their horses, starting down the rutted road. Blays lowered his voice to a hiss. "I've got a solution: a whole lot of murder."

Dante shook his head hard. "If a troop of the king's soldiers turns up dead in norren lands, do you think that makes the norren *less* likely to be invaded and massacred by the king?"

The soldiers' hooves clopped closer. "Well, think fast."

Dante's mind spun in circles. Forty feet away, the soldiers slowed their mounts to a walk. Their gazes lingered on Blays' swords. Dante gritted his teeth. "I can try to disguise them."

"The swords?" Blays whispered. "What are you going to do, put wigs on them?"

The riders were too close to respond. Dante extended his mind to the nether, the shadowy substance that lurked within all things. Few could even see the nether. Those who commanded its power could change the shape of the world, mending the wounded or killing the firm. As a last resort, Dante would turn it on the king's soldiers pulling to a stop in front of the halted wagon. If they hid the bodies well enough—and the cold pine forest was bleak enough to conceal an entire city of the dead—there was the chance, however fleeting, the soldiers' deaths would be blamed on the snows or the bears instead of the norren Dante was trying to free from the king's yoke.

For now, though, he had a better idea.

The lead rider had a permanent squint; winter lingered on its deathbed, but his face was tanned and chapped. It was the face of a man who'd spent most of his forty-odd years in the wilds confronting strange men. He jerked his bristly chin at the wagon. "What are you carrying down the king's roads?"

"It's a surprise," Blays said.

"Surprises are meant to be opened." The man gestured two of his men around the back of the wagon. "Rip it apart."

"There's no need for that." Dante hopped down from his seat. Two of the mounted men drew swords with the whisper of steel on leather. Dante held up his hands. "I'll open it for you. It's just a little wheat. Nothing wrong with a little wheat, is there?"

"That depends on what's under the wheat. More wheat? Or something shiny and silver?"

"Who would bake bread out of silver?" Blays leapt down from the wagon to join the others at the back. "You'd break a new chamber pot every morning."

The man didn't look his way. "Some like to hide their coin beneath their grain. To muffle the annoying clink, no doubt. Not to avoid King Moddegan's taxes."

"No doubt," Dante muttered. He focused his mind and sent the nether winging to the wagon, coating its contents in a thin layer of illusion. A soldier pulled aside the oiled canvas, revealing long boxes stacked high. He lifted one of the lids with a squeak of wood. Instead of revealing the long killing steel of swords, the soldier stared at a box piled high with dusty brown wheat.

Dante held his breath. The soldier gazed blankly at the grain. He nodded. Dante willed him to turn away, to drop back the canvas and go on his way.

Instead, he plunged his hand into the fake grain.

Steel clanked. The man screamed and yanked back his hand. Blood flowed from a gash across three of his fingers. In a panic, Dante let the nethereal illusion fall away. The shucked wheat disappeared, replaced by the reality of the seven-foot swords filling the box.

The commander's mouth fell open. "Weeping wounds, what is happening here? Where did the wheat go? What are you doing with a cartload of norren swords?"

Dante flung up his hands. "Well, you see—"

From beside the road, a voice rumbled like falling stones. "We're taking them away from norren clans who would put them to no possible good use."

Dante whirled. A lean and shaggy bear stepped from the pines, seven feet tall and dressed in travel-worn deerskin. He jerked back from the monster, drawing the nether to him in a dark rush. The bear smiled. Dante cursed silently. The man was a norren, of course: impossibly tall, with thick shoulders and an even thicker beard that rose to just below his eyes. Coin-sized ears poked from his thicket of hair. No matter how many days Dante spent among them, their sheer inhuman size could still catch him off guard.

"I am sorry I was gone for so long, my lords," the strange norren said. "Is everything all right?"

"Where have you been?" Dante improvised.

"I thought I heard the call of the Clan of the Whipping Reed," the norren said. "They hunt these woods. I didn't want them to hunt us as well."

The commander squinted up at the norren. His hand moved to his sword. "Who are you?"

"My name is Mourn," the norren said. "But I doubt that is what you mean. *What* I am is the slave of these fine men. I am sorry if I startled you."

"Got your papers?"

"I'm sorry, we left our office in our other wagon," Blays said. "He's registered in Yallen. That's where we're taking these swords."

The commander stared at the blades gleaming in the winter sun. He shook his head hard enough to dislodge his own squint. "You said you were hauling wheat. I saw wheat."

"I am a hedge wizard," Dante lied. "You see?" He snapped his fingers; the wheat materialized atop the swords. Another snap, and it disappeared. One of the soldiers swore. "The primitives in the clans look at me as a god. Much easier to convince them to turn over their arms when you've got divine right on your side."

"And you think you can trick us as easily as the savages? What are you trying to hide?"

"In the Norren Territories, steel is worth more than gold." Mourn leaned forward as if disclosing a secret. "The king's own soldiers have been known to sell swords back to the same clans they confiscated them from. It's a sad thing. Except for the soldiers, I suppose, who now have the money to finally make themselves happy."

"I've heard of that," one of the redshirted soldiers nodded. "There's no law out here except what we enforce."

"That's right," said the commander. "So who authorized this?"

"Lord Wallimore of Yallen," Dante lied smoothly. He patted his pockets. "I have his writ right here." Paper crinkled from his doublet. He removed the sheet. It was a purchase order for raw iron from a border-town, but before he unfolded it, he overwrite it with a flick of nether. The illusory note was brief, to the point, and concluded with the signature of the nonexistent Lord Wallimore.

The weathered commander read the note, nodded, and passed it back to Dante. He jerked his head at the soldier's bleeding hand. "Your deceit hurt one of my men."

"I'm sorry about that. Keeping our country safe carries constant risk." Dante frowned and drew on the nether again. This time, he sent it flocking to the wounded man's hand. The wave of shadows washed away the gash like a trench dug below the tideline. "Better?"

The man yanked back his hand, shaking it. "Tickles!"

Dante turned back to the commander. "Does this square us?"

He squinted between Dante, Mourn, and the wagon. "You're doing the king's will. Now get these arms out of here before a clan cuts your throat and carves your bones into spears."

"You got it," Blays said. He leapt back into his seat behind the driver, who'd watched the exchange without a word.

Dante gestured to the norren. "Come along, Mourn."

As Dante slung himself in beside Blays, Mourn climbed up on the running boards, tilting the carriage under his weight. The driver flicked his reins. The horses leaned forward, yanking the carriage behind them. Dante unclasped his cloak and shucked it off his shoulders. Despite the freezing air, his skin was as hot as a stovetop.

He didn't look back at the disappearing soldiers. "What just happened?"

"Our quick-thinking slave just saved the day," Blays said. "Hey, that reminds me. When did we get a slave?"

"I'll ask him the moment I stop shitting my pants. Do you have any idea how close that was?"

"They couldn't *prove* we're bringing this stuff to the norren."

Dante snorted. "Which wouldn't have stopped them from arresting us for treason and torturing us until we revealed Narashtovik's spent the last five years funding armed norren rebellion."

"Maybe not." Blays patted his swords. "But these would have stopped them from living, which would have put a bit of a damper on any arresting and torturing."

"And left us with a pile of corpses to deal with instead."

The wagon bounced between the pines. Dante glanced over his shoulder. Given that norren men's beards grew like spring grass, it was tough to gauge their age, but Mourn looked no younger than himself—early twenties, perhaps. Mourn caught him staring and nodded back.

They spoke little over the next couple miles. Sunlight trickled through the pine needles, pale and bitter. Soon enough, the light dried up like morning rain.

"What do you think?" Blays pointed into the twilit woods. A couple hundred yards off the road, a log shack stood beneath the trees. "Won't do any better than that tonight."

Dante nodded and directed the driver to turn off the road. The shack's roof was half collapsed, but it was empty of humans and animals. Half-melted snow lay across half the floor. Dante helped towel off the horses, gazing steadily at Mourn.

"What happened back there?"

Mourn looked up and shrugged. "You were stopped by kingsmen. They questioned you about smuggling, then let you go on your way."

"Yeah, I remember that. Along with when a total stranger leapt out of the woods and lied to save our asses."

"I didn't leap."

"All right. You strode from the woods, without warning, to assist three total strangers."

"You're not strangers."

Dante threw up his hands. "I've never seen you before in my life!"

"I've seen *you*," Mourn said. "You've been down here for months. Bringing us things. Things that could get you in trouble. I know what you're trying to do for my people."

"Wrong," Blays said. "We've been down here for years."

Mourn stiffened, face going slack with horror. "You're right. I've only *seen* you here for months. I'm so sorry."

"I was just fooling with you," Blays frowned. "Don't take it so seriously."

The young norren drew back his head in reproach. "Speech is a dangerously imprecise form of communication even when we try to be as exact as we can be. If we're sloppy on purpose, who knows what disasters might come of it? Nobody, that's who. Nobody mortal. Unless there is a soothsayer somewhere I don't know about."

"Well, talking's the best system I've come up with so far," Blays said.

"If you've watched us that long, you must live around here," Dante said.

Mourn nodded. "Sometimes. My clan ranges more widely than most. That I know of. You would think it's nice, but you can only see so many hills before they all become the same hillish blur."

"Which clan is that?"

"I belong to the Clan of the Nine Pines."

"Oh no," Blays said.

Mourn cocked his head. "Do you know of us unfavorably? You must. Otherwise, a groan must mean something different to you than it does to me."

"It's not your clan that's the problem. It's what you've got."

"We don't know they have it," Dante said. "We don't even know if it's real."

"You're right, I'm being sloppy," Blays said. "It's not about what the Nine Pines may or may not have. It's about Dante's monomaniacal desire to have it for himself."

"If the Quivering Bow is real, we could use it to threaten the king into leaving the norren alone forever and destroy the whole capital if he doesn't. What's so monomaniacal about that?"

"Ah," Mourn said. "The Quivering Bow."

"Well?" Dante said.

"Well what?"

"What else could I mean? Do you have it or not?"

"I'm not going to just assume that's what you meant," Mourn said peevishly. "Anyway, if we have the Quivering Bow, I am not aware of it."

Dante's face fell. "Oh."

"But there is much about my clan that I am not aware of, because I am young, and they don't tell me things because young people can't be trusted with wisdom. Which makes no sense to me.

How can young, foolish people become not-young, not-foolish people if you never expose them to wisdom?"

"By hitting them?" Blays said. He smacked his horse's freshly-toweled flank. The smell of animal sweat competed with the frosted pines. "Anyway, in a few minutes it'll be too dark to tell what's kindling and what's a snake. I don't know how much you guys know about building fires, but those aren't ideal working conditions."

He wandered off to gather small branches for the night's fire. Small birds settled into the darkening trees, silhouettes on skeletal branches. Dante rummaged through their catch-all pack for the spade, but the ground was half-frozen. No matter how hard he leaned into the undersized shovel, he could only scrape away a handful of dirt at a time.

"You are trying to dig a pit?" Mourn asked after a futile minute.

"I'm trying to dig a hill so we can build a fort on it and be safe and never leave." Dante scowled up at him. Although it was cold enough to see his own breath, he was sweating under his doublet. He flung down the spade. "Forget it. It'll be morning before I'm finished with this."

"Perhaps I can help." Mourn knelt and picked up the small shovel. His thick shoulders bunched as he drove it into the ground, dislodging a healthy load of black earth. He glanced up. "How large would you like your pit?"

"Fire-sized," Dante muttered.

He dug steadily and contentedly, dislodging a half-frozen mix of dirt, leaves, old needles, and dormant grass roots. The smell was earthy and gently rotten. Once, the iron wedge of the spade bent on a rock; Mourn gripped the point and the handle in his heavy hands, bore down, and straightened the bend right out.

"You've already saved our lives," Dante said, "or at least from a load of trouble. So I'm loath to ask you another favor."

Mourn flung another scoop of dirt. "But you would like me to ask my chieftain if we possess the Quivering Bow."

"Would you?"

"Would I? That is a good question. The asking costs me nothing in a physical sense. On the other hand, if we don't have it because it is imaginary, I could be mocked by my entire clan." He sat back and pierced Dante with his gaze. "What would you do with the bow?"

Dante froze. Could he really just say it out loud? To a total stranger? On the one hand, Mourn was a norren himself. He would make for a very unlikely traitor or spy. On the other hand — what if he was?

The truth would be a risk, then. But if there was any chance they had the Quivering Bow, it was a risk worth taking.

"We'll use it to free the norren from slavery," he said. "To gain your independence. And that of my homeland of Narashtovik as well."

Mourn stared at him beneath the blackening pines. "I will ask them."

"Ask who what?" Blays said, returning with an armload of branches, twigs, and yellow grass.

"What took you so damn long with the firewood," Dante said.

"Well, it's not like this stuff just falls off of trees."

Blays knelt over the firepit and arranged the kindling. He groaned as Dante and Mourn struck out the details of when the two humans would meet the Clan of the Nine Pines. Owls hooted through the barrens. Night stole over the woods, as gentle and cold as ancient ghosts.

"You two are a couple of chowderbuckets," Blays said as they layered their blankets inside the half-ruined shack. "There's no such thing as a bow that can shoot down walls."

"You should be in favor of this," Dante said. "If the Quivering Bow *is* real, and we get ahold of it, it'll save us years of work. No more camping out in gods-forsaken woods delivering swords to some clan that might turn them on their clan-enemy as soon as we turn our backs. Not when we can say, 'Hey, King Moddegan. Release the norren—and us too, while you're at it—or we'll bury you under a thousand tons of your own palace.'"

"Huh," Blays said into the darkness. "Any chance we can do this meeting tomorrow, Mourn?"

There wasn't. Mourn claimed the Clan of the Nine Pines was too far away. Instead, the three of them would reconvene in three days at the old norren ruins on Kerrin Hill. In the morning, he said his farewells. Dante and Blays hopped on the wagon and made their delivery.

Three days later, the two of them climbed Kerrin Hill under cover of night. Mist curled up the hillside. A face loomed downhill, obscured by gray vapor and black branches. In fact, between the distance and the gloom, Dante couldn't be certain there was a face at all—that pale, unflinching shape could be a patch of trunk rubbed of its bark, the wilting white flower of a five-foot shrub. He glanced at Blays. The blond man was tracing an obscene drawing on the mist-slick surface of a fallen stone. When he looked back, the face was gone.

"I think someone's following us."

Blays added another curve to his outline. "No one is following us."

"What I'm proposing is the radical idea that they are."

"For one thing, you can't really be *followed* when you're just standing around. For another, we're six miles from nowhere in a graveyard that hasn't been used since we started putting points on the ends of our sticks."

"It's not a graveyard."

Blays smacked the table-sized stone with his palm. Dozens like it littered the hilltop, a handful of others still standing upright, weathered and patchy with lichen. "Then what do you call this?"

"A rejected bed." Dante peered into the mist. The weather had warmed in the last three days, shrinking the snows and feeding the fog. Streamers wafted between the pine needles, carrying the mud-and-clams scent of the river with them. "It was a holy place, once."

"Whatever it is, I'm cold as hell. Does Cally even know about this little mission of yours?"

"More or less."

"Oh really? I'm guessing that 'less' is going to be upset to learn it's being used in place of 'not at all.'"

Dante put on his haughtiest voice. "The purview of my authority is as far-ranging as its cruelty and you would be wise not to disrespect it."

Blays smeared his forearm across the sketch he'd drawn in the dew. "Wasn't Mourn supposed to be here an hour ago?"

"Yeah."

The shape reappeared among the pines, oval and unmoving. Too pale and small to be Mourn. Dante leaned forward on the stone he'd seated himself on. Blays shoved his shoulder, spilling him into the sodden grass.

"If you're that concerned with being watched, let's go ask that guy what he's doing here."

"You can't just *ask* him."

"Of course I can." Blays stalked downhill. "If I don't like his answer, I can punch him, too!"

Dante hustled after him, boots skidding in the grass. Instinctively, he reached for the nether, drawing the dark power from the shadows of rocks, the undersides of leaves, the night air itself. It coiled around his fist, so perfectly black most people couldn't see it at all. Blays swished through the carpet of brown needles, one sword swinging from his hip, the other bouncing from his back. Dante threaded through the gnarled trunks. By the time they reached the base of the hill, the stones at its crown were blurs in the mist.

"Well?" Blays said.

"If the watcher *was* here, you probably spooked him."

"Sounds like he'd deserve it, creeping around in the fog like that."

Dante turned in a slow circle, scanning the trees for movement, flashes of color, but saw nothing but the pressing gray air. A stick snapped among the trees. Blays' smile vanished. Dante drew the nether closer. Just ahead, a hulking figure plodded through the fog, seven feet tall, shoulders so solid he looked as if he could walk straight through the trees without slowing down.

"Hello, Mourn." Dante said. "Bit late, aren't you?"

"Aren't we all, sooner or later," the norren said. He gazed down at his sodden pants-cuffs with exasperation too deep for a sigh. His silver-and-bone earrings glinted in the darkness. "Can we do this down here? Or do we have to trek up to that fallen-down garbage up there?"

"Your people built them."

"So they claim."

"Here's fine," Blays said.

"Good." Mourn ran a thick hand over the equally thick beard

that grew from every inch of his face besides a gap around his eyes and a small patch directly below his cavernous nose. "So. About the bow."

"Yes?" Dante said.

"The clan would like to know how they can be sure they can trust you."

Dante scowled. "We've been in and out of these hills for two years now."

"Spend two thousand more and we'll be on equal footing."

"Our word?" Blays said.

"Is good for a laugh." Mourn's bovine eyes considered Blays. "Nothing personal."

"Who could take offense to that?"

Dante glared into the fog. Over a year ago, he stopped thinking of his duty in the Territories as a political favor to be discarded at the first sign of trouble; instead, he now regarded it as something he wanted to do, a cause he'd fight for even if Cally weren't forcing him to be here. He liked the norren. He believed in them. The problem was such feelings were rarely mutual. The norren, in large part, distrusted anything that came from beyond the Territories. Hell, most of the time they distrusted anything that came from the wrong part *within* the Territories, meaning anything beyond their village or their clan's roving-range. No matter how much time Dante spent here, he kept having to prove himself to each new norren and clan he met. Sometimes he built up a relationship with a group, returned six months later, and found himself treated as a stranger again, the trust he'd established eroded like a beach during the storm season. The whole experience was so frustrating there were times he wanted to smash a block down on the norren's oversized heads.

By norren standards, Mourn had been extremely trusting to date. Against his better judgment, Dante had cultivated hope his whole clan would be the same. Open. Helpful. Faced with the truth, his hopes came crashing down.

"I don't even know what the Clan of Nine Pines *is*, exactly," Dante said. "How am I supposed to know what they consider worthy of trust?"

"Oh." Mourn's disappointment was as thick as the fog. "Well,

I'm off, then."

Blays glanced between them. "That's it?"

"It's a long walk home."

Dante stood stunned, watching the norren slog into the trees. At times he believed it was all a game the norren played, these endless spirals of approval-winning and worth-proving, and that when Mourn returned home to tell this story, he'd be met with bearish laughter and grinning shakes of the head: Gullible outlanders! Would probably give their own balls a whack if you told them a man's testicular fortitude was considered an equal sign of the fortitude of their loyalty.

He shook his head. This business with Mourn and the clan was just the latest fence they'd have to hop. Under Cally's direction, he and Blays had burned two years arranging and bodyguarding shipments to and from the Norren Territories to the south—silver, swords, spears, great wains of grain. He met with village leaders, brokered peace and pacts with the human settlements on the fringes, delivered memorized messages too sensitive to be trusted to a page. Days and weeks and months spent preparing the Territories for something they would never have dreamed possible: independence from the empire of Gask.

Throughout his travels, he began to hear rumors of the Clan of the Nine Pines, who, along with the Dreaming Bear and Three-Part Falls, were widely considered one of the fiercest clans in all norrendom. But—again, according to rumor—they had something else on top of that: the Quivering Bow. When Dante asked what *that* was, the norren had smirked knowingly. Why, it was just a legendary weapon whose arrows sent enemy walls shivering down like the banks of a flash-flooding river.

From that point on, Dante learned all he could about the Nine Pines. Which wasn't much. Like most of the other clans, they were nomads. They traveled on foot, were rarely seen, and almost never spent time among the civilized city-dwelling norren. In the past, the Nine Pines' paintings sold for sums that could have established estates. In present times, they were said to forge swords that never lost their edge.

That in itself was interesting. But what had really snared the bunny was the bow. A bow that maybe—probably—didn't exist.

When he first voiced his interest to Blays, Blays had dismissed the whole thing with a broad swipe of logic: If the bow were real, why wasn't the Clan of the Nine Pines picking their teeth with the king's bones right now? To Dante, that didn't prove anything. You couldn't free a people or conquer an empire with a single weapon, no matter how powerful that weapon may be. You needed soldiers. Lots and lots of soldiers. Most clans only had forty or fifty of those. And the fact the clans weren't exactly fond of banding together was perhaps the main reason so many of their people were enslaved across Gask.

Still, in the months since learning about the bow, his hope had cooled. Until he met Mourn, the first member of the Nine Pines he'd seen with his own eyes. Because what if the bow were real?

"It's all bullshit anyway." Blays' virtual mindreading had grown increasingly common—and somewhat unsettling—the more time the two spent with each other. "If it comes to war, our best weapon's going to be stabbing. Lots of stabbing."

"That's your answer to everything."

"That's because it's such a good one. Now can we get out of here already?"

Dante stirred fallen needles with the toe of his boot. "I'm sick of these games. If they'd drop all the ritual and let us do what we're here for, we'd already be hoisting their flags over the ramparts of Setteven."

Blays gave him the sort of frown reserved for the unanticipated expulsion of something that was just in your body. "Then cut through the games, dummy. Follow Mourn back to them."

"The clan would not care for that at all." He scanned the forest floor for anything white. "Hope you've got your chasing shoes on. Now help me find something dead."

"I'm beginning to hate those words."

"If it makes you feel better, it can be alive."

"Until you get your hands on it."

"If the rabbit's family comes seeking satisfaction, I promise to stand as your second." Dante stooped and shuffled through the damp mulch. Finding a spare body, he had long ago learned, was much trickier than common sense tells you. In a world of living things, you would imagine the ground would groan with the fallen dead, that beneath the forest's skin of leaves and needles would lurk a second layer of bones and fur. But animals occupied a small corner of any given space. They were so rare, in fact, that when they dropped dead, their remains tended to get snapped up by any other creatures who shared the area. A nice enough truth when the goal is walking through the woods without plunging ankle-deep into a former muskrat. Not so nice when the goal is to put that muskrat to one last use.

Blays crunched through leaves uphill. Dante smelled fresh mold and wet dirt. Mourn was getting further away by the moment. Dante straightened, relaxing his gaze until his vision blurred. It was perhaps that very rarity of remains that made them stand out so sharply if only you knew how to look. Possibly, it was that corpses still held on to some trace of the nether, the grist of Arawn's flawed mill, that quickens all mortal life. Whatever the reason, within moments a cold, silver light glimmered at the base of a nearby pine, flickering like moonlight on a pool. Dante knelt to brush away the leaves. A faded whiff of decay rose from a scatter of small bones. Hair and sinew clung to ribs and joints. Dante smiled.

Black wisps gathered in his fingers. Needing no more than a dab of blood, he picked a shallow scab on the back of his hand, waited for the small red bubble to rise, then touched his blood to the bones. Like rain on a window, shadowy nether slid from his hands to the body. Claws twitched. As if drawn by a string, a loose femur drew to the hip. The creature stood, swaying. It might have been a rat, once. A squirrel. Now, it was a silent automaton, and if Dante closed his eyes, he could see through its perspective instead. He nodded in the direction Mourn had gone minutes earlier. The creature turned and dashed away in a spray of leaves.

Dante called Blays from down the hill. "We'll stay a mile behind him. He'll never know we're here."

"Next time, I demand a plan with less walking. Like sitting around being fed roast pork."

"I'm not sure how that forwards the cause of norren independence."

Blays shrugged. "They can figure that out for themselves."

The creature raced along the forest floor, skidding through

leaves, leaping over roots and dips, unhampered by the need to breathe or rest or slow for treacherous footing. Within minutes, it—and by extension Dante—could hear the norren threading through the brush with surprising grace. He and Blays began their pursuit.

Mist drifted between the hard-barked pines, thinning the further they got from the river. After a couple miles of woods, the forest dissipated in favor of grassy hills, the draws and folds furred by spicy-smelling pines. The light of a half-moon drenched the trailless earth. Dante's breath rolled from his mouth in thin clouds. His nose and ears numbed while sweat dampened his underclothes, which were already a good week in need of a wash.

Mourn didn't take his first break until dawn took its first pink glance at the east. Blays sat, blear-eyed, scowling at the block of bread Dante had taken along in case they didn't wind up returning straight to town after the meet.

"This stuff's hard as a brick," he said, spraying crumbs. "Tastes like one, too."

"Yet you're eating it. Remind me not to invite you to my house."

"What's that hairy jerk doing now?"

Dante closed his eyes. More than a mile away, the creature watched from beneath a bush while Mourn pried the bark from a fallen log and ate the pale grubs beneath. "Enjoying a pan of bacon. I think I can smell it—crisp meat, smoking fat."

"Gods damn it."

Mourn rose, then crouched beside a body of water that was more puddle than pond. "The wine looks good, too."

"At least tell me he looks sleepy." Blays stretched out his leg, massaging his calf with his thumbs. "I've had a few hours to think here. Which, for one thing, is a few hours we're not spending getting swords into the hands of villagers. For another, what's the point of chasing after the world's greatest bow when the whole idea is to *avoid* war?"

"Every day we're down here is a gamble. If the wrong person gets wind that we're arming the norren and brings that to the palace in Setteven, how long before the entire Gaskan Empire is marching on the Norren Territories? Three seconds?" Dante crunched into a bit of bread, chewing thickly. "Now what if we have a bow that can drop their towers as fast as you drop your trousers? Won't that give them second thoughts?"

"And you really think this thing exists?"

"A bow that can win a war by itself? What are you, an idiot?"

Blays threw up his hands. "If this is a joke, then so is the fist I'm about to put through your teeth."

Dante pulled his mind from the creature's, where Mourn was chopping long, straight branches and leaning them against the low crotch of a tree. "I just think it's worth sacrificing a couple days to confirm it doesn't exist. At least we'll have finally seen the Clan of the Nine Pines for ourselves."

"I heard they once killed an entire Setteven troop over the suggestion they start paying taxes."

"Donn told me they give their children knives as soon as they can stand. Accidentally cutting themselves is part of the process of learning to use one."

"Well, we've got to get those guys on board. King Moddegan's army doesn't stand a chance against the knife-babies." Blays blew into his hands. "I'll give it two more days. Past that, and I will begin shrieking until you admit your mistake."

Two days later—two long, cold, relentless days of aching feet, stiff fingers, and dwindling bread that didn't taste good even when his belly was empty—and Dante was ready to turn back himself. Mourn's course kept his resolve from dissolving completely: the norren was headed straight into nowhere. An eastern course into grassy hills and patchy woods too removed from the roads to see any signs of people besides the occasional hermit or roving tribe. Desolate and windy. A person could spend weeks combing these lands without finding a trace of the people he was after.

That afternoon, Mourn and his undead pursuit entered a wall of trees whose small green buds were just beginning to displace the stubborn, brittle leaves still hanging from the branches. Deep shadows pooled the ground. Mourn walked noiselessly, hardly stirring the crackly blanket of leaves. After spending a good portion of the last few years learning to do the same, Dante envied the large man's effortless skill.

Yet with the sun a hand's-breadth from the hills, its light fading from the soil like a summer rain, Mourn suddenly began scuffling his feet, tramping through great beds of leaves as if shouting his name to the world. Ahead, a quiet blue lake winked between the trees. Above its shallow, grainy banks, Mourn was greeted by a trio of tall, stone-faced norren.

"Found them," Dante murmured.

"How many?"

"Um." He stopped, ordering the distant skeleton to take a quick jaunt. Men and women sat around fires, hauled wood, reeled in nets from the shore. "Fifty. Maybe more."

"I have a thought," Blays said. "If these people are as brutal as they all say, is it wise for two strangers to burst in on their secret forest lair?"

"Good question," rumbled a voice to the left.

Adrenaline bloomed from Dante's solar plexus. He dropped into a low stance, drawing his sword with his right and the nether with his left. Blays whipped out his blades with a leathery hiss. Twenty feet away, a man stepped from the trees, young enough that his beard only climbed halfway up his cheeks, but still a foot too tall to be mistaken for a human. A cleaver-like blade hung from his hand, the weapon as oversized as his bearish body.

"We're not enemies," Dante said.

"The clan will be here to judge that in a minute."

Dante flicked his eyes closed. At the camp, men and women grabbed up swords and bows and raced into the woods, backtracking Mourn's route. He ordered the creature to follow them back. He reopened his eyes on the lone norren. "How did you alert them?"

"Josun Joh watches out for us all."

"Tell them to bring steak," Blays said. "I'm starving."

He put away his swords, a motion so smooth it was like watching a feat of actual magic. Dante, unable to draw his blade without glancing at the handle first, left his out. He didn't say another word until Mourn arrived in the dusk with a dozen other norren, each dressed in the same supple deer-leather and silver ear piercings. Surprise, confusion, and anger battled for control of Mourn's heavy eyebrows.

"Hi, Mourn," Dante said. "We followed you."

"I would have seen you from a mile away."

"That's why we stayed two miles behind."

The other warriors regarded Dante with blank eyes, thick swords held before them. Dante had guided the dead watcher into some shrubs behind him. He blinked, glimpsing a silent woman stalking straight for him, a knife gleaming in her hand. Without turning, Dante knocked her to the ground with a club of nether, forceful enough to rattle her plate without cracking it.

"I am Dante Galand, council member of the Sealed Citadel of Narashtovik. We're here for the cause of norren independence."

"I'm a guy in the forest," said a middle-aged norren whose left cheek was nearly beardless for all the scars. "And you are a long way from Narashtovik."

"Consider it a sign of our sincerity," Blays said.

"'Sincerity'? You have strange words for 'trespassing,' strangers."

Slowly as a stalking cat, Dante drew his lowered blade across the back of his left hand. The cold metal bit into his skin, replaced by the warmth of a fresh wound and the hot blood dripping from the edge of his palm. Nether flocked to the fluid in swerving twists of darkness.

"You know why we're here," he said. "With that bow, we could guarantee Setteven wouldn't dare set foot in the territories."

"There is a problem," the scarred man said.

"A problem the severity of which depends greatly on your perspective," said a female norren, no shorter than the males yet significantly less hirsute. Her eyes were as orange as a harvest moon. "From your perspective, it is not so auspicious at all."

The scarred man waved the point of his ponderous sword at knee-level, as if it were too heavy to lift without great cause. "Strangers who come to the Clan of the Nine Pines are required to leave as ash on the wind."

A dozen norren lifted their weapons. Further back among the trees, others nocked arrows, sighting down the shafts.

"Why does everything have to be a fight with you?" Blays said sidelong. He bared his teeth and raised his blades. Dante summoned the nether to him in a great and hungry rush.

For months, he had spent his free hours practicing the creation of lights and illusions—bending the nether into gigantic patterns, letters, and symbols that could be seen and interpreted from miles away. If some of Narashtovik's priests and monks were placed along the border, they could fling up the signs at the first sight of Gaskan troops. Other scouts could then recreate the signs with fires and mirrors, passing the information deeper and deeper into the territories. Enough of these signalmen in the right locations, and in the span of hours, crucial news could be transmitted hundreds of miles to Narashtovik and the territories. Those in the path of the coming storm would be given precious extra days of warning.

This was the theory. In practice, men and women able to bend the energy of ether and nether were somewhat too rare to exile to mountaintops across the countryside. Yet the potential of this notion compelled Dante to look past the impracticalities, and he'd spent many nights, when he wasn't too bone-tired to do anything at all, turning the darkness of the nether inside-out, painting the air with blazing red letters spelling "BLAYS IS DUMB" or with crude animations of the blond man getting repeatedly whacked on the head by a succession of hammers. It was a challenging task, more subtle than skewering an enemy with a sudden spike of raw energy, and at first his concentration had been unable to sustain a moving image with any level of clarity for more than scant seconds. Yet he kept at it. Recently, he'd been able to illustrate whole (if short) stories above his head while grinning norren bards chanted the poems his pictures matched.

He hoped it would be enough.

With the clan's warriors closing in, he dispelled the creature that had dogged Mourn for two straight days. A light bloomed amidst the darkened treetops. The norren tipped back their heads, eyes narrowed. At first the image in the sky was nothing more than simple color, silvery yet soft to the eye, but it quickly took on the shape of a young boy: black-haired, blue-eyed, his features, even at the age of five, sharp enough to skin a pear.

High in the air, the glowing boy toddled through windy fields, overturning rocks at the edges of streams. By candlelight, a middle-aged man wearing a cassock and a kindly if impatient smile ran his finger along lines from a book of fairy stories. The next moment, the boy grew chest-high on the man, reciting unheard words from a book three times thicker. The boy grew taller yet; his dark hair flowed from his head, lengthening until it suddenly queued behind his head. By night, he walked down an overgrown lane—around him, green outlines suggested dense trees—where, in the basement of a ruined temple, he found a black book whose cover bore a stark white tree.

The image shifted again; the young man sat at a library table, reading and rereading the book's opening pages. The scene leapt to a city street, cobbles and a flickering torch. A blond-haired boy stood beside the black-haired one, sword drawn against two armed and faceless men. The dark-haired boy, face twisted in terror, threw up his hand in a theatrical gesture. The group disappeared in a globe of darkness. When the scene returned to light, the two attackers lay dead.

The images came fast—an old man lecturing the young man from inside a tomb, the blond boy with a noose around his neck, then racing away on horseback. The two boys riding north through the outlines of snowy mountains. Arriving at Narashtovik, the dead city, a sketch of ruins and a high citadel at its center. A stark-faced woman lectured from a cathedral podium; at the fringes of the crowd, the boys failed to fire their bows. But then they were inside the citadel where the woman lived and ruled; and then stood on a snowy march with her priests and soldiers, who battled rebels in a dark wood before arriving beneath the boughs of a monstrous white tree, its heavy limbs grown of sleek and solid bone.

Light flashed beneath the tree; chanting faces summoned a black door; the old man reappeared in a scrum of bloody chaos. When it cleared, the woman was dead alongside dozens of others. The image pushed in on the dark-haired boy's face, closer and closer, his blue eyes frozen on something far away, more cold and forlorn than that icy hill.

He meant to do more—their return to the hills of the territories, the grain they'd delivered to the village on Clearlake Hill, their pursuit of the men who'd slaughtered a norren wagon train—but his strength faltered. The illusion vanished. Dante dropped to one knee, panting. The norren looked down, blinking. Several dropped back a step.

"There," Dante said. "We're no longer strangers."

The scarred man glanced at the orange-eyed woman, then back to Dante. "Can you do more than find loopholes and paint pretty pictures?"

"Yes." Dante let out a shaking breath; his head throbbed, overwhelmed. He blinked the blurriness from his blue eyes, swept sweaty black hair from his forehead. "Come at me, and I'll reduce you to the Clan of the Three or Four Pines before you bring me down."

The woman gave the scarred man a small nod. "Why don't we take a walk to camp."

They led the way, distancing themselves to speak in soft, rumbling tones. Blays elbowed him in the ribs.

"I look much better than that."

"At least I omitted the warts," Dante said.

"Did you actually think that would have any chance of working?"

"It seemed smarter than fighting. I don't think a dead body can tell me where its bow is no matter how long I yell at it."

Leaves crunched underfoot, smelling of sap and must. The afterimage of his work lingered in Dante's eyes, silvery flecks that flashed whenever he blinked. A pair of norren followed them on either side, two more at their back. Blays did nothing to disguise his stare. The norren paid them no mind. Woodsmoke sifted through the budding branches.

They were directed to a patch of clear, bare earth not far from where the lake lapped softly on the muddy shore. The scarred man was named Orlen, the orange-eyed woman Vee. They disappeared inside a leather yurt to continue their conversation while Arlo, the young norren who'd detained Dante and Blays in the woods, brought out fried trout and raw greens. Blays swallowed the crackly tail, then dug into the sweet, steaming white meat with bare fingers, plucking out ribs.

"This entire trip is now worth it," he declared. "Even if we die, my ghost will agree."

Dante dug his thumbnail against the scraps of green onion in his teeth. "I think we've reached the point where if they wanted to kill us, they'd kill us."

"Maybe we're being fattened."

"They're nomads, not cannibals."

"Maybe they're branching out."

Around them, the norren ate their own meals, stopping at the end to rip off the heads of cooked fish to suck out the eyes, then flinging the bony remainder into the lake.

"Imagine those fish are you," Dante said.

Orlen and Vee emerged from the yurt and approached the main bonfire. Without a word, ten others joined them. The rest of the clan didn't look up, continuing to pick their teeth with fish bones and mend the nets they'd pulled from the lake. Dante raised his brows at Blays and joined the norren at the welcome heat of the bonfire. Orlen stared at them without blinking, even when the shifting wind drove stinging smoke into his eyes.

"I don't know what you've heard about us," the scarred chieftain said finally. "Likely you have heard several things. When a thing is unknown like our clan, people will rush to fill the void of knowledge with whatever stories they like best."

"We understand you want the same thing we do," Dante said. "An independent norren state free of tribute to or dependence on the nation of Gask."

"Vague enough to be a diplomat," Vee said. "Watch out for his promises."

Dante scowled over the fire. "We know your clan has a long history of resistance against the capital. That's all we *know*. We've heard you possess a weapon called the Quivering Bow. If it does what rumor says it does, I think it could be a critical piece in forestalling a war—or in winning one, if the nobles at Setteven decide they've had enough of what's gone on down here."

Orlen inclined his head. "The bow. Yes."

"Then it's real?"

"It has been a relic of the Clan of the Nine Pines for so long none of us actually knows how we got it."

Vee folded her large hands. "Perhaps it was strung with the guts of patriarch Boh's first son. Or maybe we stole it from lesser people who weren't worthy of it."

Dante's head tingled. "It can do what its name says, then. Shake down walls."

"If you know how to use it," Orlen said. "And if you will use it to help free our people, you may have it, because what greater purpose could it serve? But there is a problem with it."

"Not an insurmountable problem," Vee added. "It is not like the problem of why we are born only to suffer and die."

"Really, a rather minor problem. A dim constellation in the vast starscape of all that is wrong."

Blays pressed the heels of his hands to his forehead. "Have you ever considered this problem only exists because you're too busy talking about it to solve it?"

"You see," Orlen said, "we don't know where it is."

2

"I see," Blays said. "Do you remember where you put it last?"

Orlen narrowed his eyes. Smoke rose from the fire in white walls, screening the stars. "In the hands of a Gaskan lord."

"What!" Dante said.

"It was taken, along with every member of our cousins the Clan of the Green Lake, some weeks ago. When was that, Vee?"

Vee tapped her hairless chin. "Three weeks ago. That was when we found the lake-crabs, remember? On the way back from finding the bodies of our clan-cousins. The empty yurts. The wailing young who'd hidden in the woods."

"Oh yes, the crabs. You do not often find the lake-crabs. I had begun to think they had all died out, or at least moved to another lake."

Dante pressed his fist against his lips, waiting for his anger to subside enough to open his mouth. "If the Quivering Bow has been taken, I pledge our immediate support to getting it back."

Blays cocked his head. "I call foul on that pledge. *My* support is thoroughly undecided."

"If that bow has fallen into enemy hands—"

"Yes, yes, then we'll all spend our next Falmac's Eve watching the bunny races in hell. I'd like to at least know why the clan hasn't already gone after the bow—and their cousins or whoever—before promising we'll do what they won't." He glanced at Orlen. "No offense."

"None taken," the man said. "We were simply waiting on the word of Josun Joh."

"Josun Joh?"

"As in the god," Dante said.

"Oh," Blays said. "*That* Josun Joh."

"He looks out for the people, shows them the way when they're lost. Despite only having one eye."

Orlen nodded. "He lost it in a bet. Over whether he could put out his own eye."

"I thought it was to use it as bait to finally catch Sansanomman, the eternal catfish," Vee frowned.

"That doesn't make any sense."

"You say you *were* waiting?" Dante cut in.

"Today, Josun Joh spoke to me," Orlen said. "Tomorrow, we move."

"Then I'd like to come with you. I can't speak for my friend."

The two norren leaders exchanged an unreadable glance. Orlen considered the fire. "Josun Joh said we'd find an unexpected and powerful ally. If you help us recover our cousin-clan, you may have the Quivering Bow."

Dante extended his hand. "Agreed."

"Good." Orlen waved his thick hand. "Now please leave the fire and go to your tent. Outsiders aren't allowed here."

Dante forced his eyes not to roll. He stood. "I understand."

Mourn appeared beside the fire. "Your yurt's over here. It doesn't smell very good."

He was right. Inside the deer-leather tent, its fluffy cloth padding smelled musty and faintly fishy, conditions made worse by the fact it was notably warmer than the outside air. Dante conjured a soft white light to illuminate the bare interior. Blays slung out his blanket and sat down with a sigh.

"This whole thing could be a wild goose chase, you know. And I don't see how a wild goose is going to do any good if the Territories get invaded."

Dante licked his thumb and smudged away the black fringes of the fresh scab on his hand. "Even if we don't come out of it with a weapon of awful power, rescuing their cousins will only strengthen one of the nastiest fighting units in the entire region. It's the opportunity to put down a group of norren-slavers, too. How is there any downside?"

"First, we don't know the timescale. Second, if Cally needs to reach us, he may as well shout up his own ass for all the good it'll do him."

"Since when did you care about what Cally wants?"

"It's not Cally I'm concerned about." Blays gestured at the wilds beyond the yurt wall. "My worshippers will have a tough time reaching my grave if I'm struck dead in some stupid forest."

"A long trek will just prove the purity of their faith."

"True enough. Make it a tasteful marker, though. No more than twenty statues of weeping women."

Dante woke in the predawn darkness to the sound of feet squelching in the mud. He brought the nether to his hands, lying silent, until he remembered he was among a strange but hospitable people. He had been dreaming of walking through a forest like this one, but beneath the layer of leaves and grass lurked a gaping abyss, and his feet kept plunging into the open nothing, exposing them to the unseen and unknown beings lurking beneath.

Outside, looming silhouettes stalked the shoreline, rolling up yurts and drawing in the nets. Others knelt beside flat rocks, spread cloths to soak up any dew, and smoothed yellow parchment atop the cloths, preparing for the dawn light considered best for their stark line-paintings. Smoked fish carried on the cold breeze. When Dante returned from relieving himself, Mourn waited by the tent. He had clearly been designated the go-between, the buffer between the strangers and the tight circle of the clan.

"We move in an hour," the norren said. "Assuming you want him to come, alert the snoring thing you call your friend."

Blays groused and hacked like an angry duck, but calmed down quickly over a breakfast of dried fish and herb-crusted bread. Minutes after dawn, the clan split into two parts: the young warriors and hunters ready to track down their cousins of the Green Lake, and those who'd stay behind—those too old, young, or injured for travel, along with a small contingent of the battle-ready to provide for them and see them from harm. There were no tears shed, no speeches or goodbye ceremonies. The travelers simply walked from the lake while the remainder continued to mend nets, add brushstrokes to parchments, and pluck herbs from the boisterous woods.

"Now that's a farewell party," Blays said. "Did anyone even

bother to look up?"

"Either we'll be back or we won't," Mourn said. "What's there to get so excited about?"

"Rum? Corsets? The promise of rest at the end of a long day's travel?"

"Fleeting distractions from the only thought worth having: you're going to die."

Blays glanced from him Dante. "You two should talk. You're like two peas from the same moldy, withered, sprouted-from-a-grave-at-midnight pod."

Dante snorted. "Death's inevitability makes it the very thing *least* worth thinking about. You don't see hermits retiring to mountaintops to contemplate the nature of smelling bad after a hard day's work."

Mourn exhaled through his nose, the steam of his breath condensing in his mustache. "Well, you'll have plenty of time to think about how wrong you are once you're dead."

Birds twittered from bare branches. Warmthless sunlight fell from the canopy like an old acorn. When the group stopped to rest before midday, a quartet of hunters quickly returned with a steaming boar. The clan fell upon it, skinning, gutting, and butchering. A broad-shouldered middle-aged woman who Dante thought but wasn't certain was Vee's sister allotted slices of liver and raw muscle to everyone on the march—Blays sucked his down so fast Dante doubted he'd chewed—then handed off the remainder to be packed in thick fern leaves. The clan resumed the walk two hours later.

The pace was steady and perhaps comfortable by norren standards, but to Dante, whose legs were several inches shorter, it was just this side of grueling, worsened by toe-grabbing roots and heel-sliding slicks of rain-rotted leaves. He had to soothe his physical exhaustion with draughts of nether every couple hours, a tradeoff that left his muscles relaxed and unsore but which left something at his core lacking and ground-down—not his spirit, but something with more physical weight. Something more like his wind. He could see the strain in Blays' face, too, the limp he tried to conceal as the sun shrank and his blisters swelled. Blays would never complain about anything real, of course. Not in earshot of Dante, the norren, or any other being with a set of ears and the capacity for speech. When he slept, Dante swept the swelling from Blays' feet, then collapsed into unconsciousness himself.

By the second day, they were some forty miles from the camp by the lake and sixty miles or more from the village where, until rumors of the bow ripped them away, they'd been drilling norren militia to stand against cavalry. Too heavy to ride anything but the biggest workhorses, norren had as little experience defending themselves from mounted riders as Dante had defending himself from rainbows.

"Quite the walk," Blays said once they'd pitched their yurt and sat down to rest in the twilight. "It's enough to make a man question where he's going."

"After the one thing that can make a difference."

"Wild geese?"

"A stick. Specifically, a curved one that can destroy a fortress in a single shot."

It was a concept, however simple, he hadn't been able to completely convey to Blays, at least not in terms the blond man found convincing. Cally had first laid it out to Dante a year and a half ago on a brief return to the Sealed Citadel in Narashtovik, a summer visit where the bayside humidity was nearly intolerable even at the top of the high, breezy tower where Cally liked to literally look down on the citizens shouldering each other aside in the narrow streets beyond the Citadel walls. The sapling-thin old man hadn't spoken for some time after Dante joined him on the stone balcony, which was fine with Dante; so long as he was standing still, he could almost stop sweating.

"How do you fight a war that isn't a war?" Cally said at last. "More properly, how do you avert the war in the first place?" He ran knob-knuckled fingers through a beard he refused to comb despite years of protests from the servants tasked with making the Council look properly holy. "Think of it this way: a man with a club only has to shake it around and scream a little to convince the man without a club to back down. We're the man with the club, but we don't actually want to strike Setteven, the unarmed man. Just to menace them into doing what we want, i.e. letting the norren do whatever *they* want."

Dante frowned. "But in this case, the other man is actually many thousand men, and instead of being unarmed, they're actually carrying an army's worth of swords, spears, bows, axes—"

"Yes, well, no need to get literal. It's about the *idea*. It's about convincing them they *feel* like a helpless man while believing we're waving about a frightening and lethal club."

"Have you ever considered writing a book? It would be a shame for this wisdom to be lost to the ages."

Cally's brows arched into a scowl, a movement which, given their shrubby mass, might have forced a lesser man to sit down. "I am trying to impart to you a philosophy of preparation that could save the lives of thousands. You could at least pretend to take it to heart."

"I'll take it to spleen."

"As there's no chance you'll take it to brain, I will consider that good enough. The point is we couldn't possibly win a conventional war of army versus army. The alternative, then, is to explore all the ways to fight that aren't conventional—to find new clubs, and to steal them from the enemy."

Despite his efforts to wind the old man up, Dante had taken the idea to at least one and possibly several of his organs, and felt confident Cally would approve of his current detour. It was, after all, the pursuit of a very large and nasty bludgeon. If Dante had passed the opportunity by, Cally would no doubt have spent more time yelling at him than he would have spent chasing down the bow.

"You champion ideas like this all the time," he told Blays. "I think the only reason you're against it is because you didn't come up with it yourself."

"I'm just tired of being in the dark here." Blays elbowed Mourn, who gave him a glare that could strike fire in a downpour. "Josun Joh told you anything about when we might stop walking and start arriving?"

"Don't mock him."

"Well?"

"Any day now. The next one, I'd think."

Dante didn't allow his hopes up, but the next morning they intercepted the river where it weaved between modest hills and short cliffs, a quarter mile wide and as gray as the clouds overhead. A dirt path followed the shoreline. Within miles, the clan stopped. Vee and a pair of warriors continued on to a cluster of dark holes speckling a rocky cliff above the stretches of flat green land bracketing the shores.

"Cling," Mourn explained. "Home of the man who can point us toward our cousins."

Blays nodded. "Who aren't here themselves."

"Oh no. Do you expect everything in your life to be that simple?"

"No, but it's easier to complain as if I do."

Vee and the others returned a half hour later; though they made no specific announcements about it, Dante gathered that the coast had been cleared. The Clan of the Nine Pines moved on as a whole, slipping double-file down the hard-beaten path to Cling. From a distance, Dante hadn't seen anything but the caves, and had marked the place as a literal backwoods—just one step up, civilization-wise, from the nomad-warriors he traveled with. Closer, though, he could see docks and barges past the trees at river's edge, and smelled that particularly potent brew of hog shit that only arises from organized farming. On the other side of the path, the fields were empty, brown, and tilled. The path switched from dirt into a bizarre foreign material. Dante could see no seams in it, suggesting a single sheet of hard-fired clay or the like, yet the path's solid mass couldn't be anything but stone. He said as much to Mourn.

"Best roadmaster in the territories, Codd," the norren said. "It's a wonder the humans haven't kidnapped *him*."

Despite stooping for a closer look, Dante could only make out a handful of seams separating the stones that formed the road; most were artfully concealed as part of the sandstone's grain, with others too fine to see even when he knew they must be there. Nor did it try to imitate the straight lines of many well-paved roads. Instead, it followed the subtle contours of the landscape with the same integrity that the river followed the low places through the hills. Indeed, given its appearance as a single flow of stone, it was possible, if you looked at it in the right way, to see the road as another river, a heavy creek from a realm where frozen water didn't form ice, but stone.

He grew dizzy and straightened up. "This must have taken an eternity to build."

"Codd doesn't build. He *sculpts*."

"Sorry," Dante said. He should have known better. When it came to tangible objects like the road, norren approached their craft with the same dedication and piety as a prophet approached his lord. He had once seen an old woman go on carving a soapstone owl while her house literally burned down around her. Only when she passed out from the smoke had her son been able to drag her from the flames. "I've never seen anything like it."

"Of course you haven't."

Ahead, Orlen came to a stop. The clan stood in a square as finely cobbled as the road, a shallow bowl of seamless stone, the natural colors of which painted a vast mosaic of a salmon, its upper jaw as wickedly curved as a hawk's. At one end of the plaza, a single boulder, smooth and rounded as a river pebble, served as a podium or dais. Wooden shops ringed the plaza, some utilitarian, some elegantly simple, but beside the mastery of the plaza and the roads feeding into it, all equally forgettable.

The land between plaza and river was grassy and empty. Probably a field for festivals, prayer, and whatever else drew the crowds. The clan set camp in a field between the docks and warehouses. Flat-bottomed boats drifted downriver, bulging with barrels and tarps. Uphill, the black eyes of caves gazed down on the mild bustle of the port town. While the rank and file warriors spread blankets and rolled out the yurts, Orlen and Vee started up the road switchbacking Cling's highest hill.

Blays visored his hand against the afternoon sun. "Where are they off to?"

"To see the mayor about the kidnappings," Mourn said.

Dante gestured uphill. "Then let's go."

"Oh, that's not allowed."

"How are we supposed to help track down your cousins when we can't question the only people who know where they went?"

"By letting Vee and Orlen ask the questions themselves. And then by following them."

"To hell with that." Blays took off jogging. "And not the hell for fun people, either."

Mourn dogged their heels, running close enough to trip them. "You can't go up there!"

Dante didn't look back. "Our upward progress suggests otherwise."

"Pedantically speaking, you can move up this hill. But don't say I didn't warn you when they throw you back down it. Because that is what I am doing right now."

They caught the two clan chieftains before they were halfway up the switchback. Vee gazed at Mourn with distilled reproach, her orange eyes withering him. Orlen coughed into his hand and then considered the contents of his palm as if they contained a half-ruined map.

"No," he said.

"No what?" Dante said.

"Further."

"Why on earth not?"

"Because you are a human, and this is norren business for norren ears."

At first he thought this was a strange joke—in contrast to every other part of them, the ears of norren were bewilderingly small, coin-shaped and often lost beneath their tangled hair—but Orlen and Vee were staring at him with the gravity of a prince's funeral.

"I'm aware of your tradition," he tried, "but given how many lives may be at stake, I think an exception—"

Vee shifted forward. "The next step you take up this hill will be your last with the clan." She drew her brows together. "That sounded more ominous than I meant. I didn't mean we'd throw you down the hill. Just that you'd no longer be permitted to travel with us."

"This is stupid," Blays said, but apparently had nothing more convincing than that. Considering the affair settled, the two norren chieftains turned and continued uphill.

Mourn folded his arms. "See how futile that was?"

"So what now? Sit around and wait to be told what's next?"

"No," Mourn said. "You don't have to sit."

But Dante was tired from yet another day of relentless walking, so sitting beside his tent in the field was exactly what he did, at least until he nodded off, at which point he slumped around waiting for word from above. News arrived after nightfall when Blays shoved him all the way over, jarring him awake. Orlen and Vee had returned from the hill.

He rousted himself, knees popping, and headed to the shoreline. Boar roasted over a firepit, smogging the air with rich, crackling meat. At the water, bulky silhouettes cast nets fringed with small rock weights. The two chieftains sat on their heels by the fire, gnawing pork, wiping their greasy faces with their sleeves. Dante sat across from them.

"Did you find anything out?"

"Yes." Orlen thought for a moment. "That the mayor had nothing to say on the matter."

"But I thought he'd seen them."

Vee wiped the back of her hand across her mouth. "He said the slavers didn't pass through here after all. Which doesn't tell us nothing. It tells us the slavers didn't pass through here."

Frustration welled in Dante's throat. "I thought Josun Joh told you to come here for answers."

"He did."

"And here we are," Orlen said. "Which is closer than we were before."

Vee raised her right fist and held it to her ear. "Where we'll wait to hear from Josun Joh again."

Dante nodded, too wound up to speak. Blays gestured downriver. Dante followed him along the pebbly shore, where the smell of wet moss and faint fish carried on the river's gentle waves. Mourn walked some ways behind them. When they paused, the norren did too, crouching beside the water and pretending to investigate the rocks. He pursued Dante and Blays all the way to the other side of the piers where the town ceased and the waterfront woods resumed.

Dante stopped there, gazing out across the wide black river. "I'm beginning to think they *should* be enslaved."

"Is this because they live longer?" Blays stooped. He picked up a pebble and slung it over the flat waters. It sunk without a single skip. "They think they can just wait around for a god to billow orders from the clouds?"

Dante stared at the steep hill beyond the plaza. Skeins of smoke curled from its crown, venting the hearths of the homes in its side. "Does encamping their warrior-band in the middle of town strike you as unusually aggressive?"

"The kind of thing you'd do when you wanted to provoke answers from someone who doesn't want to give them?"

"Exactly."

"Maybe." Blays skipped another stone. "Can you really see them turning on each other?"

"I don't know. The norren aren't exactly a unified people."

"But they've hardly been clawing at each other's throats the last few years."

Dante glanced upstream, where Mourn was kneeling, butt on his heels, and staring out over the water. "Still, if waiting around is their only goal, there is plenty of non-town space for them to occupy instead."

"So let's go feel the mayor out for ourselves."

"What about our shadow?"

Blays knew better than to glance at Mourn. "Point your finger at him and make him fall down."

"That isn't how it works."

"Yes it is."

"All right, that's basically how it works." It was, in the scheme of things, a simple task, with no need for theatrics or even any blood to feed the nether. Dante squinted at the mossy rocks, the waves slurping through them. The nether pooled in his hand like the shadow of quicksilver. For Blays' benefit, he pointed at Mourn as one would point out a thief. The kneeling norren leaned forward like a toppling tree, spilling facefirst into the grass. "Wait. Do you even know where the mayor's house is?"

"Of course. When somebody tells me I can't come with them, the first thing I do is watch where they go."

They headed back for the plaza. Light and laughter poured from the windows of the public houses; a longboat had pulled in during their walk along the shore, its crew beelining for the likeliest sources of liquor. It provided more than enough cover for any noise Dante made skirting the square. Was he being paranoid?

Orlen and Vee wouldn't let them up to see the mayor themselves. They'd assigned Mourn to follow Dante and Blays wherever they went, presumably as much to keep tabs on them as to ensure their own safety, but why let the pair of humans come along at all if the norren chiefs didn't consider their presence useful? As usual when dealing with the norren approach to outsiders, Dante felt like he'd nodded off in the middle of a carriage ride and been dropped off in strange streets with no idea which way was north.

He started up the switchback at a swift but unremarkable pace. Cave-houses sat in the rocky face of the hill, doors cut to fit the irregular contours of the caves' natural mouths. Torch sconces projected from each side of the doors, some lit, illuminating the path ahead and the family names painted in gorgeous runes above the entries. They climbed until Dante was panting and Cling lay below them in the haze of the river-mist. Torches flickered around the salmon-mosaic in the central plaza.

"Just ahead." Blays nodded to a cave-door little different from the dozens below it or the handful above. It wasn't that late, perhaps an hour past supper-time, but Dante was suddenly aware of the questionable etiquette of barging in on a city official under dark of night. Blays promptly resolved this dilemma by planting himself in front of the cherrywood door and knocking like the hand of Death himself.

Faced with the sudden prospect of confronting the mayor, Dante wished he could run right back down the hill instead. Positions of leadership in the norren territories were filled through a process that baffled human commoners and horrified the nobles. In contrast to the process of power-accumulation typical to human government—birthright, nepotism, wealth, and well-paid armed killers—norren men and women were promoted to chieftancies, mayordoms, and regional stewardships based solely on the public perception of and appreciation for their opinions. Not their political opinions, either. Nobody cared what a man had to say about taxes or trade or the distribution of the commons. Or anyway, if they did care, it wasn't over the political positions themselves, but rather for the theophilosophical reasoning that had led the leader in question to take those positions in the first place.

Most of the time, it was even more abstract than that. Say a young woman appeared to live a noble, upright life among her clan. She also had bright, wise things to say about the holy scrolls and the right way to lead a well-lived life—and her deeds matched her words. These things would be noticed by her clansmen. Tucked away. And if a crisis struck—if the current chief died, or went mad, or had a philosophical revelation indistinguishable from madness—that bright, noble young woman might find herself elevated to the chieftancy in the blink of an eye.

How the public reached these decisions as to whose integrity was greatest and whose position was most convincing was as nebulous as it was sudden. Sometimes there was no open discussion at all, yet with less warning than a flash flood, a formerly beloved clan-chief wound up replaced. Most perplexing of all, most leaders *welcomed* being replaced. To the norren, leadership was a burden, a leaden net of unwanted responsibilities, judgments, arbitrations, and bureaucratic wheel-spinning that left them precious little time to pursue the highest virtues: arts, craftsmanship, and tribal warfare.

Meanwhile, the few norren who desired political office were typically those who lacked the brains to ever be granted it. Many of the most thoughtful spoke little at all, preferring to be thought of as mentally crippled rather than exposing the wisdom of their philosophies and thus putting them at risk of a sudden promotion to power. And the more cunning leaders, upon discovering firsthand how unpleasant the demands of the crown, scepter, or wolf's-head could be, took to deliberately espousing theories of life and scripture that were flawed, flagrantly heretic, or outright nonsense, hoping to have the mantle snatched from their shoulders and draped over those of some other sucker. Often, the public saw through these deceptions and played along anyway in a stubborn effort to call the chieftain's bluff.

The result was twofold: the policies of clans, villages, and territories could suddenly become bizarre or outright self-destructive, leading to regular turnover at the top and a widespread degree of low-level chaos that the regimented politics of the capital in Setteven found laughably easy to exploit (and which Dante found maddening to try to keep up with). And in the rare cases when a mayor or chief stuck fast to his or her position for years or decades, their realm might be stable, but the leaders themselves were often resentful and bitter of their responsibilities—sometimes poisonously so.

The man who opened the door was one of the latter.

Old even by norren standards, gray colored the mayor's head, brows, and beard. He was lean like jerky is lean, but had lost none of his 7' 6" height to old age, or in any event had plenty to spare. As he towered two full feet above, Dante suddenly understood how it felt to be a dog that's just been discovered snatching up the roast.

"Are you the mayor?" Blays said.

"Are you knocking on the mayor's door without knowing who the mayor is?"

"We're friends," Dante put in quickly.

"Doubt that. Don't often feel like taking a hammer to the heads of my friends."

"We're here to help. A clan of norren was taken as slaves—"

"And now they're gone, and the rest of us still got to look out for ourselves." The old norren lowered his face inches from Dante's, filling him with the same vertigo that might come from being stared down by a mountain peak. "Unless you're looking to become a part of my doorstep, get off of it."

Blays stood his ground. "If you change your mind, we'll be sleeping on your town's lawn."

Something shifted in the old man's eyes. He closed the door hard enough to make Dante blink. Laughter trickled up from the plaza far below.

"He's got my vote," Blays said.

"He's hiding something."

"Tall as he is, he could be hiding a pike up his ass and you'd never be the wiser."

"That would explain the general tightness of his character." Dante kicked a pebble down the trail. It bounced awry, bouncing over the edge and clattering on the stone incline below. "He knows something. That's why the clan came here. That's what he meant about looking after themselves now."

"Sounded like typical norren fatalism to me."

"I think he thinks talking would put him in danger. Maybe pose a risk to whole town. If so, how do we make him talk?"

"I predict he's impervious to threats."

"*Physical* ones."

A smile began to spread on Blays' face. "Bribery? Blackmail? We don't even know the guy's name."

"Then it's a good thing we have absolutely nothing better to do than plot and scheme to ruin his life."

"I'm sure you're aware that tradition and logic dictate the best place to scheme is in a pub."

"My thoughts exactly."

"Wait, really?"

Dante nodded downhill. The lanterns of the public houses flickered over the sprawling stone mosaic. "If there is one thing you can always find in a pub, it's people willing to badmouth public officials."

"We'll have to be careful not to draw suspicion. I'll disguise myself by getting drunk."

No less than three public houses stood in the square. Dante chose the loudest, a two-story structure with a ground floor of clamshell-studded clay bricks that must have been fired from river mud. Its upper level was unpainted pine boards; that and a visible slant to many of its windows marked the second story as a later and somewhat hasty addition.

An old man poked at meat grilling over the fireplace. Scents of fish oil, beer, and sweat miasmaed the wide room. Though few humans peopled the norren lands, the pub's patrons, like those of any decent port, were a diverse bunch, evenly split between human and norren. The furniture didn't reflect this democratic spirit. Human legs dangled from chairs built for much larger bodies.

Blays ordered while Dante found a promising seat at the end of a long table just high enough to make resting his elbows on it entirely awkward. The wooden bench was worn shiny and smooth from the butts of countless travelers. His pint was pleasantly bitter and just as cold as the wintry air outside. Blays bought a platter of steaming, flaky white fish, nearly doubling the price with a side of extra salt.

Dante had expected the dozen-odd norren and humans at the table to begin criticizing, insulting, and slandering the mayor at a moment's notice—from their supple leather coats, they were native to the territories, if not Cling itself—but three pints and an hour later, he had nothing to show for himself but a decent buzz. Blays seemed happy enough, chatting away with a shaven-headed norren about various flavors of norren beer, a topic which, given the hundreds of varieties of norren wheat (they approached the cultivation of their staple crop with the same rigor and vigor they brought to their art), could fill a solid month of discussion, and Blays gave every indication of doing just that.

"Excuse me," Dante finally said to the gray-bearded norren to his right. "Can you tell me who's mayor here?"

The man didn't look up from the chipped clay mug he'd been staring at the last five minutes. "Why do you ask?"

With a drunk's skill for plucking up lies as easily as fallen scarves, Dante said, "I'm looking to do some shipping here."

"You're not from here. It's obvious as a sunrise. So let me spare you the speeches about Mayor Banning and say this: he's great. You couldn't ask for a better leader. Honest. Forthright. A man who looks out for his town."

"I see."

"Put him in charge, what, forty years ago. *Stoics of Barnassus*. After he wrote that, they tried to put him in charge of the whole territory, but Cling wanted him too—hometown and all. Fought themselves a little war about it. Cling's victory inspired him to write *The Posture of Virtue Is Not Kneeling*."

"I've read that," Dante said. "He argues that taking a stand against a stronger foe guarantees the eternal blessings of both Haupt and Josun Joh. Very spirited."

The norren eyed him, drawing back in the universal gesture of reappraisal. "Should try to take a look at his paintings if you get the chance. Landscapes so real you could tip them back and pour their rivers right in your mouth."

"Really? Where can I find them?"

"Not his workshop, that's for sure," the old man laughed. "He keeps that locked down tighter than the princess' panties. Couldn't even tell you where it is." He gulped his beer. "Can't blame him, either. He'd never get one stroke down with a crowd of gogglers pressing in over his shoulders."

Over the course of the night, Dante struck up conversations with the pubkeep, another norren local, and a trio of human bargemen who made regular call at Cling. On the starlit walk back to their tent, he detoured back to the river shore.

"They all said the same thing. A man whose integrity and talent is matched only by his prolificness." He spat beery aftertaste into the slow-moving waters. "I hope you came up with something more helpful."

"Oh," Blays said. He reached down for a stone and wobbled, slapping both palms into the muck to steady himself. "That."

"That?"

"I sort of forgot why we were there." He attempted to wash his hands in the river and fell down again, soaking his pants. "I think I need to go to sleep."

Dante sighed and headed to the tent, where Blays proved himself right by collapsing into his blanket, where he stayed until well past noon. The clan was similarly indolent, fishing, napping, sketching circles in the mud, where they lit candles and knelt to pray to Josun Joh for direction. Dante, turning to more earthly forms of action, decided to follow the mayor.

Technically speaking, *he* wasn't following Mayor Banning. A dead fly was. But Dante had killed it—three, actually, but the first two were too mangled to use—revived it of a sort, and sent it after Banning the moment the mayor lumbered from his cliffside home. Seeing through the fly's eyes was so nauseating Dante puked his guts up all over the shoreline reeds, where a hungover Blays had had the same idea. Unlike the sights and sounds he received from dead animals, which were essentially the same as (if sometimes sharper than) his own, the senses relayed from the fly were kaleidoscopic and chaotic, a fractured, fisheye view of the world that careered into stomach-stirring anarchy the moment the insect took wing. The only way Dante could keep up was to lie down in the darkness of the yurt with his eyes closed and a cloth over his face, a posture which Blays imitated after just a few minutes of trying to battle the shimmering sunlight mirrored on the blue waters.

Through the fly's manifold eyes, he watched Banning take meetings with merchants. Have lunch with his wife. Have *more* meetings with merchants, followed by a meeting with a mayor from downriver, and finally, with another pair of merchants, whom he spoke with over dinner and wine before retiring home to read scriptural scrolls in the candlelight.

The next day, during negotiations with a landlord from upriver over the prospect of floating his timber through Cling, Banning rose and smashed the fly into a gooey blot. Dante's second sight disappeared with a pinprick of pain in the center of his brain. Citing exhaustion, he sent Blays to catch him a new fly, which he had back in action by midafternoon. Just in time to watch things conclude with the would-be timber baron, whose proposal was denied on the grounds it might interfere with local fishermen.

For three days, Banning did nothing but rise, meet, eat, and read. On the fourth day, rather than descending the switchback to his offices on the short hill on the north end of town, the towering norren climbed to the very top of the rise in which his house was set and continued west into the woods. He wandered along as if aimless, gazing at sunbeams, kneeling to brush leaves from stones. After a few hours, during which Dante nodded off more than once, Banning trudged to a fold in the hills where a small, simple cabin hid among the thick trees. The mayor knocked on the door. A young norren appeared, smiling, and handed Banning a wide, flat object bundled in cloth. Paint smeared his hairy arms.

Dante opened his eyes and went to get Blays.

"He doesn't paint his own paintings," he explained. "He doesn't have time. He's so busy running the town's affairs he has some kid do it for him, then picks them up when they're done."

"So what?" Blays picked pulled chicken from his teeth; still traumatized from their days-long march of crusty bread, he'd made it his mission to try the fare of every stall, inn, and bakery in town. "Every master in Bressel does that."

"We're a thousand miles from Bressel. To the norren, the things you make are a reflection of your soul. That's why it's such a big deal. Passing off someone else's work as your own is like plagiarizing the *Cycle of Arawn*."

"A great way to get lynched by humorless scolds?"

"And to get him to talk."

"Now?"

"He's miles from town. We can catch him on the way back."

"What about him?" Blays nodded at Mourn, who idled at a bakery across the plaza, crumbling bread into his mouth. Out of shame or confusion, the young norren hadn't mentioned suddenly falling asleep the other night, but he hadn't ceased following them, either.

"Let him follow. If Banning tries to kill us, we'll have a witness."

Blays went back to the tent for his swords. While he was gone, Dante sat down and closed his eyes. Banning was still in the woods to the north, traipsing Cling-ward with the help of a tall staff, a package tucked gently under his other arm. Dante didn't bother fetching his own sword. He doubted Banning would attack them outright, whether in feigned outrage to their accusation or to stop them from telling others, but if Dante was wrong—and given how seriously the norren took these things, there was always a chance—his middling swordplay wouldn't be much use against the towering mayor.

They puffed their way up the switchback road, then followed the dirt trail traced across the hill's flat crest. Mourn lagged a hundred feet behind, but once the trail gave out and the two of them cut across the high brown grasses of the open field, the young norren jogged to catch up, his face dark with annoyance at being forced to run after his troublesome human charges.

"Where are you going?" Mourn said when he reached their side.

"Our daily stroll across the middle of nowhere," Blays said.

"You're not supposed to leave town."

"And my mother didn't want me to grow up a swordsman like my dad, either, but that didn't stop me from disgracing her dearly departed memory."

"Turn around and get back to your tent."

Dante scowled over his shoulder. "If you'd like to try to stop us, please let me know where to send your remains. Now go back to town and beseech Josun Joh to tell you what to do next. It's worked great so far."

"Josun Joh's words are real." Mourn's voice sounded so hurt Dante almost stopped.

"You've heard him?"

"Not me personally. Vee and Orlen do most of the talking."

"Then how do you know they're not making it all up?"

"Some summers ago, the clan headed to the highlands to wait out the heat. The peaks are high and jagged there, ready to tear open the belly of any stupid and lazy clouds who get too low. But it was dry there too, because sometimes the gods hate us. And who can blame them, when every smart lad in the land is ready to denounce their very existence." Mourn waited a moment before going on. "We were gathering jen-nuts when Orlen went stock still. Josun Joh had spoken to him, he said. There was a fire past the western ridge. We needed to move.

"We traveled east. Within an hour, the fire jumped over the ridge and swept over the valley where we'd been earlier that morning. Maybe we'd have had enough time to get away. But we were on foot, like always, and fire can outrun any man when it's hungry enough."

"Orlen probably smelled smoke," Dante said.

"When Josun Joh spoke to him, the wind was blowing westward."

"So he saw the smoke. Fire has a unique property of being visible."

Mourn tromped through the weeds in silence. "At least tell me where you're going."

Blays touched the pommel of the sword at his hip. "Oh, just to kick the mayor until the stars whirring around his head show him the sign to tell us where the hell your cousins are."

"I think Vee hates me," Mourn declared. "Why else would she assign me to you two?"

"Maybe she hates *us*."

"It's a stupid thing, really. You're running off to gods know where, and what am I supposed to do to stop you? Attack you? I don't think any good will come of that. Except for the local worms. So I'm supposed to run off and tell mommy and daddy like a spited toddler?" Mourn shook his head at the state of things. "You know what, to hell with them. If they want to guard you, they can guard you themselves. We're beating up the mayor? Let's go beat up the mayor."

The hill sloped down into a low forest of birches and young pines. Star-shaped yellow flowers dotted the roots of the trees. Dante shut his eyes to glance through the fly's and tripped into a pile of pine needles. Smelling sap, he kept his eyes shut.

"Are you okay?" Mourn said. "I think he's dead."

"I'm not dead." In the fly's fractured vision, dozens of Bannings hiked up the side of a hillside more or less identical to their own. He ordered the fly up, stomach lurching. He managed to prevent himself from puking until the bug had located them among the trees, confirming the mayor was no more than a half mile away. When Dante was finished, he kicked pine needles over the hot, sour mess, gargled with cool water, and gestured down the hill. "Stop staring at me and start looking for our man."

They need hardly have bothered. Within a minute, Banning began singing to himself, an eerie, droning tune that carried down the hillside like the honking of morbid geese. When Dante stepped in his path, the spire-tall norren stopped less than a foot away. Dante tensed, preparing to fling himself out of the way.

"I know you." Banning's face darkened. "Just because the cliff isn't here doesn't mean I won't throw you down it."

"You should at least hear what I'm about to say," Dante said. "Then some people might even not blame you for what you've done."

"Talk sense or talk less."

"That package under your arm. Is your name on it?"

Banning didn't glance down. "It's the last stroke I make."

"Typical of most artists, I imagine. Except, apparently, the man who actually paints yours."

The mayor's gaze was as still and deep as a lake. "Pick up a weapon."

Dante cocked his head. "What?"

"So I don't have to say I killed an unarmed man."

Sudden anger rippled through Dante's veins. With it came the nether, great pools he gathered in his hands. With a thought, he shaped them into shadowy ropes which looped around the tree branches and clawed at Banning's rugged face. The air dimmed like an instant sunset. Dante gave form to the nether for those who couldn't see it, viscous, liquid shadows that dripped from his hands like reluctant blood.

"I could have threatened you with violence," he said softly. "But I could tell at a glance it wouldn't work, and I'd have to either back down or hurt you, which I don't much like to do. But if you don't answer my questions about the missing norren, I *will* tell the city where your masterpieces really come from. You'll be exiled from Cling to die as an old man in a place you do not know."

Anger flowed over Banning's face, followed by a quiver of fear that was clearly visible beneath his thatchy beard. "If someone were to have up and enslaved a clan, you think their fellow norren would be happy to point those people out."

"Unless?"

"Unless saying such would threaten the ones that they hold dear."

"I see."

"Maybe even an entire town."

Dante let the taut branches relax. The shadows faded from his hands. "Then I'll put myself on the line, too. I'm from Narashtovik. I'm the agent of Callimandicus, highest priest of Arawn. I'm here to help."

"Narashtovik is a part of Gask like anywhere else."

"And if the capital finds out we're here, we'll be invaded the minute they're finished with you."

Banning slung the wrapped painting onto the forest floor. "Tell them anything you like. I don't give a damn about my reputation. And I don't know who took your people or who they sold them to." He stepped on the package. The wooden frame cracked beneath his weight. "But I do know who took them downriver."

"Who?"

"You give me your word."

Dante nodded. "No one will know who told me."

The old man grinned, a savage thing that bristled his beard like a wall of thorns. "Oh, I want the ones who did it to know. What I want you to promise is you'll scream my name before you kill every last one of them."

3

Haggling for the barge strained Dante's patience as hard as the days-long process of watching Banning's meetings. Before he could even begin to bargain with the captain, Dante first had to convince Orlen and Vee that hiring a boat was necessary to begin with, a requirement that seemed self-evident to him—when your quarry is river pirates, you won't have much luck hunting them down on foot—but which took the better part of the night to hash out. By the next morning's walk to the docks, he was ready to give up on talking and try hitting instead.

River pirates. It was simple enough that Dante considered it a major blow to Josun Joh's credibility that the mercurial god hadn't passed that info along directly rather than shooing them in the vague direction of a recalcitrant old man. But once Banning had been ready to speak, he'd spoken like he might never have the chance to speak again.

The slaveship had docked in Cling just over a month ago. The dockhands had seen the eyes glittering from the darkness belowdecks. There had been talk in town, when the pirates debarked, of slaughtering them then and there, but none of the captives were known to be family of anyone in Cling, and it had been pointed out that these weren't just a slapdash rowboat of common pirates, but the Bloody Knuckles, a multi-vessel armada headed by the three-decked galley the *Ransom*. The last village to threaten the Bloody Knuckles had been so thoroughly robbed, raped, murdered, and torched that six years later the only remnant of the settlement were the cinders of its dead and the nightmares of their relatives.

And so a conspiracy of silence had been enacted by the town of Cling—or those few who knew about the slaves, anyway, a shortlist including the dockside witnesses, Banning, and a handful of the port's elders and most highly-feared warriors—which Banning didn't break until witnessing Dante summon the nether from the forest floor. In that moment, he decided the Clan of the Nine Pines and its two human allies had a real chance to wipe out the Bloody Knuckles in a single blow.

If only Dante could afford a boat.

In theory, he had access to the full treasury of the Sealed Citadel of Narashtovik. The city had grown substantially in the last few years, propelled by Cally's new policies and the refugees from the war with Mallon, who, finding abandoned homes available for the taking in the city's outer rings, had flocked by the thousands to the foreign city, bringing new businesses, trade routes, and labor in equal measure. Despite Cally's covert funding of the operations in the Norren Territories, the city was rich by any objective measure.

In practice, Dante couldn't just sign his name to a receipt of credit for the same reason a traitor can't stroll into the palace with a smile and a wave. Strictly speaking, he *was* a traitor. To Gask, anyway. He had plenty of silver cached in their base of norren operations in Dunran, but that was 150 miles overland in the wrong direction, and even on the horses he couldn't afford, making that trip would set them back at least a week on a venture that was already weeks behind. He and Blays had enough on their person to buy decent lodging and board for a couple weeks apiece, but that was hardly enough to rent a boat and its crew for a journey of 200 miles or more with a passenger manifesto of some thirty armed warriors. The clan, meanwhile, had essentially nothing (with the exception of an armory of immaculately forged swords, which were priceless in the very real sense they refused to sell them). In the end, Dante had to resort to requesting credit from Banning, who agreed readily, going so far as to refuse all offers of repayment, be they sooner (wealth recouped from the pirates) or later (the weeks it would require to get word to Cally and hard funds).

By the time all this was arranged, the crew of the *Boomer* was already drunk, and Captain Varlen, a stout man whose barrel-shaped body looked like it could serve as a ship of its own if properly hollowed, showed unusual concern in insisting they not shove off until the crew slept off their rum, wine, and beer. Dante boiled with the specific annoyance of a delayed journey. To occupy his mind, he practiced with the nether inside the yurt, forming images of Blays falling off a variety of cliffs, treetops, and towers.

Mourn woke him shortly after dawn and they tramped down the pier to the *Boomer*, a nondescript grain barge with a flat bottom and a single deck, below which spilled wheat was lodged into every corner and cranny. The clan, evidently confused by the concept of boats, set about erecting their tents belowdecks while Captain Varlen shouted the vessel into open water. A solid sheet of gray clouds tarped the sky. A low wind rippled the sails, chilling Dante at the side railing where he watched them depart from Cling. On the receding docks, men lugged bales and barrels from and into waiting ships. The steep hill rose behind town, pocked with doors, slashed from top to bottom with the zigs and zags of its seamless, perfect road. Varlen nudged the barge to the middle of the river, clearing them from the port town's miasma of river muck and feces. Cling disappeared behind a bend.

Dante had always wanted to take an extended trip via water, but he was soon glad he hadn't. In a word, it was boring. In another word, it was repetitive, a slow-scrolling vista of shoreline trees, short hills, and sudden cliffs with rocky piles collected at their bottom. Shacks dotted the banks every mile or three. Every few hours, the current pushed the *Boomer* past a norren village. Their high, conical roofs, designed to keep the snow off, jabbed from the shores like pins in a knitter's cushion. For two days, this was all Dante saw, and though he wasn't one to bore easily, the trip was doing its best.

His condition wasn't helped in the slightest by the clan warriors, who continued to treat him and Blays like off-duty farm dogs—fed occasionally, otherwise ignored—despite the fact that if not for them, the clan would still be sitting on a muddy bank waiting for their one-eyed god to stop chasing female mortals long enough to clue them in about where to go next. (When he'd brought that very point up, Orlen had brushed it off; Josun Joh had sent them to the right place, he said, but left it up to them to find what they'd come for.) The exception was Mourn, who now spoke to them regularly, readily answered questions, and generally showed all signs of having abandoned his task of minding the two humans. Possibly because they were trapped on a boat, where the only opportunities to sneak off into trouble involved getting very wet. Still, Dante thought Mourn's shift in priorities was genuine.

"Somebody do something already," Blays said from his seat on an out of the way portion of the deck. "I'm so bored I'm about to start counting my own fingers."

"You have ten," Mourn said.

"Don't be so sure. I've been drumming this deck so hard I might have worn some of them down to the nub."

"You could try watching for pirates," Dante said.

"Oh, look, there aren't any."

"Try napping. You're cranky enough."

Blays pounded his fists on the deck. "But I don't wanna nap!"

Dante laughed. "We could...tell stories."

"That actually doesn't sound horrible." He glanced up at the overcast sky, whose threats of rain had gotten as tedious as the scenery. "What about this Quaking Bow? It would be nice to have some idea exactly why we're sailing after a band of professional murderers on this terribly fearsome wheat-bucket."

"The *Quivering* Bow."

"I don't care what it's called. I care about a graphic recounting of all the things it's destroyed."

Dante gazed at a gray granite cliff, its face striated with white. "I'm not sure I know any true stories. Some legends, perhaps."

"I don't care if it's true or false. All I want to hear is how a bow convinces a castle to blow up."

Mourn lowered himself from the barge railing to sit on his heels. "Tell him about how the Quivering Bow got made."

Dante shrugged. "I don't know how the Quivering Bow was made."

"Everyone knows how the Quivering Bow got made."

"I didn't grow up in Gask, Mourn. I hadn't even heard about the Quivering Bow until a year ago."

"Then I'll tell him how it was made. And you. Wouldn't do at all for you to have the thing and not have any idea what went into making it. Is that a human thing, rushing off to use things up without caring where they came from?"

"I think it's a Blays thing," Dante said.

Blays pressed his palm against his forehead. "Right now, the Blays thing is praying you both die if you don't get on with it."

"You should pray for *yourself* to die," Mourn said. "Then you'd get to do something really interesting." He cleared his throat and frowned down at his hands, which he'd placed palms-down on the hard wood deck. "I'll take a wild guess that you haven't heard of Corwell, either. Thought not. He's only the half-mortal son of Margon, brother of Josun Joh himself. The first thing I would ask is why Corwell is *half* mortal, but then again I wouldn't need to ask, because I actually have an education."

Blays rolled his hand through the air. "Get on with it before your education and the body that holds it find themselves at the bottom of a river."

"Margon had a thing for norren women. The bigger the better. I think this is because he was a small god. Small like you, I mean. This meant he had nimble fingers and was very good at making clocks and flutes. And in picking the locks of sleeping norren women. Which he did. A year later, Corwell was born.

"Corwell, being half-mortal, wasn't allowed in the heavens. Kind of for the same reasons you're not allowed to speak to Orlen, really. Instead he grew up among norren, where he used his norren strength and divine quickness to become an archer so fine he could shoot out a hawk's eye from so far away the hawk couldn't see him. This won the heart of Velia, a woman everyone agreed was the most beautiful norren born in seven generations.

"They married. They were happy. But Margon wasn't, because Corwell had gotten to Velia before he could. So he crept into their house one night and stole her. Which, can I pause for a moment? That's not really acceptable in any form. A dad's supposed to be an example for his sons. I don't think anyone wants their sons to grow up to be a kidnapping rapist."

"Maybe he just wanted to keep the family business alive," Dante said.

"I would guess he was just selfish, but to each his own. Naturally, Corwell found it as despicable as I do, but couldn't do anything about it, because Margon lived in a tower of solid iron with a top so high it was lost in the clouds, and the tower itself stood on a mountain so high it makes you too dizzy to stand. Corwell only made it up because he was half-god, but as much as he pounded on the tower's walls, he couldn't leave a scratch. It just gonged like a giant bell, resounding through the clouds, which was probably a good thing, because when Corwell, in his completely relatable despair, flung himself from the mountain, his uncle Josun Joh had already been drawn there by the bell, and was able to catch him.

"Josun Joh offered to help, because unlike Corwell's own father, he is a man of principles and upright character. Plucking a seedling from the base of the White Tree, he bent it into a bow, stripping its leaves—this was a fairly normal tree, unlike its hideous progenitor—to be tied into a fan. He gave these to his nephew and told him the tower's outer wall was invincible, but that it was just a shell around a very normal stone structure. If Corwell could fire an arrow through the single window just below the tower's peak, he could strike the inner stone, sending the whole thing crumbling down.

"So Corwell went back to the iron tower and called to his father Margon, who didn't even bother to come out and explain himself, which again shows you what kind of man *he* was. Corwell waved the fan, blowing away the clouds. He drew back his mighty bow and sighted in on the window, which was just a black speck so tiny you couldn't even see it, let alone shoot an arrow through it. In fact, it was so far away it took a full minute after he released his arrow for it to fly right through the distant window.

"Once more, the tower rung like a bell. Its note was so strong it knocked the birds from the sky. Half the mountain slid into the sea, which probably killed a lot of people if anyone lived on the nearby islands. And the tower itself crumbled, dashing down in a hellstorm of thudding stone and screaming iron. Horrified that everyone in it was dead, Corwell waved his fan, flushing the dust out to sea, and found Velia alive under the broken body of his father."

Mourn frowned again at the backs of his hands. "Which sounds like a happy ending, except when you think about it Corwell killed his own dad and Velia was abducted and ravished by her husband's father, which she couldn't have been too happy about either. But that's how Corwell got the Quivering Bow, and at least nobody ever bothered him or his family again."

"Neat," Blays said. "No one will want to mess with us then, either."

"Now do you see why we're after it?" Dante said.

"Sure. Sounds like we'd be invincible. So why not go after the Hammer of Taim while we're at it? Or find a way to catapult the sun straight into Setteven?"

"Origin stories are always exaggerated. If you don't buy Mourn's, I know one I think actually happened."

"I wasn't just making that up," Mourn said.

"All I'm saying is—"

"These are things we believe, you know. I don't know where you're from that you don't even pretend to take them seriously, but it must be a rude place. Many shoving-related deaths."

Dante glared off at the cliffs drifting by at the speed of the current. "I don't know what's true and what isn't. If the bow's real, then maybe Corwell's story is, too, along with the one I've heard. It's about a norren named Wenworth, who only died about fifty years ago, so—"

"Wenworth the Mole died 56 years ago."

"—it's at least reasonably trustworthy. In short, Wenworth was a norren warrior exiled from his clan after his younger brother convinced them he'd burned down their ancestral shrine—but his brother stole some of the relics from the shrine, and sealed them up in a stone tomb. A tomb in which his treachery would soon cause him to be interred.

"It began from jealousy. Wenworth and his brother Bode were sons of the chieftain, and Wenworth, as the elder, was naturally in place to—"

"All hands!" Captain Varlen bellowed from the barge's aftercastle. "All hands take arms!"

A sailor leapt on the mainmast, climbing hand over hand up the rigging. Others rushed for the ship's bow or passed around spears stored in a closet on the face of the stern's castle. Dante rose and peered across the gray waters. Small waves smacked the hull.

The men called back and forth, adjusting sails, swinging the *Boomer* starboard and angling it at the eastern shore. Norren warriors swarmed up the ladder from belowdecks. Dante and Blays exchanged a look, then jogged to the bow and up the steps of the aftercastle, where Varlen relayed orders to a bald, gnomish old man who in turn barked them to the crew in a voice far larger than his wiry body would seem to allow.

"What's happening?" Dante said to the barrel-chested captain.

"Someone's distracting me from my duties," the captain said.

"If you think you see pirates, we need to know."

"No pirates."

"That's good," Blays said.

"Just the bodies they left behind."

Varlen nodded across the river and resumed jabbering at the gnomish man. Upriver near the far bank, something flat yet jagged floated a short distance from shore, a plane interrupted by sudden snagging upthrusts of snapped wood.

"Is that a shipwreck?" Blays said. The captain nodded. "Then what are we doing sailing *away* from it?"

"Avoiding a trap." The burly man pointed to a steep rise, its top lightly wooded, where the river curved downstream. "Such as a man left ashore on yonder hill, with a signal-mirror ready to flash the vessel hidden around the bend."

"So what? We've got to check it out."

"Anything worth taking's already been took by the ones that burnt their ship."

Blays rolled his eyes. "To help the survivors."

"That isn't a part of our mission," Dante said.

"Our *mission* is to help the people of these lands. When you're brought to Arawn's hill in the sky, don't you want to be able to point to a *few* good deeds to balance out all the killings?"

"Arawn doesn't judge."

"Well, he should. And we should, too." Blays turned to Varlen. "Take us to the wrack."

"That thing looks days old. The only comfort they'll need is a burial." The blocky man rubbed his stubble. "Well, you're paying for this trip. But one whiff of anything fishy and we're shoving off."

"Cowardice isn't a free meal," Blays said. "It isn't something we should be lining up for."

He turned on his heel, brushing shoulders with Orlen, who'd joined them on the aftercastle. Dante followed Blays down the steps. The gnomish sailor roared out new orders. Men clambered the rigging, tacking the sails to swing the barge larboard. Blays set up position on the bow, swords sheathed. Mourn procured a bow and hastily strung it. As they neared the wreckage, Dante kept one eye downstream for enemy boats, but the waters were empty, gray as the clouds.

The wreck, it turned out, wasn't drifting so much as lodged in the rocks and mud ten yards from shore. Its hull stopped a few feet above the water, charred and broken. Submerged white sails flapped in the current like bleached seaweed. Wood creaked on rocks. Soot and rot rolled over the clammy, muddy smell of the river. Varlen anchored and set his crew to preparing the *Boomer*'s single life raft, which had just enough room for Dante, Blays, and two sailors manning the oars. Though the wreck was as silent as the clouds, Mourn crouched over the *Boomer*'s rails, bow at the ready, joined by a dozen other warriors of the clan. Two crewmen dipped their paddles into the cold water and pushed the rowboat forward. The tiny vessel rolled on the waves, swells thudding hollowly against its wooden sides.

The deck of the wreck angled from the waters. One of the rowers reached for the damp railing and guided the rowboat in. They tied off, startling a crowd of crows, who hopped further down the ship and resumed pecking at a blackened arm tangled in a wrist-thick rope.

Dante crawled past the crewmen, grabbed onto the railing, and eased onto the slant of the deck, boots slipping on the slick wood. He braced himself and gave Blays a hand up. A few feet to their right where the deck met the water, a pair of legs lay on dry wood. The man's upper body swayed in the water, shirt billowing around his bruised and pale skin.

Dante crouched down, breathing through his nose. "This does not look so good."

"That's because it's a wreck," Blays said. "Anyway, it doesn't matter if they're all dead. The important thing was coming here to check."

"Well, look at you. I'm surprised you could coax that high horse into the middle of a river."

"Sorry to interrupt all the beatings, threats, and killings to *help* someone for a change."

Downed sails and charred, shattered wood blanketed the deck. Reddish-brown ovals stained the canvas. Blays curled a rope around his forearm and used it to brace himself as he half-climbed, half-walked up the deck toward the stern, where an open hatch gaped into darkness. He leaned over its edge, wrinkling his nose.

"If smells can kill, I hope you're ready with my eulogy." He unwrapped the rope from his arm and slid it down the canted deck to Dante.

"I'd be honored. You *are* an overweight nun with a drinking problem, right?" Dante coiled the rope around his arm and scrabbled up the creaking planks. At the hatch, the stink of fresh death churned his gut. Water lapped gently in the darkness. Still clinging to the rope, Dante rolled onto his back, rooted through his pack, and emerged with a dull, semi-opaque marble. He rubbed the torchstone between his palms, periodically blowing on it as if it were a colicky fire, until a strong, pale light bloomed from the stone. Dante leaned over the hatch rim and lowered the stone into the gloom. Ropes, broken casks, and shards of pottery scattered the planks some 15 feet below. Bodies lay propped against pillars or crushed between barrels. His nose already acclimating to the scents of decay and exposed guts, Dante smelled old smoke, coppery blood, and the sharp, irritating tang of oil. From the darkness beyond the stone's reach, something stirred the broken jars.

Dante jolted back from the hatch, scrabbling to catch himself on its edge before he slid down the deck. "There's something down there."

"A cargo hold has cargo? This is a discovery right up there with fire."

"Something alive."

"Oh." Blays gazed down at the opening as if suddenly regretting the entire venture, then grabbed the rope, scooted toward the deck railing, and started knotting. "This river just has fish in it, right? Nothing with tentacles?"

"I feel like a large, tentacled object will pretty much go wherever it pleases."

"Why do I always forget to bring a trident?" Blays tested his knot with a tug, then slung the rope's free end down the hatch. It struck the bottom with a damp thud. He gestured down the pit. "Well, you've got the light."

Dante frowned at the gloom. "I could just hand it to you."

"Too much work. Get climbing."

Dante scowled, clamped the stone between his teeth, and grabbed hold of the rope. For all he'd seen and done—the fights, the battles, the deaths—he was still afraid of the dark. Not in a rational way, either. He was less scared of whatever was really down there than of all the things that couldn't be: the venomous monsters, the clawed horrors, the spider-faced giants that would lurch from the darkness the moment he turned his back. But this wasn't a fear he could voice to Blays, so he lowered himself hand over hand into the damp chill gloom.

As the rope swung with his weight, Dante glanced frantically from corner to corner, splashing the hold with the stone's white light. It rushed over shattered wood, burst barrels, bubbly green glass. His boots touched the floor. He shuffled through the debris towards a chest-high crate that was gouged but intact, then hunkered down and pressed his back against it.

"I'm down," he called.

Feet dangled through the hatch. Blays leapt straight down, the rope threaded through his elbows, slowing him just enough to stave off injury when he thumped to the planks. The boat groaned, grinding on the rocks, broken glass jangling in the darkness.

Blays threw his arms out for balance as the ship settled into a new angle of rest. "Possibly not a great idea."

"Not unless you're *trying* to drown. In which case please ask me first." Dante glanced up the sloping boat. At the gray limits of the torchstone's reach, a man lay facedown beneath a mass of loose barrel staves and hoops. Other than Blays' disturbance of the rubble, Dante hadn't heard anything since descending besides the smack of waves against the hull. He crept across the floor and knelt beside the body. The man's wrist was cold as the river. Dante turned downslope. Beside him, Blays eased through the ruins, pointing at a pair of legs jutting from a mound of broken crates and spilled white cloth. Dante stepped through the tacky, rusty stain around the body and crouched beside one foot. Tugging up its pant leg, the shin was white and cold.

There was no need to check the third man for warmth or pulse. He slumped against the curved inner wall, head missing from the nose up. Dante moved past, smelling cold, stagnant water. The torchstone's white light glimmered on the black pool that was the back half of the sunken boat. Broken boards and whole barrels floated there, circling in an unseen current. He suddenly felt very cold.

"Okay," Blays said. "I've seen enough."

Dante stared into the black water. He thought he could see something moving there, a serpentine, twilight shape that could only be seen in glimpses from the corner of his eye.

A voice moaned from the darkness.

Dante nearly dropped the stone. Blays yelped. "Remind me never to do anything good again."

They found her curled tight under a shroud of sodden, dirty cloth. Dark-haired, a few years older—mid-20s. Her bare arms were as ropy as the rigging, but her cheeks were sunken, her skin as pale as the sails swaying in the current. A bloody bandage held her left leg together.

"Go get help," Dante said. "I'll see what I can do."

Blays' footsteps faded up the slope. Dante drew his knife across the back of his hand. The nether reacted at once, restless in this borderland between air and water, light and dark, life and death. He took hold of the woman's wrist, which pulsed heat like a stove. Shadows flowed down his arms, sinking into her skin like rain into sand. She coughed so hard her shoulders lifted from the deck. He turned her head sideways to let her dribble phlegm onto the damp wood.

He breathed slowly, drawing the nether from the black pool, from the shadows under casks and crates, from the bodies of the dead. The heat of her skin ebbed. He checked the wound on her leg. It was red as a rose, inflamed and oozing blood. A white shard of bone projected from her skin. For now, he left it, along with her pain, fighting her fever instead, her soul-deep chills, the things that threatened to devour the final remnants of whatever spirit still clung to her bones.

She hadn't awoken by the time the crewmen from the *Boomer* arrived. Nor even when they built a stretcher, strapped her to it, and lifted her into the waning daylight of the topdeck. The rowboat shepherded Dante and the woman back to the *Boomer*, then turned around to pick up Blays and the other hands who'd helped with the rescue. Dante settled her into a cabin on the aftercastle and summoned the ship's barber, who set her leg and cleansed the wound.

That, at last, was enough to wake her. Dante called the shadows to soothe her pain. She collapsed into the sheets, sweating and unconscious.

Back on the open deck, Blays puffed his cheeks with a sigh. "Think she'll live?"

"Yes, in the sense that she hasn't died while we're talking. Past that, I give her even odds." Dante glanced at Captain Varlen, who stood with arms folded. "We should question her next time she wakes up. She might be able to point us in the right direction."

Varlen squinted his small black eyes against the sunset. "Need to get away from the wreck. Night's coming."

"Meaning?" Dante said.

"Meaning dead sailors become unruly jealous of those who aren't."

Dante was too tired to argue. The *Boomer* weighed anchor, steering for the river's middle. He sat watch over the woman but quickly nodded off. An hour later, heavy knocking jolted him from his seat. Orlen shoved open the door before Dante crossed the tiny cabin.

"What's going on here?" the chieftain demanded.

Dante moved to block the massive man's entry. "Since when was I allowed to speak to you?"

"Since you ordered we stop. Are we currently standing hip-deep in dead pirates? *That* is when we stop."

"That woman is near death. Unless you'd like to beat her there, lower your gods damned voice and get out of this room."

Orlen's scarred cheek twitched. He backed from the cabin, lowering his shaggy head to clear the doorframe. Dante followed him outdoors. The clouds had cleared and stars reflected from the waters.

"I should know by morning whether she'll wake up," Dante said. "If she does, she may know where the *Ransom*'s gone."

"Away. And we need to follow."

"What if we pass right by in the night? Or worse, *they* run into *us*?"

The norren shook his head. "Josun Joh has spoken to me. The *Ransom* is more than a hundred miles downriver."

"Forgive me for preferring to get the facts from an actual witness."

"Josun Joh is both actual and a witness. Every day we dawdle takes our cousins of the Clan of the Green Lake another day away." Orlen closed his eyes and nodded. "We sail on."

"We're not going anywhere. I'm the one who paid the captain."

Orlen gave him a tight smile and started up the aftercastle stairs. Dante returned to the cabin. A few moments later, shouts rang up from above, followed by the angry thumps of a 350-pound norren descending the stairs.

The woman woke before Dante did, rasping for water. He returned with a full mug. She gulped it down without stopping, then fell back among the bedclothes, gasping. "Who are you?"

"My name's Dante. What happened to your ship?"

Her sunken eyes dwindled further in their sockets. "We were attacked. A war-galley."

"The Bloody Knuckles?"

"They wore red sashes over their hands. I thought it was strange. Bad for one's grip."

He smiled. "You're a fighter?"

She gazed down at her leg, where fresh bandages wrapped her compound fracture. "I doubt that title can still be applied."

"We don't know that yet." Dante retrieved his small knife belt and placed it against the back of his left hand. She stared. He cleared his throat. "This will look weird, but I promise you—"

"You're a sorcerer. A netherman."

He cocked his head. "Would you like to see?"

She nodded. He leaned forward and neatly sliced the bandage from her leg. After a long breath, he cut a fresh line next to the scab on his hand, calling out to the nether. Her thigh was warm to the touch. He shut his mind to everything but the cold flow of shadows and the heat of her broken leg. Tendrils of nether disappeared beneath her skin, prodding, exploring. She hissed through her teeth. Linked to her leg, he could feel its raw edges, its jagged breaks, the mewling pulse of snarled flesh. As gently as he knew how, he guided the torn-up pieces to match the unbroken whole of her other leg.

She arched back into the blankets, sweat popping across her skin. Beneath the red mess of her wound, bone met and hardened together like an icicle that's reached the bottom of the sill. Before the last of Dante's strength gave out, he pulled her punctured flesh together, meat and veins knitting into a thick pink scar.

He dropped, catching himself on his palms. The room smelled like blood and raw beef. For a while, there was no sound but their breathing and the rock of the waves against the boat.

"Don't you dare try to walk on it," he said eventually. "Unless you want me to break the other one."

"What just happened?"

"The resumption of your sword-slinging career. You can thank me by explaining who attacked you, what they wanted, and where they went when they were done."

Her name was Lira Condors. She was, to Dante's mild surprise, a mercenary, hired by the former *Notus* for guard duty. The attack, to the best of her knowledge, had come three days ago. The galley appeared in the night without warning, ramming their stern below the waterline and backbeating its oars to disengage. The *Notus'* captain tried to take them into shore, but arrows rained down on the decks; as sailors jumped overboard, arrows slashed into the black water around them. Lira had gone belowdecks with a handful of survivors, where she hoped to make her stand and wade in pirates' blood, but the ship had been rammed again, and she was struck by a falling crate. She woke to smoke roiling down the hatches. Her leg was broken, the ship was sinking, and everyone else was dead.

Unable to climb or even stand, Lira clawed her way through the rubble to the water pooling at the back of the hold, where she wetted down sheets and used them to mask her mouth against the smoke swirling down from above. For hours, she slept fitfully atop a crate, waking when fire and flooding plunged the ship's bow into the rocky river bottom. The flames went out. Below the hatch, she tried piling up crates into a makeshift staircase, but she was far too tired; she tried tying a thin rope to a knife and hooking it over the edge, but it never lodged deeply enough to hold her weight. Instead, she curled up in the cotton sheets in the dark and the cold, where she resolved to die.

"You saved my life," she finished. "That makes it yours."

"Excellent. I could use another life or two."

A vein stood out from her pale brow. "I'm not kidding. I literally owe you my life. I'm pledging it to you in repayment."

Dante frowned. "Let's not go pledging anything while we're still too dizzy to recite the alphabet."

"Are you saying my life isn't worth having?

"You don't know the first thing about why we're here. We could be sailing off to slaughter every baby in Gask. How would your life look then? Pretty baby-killery, I'd wager."

"What *are* you doing here?"

He looked away. "Hunting down those pirates. Probably to kill them all."

She laughed, a throaty thing that transitioned quickly to a cough. "I'm not going anywhere. And not just because my leg would rebel and declare its independence from my body."

Dante set all this aside and pushed on to whether Lira had an estimate for the Bloody Knuckles' numbers (roughly forty armsmen, but certainly additional oarmen, too, though they were quite possibly slaves); whether the *Ransom* had any distinguishing characteristics (unusually large for a riverboat, with a figurehead composed of two massive horns or tusks); and whether her ship had any warning at all as it approached (no—it was as if the night had disgorged it whole). With that, he nodded, patting her unhurt leg.

"Thank you. This could be a tremendous help."

"Do you really mean to destroy them?"

Dante smiled. "You should see what we have downstairs."

Blays waited outside the cabin, peering through the doorway as Dante exited. "She's awake?"

"And overflowing with useful intelligence about the Bloody

Knuckles." He gazed about the crisp cold morning, searching for the captain. "I think they carry a sorcerer with them."

"Oh? Did she relate stories about a perversely morbid youth with a handsome, dashing friend?"

"The *Ransom* sounds sneakier than the Mallish pox. Maybe it's got an expert crew—and maybe they have someone who can make a whole ship disappear."

After relaying Lira's info, it required little work to convince Varlen to double the night watch. Even so, Dante napped through the day, rising at the red clouds and shadowy cliffs of dusk to sit in the prow. He asked Blays to join his nightwatch; with no discussion whatsoever, Mourn joined them, too, providing blankets and black tea to buttress them against the cold night winds, acts which bought Dante's favor well enough not to tell the norren he was completely unnecessary. Not that the whole business was anything but a hunch—but the river was wide enough and the *Boomer*'s crew knowledgeable enough of it to sail all night, cleaving to the river's middle, sails stricken, propelled by the current.

Dante stared every time a fire gleamed in the darkness, imagining lamps hanging from the prows of enemy galleys slinking through the night. But they turned out to be nothing but campfires, of course, travelers along the road that paralleled the river, or the lanterns of the villages spotting the banks every few miles. The river tricked him, too: the wash of the waves was as regular as the stroke of oars, and for long stretches he strained his ears against the darkness, peering for glimpses of the ship that must be bearing down upon them, its shining ram plowing a foamy furrow through the waves.

"Tell me more about Josun Joh," he said to Mourn one night, as much to break himself from these paranoid visions of midnight fleets as to better understand the norren's relationship to their god. "Does he speak to everyone?"

Mourn glanced up from his papers; he was working on a treatise that the movement of the heavens were fueled by a regular input of sorrow, which was why the gods had created man in the first place. "No."

"Then who does he speak to? Orlen? Vee?"

'Mostly. Not exclusively." He blew on the ink shining on his parchment. "He speaks to travelers sometimes. Scouts. He's sympathetic to anyone alone and away from home, you see."

"When he speaks, is it just to the one person? Or can he be heard by anyone standing nearby?"

"Only the recipient. Why?"

"I'm trying to figure out whether anyone can vouch for what's claimed to be said."

"In other words, could Orlen be making up visitations to advance his own agenda."

"More or less." Dante grinned. "Neither more nor less, actually. Exactly that."

Mourn set down his papers and gazed at the black waters with an expression that was cousin to a frown. "Humans do that, don't they? Put themselves ahead by making up whatever they want about their most sacred beliefs. Cheapening everything with false prophecy. Well, we don't. Not about Josun Joh. When he speaks, it's to save our lives."

Dante's natural instinct was to question that—in fact, to mock it—but there was an earnestness to Mourn that made his claim approach credence. It wasn't that norren never lied, or were too rarefied to consider manipulating others through their beliefs. But there did seem to be a level they just wouldn't stoop to. Perhaps it came from being bullied, enslaved, and slaughtered by the kingdoms of men for so long that the notion of betraying each other's deepest trusts had become as anathema as barbecuing your own newborn. Perhaps they were simply different, baked from a different blend of the nether that rose in men's souls. Whatever the case, it wasn't that Dante could rule out the idea that Orlen could be lying. He just didn't think it was the *most* likely explanation.

He slept at dawn, rising a few hours later to check on Lira, whose face, once paled by the experience of looking Death in the eye, had resumed an olive shade rather close to Dante's own. Varlen had seen no further sign of shipwrecks. That afternoon, they set to port in Honder, a thriving norren city with a healthy human minority, a city that embodied the late days of winter: a cliffside place of mist, frost, and starkly high, cone-capped towers. There, they took on fresh water and the crew swabbed belowdecks while the clan, smelling rather righteous after days cooped downstairs, bathed in the frigid waters, splashing and laughing at each other's hairy bodies. Dante, Blays, and Mourn checked in at a portside tavern for word of the Bloody Knuckles, finding the news matched Orlen's word from Josun Joh—the *Ransom* was last seen far downstream, by all indications bound for Gask's human lands.

That was enough for Blays, who retired for a nap once the stars turned to the small part of the morning. Dante remained in the prow, accompanied by a blanket and tea gone cold. In his heart, he knew he was only feeding his own unreason; the captain had his own sailors out on watch, men plenty used to the noises and darkness of the riverway, less prone to imaginary glimpses of hostile faces or cruelly curved figureheads appearing from the misty drapery. Even so, he remained, watching the waves, using the idle hours to contemplate the ways to let Setteven know the bow was in service of supporters of the norren without exposing that it was specifically Narashtovik doing the supporting.

Hours later, darkness moved on the waters. Dante leaned forward, as if that would bring him any closer to what he was seeing, blanket slipping from his shoulders. The mist had thinned to something more felt than seen, and the gappy clouds showed stars by the dozen. It wasn't a shape *on* the water that was dark: it was a patch of the water itself, blank as a cave. Nearby waves flashed pricks of reflected starlight. Waters had strange textures to them, of course. Dante had spent enough time looking down on Narashtovik's bay to see the ocean, through some function of the light, banded with light and dark strips of blue. At times, parts of the surface nearly boiled with fury while others washed on as flatly as a table.

Running bodies of water, in other words, didn't make a ton of sense to the eye, particularly when you've been staring at them for minutes on end. But after several more minutes, the black patch was demonstrably closer—Dante had fixed its position to a rocky outcropping on the left bank, and while the *Boomer*'s course had taken them nearer the patch, the darkness had moved, too, advancing past the swell of rock.

Against the current.

In the gloom, it was hard to place its precise distance; it was only slightly darker than everything else and its amorphous edges blended with the rippling river. Less than a mile away, though. Perhaps as little as half that, and growing nearer. He'd never worked the nether at such a distance—the further away you got, the clumsier and more draining it became—but he brought the shadows to him nevertheless, condensing them in his hands and unspooling them in a dark thread that reached across the water towards the coming darkness. When the thread intersected the patch, the nether disappeared, fizzling away from his command.

Dante's blood ran cold as the river.

With a focus fine as a needle's tip, he tried again. When the forces intersected, he was ready for the unseen attack, holding fast to his thin thread of nether and probing beyond. The black patch was nether, too: a vast cloud given color and shape, obscuring anything that lurked within it.

He withdrew. He pried open the scab on his hand. The nether filled him like a deep breath after a long dive. He lanced toward the nethereal fog, driving into it with all he had, shredding and rending its ties to the physical world, driving it back to its lairs in the dark places of the world. In its place, he shaped a starburst of cleansing light.

In the ghastly white noon some three hundred yards away, a galley slashed through the sluggish current, light glinting from its heavy bronze ram. Above, two wicked horns curled from its prow.

4

"The *Ransom*!" he shouted. "The *Ransom* is here!"

He needn't have bothered. The night watch had already begun to cry out, first in wordless animal surprise, then in the coded language of a ship at war. Ahead, the *Ransom*'s oarsmen redoubled their beat, thrashing the waters. Varlen's voice boomed through the night. The ship lurched starboard.

Dante pounded up the aftercastle steps. "They're going to ram us!"

"No shit," Varlen rasped.

"Flaming arrows, too."

"Oh shit."

"And a sorcerer."

The captain flung up his pudgy hands. "Lyle's bruised balls! What hell have you sailed us into?"

The *Boomer* continued to veer right. A hundred yards away, the *Ransom* matched course, its captain roaring orders that echoed between the cliffs. Against all instincts of self-preservation, Dante raced down the steps towards the prow, joined along the way by an armed and sleep-angry Blays.

"What's going on?" Blays called.

As he raced by, Dante gestured to the men hauling ropes and canvas through the rigging. "I think those shouts translate to 'We're about to be murdered.'"

He pulled up to the railing. Blays leaned over next to him, gaping at the oncoming vessel. "It looks like we're about to be rammed."

"Yep."

"Then what the fuck are we doing up here? Drawing them a target?"

"We're here to stop them." Water splattered from oars, spilling off the *Ransom*'s glinting ram. The galley closed, impossibly fast yet horribly slow. A lone silhouette ran from the rail of its high topdeck. A voice bellowed through the darkness; the oars retracted from the water, slipping smoothly through the slots in the hull. The ship hurtled closer and closer, as massive as the wing of a castle. Dante grabbed hard to the rails.

The *Ransom* gashed by mere feet away, near enough that anyone on its deck could have leapt down to the lower *Boomer*. Its crew was braced for impact, though, and Dante didn't see a single enemy face as the ship's slick wooden hull whisked by, stirring the cold freshwater air. The *Boomer*'s crew groaned in relief at the miss. The topdeck of the *Ransom* blossomed with a string of tiny orange fires.

"Get down!" Dante shoved Blays to the deck and followed him down.

Blays socked him in the shoulder. "Ask next time!"

Lines of light creased the sky. The flaming arrows whacked into the deck, slashing through the sails. One thumped into the prow feet behind Blays. A man fell screaming from the rigging and thudded on the deck.

Men with buckets rushed to douse the flames. The warriors of the Clan of the Nine Pines swarmed from below, bows in hand. Others carried heavy furs taken from the walls of their yurts which they draped over the railings. The archers took up behind the makeshift screens, pelting the men on the *Ransom* with return fire. Dante narrowed his eyes and focused the nether. Flame leapt up from the rear of the enemy vessel. It was quenched before Dante made it five steps toward the stern.

The two boats carried their opposite ways, firing arrows back and forth across the widening gap. The *Ransom*'s oars dipped back in the water and the ship began the slow business of circling around. Dante neither saw nor felt further sign of the Bloody Knuckles' sorcerer. By the time the *Ransom* came about and took up chase, the two boats had fallen out of bow range; the enemy still took the occasional shot, gauging range with their fiery arrows.

"Ugly," Blays said.

"What?"

"The deck of this ship once they start boarding it."

"Suppose I'd better fetch my sword." Dante started for the staircase down. "Oh, don't forget. Leave at least one of them alive to torture the slaves' location out of."

Blays' mouth quirked. "Do you have to put it like that?"

The planks were slick with water, scarred with scorches, and prickled with arrow shafts. Dante hadn't been belowdecks in a couple days and the stench of sweat was thick as mud. Torn-apart yurts scattered the floor. Clansmen loaded their arms with swords and spears and thudded upstairs. Dante found his sword in a chest near the rear and returned to the surface. Arrows whispered from the norren archers, who'd relocated from the larboard railing to that on the back of the aftercastle. Others hid at the aft's base, the wooden rise sheltering them from enemy fire, and emerged to batter down any fresh flames with their furs. Blays was there too, along with Mourn, who carried a curved, single-edged blade.

"You might want to get belowdecks," Dante said.

Mourn glanced up from rubbing his sword with a rag. "Why would I want that?"

"To avoid anything unpleasant. Such as dying."

"I would rather die than hide downstairs to listen to the screams of my clan."

"That's the kind of thing that sounds a lot less noble when you're moaning in the blood with a sucking chest wound."

Mourn cocked his head, meeting Dante's eyes. "I'm not trying to be noble. I would literally prefer to die fighting for my friends and blood-family. Why would you suggest I wouldn't? Do you think I would enjoy crying in the dark?"

"Forget it." Dante climbed the steps to get a glimpse of the *Ransom*. It was closing rapidly, oars circling through the water while the *Boomer* relied on currents and a rather slack wind. Not that they were trying to outrun the Bloody Knuckles, so far as he knew. In fact, he had the impression that appearing to flee at full sail was a mere ploy to keep their would-be predators on the hunt. To avoid the ram too, he supposed. He was no admiral.

The next few minutes were confusing ones. Dante waited behind an open door while the archers fired and crew strained with the rigging. Three men jogged down the aftercastle steps bearing a grimacing norren, an arrow projecting from his ribs.

"Lay him on the deck!" Dante rushed into the open deck. The men stopped, glancing between each other as if he were a stranger in the street. Dante circled in front of them. "Put him down, gods damn it."

They stretched the wounded man on the damp planks. Dante knelt, stripping the norren's shirt away from the arrow buried in the side of his furry chest. Blood slid to the wood. The man's eyes were open and moving, but he did no more than grimace as Dante tested the arrow, then yanked it wetly from the wound. Dante slung it aside and clamped his hands to the bleeding. Within moments, the blood stanched, scabbing.

Dante rose, wiping his hands on his pants. "Get him below."

"Will he be okay?" one of the clan warriors asked.

"He's less fit to fight than a dropped baby bird, but he'll be fine."

The norren knelt to offer the wounded man his shoulder. They limped towards the stairs. On the castle, men shouted. The *Ransom* loomed above the railing, oars pulled in as it swung alongside the smaller craft. Hooks and grapnels arced from the pirate vessel, clunking into the *Boomer*'s planks and rails. Sword-bearing norren charged to the railing to hack at the ropes drawing the two ships together. Arrows whisked from above, dropping two warriors and driving the others back.

Men with knuckles wrapped in red cloth vaulted down the eight-foot rise between the ships. The norren met them, heavy swords hammering the pirates to the deck. Sabers and short swords flashed in the enemy's hands. Norren dropped along the line. Blays charged a tall, ragged-haired man, intercepting the enemy's incoming thrust with his left-hand blade, flicking his wrist and elbow in an upward snap. The parry deflected the pirate's sword past Blays' shoulder; Blays' right-hand weapon buried itself in the enemy's gut. Dante moved to Blays' flank. A spear jabbed at his ribs. He battered it down with a clumsy strike, then thrust out his empty hand. The nether punched straight through the spearman's neck. He collapsed into the railing.

Nether speared down from the upper vessel, knocking three clan warriors from their feet. Blood pattered the deck. Above, a man in a long coat with a single stripe of hair atop his shaved head raised his hand in an eagle's claw. Dante fell back from the clanging melee, lashing a bolt of shadows at the chest of the man in the coat. The sorcerer's face blanked in shock. He jerked backwards, blasting raw nether at the incoming force, dashing it into the night. His gaze snapped to Dante. A rush of piercing energy followed. Dante knocked it aside with a wedge of shadows. They struggled this way for some seconds, needles of nether twining around one another and boiling away into nothing.

Dante eased his resistance, falling back a step as the other man's dark tendrils wormed forward. The man in the coat smiled. Dante lashed out for the *Ransom*'s railing instead, pelting the man with a hail of hard splinters. His focus collapsed. Dante drove forward, lancing the man's heart with a bolt of raw force.

To his right, a blade flicked at his face. Blays intercepted with crossed swords, scissoring the enemy weapon into the planks, then rolled his forearms, swinging his blades through a tight circle and snapping them into the attacker's jacket-padded collarbones. As the man staggered, Dante took him under the ribs with his sword.

Humans and norren flopped and bled. No member of the Bloody Knuckles remained standing on the *Boomer*. The norren warriors sheathed their swords and clambered up the ropes marrying the two vessels, archers covering them from below. Dante climbed up, too, but the *Ransom*'s topdeck was nearly empty. As two small skirmishes broke out, a handful of men with red-wrapped knuckles fled belowdecks or leapt off the side.

"Think you've got this?" Dante said to Blays.

"Considering I've got thirty sword-wielding norren monsters on my side, I'm going to say yes."

Blays raced to catch up with the pursuing norren. Dante slid back down the rope to the barge, treating the wounded until his command of the nether faltered and the shadows refused to venture from their crannies. His nerves felt as raw-scraped as a fresh hide. By the time the battle finished, the five surviving members of the Bloody Knuckles matched the total number of Nine Pines dead. Their original numbers had been roughly equal, but that was the nature of armed conflict, particularly in smaller scale, where an advantage in strength, size, and the sudden removal of the enemy's nethermancer could be exploited for an overwhelming victory. The man in the long coat had been the cornerstone of the Bloody Knuckles' terror. There were likely just a few hundred men and women in all of Gask with any real talent in the use of nether or ether, and mere dozens with the skill to match the dead man's. Combined with the pirates' willingness for stark and sudden violence, it was no wonder they'd terrorized the local waterways for over a decade.

Orlen's response to the pirates was no less violent. The few who tried to hide among the oar-slaves were quickly ratted out, then just as swiftly executed and flung over the side of the galley. The five survivors were brought to the *Boomer*, where the deck was still being cleared of bodies and swabbed of blood. A man with a shaved head and a bleeding, smashed nose was forced to kneel in front of Orlen. The norren chief's heavy sword hung from his hand.

"I'm going to ask once, because the question is so simple failing to understand it will tell me you have no brains to spill. One month ago, you took possession of a group of norren of the Clan of the Green Lake. Where did you take them?"

The man hawked blood on the planks. "Their rightful owners."

Orlen's sword flashed in the torchlight. Pink matter spattered the deck. Orlen blinked at his sword in surprise.

"Oh. Brains! I was wrong." He beckoned to two warriors, who thrust another pirate to his knees. Orlen stepped forward. "Where did you take the norren of the Clan of the Green Lake?"

The man tried to wriggle away. He toppled, crashing to the floor. "Dollendun. One of the beefers there. Uglier than dysentery. Name's Perrigan. Don't know from there."

"Thank you," Orlen nodded. He slit the man's throat. The man gaped at him, eyes bright with betrayal. While he bled out, the warriors took their blades to the other three survivors, dumping their remains into the river.

"Seems wrong," Blays muttered.

"I know," Dante said. "Should have at least interrogated them properly."

"I'm talking about the part where they were butchered like hogs. Treasonous hogs. Hogs who tried to stick their hog noses up the farmer's daughter's skirt."

"They were murderers."

"We don't know they *all* were. There must be *some* good pirates. Maybe we executed the guy who wanted them to change their wicked ways."

Varlen cleared his throat. His face was haggard and sooty. "We got a few things to figure out before weighing anchor. The *Ransom*, for instance—"

"Will be scuttled," Orlen said.

"Hold on a minute. That thing is a proper galley of war. You could threaten a barony with it. You taken a look at the old lady you're standing on?" He gestured to the *Boomer*'s slashed sails, its torched canvas and smashed rails and bloodstained decks. "I'll be lucky to break even from what you paid me. The point of pirate-busting is to thrust your hands into their deep and jingly pockets."

"Thrust away. The ship itself was a vessel for killers and slavers, who can continue to enjoy it as their tomb."

Varlen rolled his thick lips together. "You hairy bastard. This is dumber than a cotton bottle."

Dante wasn't surprised. As a whole, norren tended to treat wealth with indifference or disdain, particularly the clans, who were perfectly able to fend for themselves. When it came to the galley slaves waiting below the *Ransom*'s decks, however, he had no idea which way Orlen would break. He could see the norren chief, without a whiff of hypocrisy, ordering their slaughter as accomplices; just as likely, he would treat them as his most honored guests, leading them by the hand into the daylight and striking off their chains.

Instead, Orlen went to bed, leaving Vee, Varlen, Dante, and Blays to hash out an agreement that the slaves be freed and offered the option to sign on with the captain's crew; he'd lost three men to stray arrows. The families of the dead crew, meanwhile, would be compensated with whatever was found on the boat, minus half to be divided among the former slaves to give them a chance to make it once the *Boomer* made port in Dollendun. It was the kind of compromise that left both parties mad. Vee was talked out of whippings for the slaves (she considered the lashes cleansing, for the slaves' own good). Meanwhile, Varlen demanded all the *Ransom*'s wealth; Blays reminded him he'd had more than a little help wiping out the Bloody Knuckles, the most-hated local raiders of the last generation, and that by the way, greed had been the Knuckles' chief motivation, too.

By the end, Dante was frustrated, impatient, and exhausted, but helped search the captured ship anyway, both to ensure the agreement was honored (the ship's crew was noticeably more sullen than before the battle, giving the norren long looks of barely-concealed resentment) and to make a personal search of the captain's cabin, where he overturned drawers, smashed open chests, and knocked on walls for secret compartments until Blays asked him what the hell he was doing, which took several minutes longer than Dante expected.

"Somebody knew something." Dante stepped back from a bolted-down desk, surveying the scree of papers, gold-plated trinkets, and strings of what he suspected were knuckle bones hanging from the wall. "If the *Ransom* just attacked every ship heading downstream, the traders would have dug themselves a new river years ago."

"Think somebody tipped them off?"

"Unless Josun Joh is playing both sides, how else would they know to attack the *Boomer*?"

"So you're looking for evidence of this little theory," Blays said.

"Yes."

"Hard proof that someone told them we were after them and let them know how to find us."

Dante set down a curved ornate knife and stared at Blays. "Why the hell else would I be tearing the room apart? Should I go try yelling at their corpses instead?"

"Oh, just thought you might be interested in this."

Blays passed him a thick, grainy piece of paper, folded twice. Inside was a sloppy, almost childish drawing of a barge, wide and single-masted. It could have been any of the cargo vessels plying the river, but its prow extended into a figurehead of an owl, wings swept back, preparing to launch into flight.

"What are they doing with a drawing of the *Boomer*?"

Blays nodded. "And who drew it?"

There was, of course, no signature. No words whatsoever. The only way to determine the sketch's authorship would be to force everyone in a 500-mile radius to draw another barge and compare the output to this child's scrawl on a fuzzy sheet of pulp. In practical terms, that plan was only slightly better than attempting to snag the sun in a net and putting it in his pocket so Dante could have toast wherever he went.

They found nothing else of interest. The galley-slaves, a mixture of norren and human men, were transferred to the suddenly crowded *Boomer*. The *Ransom* was made to drop anchor. Clansmen piled the bodies of the Bloody Knuckles in its hold, spilled oil over them, and splashed its topdeck to boot. The grapnels joining the two ships were severed. The *Boomer* weighed anchor, letting the current carry it away. In the first light of dawn, a woman of the Nine Pines ascended the steps of the stern, bent her bow, and sent a flaming arrow winging toward the *Ransom*. It snapped into the topdeck, fire dwindling until it looked like it would wink out completely: then an orange wall flared across the former slaver. Thick white smoke roiled into the sky.

Dante emerged from his cabin late that afternoon. Mourn quickly informed him both Orlen and Lira were waiting to speak to him. Dante drank some tea, stretched the soreness from his muscles, and went to see Lira. Her cabin's scent had the moist, mushroomy pall of the wounded, but she looked better already, a touch of pink to her broad cheeks.

"You killed them without me," she said. Accusation gleamed from her eyes.

"Would you have liked us to drag them in here for you to club from your bed?"

"You could have brought me out to watch."

"There were no guarantees we'd even win. If just one of them had broken through, you would have discovered that steel tastes a lot like horrible pain."

"I've been cut before." She gazed out the cabin's round window.

"I hoped to be healed when you caught them. To pay them back. And you."

"The info you gave me about the attack on your ship is the reason we're here talking instead of sitting at the bottom of the river waving to each other for eternity."

"Still. I'll pay you back."

He folded his arms. "Enough of this 'debt of honor' nonsense. You don't owe me for saving you any more than you owe everyone else on this ship for not stabbing you in your sleep." He gestured in the vague direction of the other cabins. "Anyway, it was Blays who made us go to the wreck."

"Then my debts just doubled."

"For the love of—"

"Don't think of my life as dedicated to you. Think of it as dedicated to goodness. Your act deserves praise. Support. Protection. My debt's not to you, but the ideal your act of rescue embodies."

Dante narrowed his eyes, seeing her in a light completely separate from the waning rays angling through the window. "I'm not all good."

She leaned back into her blankets, weary. "Then may my devotion be a double-edged sword that inspires you to do better."

His reasons for objecting weren't yet shaped well enough to hammer into words, so he left it at that. It wasn't that he disagreed with the premise of a personal loyalty that ran so deep you'd put your own life in harm's way. He supposed he'd done that for Blays. More than once, in fact. Often enough that Dante's just afterlife would feature a full servant-crew composed entirely of Blayses. Meanwhile, he might not give up his *life* for Cally, but he'd probably give up a leg or an arm. His left arm, at the very least. For semi-friends like Mourn, he'd sacrifice a finger or two. Even for strangers—a woman being beaten in the street, say—he'd risk a black eye or a bloody nose, although he reserved the right to complain about it later.

But Lira hardly knew him. If she were serious, in a sense she already *had* committed suicide for him, submerging her identity and desires beneath a sea of principle. He and Blays protected and fought for each other because they believed in the same causes. Sure, the original cause they'd fought for had been basic self-preservation, but that was a pretty good one, he thought. On a deep-down level, Lira's desire to rid herself of her own personal goals disturbed him.

He headed belowdecks to snag Blays and find Orlen among the close, smelly yurts. Orlen insisted they head back upstairs to the foremost section of the bow, which aside from the ship's cabins was perhaps the one spot on the *Boomer* with any major privacy: not only could they see anyone approaching, but the rustle of water around the prow cushioned their words from anyone wandering too close.

Orlen sat on his heels and gestured them to do the same. "I think it's time to clear the air."

"Or at least to choke it with a different brand of smoke," Vee said.

"There aren't to be any more secrets."

"Certainly *less* secrets," Vee said. "We might inadvertently maintain secrets we weren't aware were secret."

Blays stared dumbly. "I hope the melted substance in my ears is wax."

"In short," Orlen said, "it's time we pool resources. Work together. Achieve as one."

"I'd complain that it's about time," Dante said, "but it took so long to arrive I'm too puzzled to resent you."

Vee screwed up her orange eyes and gazed up at the gently flapping sails, which had been restored, with gruesome stitching, to an approximation of their pre-battle wholeness. "There are two reasons. At least two reasons. We may have others."

"First," Orlen said, "for the Clan of the Nine Pines, trust needs more than a handshake. I'm sure this seems quaint to you, or a series of pointless hurdles, but that is because when you look at yourselves, you see Dante the Noble and Blays the Also Noble. But when we look, we see two of the species that has enslaved so many of our own."

Vee nodded. "Better to look like the hole of an ass than to look from behind the bars of a cage."

Dante tapped his thumbs together. "That's all well and good, but wasn't the business at Cling enough to earn your trust?"

Orlen frowned, rippling his beard. "For blackmailing a mayor?

Anyone can do that. Not everyone can save our ship from being rammed."

"Specifically," Vee said, "only you did."

"And fighting alongside the clan is, in a sense, to become a part of the clan."

Vee nodded again. "But only in a sense."

Blays twirled his hand in a let's-move-it-along gesture. "Let's get to the second reason before we forget what we're talking about and who we are."

"We're about to pass into human lands," Orlen said. "We'll need humans to move us forward."

"Our trust will still be circumscribed," Vee said.

Blays cocked his head. "Well, you should at least get it drunk first."

"What more can we do?" Dante said. "Should I put the king of Gask in a headlock and knuckle his scalp until he renounces norren slavery forever? We're here to help."

Orlen nodded, eyes closed. "So you keep repeating. We're very grateful. There is no question of your sincerity."

"The question is whether Narashtovik might be angling for independence of its own," Vee said.

Dante smiled in disbelief. Not at the question itself. The question was good enough that Dante had considered it several times himself. Cally's entire support of norren independence stemmed from a single promise to a single norren who'd helped Cally reclaim his seat at the head of the Council of Narashtovik. That debt deserved repayment, no doubt, but if that *were* the only source of Cally's motivation, the scale of his repayment was somewhere between generous and a level of insanity normally associated with bottling your own urine.

Maybe the old man just believed in liberty. In Cally's own cynical way, he did believe in the principle of self-rule. At the very least, he thought it was pretty stupid to decide rulership of an empire based on which blueblood's family tree had the most tightly-snarled and inbred branches. But neither was Cally a banner-waving proponent of the islands south of Mallon, where they appointed leaders based on some sort of common vote—when the matter had once come up in passing at a council meeting, Cally had dismissed the notion by asking "Why not just put a pig in charge?"

In other words, Cally wasn't leading the charge for norren freedom on the basis of principle alone. To further muddy the waters, the old man bristled whenever some new tax or formality had to be paid to the palace at Setteven, forcibly dispelling any illusions he held of Narashtovik's autonomy. Dante had no doubt this resentment fueled Cally's dedication to freeing the norren from their sometimes literal yoke. And if that were true, it was easy to imagine Cally had another motive in mind: that if the Norren Territories gained independence, Narashtovik could easily follow.

"Outrageous," Dante said to Vee's accusation. "Cally's done nothing but help the norren."

Orlen glanced between the two humans. "It is settled."

"Great," Blays said. "Then in honor of our newfound mutual trust and appreciation, I'd like to let you know one of your people is a dirty, rotten turncoat."

Vee didn't move, didn't even lean forward, but her presence seemed to increase in the same way the full moon grows larger the closer it comes to the horizon. "If this is a joke, human humor is stranger than the beasts that wash up from the deep sea."

"It's no joke. Except maybe one of those cosmic ones."

"Then be very, very precise about what you say next."

The corners of Blays' mouth tucked in a subtle way that usually presaged the breaking of objects and sometimes people. Without removing his eyes from Vee's, he reached into his pocket, removed the drawing, and smoothed it on the deck, holding it in place against the steady breeze of the boat's passage.

"We found this in the captain's quarters on the *Ransom*," Blays said. "Either Banning hedged his bets and warned the Bloody Knuckles they were about to have to rename themselves the Bloody Spinal Stumps, or someone from the clan wanted to give them an extra-sporting chance."

Vee surged forward. Orlen barred an arm across her large chest. Her face hung before Blays like an angry moon.

"Excuse her," Orlen said. "She is a staunch advocate of Vorgas' Three C's."

"Vorgas' Three C's?" Dante said.

"Clarity of thought, clarity of speech, and crushing the skulls of those who slander your clan."

"Then let's add a fourth: Considerately not assaulting your dear, dear allies."

Vee relaxed to her original position. "Your proposition is not a binary either/or. There is also the possibility someone saw you bumbling around Cling, recognized the clan, and surmised our purpose."

"Fine," Blays said. "It could be literally anyone, up to and including me and my evil twin I've never met. That's a very useful way of honing in on who actually did it."

"We will keep our eyes open," Orlen said.

Vee restrained a sigh. "And conduct our own investigation. It will have to be a passive one until more information allows us to turn aggressive."

Dante nodded. "Unless there are any more accusations or fists to be thrown, what, then, do you have for us?"

Orlen glanced over his shoulder at the wide gray river. "Where this river passes through Dollendun marks the border between the Norren Territories and Old Gask. Are you familiar with the border?"

"Big black line, right?" Blays said.

"Very invisible, in fact, but people behave like their nightmare's own nightmare waits for any who cross from one side to the other. Norren do, anyway. Humans are free to cross the river as they please."

"So you've enlisted us for any duties on the human side."

"Which we believe will be considerable. This man Perrigan is a beefer, meaning a trader of meat, meaning a dealer of norren slaves. We'll need you to find out who he sold our cousins to."

Dante scratched the base of his neck. His hair was getting long again. "Do you expect that will be difficult?"

"How should we know?" Vee said. "Do you think we've met him before? Perhaps he is a braggart, and will tell you for the swell of telling you that he is a man who owns other, lesser men. Alternately, the secret of a client could be a thing he wouldn't reveal on pain of pain."

"Again, very helpful to have such hard details," Blays said.

"Now we know he could react in any conceivable way."

Orlen ran his thumb along his scarred cheek. "We'll send clan-warriors with you to pose as servants. They can help with any unexpected situations."

"Or attempts to murder you," Vee said.

"We'll take Mourn," Dante said.

"We will send Gala, too. She is one of our finest warriors."

"I think Mourn will be sufficient."

Orlen pressed his palms together and glared at Dante over his fingertips. "One servant among two men of means will diminish you both. Gala goes, too."

Dante held up his hands, already regretting being brought into their outer circle of trust. "Fine."

"Good. We are scheduled to arrive in Dollendun late tomorrow morning."

"That's it?" Blays said.

Orlen gave another of his monkish nods. "There is only ever so much."

Dante stood, knees popping. He wandered with Blays along the railing, stopping once they were out of easy earshot of the norren or any idling crew.

"That last thing didn't even make sense," Blays said. "And did you get the impression they were pushing another babysitter on us?"

"Guaranteed. They still don't trust us."

"Maybe they're right not to. I've always wondered why Cally was so interested in this whole business. The only reason I've never pushed him on it is because he's finally doing something I agree with."

They hunted down Mourn to bring him up to speed and to pump him for more information about the border city of Dollendun. The Clan of the Nine Pines almost always stuck to the wilds, hunting the hills and fishing the lakes, but the clans frequently delegated unpartnered young men to roles as wandering scouts, both for the specific purpose of keeping up on the doings of rival clans and for the much broader aim of seeing whatever there was to see. As it turned out, Mourn had also spent a couple weeks in Dollendun, which was two more weeks than Orlen or Vee had spent there. According to Mourn, it was, for the most part, your typical large city: a scab of nobles, wealthy merchants, and shipping tycoons crusted over a great messy wound of laborers and peons.

The difference was Dollendun was literally split down the middle, norren to the Eastern Shore and humans to the Western, and the only norren allowed to cross westward were slaves—in other words, some tenth of the total populace of Dollendun, a figure Blays found incredulous ("Why don't they just flex their biceps, pop their bonds, and start smashing skulls?") and Dante found dubious. With that many slaves running around, how could you tell which norren on the Western Shore were owned and which ones were free?

Mourn explained. Slaves were branded on their right cheeks. All norren citizens were lawfully obligated to restrict their beards to an inch in length so the slaves couldn't comb them over their brands. Any norren man with a longer beard could be arrested on sight and (in the best-case scenario) deported to the eastern banks. Permits were allocated to allow norren leaders, traders, and diplomats to handle their business on the human side, but there were never more than a few dozen permits active at any one time, and even the permanent ones—most were day passes—had to be renewed annually at a steep fee. And yes, free norren had tried to thwart this system by branding themselves, wandering the Western Shore, and passing as slaves out on the errands of their masters, but all brands were registered at the Chattelry Office. Meanwhile, norren sporting unknown brands were eligible to be captured and held in the Office's cells, and if they weren't claimed within a month (at the cost of a claimant fee and, naturally, a second fee for registry of one's brand), to be auctioned at the monthly market to the benefit of Dollendun's coffers.

In short, challenge the system at the risk of your eternal freedom.

Other than being regularly invaded by Chattelry Office agents in pursuit of escaped slaves, the Eastern Shore *was* essentially left to its own affairs, however, meaning it bore but a superficial resemblance to the standard human sprawl of urban trade, labor, appointed offices, and law enforcement. Rulers were determined through typical norren process, i.e. their murky theo-philosophical sparring grounds. But East Dollendun was special among norren cities in that it was the only one to be truly *massive* in the way Setteven was massive, or Bressel, or (of late) Narashtovik itself. This allowed for a phenomenon unique among all the Norren Territories and thus probably the world: the Nulladoon.

"Oh come on, you can't just stop there," Blays frowned. "You wouldn't be telling us if it wasn't important."

"It would take too long to explain," Mourn said.

"We won't reach Dollendun for nearly a day."

"That's what I just said."

"Then be brief," Dante said. "It might be important."

Mourn screwed up his face. "It's like...a game of dice."

"That doesn't sound that involved."

"That runs the city. And instead of the exchange of money, it determines the exchange of items and nulla."

Blays glanced away from the grassy riverbanks. "Nulla?"

"How can I explain the Nulladoon if you don't even know—" Mourn interrupted himself to sigh and lean his heavy arms upon the *Boomer*'s railing. "It means...craft-favors. IOUs, sort of, but instead of money, it can be whatever the norren making the promise is famous for—swords, tapestries, dances."

"Dances?"

"I told you, it's complicated."

Even this bare attempt to summarize the Nulladoon put Mourn into one of his moods. Dante had spent enough time in the territories to know what nulla were, but he had little inclination to attempt to wheedle, cajole, or flatter Mourn into explaining exactly what the Nulladoon was, particularly when belowdecks smelled like bandaged blood and infection, evidence of nearly a dozen wounded warriors suffering from everything from scrapes and bruises to deep sword wounds and one broken arm. By the time Dante finished treating them, the warrior's arm was free of its sling. Stitches were trimmed from slashed arms and bellies. Sweaty brows cooled and relaxed. If it came down to it, he expected each one could lift a sword by the time they debarked in Dollendun.

The leadup to their arrival was an uneventful passage of forested shorelines. Through the bare branches, metal clanged and axes chunked. After the frost, bitter winds, and shadowed pockets of snow on their long descent from the hills, the hard, cool sunlight of Dollendun felt like a tepid relief. So too did the return to a proper city, even a foreign one. Docks choked the river on both its east and west, and the smoke of countless chimneys mingled into a single cloud above the river, but otherwise the shores of Dollendun looked like two different countries. On the west, wood cottages sprouted on the outskirts, often built right on to the walls of preexisting houses. Past a high stone defensive wall, the buildings leapt to three and four stories in height, crowned by the high, snow-shedding peaks typical of Gaskan construction. Houses stood wall-to-wall, so straight and narrow an arrow shot through one window might well pass straight through another on the far side. Except on the hastiest houses, those that leaned like beer-blinded longshoremen, the windows were ovals, ringed by dark wood that stood out from the blond pinewood walls and occasional splash of whitewash. Three hills stood at a reproachful distance from the urban crush, lush green courtyards visible between round-towered manors of clean white limestone.

There were no such manors on the eastern side. No defensive walls, either. In fact, there appeared to be very little of stone at all, aside from some homes dug straight into the sides of the hills. Rather than cottages and shacks, the space between the surrounding meadows and the city proper consisted of tents, yurts, and other nomadic repositories. Sophisticated multi-family shelters with patterns and illustrations stitched into their oiled leather sides mixed with the crudest of pine-branch lean-tos. Further in, the round-windowed wooden houses rarely rose above two stories.

"Hey Mourn, your people's side looks like shit," Blays said.

The skin crinkled around Mourn's bovine eyes. "Hey Blays, your people's side looks like it uses the people from my side as beasts of burden."

"I'm not criticizing."

"Well, I am."

Varlen and crew guided the *Boomer* to a dock big enough to tie the barge up. The clan had all but completely unloaded their gear by the time Dante finished reexplaining the situation to the stout captain, who was affronted that Dante couldn't be more specific about how long they'd spend in town than "a day or several." The river smelled of sewage and mud, sludgy vegetables and used cooking oil.

To preserve the ruse they were a common barley barge with the usual assortment of random passengers, Dante stayed onboard along with Blays, Mourn, Lira, and Gala, who stood just under six and a half feet tall—practically a dwarf by norren standards. Despite her stony muscles, she was almost thin, too. With the rest of the Clan of the Nine Pines departing through the streets to camp out on the edges of town, the *Boomer* shoved off, tacking across the river to tie up at another dock and discharge its remaining passengers. Dante and crew donned hooded winter cloaks and descended the pier to the streets of Western Dollendun.

The city was, at a glance, no different from all major cities. Men and women rushed along with a haste that seemed absurdly self-important to the outside eye, particularly when most of them were probably on their way to hold foolish discussions over too much tea or to broker business deals they would regret the moment they lay down to sleep. It was the sort of jostling, steaming hustle that exasperates everyone involved, leading to behavior that ranges from the annoying: people slinging elbows; carriage wheels throwing mud; what self-important pricks—to the potentially lethal: the reckless, wild-eyed speed of the horse-teams, who could easily crush a man if he didn't hear the driver's shouts, and who drove as if arriving thirty seconds early to their appointments would make the difference between laughing from the castle's roof and dying in the shit-caked gutters. Annoying or outright dangerous, these conditions struck Dante with equal irritation.

Dollendun was, in short, exactly the same and exactly as different as every big city in the world. It was unique in its particular blend of spices, smoke, and waste. It was identical in its bustle, the urban pace someone from nowhere would dismiss as a fine place to visit but not live, while visitors from other big cities would peg as interesting, in its own quaint ways, but not half so much as wherever *they* were from. In Dante's case, it wasn't as large as Bressel or as historically, almost mythically charged as Narashtovik. Still, it was a *city* in the way all non-cities aren't, and he breathed the air as if it were the vapors of a cleansing tonic, observing shops and citizens as if they held secrets he'd never uncover. By the time Blays selected an inn entirely at random, Dante was already regretting a departure which would inevitably come too soon.

The three-story structure's eaves and cornices were heavy with elaborate Gaskan Old Empire leaf-carvings, but the inside was drafty and stained. Perfect for maintaining appearances on a limited budget. Dante and Blays got pleasantly drunk, which is what one does in new cities, particularly when plying locals and regular passers-by for information, but learned nothing revelatory about Perrigan the beefer, other than that he resented the slang term for his profession and that he lived on Sounden Hill. Dante woke with the sun nearly full overhead. His mouth tasted like soured beer. Mourn watched reproachfully from the common room, munching on bread and celery. Dante dispatched a letter of introduction to one of the messengers trotting up and down the boardwalks, then returned upstairs to wake Blays, a task every bit as dangerous as wandering into a pirate's ambush.

Their subterfuge was simple. They'd pose as Mallish aristocrats resettled in Gask in the hopes of trebling their fortunes shipping tea from the valleys of Gallador to the busy southern ports. All they needed was labor, which they'd heard the norren provided in spades. Perrigan replied via messenger that evening for a meet on the following day.

"It's been so long since we've been somewhere proper," Blays said that night, as if he'd needed a full day to absorb the shift from wind-swept grass and birded hills to bustling city. "The clan won't mind if we dawdle on their cousins, will they? What's three more days in chains to people who expect to spend their whole lives in them?"

Mourn gazed over the foamy tower of his beer. "If Vee heard you, she'd split you like a log. Not a log she liked, either."

"Well, Vee's not here, is she?"

"I'm making a decision in my capacity as leader." Dante glanced at Gala, who hadn't said four words since they'd stepped onto the docks. "I declare this beer is for enjoying, not arguing. We'll see what happens tomorrow."

Beyond the greasy oval windows, wagons hauled grain and

clay and stone and hay to the houses on the hills.

The carriage arrived on schedule the following noon. Mourn and Gala held the doors while Dante and Blays seated themselves on the hardwood bench. The norren gave slight bows, then circled to the back of the carriage and stepped onto the running boards. The vehicle's body groaned and lowered under their weight.

"Why can't they sit in here?" Dante said.

Blays peered at him from the corners of his eyes. "Because they'd squish us to death? Oh yes, and they're slaves?"

"It was rhetorical." Out the screened window, humans came and went, hopping over piles of horseshit and stopping outside of teahouses to snag passing friends by the collars and grin in their faces. Around them, silent stooped men carried sacks and letters, faces grim and grimy. Norren strode on errands, too, bearded lighthouses among the seas of humans. The giants' cheeks were cut close or shaved bald, showing shiny pink lines, letters and simple icons.

The carriage swung uphill. Gala and Mourn stepped down to trot along behind. A paper fluttered from a high window. In a narrow gap between houses, a norren sat in the mud, clutching his bloody face. The road leveled out. The crush of structures cleared out in favor of wide lawns, green shoots pushing past the brown of winter. Dante pressed against the carriage door as the driver swung onto a cobbled road. Ahead, the pavement reeled straight toward a white stone manor that could have served as the keep of some towns. Whip-thin trees lined the path and the house's front, their branches blue-green and needly.

A bald man in outdated formal wear received them in the echoing foyer. Mourn and Gala were seen to the servants' quarters. Sunlight gushed through the windows, illuminating swirling dustmotes. Two fires snapped in the manor's central hall. Dante accepted a padded red seat in front of one hearth, where he warmed his hands and gazed across the wall tapestries: stitched portraits of middle-aged men, most of whom showed grass-green eyes and regally aquiline noses. Their beards were a timeline of high Gaskan style: trim, pointy triangles; then aggressive, full-face snarls that would have driven off a bear; finally the cut of the previous generation, square sideburns which continued perpendicular from the earlobe to connect to a straight, manicured mustache.

"Warm enough?" Behind them, a tall, green-eyed man clicked across the stone, his padded coat clinging smartly to his chest. His coat was green as his eyes and divided into neat squares by glossy black stitching.

Dante rose. "Lord Perrigan."

"Lords Winslowe and Lionstones," he greeted Dante and Blays in turn. Dante quashed his frown at the names Blays had given. "I'm honored you'd look to me on your expansion to Gask."

"The loftiness of your reputation competes with the peaks of the Junholds," Blays said, entirely straight-faced.

Talk turned for some minutes to the common ground of all wealthy strangers—whether they enjoyed their trip, had they yet been to Dollendun's Frozen Gardens, the shortsighted taxation policies of their respective rulers. Perrigan's self-deprecating discourse on the nature of success in business, which he compared to a blind shepherd repeatedly driving his flock off a cliff, then crowing in triumph after one of his fallen sheep broke open a vein of gold, was charming enough that Dante temporarily forgot the lord had built that fortune on the literal backs (as well as hands, legs, and sinews) of hundreds if not thousands of norren slaves.

"Fifteen or twenty," Blays said once the topic finally turned to their own business, specifically the number of laborers their tea-growing operation would require.

Perrigan raised his thin black brows. "Then you hardly need even my modest expertise. You could fill that order at the back-market on your way home."

"That's just for the initial outlay," Blays said. "It's all about feasibility, you know. The sustainability of the strategy. We *could* wait another three or five years and plunge whole-barrel into the operation, but who knows how diluted the market will look by then, you know? Whereas if we start now, well, the leverage cranks itself."

"Of course."

"In which case we'll need a regular supply of bodies," Dante said.

Perrigan gazed across the faces of his ancestors on the wall tapestries. "Strong backs are always in demand, of course. But we may be able to arrange an annual contract."

"Not all of our investors are as confident as we are. We were hoping to make a strong initial splash."

"Nothing opens a man's eyes like having water dashed in his face," Blays added. "We heard you were in possession of the entire Clan of the Green Lake."

"Ah." The man leaned back in his padded chair, smoothing his rich green coat. "Fearsome warriors. Their ploughshares are as fierce as their swords."

"So you have them," Dante said.

"No."

Dante's face fell. "Do you know who does?"

"Naturally. I'm the one who sold them."

"We were hoping to make the buyer an offer. With workers such as those—"

"I'm afraid not," Perrigan cut in with a regretful smile. "Let's leave it at that."

"We're all gentlemen here." Blays drew back his head, shoulders straightened. "Surely we can make a gentleman's agreement not to tell any other men, gentle or otherwise, that the name of a certain other gentleman was disclosed here."

"It's easy enough to earn money. Much harder yet to earn a reputation. I bank on my integrity more deeply than any credit. The deal was made in private, and there it must remain."

"There must be some arrangement we can make," Dante said, thinking quickly. "We're not just men of business. We're men who make things happen."

"Oh, no doubt. So when I say the matter is closed, it is with trepidatious hope you do not use those powers to *do* against me."

Along the walls, the eyes of the tapestries swung to focus on Perrigan. Their gazes grew steely, glaring; beards bunched as jowls soured into frowns and sneers. Their lips began to move, muttering silent condemnations, the dark rhythms of curses. The movement caught Perrigan's eye; he did a double take, staring expressionlessly at the displeasure of his ancestors, their shaking heads and curled lips. Like that, they stopped, once more still stitching hanging from the wall.

"You don't see that every day," Blays improvised. "How often do *all* your relatives agree on anything?"

The last wisps of nether fell from Dante's grasp. "That depends on who is convincing them."

To Perrigan's credit, he met Dante's eyes, his cheeks and brows showing mere hints of strain. "What is this supposed to prove?"

Blays smiled. "How crummy your afterlife would be if you suddenly joined them."

"It's not a threat," Dante said. "Just a display of the powers we could put at your disposal."

"I'm a wealthy man." Perrigan smoothed his mustache, and with it his face. He gestured to the high stone walls, the snapping fires, and finally the tapestries, where his gaze lingered, hardening into a resentful scowl. "My face isn't beside my ancestors'. That's because the only one worthy of capturing my likeness to hang along my forefathers refuses to do so on account of the grounds by which I made the wealth that would pay her. Her name is Worring. She lives on the east side."

"And if we acquire her service?" Dante said.

"You'll also acquire the buyer's name."

Their departure was as chilly as the air outside the manor. A servant closed the groaning doors.

"You know, we could just ask one of them," Blays gestured toward the servant. "They'll usually respond to beatings."

Dante buttoned his coat to the collar. "The few who know would probably be killed for speaking. Let's see Worring and see what happens."

Their carriage waited. As Dante piled in, Mourn leaned in to the norren driver and exchanged a few words. The horses trotted down the path, wheels grinding loose pebbles. From the hilltop, Dollendun stretched for miles, bifurcated by the silvery band of the river. The carriage swung a sudden left down an alley of tight-packed houses and descended another hill into a wide plaza of packed dirt and trampled grass. At the square's fringes, humans jabbered to each other, scribbling notes, exchanging them, frowning, and then scribbling a fresh note, often to the exact same reaction. Behind them, norren crouched in cages of thick wood and pitted metal. Many were half-naked, others shoeless. A fat man lumbered forward, leaning against the weight of the bucket hanging from his hand. Water splashed over his shoes. He slopped the bucket across the floor of one cage, rinsing waste onto the muddy ground, then turned and waddled back toward the fountain at the plaza's center.

Men in padded cotton coats milled about the grounds, pausing in front of occupied cages. Then, with their hands on their hips or chins, they appraised the captive subjects from tip to toes. Equally well-dressed sellers approached to point out abundances of muscles and teeth. As their carriage cornered down another alley, an eye-patched man, accompanied by two others brandishing spears, swung open the bars of a cage and shouted its occupant into the sunlight. Blays, who rarely stopped talking even after years of travel together, didn't speak until the carriage wheels clicked onto the mortared stone of the bridge.

The eastern shorefront was a profusion of shops, warehouses, and public houses from whose open windows wafted spiced tea and spicier tobaccos. Dante called a stop outside a shop with a carving of a loom above its door and rugs piled in its windows. Mourn hopped down and went inside while Gala watched the street, sword on her back. Mourn emerged a minute later and fed the driver directions to Worring's.

Her shop stood in the middle of a cockeyed street so narrow they had to debark the carriage and continue on foot. The building's squarish design, slightly flared at the top, suggested it had once been a yurt long since plastered over with timber, and its cramped, dark interior only confirmed that. The close air was heavy with the smell of soap and dried linen. Dante seated himself on a bench a few inches too high, where he was joined by Blays and Mourn, and kicked his heels.

Between the three of them, there was scarcely space to turn around. Though Dante had spent little time in Narashtovik in the last few years, and littler time yet attending to the ceremonial and social sides of his post as one of the twelve-person Council there, he'd nonetheless acted as a man-about-town on more than one occasion. Often enough to think Worring's shop was all wrong for her apparent stature. The floors of finest artists and craftsmen were supposed to be open and airy, intentional *wastes* of space which called all the more attention to the sparse examples of their work on display (and thus how valuable these few pieces must be). By contrast, Worring's main floor was a crush of raw fabric, loose threads, and steel needles, the unfinished materials lumped in piles around the finished work.

Work that more than justified the urgency of Perrigan's vain request. Most of Worring's tapestries showed landscapes and cityscapes: misty hills, dignified white rowhouses, and the primally civilized hill-homes of the norren. A minority displayed the faces of human men and women, most in three-quarter or full profile, but a few straight-on, their gazes so superior and regal they made Dante feel as if he'd loudly farted. Yet there was a softness to their eyes, too, a mitigating light that suggested all was forgiven, that we are, after all, all human, even those of us whose blood runs blue as the sky. This liveliness was shared by the landscapes and cityscapes; when Dante glanced away or an unseen draft ruffled the room, the rivers and lamps and stars twinkled. In short, they were amazing. He had half a mind to hire Worring's services for himself.

After the clearing of a throat or two, a thin norren woman emerged from the back room. At six feet tall, her brown eyes were nearly level with Dante's, or at least as close as he had ever come on a norren. Her bare arms could easily pass for human as well—though one that got plenty of exercise, say a water-carrier or a widow who'd taken charge of her late husband's farm. She indicated her three guests. Her hands were as swift and precise as a professional swordsman's.

"I know why you're here." She seated herself behind her cluttered desk. "You want me to build you an airship."

Dante blinked. "We're here about a tapestry."

"Well, you're obviously not here for the jokes. I can spare five minutes. Please don't waste them."

He launched into an extremely abbreviated version of what had brought them to her. The woman cut him off as soon as he got to Perrigan's name.

"Absolutely not."

"I don't think you understand." Dante glanced toward the closed door, as if spies might have their waggling ears pressed to the other side. "If we do this for him, he will give us the location of an entire clan of slaves. Slaves which, if we have our druthers, won't be slaves for long."

"Then beat it out of him."

"That's what I suggested," Blays said.

"This is true," Dante said. "It's much easier to wrest dozens of unwilling captives from their baronial owner when you're arrested or dead."

Worring's brown eyes didn't sway from his. "You're not going to guilt me into this. You know what Perrigan does. The only work I'll ever do from him will be sewn from his own hide."

Dante sighed inwardly, wishing he had the power to annihilate the entire kingdom of Gask, Norren Territories and himself included, and thus avoid another single moment of this self-defeating nonsense. "I know the perspective must be very skewed from a horse that high, but I'm trying to help."

"And I'd help you if I could. But immortalizing that man would violate every principled bone in my body. Unfortunately for you, that's all of them."

"Well." Dante rose, feeling like he weighed a thousand pounds. "Your work is exceptional."

He left to meet Gala in the crooked alley. Blays glanced back at the shop. "Is it time to go beat a nobleman?"

The idea was tempting as a basement-cooled beer after a long day, but Dante shook his head. "That's our last resort."

"I didn't realize we had any other resorts."

"Mourn, I need you to tell me more about the Nulladoon. Gala, I need you to find out to what extent Worring participates in it."

"It's a little like chess," Mourn said.

Gala shook her head once. "More like hearts. Or plock."

"I was getting to that."

"I thought you said it was like dice," Dante said.

"That too." Mourn tipped back his head and considered the high, patchy clouds. "It also resembles an argument."

"An argument?" Blays said. "How's that?"

"Mostly because it is one."

Dante exhaled audibly. "I think I need to see this. Is there somewhere we can sit down and play a round?"

Mourn shrugged his broad shoulders. "Oh, just anywhere."

The norren man gave Gala the name of a public house and directions to it. She nodded and strode down the alley. Mourn led them toward the docks. Baked vegetables and potatoes steamed from vendors' stalls, tickled with herbs from all over. At a thoroughfare, norren drove mule teams or simply hauled the wagons themselves, leaning into leather straps tied to flatbeds bearing bricks or chopped wood or burlap sacks. About one out of ten women showed brands on their cheek. Mourn led them into a busy tavern with two leaping salmon painted above its door. Inside, norren partook in the standard drinking, laughing, gossiping, and news-chasing, but an unusual number of the crowd were gathered at the back, peering over the shoulders of three men seated at a wide table.

Blays bought pints. Mourn went to speak to the bartender and came back with a set of battered wooden cases. Dante sipped beer, cold as the street and just as bitter.

"Nulladoon," Mourn said, unprompted. "First, you have a board."

"Well, that sounds easy enough," Blays said.

"Most things do when you have no idea what you're talking about." Mourn rubbed the thin strip of bare skin between his brows and hairline. "Sorry, I'm under a lot of stress here. There are classical map arrangements some players specialize in, but you can arrange your tiles freeform, too, with opponents taking turns until the map's complete. Pieces are affected by elevation and water and so forth."

He unsnapped the hasps of one case and fanned out a handful of flat wooden squares, most painted blue or green. From a second case, he drew several wooden figures, worn and chipped but still identifiable as archers and spearmen and scouts.

"Then they are your pieces. Like chess, they all move and attack in their own ways, but they can do other things, too." Mourn pulled the twine from a deck of cards and spread them out. Dante didn't recognize a single one. "Then you have cards. Your opponent does, too. You *both* have cards. Cards affect units and conditions like weather and you can use them to provoke your opponent into using, losing, or giving you some of *his* cards. Think of them like ploys. Battlefield gambits."

He stared at the array of equipment. Dante picked up the cards and leafed through them. "Where does the argument come in?"

"Everywhere," Mourn sighed. "Each turn also involves an ongoing philotheosophical debate. Like the maps, they can be classic topics or decided on by the players. The soundness and originality of your argument influence play similarly to the cards."

"You're just making this up, aren't you?" Blays said. "Arguments? So after you've shouted at each other for a bit, the other guy's just going to say 'Oh, good point. Here's my king'?"

"The merits of each player's arguments are decided by one to three arbiters. If the argument's that good—or that bad—the spectators weigh in. A biased arbiter won't stay biased for long. Not unless he enjoys black eyes." Mourn glanced to the back of the room, where men roared with abrupt and unified triumph. Once it quieted, he went on. "Victory is achieved through wiping the other guy out or forcing him to concede. The winner collects his nulla, the terms of which are decided before the match."

Dante looked up from a carving of a fanged, long-nosed beast. "That's the idea. All I have to do is beat Worring in a match. Perrigan gets his tapestry, we get our name."

"Before we get any deeper, I think we should talk about something," Blays said. "Like what the hell this has to do with why we're here."

Mourn clicked the tiles against the table. "It's a good plan. It's also a very bad plan."

"Start with the good."

"If Worring plays—and they all do—she'll abide by her debts."

Blays quirked his mouth with doubt. "She'll break her personal rule about 'No dealing with abominable slavedrivers' to stick by the rules of some game?"

"Yes," Mourn said. "And if that doesn't do it, the threat of fines, beatings, and in extreme cases enslavement should convince her instead."

"So what's the bad?" Dante said.

"You can't possibly win."

"Of course I can."

"How long have you been playing Nulladoon?"

"Well, never."

Mourn gestured to the spread of pieces, cards, and tiles. "Never. You've been playing for never. Which is funny, because most of this city's been playing since always. Since they were kids."

"Big deal," Blays snorted. "We can just cheat."

Mourn went as still as one of the wooden units. "You can't cheat at Nulladoon."

"I can cheat at anything. I'll cheat you right now if you want. What would you like to be cheated at?"

"It's...*sacred*. It's not something you do."

Dante leaned in, matching the low tones of the norren man, if not his awed disgust. "Mourn, what does it matter? We're talking about saving your cousins' lives. Is that less important than the rules of a game?"

The norren exhaled until his whole body slumped like a discarded shirt. "I don't like this."

"Me neither," Blays said. "It's more tangled up than spiders playing tag."

Dante reached for his beer. "If you can think of a better way, I'm all ears."

"I can think of twenty."

"That doesn't involve punching, stabbing, or us being jailed."

"I can't think of any."

Dante took a long drink to hide his smile. He couldn't think of anything less convoluted, either, but in point of fact, he *wanted* to play. He'd been allured by the Nulladoon from the moment Mourn mentioned it, and hearing its rough details had hooked him all the harder. It was clearly a game you could get lost in, endlessly variable, with strategies within strategies, all of which might be compromised or annihilated by the wrong stroke of luck, leaving you angry yet determined, obsessed to play again and prove that when the game is *fair* you cannot be beat. He looked forward to studying its facets and depths with an intellectual eagerness he hadn't felt since discovering the *Cycle of Arawn*.

After several complaints he was hardly an expert, Mourn relented and agreed to teach him. Mourn arranged the map in one of its simplest variants, led Dante through a quick overview of piece selection (just as customizable as the maps), then proceeded through what he warned was a dumbed-down game. Though it was clearly an expository match, with Mourn constantly pausing to explain a rule and its limitless permutations, exceptions, and contingencies, it nonetheless drew a steady stream of onlookers, many who seemed as interested in the fact a human was learning their game as in the outcome of the halting match itself. Mourn had no trouble enlisting a trio to arbitrate the scoring of their debates.

And those were the stumbling block. Dante grasped the core combat at once—a rock-paper-scissors-style system of engagement with just enough intrinsic complexity to allow for in-depth strategy in every situation. By their second game, several of his gambits drew appreciative nods and chuckles from the crowd. Yet each skirmish—every single godsdamn one—resulted in the loss of a unit, territory, or both, overcome by modifiers from Mourn's cards or his victories in debate. Dante simply didn't know enough. He knew most of the key players, Josun Joh and his host of brothers, cousins, and enemies, and when it came to philosophical concepts, he was easily Mourn's better. Yet he didn't know enough of norren theosophy to marry the general to the specific. It was beyond frustrating.

Gala returned in the middle of their third match. "She plays."

"Finally some good luck," Blays said.

"Not really. They all play."

"Told you," Mourn said. He advanced his swordsman. After a brief exchange of modifiers, Dante removed his ice-drake from the board.

After his third loss, Dante dropped from his oversize seat to go update Orlen on their situation (Gala had arranged a note-drop under one of the piers) and warn him it could be days or even weeks before they moved on. He penned a letter of aid to Perrigan, too, alerting him Dante believed they'd secure his tapestry soon enough but that he'd first need access to as many libraries of norren-lore as Perrigan could get him into.

He resumed play. Mourn's style was plodding and defensive, advancing his pieces with stubborn deliberateness until his advantage was too overwhelming to break. His style of debate mirrored it, carefully laying the groundwork and initial conditions (that history showed Josun Joh was in Canwell on the third day of the third year) before unleashing his conclusions in an ironclad case (and thus couldn't have been the father of Kandack, whose mother had, on the day of the boy's conception, been across the land in Merridan). Dante tried a range of guiding strategies before settling on his standard, a deceptive style that appeared cautious yet relied on massive risks taken right under Mourn's oversized nose. These efforts panned out often enough to turn the tables more than once, but by the time the two of them were too tired to go on, Dante still hadn't won a single match.

Letters of recommendation arrived from Perrigan the next day. Dante split time between the two banks of the river, playing Nulladoon in the east and reading norren scripture in the west. On the third day of play, Dante retreated his main force to a steep hill, leaving a contingent of swift, light-hitting drakes trapped behind Mourn's infantry wall, doomed before the next turn.

But during that turn's debate, Dante tricked Mourn into a confession that the traditional sacrifices to stall Ferrow's wrath weren't rams, they were deer. Using that as the hinge for his conclusion that Ferrow's domain was not with herding nomads but instead among wild hunters, Dante racked up enough conditionals to send his lone remaining swordsman into a berserk fury. Mourn lost three units before the berserker fell, along with the center of his line. Peppered by Dante's hilltop archers, harassed and ensnared by the hit-and-run drakes, Mourn removed the last of his pieces from the board four turns later.

The audience applauded and whooped. Significant fun was made of Mourn's loss to a scrawny human outlander. Mourn's smile was as slow as his advance across the battlefield.

"Good move," he said. "Now why don't you play someone who actually knows what the units with the spiky things are called."

Dante slouched back in his chair, heart thudding. "But I don't have any nulla to wager."

"You're so dumb you'd probably forget what food is for," Blays said. "You're the best healer in town. Bet with that."

Despite the potential for humiliation at the hands of a human, when it came to Nulladoon, the standard norren suspicion of outsiders evaporated altogether. Within minutes of announcing he was looking for a match, Dante had enough appointments to fill out the day. It wasn't simply the novelty factor, either. Word had somehow spread that he'd healed several members of the Clan of the Nine Pines after a ferocious battle, and that his healing-nulla could cure anything short of death itself. In a city as mean, pestilential, and backbreaking as Dollendun, challengers lined up like he were passing out free wine.

He lost, of course. The first game was a war of attrition; he couldn't keep up with his white-haired foe's subtle modifiers and wily wisdom during disputes. He played his second game against a young woman, but the match collapsed in less than twenty minutes when Dante's opening charge (intending to attain an initial strength advantage he could then leverage murderously through strangulating conservatism) died on enemy spears. The third match lasted right until midnight, however, a back-and-forth tilt that saw him and his rival switch not just tactical but geographic position several times, a game of reversals and re-reversals so captivating that the pub's owner began to complain his patrons had forgotten how to drink. When Dante's final piece—a battered sorcerer—finally dropped, there were as many sighs as cheers. Dante's opponent, a middle-aged potter, immediately bought him three beers.

But it didn't matter that he lost, except for the time he lost when winners cashed in their nulla-writs and called him away to soothe a sister's pneumonia or heal a father's broken wrist. Dante didn't resent the lost time. He didn't need to become the best. Not after he figured out how he could cheat.

While card-play was a single dimension of the game, it could provide a big enough advantage to overcome many slips of tactics and strokes of poor luck. If Dante could see his opponent's hand—through his connection to a dead fly on the wall, say, or better yet, a lizard, something small enough to escape notice but which at least shared his basic senses—he could overwhelm that field of the game, flushing out the opponent's hand while strengthening his own, anticipating their movements and preparing his counters moves in advance. In one private test with Mourn (Blays acting as a hapless arbiter), it worked so well it was nearly *too* obvious. They tried again, with Dante playing his cards with just enough deliberate mistakes and oversights to pass muster.

He continued playing, reading, analyzing, discussing. He won his first competitive match, earning a minor nulla from a silversmith, which he cashed in for the forging of a unique Nulladoon piece: a thin, unimposing sorcerer, one outstretched hand painted with charcoal shadows. Gala poked into Worring's playing habits, learning the weaver participated in at least one match a week and sometimes binged for several straight days.

It was absorbing. Engrossing. Addicting. Some part of him wanted to forget the Quivering Bow existed, to give up his very council seat in Narashtovik to continue matching wits in the smoky taverns of Dollendun's norren shore. This was a fantasy, of course. Across town, the Clan of the Nine Pines waited in their tents. Somewhere in the heart of Gask, the Clan of the Green Lake waited in their chains.

Within a week, he won as often as he lost. That achieved, he began to cheat, at first a single glance at their starting hand through the eyes of a spider hanging from the wall, and in later games continuous looks at their changing cards. Still, he didn't win every game. But he took most, and many easily. It earned him many nulla, too, of all stripes and shapes—a smallcask of homebrewed beer, a wavy-bladed dagger, labor from carvers of wood and stone, which he promptly turned in for more figures for his expanding Nulladoon set.

But victory robbed him. When his opponents clicked their pieces into their wooden boxes, frustration or sad self-disappointment creasing their bearded faces, he had to turn away or risk blurting his deception. When norren recognized his face, called him by name, and bought him drinks and meals, his stomach turned with inward disgust. He had to end it.

Two weeks from the night Mourn had won their first match, he issued his challenge.

He had no doubt Worring knew his motives, or at least what he would ask if he won. But denying a public challenge was a disgrace, one that could lessen the perceived value of the denier's crafts or skills (were they afraid they made unworthy gifts?) and thus the social standing of the denier themselves. Worring accepted. She set a date for Wednesday night, three days hence.

"What happens if you lose?" Mourn asked that night. They'd

headed upstairs to Dante's room to unwind and go over the ins and outs of Worring's standard strategy. Pieces and cards littered the board, scattered between chipped beer mugs.

Dante shrugged. "Convince her to see reason."

"She won't."

"Then I'll keep coming back."

"She won't see you," Mourn said.

"Then I'll make myself look very, very scary." Dante lifted his palms. "What do you want me to say? Maybe there won't be anything I can do."

"Well, I just wanted to know if you'd considered that possibility. I think it's an important one for everyone to spend some time thinking about." The norren knocked an unpainted wooden archer on its side. "Lots of time, to be quite frank. It's always less disappointing that way."

"What's your nulla, anyway?" Blays said from his seat in the window.

Mourn glanced over. "What?"

"Your nulla. You all have one, right? So what's yours?"

"Oh." Mourn cupped his hands together, forming a box, then peeked inside, as if expecting to find the answer. "Well."

Dante frowned. "I thought you guys start in on your calling before you learn how to shake a rattle."

"The thing is, the quality of my work doesn't yet match up to my personal standards."

"Oh, come on." Blays shoved off the window sill and refilled his mug from a pitcher on the table. Foam spattered the board. Mourn scowled and toweled it up with his sleeve. Blays look a long swig, foam mustaching his lip. "We're all friends here. If I'm going to mock your lack of skills, it'll be to your face."

The norren rubbed his beard. "Arrowheads."

"Fletching? That's great. Nothing badder than a man who makes his own weapons."

Mourn shook his head. "Just arrowheads. There's a lot to them, you know. For instance, you humans favor metal heads exclusively, but obsidian arrowheads are frightening. Sharp as a razor but they'll break off inside your gut if you try to pull them out the wrong way. On the other hand, rock isn't what you'd call malleable, and I for one think the entire arrowhead industry is conservative to the point of absurdity. Why are we so locked into the *triangle*? What about a crescent shape? Much better for attempting to sever distant ropes, I say. And what if you shaped them so they whistle in flight? There'd be no need to carry a bulky old horn onto the battlefield."

Blays nodded thoughtfully. "I'd make my nulla sex."

Mourn reddened beneath his beard. "It doesn't work that way!"

"It can be anything, can't it?"

"It has to be something tangible. Something you can *hold*."

"Oh, there'd be something to hold."

Mourn snatched his mug from the table. "It can't just be an experience. Other people have to be able to see it."

"What about poems?" Dante said.

"What about them? You can write them down, can't you?"

"That seems like a cheat. Most poems are recited."

"I don't see what's cheating about it."

"What if I give you a drawing afterwards?" Blays said.

Mourn glared into his beer. "You're not taking this seriously."

"How about dancers?" Dante said. "You said dances could be nulla."

"Those are public. Other people can see and confirm the value of what you're receiving."

"Look," Blays said. "If I've dedicated my whole life to sex, I think I'll be good enough at it that it'll be no issue to throw a sheet across the plaza and—"

"I don't think they would appreciate a solo performance," Dante said.

Mourn rose, swaying. "I'm going to bed."

Three days came and went like the boats at the piers. It was time. Worring didn't care about the venue, so Dante had arranged to hold it in the pub where he'd learned to play; he was comfortable there, and the playing-stations lined the back wall, providing ready perches for a spying spider. Worring arrived alone, seating herself opposite Dante. The crowd closed in behind her, pointing at specific positions on the table despite the fact not a single tile had yet been laid. Worring withdrew a glossy teak box from a purple velvet sack. The case's latches snicked. She arrayed her pieces, soapstone warriors and beasts dressed in minutely sewn clothing: leather armor, cotton trousers, and brown boots laced with single lengths of thread.

Finished, she gazed at him over the table. "I hear you're among the best human players of your generation."

He shrugged, stacking tiles with wooden clicks. "When the right cause inspires me, I'll see it through at any cost."

"What cause led you to pushing toy soldiers around a fake map?"

"One of those casual injustices that has been going on for so long that speaking about it in polite company brands you a fanatic."

"Ah. That narrows it down."

They agreed on a map (Lakepatch, a common terrain where the many ponds funneled action into the killing fields of open meadows), piece allotment (standard-three, a skirmisher-heavy default, which they modified with an allowance to swap out any two units), and the terms of the nulla.

"A tapestry," he said. "Choice of subject decided by me."

Her brown eyes met his. "It's said you're a healer."

"Once you cause enough wounds, you get a pretty good idea how to fix them."

"My father was enslaved for debt a few years into my apprenticeship. They worked him in the fields. One day they were short of oxen, so they made him pull the plow. He tripped in a gopher hole and broke his leg." She laid her first tile, holding his gaze. "They didn't bother to set it. He still can't walk."

"Old wounds are harder work," he said. "But if I can, I will."

The arbiters—to reduce the risk of rogue decisions stripping him of victory, Dante had insisted on three of them—introduced themselves and sat. The audience placed bets of drinks and money and sometimes small nulla of their own. Mostly, they watched with open grins as the final piece was placed and Worring opened, drakes zagging along one side of the board while her archers and gnomes ducked in and out of cover. Dante advanced to intercept, his forces aligned in a shifting sickle, striking from both points of the blade as Worring rearranged her defenses from one side of the field to the other.

She gave a small smile. "You fight like a human."

"What does that mean?"

"I have no damn idea what you think you're doing."

He smiled back, then played a run of cards. By the time he completed the side game, he'd depleted twice as many of her cards as he'd spent, snagging a crucial modifier to his sorcerer's armor. The figure was a tentpole of his strategy, obliterating anything that came too close, yet it had already been bloodied to dangerous levels by the regular pelting of her archers, who fired behind the safety of lakes, clad in nothing stronger than their brown cotton robes.

"Take a break?" he said an hour later. Their forces were on the verge of a critical, all-out melee. For the last several moves, her gnomes had harried his norren frontliners, dancing forward to the very point of overextension before drawing back into the protective range of her archers. He'd withdrawn his sorcerer early on to preserve it as he maneuvered his bear-cavalry to block those damned gnomes. Recognizing his ploy, she'd arranged her troops into jagged yet subtly intricate lines of defense that could snap shut like a cougar's jaws.

"No running off for advice from your friends," she smiled.

His own smile was as tight as her deployment. "Just for a drink. Want one?"

"A beer." She tipped her head at the laughing throngs, foam drying on their beards. "If there's any left."

He shouldered through the crowd, face brushed by bulging bellies and sweaty arms. It stunk like men who've spent too long working, playing, or both. He smiled at strangers' encouragement, their playful taunts, and returned from the bar with two heady mugs.

Play resumed. A discussion of the moral implications of Lord Jonn abdicating his throne (and thus abandoning his responsibility to his subjects) to save Lady Herren from the underworld resulted in a rhetorical stalemate—Dante argued his duty to his war-threatened kingdom outweighed his duty to his wife, while Worring argued that a man who won't attempt to save that which is dearest to him is unfit to rule a kingdom in the first place. On the board, Worring advanced and retreated methodically, rhythmically, her drakes weaving among his lines like a shuttle through the loom.

At times her forces showed patterns with no identifiable strategic goals, as if she were playing more for the aesthetics than for the thrill of the challenge or the nulla-favors earned from victory.

Dante leaned back in his chair.

Until now, he had been thinking of the game purely in the abstract, analyzing it within the strict rules of its own internal logic. Position his spearman just so, as to block the enemy's drakes. Keep his slingers in motion, reducing oppositional accuracy. Play his card of Blood Debt on the same turn the bulk of his norren swordsmen were in position to strike. On some level, he'd realized the game must have emerged as a way for citybound norren to settle disputes their earlier, wilder, free-ranging ancestors had settled (and still did, in the case of the Nine Pines and others) through blood and steel under harsh and silent skies. But there was another level to Nulladoon, too. It wasn't just a practical game. It was a game of the norren's own spirit, a celebration of their talents, their skill with their hands and their sheer love of fun for its own sake. A chance to express one's own being and witness another in similar expression. And then, in victory or defeat, to give or receive something tangible, if only the memory of a wonderful dance or song, and so appreciate each other all over again.

This understanding lent him no tactical advantage. Knowledge of her cards was enough to slip the noose around her neck; Worring was highly skilled, but not one of the highest masters, and when his bear cavalry pressed her gnomes against the shore of a lake, the pesky skirmishers were eliminated to a man. But when his sorcerer finished its turn and Worring extended her finger to topple her last drake, Dante knew he hadn't allowed her to see the nature of himself. Worse yet, perhaps he *had*. He hadn't played the game. He'd cheated.

And he had won.

5

Perrigan's smile made Dante want to wring his well-bred neck. The man held the parchment at arm's length, as if he didn't want Worring's bare signature to come too close and taint him. After a long moment of admiration, he rolled up the writ of nulla, stuffed it in his desk, and turned that smile on Dante.

"I sold the Clan of the Green Lake to Lord Cassinder of Beckonridge. The estate is some miles east of Setteven. If he hasn't broken up the sale—and I believe he'd just sunk his latest mine, so I don't see why he would—you'll find them there."

Dante thanked him stiffly. "Let's hope the right price can convince him to part with them regardless of his plans."

Perrigan turned to gaze at the woven faces of his ancestors hanging from the wall. "Well, there's always a price, isn't there?"

"And often a later one to boot."

The lord gave him a curious look, but Dante turned on his heel. The carriage descended through rowhouses and a crisp sunlight that was too early in the season to be warm. They rattled over the bridge, smelling freshwater and windborne pollen, and halted in a plaza on the eastern shore. He relayed Perrigan's intelligence to Gala and Mourn.

"Go tell your clan to get ready to move. I have one last thing to do before we leave."

"Don't tell me it's another game," Blays groaned.

"I hope you didn't have plans for the rest of the week."

"What!"

"It wasn't that boring, was it?"

"Two weeks of watching you read books and play an even

dorkier version of chess? I'd have more fun learning to piss through my eyeballs."

Dante's grin faded. "No more games. Just one last debt."

As they entered her dark shop, Worring's face folded as fast as her troops had in the final battle. "I already know what you want."

"And for that I'm sorry." Dante met her eyes. "But I didn't come here to claim my nulla. I'm here to pay you mine."

She laughed, deep and bitter. "Beaten by a human who doesn't even know the rules. D'you think I'd be shamed more or less if I killed myself before I finish your order?"

"I know the rules perfectly well. Now close this shop and take me to your father."

Worring drew back her head. "He lives on the far north of town."

"I spent a fortnight playing games. I think I can fit a few more hours into my busy schedule."

Even so, Dante hired another carriage, spending most of what little he'd gained selling nulla and placing side bets on other games. Wheels splashed mud and other substances across unpaved streets. A score of hammers rang from a dozen anvils. The metallic clanks faded by the time shacks replaced the proper houses. After a half mile of dirt alleys and thatch-roofed, single-room homes, Worring called a stop in front of one no different from a thousand others.

She stepped into the cold dust, pausing before a door that fit worse than an older brother's hand-me-down trousers. "Give me a minute."

She slipped inside, tugging the door several times before it squeaked shut. Low tones filtered through the drafty wallboards, one voice female, the other male and coarse as a raven. Clinks, shuffles, and clatters overcut the talk, as if many small things were being converted into one large pile.

"I think she's into you," Blays said.

"I highly doubt that."

"Who else cleans just because a near-stranger comes to their house?"

"Women," Dante said. "A good deal of men, too. Just about everyone, in fact, except those whose servants do it for them. We need to get you out more, don't we?"

"Not if it's to the sort of places where people *clean*."

The door opened, pouring sunlight into a single tight room. A blanket covered thigh-high lumps piled along the back wall. A rickety stove pumped smoke up the narrow chimney of fieldstone and clay, pouring heat into the sievelike shack. A pale leg projected from a cot half-visible behind the doorway.

The norren it belonged to was well past middle age. The gray of his beard had begun to seep into his dark brown hair, coloring it like milk dribbled into unstirred coffee. He had the usual flabbiness of age, but his right leg was a bony broomstick beneath grimy pants. The room smelled faintly of urine.

"My father Shone," Worring said.

Dante introduced himself and Blays. "Your daughter's work is spectacular."

"No doubt," Blays said. "I stared at one weaving of a lady so long I feared she'd reach out of the thread and slap me."

"Well, she stole all she knows from me." Shone struggled to swing his legs from the cot, bracing himself on a block of wood that served as a table.

"Please don't get up," Dante said. "That's why I'm here."

"To gape at a cripple?"

"Sir, I can assure you—"

The old man held up a roughworn palm. "Shut up. Worring told me why you're here. She's expecting a miracle."

"And what are you expecting?"

"To learn one more time that 'I told you so' is always more satisfying in your head than spoken aloud." He lay back on the cot, glaring at the bare, cobwebby rafters. "Let's get to it."

"You might want to leave," Dante said to Worring. "I expect this will hurt."

It did. The knee was hard and knobby as dry coral. To set it, Dante first had to rebreak it, dissolving the old mending with hard rasps of nether. Shone screamed, sweat trickling through his ashy beard. Blays helped hold him down, offering gulps from a flask. Once the knee was disjointed—to the nether's touch, it felt like loose pebbles among an internal creek of hot blood and lymph—Dante aligned the old break as cleanly as he could, filling the gaps with nether-prompted growths of new bone. Most of Dante's intensive work had been done on the vibrant young, on warriors and soldiers (not to mention himself and Blays), and the old man's flesh and tissue responded sluggishly, accumulating and binding only through Dante's constant, steady focus on the nether. Grain by grain, the bone returned.

After some time—a half hour, perhaps twice that long—Dante plopped on the floor, as sweaty as the old man. As for Shone, he regarded Dante coolly, as one watches a lone wolf from across an open meadow.

"Why did you come here?"

Dante wiped his sleeve across his forehead. "Your daughter's a very fine Nulladoon player, too."

"That she got on her own. Damn game ran me right out of business." Despite the old man's cynicism, a decade of anticipation was etched on his face. Shone swung his leg off the bed. The skin around his eyes relaxed. "Josun's toes, son. A man who can do what you do's got no business wasting time with games."

Dante smiled and stepped outside. Worring pulled her finger from her mouth and spat a ragged bit of nail into the dirt. "Well?"

"Better," Dante said.

"Such modesty," Blays said, eyes rolling. "That old crank will be fit enough to kick your ass again in no time."

"Maybe you can come see for yourself." Worring glanced toward the door. "If you come here again."

"Soon." Dante climbed inside the carriage. In the moment, he meant it: he and Blays could come back here on their return from the estate outside Setteven. He'd like to play Worring again, a rematch where he competed without the knowledge of every one of her cards. He would even enjoy losing, he thought, and if he won, to have a weaving made for himself.

But he wouldn't return for years. When at last he did, Worring would be old herself, and retired from the tables, even friendly matches. She would tell him how Shone had healed: walking to the shop with her each morning, this time not as her master but her partner, his earnings from weaving just keeping up with the nulla he incurred from gaming. He would die three years before Dante made it back to Dollendun.

~

While Dante played, the others had worked. The *Boomer*'s sails were whole and white. Bright blond wood stood out from the railing where wind- and spray-chapped timber, smashed in the battle with the Bloody Knuckles, had since been replaced. More surprisingly, Lira stood on the deck to greet Dante.

"Leg better?" he said.

"Fit to start working off my debt."

"Saving you was my idea, you know," Blays said. "If he doesn't want to boss you around, I'll bear that burden for him."

She swept breeze-blown hair from her face. "But I do owe you."

Blays raised his brows. "In that case, you should know I can do my fighting on my own. It's other realms where it helps to have a partner."

"I don't know," Dante said. "You seem plenty capable of handling that on your own, too."

Orlen was striding across the deck on a beeline for him. Dante met him halfway.

"Good work of it," the chieftain said. "When we heard the lord refused to name his buyer, we began our battle-prayers to Josun Joh."

"Hope nobody went stir-crazy during the wait."

"We are accustomed enough to waiting. That's what we do all winter. What we're not accustomed to is other people fighting our battles for us."

"Good," Dante nodded. "Because whenever I rescue a clan of slaves from the bottom of a mineshaft, I prefer to do it with thirty howling warriors at my side."

"It may not come to that." The tall man smiled. "But I hope it does."

The *Boomer* pushed off that same day, negotiating its way through the pilings and river-traffic of rowboats and flat-bottomed schooners. An hour later, Dollendun was a black mass of buildings to their back, a blocky forest of stone and hard-fired mud. Dante had a firm enough grasp on Gaskan geography to know the Cricket River on which they'd been sailing this whole time was a tributary of the Rommen that ran through Setteven, meaning they could more or less float the whole way to Beckonridge, debarking however many miles away to complete the journey overland. What he didn't know was how far that was. Varlen reported it was just over 250 miles—less than a week's journey, if they sailed through the nights and made minimal stops.

Dante had spent twice that long at Nulladoon, but the remainder of the trip felt much longer. Towns drifted past, but none nearly as large as Dollendun. Barges came upstream and down, and on two occasions the oars of war-galleys slashed the gray water, but neither vessel showed the faintest sign of interest in the *Boomer*. Even the land seemed to grow bored, flattening into an endless prairie of winter-yellowed grasses, hawks circling and screeching, mice and gophers ruffling the fields on their hunt for seeds, the skies clear and cool, but not quite cold and far from warm.

He got out his boxes to play some desultory games of Nulladoon with Mourn, but he was missing pieces and tiles, and the game suffered for it. He watched Blays and Lira practice swordplay on the deck, their blades glinting in the sunlight until the fighters' faces gleamed and their chests heaved. Lira limped, but was able to lean and feint through all but the most delicate footwork. Out of eyeshot of the major towns, clan warriors took to the decks, too, sparring or just sunning themselves to break up the closeness belowdecks.

On both banks, the land rose, first into yellow hills, then high bluffs with pale green shrubs and scraggly pines. The sides of the gorge were so steep Dante could see bare rock slanted in layers, great crumbles of loose stone mounded around the feet of the cliffs. The way grew fraught with sudden bends and jutting spurs of rock; Dante stayed up through the night, lighting the way from the prow with a white beam that flowed over black waters and cliffs. Snow capped the heights and the shadows where the sun rarely touched.

The *Boomer* emerged from the gorge into brackets of pine-heavy hills. The air was wet and dense and deceptively cold, a damp hand that snatched your warmth while you weren't looking. That night, Varlen put to port in a small town where the docks were slick with algae and the log houses were fuzzy with moss. He returned from the dockmaster to confirm this was their port.

Orlen held the troops belowdecks until all the town's lanterns but those on the docks had been extinguished. Then the warriors padded down the gangway single-file, as silent as snow, and gathered a short way into the woods. Dante, Blays, and Lira were the only humans to join them. The rest of the crew remained onboard the *Boomer*; according to plan, the ship would shove off in the morning, then turn around after two days to rendezvous with the clan and its cousins upriver in something like a week. If Captain Varlen hadn't seen or heard from the clan in a fortnight, he'd be free to leave without further obligation.

The clan slipped into the forest along a plain dirt road that was frequently muddy and patchy with holes. Scouts returned to let them know the way ahead was clear. Vee estimated a two-day march to Beckonridge. Along with Orlen, she dropped back from the body of warriors to speak to Dante and Blays alone, glaring at Lira until she took the hint. With a cold nod, Lira dropped back further yet, out of range of their murmurs but close enough to watch their backs.

"We expect the situation at Beckonridge to be much the same as Dollendun," Orlen said.

Vee glanced in the direction of a hoot from the darkness. "Except in the sense that everything will be different."

"But once again, a full body of warriors will be unwelcome, so we must present a human face instead."

"Don't worry, we're experts at pretending to be what we're not," Blays said. "Like bathed."

"We'll use the same story we did in Dollendun," Dante said. "Less suspicious. And with the added bonus of not requiring any more work."

"I can't agree with that fast enough."

Orlen pulled his soft leather collar tight against the cold. "As before, taking Mourn and Gala should—"

The chieftain collapsed to his knees. In the darkened roadway, his head spasmed side to side, earrings flashing, as if he were attempting to shake a demon out of his skull. Spittle gleamed in the corner of his mouth.

Dante knelt beside him, reaching for the nether. "What's happening?"

Vee slapped his hand away with enough force to crack walnuts. "You mustn't touch him. Josun Joh is upon him."

Orlen's violent jerks subsided to irregular twitches. He was overcome by a stillness as perfect as the meditations of the supplicants of Urt. His eyes flicked open. "Josun Joh says the Quivering Bow is in the highest place; the Clan of the Green Lake in the lowest. Yet if one has two hands, both may be taken."

"You know," Blays said, "Josun Joh might get more done if he said things that made any damn sense."

"The meaning of his words often comes later, in singular moments of clarity." Orlen stood, wiping his eyes. "We'll understand soon enough."

The march was pleasantly uneventful. Scouts watched for carriages and riders; at their whistle, the clan melted into the woods like a morning fog. On the second day the westward path sported a northern fork, leading them through shallow, rolling hills and the sharply sweet scent of pine.

"You realize we're showing up on foot," Blays said when the scouts returned with word the manor was less than five miles away. "They're going to think we're the type of people who show up on *foot*."

"Leave it to the norren to forget the wealthy treated their feet as the decorative bulbs at the end of their pants," Dante said. "We'll tell Lord Cassinder we were robbed."

"That will never work."

"You're right. Much more credible that we walked a thousand miles from Mallon before suddenly realizing what we'd left at home: horses."

"Come on," Blays said. "Who's going to believe *I* could get robbed?"

Dante nodded. "We'll tell them you look strong, but inside you beats the heart of a coward."

"How about this? You thought our map was actual-size, and declared we'd have no need for horses."

"We're the type of noble who boasts as much as he drinks. We decided to walk from the river to remind ourselves of ancient days, to partake of the brisk forest air, and to feel the strength of our legs beneath us."

"Suppose we'd better get drunk, then. To get in character."

The pair of forward scouts returned. Beckonridge was scant miles ahead. Orlen led the clan off-trail into the woods single-file. The last member dragged a stone-filled sack behind her to confuse their tracks. Miles out of sight of the manor, the Nine Pines bivouacked near a minor creek trickling between the ferns and the mossy roots of colossal red trees. Warriors turned their axes on saplings and low branches, raising inconspicuous lean-tos while Vee and Orlen rehashed the plan. There existed the fair chance that, as visiting aristocracy, and foreign ones at that, Dante and Blays would be taken in as guests, and might find it difficult to slip away; in that event, their "servants," particularly Mourn and Gala, would find it much easier to sneak away and get word to the rest of the clan about what was happening inside. The clan itself, meanwhile, would investigate the mine as best they could while exploring the woods for escape routes and sound places to defend from in the event enemy riders overtook them. That was it; the rest was left to chance, or rather, to their ability to improvise on the fly.

Dante sent Lira and Mourn ahead to announce their presence, then cleaned up in the ice-cold creek as much as he could stand. He dried himself with a blanket and gathered up his things. Horse droppings littered the path through the pines.

The forest ended on the ridge of a low hill, Beckonridge spread in the valley below. For administrative purposes, the place was a single household, yet in practical purposes it resembled a small village. The manor itself was a giant stone structure, L-shaped, with four floors of windows and several towers rising another three stories above that. At a tasteful distance, smoke poured from a smithy, the rhythm of clanging metal trickling through the damp air. A barn and stable sat close together. A number of other simple wooden structures were arranged here and there, housing for servants and resident employees. The dirt road continued past all this, widening as it climbed the ridge on the valley's opposite side.

Gala walked with them, scanning the open fields as if she expected the old tree stumps to rip themselves from the ground and tear Dante and Blays limb from limb. Dante saw no hint of Mourn and Lira, which was either a good sign or a very bad one. At the manor, a servant waited before iron-banded double doors that could have resisted most armies. The woman led them to a warm receiving room, thick with carpets, a full shelf of books, and the scent of woodsmoke, where she explained that Cassinder was currently at the mines but would return shortly. Lira and Mourn were brought to the room a few minutes later, taking up properly studied positions along the wall.

"See anything interesting?" Dante asked.

Mourn nodded enthusiastically. "A rather nice rendition of the confluence of the Cricket and Rommen."

"He said interesting," Blays said.

"If you're referring to things you can eat, the answer is no."

"There's always *something* to eat. It just depends on how much you want to chew."

They spent the next hour leafing through picaroon novels and poking at the reluctant fire. At last, the door opened. In it stood a shortish man in a quilted pine green undercoat and the blotchy complexion of one who's been riding in the cold. His blond hair was cut severely short, a glowing fuzz above the sharp angles of his face. To Dante's surprise, he introduced himself as Cassinder; Dante had expected your typical middle-aged and doughy-middled lord, not a thin man nearly as young as himself.

Cassinder blinked at the books spread on the low table. "There is no tea."

"In all the world?" Blays said. "Have you checked under the bed?"

"Excuse me. I will return with tea."

Cassinder did just that, personally bearing a bronze tray carrying five green-glazed mugs and a steaming clay pot. He set them on the table and poured each full, offering one not just to Blays and Dante, but to Lira, Gala, and Mourn as well.

"I'd heard this was a strange land," Dante said in his best blustery, jovial, bring-me-a-beer-and-the-nanny voice. "But not so strange that you serve the servants."

"Everyone gets cold." Cassinder took a step from the table and gazed between his guests in the ritualistic Old Gaskan acknowledgment of presence that might well have been lost on Dante if he really were a traveling Mallish lord and not in fact a Mallish transplant who'd spent years attending dozens of versions of this same traditional tea-greeting. Considering his station, Cassinder's version of the ritual was extremely stripped-down yet respectful, a return to its historical origins. In other households, Dante had seen lords nod briefly at their guests while ignoring the servants pouring tea from emerald-crusted pots into delicate silver cups.

Dante slurped tea. "Some excellent weed-juice you got here."

"We grow it ourselves."

"Funny, that's exactly why we're here. But I'm getting ahead of myself."

"I will not be insulted if you want to cut straight to the point."

The lord had a soft way of speaking that made you focus on every word. Dante suspected this was deliberate. Dante grinned and made another bonhomie-heavy insight about how nice it was to cut the crap, then launched into their cover story about needing to put the best possible laborers in front of their skeptical investors—specifically, the figures of the fabled Clan of the Green Lake.

"They are, unfortunately for you, not for sale." Cassinder said. "Have you seen any of the Clan of the Green Lake?"

"Not personally."

Blays grinned. "Although we've heard so much about them I could believe there *are* no other norren."

Cassinder gazed at the cooling teapot. "To southern eyes, they look no different from any other norren."

"What's the difference to northern eyes?" Dante said.

"Their beards are slightly reddish."

"That's it?"

"That is what I said."

Blays cocked his head. "Then why are they so important to you?"

Cassinder refilled Blays' tea. "They and their nomad cousin-clans are open supporters of norren independence. The message they send from down my mine is worth more than anything you can offer for them."

"Don't be too sure about that," Blays said. "In Mallon, our gold grows as thickly as wheat. Our bread weighs eighty pounds a loaf."

"Then I am surprised you have come all this way for norren

when your own farmers must have the musculature of elephants."

"Are the norren so likely to rebel they need reminders of their place?" Dante said. "From what I hear they're so busy exchanging treatises and crafting cups they can hardly run a village."

Cassinder laced his fingers together, gazing at his paralleled thumbs. "The norren are restless. If they push much more obviously, several clans will soon be headless."

"Sounds like you've got them under control either way."

"I will not sell my stock. I will consider pressing the matter any further rude."

Dante drew back, palms raised, eyes downcast. "Not our intention at all, sir. But I hope you won't consider it rude if I ask to see them, so that when I look for stock elsewhere, I'll know for myself how close my purchase comes to the finest clan-warriors in Gask."

"It is not rude, merely pointless. But you are guests. We will go to the mine tomorrow morning."

Neither his expression nor posture changed, but there was a sudden absence to Cassinder that made it perfectly clear their discussion was done for the day. Dante made a show of stretching, remarking how long the day had been. Cassinder nodded and excused himself. He was replaced by a pair of servants moments later, one of whom led Lira and the two norren to the servants' wing while the other showed Dante and Blays up a stairwell so plushly carpeted they couldn't hear their feet at all. The walls were empty of paintings, cloth hangings, statues, any of the usual trappings of status and wealth. Their two guest rooms were similarly spartan: a bed, a reading-chair, an end table, then nothing but carpet and blank walls, interrupted only by a fireplace. Dante visited the water closet, then returned to Blays' room.

"What do you think of our host?" he said in Mallish, as if Cassinder might have his pale ear pressed to the door.

"That he was born three months premature."

"The fact his fellow bluebloods haven't killed him and claimed they mistook him for a fox makes me think he's close enough to the throne to smell King Moddegan's sweat."

"He's a second cousin or something. Are you telling me you didn't know that?" Blays turned to the waning sunset beyond the window. "Good work down there, by the way. You almost convinced me you can hold a normal conversation."

"What? I can talk to people."

"The same way a fish can wriggle out of a boat. Lots of flapping around, and someone's going to wind up all slimy."

"If I had a club, it would be on its way to your skull right now." Dante glanced up at the plain ceiling. "Where do you suppose the Nine Pines' bow is?"

"The armory?" Blays jerked his chin at the bare walls. "Judging from the other furnishings, it'll be the only thing there."

"Josun Joh said it would be found in a high place. If the Green Lakes are at the bottom of a mine—the low place—where would that put the bow?"

"At the top of a mine?"

"That is definitely not the answer."

"At the top of an anti-mine."

"Of course!" Dante said. "By coincidence, it's rumored your brain is hidden there, too."

"The attic, if this place has one. Or one of the towers. What do I look like, a Pennish bow-hound? We'll ask for a tour and see what there isn't to see."

Which was actually a decent plan, given that it was low-risk, unsuspicious, and might even involve a helpful friend or servant stopping to specifically point it out—with the implication that "Here is the Quivering Bow, a norren artifact of unsurpassed power, so what does it say that it's now in the hands of our esteemed lord?" Alternately, their tour leader might go the opposite route, conspicuously leaving a part of the manor unshown to avoid revealing their secret weapon to Mallish eyes. Either way, the search would be narrowed.

Cassinder was gone again in the morning. Something about overseeing the latest extraction, said to be especially rich. Dante asked for and was reluctantly granted a tour of the household by its majordomo, a man near fifty with thinning gray hair and the tight, clipped gestures of a former soldier. He led Blays and Dante through the manor's numerous wings, floors, and cellars, pointing out ancestral heirlooms (an engraved chalice, a sapphire ring, a broken arrow, which excited Dante until the majordomo explained it had been retrieved from Cassinder's great-great grandfather after the battle of somewhere-or-other); the home's notable additions (along with which estate-owner commissioned them and which architect designed them); and an endless procession of guest rooms, which were of interest not for *what* was in them (nothing, for the most part, though a handful were appropriately if archaically furnished), but for who had once slept in them, a list of historical so-and-so's whose names Dante forgot as quickly as the balding man recited them.

"Is there an armory?" Blays said as the majordomo returned them to the carpeted but otherwise blank hallway that opened to their rooms. "Any legendary weapons of yore? Nothing restores your sense of wonder like looking at a sword that's killed a king."

"Unfortunately, there is nothing like that in the house itself," the man said. "With Lord Cassinder's permission, perhaps you might see the collection in the tower." He glanced down and to the corner. "Yet as with the house, the contents are...austere. Our lord is ever a minimalist."

Blays took an expression of mock affront. "Except in his hospitality!"

"Of course."

The man left them to the quiet house. Cassinder returned by noon, flushed from the chilly ride. After convening downstairs along with the various servants and attendants of both parties, he offered Dante and Blays a carriage for the ride to the mine.

"Horses or our own feet," Blays said, continuing the bravado. "Carriages separate a man from the world. You know what you get when you're separated from the world? Soft. And white enough to read by."

Dante expected one of the man's chilly rebuffs, but Cassinder responded with a fragile smile. "It will be done."

His people scattered for the stables, bringing back two fine-looking horses (for all the riding Dante had done between Narashtovik and the Norren Territories, he still couldn't tell any equine differences more specific than mare or stallion) and an adequate if less nobly statured mount for Lira. Gala and Mourn were left to accompany on foot. Cassinder's troop consisted of three mounted men and two unmounted norren of his own, who carried large packs on their broad backs.

The trail curled up the hill. To both sides of the dark dirt, grass and ferns glistened in the sun, still damp. Vapor trailed from the horses' nostrils. Cassinder ranged ahead. From most nobles, Dante would take this as a sign of arrogance—the light, ongoing cruelty of constantly reminding everyone around him of their place—but Cassinder's long gazes over the green fields and his nature in general suggested he was simply the type to wander ahead because he was lost in his own thoughts. He was an odd duck, a strange bird among the social beasts that made up the aristocracy, and if Dante didn't have more pressing matters on his hands, he would have tried to get to know the young lord.

"Do you do any fencing?" Dante said instead, trying to steer their host into martial matters. "Boxing? Archery?"

"I train with the besette," Cassinder said, referring to a reed-thin blade that hadn't been popular in Gask for at least three generations. "It is a weapon of finesse."

"Just that?"

"It only takes one weapon to kill a man."

Blays pushed out his lower lip. "If you don't care about having fun, sure."

"Killing is a tool, not a sport." Cassinder blinked, then offered that same fragile smile. "I am sorry. My mother once told me I'd have to learn a blade to protect myself from my tongue."

"Smart woman."

Dante pried further, but Cassinder's responses turned monosyllabic until the lord shifted the discourse to chummy small talk—their trip, their families, etc. The hill apexed and began a shallow downslope into a valley cleared of trees. Trying to clear the lush landscape of all growth would have been futile, however, and the ground remained fuzzy with bushes, weeds, ferns, stump-mosses, and fungus. A few miles further along the road, the land swelled again. Atop its high crown, a narrow tower jutted into the sky.

"Is that where you keep your armory?" Dante said without thinking.

Cassinder looked at him from the corner of his eyes. "My armory?"

"Your man gave us a tour of the household. We wanted to see the family arms, but he said they were kept in a tower."

"The original site of the house." The blond man swayed with the roll of his horse. "But it is not a good time."

"Are you that busy? Surely one of your people could show us up."

"The steps to the top are in disrepair. Reaching the armory is currently impossible."

"Damn," Blays said. "When are they going to invent ropes already?"

Cassinder gazed at the finger of stone on the hilltop. "You would only be disappointed. There is only one item of note, acquired so recently it has not yet been given a proper display."

Whatever Cassinder's claims, the tower looked intact and unblemished, an impression Dante confirmed when they crested the hill and rode under its noon-shortened shadow. It was a simple construction, smooth walls of white stone flecked with brown and yellow, its curves broken by narrow arrow-slits. The single door was average in size, but its ring handle was bulky enough to brain a bull. Cassinder stared past it as they advanced. Dante caught Blays' eye and raised his brows at the silent tower.

They reached the mine within the hour. It sat halfway up a hill, a dirty sprawl of scaffolds surrounding a cavelike tunnel into the stone. Norren emerged with buckets, shoulders bent, dust sifting from their hair. Others turned the wheel of a listless windmill, siphoning water from the depths. Smoke poured from the chimneys of a smelter. A single long barracks stood a few hundred feet away. Men with swords and bows laughed, arms folded over their chests, sparing glances at the lean norren hauling rubble and ore up from the torchlit tunnels.

Cassinder turned his horse sideways to watch the proceedings. Near the barracks, a one-armed norren tended pots above a firepit. A woman limped up to set a water bucket beside him. Others emerged from the smelter, trudged to a clearing by the mine's entrance, and hefted buckets, arms and backs straining, before returning to the smoking building. They showed no expression but the occasional wince. Over Dante's shoulder, the faces of Mourn and Gala were coldly blank.

"It is a pinnacle of the intersection of purpose and meaning," Cassinder said softly, as if to himself. "The labor of would-be traitors is instead turned to extracting the silver of one of the nation's wealthiest new mines. In this way, their treasonous spirit is converted into strength for the very country they would sabotage."

"Pretty fit punishment," Dante said.

"It's not a punishment."

"I didn't mean to imply they're not treated well."

Cassinder shook his head, features contracted into something sharp and eager. "You misunderstand. It is a sign."

"Looks like hauling rocks to me," Blays said. "I don't know what that's a sign of. Other than a lifetime of shit-work."

"How do we know the things we do are right?" Cassinder said. "Praise from others? But they are just men, their vision and wisdom limited by a mortal span and the circumscribed perspective that comes with it."

"Well obviously."

"Others look to inner praise. The righteous pride one feels when one has done well. There is nothing purer than one's own spirit."

"But we're just men ourselves," Dante said.

Cassinder's head snapped down in a nod. "Exactly. Exactly. The praise of mortals—weak, flawed, rotting—cannot be trusted. Whose can? That of the gods. The heavens. But they do not speak to us. Not in words like these. They operate by *signs*." He gestured to a dust-blackened norren as the worker staggered to a stop, dropped two buckets with a hollow thump, and gasped for air. "The heavens are symmetry. Perfection reflected and reproduced. The dirt in those buckets becomes pure silver. So the dirt in that man's rebellious soul becomes the power of Gask. Between this symmetry, we glimpse the approval of Arawn."

Dante had to literally bite his tongue to prevent himself from launching into an extensive, *Cycle*-quoting counterargument that Arawn doesn't in fact care about the acts of men at all—that we are all derived from and return to the same stuff, the nether, the grist of Arawn's mill, and so our time spent as men doesn't seem that significant to him at all. Instead he said nothing. He was all but certain the Quivering Bow was locked in that tower with its "broken" steps. If he did nothing to impinge on his host's goodwill for two more nights, the bow would be his.

"You did not come here to see me speak," Cassinder smiled into the silence Dante had inadvertently let grow awkward. "Careful inside. There are rocks."

Dante laughed, but Cassinder's quickly-hidden look of puzzlement suggested that hadn't been a joke. He provided them covered lanterns and warned them to let him know if the flame changed color, particularly green or blue. That much sounded exciting, but otherwise the mine looked exactly the way Dante would have guessed: stone tunnels, boards planking the walls and ceilings to lock in loose rocks, grit and dust and sweating men bunching their arms to assault the walls with heavy picks. Other norren gathered the rubble into buckets and lugged it up to the light. No surprises except the silver ore itself, gnarled rocks shot through with shades of rust and blue.

Yet the banality of it all was a sign of its own. The norren struck the wall, rested a moment, struck the wall, rested. Others knelt among the clouds of dust and swept up loose rocks. It seemed suddenly foreign, even monstrous, that Cassinder should *own* men the same way he owned their shovels and buckets. Not that Dante was alone in this thought. There were abolitionists wherever there were slaves. Its wrongness was simply obvious to him now in the same way his acceptance of it had been obvious earlier that day. The servants at Narashtovik's Sealed Citadel, were they slaves or paid hands? Dante had no idea. In the darkness, his cheeks flushed red.

He didn't speak much on the way back, which surely suited Cassinder fine. The midday sun was full but so lacking in warmth Dante could still see the foggy ghost of his own breath. The echoing halls of the house at Beckonridge were nearly as cool as the outdoors, but the fire in his sparse room had been kept stoked in his absence by able servants. The room was so hot his skin itched.

"What do you think?" Dante said, shedding his coat and stripping off his doublet.

"That you should do more pushups," Blays said.

"About the bow, dummy."

"That just maybe it's up in that tower he refused to let us see inside."

"I agree with you. Which makes me very scared."

Blays gestured at the squeaky-boarded floor. "How much

longer can we depend on a nobleman's hospitality towards his own kind? Cassinder's the type of guy who wouldn't let the friends he doesn't have stay more than a few days."

Dante circled the room, as if the motion would unwind the contents of his head. "We'll move tomorrow night. That will give us another day to search and the clan to prepare. Get your stealing shoes on."

"Who says I ever take them off?"

Dante passed word of the decision to Mourn, who promised to deliver the message that night. Dante didn't tell Gala or Lira, the former because he didn't think she'd care one way or the other, and the latter because Lira's earnest loyalty (she'd done nothing but play the part of a servant since arriving at Beckonridge) and almost too-convenient method of meeting them on the river had Dante privately concerned she might not be who she said she was. Which was perhaps paranoid, given the broken leg and the starvation and all, but if her life-debt nonsense was as heartfelt as she claimed, she would happily follow them into the gall bladder of a firesquid. By contrast, accompanying them on a midnight break-in to a crumbling tower would be no trouble at all.

In the morning, a bleary-eyed Mourn told them word had been passed, with Orlen planning to raid the mine at 1 AM. In case the clan and Dante's party stayed separated, they'd reconvene at the *Boomer*. Dante and Blays spent the day pumping Cassinder's servants on the history and lore of Beckonridge, recruiting Mourn to do the same from his side of the social strata, hoping to induce a revelatory brag about the bow. In this way, they coaxed the majordomo into confessing the estate's purchase of the Clan of the Green Lake had come with the acquisition of a weapon of "no small power." When Dante pressed for details, the man implied in the politest and most deniable terms that Dante might be a lord, but he was still a *foreign* lord, and it was not the majordomo's place to reveal what might well be considered a secret of the state.

Still, besides being shot with the bow itself, it was the best confirmation Dante could have hoped for. He went to bed with the same childlike anticipation he'd once felt for Falmac's Eve. Much like that day of meat pies, fermented cider, and tiny wooden one-eyed idols, it would probably all be over before he knew it.

He met Blays in the hallway at midnight, or as close to it as he could reckon by the stars. Except for the sporadic crackle of fireplaces, the manor was silent and all but completely dark; the wall candles had burnt out or been put out, leaving the starlight to fight its way through windows that had iced over in the night. Dante crept down the spiral staircase, feeling the way with his feet. If they were intercepted by anyone with the courage and authority to question them, Blays' idea of a cover story was they were meeting with Lira in order to arrange a surprise feast for their host—a story which they would, through awkward phrasing and embarrassed glances, in turn imply to be a cover for your typical perverse aristocratic sex with the help—but by the time they met Lira in the servants' kitchen and its faded yet cloying scents of rendered fat and boiled beets, they hadn't seen another soul.

She led them into the biting night. The dirt road was frozen underfoot. Frost glittered from the weeds. Dante heard no baying of hounds, saw no sudden lighting of lanterns. Under starlight, they'd be nearly invisible. He kept the nether close. Its cold pulse mirrored his own. His breath swirled from his mouth, hanging in the damp air. Mourn and Gala waited for them beyond the first ridge, swords on hips.

"The clan will move soon," Mourn said. "Don't expect subtlety."

Blays snorted. "You guys are seven feet tall and weigh as much as a statue of yourselves. I don't think you do *anything* subtly."

"This isn't just a rescue," Gala said. "It's vengeance."

"Good," Dante said. "Then Cassinder's soldiers will be too busy dying to notice we're stumbling around in their tower stealing their things."

He could see it already, a fingerlike silhouette rising from the opposite rim of the valley. He wanted to run to it, but maintained a brisk walk instead. The tower arrived soon enough. Standing beneath its hundred-foot rise of white stone, Dante could feel every ounce of its weight. Its very star-cast shadow pressed on him, simultaneously holding him down and compelling him onward. He pulled the door's huge iron ring; the door didn't budge.

"What would you do without me." Blays knelt beside the lock, an outrageously huge pad that could be repurposed as an anvil at a moment's notice.

"I'd ask Mourn to smash the lock right off," Dante said. "I assumed picking it would make less noise, but I forgot that would leave your mouth as free as ever."

Blays unfolded a leather case of narrow metal prods, hooks, and squiggle-tipped wires. When they'd first met, Blays had been a devoted student of the school of "bash it once, and if that doesn't work, bash it harder," but over the last year or two he'd taken to practicing methods that left locks, knobs, and hinges intact, recognizing that much of their work in the Norren Territories was the kind that must be denied rather than gloated about. His interest in the skill had doubled at a party in Narashtovik at Duke Abbedon's manor which Dante's position on the Council forced them to attend. On hearing the Abbedon kept his best wines beside his own bed, Blays went upstairs, trailed by a young lady he'd been after all night. The duke's bedroom bore not one but three locks, but Blays had them off in seconds, so impressing the lady that it took no kits or tools whatsoever to pry her from her dress then and there.

Beneath the white tower, Blays set to his task with uncommon sobriety, methodically wiggling a number of thin rods into the lock's keyhole, squinting into the empty night as he poked and worried the tools about its raspy interior, guided by touch and sounds far too arcane for Dante to differentiate. Exhausting one pick, Blays swapped it out for another and leveraged a third thicker tool into the tumblers and latches lurking inside.

"I don't think this is happening," he said after a couple minutes of jiggling and prying. "I guess we'll just have to forget the bow, renounce our beliefs, and return home to retire as farmers." Blays reached down for an L-shaped rod with a crooked little tooth at its end, inserted it into the pad, and torqued his wrist. The lock squeaked. Rust flaked onto Blays' hand. He slipped the opened pad from its loops and dropped it in the grass. "Oh. I forgot I'm the greatest."

"Congratulations, you have the skills of an eight-year-old orphan." Dante stepped into the darkness and lit a candle with a flicker of nether. The others crowded in beside him, accepting candles of their own. A wooden ceiling hung some twelve feet overhead, penetrated by a staircase that ascended into darkness above.

At its other end, it descended through the floor to an even deeper blackness below. Melted remnants of candles sat on the floor. Burnt-out torches rested in wall sconces. The ground floor was bare except for a large wooden plank to bar the door and a few sacks of what was, judging from the mice droppings, likely to be grain.

"I could only find the rope," Mourn said, extracting it from his pack. "I hope it's enough to get past the upper stairs."

Dante tipped back his head, peering into the drafty heights. "I doubt there's anything wrong with the stairs at all. That was just a cover to keep us out."

"Still, it's a depressing thought to come hundreds of miles and wind up ten feet out of reach of the object of your desire. I don't know what I'd do. Jump from one of the windows, I bet."

"Me too, but only because of the shame of lacking basic problem-solving skills. Get moving."

Dante led the way up the steps. The stairwell was so tight Mourn and Gala not only had to duck, they had to turn their shoulders, too, filling Dante's head with nightmare scenarios of one of them slipping and getting so thoroughly lodged between the steps that those above them on the stairs would be trapped, left to starve to death—or forced to burrow their way to freedom through a mass of hair and blood. After a complete turn, the stairs opened into a round, plank-floored room. Drafts blew in through the arrowslits, disturbing Dante's candle. This room was largely empty, too, besides a few rotting chairs blanketed with cobwebs and an old set of dishes which weren't glazed but had instead acquired a fine finish of dirt.

The following floors were just as barren. The tower's furnishings, in fact, gave every indication it had been in disuse for years now, if not decades, and that the last owners to put it to use had employed it as the watchtower/fortress it had clearly been built as.

Then, some eighty feet up, the steps became a blank black space. Dante shoved his hands against the close walls, swearing, bracing himself against a vision of the fumbling body that would push him over the broken steps.

"Hold it!" His voice echoed up and down. Blays nudged him,

peering over his shoulder at the spot where the steps disappeared, a void that stretched beyond the curve of the staircase. Vestigial lumps of stone projected from the walls along the missing steps' former path, but these were just a few fingers wide and obviously crumbly even by the meek candlelight.

"No problem," Blays said. "Mourn, get up here and throw me."

"What?" Dante said.

Blays gestured at the yawning gap. "He throws me, I land on the other side, we all praise my name."

"You can't even see the other side."

"Are you suggesting it's not there?"

"I'm suggesting you will fall and break whatever parts of yourself you land on."

"I'll cling to the wall. Like a handsome raccoon."

"Raccoons, known worldwide for their proverbial jumping ability." Dante pointed at the cracked stone jutting from where the stairs had set into the wall. "At least try that before your leap of faith."

Blays crouched down, forcing Dante back a step, and leaned forward to test the jagged stone remnants with his fingertips. Parts were wide enough for a firm toehold, perhaps for a whole shoe, but in long gaps the broken steps were flush with the sheer wall. Dust and sand sifted down into the darkness, sprinkling on the stairs a spiral below.

"I don't know about this," Blays said.

"Two seconds ago you were ready to send yourself smashing straight to hell."

"Yeah, but that would have been over in a second. All this creeping along, waiting for the ledge to crumble underneath me...it seems kind of stupid."

"I'll do it," Lira said from behind them.

"You're not doing anything." Dante looked in vain for a fly or spider he could kill, restore to unlife with the nether, and use to scout the stairs ahead. "If you want to be helpful, start composing Blays' eulogy."

"Remember to include a line about how I'm 6'9"." Blays ran his hand down his mouth. "All right. We tie the rope around my waist. I try to scooch along the side here. Mourn holds tight to the free end of the rope while Gala sets up below to catch me if I fall."

"Meanwhile, Lira and I will shut our eyes and pray." Dante stepped away from the broken steps, pressing his back against the wall. "Let's do this."

It took a full minute of awkward shuffling, retreating, and bumping around before Gala made it to the full turn below where Blays might fall and before Blays and Mourn got in position on the lower edge of the gap. Dante took up beside Gala and sent a small white light up to the broken steps directly above them, eyeballing exactly how much of the staircase was missing. Even from below, it wasn't easy to tell—the missing portion was a good twelve feet overhead, and the tight spiral quickly stole the ascending steps from view, making it more than possible there was another broken stretch further up—but he guessed some eight horizontal feet of stairs were missing. He anchored the white light above the ledge where Blays would cross, then slipped downstairs past Gala, keeping the nether close at hand in case of a fall. The whole stairwell smelled of fresh sweat and the sweet wax of burning candles.

"All set?" he called.

"I still think I should jump," Blays echoed.

"If you fall, use your last thought to pretend that's what you did."

"Make sure your head's out of the way. I don't want to get impaled."

Leather scuffed stone. Blays grunted. His leg extended into view, tapping down on the cracked ledge. Dust speckled into Dante's eyes; he turned away, blinking hard. His light above flickered.

"Lyle's balls!" Blays yelled. "Let's wait until the next time before we try this in the dark, huh?"

"Just trying to add to your legend." Dante redoubled his focus, restoring the full glare of the white light. Blays clung to the wall, palms spread, his feet turned sideways for maximum surface area along the narrow, irregular, rising ledge. A rope trailed between his waist and Mourn, who'd installed himself at the lower edge of the gap, his feet and shoulders braced against the walls. Blays took a minor step forward, dragging his back foot after. Inch by inch, he struggled on, pausing regularly to strengthen his toeholds and dig his fingertips into the crannies between stones, grimacing, panting hollowly over the ticking sound of falling grit.

His next step led him to a proper foothold, a flat chunk of step protruding a full foot from the wall. Blays extended his front foot and stepped onto the widened ledge.

"Whoa!" He threw out his arms. Dante cringed, throwing his hands above his face. Blays chuckled brightly. "I'm fine. Good to see where your first instincts take you, though."

Blays caught his breath, then carried on along the narrow lip of ruined steps. Within a minute, he reached the far side. Dante maneuvered around Gala and climbed up to the edge of the gap.

"What now?"

Partly occluded by the curve of the stairwell, Blays jerked his thumb upstairs. "There are some sconces and stuff on the walls. If I tie one end of the rope up here and you secure the other down there, it should be a lot easier to cross."

Dante frowned. "If they don't pull right out of the walls."

"Well, you don't have much choice. If you stay down there, I can tell everyone you're a coward *and* have three witnesses to back me up."

Blays disappeared upstairs, rope dragging along behind him. He returned seconds later to sling the loose end downstairs. Dante caught it and wound down the steps until he located a wall sconce, then knotted the rope tight around its upturned iron fingers.

He began the crossing before he could have second thoughts or face further taunts. Aided by the rope, against which he could lean most of his weight when toeholds were sparse, he proceeded quickly, heart racing; grit twisted under his soles as the rope's rough fibers chafed his palms. He stepped onto the solid ground of the far side with physical relief.

"I think you've got a future in the carnival," Blays said.

"I've got plenty of experience working with freaks."

"Stop!" Mourn called, strangled.

Dante whirled. Through his beard, Mourn was pale, features pulled in a tight rictus.

"We're only kidding," Dante said, confused yet gently. "You don't have to—"

"Don't go upstairs."

"What are you talking about? We're fine, Mourn. We're not going to turn around with the bow right up these steps."

"I just heard from Josun Joh."

Dante rolled his eyes. "Josun Joh's less reliable than a choleric's bowel movements. What's he got to say this time? That by 'the highest place' he meant the bow's been stolen by eagles, and we'll have to enlist the Vulture King to get it back?"

"He says we've been betrayed and Cassinder's personal army has surrounded the tower downstairs."

Blays blinked. "That's...specific."

A prickling, dreadful heat washed over Dante's skin. "This is a thing that's happening now?"

Mourn's eyes were bright beneath his heavy brows. "Look outside."

An icy wind knifed from upstairs. Dante headed up, Blays on his heels, into a dusty and cobwebbed storage room. He dimmed his light until the chests and sacks littering the floor were dim shapes of black and gray. Beneath the torn flaps of a burlap sack, a glimpse of tightly-sheafed arrows sent his heart thumping. He moved past them to a window of tall sectional glass with a couple broken panes. Stars twinkled silently over the black field. Dante extinguished his light, Blays his candle.

"See anything?" Dante whispered.

"A bunch of dark stuff. Think Cassinder's army is made out of coal-men?"

"Wait." As his eyes adjusted, he began to pick out movements that couldn't be ascribed to breeze-ruffled weeds. Starlight glinted on steel. Eighty feet below, a row of men kneeled across the road from the tower's front door. "Mourn's right."

"You're sure? Because that would mean bad things for us. Stabby things."

"Twenty of them. Maybe more." Dante retreated from the window and relit his candle, crouching to hide the light from the soldiers below. "It's all right. The bow's up here. We can use it to escape."

"There is no bow." Mourn's voice filtered up the stairway, ethereal, dolorous, shamed.

Dante returned to the top of the gap in the stairs. Mourn hadn't moved. "Their soldiers are at our feet, Mourn. Very soon, they're going to come up this tower, or set a fire below, and you will be roasted like a very hairy and treasonous pig. Now tell me what you're holding back."

The norren looked down at his heavy palms. Fear and doubt added years to his face. He closed his eyes. "There is no bow. Or anyway, if there is, it's just a bunch of legends that built up around a very normal weapon. When you came in questing after it, Orlen let you believe it was real."

"What?"

"He saw what you could do. That you're a sorcerer. He thought he could use you to—"

Gala rose behind the seated Mourn, blade in hand. "That's enough."

Lira's sword flashed from its sheath to point at Gala's back. In the same instant, Dante shaped the nether into a swirling black ball. "Silent. Or you die."

Gala's face took on a resigned smile. "I don't fear death. I do fear my clan."

"We're going to die down there anyway, aren't we?" Blays shouldered past Dante, nearly toppling him down the empty gap. "What does it matter what we know? Our brains aren't tea leaves. When our skulls get split, all that will leak out is a bunch of goop. So sit your giant ass down and let the man talk."

Fleetingly, Gala's smile widened. She lowered her curved blade, sheathed it. "Fine. If he wants his final act to be to dishonor his clan, let Josun Joh judge him."

Mourn kept his gaze on Dante. "Orlen was using you to get back the cousin-clan."

Dante swallowed against the tightness in his throat. "And now he's sold us out to the enemy while he rescues his people from the mine."

"No!" Mourn's face jerked up, tight with pain. "Orlen just wanted your help. He didn't think he could secure it without making you believe you'd get the bow. You were sold out to Cassinder by one of our other clansmen. He thought it was the only way to get his family back. He's the one who tipped off the Bloody Knuckles, too. Once he saw we were poised to take back the Clan of the Green Lake ourselves, he confessed to Orlen and Vee."

"Is that it?"

The norren's gaze flicked past his shoulder. "The raid on the mine is real. So is the timing."

"Meaning there's hope of an even bigger distraction." Dante glanced at Blays. "What do you think?"

"That they'll kill me over my dead body." Blays grabbed hold of the rope and searched for a toehold down the ruined steps. "We should get downstairs. Block the door or see if we can make a run."

"I'll be right behind you." Dante turned and jogged back upstairs. His mind whirled with anger and the helpless sense of being duped, of illusions torn away like shabby clothes. But there was no time for the self-pity or humiliation that welled beneath his outrage. On the upper floor, he lit his remaining candles and hurriedly placed them throughout the room. Cassinder's forces thought they had surprise on top of numbers. No reason to disabuse them of their own illusions.

The others had already disappeared downstairs. Dante hardly slowed on his way across the rope spanning the gritty ledge. On the other side, he lit his feet with tiny white lights to show him the way and hurried to the ground floor, where the others waited in starlit darkness.

"I count about forty versus five." Blays slid down from the narrow window to give Gala a pointed look. "Or should that be four?"

She shrugged her broad shoulders. "I hope to see my clan again."

"With that kind of enthusiasm, let's bump it up to four and a half. We could just let them siege us. Mourn and Gala are very large, so it should take several weeks to eat them."

"We need to run," Dante said.

"I'll lead the charge." Mourn gazed at the black window. "To erase my betrayal, I'll try to absorb as many arrows as I can."

"You getting shot to death is not a plan." Dante crept to the window. Beyond, silhouettes of soldiers arranged themselves on the other side of the road. A picket of three or four troops waited further down the road toward the mine; presumably a similar group was blocking the opposite route to the manor. More than two hundred yards of open downhill slope separated the tower from the pine forest to the west, the obvious place for Dante to lose their pursuers—or to string them out and battle them in clusters rather than en masse. "Suppose they've got cavalry, too?"

"In reserve at best," Blays said. "A horse snort carries pretty far at night."

"So the good news is the cavalry might trample the arrows right out of our backs."

"Can you make us invisible?"

Dante shook his head. "Too complicated. I would have to match the illusions to whatever was around us. On all sides. Constantly."

"Is that all?" Blays gritted his teeth. "But you could make illusions *of* us. Which could run out to do battle, swords in hand."

"While the real usses make a break for the woods."

"While you wrap us up in one of those balls of darkness. Like back in Bressel."

"Wouldn't be able to see where we're going. We'll trip constantly. The'll be on us in seconds."

"Will you stop making this so damned hard?" Blays laughed. "So we hold hands. Mourn's in the middle. I'm at the front. You focus on keeping the sphere centered around Mourn's big head, keeping the darkness just wide enough so I can peek out the front and make sure we're not about to plunge into a ditch."

"That is insane." Dante laughed, too, waving one hand in dismissal. "Don't bother to ask. No, I can't think of anything better."

Lira shook her head. "I don't understand a word of what you two just said."

"Don't worry, neither did I," Blays grinned. "Just hang on to my hand and cut anyone who tries to take me away."

"Are those the same orders you'd give a man?"

"I don't know. Become one and we'll find out."

Dante wasn't troubled by the idea of maintaining the shadowsphere during their run. In that alley in Bressel, the ball of darkness had been the very first time he'd used the nether—in fact, it had appeared completely by accident, a physical manifestation of his quite conscious desire to escape the men who'd been pursuing them. In much the same way he could hold a conversation while watching a play, he was certain he could keep up the sphere and their illusory doubles even while being tugged along blind down a hill. If he tripped, however, or inhaled a fly, all bets were off. Then it would be them, in the open, before some forty armed men.

There was just enough space in the tower for the five of them to string themselves out hand in hand. Dante conjured the shadowsphere, concealing them inside a ball of perfect black. He shrunk the sphere until Blays called out that he could see, then held its size in his mind, memorizing the influx and arrangement of nether that would keep it at its present circumference.

When he let the sphere fall away, the starlight was so crisp and silvery he could see the faces of the soldiers across the road. Dante drew the wavy knife he'd won at Nulladoon and traced a stark red line down the back of his arm. Nether fed on the blood as it ticked to the floor. One by one, he shaped the shadows into doppelgangers of their waiting crew. The matches were far from perfect — their flat eyes and chunky hair would easily be discredited in direct sunlight — but under full night, the hulking forms of two norren would be unmistakable. He finished the illusion with two human males, one blond and one dark-haired, and a woman with her long brunette locks clamped tight in a ponytail. Lira watched her double walk to the door with the strange half-smile of someone who's just heard something unspeakably rude.

"Well," Dante said slowly, his focus splintered between the five stiff figures. "I hope I don't die with a stupid look on my face."

Mourn lifted the board braced across the entry. Dante leaned into the heavy wood door and flung it wide, leaping back into the safety of the tower. Someone whistled sharply from the enemy lines. Dante narrowed his eyes. The five images hunched down and crept out the door, one by one.

"Stop!" a man called from outside in a clear tenor.

Dante straightened the figures and sent them racing north, paralleling the road to the mine. The man repeated his order. The five real people gathered just inside the tower doorway, linking hands, Blays at the front, Mourn in the middle. With the illusions fifty feet away and gaining distance fast, Dante summoned the shadowsphere to center on Mourn's head. Total blackness painted his eyes.

"Go!" Blays hissed.

A moment later, Mourn's thick hand yanked Dante forward; his right arm jangled, tugging Gala behind him. His feet swished into the weeds. Dante could no longer see the illusions except in his mind's eye, where they pumped their feet and sent horrified glances at every shout and command of Cassinder's troops, but he heard the arrows slashing the air, the thump of soldier's boots in sprinting pursuit. His own foot slipped in the damp grass; the shadowsphere flickered, allowing a ghostly glimpse of sword-bearing men charging away after the illusory silhouettes. For an instant, both of Dante's feet left the ground, his arms straining between the two norren's unholy strength, and then he found his footing and ran and ran. He redoubled his focus. The shadowsphere returned to total darkness.

His feet struck packed dirt, jarring painfully. Some ways to his left—what he hoped to the gods was the south—hooves thudded the turf. Then he was back in the grass, feet churning. Mourn grunted in pain but didn't break stride. Up the road, a man cried out a string of incredulous profanity.

Dante kept hold on the doubles and the shadowsphere. The confusion spread to a babble of voices, each soldier demanding, in his own specific phrasing, to know what in the nine hells was happening. Dante relaxed his hold on the sphere. Across the road and a couple hundred yards toward the mines, a man poked his sword into one of the false norren and waggled the weapon from side to side. Dante sent a final pulse of nether to the images. They popped in a rainbow-hued burst of silent light.

Men cried out in surprise. The woods waited just ahead, thrusts of pines mixed with harvested stumps that could easily break an ankle. Dante dropped the shadowsphere completely. His hands slipped from Mourn's and Gala's. Behind them, men scattered across the grass, hollering frustrated updates; torches flared, casting yellow light and long shadows. Dante pounded into the fringes of the wood. For a moment, he thought they might escape without being seen at all.

"In the trees!" a man shouted. "Right there!"

Faces swung to stare their way. Men broke into dead runs, torches flapping, swords in hand. Archers set their feet. Moments later, the first arrows hissed through the leaves, smacking into trunks and burying shafts half a foot into the damp earth. Blays swore and veered left through the pines, then swung into a sharp right. Lira began to limp.

Blays fell back with her, and after a moment's hesitation, so did Dante. The two norren slowed to a jog as well. Torches flashed between the trees, closing. It was a matter of time.

Yet the chase had strung out Cassinder's soldiers, house-guards with little discipline. Feet thrashed through weeds and leaves. Blays stopped and whirled, ripping his swords from their sheaths. The nearest guard was a good twenty feet in front of the others; his eyes widened as he pounded down the slope, unable to stop.

"Is this how you treat your guests?" Blays' sword sent the man's head spinning into the grass. Three more soldiers rushed down the hill. Dante flung a bolt of nether through the closest man's chest. The soldier's breath left him in a horrid groan. He crashed into the undergrowth, skidding facefirst. The two other stopped, faces painted with sudden fear, torches crackling. Bursts of shadows leapt from Dante's hands. Blood flashed in the starlight. The two men gurgled in the ferns.

"For Beckonridge!" a man screamed from up the slope. Ten soldiers spilled down with him. Something heavy thumped behind Dante. Gala lay in the grass, an arrow jutting from her skull.

Mourn lifted his gaze from the body. Wordless, he strode forward, raised his heavy sword, and slammed it down on the first man to reach him. His opponent blocked with a high, crossward slant. Steel banged on steel; the man's sword shot out of his hand, thudding to the dirt. Mourn's next blow cut straight through the man's warding arm and halved his head.

Swords and blood and screams moiled in torchlight and darkness. To Dante's left, Blays punched his sword forward to meet an incoming blade, the weapons straining between their chests. Blays dipped his offhand blade, jabbed the soldier's foot. The man yelped and fell. Blays stabbed him without looking, parrying the thrust of another guard. A man rushed Dante, straight sword aimed at his chest. Dante intercepted with his own, dropping back two steps from the man's downhill momentum, and sent a spear of nether battering through his ribs.

Beside him, Lira feinted, feinted again, then stumbled. As her opponent closed with a downward stroke, she lunged forward—the stumble, too, had been a feint—angling to the outside of the man's swipe and driving her own blade through his stomach.

Uphill, a mounted man stopped his horse and turned it sideways. His downy hair glowed in the torchlight. Shadows flocked to Dante's fingers. He danced back from a man with a spear, putting Mourn between them, and winged a dark bolt for Cassinder's midsection. White sparks burst from the lord's stomach. Cassinder cried out, slumping from his horse and collapsing to the ground.

"Your lord is dead!" Dante summoned a point of light high above his head, so bright and piercing he thought he could see the soldiers' skulls through their skin. "Do you want to die with him?"

Cassinder's guards shrunk back. Several bolted for their master lying motionless in the grass. A bow whispered; an arrow gashed through Dante's left ear.

"I say we try the running again," Blays said.

Mourn sheathed his sword, grabbed up Lira, and slung her onto his back. She blinked, hoisting her sword to keep it from slashing the giant man. Other than the blood dripping down her temple, Gala still hadn't moved. Dante turned and ran down the hill.

The land dropped sharply. Every step threatened to spill him. Mourn somehow matched pace, Lira bouncing on his back. A handful of arrows hissed past. The guards resumed the chase, torches winking behind trees, but between the skirmish and those who'd stayed behind to tend to Cassinder, the pursuers were less than half the number that had gathered beneath the tower. That, perhaps, explained why they stopped five minutes into the chase, their fires shrinking with each step Dante took through the wet grass. Dante heard nor saw any cavalry, either—the slope was too steep for horses, the night too full—but suspected they'd patrol the roads for days.

Still they ran, leveling out and splashing across a frozen creek, then climbing through slippery pine needles and frost-glittered ferns. At the top of the hill, Mourn called for a stop. Blays bared his teeth, breathing hard. He gazed downhill and planted his hands on his hips.

"Well, I don't think we have to worry about starting a war anymore."

"What are you talking about?" Dante said. "That was a disaster!"

"Exactly." Blays nodded down the slope. Dante turned. At the mines miles to the north, a great fire glared in the night, gouting white smoke. Far south, a second fire burned from the manor where they'd spent the last three nights. "I'd say the war's already begun."

6

"Well then," Dante said. "Let's be on our way."

Blays blinked in the moonlight. "Did you hear me? That war we were trying so desperately to avert? Here it is!"

"Right now, I'm a little more concerned about that." Dante tipped his head to the woody valley, lightly smeared with mist and smoke. Beagles howled from the trees. "I don't think I'll be worried about a war after I'm passed through a dog's belly and deposited on some lord's lawn."

"You think being a pile of shit's going to save you? That will just make it easier for Cally to stomp you."

Dante offered his hand to Mourn, who looked cadaverous beneath his beard. "Sorry to part this way. Perhaps we'll meet again."

Mourn stiffened. "I thought I might come with you."

"We're going back to Narashtovik. We're done with your clan."

"I'm afraid I am, too."

"What are you talking about?" Blays said. "You can't just run off on your clan."

The norren tipped back his high chin, frowning down on them. "I can do whatever I want. I can jump down this hillside if I determine that to be a rewarding course of action. If you wouldn't consider me a millstone around your neck, I'd like to come with you."

"We could use your help with her anyway," Dante nodded at Lira.

Lira raised an eyebrow. "I'll be fine. It's a sprain, not an amputation."

"Lyle's balls, I'm just saying you can't run at a time when we may need to. Can we get a move on?"

She nodded, mollified. Dante cut east down the slope, reckoning by the stars and the twin columns of smoke. His footsteps stirred the scent of pine needles and minty wintrel leaves. Even with Lira leaning on Mourn's shoulder, the huge man moved lightly, stepping over low branches to leave them undisturbed. Not that it would help if the dogs caught up with them. If that happened, Dante would have to resort to methods that would provoke some very sharp words from Blays.

The canopy closed above their heads. Birds peeped from the darkness. The howls of the hounds faded, miles away. Chasing the Clan of the Nine Pines, then. Dante expected the clan could take care of itself.

It had certainly taken care of his own small contingent. Orlen and Vee had played them like a hand of two-bluff. Oh, you're looking for the Quivering Bow? Right this way. It happens to have been stolen by our worst enemy. If you'd like it back, all you'll have to do is everything we ask.

Dante had let them lead him by the hand like a child crossing a thoroughfare. That knowledge tingled in his gut and prickled down his skin, hot and nauseating. In the cold, he felt his cheeks flushing. He'd let himself be swindled, blinded by a fantasy of a bow that could turn the tide of war by itself. Cassinder had done the same, letting his people feed Dante vague hints of the lord's wondrous new weapon, baiting the trap for Dante to make his move.

Blays was right. The burning of Cassinder's estate would spark the very war he'd been trying to stave off. And yes, in all likelihood, that war would have come at some point no matter what they'd done. Gask wasn't going to just shrug as its norren vassals shucked their chains and began governing themselves. Eventually, it would have come to blows. Many thousands of them, in fact.

But it didn't have to come so soon.

The stars had shifted by degrees by the time they struck camp. Fog dripped from the pines, pattering the tarp strung above their heads. Dante had a look at Lira's leg. The healing wound was scarring nicely, but the skin around was swollen and pink. He soothed the ache with a flood of cool nether, then did the same for her sprained ankle.

No one had even bothered to suggest striking a fire. Blays passed around hard sausage and harder bread, crumbs falling from his lips. He thunked down in front of a tree and leaned against its mossy trunk.

"I don't see why we're bothering to run," he said. "Not when Cally's just going to glare off our heads the moment we step foot in the city."

"He knew the risks." Dante gestured in the direction of the Norren Territories. "This whole enterprise was his idea."

"And I think it was also his idea that we not take a torch to one of our enemy's bluest bloods."

"Then he probably shouldn't have sent us."

Blays grinned. "You know, he might actually buy that."

"Who is this Cally?" Lira said. "Another enemy?"

The pair laughed. Blays rubbed his mouth. "I don't know. Do you think a dog considers its worms the enemy?"

Dante tipped his head. "I'd say he's more like a bull who can't tell the difference between the flies and his own hooves."

"I don't follow your path," Lira frowned.

"Cally is the lord of the Sealed Citadel and head of Arawn's Council at Narashtovik," Dante said. "I know him from our homeland. He taught me most of what I know. About the nether, anyway. I wouldn't even want to know what he thinks about art or women. He's an extremely clever and capable leader who runs things in a way that would probably look outright blasphemous to the attendees of his weekly masses. In short, he's cunning, demanding, and unpredictable—but I know him well enough to guess he'll be madder than he's ever been."

"But you were pursuing a just cause. Freeing the people you want to protect. Won't that count for anything?"

"If anything, it'll make him madder."

Blays laughed again. "Anyway, we weren't blazing the trails of righteousness. We were chasing a fairy story."

Dante fought the flush down from his face. "Which won't help."

Lira's face slowly went blank. "Might he try to harm you?"

"He's no Vartigan. He won't stuff our intestines with pork." Dante took a bite of cold sausage. "But to redeem ourselves, he'll probably expect us to do a series of very dangerous things."

Blays scuffed his boot across the dirt, kicking away stray stones. "Then again, that's what makes it so much fun."

Lira nodded, but the lines on her brow and lip suggested what she left unsaid. Dante gazed into the dark woods. Mice crept through the leaves. Every few minutes, an owl screeched like it was calling from another world. He hadn't heard the dogs in a couple of hours. They were miles east of the manor. He wondered if Blays would accept first watch. His use of the nether back at the tower had frayed his nerves; he might pass out soon.

"Do you really think this will lead to war?" Mourn said.

Dante looked up. The norren hadn't said a word in more than an hour. "How closely do you monitor the political sentiment in Setteven?"

"I follow my clan." His beard twitched unreadably. "We keep to ourselves."

"Well, the king's not dumb. Setteven knows what's going on. They can see the norren are gearing up for independence. But we've been very careful to deny them any explosive proof. Tonight, with the assistance of a contingent of humans from Narashtovik, an outlaw clan broke into a nobleman's manor deep in Gaskan lands, made off with his property, and killed any number of human citizens in the process."

"Which other human citizens will take offense to."

"Popular opinion is a form of currency," Dante said. "Tonight, we dropped a gold brick in their laps."

The norren nodded. Through their talk, he hadn't quite met Dante's eyes. His gaze began to drift toward the center of their camp, where they might have built a fire if they weren't eluding pursuit.

"So what's the plan tomorrow?" Blays clapped. "Some light robbery? Fatten our purses enough for three horses and an elephant for that one?" He jerked his thumb at Mourn.

"I thought we'd go downriver," Dante said.

"Northwest."

"That's the way the river goes."

"We are talking about the same Narashtovik, right? The same one that's thoroughly northeast?"

"Hundreds of miles northeast. The distance between which may be thick with people looking for our faces."

"Take the river to the port's at its mouth, then sail back to Narashtovik." Blays narrowed one eye at Lira. "What do you say?"

"Yallen's a busy port," Lira said. "Whatever you think is best."

Mourn didn't glance away from his imaginary fire at camp's center. "I've never been this far north. Unless my parents took me here while I was very small. But even if they did, I don't remember anything that would make my input worthwhile."

Blays shrugged. "I like ports. No one stays there too long for you to get sick of them. And if they do, you can just ship yourself off instead."

Whether or not the rest of the group agreed, that ended the conversation. Dante found his head snapping upright; he'd nodded off.

"I'll take first watch," Mourn said, meeting his eyes for a moment. "For now my brain would rather think than sleep."

Dante didn't pretend to protest. Sleep rolled over him as sudden and unstoppable as a landslide.

He spent most of the next day's walk to the river thinking about what he'd say to Cally. Maybe that was part of his motivation for wanting to sail home rather than taking the overland route: on a boat, you were much more likely to be wracked on a reef or enslaved by pirates or stranded on an island beyond sight or hope of shore. Some ships just disappeared completely, like they'd sailed beyond the rim of the world. If he got lucky, maybe the same thing would happen to him.

Ultimately, there wasn't much *to* say. He could play up the idea they were primarily involved to help the two clans and thus earn their loyalty, but he'd still have to explain about the Quivering Bow. Cally would find out somewhere else anyway. For him, ears sprouted like mushrooms. Dante and Blays weren't the only ones he had gallivanting around the Norren Territories. Somburr was out there as well, and he had an entire network of scouts, spies, and informants. Anyway, Cally would have planned for the contingency of sudden war. It was not in his nature to assume all would follow his most ideal plan.

Still, Dante did not look forward to bearing the bad news.

The river was wide and gray and cold. Smooth rocks clattered along its muddy banks. Fishing villages poked from the mist every few miles. At dusk, the lanterns of a modest town glimmered over the black water. Their group encamped a quarter mile from the road with the intention of enlisting passage downriver in the morning. Given their combined coinage could be held in a single palm without spilling, Dante wasn't certain *how* they'd hire their way, but there was always violence.

Though they'd seen no sign of pursuit during the day, Dante once again ruled out a fire, no matter how badly his feet and legs ached from the walk. The others were quiet and heavy-lidded, lost in their own thoughts of future days. Dante conjured up a small figure of light and shadow, sculpted its hair into Blays' tight crop, and shaped a tiny scabbard on its back and hip. For the next several minutes, he sent the figure bumbling over leaves, pawing through the grass, and scrabbling up trunks and limbs, each quest ending with an abrupt fall, be it of the figure to the ground or a spectral boulder on top of the figure, until Dante sensed his audience growing tired. With a flourish, the figure drew its swords, one white and one black, cocked its head in confusion, then drove both blades through its own ribs. It disappeared with a pop and a wisp of shadow.

"I think you're in the wrong line of work," Blays said. "You should be touring taverns."

"I thought it was funny," Lira said.

"Thanks." Dante was surprised at himself; he wasn't normally the type to care about morale. The task itself should be important enough to command the focus of whoever pursued it. Perhaps he was trying to distract himself, too. He and Blays had been playing this shadowy business for years. Getting weapons to the scattered clans. Forging relationships and alliances. Traveling in disguise as merchants and field workers and Mallish pilgrims, all the while looking to subvert the Gaskan lords who claimed the norren hills. In its way, it had very much been a game, like children dressing up as pirates and bygone heroes, or concealing themselves with branches and cloaks while their parents pretended not to see them.

All this was about to change. There would be no denying the realness of their actions once wheatfields burned and smoke rose from the ashes of ten thousand homes. Dante had seen plenty of skirmishes. One time he'd even fought in a proper battle with a few hundred to a side. They'd piled the dead in pyres and choked on the greasy clouds. What would the Norren Territories look like a month from now? A year?

"I could tell a story." Mourn stared into the empty center of the camp. "If you are people who find stories entertaining."

Blays gave him a skeptical look. "I prefer to be entertained by boredom. Stories and music just bores me. Which then entertains me. Which then bores me and—hold on, my head's about to burst."

"Is that a no?"

Dante smiled with half his mouth and gestured at the bare earth beneath their dewy tarp. "Does it look like you'd be interrupting our great works? Out with it."

Mourn's watery brown eyes flicked between the group. "Okay. But promise you'll tell me if it gets too long."

Blays mock-scowled. "Please, Mourn. There's a lady present."

"This is from a very long time ago. From before the animals forgot how to talk." He pursed his lips. "Or maybe we just forgot how to talk to them. That seems equally likely, doesn't it? How come it's always *their* fault? Pretty arrogant of us talking creatures, if you ask me."

"Getting long," Blays warned.

"Back then, crows lived in big flocks. Fifty, even two hundred at once. They sang to each other because they thought it was fun. Their voices were different then, too. Not all nasty and mad. Instead, some had voices like thick blankets after a night in the snow. Others had voices like fast streams after a run through summer hills. For a long time, the flocks lived alone in the pines, singing to each other. Talking.

"One day, a lost traveler wandered into their woods. He heard the crows singing. Talking. He tipped back his head, more lost than ever in their music, transfixed until that night when they roosted in the boughs. The traveler found his way home to the lowlands, and he told the others what he'd heard.

"Soon, all kinds of travelers climbed to the high forests. They listened to the crow's song, too. After a few weeks of watching his fellow villagers climbing up and down the mountains, a clever man decided to catch some crows and bring them back to town so he could charge people to hear them sing. At first, he couldn't catch any of them. The crows knew the forests so well they could have escaped even with a broken wing. But the man came back with his nets every day, and finally, he caught two crows. He brought them home and opened a little theater, and all the other villagers came to hear the crows sing. To hear them talk.

"But that didn't stop the people from hiking up the hills. Other men wanted to open little theaters of their own. Soon, everyone in the village wanted a pair of crows for their own home. For pets. To ease the hours on their farms and mills. More and more crows left in cages.

"The old birds in the flocks didn't know what to do. The people kept coming, more and more of them, and they had cunning nets and snares. They were patient, too. They hid in the trees until the crows landed for the night, then snatched them up in bags and carried them off to distant lands."

Mourn paused, running his hands through his thick hair. All the while, he'd stared into the imaginary fire, even squinting as he spoke, as if warding away the glare of flames that weren't there. He let out a long breath.

"But a young crow named Nonn was getting angry. Like all crows, he knew they weren't born with their sweet voices. Their soothing songs. Berries grew among vines that lived in the crowns of the pines, and if you ate the berries, the roughest voice grew as smooth as glass. Nonn wanted to tell the people about the berries. If they grew them for themselves, they could eat them and sing to each other instead of coming to steal the crows away from their homes.

"The elders exchanged one look, then locked Nonn up in a cage of their own. They refused to let him out until he promised not to tell. The people kept coming. Stealing crows. Sometimes whole flocks. The old crows accepted this, because most escaped to have more fledglings and keep their flocks alive. When Nonn grew sick of his cage, he made his vow to the elders. He was released. He kept his vow. Perhaps it could have lasted this way forever, a few crows lost here and there to greedy hands while the luckier ones lived on. But one night on a hike up the mountain, a man dropped his lantern. Flaming oil boiled up the trunks. The whole forest burned to the ground.

"The crows had wings, so the flocks flew together to a new forest. But this forest had none of the vine-berries. Soon, the crows lost their cool song, their warm words. They croaked and squawked. To their ears, the sound was so hard and ugly they couldn't stand to hear each other speak. The flocks broke apart. They stayed apart.

"Now crows live alone. They glare at people from the branches. And when a man grows too close, crows curse and spit until he goes away."

Mourn didn't move, but he seemed to shrink in the silence that followed his story. Lira nodded, eyes downcast. Blays' brows knit together and stayed tied, unusually serious.

Dante watched Mourn. "I haven't heard that one before."

The norren didn't look up. "What did you think?"

"I liked it. Very much."

"I mean about Nonn. Do you think he should have told the humans about the berries? Or should he have kept quiet like his flock wanted him to?"

"The whole damn forest burned down," Blays said. "Of course he should have told them."

"But he vowed not to," Lira said. "Could you betray your people like that? I'd rather hang myself."

Blays cocked his head. "Can crows get hanged? They seem awful light."

"It can't be done." She rose and paced the cleared ground, head rumpling the underside of the sagging tarp. "Your loyalty is all you have. If you forfeit that, you burn the forest of your soul."

Mourn watched her, expressionless, then slowly turned to meet Dante's eyes. "What do you think?"

Dante held up his palms. "I can't say. Yeah, the forest burned down, but Nonn didn't know that would happen. Judging from hindsight is like betting after the fight is won."

"What would *you* have done?"

"If I thought it was the right thing to do?" Dante shook his head. "I would have brought the berries down myself and broken the wing of anyone who tried to stop me."

Mourn laughed through his nose, mouth maintaining its blank straight line. "If I had to bet, which I don't, I bet you would." Cavernous sorrow opened across his face, then disappeared. He smoothed his beard. "Josun Joh doesn't speak to us."

"That doesn't mean he frowns on what we're doing," Dante said.

"Anyway, gods can't speak to you every second of the day," Blays said. "He's probably off doing godly things. Screwing a goose or whatever."

"I don't just mean *us*," Mourn gestured across the small camp. "He doesn't speak to anyone. Well, I can't state that as fact. Maybe he really does speak to some people. We probably think they're crazy, though. But he certainly doesn't speak to me. Or to Orlen or to Vee."

Dante glanced between the others. "What are you talking about?"

"I said we don't speak to Josun Joh." Mourn reached for his silver and bone earring, carefully unclasping it from the rim of his coin-sized ear. He extended it to Dante, gaze level. "We speak to each other."

Understanding hit Dante as quickly as the memory of a chore you were supposed to have handled the day before. Acceptance took significantly longer. Such a thing couldn't exist. It was just as imaginary as the Quivering Bow. And possibly just as powerful.

"What the hell does that mean?" Blays scowled at Dante. "You look like you're about to kiss him with your eyes. And find out whether those eyes have tongues."

"Um," Dante said. Mourn just gazed back. Dante hesitated, mouth half-open. Mourn couldn't *really* be saying that. If Dante said what he thought Mourn meant, he'd look like a fool. A child. The kind of simpleton who believes every story he hears about fairies, dragons, and the sexual prowess of men from the Golden Coast. "Are you saying what I think you're saying?"

Mourn nodded.

At last, Dante shook his head. "I don't know what you'd call it."

"We call them loons," Mourn said.

"Of course you do," Blays said. "Now tell me what they *are* before I embed you in this tree."

"If I understand correctly," Dante said slowly, "loons are a way of speaking..." He glanced at Mourn, who nodded. "...across great distances."

"Correct," Mourn said.

Blays rolled his eyes and flung up his hands. "So? Battlefield trumpets can do the same thing."

"Is there any limit to how far they can talk?" Dante asked Mourn.

"Not that I know of," the norren shrugged. "But I don't know much about loons besides they exist."

Dante turned to Blays. "If you're capable of anything besides flapping around like a salmon, *think* for a moment. If we had a set of these, we could tell Cally what happened right now. As soon as he got done shouting at us, he could then tell *us* what to do next." He gestured at the dark woods. "If we had loon-equipped scouts across Gask, they could report the moment some lord levies his troops. If we posted them along the river, they could tell us the instant Gask's armies cross into the Norren Territories. We would know every step of their advance as they took it. Meanwhile, their reports would lag behind—by hours, days, weeks."

Blays' head tipped so far back he looked straight down his nose. "I can see how that could be useful."

"Forget that Quivering Bow of yours," Lira said. "It sounds like you've found something even greater."

Silence retook the camp. Again, Dante thought of his future. From their downcast faces, he knew the others were doing the same. This time, however, it was not with unease and mounting dread, but with wary optimism. Like spotting the hole in a rickety bridge before it plunged him into darkness. If he was careful, he could still find a way to the other side.

But that was only true if he learned to harness the loon. To make more. He looked up from the bit of bone and metal. "I'm going to need this, Mourn."

"I know."

"I may have to take it apart. Or break it. For all I know I'll have to eat it."

The big man raised his bearish shoulders. "Do whatever you

want with it. It won't be speaking to me again."

Dante worked through the night.

He hadn't meant to. It was just that, after what could only have been an hour and a half with the loon—two at most—he looked up to see the gray-blue breath of predawn warming the trees of the eastern shore. He sat back on the dirt, suddenly bone-weary, as much from nether-spending and lack of sleep as from the knowledge that he likely wouldn't get any rest until they were snuggled into a cabin on a barge, punt, or river-schooner headed for the sea.

The loon had resisted him. Any artifacts powered by nether or ether were excessively rare. The only one Dante owned was the torchstone, a source of light as portable as a coin, immune from the dangers of blowing out or setting unexpected fires, and capable of glowing brightly for a couple hours before it needed some sleep of its own. Dante hadn't yet explored much artificing himself. He was aware of some theory, sure. The main problem appeared to be that the raw energy of nether and ether was notoriously difficult to bind to the solid matter of bone or rock or steel. It tended to slip away, to leach through cracks, to boil off. Eventually, for all your hard work, you were left holding a perfectly ordinary jewel or amulet or dagger. Fickle, shifting nether was particularly difficult to work with. Ether was more stable, more pure and abstract, in a way, and if you were clever enough, it wasn't impossible to bind the energy of ether-generated light to a stone meant also to generate light.

For Dante, however, trying to wield the ether was like trying to wrestle a full-grown tuna to shore using nothing but his elbows. He didn't know why the ether resisted him so strongly. Maybe his inborn talent for handling the nether had come at the cost of being able to work its stabler counterpart. Not everyone who could work nether could work ether, and vice versa. Even among those who could handle both, most found one far easier to work with than the other, and thus specialized in it. In fact, if Dante devoted years to learning the ways of the ether, there was a fair chance he could learn to harness it. But why spend all that time learning to walk with the ether when he could already fly with the nether?

A decision he regretted quite bitterly now that he was faced with the loons. As the others had bedded down on the hard dirt, he walked a short way from camp and delved into the loon. Physically, the main body of the earring was a single knuckle-sized talon or tooth scrimshawed with norren runes too fine to read. A short silver chain contained two pea-sized bones, one shaped like a wishbone or stirrup, the other resembling a C or the curve of a jaw. The chain connected the talon to a silver icon resembling an arrowhead; Dante suspected it was a stylized pine tree. On its back, a blunt hook helped secure the arrowhead to a fold of the inner ear while allowing the talon to dangle free. Meanwhile, a clasped ring would connect it securely through Mourn's piercing.

Dante closed his hand over the loon and shut his eyes. He breathed slowly, deadening his thoughts, focusing on the feel of moonlight on his skin, the taste of the wind, the noise of the stones. Nether pooled around his hand and sunk through his knuckles. Where it touched the loon, his inner eye saw its shape. Threads of ether wound through both silver and bone, the hair-fine strands as bright as sunlight on a pane of glass. His mind-sight swam closer and closer until each thread loomed as big as a rope. Perhaps it *was* a rope—at closer look, what appeared to be a single thread was composed of hundreds of other minute fibers. He moved closer yet, examining a fiber, and saw it too was woven from hundreds of threads of its own...

He pulled back, dizzy. The bright white threads faded. The loon was a simple thing again, a physical trinket of metal and bone. It felt like short minutes had passed. In the gaps in the canopy, the stars had leapt a quarter of the way across the sky.

He closed his eyes and delved again. Did the structure of these threads within threads lend the item its power? Or did that just happen to be the form that power took when the ether that formed them bound to the matter? This time, he kept his focus broad. The gleaming white threads converged at three distinct points. One node met inside the tiny wishbone. The other met inside the tiny C. The other was less densely-packed around the blunt hook on the backside of the arrowhead, more resembling a tight net than a solid ball of ether. Other threads tangled through the earring as well, sparse by contrast. Structural support, perhaps.

Subjectively, he spent an hour or so poking at the loon with delicate probes of nether, exploring crannies, turning it over for a better feel for its whole. And when he emerged, the dawn approached the eastern shore.

He rose to urinate, then rooted through his pack for his water skin and a torn-off handful of bread. Long stale. At least the humidity kept it moist. Then he fitted the loon to his ear, holding it in place—he had no piercing himself—and listened.

A minute later, he'd heard nothing but the pinejays greeting the sun. He waited for Mourn to wake up, empty his bladder, and gargle a mixture of water and salt, then held up the loon. "You both hear and speak through this?"

Mourn tipped his head to one side. "I used to."

"Was it always active? Or did it only speak to you when someone had something to say?"

"It spoke like an old monk. Rarely, and only when telling me what to do."

Dante smiled. The others woke soon, stretching, rubbing their limbs. Blays spit the dryness from his mouth. Lira stretched and executed a choreographed set of martial exercises. After a cold breakfast, they cut through the woods toward the town on the river. Dante's head felt like a bruised cloud. They paused at the edge of the woods. Gray light touched the wet timbers of the town. A few pedestrians mingled with the mule teams hauling sacks and wagons to and from the piers. Smoke rose from the chimneys of pine-board houses.

"Look like anyone's planning to kill us?" Blays said.

Dante squinted. "No more than usual."

Lira frowned between them. "That's usual?"

"We have an unfair share of detractors."

Blays hoisted his sword belt up his hips. "Probably because I'm so pretty."

Two barges creaked at the piers. A rowboat inched downstream. Seagulls soared over the gray waves. Dante's pockets felt very light. He needn't have worried. Down on the docks, where the water smelled like wet rocks and fish bones, Blays haggled with a bargemaster. The captain expected a load of coal and timber that morning. He'd be taking it all the way to Yallen. Shorthanded, he offered the four of them passage in exchange for helping to load the barge and guard it from pirates on their way to the sea.

Dante teetered on the planks of the dock, gazing forlornly at the broad barge. "I could use a nap."

"That's what nights are for," Blays said. "If you plan it right, you can even get two or three good naps in a row."

"I was working on Mourn's jewelry."

"Is that all it takes to make you swoon? If Lira gave you a pair of her bloomers, you'd die of starvation."

Lira gazed pointedly toward the river. A pink blotch appeared on her turned cheek. Dante left for the nearest inn, a two-story place with a flagstone-paved porch and a mast rising from its roof, a towering trunk of pine stripped of all branches and bark. The wood was lacquered smooth, shiny under the overcast skies.

The innkeeper was in the process of blessing plates of eggs and potatoes and bread, flicking drips of water over the steaming bowls, then snapping sprigs of wintrel and depositing them in a small wire basket suspended over the hexagon of candles at the center of the table. Toasted mint filled the warm room. The innkeeper said a quick prayer to Arawn, then finished the rite by blowing a pinch of flour mingled with black sand—the grist of Arawn's broken mill—over the candles. Dante watched, transfixed. However many times he saw such open worship of Arawn, he couldn't help his shock. Back in Mallon, it would get the man tortured at the least. Probably, he'd never be seen again.

Dante rented a room for the day and collapsed into the straw mattress. Lira knocked an hour later. He rose confused and aching, feeling worse than before. Down at the docks, mules and wagons crowded onto ramps, unloading cords of wood and crates of coal.

A crewman with a salt-and-pepper beard gave Lira a wink. "No need to dirty your hands, ma'am. Prefer a tour of the ship instead?"

She stared him down. "Do you think my breasts get in the way if I try to lift a crate?"

The man backed off with his palms raised, muttering an apology. Behind Lira's back, Blays shot Dante a smirk.

It was the last smile Dante would see for some time. The next two hours were a monotony of picking up a cord of wood, crossing the flat gangplank, and tromping downstairs to one of the holds. Dante's leather gloves and the front of his doublet grew crusty with resinous sap. Blays was panting within a few minutes, too. Lira shuffled back and forth and up and down, face gray with pain, pausing regularly to catch her breath and rest her leg. Mourn came and went without slowing down, strong as a flood, inevitable as the tides.

Before long, Dante lost track of everything but the lessened gravity of setting down a bundle of wood. Two hours later, he rose to the docks and blinked in confusion. They were empty. Removed of everything but stray twigs, flakes of bark, and black patches of coal dust.

They were done. So was he. Ensconced in a hammock belowdecks, he slept until darkness. On waking, his body was sore from neck to soles, but his mind felt as if he'd just emerged from a warm bath. For several minutes, he did nothing more than breathe the cold air, smell the clean water, and listen to the soft slap of waves against the hull. Then he retired to a quiet corner of the empty deck and considered the loon until dawn.

Examining its physical and ethereal structures wasn't doing him any good. He didn't know enough about artificing to tease any meaning from the knotted and netted lines of ether. Instead, he needed to approach the loon from a theoretical standpoint. If he understood the thinking that allowed it to be created in the first place, he could, if nothing else, present Cally with a framework to allow the old man to duplicate the earring's function.

Not that this was any easier.

What did the loon do? It sent your voice and allowed you to hear back from someone who might be hundreds of miles away. Earlier, Mourn had informed him the effect was instantaneous, or something very near it. So its principles didn't rely on those of noises that carried long distances—thunder, for instance, could be heard miles from its source, but it could take several seconds after the lightning for the roar to reach your ears. If a trumpeter sounded his horn across a valley, you wouldn't hear the first note until after he finished blowing. Sound traveled fast, but it wasn't instant.

That implied the distance itself was somehow shortened. As if a piece of the speaker and the listener had been embedded in the loon, so when the speaker spoke, the loon spoke with him, however far away he might be. Mourn dashed that theory, too. According to him, a loon could be used by anyone. That was part of why the Clan of the Nine Pines kept their secret so close. Any enemy could listen in as easily as a member of the clan.

Alternately, the loons themselves were perfect duplicates, identical twins who resonated as one. But Dante'd never heard of such a thing. You couldn't just copy a *tooth*. Silver cast in the same mold from the same ingot did not make the pieces the same. He couldn't rule out the idea completely, but as a solution, it didn't compel him in the slightest.

Four days cycled along. Blays gambled with the crew by nights, winning more than he lost. It wouldn't be enough to buy them passage on a ship to Narashtovik, but at least they'd be able to pay for food and lodging while they worked out those logistics. Lira fended off the advances of sailors and paced around the deck to keep her leg limber and strong. Mourn whittled arrowheads from scrap wood, embellishing his pieces with hooks and grooves and jagged edges.

"Is that supposed to kill someone?" Blays said, leaning over a piece shaped like a devil's sawblade. "Or circumcise him?"

Mourn frowned up from his makeshift workbench. "What's a circumcise?"

Blays grinned. Dante walked off before he could explain.

After the turmoil of the last few weeks, the peace of their passage downriver was like an evening beer after a day behind the plow. Occasionally they were called on to haul cargo to the piers of various villages and towns, but for the most part, those four days passed in total quiet. The morning of the fifth day since they'd hopped ship, the river widened until a mile of water separated its shores. Craggy islands jutted from the slowing current, furry with pines. The western shore neared as the river swung due north. Smoke curled from the damp trees. Sections of forest disappeared in favor of dark brown fields and young green shoots of winter wheat. Above an inlet protected by a high spar of limestone, docks jutted into the gray water. Downstream, three more barges coasted toward the sea; a two-deck galley thrashed the water with its many oars.

They reached Yallen by mid-afternoon. The city consumed the western bank of the delta. Two high-arched bridges spanned the sluggish water, connecting the larger islands and the eastern shore with its smoky tents, shacks, and furnaces. Masts piked the river, clustering thickly on piers that bustled with sailors and merchants and travelers. Instead of a wall, the city was banded at intervals by greasy canals some forty feet wide and spanned by low wooden bridges. Flat-bottomed boats navigated the canals with poles or ropes strung along the brick-lined walls. Inland, three hills considered the sprawl, their crowns heavy with towers and high wooden manors. Beneath, three-story row houses stood shoulder to shoulder, capped by sharply canted roofs of tar-sealed pine. The shining gray sea waited beyond the last of the islands. Dante smelled salt and shit and the cold of northern waters.

"What do you think?" he said to Blays, who watched beside him.

"It looks," Blays said, "like a place where things happen."

"I think it looks like a place where *you* figure out how to get us a boat."

"Why do I always have to be the one who gets things done?"

"I'm sorry," Dante said, twirling the loon between his fingers. "I've been a little busy trying to save us all from decorating the spires of Setteven with our skulls."

Blays snorted. "You've got nothing to worry about. Your skull's too ugly to show in public."

"Seriously, do you have any ideas?"

"I have a very firm thought, in fact."

Dante raised his brows. "What's that?"

"That you should shut up and let me do my thing."

The barge angled toward the crowded docks. A couple hundred yards from the crush of ships, an oared tug-pilot met them in the waves. Ropes flew between the vessels. Ashore, a team of oxen churned their hooves in the mud, guiding the barge in to port. Hulking norren and well-tanned men coiled ropes, lowered barrels, and argued on the briny planks.

Dante pulled up the cowl of his plain black cloak. The barge squeaked against the dock. Sailors flung ropes over the railing, followed by their own bodies. They landed lightly and tied knots as nimbly as the toe-dancers of Sweigh. Across the deck, Lira climbed into the sunlight. Dante moved to intercept her.

"There's a fountain at the far end of the plaza," he pointed, then pulled her behind the safety of a cabin wall. "The one shaped like a leaping salmon. I want you and Mourn to wait there while Blays and I see about finding us a boat."

The creases of a subtle insult crinkled her eyes. "Do you consider us baggage?"

"Baggage?"

"Bulky objects to be set aside whenever you plan to put your hands to use."

He frowned. "I consider you flags. Conspicuous things to be waving around when I'm worried about being found and flayed by the agents of a wealthy lord."

She regarded him for some time. "You won't learn to wholly trust us until you put us to use."

"We'll see about that as soon as we're out of increasingly hostile territory. For now, trust *me* and go wait by that damn fountain."

Sailors and stevedores hollered back and forth. Once more, the four of them pitched in to help unload, sweating in the chill breeze. The last of the lumber touched the dock an hour before the sun would touch the western hills. Packs shouldered, Dante and Blays thumped down the planks to the relatively dry land beyond the docks, a sodden square of wide-spaced cobbles choked with mud, sand, manure, and well-trampled grass. Taverns, public houses, and tailors fronted the square. Blocky warehouses rose behind them.

Mourn and Lira entered the crowds and crossed toward the fountain with the salmon. Beneath his hood, Dante scanned the throng, easily distinguishing the sailors in their tight leggings from the locals in their knee-length fur coats. No one seemed to be paying any special mind to the norren and the woman.

By the time Dante turned away, Blays had already flagged down his first sailor and asked which ships were Narashtovik-bound. The sailor chewed his beard a moment, and then, his breath smelling of yeasty beer, rattled off the names of three vessels that would depart the next day.

"Where are they docked?" Blays said.

The sailor scowled. "Seems to me anybody who knows that would be some kind of expert. You know the thing about experts?"

"They have expertise?"

"And they don't give it away free."

Blays' brows muddled, then he laughed. "They sure don't. For your time and trouble, most honored bosun."

He passed the bearded man an iron two-penny. The sailor ran his thumb along its clipped rim.

"The *Boon*'s at Pier 15. The *Vanneya's Song*'s at Farry's Punt. Can't miss it," he said, pointing downstream to a dock that bent from the shore like a misshapen Y. "And the *Bad Tidings* is berthed at the Westlong Docks." He gestured further downriver, then squinted between Dante and Blays. "Might not want to hop ship just yet, though. Hear bad things are coming Narashtovik way."

"Like what?" Dante said.

The man shrugged, gazing off to sea with weighty significance. "Arawn's own dead. Sent to right the heresy of that old man in the tower." He shrugged again. "Anyway, that's what they say."

"Zombies?" Blays said, hushed. "My goodness. I'm going to need a bigger sword."

Pier 15 was just a short ways down the muddy banks. The *Boon* was a large longboat bearing a single square-sailed mast and a high bank of oar-holes, but one of its mates informed them it was all booked and refused access to either of the ship's quartermasters. Marine-green kelp swirled in the cold estuary. They thumped down the salt-whitened planks toward the bent protrusion of Farry's Punt. There, sailors dangled on ropes over the railings of the *Vanneya's Song*, gouging barnacles from its high hull with flat iron chisels.

"Taking passengers?" Blays hollered from below.

Without turning, a soldier jerked his thumb at a rope bridge bobbing softly in the low swells. Dante frowned, waiting for more explicit permission. Blays strode forward and threw himself onto the ladder.

From the ship's deck, Dante had a clear view of the longboats, galleys, barges, caravels, and sloops snarling the docks between them and open sea. Inland, a seaborn breeze dragged chimney-smoke across the steep roofs of the city. Blays rapidly learned two of the *Song*'s quartermasters were ashore in taverns unknown, but the third remained in his cabin. Blays knocked on his well-cleaned door without hesitation. A middle-aged man opened it a moment later, his scowl deepening the heavy creases around his eyes, one of which was clamped tight around a thick glass lens.

"We'd like passage to Narashtovik," Blays said. "We have—"

The man's lens flashed. "Four rounds and four pennies per body."

"Well, you see. We don't have that. But we do have someone in Narashtovik who would happily—"

"Four rounds and four pennies per body. To be paid before your boots hit the deck."

Dante bared his teeth. It was easily three times what they had on hand. "Perhaps we could strike a bargain for other services."

The man's vowels were flat with an eastern accent Dante couldn't quite place. "Four rounds and four pennies per body."

Blays' spine stiffened. "You, sir, have just lost a customer! *Four* of them!"

He turned before the quartermaster could inject another word. They descended to the dock, which was suddenly chilly and thick with the scent of overripe fish.

"They don't leave until tomorrow," Dante said. "That gives us plenty of time to locate a few pockets heavier than our own and relieve their owners of their burden."

Blays nodded, distant. "I don't know. That could attract attention."

"Since when did you consider that a bad thing?"

"Since legions of soldiers might be on our heels. Not to mention the grumbling we'd face from Lira."

Dante waved his hand. "She's so high on her horse I doubt we'd hear a word of it."

"Anyway, just because crimes are fun and easy doesn't mean I always want to do them." Blays gestured downstream in the vague direction the sailor had indicated for the Westlong Docks. "Besides, we've got at least one legit chance left."

Dante considered him a moment, then headed down the docks, swerving around an inborn oxen team and the spittle flying from their driver's lips. A quarter-mile walk took them to a rather less-peopled stretch of warehouses and half-paved streets. Grains of wheat and corn speckled the muddy alleys. Planks lay between the stone streets and the doors of the blocky lofts and silos. Broad, flat barges wallowed in the waters beside the thick piers. Mussels and dark green slime coated the pilings.

The *Bad Tidings* was one of the few sailboats at the Westlong, with one high mainmast and two smaller and well-mended sails snapping in the steady offshore wind. Blays hollered more than once before a sailor in a knit cap popped up on its deck. The crewman let them aboard to see yet another quartermaster, a man in his early 40s with a beard thick enough to raise robins in. His name was Mart and he was blunt but reasonable; over the course of a few minutes, Dante and Blays bargained him from a fare that outstripped the official on the *Song* and down to a mere three rounds and change apiece—still more than double what they had on hand.

"I'm sorry, but that's as low as reason allows." Mart reached for a much-scribbled scrap of paper. "If you change your minds, we'll be here until tomorrow afternoon."

Dante sighed through his nose. "I hope by then to be able to take advantage of your generosity."

Blays glanced out the porthole. Sunset's last red spark trickled through the bubbly glass. He leaned from his chair and slapped the wooden floor. "What are you hauling here?"

Mart glanced up, eyes sharp. "Barley. A whole lot of barley."

"Got rats?"

"Does the king's mistress have crabs?"

"That would explain the pettiness of some of his recent policies. Maybe we can offer you something besides money." Blays tipped his head toward Dante. "My friend here is the finest rat-catcher in the land. Possibly in all the lands."

Mart smiled indulgently. "Is that so?"

"So they say," Dante played along.

"Here's my proposal." Blays leaned forward conspiratorially, patting Dante on the shoulder. "My friend Blegworth goes down into your hold and goes to work on your rats. If he clears them all out, we get free passage. Us and our two companions. But if he leaves a single rat alive, we go on our merry way, and you still have a whole lot less rats in your hold."

"I'll need complete solitude," Dante said. "The presence of others might scare the rats into their dens."

Mart jutted his lower jaw. "So you can steal the rum? Or set fire to the entire hold? What then?"

Blays held out his hands. "Then you and your crew stab us until you feel justice is served."

The quartermaster laughed for the first time. "I can't tell if you're arrogant or insane. But it sounds like I win either way. If you can get rid of all the rats, the trip is on me."

They squared off the details; the crew was still in the midst of relocating goods, refreshing supplies, and patching sails, but Mart claimed he'd have them cleared out belowdecks by 11th bell of the evening. Dante climbed down to the deck and headed offship.

On their way to meet Mourn and Lira, Blays stepped over a grassy pile of manure. "So can you actually do that?"

"I have no idea."

"Fantastic. Do you *think* you can do it?"

Dante slowly shook his head. "I have an idea. I can't say whether it's a good one."

"If it were I would be highly skeptical it was yours."

"Thanks for volunteering me, by the way. If I can't pull it off, I expect you to sell your body for the cause."

Blays snorted. "If I did that, we could buy our own boat."

"Then get to work." Dante detoured around a ring of hooting bystanders. In their middle, two men swayed and postured, throwing more insults than punches. "What did you call me back there? *Blegworth*?"

"You look like a Blegworth."

Lanterns sputtered from plaza poles and the cabins of boats. Blays waited at the plaza's edge while Dante rendezvoused with the others. Water sprayed from the mouth of the stone salmon on the fountain. They accepted his explanation with little comment. Mourn looked tired, Lira stiff. For whatever help it would be with their lodgings, Dante passed over his comically light purse.

"Meet back here at dawn," he said. "I'll be the one who smells like rats."

Lira tilted her head. "What exactly are you doing out there?"

"What I do best: exterminating."

They parted ways. With several hours to kill, Dante and Blays meandered the nearby streets, eventually settling in at a thriving tavern. Rather than tables, deep shelves stood at rib-height along all four walls. A vaulted ceiling with naked beams allowed space for a sort of shack in the center of the room, where men lined up to step through a curtain, spilling a fan of bright green light across the tavern floor. They emerged a minute later with mugs in hand. At intervals, smoke jetted from the pipes protruding near the top of the shack, smelling of kelp and orange rind and bitter larret root.

Blays pressed iron into Dante's hand. "Go buy us some drinks, will you?"

Dante frowned at the hissing shack. "Why me?"

"Because I'm paying. And because I'm bigger and I'll shove you around if you don't."

Dante joined the roped-off line. It moved quickly. Each time a man came and went through the curtain to the shack, green light washed the floor. Soon, it was his turn. Inside the shack, green light gleamed from bottles of all colors of the sea—blue, gray, green, and black. A very average-looking man tapped his fingers behind a short bar. Dante stared at the source of the light, an unwinking stone suspended a few inches from the ceiling.

"Is that a torchstone?"

The man didn't glance up. "That doesn't sound like any drink I've ever heard."

Since they were within spitting distance of the Houkkalli Islands, Dante bought two anise-flavored kaven and found Blays parked at one of the drinking-shelves. Past the gritty glass windows, the bustle of daily labor shifted to the whoop of nocturnal play.

"What do you think?" Blays asked once they'd drained their second mugs. They'd been talking around the war for the last few minutes. "I mean, what do you *really* think?"

"What do *you* think?"

"I think everyone's full of shit. Hot, windy shit. Wait, that's pretty gross." Blays tipped back his mug, dislodging another couple drops of rosy liquor. "I think Setteven gins up an ultimatum, the clans huff and puff for a couple weeks before backing down and accepting their demands, and Cally plays it as dumb as he can to continue the illusion we're keeping our noses clean. Nobody *wants* a war."

Dante gazed out the greasy window. Low clouds had encroached with the night and a misty drizzle dewed the cobbles. "I think Setteven's growing increasingly displeased with the unruliness of the eastern branches of their kingdom. I don't think they'll discard the opportunity to put us in our place."

Hours plodded by in that bovine way time takes while waiting on an unwanted task. Dante sipped his way through his third cup. 10th bell rang from the spires of Taim. A half hour later, he cut Blays off and started back for the *Bad Tidings*. The ship was so quiet you could hear every wave rippling against its hull. Thousands of pounds of sealed wood creaked and popped. Up top, Mart waited for them, flanked by four sailors armed with straight swords.

"The hold is all yours." He gestured to his men. "If you try anything funny, you're all theirs."

"Just them?" Blays said.

"And I'll require your swords."

"Ah." Blays reached for his buckles. "Well, that might even it out."

Dante passed over his sword and his two larger knives. Mart nodded to a crewman as tall and thin as the mainmast, who moved to pat Dante down. Dante clung to his last blade, a pick as short and slender as his little finger.

"I'll need this one."

Mart chuckled, expression unchanging. "That's how you'll be rid of them? We leave tomorrow. Of this year."

"See you at dawn." Dante smiled with half his mouth. He nodded at Blays. "Cover the top of the stairs. No humans are to come down nor rats to come up."

Blays crossed his thumbs in the salute of the Bressel armsman's guild he'd never actually been fit enough to join. "Of course, my liege."

Dante stepped over the rim of the hatch and clumped down the stairs. The main chamber of the lower deck was a square roughly thirty feet to a side, lit by a single smokeless catchlamp at both ends. Barrels lined most walls, blocked and chinked in place. It smelled of fresh beer and stale water and the acrid stink of small mammals. Barley gritted underfoot. Something small rustled from the gloom. Large serving-tables took up the remainder of the room. Small cabins filled the aft with a galley and chain locker at the fore, the iron links of the anchor lying heavy on the floor.

A second set of stairs descended to the main hold. This was split between three main spaces front, middle, and rear. It was pitch black; Dante drew out his torchstone and breathed on it until white light expanded over the casks, barrels, sacks, crates, and chests. Some sections were packed higher than his head, held fast through arcane packing techniques that required few if any ropes or restraints. White grain dappled the deck. So too did tiny black droppings.

He would work his way down. The creatures of the dark always descended in times of crisis.

He ascended to the lower deck and knelt beside the stairs. He drew the slender knife and traced a line of blood across his left forearm. He'd never summoned the nether on open water before, but if it differed from the sources on land, it was too subtle for his eyes—the same mothlike shadows fluttered from the cracks and corners, coating his hands, turning gently as they waited to be shaped. He rubbed his thumb against the torchstone until it faded, leaving him in the weak light of the catchlamps.

It didn't take long. Submerged in the nether, his sense of time was somewhat blurred—destabilized, perhaps, by the eternal cycles of the shadows—but no more than five minutes could have passed before the first rat crept from the maze of cargo. It moved in stops and starts, stopping to haunch back, nose and whiskers twitching, before it lurched forward to snatch up a stray kernel of barley and crunch it down to nothing.

Dante stilled his mind and struck the rat with a narrow spear of nether. It flopped to its side, legs kicking, smearing blood across the timbers.

All creatures great and small carried a pulse of nether within their skin or shells. By the *Cycle of Arawn*, all life itself was netherborn, brought to motion by the black grist ground from Arawn's cracked mill. With his fear and rage and pain, man carried the most nether of all, but if Dante made himself go quiet enough, he could feel the thin thread waning in the struck rat's veins. Even once each of its organs went still and dark, the nether didn't disappear. It simply quieted, too. Dormant. Only when the body decayed and dissolved would the shadows also pass away into the earth.

Dante seized this snoozing nether, melding it with a strand of his own. With a thought, he returned the rat to its feet, where it waited in perfect undead stillness.

Go, he told it. *Find the others. Bring them to me.*

It skittered into darkness. A moment later, a short, inhuman shriek pierced the silence. Fur whispered on wood. The undead rat backed into the cleared space around the steps, tugging a fresh corpse along in its teeth. Dante brought this one back to its feet, too. Before he ordered it away, he closed his eyes and shifted his sight into it. Vertigo bent his head—he looked back on himself, terribly tall even when kneeling, a pale-faced giant whose features were sharpened with the cruelty of one whose role is to kill. He sent the rat his command. His second-vision swung as it turned on its claws and raced into the towering alleys of crates. Its whiskers tickled along the splintery wood. It reached the wall of a cabin and squeezed into a crack that would be invisible to a standing human. Dante felt it rustling among loose shreds of chaff, splinters, and the browning rinds of lemons. In total darkness, its teeth clamped down on something hairless and pink. The baby vermin screamed. Dante opened his eyes and gazed at nothing.

It was dawn by the time he returned to the deck. Mart raised thick and skeptical brows, then lowered his gaze to Dante's left arm, laced with paper-fine cuts and crusted with rusty layers of blood. The man's face softened into something that might have been concern.

"Sleeping Arawn," Mart said. "Did you challenge them all to a fistfight?"

Blays shouldered past the quartermaster, puffy-eyed with the grueling sort of hangover that comes from burning off one's liquor without the help of sleep. "Well?"

"Well what?" Dante said.

"Did you get all the rats?"

"Oh, that? I ferreted out the last one hours ago."

Blays gaped. "Then what have you been doing down there all that time? Napping? I want to nap!"

Dante let out a long breath. "I understand the loons."

7

Fortunately, Mart brushed that off as the delirious statement of a man who's spent hours in the dark with no company but his thoughts and a growing heap of dead rats. As hand-counted by a teen boy who was clearly on the outs with Mart, these totaled 240 all told, a bleeding and mutilated heap that had the growing crowd of sailors eyeing Dante with some emotion between respect and disgust. Mart took a tour belowdecks while Dante leaned against the railing and let the ocean wind wash the scent of blood, fur, and feces from his nose.

Mart thumped up the steps a few minutes later. He leaned against the rails beside Dante and gazed seaward. "The fact of the matter is there's no proof of your achievement."

Dante turned, incredulous, and gestured at the mountain of motionless rodents. "What do you call that? Coincidence? Did I smuggle them aboard in my pockets?"

Contempt hardened Mart's eyes, quickly fading. "Our agreement insisted you kill every single rat."

It took a moment for this to penetrate the fog of sleeplessness around Dante's mind. He stiffened. "And there's no way to prove they're all dead."

"Not without tearing the ship apart board by board."

"I see." He supposed he should be angry. He supposed he would be, after he'd had some sleep. After the *Bad Tidings* had sailed away.

"But if I left you ashore, my crew would tear *me* apart board by board." Mart nodded to the idling men. One scooped up a rat and waggled it in a bearded man's face, earning himself a meaty punch in the shoulder. The rat bounced from the deck. Men laughed. "You've earned your passage."

"You could have told me that from the start."

"I could have, but I didn't." He gave Dante a long look. "Regardless, if we arrive in Narashtovik and discover you've missed any, I can simply pass your debt along to Callimandicus."

That wiped the fog from Dante's brain. "If you want a safe trip, I wouldn't speak a word of who we are."

"I'm not going to give your name away. I'm responsible for all my ship's cargo, human or otherwise. Now fetch your friends."

He did just that. At the fountain of the salmon, Lira and Mourn looked enviably well-rested. Back on board, they were shown to two cabins belowdecks—one for the three males, one for the lady.

Lira's jaw drew tight. "I am sworn to protect this man." She inclined her head at Dante. "I can't do that isolated in my room."

The young sailor ducked his eyes. "Ma'am, barring storms or giant squid, I think he'll be perfectly safe. After seeing what he's done to those rats, nobody's going want to find out what he'd do to a human."

That only raised further questions from Lira, but at least it settled the arrangement of sleeping quarters. Dante meant to see the ship's departure into open ocean—he'd sailed enough rivers, but never the sea—but on settling into his down mattress to rest his body, the rest of him quickly followed suit. By the time he woke in early afternoon, the shore was a far line of pine green across miles and miles of whitecapped gray.

According to a crewman whose superhuman focus on reining in his flapping sail may have been due to the fact he'd lost two fingers earlier in life, the trip to Narashtovik would take six days, allowing for the wind and their planned stop in port at Kannovar. All told, they'd span a good 400 knots, which struck Dante as a miracle. Even with good roads and spare horses, traveling overland would have taken them more than twice as long and been far more dangerous. In fact, the duration was perfect. Six days ought to be plenty of time to confirm his operational theory of Mourn's loon. If Dante was equal parts lucky and dedicated, he might even have a fresh one to show Cally. If anything could blunt the old man's wrath, it would be an item of immense practicality that came wrapped in the priceless ribbons of secret lore.

Lira happily lent him the privacy of her cabin. She sat outside on a stool while Dante set to work. The boy who'd shown them their cabins turned out to own a two-book library consisting of the *Cycle of Arawn* and a picaresque novel about pirates who spent more time clinging to the wreckage of their ship than in committing any actual piracy. He lent Lira the book without a second thought, and even through the closed door, Dante could occasionally hear the rasp of pages or Lira's warm, low chuckle. Besides that, however, his only distractions came from the pitch of the ship, which his stomach hadn't begun to adapt to, the occasional holler from the crew up above, and rarest of all, the carrying cry of the huge-winged birds that scoured the ocean's surface for prey.

In truth, the rodent body count had been 246. Dante had slipped six of the smaller adults into his pocket before rising from the slaughter to show Mart his catch. Because he had a theory. If his theory proved seaworthy, he expected he'd need more than one body to refine it before landfall.

The idea had arrived from a special kind of nowhere, a place no other human had been: from inside the dead rats' own heads. Yet the concept was simple enough Dante could have put it together years ago.

When he was linked to the body of a rat, he could sense whatever they sensed. See what they saw. Hear what they heard. Assumedly, he could taste what they tasted. This worked whether they were in the palm of his hand or miles away. Essentially, they were doing the exact same thing the loons did.

He borrowed, requisitioned, and gathered more than just the dead rats. In addition to these, which lay in neat lines atop a cloth on the cabin's floor, he had a hand axe, his small knife, a tin spoon, the strips of what had once been one of his older shirts, and perhaps most important of all, a bucket of water. He separated one of the rats from the others, took up the hand axe, and severed its head less than expertly. With a concentrated effort to ignore the noises and smells his next actions made, he used the knife to peel away all the skin, flesh, and tendons from the skull, then picked the axe back up and whacked it once along its long axis. A splinter of bone pattered across the pinewood floor. He noticed the smell then, the thickening blood and hours-old flesh, and opened the small round porthole. After a few breaths at the window, he raised the axe again.

The next strike split the skull from snout to base. Pink mush splattered the deck. The bone hadn't broken completely along its bottom edge; Dante cracked it in half, then used the spoon and knife to dig out everything he could reasonably extract. Uncertain the leftovers would be of any use, he set these aside on one of the cloths, then spent a long time cleaning his hands and the two pieces of mostly-empty skull.

He knelt beside the mess and brought forth a palmful of nether, which he sunk into the bones like a wave into sand. He reestablished the nethereal link between the two halves, then opened another line between himself and the half he dubbed the "Ear." He set the Ear to his own ear, aligned the earhole of the second piece (which he thought of as the "Mouth") to his mouth, and said "Hello." Had he heard—? He put the Ear to his other ear and tried again. As previously, the word sounded strange, somehow distorted, but not conclusively different from whatever he was hearing aloud.

Perhaps it was simply too close for his senses to separate the sounds. He cracked the door. Lira looked up, closing her book around her finger. Dante flushed with sudden embarrassment.

"Lira." He held out the Mouth. "I need you to do something for me. I'm going to go back into your room. Three seconds after I close the door, say something into that."

She reached out for the cracked bone, then jerked her hand away. "Is that a rat's skull?"

"Of course not. It's one half of a rat's skull."

"What am I doing with one half of a rat's skull?"

"Helping me win a war."

She considered him for a long moment. "Are you being serious?"

He held up his palms, discovered the underside of one forearm was globby with gore, and hurriedly wiped it off on the leg of his pants, which he immediately regretted. "I'm sure this looks very strange."

"It looks like you've decided to become a butcher. Or a pervert.

Or some combination of the two."

"You don't have to touch it." He bent and placed it on the floor. "Just speak into it. Directly. Where the ear would be, ideally. Oh, and don't speak loudly enough for me to hear what you're saying through the door. Understand?"

"As much as that's possible."

He closed himself inside the cabin and held up the Ear. Three seconds later, he heard Lira murmur "If you're hearing this, then perhaps you're not crazy"—but rather than hearing the words through his ear, the way Mourn had described the loon as functioning, he heard them inside his head, the same way he'd perceived such things when he was piloting the dead rat around the hold to hunt down the living. He returned to the hall.

"I spoke into it," Lira said with the unconcealed disgust of a childless adult watching another person's kids paw through an apple cart.

"I'm not crazy."

She blinked at him. "Perhaps not."

He took the Mouth and went back inside her room to kneel beside the mattress and think. So it was possible to take pieces of a skull, link them together, and share the senses experienced by one of those parts by the other pieces of the whole. In a sense, then, he had just created a very poor loon: it was one-way, only he could use it, and it would cease to function the moment he dropped his focus from the link between Ear and Mouth. Still, it felt like he was onto the principle. Now all he had to do was refine it.

He understood how to solve the one-way problem at once. If he could be either a Mouth or an Ear, either to able speak or hear, all it would take to be able to do both would be to combine two sets of these things. To create a linked Mouth A and Ear A, a second Mouth B and Ear B, then combine Mouth A and Ear B into one loon and Mouth B and Ear A into another such that words spoken into one loon would be heard through the other and vice versa. He did just that, axing his halved skull into quarters so each fraction contained part of the original structure of the skull's ear port. He then formed two proto-loons and had Lira speak into each in turn while he listened from the cabin. He could hear her through both pieces. She couldn't hear him, of course, because she lacked any link to the loons herself, but if he could solve that problem, all that would remain was to make the items permanent.

Day faded from the porthole. He opened the window and flung the rat's headless body and bits of brain into the sea. He hid the intact corpses as well as his skull-pieces in his pouch, wishing for some ice or a cool hole in the ground. They were already starting to get a bit squishy. He cleaned his tools and his hands in the reddish water and then sloshed that out the window as well, splattering just a bit on the interior wall.

Feeling work-worn but energized, he went to the second cabin to find Mourn, whom he engaged in a makeshift game of Nulladoon using pieces cobbled from stray barley, pennies, and bits of cork, with clay tea plates standing in as terrain. They set up on one of the common tables belowdecks. Before the end of their second turn, a pair of offduty sailors stood over their shoulders, brows knit, asking questions about the intricacies of play. Soon, most of the free crew stood about them, placing bets over mugs of watered rum.

Dante lost, drawing sighs and curses from those who'd wagered on him and cheers from the opposition, but he grinned anyway. He'd already determined the shape of the puzzle of the loon. Now it was just a matter of filling in the pieces.

They made port in the Houkkalli Islands two days later. Dante scowled at the jagged crags and churning windmills. He was no closer to any solutions. Whenever he tried to load up his loons with enough nether to keep them functional after he dropped his focus, the bones leaked his shadows like a punctured waterskin. He'd done no better with the problem of getting the loons to make audible noise rather than restricting their transmission to the braincase of their creator. In fact, on dwelling on *that* problem, he'd only discovered another: that unless he wanted the loons to yammer aloud to everyone in earshot, he needed to find a way to make them whisper to their intended recipient alone. It was a reminder, and not a welcome one, that for all the ways he'd learned to command the nether—to forge killing spears, to make the dead walk, to bend reality to illusion—he lacked the scantest understanding of many of its subtleties. For him, trying to make anything permanent was like pouring water on a flat floor and expecting it to take the shape of an angel.

"You look," Blays said beside him on the windy deck, "like someone's been squeezing your nuts all night."

"That would be bad?"

"Maliciously."

Sailors called back and forth, trimming the *Bad Tidings* to angle it toward the island of cliffs and cold marshes where round houses hunkered in the wind.

"It's the loons," Dante said. "I know the effects I need, but I have no idea how to create them."

"Well, that's a bit of luck then."

"Yes. About as lucky as a starving man with a net and no ocean."

"No, I mean that we're here. In Keyote." Blays gestured to the modest city of stone homes and wood huts buffeted with shedwind stalks, tall reeds which held uncannily still in all but the harshest gales. "The Hanassans have their temple here. On Mount Sirini. You know, I don't get why mountains are so popular among the monks. Like it's such a feat of piety to walk up a hill. Anyway, the Hanassans know everything."

Dante cocked his head. "How do you know about the Hanassans?"

"What, you're the only one who gets to know things? They were my favorite as a kid. Used to make my mom tell me stories about them every night."

He considered this a moment, then shook his head. "Even if they could help me, which they can't, they wouldn't want to."

"We'll be in port all day," Blays snorted. "What else are you going to do? Dress those little rats of yours up in bonnets and booties?"

Dante laughed, flushing. Once the *Bad Tidings* had completed the rather tedious process of nosing up to the deepwater docks and tying off, he clambered down the ladder and made for town. He knew very little about the Houkkallians other than that they rarely left their homeland, they favored fur hats from the skin of a biskin (a ferocious bear-like predator that, as far as Dante knew, didn't actually exist), and it was virtually impossible to tell whether they were serious or pulling your leg. He couldn't even trust the directions to Sirini Temple he got from a local stevedore — "Walk up the mountain until you can't walk any more."

Just in case the stories of the biskins were true, he took his sword with him, but left Blays and the others behind. This mission had the feel of a pilgrimage or an embarrassment, and either way it was best faced alone. The streets were paved with broad slabs of basalt with irregular sides but which fit together with minimal cracks between, as if they'd all been snapped off from the same massive table of stone. Live shedwind lined the paths to most houses, their straight green shoots eight feet tall. The road climbed a rolling hill. Behind him, the sails of the *Bad Tidings* gleamed white against the glittering gray sea.

The town and the pavement ceased abruptly. Round stone farmhouses stood off the dirt road. Fields of green and brown stretched for half a mile or more; at their borders, dark firs rose in a towering kudzu. Ahead, the road led straight to the tallest of three modest mountains with white-painted peaks. The nearest mountain was banded with alternating shades of green.

Dante saw why an hour later. With the ground rising beneath him, the madly hissing forest that had swallowed the path suddenly vanished in favor of motionless fields of shedwind. A couple hundred yards later, the forest resumed, only to cease just as abruptly for more shedwind some ways past that. Meanwhile, waist-high stone dogs bracketed the road at the border of each change. They had the straight spine and pricked ears of the watchdog of Mennok, but the statues' ears were decidedly foxy, their tails flaring and puffy. The eyes were simply hollows in the stone, but their sockets canted in a cunning expression. Which made no sense at all. Mennok was as somber as it got, his distanced gloom untouched and unaffected no matter how chaotic the earth or heavens became. The fox of Carvahal, meanwhile, *lived* to cause trouble. To play gods and humans against each other in any combination. He'd probably trick the trees if he could. Combining these two icons into one watching, laughing canine was either blasphemous or an incomprehensible joke.

The alternating bands of firs and shedwind continued for four or five miles. Just when Dante thought the path would never end, it did. A flat and grassy plateau abutted a sheer black cliff. Crumbled basalt slumped against the cliff face. The road branched four ways, leading to four caves set into the vertical stone. Thirty yards ahead, a man stood across the path, dressed in furry leggings and several layers of jackets.

"So you made it."

"Is this it?" Dante said. "The temple?"

"You were expecting lofty spires?" the man said without smiling. "Delicate stained glass that paints the floor in rainbows?"

In truth, Dante had expected something quite like it. "Are you waiting here for me?"

"Anyone who'd walk up a mountain must have an interesting question."

"What if he doesn't?"

"Then it is fun to laugh at him." The man touched his blond beard. "What is your question?"

Dante went as still as the shedwind. What *was* his question? He couldn't flat-out ask about the mysteries of the loon; if its secrets got out, their entire advantage would be nullified, leaving them to face the armies of Gask with nothing but inferior numbers and prayer. Anyway, what would this cave-dweller know about the nether? Of bending it to form artifacts that could outlast an age?

The man tipped back his head, as if reading Dante's mind. "You came all this way without knowing your question?"

"Maybe it's too complicated to pose simply."

"Maybe you're too simple to make *it* simple."

Dante tightened his jaw. "What do you know about the nether?"

"Whatever it allows me."

"Nice dodge. Has anyone who knows what they're talking about ever fallen for it?"

The man stuck out his hands at arm's length, face contorted in revulsion. Black slime dripped from his fingers, pattering soundlessly on the dirt path and evaporating like water on a griddle. The viscous slime climbed his forearms, swallowing his elbows and then his shoulders. As it slithered up his neck and began to form a black mask, the man went motionless and smiled like a painting. The nether disappeared.

"Oops," he said.

"I spoke too fast," Dante said. "But that display was awfully fast itself. My problem lies in making such things last."

"A lasting mark," the man nodded. "The concern of every young man. And likely every young woman, too. But they hide it better."

"If the nether comes from my hands, how do I make it stay once I take my hands away?"

The man tipped his forehead forward, frowning. "You think the nether comes from your hands?"

Dante blinked. "That's not what I meant."

"Strange. Because that is what you said."

"Well, where do you think it comes from?"

"Me?" The man looked genuinely surprised. "Oh, I believe I'm Arawn in human skin. I have yet to be proven wrong."

"Do you know how to get it to stick to a thing?"

"This is no longer interesting." The blond man nodded downhill. "I think you belong back there."

"Already? But I came all this way."

The man raised a brow. "It really isn't *that* far, you wimp. Now move, for I have praying to do."

Wind gusted through the plateau, stinging Dante's eyes with grit. The man didn't seem to notice. Dante waited for several awkward seconds, then turned and started back down the banded mountain.

In town, he found Blays ensconced in a bench recessed into the floor of a tavern just past the docks. Blays smiled over a stein of kaven so heavily spiced it must have been brewed locally.

"Well?" he sipped. "How'd it go?"

Dante shook his head. "I think he made fun of me."

"Is that it?" Blays said. "I could have done that right here and saved you the trip."

By the time they finished at the pub, Dante had a hard time climbing the wooden ladder back to ship. In the cabin, Mourn snored on the bunk across the room, his hairy shins jutting from the edge of the bed. Blays banged through the door and flopped into bed with his boots still on. His phlegmy breathing soon joined Mourn's.

Dante hated the oracular speech of monks and priests. If you used enough vagaries and poetry, you could make anything sound profound. *The wise man heavies his plate with eggs, for the wisdom of the unborn is unbound by perspective.* Either the blond man knew how to help him, and should have said so explicitly, or he didn't, and should have been equally explicit about that. No wonder so little ever changed. When people weren't lying outright, they peddled half-truths and obscurities.

Next morning, Blays woke with a scowl. He slung his feet off his bunk and crinkled his face. "Did I step in something?" He squinted at the soles of his feet. "Did I *sleep* in something?"

"Just yourself," Dante said.

When Blays left for breakfast, Dante quickly took his satchel of rats next door, confirmed Lira was out, then occupied her cabin to chop up the rodents' bodies, clean out their skulls, and dump everything else into the sea. He spent all morning and afternoon with the nether, saturating the fresh bones with shadows that melted away the moment he turned his mind elsewhere. How could he possibly convince it to stay? If it was a spirit, an essence of the thing to which it was attached, how could he force it to stick to an object it didn't embody?

Sunset bathed the cabin red. He left Lira's room for his first meal of the day. He intended to return to his work, but Mourn asked for a game of Nulladoon, and as he wavered, three other sailors eating at the table goaded him to accept the challenge. Mourn's play was careful and thorough. In the end, his last pebble was too strong for Dante's final orange seed. By the time they dissected the game over two beers apiece, Dante was too tired to even think about nether or bones or cryptic monks.

That left him two days until Narashtovik. Two days to find something to bring to Cally's door besides apologies and empty hands.

He paused mid-stride on his way to the plank that served as the head. Empty hands. Empty hands he filled with nether. Was that what the monk had meant with his question about the nether's source? Because his hands weren't quite empty: they possessed a drop of nether themselves. If he honed his focus like the point of a pen, he could draw the substance from his palms like a line of ink.

If he then spent it, it returned in the next hour or day, didn't it? There was a reason he felt drained from practice and refreshed with rest. It was no different from the way his physical strength wore away and then returned. Presumably, any object that contained nether would regenerate it — or rediscover it? — with enough time.

Heart thumping, he spread out his assortment of bones. He sucked nether from the walls and himself, spinning it into the veiny network that connected him to the dead rats' dormant senses. And then, with all the care of a hobbyist mounting a butterfly or a traveling barber pricking the cataract in the eye of a patient, he drew the droplets of nether from the bone itself and used them to smooth a tight sheath around the shadows he'd drawn from himself.

He held his breath. If he could have, he would have held his heartbeat. Gently as sleep, he removed his focus from the pair of loons. The veins and their sheaths stayed in place. For a minute, Dante did nothing but watch. Nothing changed. Nothing faded or slipped away into the crevices it had been called from. At times, the sheath glimmered darkly, as if rippling under a pale moon, but Dante saw no movements of any other kind, and detached from the loons, he couldn't feel them, either.

Not with his mind, anyway. The two loons lay on an old cloth on the floor. He touched the nearer one as cautiously as if it had just been plucked from a boiling pot. He felt nothing but bone. He lifted it to his ear. Heard nothing but the dumb hiss of a cupped seashell. He brought it to his mouth, paused to think, and said "I don't—"

"I don't—" said the loon still resting on the cloth.

Dante sprawled back, banging his spine into the side of the bunk. He crumpled forward in pain. Several seconds later, when he was fit to walk again, he snatched up the second loon, burst from the cabin, and plowed through the neighboring door. Blays sat straight up, bedsheets flapping, and pawed at the recessed shelf beside his bed, rattling his scabbards.

"I've got it!" Dante said.

Blays glowered, face puffy. "Unless 'it' is an unstoppable fire, or a giant hole in the floor, you can tell me about it later."

"Take this." Dante pushed one of the loons at Blays' groggy face.

"What is this? It looks like a bunch of bones wrapped up in string."

"It is. Now stay there." Dante ran back outside and slammed the door, drawing a stare from Lira, seated a short ways down the hall. He ducked into her room, closed the door, and brought the loon to his mouth. "Blays Buckler prefers the company of aquatic mammals."

"Holy shit!" Blays' voice piped from the bundle of bone in Dante's hand, followed by a painfully loud clatter. Something hard scraped against wood.

"Are you dropping my priceless artifact?" Dante said.

"No! I mean, it talked! I mean, *you* get hard from dolphins."

"I will now be accepting nominations for sainthood. Of me."

"That requires proof of godly ancestry," Blays said through the loon. "No more than four generations removed, if you can trust my mom." The door to Lira's cabin jarred open. Blays wandered inside, still speaking into the loon held in front of his mouth. "Which I do. Because she also told me I was the handsomest boy in Mallon."

"Close the damn door," Dante said, hustling to do just that. "So there now exists the non-zero chance Cally won't use us to mulch his garden."

Blays turned the bundle of bone and string over in his hand. "I'll admit this is impressive. Not impressive enough to redeem yourself for sparking a war. But probably impressive enough to get you off the hook if you'd slept with his sister."

"Cally's sister would be a hundred years old."

"And no doubt bearded. But hunger turns stones into soup."

"Once I had the idea, it really wasn't that hard to piece together." Dante reached for the other loon, holding one up in each palm. "It's based on the same principle I use to delve into the senses of dead animals. Through forming two such linked pairs, then splicing those pairs together, you more or less have the basis for a functional loon. Except only I can use it, because I'm the only one with the nethereal link. If I then go on, however, to exploit the object's own inborn nether to support the structure instead of using my external focus to do so, it turns out that—"

"Fascinating," Blays said. "Now shut up and let's tell the others. Except not like that, unless you're sick of them and want them bored to death."

Dante glanced at the closed door. "I need to ask Mourn a few questions. I don't think Lira needs to know, though."

"Why not?"

"Because I don't really trust her."

Blays raised his brows. "Of course not. It's not as if she's pledged her life to you."

"I pledge to serve you bacon shaped to spell your name every morning so long as we both shall live," Dante bowed. He straightened and met Blays' eyes. "Guess who's going to be deeply disappointed tomorrow morning?"

"Come on, she's been nothing but trustable. She could have turned us in to Cassinder's people any time in the last week."

Dante took another look at the door. "Unless she's holding out for an even bigger reward for bringing them a working loon."

"Fine, she gets to know nothing," Blays said. "But only because it's a genuine war secret."

Dante went to fetch Mourn and found him wave-watching from the bow. Empty gray waters rolled to the eastern horizon. To the south, far white hills slept under new and gleaming snow. A steady wind assaulted Dante's ears. One of the crew struggled with the rigging of the mainmast; atop the stern, another two argued with the rotund captain. The deck was otherwise clear. In the isolation, Dante gave Mourn a quick demonstration of his loons.

"I can hear the wind coming out of both of them," Mourn said after a moment. "The clan's loons spoke directly into your ear, and only when someone had something to say."

"Well, I'm not done." Dante wrapped the bones in cloth and tucked them away. "I just wanted to see what you thought."

"Why would you want my opinion? I didn't have anything to do with making them. The only reason I know about them is because I had the privilege of being born into the Clan of the Nine Pines. I may as well build a castle and ask that gull over there what it thinks."

Dante frowned out to sea. "I think we should rename you

Cheer."

He wanted to construct a second set of loons and confirm his success with the first wasn't some confusing fluke, but he still wasn't sure what would come of the first. Besides, despite having sailed for several days, he'd spent less than an hour with the ocean. So he sat down beside Mourn, legs folded, and watched the incoming swells, the subtle tilt of the horizon as the *Bad Tidings* climbed each watery hill and slid down the other side. Waves hissed and splattered. A cold and constant wind grazed his face and forced its fingers past his collar. He reached his mind out toward the pair of loons every two or three minutes, unable to stop himself despite knowing there would be little or nothing he could do if the delicate nether-sheaths began to crack. Still, this ceaseless doublechecking reassured him, releasing a growing pressure that began in his head and slowly filled his gut.

An hour later, he checked the loons and found the nether was gone. He brought one to his mouth and spoke. He heard nothing but his own voice.

The nether had simply disappeared, reducing the loons to inert matter. He returned to Lira's cabin and assembled another functional pair, but an hour later, it too reverted to dumb, simple bone. He tried again, watching the third set without interruption. A little over an hour later, shining white cracks appeared in its shadowy sheath. The cracks thickened little by little; without warning, the black case burst apart. The trapped nether that linked the bones together dispersed at once, absorbing into the rag and floor beneath the loon.

Nothing he tried that day made any difference. He stayed up late and woke early. His head was heavy, but he forced himself to get up, wash his face, and return to work. Something strange had happened with the broken loons: the droplets of internal nether he'd used to form their sheaths had returned, but were unshaped. He took that nether and reforged it into fresh sheaths, wrapping these around new globs of nether drawn from foreign sources. An hour later, however, the sheaths collapsed again. Dante fell back on the cot, exhausted. What good was a loon that could only last an hour?

Late that morning, bells and shouts yanked him from his labor.

Narashtovik grew on the horizon. Within hours, he'd be brought before Cally and held accountable for setting off the war.

8

Not long ago, Narashtovik had been called the Dead City. It was known as such even among its own citizens—what few remained, anyway. No one thought anything of the ghastly appellation; that was simply its name, earned through centuries of warfare and sackings that had reduced the city's outer rings to crumbling ruins. For those who stayed, it was a home, no more and no less, and while it was true that you could find ribs and skulls if you chose to poke through the fallow houses on its fringes, life at the core of the city was still normal enough.

Things had changed since Samarand's aborted war against Mallon some six years ago. The pine forests that infiltrated the city's old borders had disappeared, cleared for timber and tilled for crops. Fresh-cut wooden homes replaced most of the old stone ruins. The rasp of saws was like steady breathing; the rap of hammers a heartbeat. To the north, a high green hill considered the city, the site of the cemetery where Larrimore was buried. Past the outermost homes, the Pridegate circled Narashtovik's interior. Further yet, the Ingate that surrounded Narashtovik's oldest quarters was hidden behind steep black roofs, but at the city's very center, the staggering spire of the Cathedral of Ivars punctured the sky. Beside it, the keep of the Sealed Citadel rose like an upthrust fist.

As far as Dante had a home, Narashtovik was his. He hadn't seen Bressel since before the war, and anyway, he'd hardly lived there a handful of weeks. Before that, he spent his childhood and middle teens in a farming village in Mallon's breadbasket. Memories of his youth were a golden haze of streams and fields. Since leaving, he rarely thought of it.

Because in a way, he had been the midwife to Narashtovik's rebirth. He'd helped put down Samarand's holy war on Mallon. The refugees and survivors of that aborted conflict flocked to time-withered Narashtovik, making their claims on half-ruined homes that had lain empty for generations. When he wasn't busy on council business or one of Cally's endless errands, Dante enjoyed exploring those abandoned homes. They felt secret, sacred. Yet he'd been happier to see new families making them their own. Between the chimney smoke and fresh fields, it was clear the city had swelled all the more in the two-three years he and Blays had spent arming, supplying, and scouting the Norren Territories. Dante had missed that growth, that bustle, the knowledge he could step out into the street and see or buy or experience whatever he wished.

So he was worried about Cally's reaction to their news. And fearful of whatever fate might befall the city in the next months or years. But he was also glad, plainly and rightly, to be home.

"Think it still stinks?" Blays said beside him on the deck of the *Bad Tidings*.

"Absolutely."

"Figure out those things of yours?"

Absently, Dante touched the cracked bones in his pocket. "Not by half."

"Well, we're still a ways out. Plenty of time to finalize your will."

"It's not going to be that bad. Maybe he hasn't even heard."

"You're leaving me all your stuff, right?" Blays said. "Because I'm going to say you are anyway."

There was no point in a last-gasp scramble to perfect the loons. Dante was simply out of ideas. Instead, he descended to his cabin, nodding to the scurrying sailors belowdecks, and packed up his spare clothes and blanket and the cracked skulls of the rats. Back abovedecks, the *Bad Tidings* slipped past the western banks of the bay where a thicket of grounded ships rested in the silt where the river met the sea. There, an impromptu neighborhood had assembled among the wracks. The ships' sails were long gone, the bronze and iron stripped from figureheads and railings. Instead, clean white laundry flapped from masts. Residents jogged across planks nailed between half-submerged decks. Improbably, smoke curled from more than one of the grounded cabins; slant-walled shacks clung to masts and forecastles. The last time Dante had seen the bay, the old ships had been completely uninhabited, their hulls crusty with salt, gulls piping from rotten rigging.

"I almost hate to make port," Mart said behind him, startling him. "We're bound to pick up some new rats."

"So you're happy with the outcome of our arrangement?" Dante said.

"Happy? We'll have the only shit-free barley in all of Gask."

"You must be very proud."

"I've got half a mind to pressgang you." Mart's eyes glittered above his beard. "But then the sensible half suggests my body would wind up piled with the rats."

The boat came to port and sailors debarked to tie her off. Over the last few weeks, Dante had become so familiar with the process he could have pitched right in. By the time the crew secured the gangway to the dock, a crowd of longshoremen, merchant's aides, and would-be travelers had gathered at the base of the pier, babbling and jostling, breath visible in the harsh light bouncing off the sea. A queue of carriages idled in the open square beyond the waterfront, but Dante decided to walk. No need to hustle to his fate.

Few norren lived in Narashtovik, and Mourn drew more than one look as their group thumped down the damp pier toward the waiting crowd. His hulking presence was enough to open a gap in the throng. Dante led the way, composing his route to the Sealed Citadel. Canden Street would be the shortest, but it was the first day of Thaws, and the main streets would likely be clogged with a plague of potters, tailors, and shoppers all looking to—

Metal flashed from the forest of fur coats. A short man plunged from the crowd, knife darting forward, his gaze locked on Dante's chest. Too late, Dante grabbed at the nether, his panic whipping it into a charcoal froth. The man's arm straightened, preparing to drive the blade home.

Lira flung herself forward, ramming her shoulder into the man's ribs. They thudded to the boardwalk, hands locked together, grappling for the knife. Lira rolled the small man onto his back and flicked her fingers at his eyes. As he flinched, she clamped both hands on his knife hand and twisted his wrist toward his body, bearing down hard. The man screamed. His wrist gave with a fleshy pop. Blays' sword snaked past Lira and speared the attacker through the left lung.

The retreat of the crowd left Dante in the middle of an empty circle. He stood there, shaking, as pink blood burbled from the attacker's mouth, the man's broken wrist flapping against the boardwalk.

Blays pulled his blade from the dying man's ribs with a wet *shup*. "I didn't think Cally would be *that* mad."

Jittery fury flooded Dante's veins. He knelt beside the assassin and grabbed him by the collar, yanking his head from the pier. "Who hired you?"

The man blinked, glassy-eyed, and coughed thickly. Dante shoved him down by the collar, banging the back of his head into the planks. "Was it Cassinder? All you have to do is nod."

The assassin choked, coughing bubbly pink blood over Dante's heavy cloak. He fell back, spasming, fishlike.

"He looks pretty dumb to me," Blays said. "Let's ask his pockets instead."

He crouched on the other side of the body and turned out the pockets of the man's cloak and doublet and trousers, revealing three more knives, one long and two small, a handkerchief, a plain leather purse clinking with coins, a bag of dried venison and cherries, a sewing kit, comb and scissors, and a pinky-thin vial of a viscous, black-brown liquid. Boots jogged the planks. Two armed men hurried down the pier, dressed in the black leather and silver trim of the city. They stopped cold when they saw the body. Drawing swords, they shuffled forward, right feet extended. Blays pocketed the vial.

Dante stood, sleeves foamy with blood. "This man attacked us."

The guards' faces were drawn with angry caution. On seeing Dante, the expression of the man on the right shifted to relieved recognition. "Are you all right, my lord?"

"I'm fine." Dante nodded to the knife Lira had knocked down the planks. "Be careful with his blade. It may be poisoned."

Another pair of guards arrived to handle the crowds and the corpse. The first pair led Dante and crew through the holiday-busied streets to the nearest guard station, a tight-quartered space inside one of the three-story towers that rose at intervals from the Pridegate. There, Dante answered questions (which he mostly ducked; he'd pass his suspicions about Cassinder along to Cally during his dressing-down) and waited around for a half hour until yet another guard arrived to inform Dante and Blays their presence was required at the Sealed Citadel. As if fearing they'd attempt to flee, this latest guard accompanied them from the tower into the rising hills beyond the Pridegate.

Children wove through the crowds, their dark hair threaded with grassy crowns. Men stopped at public houses while their wives eyed bright fabric and bought pies stuffed with the first and hardiest harvests—frostpeas, Gaskan squash, turnips. Most of the buildings here had been occupied and maintained even during Narashtovik's leanest times, and showed little of the recent patching and reconstruction that dominated the structures beyond the outer wall. Stone gargoyles guarded the rooftop gutters, silently judging the boisterous humans below.

"Thank you," Dante said to Lira. It was the first moment of semi-privacy they'd had since the attack. "I suppose that makes us even."

She shrugged, gazing across the revelers. "An action done in the name of duty is never the equal of one taken freely."

He gave her a long and skeptical look. "Are you talking about snagging you from that boat? We did that to find out where the Bloody Knuckles had gone. Saving you for information is no different than you saving me because of some crazy debt."

"What if I walk away and you're killed five minutes from now? My debt wouldn't look so repaid then."

"It's no fair if you keep changing the rules."

They passed under an arch of the Ingate, a second ring of solid stone which had separated nobles and well-landed merchants from the decay that beset the city for so long. Inside, the streets were rather more subdued; families strolled together between the bright tarps shading the stalls and carts gathered at every intersection and plaza. Dante could have differentiated the traders past the Ingate from those outside it even without the fine dress and casual pace of their clientele. Outside the Ingate, carts were piled high with cloth and toys. Inside it, velvet-topped displays held a bare sprinkle of goods—a half dozen rings, say, gleaming amidst the empty space of their surroundings.

A wide stone avenue climbed the city's central hill. The endless shadow of the cathedral fell over Dante's face. Across from it, a towering citadel gazed down from behind its unscratched walls. Dante wore none of the trappings of his station, but before he could introduce himself at the Sealed Citadel's iron gate, it raised with a series of heavy clanks.

"What, they don't even ask your name?" Blays said as they crossed into the courtyard. "If I'd arrived by myself, I'd be waiting until the walls fell down."

Gant waited just inside the courtyard, pale enough to look as though he walked between sunbeams and narrow-shouldered enough for Dante to believe he did just that. The majordomo bowed, back curved in that particular Narashtovik fashion.

"My lord Dante. It's been too long."

"I know, Gant," Dante said. "Hello and goodbye."

Gant tilted back his face. "Goodbye?"

"Figured I'd better say it now, since Cally's about to murder me. Is he up in his chambers?"

"I believe so. And I don't believe he will murder you, my lord. No matter what you've done this time."

"Oh, I don't know." He gestured to Lira and Mourn. "I've got two guests, as you can see. Will you find lodgings for them?"

"At once." Gant bowed and bobbed his head in a fashion that perfectly intimated Mourn and Lira should follow him up the stairs into the keep. Dante followed, too, but as Gant swept the others through the quiet foyer on his way to the guest rooms at the rear, Dante and Blays curled up the main stairwell instead.

"Well," Blays said, the single word echoing up the stone steps.

"Well," Dante agreed.

"You don't *really* think he could..?"

"No, I don't think so. Cally's a tyrant, but generally not a violent one."

"That's a relief," Blays said. "Except for the fact that means we have no idea who just tried to kill you."

Dante saved the rest of his breath for the stairs. Cally kept his quarters at the very top of the keep. Dante had no idea how the old man managed to climb up and down the stairs all day long. It probably involved demons. Big ones.

At last they reached the upper landing. A black carpet striped the hall. Tapestries illustrated and insulated the walls, weavings of Arawn at his mill and the starry arrangement of the heavens. Cally's double doors were closed but unlocked. As Dante opened the door, a wintry breeze knifed from the open balcony and cut past his face. Dante's boots sunk into the cushy black rug. The woman to occupy the room prior to Cally had busied it with pious marks of her station as High Priestess of Arawn: holy books, candlesticks, intricately illuminated parchments, and silver statues of the White Tree. On moving in years back, Cally had hollered "Look out below!" from the balcony and then flung most of the room's contents straight out the window. Now his chambers most closely resembled a scribe's den—bookshelves along both walls, black grenados of ink gleaming from the door-sized desk, great nests of parchment and quills and quill-snips and jars of white blotting-sand. That left the room's center quite empty. So, too, was the stuffed red chair at the far end of the room. The fireplace was cold and dark.

"Suppose he's invisible?" Blays said.

"No, I suppose he's quite visible. In a place that isn't here."

Dante left to track down a steward. The third man he found knew where Cally was—among the ruins on the outskirts of town—but balked at leading them there until Dante reminded him that dusting the mantels was several rungs less important than a direct order from a member of the Council of Narashtovik. After that, the man led them back downstairs and into the streets in a southerly course. Past the Pridegate, as many houses were ruined as intact. Many lots were nothing but snow, grass, and mounded stone. Twice, explosions boomed through the ruins further to the south.

"That's him, isn't it?" Dante said.

The servant didn't glance over. "I couldn't possibly say, my lord."

"That's definitely him," Blays said.

The steward led them into a patchwork field of snow and grass. One wall of a farmhouse stood between a slew of old stones and rotten timbers. Beside it, a solid chimney rose thirty feet into the sky, freestanding and intact. The servant led them toward its massive hearth. The ground around it was scorched. The cold wind stirred the scent of something burnt and sharp. A hinged door of iron had been bolted to the base of the chimney. It was also scorched.

"My lords," the steward said.

"Yes?" Dante said.

"I have taken you to Callimandicus. May I return to the Citadel now?"

Blays knelt and touched the patina of charcoal around the chimney. "Ye gods, we're too late! He's blown himself to hell!"

Two skinny legs thrust from the entrance to the chimney, wrinkled and bare. They were accompanied by a muffled, echoing voice. "Who goes there?"

"A confused person," Dante said.

"Two confused people," Blays said.

"Oh," the voice said. "You two."

The legs kicked, toenails scraping soot from the chimney walls. Ash sifted to the blasted ground at the chimney's base. The old man tumbled to the ground with a grunt. Cally blinked at them in the overcast sunlight, soot smearing his cheeks and his tangled beard. Between the black of the ash and the white of his beard, his eyes gleamed from his cheeks like captured sky. His bare legs sprawled, liver-spotted and hairless. A long shirt draped past his loins.

"What happened to your pants?" Blays said.

"My—?" Cally glanced down at his legs. "Oh. Lost those about an hour ago."

"Doing what?" Dante said. "Or is that a question I should leave in peace?"

"Doing this." Cally collected himself from the fireplace, careful not to bang his head on the brick of the overhanging hearth, and padded to a cart parked halfway across the field. There, he loaded a wheelbarrow with two sacks; one small and shifting with something like sand, the other big, clanky, and bulging with what sounded like crockery.

"Wheel this over for me, would you? Crawling up chimneys is hard work."

Dante muttered and leaned into the wheelbarrow. Back at the chimney, Cally tossed the small sack into the soot at its base, then gestured at the bag of dishes. "Get those out and pile them up, would you?"

Dante tore open the sack, which was indeed full of dishes, and began placing them atop the smaller bag, stirring fine clouds of choking dust. He dropped his third handful, shattering crockery over the brickwork. He swore.

"No matter." Cally flapped his hand as if to wave away the dust. "It'll all be like that in a moment."

Dante shrugged and returned, with considerably more roughness, to loading up the dishes. Cally swung the iron door closed and clamped it shut with several locks, sealing the hearth.

He batted cinders from his beard. "You might want to step back. Unless you would prefer to be flung back instead."

Cally turned and ran, shirttails flapping. Dante and Blays followed. Some fifty feet from the towering chimney, Cally hunkered down in the snowy grass. Nether roiled around his hands. His tongue poked from the corner of his mouth. Shadows flowed in a river from his hands, gushing under the iron door and disappearing into the chimney.

A tremendous bang rattled the chimney, the door, and Dante's teeth. Black smoke plumed from its mouth. An upward hail of crockery vomited into the sky.

"Taim's virgin daughter!" Dante hollered.

Cally chortled, pointing at the soaring debris. "You see?"

"Very good," Blays said, rubbing his ear. "You've discovered the world's worst way to clean a chimney."

Dante goggled up at the tumbling specks. "What was in the other sack?"

Cally shrugged his bony shoulders. "Dried urine. Black sand. A few other things. That just gives it an extra shove. Most of the force came from the nether."

"What happens when it comes down?"

"Oh, yes. Well, we should probably run again before that happens." Cally took his own advice, dashing across the field with considerable speed for his advanced age. A stand of pines flanked the dilapidated farmland. Before they'd crossed half the distance to the shield of trees, jagged flecks of dishes rained down to earth, pattering the snow and plinking from stones. Cally flung his arms over his head and laughed.

Dante reached the pines and hunkered under the branches to catch his breath. Black smog drifted south on the bay-birthed wind. "What's all this about? A crusade against crockery?"

"Imagine if you aimed that chimney at, say, thirty degrees." Cally sketched its angle through the air. "What if you fired it at a formation of enemy troops? Or a fortress' walls?"

"How much nether does it take?"

"Lots. A lot of lots."

"Why not aim the nether directly at the enemy instead? A lot fewer things can go wrong then."

Cally rolled his eyes in disgust. "Except if they have sorcerers of their own. Then they snap their fingers and your big ball of nether fizzles away like dandelion seeds in the gale. But I suppose you didn't think of that."

"I suppose I didn't."

"Anyway, this is just the theoretical stage. A perfected model would be much more effective." He clapped his knobby hands. "Want to fire it again?"

"Yes, but we need to talk first." Dante blew into his hands. "Listen. Have you heard? About what happened?"

Cally's white brows shot up. "That you burned down the ancestral manor of Cassinder of Beckonridge? And he's going to talk the king into declaring war on us? Why the fuck do you *think* I'm out here blowing stuff up?"

Dante laughed hollowly. "Oh."

"His Highest Kingship Lord Moddegan has already levied a new estate tax, you know. It's enough to think he plans to pay for several thousand men to march across several hundred miles."

"It's his fault." Blays pointed at Dante. "He was chasing down the infamous Quivering Bow."

Dante whirled. "What the hell?"

"What? You'd rather he hear it from someone else?"

"I was going to ease him into it!"

"How were you going to ease me into explaining *that*?" Cally snarled. He drew himself to his full gangly height, his elbows as swollen as the gut of a freshly-fed snake. Beneath the soot, his hair and beard hadn't been combed in days or cut in months. "Well, did you find it? Or did you get diverted by a herd of snipes?"

"Regrettably," Dante said, "we discovered that it doesn't exist."

"Do you know what you've done?"

"I thought it could win the war before it began. We made contact with the Clan of the Nine Pines. They promised it was real."

Cally ran his hand down his snarled white beard. His eyes were closed, as if he were weathering a cramp. "Within the next few weeks, the king is going to issue an ultimatum. It's going to be outrageous. Possibly so much that the Norren Territories, if they accept, will wish they'd simply gone to war instead."

"I thought war was the plan all along."

"Years from now! When we were ready! When our position would be so strong even the clowns in Setteven would rather let the norren go than try to march against them."

Dante stared at the grass. Beetles crawled between the blades. "I thought I could help."

"The norren won't back down from this. Not all of them. They're too fractured." Cally turned away from the city. Bitter wind whipped his beard. "People are going to die, Dante."

"I found something else instead. Something—"

Cally raised his splayed palms to his shoulders. "The Council meets tonight. The issue, to put it indelicately, is whether Narashtovik will stand with the norren or abandon them to the warhounds of Gask."

Dante cocked his head. "How did they know I'd be back today?"

"They didn't. As it turns out, the world goes on without you. Try to make it a better place for once."

Cally's weary disappointment stung worse than any wrath. There was too much to say, so Dante said nothing. In time, they returned to the Citadel together, wordless the whole way. Pantsless and begrimed as Cally was, the gatekeepers still recognized him. Dante supposed it wasn't the first time they'd seen him in such a state.

"That could have been worse," Blays said once they were alone in the stairwell.

"Oh really?" Dante said.

"We could be dead."

Dante gazed at the musty walls. "I think I'd rather be."

"Maimed, then. Weighed down by a brick of guilt *and* two broken legs."

"Pain would be a welcome distraction."

Blays grabbed Dante's shoulder, jarring him. "Will you knock off the self-pity? This thing has hardly begun. What do we do to de-disaster it?"

"We have no choice." Dante lifted his face. "We have to help the norren. We're the ones who got them into this mess."

"Great. So quit moping and figure out what you'll say to the Council. I'll go get the molten silver."

"Molten silver?"

"To pour on your tongue."

Dante shook his head. A floor down, he discovered his long-vacant room had recently been cleaned. The bedsheets smelled like soap and the pine needles the servants pestled to scent the linens. There was no fire, of course, and it was too cold to take off his cloak, but he left his door shut and locked. For the moment, he needed isolation.

In time, he belled a servant for a bath, which he sat in until the water grew lukewarm, letting the slow work of water wear the salt and dirt from his skin. He shaved and dressed himself in the Council's colors, then faced himself in the small mirror above his basin. His jaw and cheeks had gone harder. Suggestions had become definitions.

Under normal circumstances, he was the type to plot out every word of what he might say at the meeting. To sketch the branch of every argument he could make or anticipate facing. Instead, he closed his eyes and opened his inner sight to the nether, watching it trickle through the room's dark places, its minute pools under his bed and dresser, its shining dust glittering from every surface. A servant knocked. It was time.

Dante returned to the upper floor and made for the Council's chambers. The cherrywood double doors bore the image of the White Tree of Barden, ghastly and beautiful, its trunk and limbs fused from spines and ribs, molars and canines forming its flowers and thorns. Inside, a long, plain table dominated the room. Sectioned glass windows overlooked the vivid pink sunset on the bay. Dante was among the last to arrive. Old Tarkon was already seated, his cane leaned against the table. He winked Dante's way, heavy wrinkles bunching around his eye. Hart sat, too, a mountain of a norren with thick clouds of beard swirling about his head. Olivander's head was bent in apparent prayer, muscly soldier's shoulders bunched around his neck. Joseff's ancient eyes were closed. He may have been asleep.

These were the lone survivors of Cally's uprising beneath the boughs of Barden. Some of the dead had been replaced within days: wiry Kav, whose carved features betrayed his noble birth but not his age, which must have been passing sixty; Ulev, chubby, a simple monk raised above his station; Merria, the old woman whose blue tongue would better suit a stevedore than one of Arawn's chosen; Somburr, quick-eyed and twitchy, his brown skin and elusive accent a product of one of the southern isles; Varla, who spoke as rarely as an oracle. The last to arrive (besides Cally, whose habitual lateness was more a product of indifference than a conscious display of his station) was Wint, who in his mid-30s was the youngest councilman besides Dante himself.

Assorted servants orbited the table, too. Behind Dante's right shoulder, Blays leaned against the wall. Cally ambled into the room and the Council rose as one.

"Excellent," Cally said, seating himself. "I can't remember the last time we didn't have at least one empty chair."

Tarkon pursed his lips, ruffling his beard. "Then again, you can't remember the last time you emptied your bowels, either."

"Nonsense. On matters of importance, my scribe takes the strictest notes." Cally's smirk faded. "I'm not going to rehash every detail. If you're not up to date, it's your own damn fault. In short, a clan of norren burned Lord Cassinder's estate to the foundations. In response, King Moddegan has levied a new tax. He's begun headcounts in Bonn and Lattover. Headcounts means troop counts. Troop counts mean we'd better grab our balls and run for the hills."

"The debacle with Cassinder was my fault," Dante broke in. "We led a clan on a mission to rescue their enslaved cousins.

Things turned violent."

Wint lifted a thin black brow. "I heard the search for a few missing norren was just one of the reasons you were there."

From behind Dante, Blays snorted. "Of course it was. Do you think we'd cartwheel through some lord's door, torches in hand, all for the sake of a single clan?"

"It doesn't matter *why* it happened," Cally said, cutting off any potential objections to lowly Blays speaking out of turn. "What matters is what course we take from here. If none of you want to figure that out, *my* next course is straight to bed."

The other members glanced between each other. A servant coughed. Olivander leaned forward and clasped his heavy hands on the table. "If Moddegan marches, it will be on the norren, not us."

"Sounds like the very reason we should stay clear," Wint said.

"They're counting on our loyalty."

Somburr's head jerked back and forth. "Since when is suicide the best expression of loyalty? We preserve ourselves. Stash our loyalty away. Then return it to the table when it's actually worth playing."

Tarkon rolled his eyes. "Would that be before or after the Norren Territories are converted into the world's largest charcoal bed?"

"I've met Moddegan," Kav said in his academy-honed tones. "He doesn't believe in half-measures. If we throw our sticks in with the norren, he'll burn us without blinking."

Cally grimaced. "Olivander, what kind of numbers can we muster? Reliably, I mean. You military men seem cursed with double vision whenever you survey the troops."

"Three thousand?" the big man shrugged. "A tenth that in cavalry. Between the last war and the immigrants, our infrastructure hasn't had time to rebuild."

"And what can Moddegan come up with?"

"Ten thousand by July. At the very least. Maybe double that."

"I'm no algebraist," Wint said, "but that sounds horrible."

"They'd have to thread their campaign through a narrow needle," Varla said softly. "The Dundens are often snowed in by October."

"And that snow won't fall on whatever hill we huddle on?" Kav countered.

"Why are we arguing *whether* to help?" Dante said. "We're the reason they're facing invasion. If we hadn't been stirring up trouble the last five years, they'd still be just another unhappy territory."

"'We'?" Wint said.

"The institution of this council and the higher lord we serve."

Kav gazed at the white plaster ceiling and the chandelier's twelve clusters of candles. "The key fact is that promise was made five years ago. If we were looking at the world as it lies right now, would we make that same promise?"

"Which of course has nothing to do with the fact we did make that promise," Cally said. "Anyway, the thinking here is very all-or-nothing. There are ways to aid and resist that don't involve a field of troops, a rousing speech, and a million kegs of blood."

"If we commit one man, we may as well send a thousand," Wint said. "You think they can sweep through the norren without picking up our tracks as well? With proof of our involvement and an army at our doorstep, what king in his right mind wouldn't take the chance to finally annex us properly?"

Talk went on for another half hour, but Wint's cold logic effectively settled the issue. Cally called for a vote. He, Dante, Tarkon, and Olivander favored continued support. The remaining eight decided to cease all involvement in norren matters until a later date.

While the others filed out, Dante slumped in his high-backed chair. Blays sat on the table and kicked his heels. "Well, good luck to the clans, I guess."

"This is bullshit," Dante said. "How can they just turn their backs? We've been working towards this for years."

"Maybe the norren will do all right. I'd rather break rocks with my balls than try to scour the clans from their own hills."

"You think so?"

"Well, probably not. I'd only expect to lose *one* ball fighting the norren."

Tarkon tarried with Cally for some time. With nowhere else to go, Dante sat and stewed, seething over every insipid argument and call to cowardice. Had he just wasted the last five years of his life? Had he actually made a bad thing worse? What was the plan from here? To sit in the Citadel making faces of concern while the armies of Gask stamped, raped, and gorged their way across the norren lands?

Once Tarkon left, Cally ushered out the last of the servants, retook his seat, and hoisted one slippered foot to rest upon the table. "Disappointed?"

Dante smiled grimly. "Why would I be disappointed? It's only my fault the norren are facing war. I've just been ordered not to help them. I couldn't be happier if you told me my mom had walked back from the dead."

"I see."

"I suppose you think I deserve this. Well, the norren are about to be punished far worse than me."

"Deserve it?" Cally laughed scornfully. "I'm no Taim. I don't hand down judgment from my righteous throne. By and large, everyone deserves nothing. The rightness of this belief is proven by the fact that's precisely what they get."

"Now that's a rousing philosophy," Blays said. "The kind of thing that inspires you to spring out of bed, rub the grit from your eyes, and dive right back under the covers."

Cally flapped his hand. "Listen, dribblemouth, I'm no happier about their decision than you are."

"Could have fooled me," Dante said.

"Well, the answer to that quandary is very simple." Cally reached out to lower his stiff leg from the table. He stood, cracking his knuckles. "We're not going to do a damn thing the Council says."

9

Dante blinked. "You mean to help the norren anyway."

"That quick brain is precisely why I appointed you to the Council."

"In that case, I have something to show you." Dante jogged out the door to his rooms, gathered up his satchel, and returned to the meeting chambers, where Cally and Blays passed a badly-rolled cigarette between them. Dante closed the door behind him. Under the tobacco, Dante smelled siftspring, an odor of sage and cold winter mornings. It would perk their nerves a little bit; Cally favored it when he did his deepest thinking. Dante placed a lumpy rag on the table and unfolded it, revealing several pieces of cracked skull.

Cally leaned over, smoke rising dragonlike from his nostrils. "Very nice. Bits of dead things."

"There's more."

"Yes, I saw the string, too. Those are some tidy little knots."

"Hang on a minute, you old goat." Dante stood over the pieces and summoned the darkness to his fingers. Cally glanced away from the cigarette in his hand, frowning slightly as Dante drew his nethereal connections between the bones and sheathed them tight in the bones' own power. Dante had built loons a score of times now and the ritual took him less than two minutes. Blays, meanwhile, wandered to the fireplace to poke at the embers with a brass gaff. Dante set one of the completed loons in front of Cally. "Wait here."

He unlocked the glass doors, stepped onto the cold, windy balcony, and shut himself outside. He pressed his face to the glass to watch the old man, then lifted his loon to his face. "Callimandicus!"

Cally jerked back from the table, gnarled hands twisted in front of his face. Dante chortled and went on. "This is the voice of Arawn! You are to give the one you call Dante Galand a tower! And a harem to fill it with!"

Cally gaped at the door, beckoning furiously. "Where did you learn to do that?"

"I tried to tell you." Dante locked the door behind him, shivering in the sudden warmth. "We didn't find the Quivering Bow. But we found these."

"This is brilliant. I don't understand why I didn't think of this myself." He turned the bones over in his deep-lined palm, tapping them with his yellowed fingernails, peering into the crevices between the strung-together pieces. He cackled and flicked the loon into the air, snatching it at its apex. "Two simple links! Who taught you to make this?"

"The norren who came here with us had one. I think they severed its connection when he left the clan, so I had to deduce how it worked on the trip here."

"It won't hold together for long, though, will it? Perhaps a couple of hours."

"How can you tell?" Dante said.

"Because this little wrapper you've got holding it in place is already evaporating." Cally set down the loon and sat back, beard rolling into a smile. "Still, this changes things, you know. Things are very changed."

"Do you think we have a chance?"

"Hardly," Cally snorted. "But now's not the time to be worrying about trivial things like *chances*. Get your norren up here. We have work to do."

Cally worked with the discipline of a scholar and the enthusiasm of a fieldball fanatic. He examined Mourn's earring for five seconds before declaring the tiny wishbone-shaped bone was that from the inner ear of a human. He dispatched a servant to the basements to find as many such bones as he could, then set to work on making the loons permanent. Cally had it figured out before the servant returned: the norren loons weren't always active, allowing the nethereal sheath to "re-charge," as it were, whenever they were silent. If ever the sheath were exhausted, it would collapse, permanently severing the link, but so long as the loons were used sparingly—less than an hour a day—they could hypothetically last forever, or at least as long as the physical object maintained its coherence. They could be further stabilized by employing a second sheath of ether drawn from an inorganic mineral such as the silver used in the earring. Dante could no more command the ether than he could leap and kiss the moon, but he took Cally's word for it.

The servant returned with several miniature bones and three intact skulls, one of which was still wrapped in withered flesh, its hair like dried seaweed. Cally picked the bones apart with scalpel and tweezers and quickly bundled them into two new loons. After some fiddling, he sent Dante to the balcony. With the loon pressed to his ear, Dante heard Cally's voice as a low murmur. On attaching bits of scrap silver, the old man wrangled two different sheaths, one ether, one nether. He and Dante spent a half hour running through the keep like children, loons pressed to their ears as they exchanged insults, commands, and cryptic aphorisms. Early morning sunlight splashed through the curtains. Still, Dante could hardly sleep. By the fourth time he woke, he didn't bother trying to lie back down. He dressed, dashed up to Cally's room, and knocked softly. Cally replied at once, clear-voiced, to call him in.

Dante slammed the door behind him. "Well?"

Cally grinned, blue eyes flashing. "I think I'm going to declare a holiday in our honor."

"They still work!"

"And now comes the hard part: we can't tell a soul about our godlike greatness."

"To be perfectly frank," Dante said, "I don't understand why this is a secret in the first place."

Cally raised the thickets of his brows. "Are you kidding? This is a highly sophisticated concept. Few enough know how to animate the dead, let alone sense through their senses."

"Variations of the idea, then. Like what if I killed a bunch of eagles, then returned them to the sky with a red cloth in one claw and a white cloth in the other? They could pass a message to everyone watching them in moments. Or I could park a dead rat in your room, go to the palace in Setteven, spy on the king, and then have the rat tap out exactly what the king was saying."

The old man chuckled. "Have you ever tried to make a dead bird fly?"

"Well, no."

"It works exactly as well as when a normal person tries it. As far as commanding a rat from five hundred miles away goes, have you ever tried *that*?"

"I've commanded them two or three miles from me," Dante said. "I didn't notice any loss of control or need for additional focus."

"Try it at ten miles sometime," Cally said. "Or twenty. Anyone can waggle a three-foot stick. Try holding up a fifty-foot branch sometime. Building such a speech-web would require an army of nethermancers dedicated to nothing but making rats tap-dance 'Yes' or 'No' to other nethermancers. There aren't enough sorcerers in all Gask for that."

"Then why do the loons work at such long range?"

"Those rats of yours tax your hold on the nether at every moment of the day. It's the same way it taxes a warrior to wave around his sword. Most of the time, the loons are sheathed. A sheathed weapon draws no strength from the wielder."

"I get it, more or less," Dante said. "So we've got the loons. What's next?"

"We plan your next trip," Cally said.

"I don't know about that," Dante frowned. "The last time I was let out of the house, I accidentally touched off a war."

"That's precisely why I'm sending you out to undo it. Not for a couple of weeks, of course. I'd like to let tempers cool before we throw you back into the field."

"Well, that should give me plenty of time to figure out who tried to kill me yesterday."

Cally drew back his bearded chin. "Someone tried to kill you?"

"You didn't hear? When I got off the boat. They were expecting me."

"Well, I can't say I blame them." Cally beckoned toward the door. "Now go get ready for diplomacy. Bathing was a good start."

"No sense going to the tailor just yet," Dante said. "Not before I know whether I'll need new clothes for the bluebloods, or to wear at my own funeral. Speaking of which, I'd like you to take a look at something. It might be poison, so don't eat any of it unless you'd like to make my day."

He brought Cally the vial of black-brown liquid, then found Blays eating toast and bacon and dried peaches in the dining hall. After querying two servants and a blacksmith, he tracked Mourn down in the armory, where the norren was discussing serration with the house arrowsmith. Lira took somewhat longer to locate; she had taken to the gymnasium of the auxiliary barracks, which was presently empty. Dust motes swirled in the sunlight slashing through the empty windows. Cobwebs strangled the exposed rafters. Lira practiced in the space at the far end of the barn-like barracks, short sword in her left hand, her right hand empty. She moved as slowly and fluidly as cool honey, her blade tracing crisp patterns while her free hand moved in concert, clawing, grasping, and twisting imaginary foes. At times, she exploded into furious motion, hand and sword flowing through combinations far too fast for Dante to follow. After one of these flurries, she sensed him and turned, lowering her arms to her side. She wore a light and simple shirt and sweat shined from her temples and neck.

"What are you doing with your off hand?" Dante said. "That seems pretty intricate for shield-work."

"There's no shield."

"But a lot of the time you were *leading* with it. I'll admit I'm an amateur, but that looks like the First Form for Loss of Unwanted Hands."

She sheathed her sword and ran the fingers of her left hand from elbow to wrist of her right. "Armor goes here. You need the fingers free. Combat is sensitive."

"Not in my experience. Anyway, I don't see how you'll ever get close enough to use your bare hand."

She gave him a look, then went to the wall where the wooden swords were racked. She handed one to him hilt-first. "Come at me."

He took two steps, then lunged, his longer blade keeping his body well separated from hers. She shifted her heels, thrusting her short sword left-handed over top of his. As it slid harmlessly past her side, she grabbed his wrist with her empty right hand and collapsed into the gap between them. Her sword pressed against his gut, its short length a sudden advantage.

"That's how it works." She held the pose, steel tapping his stomach, then withdrew.

With a hollow clatter, he returned the sword to the rack. "Very clever. Unless they come at you with two blades."

"Then my bare hand takes one of the knives from my belt." She swept her arm across her sweat-smudged forehead. "I'm not making this up as I go along. I spent my youth in the Carlons. Their warriors have been dealing with Anyrrian pirates for 800 years."

"I'm going to speak to the guards again about the assassin. I'd like you to come with me."

"Afraid to walk the streets alone?" she said, perfectly expressionless.

He narrowed his eyes. Was that a joke? "No, I thought I'd do the right thing and turn you in for assault. Come on. The others are in the courtyard."

He stepped into the cold sunlight while she toweled off and dressed for the wintry air. The gate cranked open as they approached. The streets were subdued; the rowdiest revelers were sleeping it off, regrouping their strength for another afternoon of beer and a long evening of whatever drinks were set in front of them. Dante caught a whiff of vomit. Urine, too, but it always smelled like that.

The guards who'd taken the body were out on rounds. The attendant in the short stone tower told Dante the body had been moved to the carneterium for storage and study. Figuring it would be faster, Dante climbed the tower stairs and set out across the top of the Pridegate. Exposed atop the stone, the bayward wind streamed across his face.

"The carneterium?" Mourn asked.

"Don't worry," Blays said. "It's just as bad as it sounds."

"Only if you have the constitution of a daisy," Dante said, mildly insulted: the establishment of the carneterium had partly been his doing. Four-odd years back, city guards had been dying in the streets at night. Throats torn. Bodies clawed bloody, hearts torn from their chests. Witnesses confirmed the attacker had been a great shaggy beast. For a few weeks, there had been something of a werewolf panic. Dante didn't buy that for a second, even after he and Blays had taken on the case and seen the shredded dead for themselves, and he had been vindicated after discovering the culprit was nothing more than a vengeful sorcerer and his undead dog.

The citizenry were glad enough, naturally, for the panic to be put to rest. What caught Dante off guard were the scribe-written letters and visits from the families of those the sorcerer and his dog had killed. Their gratitude wasn't driven by the satisfaction of vengeance or justice, but from simply knowing *what* had killed their sons and husbands. With the support of Tarkon and Merria, and aided by volunteer monks from the Cathedral of Ivars, Dante cleared the catacombs beneath the cemetery on the hill and installed equipment and storage. A small crew of willing monks was trained for a simple purpose: to investigate any strange or suspicious deaths brought to them, primarily via whatever clues could be discerned with the nether.

The "carneterium" had not been his idea for the name.

Laughter and the clatter of hooves filtered from the streets. They passed through the upper floor of a guard tower every quarter mile, where guards glanced at Dante's sapphire brooch and black cloak and waved them on. Once the curve of the Pridegate took the wall east-west, Dante descended at another tower and strode through the quiet streets. Weedy yards separated the modest houses. A high hill rose ahead.

There were no words carved above the door in the foot of the hill. Instead, a stone plaque bore the image of a millstone pierced by an angled pole. The pole's tip was astered by the four-pointed star of Jorus.

"Why do you humans insist on putting your dead in their own little holes?" Mourn muttered.

"What do you do?" Blays said. "Prop them up at the table?"

"We've seen their funerals," Dante said. "They leave the bodies on the oldest hills. If there's more than one, they pile them up in one big grave."

"I thought that was just for the people they don't like."

"We don't think our dead should rest alone," Mourn said. "If you belong to a clan in life, why should you be isolated in death?"

The dim tunnel swallowed them up. A flicker of decay wafted on the breeze. Torches burned from the rough limestone walls. A short, gritty walk took them into a foyer furnished with a handful of chairs and an end table with a small gong on it, which Dante struck. A bald monk padded into the room, nose lifted as if he smelled a pie.

"My old student," Nak smiled. "Come to lord over me with your latest promotion?"

"Someone tried to kill me yesterday," Dante said. "I'd like to see the body."

"Right this way." Nak padded down the stone halls, exchanging pleasantries. The smell of rot thickened on the cool cavern air. Nak led them to a small room; the dead assassin rested on a stained table, body stripped bare. Nak frowned sharply. "I'll fetch the natriter."

He padded off, leaving the four of them with the body. Blays sniffed. "Doesn't look so tough now."

"Nobody looks tough when their balls are hanging out," Dante said.

Lira shrugged. "People who fight naked are more frightening than those in full chain."

"I have my doubts," Blays said. "Let's put this to the test."

They were interrupted by the arrival of the natriter, a man with dark circles around his eyes and an expression chilly enough to preserve the flesh of any corpse he glanced at. Which made sense. It was his job, after all, to decide how the dead had died.

Dante nodded at the body. "What can you tell me about him?"

The man gave him a level look. "The stab wound tells me he died of a stab wound."

"Any indication where he came from?"

"A womb, most likely."

Blays paced around the body. "Look, this justifiably dead person tried to kill my friend here. Anything you can tell us about him would do wonders for our ability to continue going unassassinated."

The natriter sighed through his long nose and closed on the corpse in a single stride. He pushed back the dead man's lips. "He still has most of his teeth. Unlikely to be a sharecropper. But his hands are awfully rough to be a lord."

"Excellent," Blays said. "So he could be anyone but the poorest of poor or the richest of rich."

The man didn't acknowledge this. "The hem of his cloak smelled like wintrel."

"What did the nether show?" Dante said.

"Nothing abnormal. You're welcome to check for yourself."

Dante shook his head. "Please hang onto the body for now. Once it turns, I'd like the skull preserved. Just in case."

"Whatever you say."

Dante waved to Nak on their way out of the catacombs. Outside, the sun felt hard, the air gentle and pure.

"That wasn't half as bad as you made it sound," Lira said.

Blays rolled his eyes. "That's because we didn't go to storage."

"Did we just learn anything at all?" Dante said.

"I don't think wintrel grows anywhere but the Gaskan interior," Blays said. "So that rules out old enemies from Mallon. Or pirates."

"Not river-pirates," Mourn said. "Or land-pirates."

"Another finger pointing Cassinder's way." Dante glanced up; dark clouds mounded in from the bay, low and fast. "Or anyone who wants to get in his good graces. Which describes nearly everyone in Gask."

Perhaps it was the comfort of being home after a long journey, but Dante didn't feel all that concerned that an unknown enemy had recently tried to take his life. Then again, this wasn't the first time he'd been attacked in the street. He had a full flask of experience to draw on in comparison. The fifth strawberry never tastes as sweet as the first.

So he didn't think much about the dead man as he led the others to the Ingate tailor who handled the Citadel's ritzier garb. The sharp-eyed proprietor closed her shop and led them upstairs to a world of fur and silk and cotton. Pins and swatches and cloth tape flew as she and her two assistants fitted them for travel and court. The old woman took Mourn's fitting as a special challenge. Mourn appeared to feel the same challenge about her measuring tape sliding under his armpits and around his groin. When they left late that afternoon, snow whorled down from the clouds. In protest, the Thaws-days revelers burnt all the moths they could find—traditionally, the last days of Urt were associated with cicadas, but Dante hadn't seen a one of those since leaving Mallon—and smashed snowmen with axes and hoes.

Several days passed in complete peace. Dante spent hours discussing his upcoming diplomatic tour with Cally. He found maps of Gask's provinces, holdings, and fiefdoms, and took them to the monks for copies. He visited with a handful of Narashtovik's lords, merchants, and ambassadors, juicing them for information about the men and families he should most try to sway. According to Cally's scheme, each visitation would carry its own goals. At one manor, Dante might entreat the lord to pressure his colleagues in Setteven to ease back on any measures against the Norren Territories. In another, he might subtly ask a baron to remain quietly neutral should war erupt—or at least provide minimal aid when the king's campaign came calling for men and grain. At yet another household, Dante might do no more than attempt to gauge its master's opinion, and remind the man, with Dante's own presence, that other powers and interests populated the lands of greater Gask besides those concentrated in its capital.

Word arrived the viceroy of Dollendun and the border-towns had banned all norren from bearing arms in public without notarized consent of the local guard. Several norren had already been arrested. Two days later, one of Cally's scouts rode through the gates with news the Clan of the Broken Branch had ranged across the river to burn a slave camp to the ground. The clan left no living human behind.

"It's just a matter of time," Blays said after a long time planning routes in his room. "We ought to just dig a huge ditch around the norren lands and fill it with all the trash we can find. See if that keeps 'em out."

Dante stood from the desk, knees popping. "Speaking of trash, I'm hungry. Want lunch?"

"Five times a day."

Dante clomped down the back stairs to take the shortcut to the dining hall. The high, wide walls were a product of an earlier time, and so too were the rules of etiquette that continued to govern it. Anyone within the Citadel was allowed to eat in the hall, from the lowest charmaid to common soldiers to Cally himself. When there were lines, no favors were to be expected or granted. Most shockingly of all, perhaps, in practice it played out just like that: the few who had issue with such egalitarianism, such as blue-blooded Kav, simply took all their meals in their room or out on the town. This order amongst the classes was self-policing and easily explained. Pull rank on a servant in the hall to help yourself to the last slice of plum duck, and the next time a meal was delivered to your room, it was likely to contain an additional spicing of saliva, hair, and pestled rat feces.

So the hall bore its usual assortment of soldiers, footmen, and monks. Flatware clattered from plates and long wooden tables. Across the room, Lira faced Wint, her back as stiff as charcoal-forged steel. Wint smiled and gestured towards her waist. Her hand flinched.

"Ah." Blays strode across the wooden floor, sidestepping a servant waddling along beneath a tray of cups and bowls. Dante jogged to catch up.

"My point," Wint said, voice threading through the rattle of knives and laughter, "is why limit yourself to bodyguarding while you're awake?"

Lira didn't move. "You're proposing to hire me in my sleep."

The young councilman shook his head. "I wasn't aware your services were paid."

Her limbs went loose. Not from a deflation of tension—the alert looseness of a warrior readying her muscles to react in an instant. "Stop speaking to me."

"Is that a command?" Wint's smile withered. "Just where do you think you are?"

"Positioned in front of a rather poor view," Blays said, slipping between them like a knife between ribs. "But I bet I can pound it into shape easy enough."

Wint laughed inches from Blays' face, brows bent. "Everyone's forgot themselves today. Officially, you're a retainer of the Citadel, yes? Bound, in other words, to carry out orders from every member of the Council."

Blays' hand found the handle of his sword. "Yes, but I have notoriously bad hearing. To me, all orders sound like 'stab stab stab.'"

Nether flickered to Wint's thin fingers. "Perhaps your ears are simply clogged, and the blockage can be knocked free with sufficient force."

"Stop this," Dante said. "Nobody wants a bunch of blood in their food."

"Nothing to worry about, then. There's no blood if a man's heart just...stops." Wint winked at Blays, then turned and strode for a nearby table, snagging an entire plate of skewered beef from a passing servant.

Lira met Blays' eyes. "I can take care of myself."

"I know that," he said. "I've just always wanted to hit that guy."

"He was reaching for the nether," Dante said.

Blays snorted. "I've been around you long enough to have worked out a plan or two. Let's see how well you boss those shadows around while I'm twisting your nipple off."

Dante shook his head. Blays rapidly dropped the subject in favor of a tirade about the inherent superiority of peppered chicken and herbed kasha, but Lira was silent even by her own laconic standards. Then again, she and Mourn had been cooped up in the Citadel and its grounds for days now, sitting on their hands while Dante, Blays, and Cally schemed and mapped and planned.

"It's the last day of Thaws," Dante said. "Why don't we go out tonight?"

Blays jabbed a greasy chicken bone his way. "Not if your plan is to go look at churches. Or attend some *play*."

"My thinking was more along the lines of eating, drinking, and repeating, until our corpses have to be swept into the street."

"That's what you consider fun?" Lira said.

She came along anyway. Dante took his loon, leaving the other with Cally. Blays took an emergency flask and an emergency-emergency flask. Lira took three extra knives. Mourn took himself. Their first stop was just beyond the gates. A similar scene was about to play out in squares across the city, but the plaza between the Cathedral of Ivars and the Sealed Citadel was the most popular by far.

Three thousand people ringed a wide, roped-off circle. Twelve monks were spaced along its interior. They carried long-handled nets and foolish grins. Spectators jostled, placed bets, exchanged good-natured jeers with the monks. The sun sank beneath the cathedral roof. A gap opened in the crowd directly in front of the church's doors, revealing an elderly woman—Hallida, the institution's master. She shuffled to the center of the vast ring, head bobbing, a squirming sack tucked beneath one arm. Four men in black hoods circled counterclockwise among the monks, passing out ceremonial wine.

"Confused, blind, and chased," Hallida smiled. "At least you're not alone."

She whipped the sack away. A blindfolded rabbit wriggled in her arm. Around the circle, the monks chugged their mugs. The crowd whooped as the monks set down their cups and took up their nets. Hallida raised her free hand for silence, then spun three times and set the rabbit on the ground.

It listed like a hulled ship, careering straight for a portly monk. He swiped at it with his net, missing widely, drawing a hail of boos. A woman sprinted forward, robes and black hair flapping. The rabbit bolted between her ankles. Three others jogged to intercept, holding a chevron formation. The creature veered toward the crowd. They stamped their feet until it reversed course—and dashed straight into an old monk's net. He hefted it over his head, its long legs kicking as he raised his fist in triumph. The audience laughed, shouted, clapped.

"I don't understand what I just saw," Lira said.

"Narashtovik," Dante smiled. "Five hundred years of sieges and decay has left them a bit fatalistic."

"And weird," Blays said. "Onward!"

Last light dwindled from the rooftops. Knowing the best taverns were rarely the richest, Dante led them beyond the Ingate to one of the city's less-loved neighborhoods. In squares, people stomped the slush and shoveled it to melt beside snapping bonfires. The smell of woodsmoke on cold air always made Dante feel at peace. In front of the six-sided spike of Vaccarrin Tower, a man in a patchwork cloak made delicate hammer-strokes from atop the ladder he needed to play the ten-foot strings of his godsharp.

The pub-hunt didn't start strong. The Left Hand was too crowded to fit through the door. The Pine and Hatchet had burned to the ground. Finally, Dante settled on Kattin's, a four-story pub and inn with an auxiliary basement they opened for holiday crowds. To his surprise, several tables were open in the main room. Their group occupied one and quickly populated it with mugs of stout. Dante wasn't as enthusiastic about pubs as Blays, but for his coin, the second drink was always the best: settled in to his chair, that first rum or beer soothing his nerves, the anticipation of the evening to come. The mood of the crowd at Kattin's matched his; placid to begin with, but gradually growing more excited for no apparent reason. By the time the barbacks shoved two tables aside for a boisterous quartet hailing from the eastern mountains, Dante's toes began to tap on their own.

"I think I need to dance," Blays declared.

Dante glanced away from the short-haired blonde whose voice was as crisp as her flute. "I didn't know you danced."

"Not *well*. But that's why it's fun." He stood, chair scraping, and extended his hand to Lira. "My lady?"

"I don't dance," she said. "Meaning I don't dance."

"How stupid. How about you, Mourn?"

The norren blinked. "Do male humans dance with other males?"

"No, but they sometimes joke about it. Wish me luck." Blays swung from the table and approached the hodgepodge of men and women dancing in front of the sweating quartet. He quickly linked arms with a young woman whose white smile flashed between the black brackets of her hair. Each time Blays stumbled, he leaned in and shouted something above the music. Each time, the girl drew back laughing.

"He's very enthusiastic," Lira said.

"Especially for putting our lives at risk." Dante sipped his thick and bitter beer. "Why don't you dance?"

"I have to choose to be thought of as a warrior or as a woman. Shooting for both targets means striking neither."

"I can only imagine."

Lira laughed in the high-pitched way of someone who's very pleased with herself. "You bought it, didn't you? Not that it's entirely a lie." She peered at him over her beer. "Primarily, I'm afraid

I'd break both legs. I'd probably break a third one I didn't know I had."

Dante chuckled. The musicians finished on a stutter of hard notes. The dancers fell apart, laughing and clapping and bowing.

Lira gestured their way. "Do you dance?"

"Just often enough to remember why I never do."

The next dance involved a rhythm of boot-stomps and partnered claps that Dante couldn't begin to follow. Blays blustered through in a flurry of stinging palms and barking laughter. At the end, the dark-haired girl hugged him and left with a wave. He plopped back in his chair sweaty and grinning.

"I'm not going to ask if you watched," he said. "Saying no would only prove you're a liar."

"We conversed," Dante said. "Mostly about the best way to scrape the remains of your partner from the bottom of your shoes."

Lira clapped her mug to the table. "I should dance with you after all. I'm much harder to stomp than some waif."

Blays grinned. "Another drink first. And much more air. Then we'll see who tramples who."

Air was breathed. Drinks were drunk. The band took a breather of their own. When they returned, Blays stood up and offered Lira his hand. She accepted with a curt nod.

"What am I seeing?" Mourn said.

Dante shook his head. "A man eager to make a mistake."

Lira moved with a rhythm that more or less matched that of the fiddle. Dante thought she'd be clumsy, stiff, openly dangerous with her elbows and toes, but she danced with a martial precision that resembled a less-practiced version of the crisp mastery she showed with her forms in the barracks. Despite this, it wasn't unpleasant—through it all, she kept her limbs and muscles loose, guided by the confident hands of training and alcohol. The players leaned into their instruments, elbows jumping back and forth. The creases of concentration smoothed from Lira's brow. She flowed after Blays' lead, matching his steps and gestures as if she'd rehearsed for weeks. Dante smiled.

Two people in tune to each other and the music that brought them together. Years later, he would remember nothing else from that evening, but his memory of the dance would persist with the sharpness of splintered obsidian. Regret came with that remembrance, of course. But also the knowledge that for everything that happened afterward, that song, that dance, that moment could never be destroyed.

The final notes swept the crowd. Blays grinned, slicking his hand through his sweat-clumped hair. Lira stepped away with a small smile and returned to her chair. "I hope that wasn't too disgraceful."

Dante shook his head, laughing. "You did just fine."

Their travel plans took shape. Cally ruled out spending any serious time in the lands directly between central Gask and the Norren Territories. If it came to war, the lords there would be deluged by the king's men, incapable of the first hint of resistance. Even acting too slowly to *support* the king's army could result in the forcible appropriation of food, men, and their very titles. Cally would dispatch another diplomatic attachment to visit those lords and make carefully apolitical promises of Narashtovik's friendship. Dante, however, would be sent further afield.

His natural targets would be those distanced geographically and politically from the capital's gravity. A long ride south-southwest would take him to the plains of Tantonnen, eighty miles of grain and grassland not far from the norren hills' western edge. They had long ties to their norren neighbors; Tantonnen had been absorbed by Gask in the same wave of expansion that gobbled up the Norren Territories. Many of its farmers and baronets had never taken to the royal yoke no matter how many decades passed. It would be unable to muster much in the way of men, but if Dante could convey to its rulers that a norren victory would enable all of the eastern states to self-rule, Tantonnen might be convinced to find a way to misplace its excess grain before the king's collectors came to call.

Dante's second stayover would take place among the lakes of Gallador Rift. Some three hundred miles further west, nestled between the mountains, the lakes' merchants were rather boisterous proponents of preserving peace at any cost: "Calm waters bring many sails," or so their motto went. Dante's pursuit there wouldn't be material gains, but political ones. If he could convince the trade-nexus that a war against the norren would be slow, messy, and chaotic, the merchantmen would assuredly pressure Setteven to settle the conflict through gentler means.

The third shot was a long one. Not just in the sense of the sheer distance to the meandering inlet of Pocket Cove. At least Dante could find the place. The same might not be true of its residents. Even if he could track down the People of the Pocket, there were no guarantees they wouldn't flay him on the spot and kite his skin on the beach.

With no unforeseen diversions or delays, the trip to all these places would last two months, with much of that time reserved for introductions, dinners, and multi-day stays in stately manors. The trip back could take as little as three weeks. Less, if they were willing to kill a few horses.

They'd be back by the end of June, in other words. If he planned to take the Norren Territories before winter, Moddegan would have to commit his forces to the field around that same time.

"Three days," Cally said after reaching that conclusion.

Dante glanced up from the maps on the table in the old man's room. "What about them?"

"That's when I kick you out the front gates."

"That's hardly any time at all. Blays has had hangovers last longer than that."

Cally scoffed, flicking his beard with his fingertips. "You have an entire castle at your disposal. If you were feeling cramped, you could clap your hands and have a new house built for you by the morning."

Dante blew on the notes he'd been taking. "It just seems fast. I suppose three days is enough."

"It had better be. Because you'll actually only have two."

"What? Why the hell did you just tell me I'd leave in three?"

"You will." Cally peered down his crooked nose. "But one of those days will be spent with me. It's time you had another lesson."

Dante looked up sharply, smudging his ink. "In what?"

"Clearly it *ought* to be in patience."

"Tell me!"

"Poultry farming," the old man said. "What do you *think*?"

That was the best Dante could get out of him. He left to tell the others the plan and get started on a final list of all they'd need along the way. Despite all the details demanding his attention, his focus refused to stay put, returning incessantly to the idea like a dog to a wounded paw. He wasn't sure Cally had given him *any* proper lessons after they first met in Mallon. While Blays waited for the gallows and Dante fumed, impotent, Cally taught him the secret of blood. A tomb had served as the old man's schoolhouse. His methods, chiefly, had been insanity. But by the time he finished showing Dante how to feed the nether with his own blood, Dante had been able to carve his way through the dozen guards that stood between him and Blays. That had been some six years ago. Six years of constant practice with the nether. What would Cally be able to teach him now?

A knock jarred him from sleep. The room was blacker than nether; his headache implied it was hours before dawn. He put on a robe, opened the door, and stared murder at the waiting servant. "This had better be about the end of the world."

"Callimandicus requires you on the roof. Now." The servants' eyes widened. "His words, not mine. I meant no—"

"Shut up," Dante said. "Tell him I'll be up in a minute. And that I hate him."

He slugged down a half-empty mug of cold tea, dressed in a thick doublet and thicker cloak, and shuffled up the steep staircase to the roof. Cally stood in its center, head tipped back, beard and hair flapping in the vicious wind. Far below, smoke furled from brick chimneys. Far above, stars burned from the perfect sky. Without clouds to trap it in, all the day's warmth had been lost. A film of frost slicked the stone.

"What time is it?" Dante said.

Cally didn't turn. "Does it matter?"

"I guess I'd want to throw myself off the roof no matter what time it was."

"So you don't think it matters."

Dante huddled in his cloak. "Is this part of the lesson?"

Cally's brow darkened. His eyes were as bright as the stars. "You're wrong. When we go to extremes, your wrongness is clear.

It's the end of winter. If you were a farmer, you should be preparing your first fields now. If you waited to plant your tomatoes and peppers until the fall, October frost would kill your crops, and then you."

"That's a difference of seasons. I'm talking about an hour or three. The difference between a normal morning and a pounding headache."

"So there's no difference between hours? What about days? Will today as a day be different than tomorrow?"

Dante rubbed his eyes. "It will be longer. By a minute or two."

"If you woke at dawn both days, could you tell one dawn from the other?"

"I highly doubt it."

The old man nodded to himself. "The clouds would look different, of course. Unless something were terribly wrong! The moon, if visible, will have waxed or waned. It will be warmer or colder. The city may be awake or recovering from a feast."

"Cally, I feel like I've been swung by my feet into a wall. I don't get where this is going."

"Do you think it's coincidence our holiest text is called *The Cycle of Arawn*?" Cally waited just long enough for Dante to fear the question might not be rhetorical. "The turn of the Celeset takes 26,000 years to complete. You could chart the stars for years and see no movement. Yet Jorus won't always guide you north." He scowled at the stars. "Do you know why Urt's followers venerate the cicada?"

Dante shrugged. His cloak slipped from his shoulder, exposing his neck to the wind. "Because they're insane?"

"Because the cicada emerges once every 17 years! For 16 years and 11 months, you wouldn't have the first clue they exist. But walk in the woods at the end of the cycle and you'd think trees grew cicadas instead of leaves."

"So all the world's a cycle. Even when we can't see it."

Cally rolled his eyes. "You are terrible about simplifying things. Could you describe males without invoking balls? Tell me, when you touch the nether, does it always feel the same?"

A sudden gust of wind tore at Dante's breath. He choked on the cold air, belching. "Most of the time it's cold as a mountain stream.

Others, it's warm like—"

"That was not the type of question that should be given a literal answer." The old man shooed his hand at the stairs. "Go back to bed."

"Wait, was that supposed to be a lesson?"

"It's not my business if you can't understand it."

"I think that's exactly what a teacher's business is!"

"So go to bed. Perhaps things will look different once the sun's come up."

Dante shook his head and headed downstairs. After the freezing winds, the cool stone of the stairwell felt like a lit hearth. He'd been a fool to get his hopes up. Cally was a man of games, most of them stupid. He asked ten questions to make a single statement. What good would a bit of linguistic philosophy do for Dante just a day before a two-month trip?

He saw no more of Cally that day. Hours passed in a blur of packing and preparation. The sun set and rose just the same as it had the day before. Dante's anger at Cally's opacity persisted until it came time to leave.

He gathered in the predawn courtyard with Blays, Mourn, and Lira. They had two horses apiece and a whole pile of luggage. No trumpets met them, no honor guards. Even without such fanfare, the Council would note Dante's absence soon enough, but at least the lack of ceremony would help grease Cally's lie: that he'd sent Dante and crew out on a simple scouting mission to the Norren Territories.

Cally met them just inside the gates. A shapeless cloak obscured his thin body and wild white hair. His breath curled from his mouth. Another man stood beside him, fine-boned and trim.

"Everyone," Cally said, gesturing to the man, "meet Fann."

"Well met," Fann said cheerily, extending his hand. "Please consider me your guide through the wilderness that is foreign culture."

"Guide?" Blays said. "How different can these places be? It's all part of the same empire."

The man shrugged his narrow shoulders. "It wasn't always."

"Thank you for the offer," Dante said, "but I think we'll be able to handle a few bluebloods."

Fann cocked his head, one eyebrow raised in perfect mockery of an amused scion. "Did you know that in Tantonnen, it is considered a mortal insult to come to your host's house bearing eggs?"

"I wasn't going to bring any eggs to anybody."

"And I suppose you know every other custom, tradition, ritual, and insult across Greater Gask. Well, suit yourself. It's not as if the entire fate of norrendom depends on this trip." Fann turned to go.

"We should take him," Lira said.

Blays scratched the blond stubble on his neck. "I think she's right."

"Oh, all right." Dante glared at Cally. "I hope he's more helpful than your advice."

"You're still mad about our lesson, aren't you?" Cally laughed. "What if you die out there? You'll regret your ingratitude for eternity! Do you have any idea how *long* that is?"

"You made out like your secret would change my life."

"Maybe it will."

"Yes, in that I'll never listen to anyone over fifty again."

"Ah. Then tragically, you won't hear me say 'Here, take this for your journey.'" He pulled a shallow box from his cloak, lacquered black wood that reflected the wind-teased torches.

"What's that, a present?" Blays leaned down from his horse. "I'll take it if he doesn't want it."

"On one condition." Cally held a knobby finger aloft. "You can't let him see them until he says something nice about me."

"Deal."

The old man passed the box with a metallic clink. "Anyway, let's not make this a big to-do. I expect to see you again in a relative blink. Try not to let your failures drag you down. It won't be easy to convince others to turn against the long knives of the king." Cally bulged out his whiskered cheeks. "Then again, try not to fail *completely*. If you do, we could all die here, you know."

"I'll see what I can do," Dante said. He nudged his horse forward. It took the first step of what would be a very long journey.

10

Dante clopped beneath the gate. Its thick stone occluded the stars. He liked best the journeys that began before sunrise. They always had an air of purpose to them. An import so weighty they had to be started while the rest of the world was still snoring. Best of all, when the light finally touched the land, it showed him a different place than the one he'd woken up in.

"Where are we going again?" Blays said.

"Lyle's balls," Dante sighed.

"Really? Count me out, then."

"We're headed to the plains of Tantonnen. There, we'll attempt to—"

"I'm just fooling with you." Blays turned over the wooden box and held it to his ear. "Say, what do you think's in here?" He gave it a shake.

"Stop it!" Dante said. "That could be dangerous."

"To us? Or the mysterious contents of this box?"

"Knowing Cally, it could be both." He gestured across the empty boulevard. "If you're going to explode, do it over there."

"Like I'm going to pass up the chance to take you with me." Blays unclasped a flat metal hook, brought the box inches from his nose, and cracked open its lid. "Oh my."

"What is it? A tiny unicorn?"

"Better."

"A tiny unicorn with an equally tiny little flute, with which it is shockingly proficient."

"Close, but this is still better," Blays said. "This thing's useful."

"Really?" Dante nudged his horse nearer. "Let me see."

Blays snapped the box shut. "Uh-uh. You heard what Cally said."

"And normally you treat his suggestions the same way you would a spider crawling over your toast."

"I gave him my *word*, Dante. That isn't just something you throw away."

Dante plodded along. Mourn coughed into his fist. Dante shook his head. "All right. Cally looks very fine for a 120-year-old."

"Insufficient."

"That's a plenty nice thing to say."

"You're living up to the letter of the law, but not its spirit," Lira put in. "That's what scoundrels do."

"No one asked you," Dante muttered. He rolled his eyes at the stars. "Cally's an excellent leader. He's unorthodox but logical. Bold, too. While his particular mix of fearlessness and schemery is precisely what got us into this mess with Setteven, I can think of no one more likely to bring us—and the norren—through to the other side in better shape than where we left. Now can I see what's in the gods damned box?"

Blays twisted in the saddle to regard the others. "What says the audience?"

"Heartfelt," Lira nodded.

"I can't weigh in on whether it's true," Mourn said. "But anyone would be flattered to hear it."

Fann took a moment to register their stares. "It was good."

"I should make you put it in writing." Blays passed over the box. "You won't be disappointed."

Dante cradled the box in his lap. The lid opened noiselessly. Inside, four brooches rested on a bed of black velvet, ivory carvings of the White Tree banded by a ring of black iron. The facets of a sapphire winked from the trunk of one tree. A note was tucked into a slit in the velvet:

Variants of your new toy. Distribute as you see fit. I suggest you take the pretty one, as it will match your eyes. They may be bonded to their recipients with a drop of the intended wearer's blood.

Don't say I never did anything for you.

~C

Dante closed the box. He wanted nothing more than to pass out the loons and deduce whatever special properties the old man had woven into the sapphired brooch, but his horse had just passed the Ingate. In less than an hour, they'd depart the city. Back into the wilds.

The road spooled south through farms and forests. The first night they slept beneath the pines a quarter mile from the road. The second, they found a crossroads inn at a farming village. The third night found them in Kalls, a modest town mixed with humans and norren.

They entered the Norren Territories on the fourth day. Patchy snow dusted the open fields and low hills. A few times a day, a wandering clan appeared on a ridge or stoked fires from the protection of a draw, but offered neither greeting nor threat.

Dante had passed out one loon to Blays and, after some thought, gave Mourn and Lira the other two. Cally could always make more later. And if either the norren or the woman turned out to be a traitor-in-waiting, Dante could just destroy his, severing the links between them forever. Because the sapphire loon, it turned out, was a hub for them all: by rotating the jewel 90 degrees, Dante could choose which of the others to communicate with. Including, if he returned the sapphire to its original alignment, with Cally.

He saw no forts or walls in the Territories. Few villages or proper buildings of any kind. Nothing, in other words, that would present a threat to an incoming army.

The road turned southwest. Short green winter wheat fought the last of the snows. They crossed out of the proper norren lands and into the unsettled boundaries of the south. For a full day, they walked their mounts along flat stretches that either had been, soon would be, or were currently being plowed. Oxen, workers, and short, sturdy houses dotted the fields of brown and green. Mourn watched them steadily, tipping back his head as if trying to place an elusive smell. Townsmoke rose from the clear horizon. An hour after dark, they reached Shan, the local capital, and bought up five rooms at a fieldstone inn. Dante chafed at the price—they could easily have made do with three—but they had appearances to keep up.

Fann led them up a well-trod dirt path the following morning. With the sun approaching noon, Dante stopped in front of a roughstone manor. Three round towers filled out its body, four stories high and equally wide. Two-story connectors linked the silo-like wings. In the fields beyond, wooden barns and outbuildings stood above the young green fields.

A light breeze ruffled Dante's hair. He glanced at Fann. "I guess you should...announce us."

"Don't be silly, my lord." Fann gestured up the gravel path. "We're in Tantonnen now. If you send your servants ahead to 'announce' you, the locals will look at you like you've asked for a golden toilet."

"We should get one of those," Blays said. "I've always thought our silver seats were declasse."

"Any other helpful advice?" Dante said.

Fann tapped his delicate fingers together. "They're not fond of shaking hands. Perhaps because theirs are always so dirty. In any event, doing so will brand you as an outsider. Furthermore, deposit your boots at the door unless you would like the head of the household to deposit his between your buttocks."

"I think that's enough." Dante dismounted and crunched up the path. He thumped the knocker of the banded wooden door. A middle-aged man appeared in the doorway, stocky and stubbled, his round gut and swollen biceps placing equal strains on the fabric of his brown doublet.

"Is Lord Brant in?" Dante said.

The man smiled. "Unless I've been overthrown in the last five minutes." He turned and bellowed back into the house. "Jilla! Have I been overthrown recently?"

"You will if you don't knock off that hollering," a woman called back.

Brant chuckled and turned back to Dante. "Looks like I'm still the lord." His gaze dropped to the two brooches on Dante's chest. "You must be what's-your-name. From Narashtovik."

"Dante Galand." He didn't offer his hand.

"Thought you'd be older. Well, come inside. Your friends, too. I'll send a man to see to the horses."

Dante had plenty of time to take in the household as he picked the knots from his boots and placed his footwear beside the door. Hard winter light gushed through the windows of the large round room. The windows were glass, and fine-stitched rugs covered nearly every inch of the wooden floors, but there was a simplicity to the room beyond the informality of the baronet who owned it. Above the fieldstone fireplace, a hoe rested across two pegs, displayed as proudly as a knight's blade.

"The same one my ancestor used to first break these fields," Brant said, catching him looking. "Scrub off the rust and I'm sure it still could."

"Nonsense," a woman smiled from the stone staircase. "You'd rather churn the dirt with your own teeth than let that old thing touch open air."

"I said it *could*," Brant said mildly.

The woman was his wife, Jilla. While she made introductions, Brant trundled off to dispatch riders to inform the local lords of the group's arrival. After a lunch of pork, potatoes, and the best bread Dante'd ever tasted, Brant brought their horses back from the stable and led them on a tour of the estate.

"We'll have dinner tomorrow," he told Dante, rolling atop his cracked leather saddle. "And tonight, of course. Imagine me taking you in and then leaving you to fend for yourselves!" He laughed, voice carrying on the flickering wind. "That's when we'll speak, I mean."

"That's fine," Dante said. "Our time isn't so precious just yet."

"Still, I'll try to help you make the most of it. I have a rough idea why you're down here. I'm sure your offer will be a right one. But don't bet your winter on it being snapped up."

"Don't tell me they're afraid of the king."

"Why would they be? All he's got is an army. And a mountain of gold. And a kingdom of people who think no more about beating a norren than a donkey that's stepped on their foot."

Dante laughed. "I'll modulate my expectations accordingly."

Brant filled the rest of the day with small talk about how winter had treated him, his expectations for the approaching spring, and questions about Narashtovik, which he hadn't visited in twelve years, meaning he'd seen none of its resurgence with his own eyes.

"Last time I saw the place, it was empty as an old man's mouth," he said during their post-dinner discussion, his socked feet propped on a chair. "You make it sound like it could sit next to Setteven in the jeweled crown of Gask."

"Not quite yet." Dante sat down his beer, a blueberry- and clover-tinged lager Jilla had brewed over the winter. "But 'The Dead City' is getting to be a more ironic name by the day."

Brant nodded, uncharacteristically quiet. "Things change fast, don't they."

Dante went to bed not long after. His room was snug and draft-free. In the morning, Brant brought them to town after breakfast to show off Shan's windmills and irrigation canals. It was a simple place. Built to last. If war came, Dante hoped it spared these windy fields.

Brant's fellow baronets arrived that afternoon. Like Brant, most of the six lords showed signs of long days on the farms despite their noble titles, their forearms ropy, their faces tanned and lined. Their opinions were as large as their shoulders. Their appetites, too. At the long feast-table that took up most of the lower floor of the second wing, they sat at attention while Jilla blessed the food (a stripped-down version of the ritual that involved a couple words and a couple flicks of saltwater from her fingers), then fell to the meal like it would be their last, disassembling roast chickens and vegetable pies faster than the two servants could bring out the next dish. Steaming bread appeared by the platter: puffy white loaves; round disks studded with nuts and grains; moist, crumbly slices embedded with raisins and dripping with butter; flatbread smeared with almond paste.

Dante assumed this wealth of breads was just an extravagance of the feast, but over the next few days, he learned it was entirely standard for Tantonnen. Almost every meal involved their staple crop in some way, be it in the wrapper of boiled pork dumplings or in the pan-fried slabs that Tantonners carried as portable meals, pie-like medleys of boiled meat, raw nuts, potatoes, and vegetables all mashed up and held together with a glue of oily dough. These were the most perfect invention Dante had ever seen.

As normal for such gatherings, the lords' dinnertime talk stayed light—how the last snows had treated them, the town cloudsman's predictions for a mild spring. Finally, the farmers toyed with chicken skins, juice-soaked bread crusts, and their fourth beers of the night.

Unprompted, the oldest of the men, a thin and wind-chapped man named Raye, pointed a chicken bone at Dante. "So what is it you want from us?"

Dante swallowed beer to clear his throat. "You've heard, I'm sure, of the recent unrest."

"I'm sure."

"We're not friends of any war, but we are friends of the norren. We fear that, if invasion comes, many innocents will starve."

Raye bunched up his gray brows. "Do you think? Most I've seen do plenty well leeching off the land."

"Plenty of them live in towns just like you or me," Dante said. "If an army marches on its stomach, towns and their granaries are the stepping-stones they use to cross the river of conflict."

"Now that's a pretty metaphor," said a fat lord named Vick, his tone much drier than his beer-foamed beard.

Blays clunked down his mug. "That's because he's too dumb to say stuff straight. Thing is, civilians *will* starve. You've got food here. We want some of it and will pay money to buy it."

"Oh," Vick said. "When you put it like that, it makes sense enough."

"But not why Narashtovik gives a sheep's shit," Raye said.

"We sympathize over common suffering," Dante said. The faces of the baronets were cowlike, slump-jawed. He clenched his teeth and let a long breath through his nose. "I'm from Mallon. A few years ago, I hardly knew a thing about Arawn, except that he'd scythe off your head if you spoke his name over open water. Because anyone who *did* talk about him—the real Arawn, the Arawn of Narashtovik and Gask—got their head hacked off. Whipped, at the very least. Which is funny, because that's exactly what happens to any norren slave who decides he doesn't want to be a slave anymore. Why does Narashtovik support the norren? Because Setteven is full of shitheads. Maybe they'll march. Maybe they won't. But if they do, we want to be there to pick the norren back up as soon as the king's done stamping on their backs."

That drew a few wry chuckles. Brant smiled and scratched his neck. "None of us are too happy about those tax-mad shitheads, either. They could cut our levies in half if they weren't so obsessed with clinging to every scrap of their creaky empire." Brant leaned back, chin inclined. "I'd be happy to sell whatever wheat I can part with. But it won't be as much as you want."

"Why's that?" Blays said.

"Everyone needs bread when the swords come out," Vick said. "And when food's needed, farmers need it most of all. They're the first ones the men with swords come running for."

Dante gazed at his plate. "Leaving you with little left over to sell."

"That's the shape of it," Brant said.

"Of course," Mourn piped up, "the bandits don't help."

At some point during the dinner, Mourn had left his satellite table to stand against the curved wall, being careful not to lean against its tapestry of a deer silhouetted on a ridgeline. As a result, he was directly behind some of the lords, who had to turn their heads like owls in order to join the others in staring at him.

"Bandits, you say?" Brant said.

Mourn nodded. "The norren bandits. Unless they are human bandits doing a very clever job of pretending to be norren."

"You know that how?" Raye said slowly. "You running with them?"

If Mourn was insulted, he didn't let it show. "They've left signs all over your roads and fields." He nodded at Vick. "If you're who they mean by 'the fat one,' they're going to take your eastbound caravan this weekend."

Vick bolted up, knocking back his chair. "You *are* running with them!"

"He's been with us for weeks," Dante said. "Before that, he belonged to a clan that lives a hundred miles from here."

Brant gestured Vick back into his seat. "There anything you can *do* about this? Or just tell us things we already know?"

Mourn glanced between Dante and Blays. "That's up to my chiefs."

"How much have you been losing?" Blays said.

"Between guards, payment, and product?" Brant shook his head at the ceiling. "All told, a tenth of what I take out of the ground."

Blays drank the rest of his beer to hide his grin. "Here's the deal. We take out the bandits, you sell that ten percent to us. At half market rate."

Raye scowled. "Two-thirds."

"Half."

"Sixty per—"

"Raye, you're missing sixty percent of your brain," Brant said. "Half's a whole lot better than none." He extended his hand to Dante, then shook with Blays and Mourn as well. "You clear the roads, you got your grain."

That settled the matter. With the business of business complete, the assembly turned to the business of getting drunk. By the time Dante got to bed, head spinning, he had all but forgotten they'd pledged to rid Tantonnen of an entire clan of norren.

Hangovers made the morning slow to materialize. Dante picked over his breakfast of toast and eggs and sweet soppy cheese. Blays joined him, took one look at his plate, and set his head down on the table.

"What did we commit to?" Dante said.

Blays didn't move. "Ask that shaggy mountain of ours."

"Are we going to have to kill a bunch of norren, Mourn? Because that doesn't strike me as a very productive way of helping them."

Mourn looked up from window where he sat reading one of the manor's books. "I don't know."

"What do you mean, you don't know?"

"I mean in a very literal sense—I don't even know whether Blays is going to vomit in the next five minutes. How should I know how it will go with a gang of violent bandits?"

Dante rolled his eyes. "How were you thinking it would go when you butted in last night?"

The norren shrugged his heavy shoulders. "That depends on the clan. I'd listen if someone told *me* we'd be overrun and butchered unless I stopped stealing."

"Then all we have to do is find them."

"Not hard. Not if you know how to read their signs. Which I do."

Blays nibbled a corner of Dante's toast. "Why would they leave big old directions all over the road?"

Mourn stared at his oversized hands. "Because if you are a clan in a hostile land, that makes you a thing that is a threat. A horde of bandits. An army. But if the clan splits up, a person sees one norren. Three norren. They don't think much. If you're a chief, how do you bring your scattered clan back together when it is time to act or move? You can shout very loudly. You can set signal fires that can be seen by everyone with working eyes. Or you can leave signs so small your enemies will never know you're there."

Dante sipped his tea. "But you can find the signs to find them, too."

Mourn shook his head. "I don't need wildsigns to find a clan."

After breakfast, Dante found Brant and informed him they'd set out shortly. Brant sent a man to prep their horses. Dante located Fann, who was holding a lively conversation with the farrier, and waited for a break in the talk.

"I was thinking you might find it more comfortable to stay here."

Fann smiled slyly. "What a polite way of saying I might get myself killed."

"You don't mind?"

"Not at all." Fann doffed his round black cap. "As you pursue the art of war, I will once more turn to the art of speech."

The horses' manes and tails had been clipped and combed. Mourn led the way down the path to the main road, scanning the ruts and weedy shoulders, clinging to the saddle of his plowhorse. Wind stirred the long grass.

"See anything?" Blays said after a mile of travel.

"Hmm." Mourn leaned forward, peering into the grass. "They say the young blond one is very homely."

"And the norren wonder why everyone hates them."

Mourn twisted in his saddle, giving Blays a stony look that soon softened into a smile. "It's a good thing I know you."

Blays tipped his head to one side. "I wouldn't go that far."

They reached the road into town by early afternoon. Mourn led them east at a casual walk. A few times an hour, he pulled up, dismounted clumsily, and crouched beside a stick or sprig of grass. His examination of bits of plants and dirt reminded Dante of divination, of reading the guts of unfortunate turkeys, but Mourn moved with a stolid purpose. Mid-afternoon, he cut south from the road into an unplowed reach of crumbling hills with grassy heads and dense thorny trees in their folds.

"They're around," Mourn said. "But unless we are better at this than I think we are, we probably won't see them until they want us to."

"Why would they want us to see them?" Lira said.

"Because there is a certain joy in revealing yourself to the thing you are about to kill."

Mourn rode cautiously and inexpertly through the grass and rocks. Snows hid in the deep shadows between hills. Blue-throated birds perched on bare twigs, peeping questions back and forth. They left the last of the carefully-tilled fields behind. Here and there, huge boulders stood alone in the flatlands, as if dropped there by a forgetful god.

When people spoke of the oldest places, they often mentioned mountains. Forbidding mists and unclimbable spires. What they really meant was that mountains were pristine; no one had any business in the icy peaks except for hermits and the insane. But people could live in this undulating prairie. To Dante, the fact they chose not to—or once had, but abandoned the place long ago—made the silence and wind more primordial and unknown than the most remote crags.

Mourn got down from his horse to proceed on foot. He mumbled to himself, gazing at flattened grass, his words stolen by the wind.

"What's that?" Dante said.

Mourn glanced up. "I said they know we're here."

"Send you a letter, did they?" Blays said.

"Sort of." The norren bent down and pointed to a branch of a jagged shrub. Two of the thorns were snapped at the base, dangling by narrow fibers. "This says 'hello.' That they used thorns means it is not a pleasant hello. Although maybe they only used them because that's all that seems to grow out here."

Dante shrugged. "At least they're breaking thorns and not our arms."

He dismounted to better read the trail for himself. Except for the clan's deliberate wildsigns, which Mourn mostly had to point out himself, the usual markers were in short supply—a scuffed rock here, a stomped leaf there. The day dwindled. When Mourn shook his head at the dusk, they descended to a crease between hills and set up camp.

"Build a fire if you like," Mourn said. "If they want to find us, they will."

"That's comforting," Blays said. "Well, if we're going to be stabbed in our sleep, I'd prefer to die in a warm bed."

He and Lira stoked a small fire. Dante pan-cooked potatoes to go with their bread and jerky. He pulled second watch. When Mourn woke him to change shifts, Dante found a dead rabbit and sent it to circle the hills, but he didn't see a single norren during his watch.

Throughout the morning, the wildsigns drew Mourn further and further east. The day was a bust. After an identical dinner to their previous supper, Dante twiddled his brooch. A moment later, Cally's disembodied voice spoke into his ear.

"So where are you right now?"

Dante smiled at the old man's tangible excitement. "Chasing wild geese through the plains of Tantonnen."

Cally laughed. "This is incredible, you know. I've had to resist summoning you up every night to find out the latest."

"Same here." Dante filled him in on the negotiations with the baronets and their as-yet fruitless hunt for the norren bandits. He could almost see Cally nodding along.

"If anything big is stirring in Gask, it's so large no one knows what they're looking at yet. I'll let you know if anything changes. For now, I advise continuing your search."

"Will do."

"I bet it's cold there, isn't it? We've had the most wonderful inland breeze. Not that I've noticed in my warm little tower."

"Goodnight, Cally." Dante cut off the link. That night, the wind felt as cold as wet iron.

Wind and birds and grass and stones. Despite Cally's reassurance, the relentless landscape wore at Dante's resolve. Days in and he still hadn't seen a single norren. Besides Mourn, of course, who read tracks too subtle for Dante to notice. High gray clouds carpeted the sky. If it rained or snowed, even Mourn might not be able to continue the trail.

On the other hand, rain would mean a chance to refill their waterskins. They hadn't seen a stream since the morning before. The grass, meanwhile, had gone notably more yellow. They could always turn to the shaded snows, but even those had grown mean, shallow patches gritty with dirt. Dante sipped miserishly.

He needn't have worried. They crested a ridge. A shallow, bowl-like valley bottomed out in a deep blue lake whose octopoidal arms extended into the crannies of the intersecting hills. They led their horses through the pines and birches gathered around the shore. The waters were murky and green, but this place was so far removed from human stains Dante didn't even think about boiling his water before drinking it. The horses appeared to have no such worries either, slurping away at the algal shore.

"I don't feel like we're making progress," Dante said after they'd all had a drink and a bite of bread. "If we don't see anything in the next couple days, I think we should move on."

Mourn smiled faintly. "We won't have to wait that long."

"You sound awfully sure of yourself," Blays said.

"It's a feeling I have."

"That sounds very scientific."

"Specifically, the feeling of being watched."

"Funny you say that." Blays rolled his neck. "Because *I* have the feeling of a stiff back. And a sore ass. And that scraped-up feel your mouth gets from eating crusty old bread. All of which points to the greater feeling of tromping around an empty wilderness with no hope of finding anything more substantial than dried-up deer turds and—"

"Shut up." The voice came behind them, soft and faintly accented. Blays whirled to his feet. Dante dropped his water. Three norren stood among the white-barked birches, bows in hand. The foremost gazed steadily at Mourn with one eye, his other a scarred-up hole. "This has gone on long enough."

"You're the ones who dragged it out," Mourn said mildly.

"Dragged *what* out?" the man said. "This is our land. We do as we please."

"And apparently it pleases you to treat the humans who live here as prey."

The one-eyed man shrugged. "It's our land. So why are you in it?"

"Are you the chief?"

"I'm the one in front of you."

Mourn shook his head. "I need the chief."

"I need a new wife," the man said. "I have the one I've got."

"Then attack us now. That's the only way you'll stop us. Assuming you win. If you don't, your clan will have three less men between us and its head."

The man glanced at his two clansmen. They maintained their silence. He shook his head at Mourn. "Come with me."

Mourn rose. Dante followed behind, reins in one hand, nether in the other. The clansmen led them around the foot of the next hill. There, beside the wind-rippled waters, three dozen norren joked and lounged and carved and weaved.

"Did you know how close we were?" Dante said.

Mourn glanced over his shoulder. "I had an idea. The last few wildsigns have been lies. Unless they are so dumb they actually don't know east from west, they were trying to throw me off."

At the camp, chatter ceased. Half the men and women reached for bows and swords and spears. The one-eyed norren gestured Mourn to stop, then joined his clansmen. He approached and spoke with a seated woman in her mid-30s. After a minute, the pair walked across the springy grass and stood in front of Mourn.

"I don't know you," she said. Her braids were brown with strands of red and black.

"I'm Mourn of the Clan of the Nine Pines."

The woman nodded. "Waill. Chieftain of the Clan of the Golden Field. What do you want?"

"For you to stop attacking the farmers here."

"You're not going to get what you want."

Mourn gazed at the lake. "Why prey on men?"

"It's simpler," Waill said. "What's simplest is best."

"There's nothing best about the norren who'll starve if war comes to the Territories. If you stop your raids, we'll have the grain to save many of our people's lives."

She smiled with half her mouth, eyes lit with something much older than her years. "That's many ifs. If war comes, why not take the grain and dole it out ourselves? Who are you?" Her smile deepened. "Who says we're not already fighting a war of our own?"

"The humans with me are from Narashtovik." He gestured to Dante and the others. "This is part of their plan to help us."

"I don't know them. I don't know any humans who help norren."

"Then I think I'm finished." Mourn turned to her clansman. "Are you unswayed by my words?"

The man didn't hesitate. "I'm unswayed."

Mourn smiled at Waill. "I don't sense any sway from you."

"I am unswayed," she said.

"Damn. I hoped I was wrong." Mourn smiled. He gazed at the lake, his eyes as distant as whatever force had dumped the stray boulders across the empty lands. "Then I request sollunat."

Waill's smile broke like ice. "You're not from the Golden Fields. You have no right to succeed me."

"Not for your place. For this one boon."

Waill glanced quickly at her one-eyed clansman. He met her gaze. She turned back to Mourn, eyes smoldering. "What weapons?"

"Bow," Mourn said.

"You challenged. I shoot first."

"I know."

"Prepare." She strode back toward her clan, many of whom stood as she approached, sensing the moment. The one-eyed man went with her.

Blays gaped after her. "Is this some kind of duel?"

Mourn shrugged. "She's going to shoot at me. If I'm still alive, I'll shoot back. This continues until one of us decides to stop. Or can't voice an opinion either way. Which is taken as implied concession of defeat."

"Are you serious?" Dante said. "I thought you settled things with rhetoric!"

"Yes, but we didn't start doing that until all our best leaders kept getting shot, stabbed, and clubbed to death."

"Well, you can't just let her *shoot* at you," Blays said. "You might get shot!"

Mourn sighed. "This is the only way to stop them. Without killing them all. Or doing something else I haven't thought about. But this is the only way I know."

"Why would you do this?" Dante said.

Lira cocked her head. "Because he believes."

Dante bared his teeth. "You don't have to do this, Mourn. The war won't hinge on a few wagons of wheat."

"I get the impression we'll need every resource we can get," Mourn said. "Besides, this isn't Narashtovik. You can't tell me what I can't do." He gave Dante a small smile. "Well, you *can*. But guess how much it will matter?"

Dante had no argument. He couldn't see the future. Not well enough to know whether the grain of Tantonnen would wind up making any difference to the norren. He *could* see that if they wanted to do any real good, they'd all have to do things they didn't want along the way. To put their lives on the line. Right now, he need Mourn to take his turn.

"Good luck, then. And thank you."

"Can you even shoot a bow?" Blays said.

"Of course," Mourn said. "The real question is whether *she* can."

The one-eyed norren returned with a quiver and a bow taller than Dante. "This way."

Mourn followed him through the birches. Upslope, the hill leveled off into breeze-swept grass. Waill stood a hundred yards away, bow in hand. Mourn stopped in the open grass and tested the pull of his long weapon. The clansman removed five arrows from the quiver and stuck them point-down in the dirt.

He eyed the humans. "Step away. Interfere, and forfeit two things: Your friend's challenge, and your lives."

Blays snorted. "Well, I don't agree to *those* terms."

Dante backed off ten yards, where he stood with Lira and Blays. Across the hill, Waill licked her thumb and raised it to the wind. Downslope, the Clan of the Golden Field watched tight-faced from the knee-high grass. The one-eyed norren looked to Mourn, who nodded, and then to Waill, who did the same.

Waill raised her bow, arrow pointed straight skyward, then

drew back and leveled it at Mourn. She held there for several seconds. Dante willed her shot to fly foul—for her elbow to twitch, for the wind to gust, for the arm of Josun Joh to reach down from the sky and squish Waill into the dirt. She let fly.

The arrow whipped above the grass. It struck Mourn's chest with a wet smack. He collapsed to the ground.

Soft groans rose from the watching clan. Dante raced to Mourn. Nether flocked to his fingers. The norren lay on his back, blinking, face white beneath his beard. The arrow jutted from his ribs.

"Get away," he hissed.

"You've got a fucking arrow in your chest!"

"This isn't over." Mourn rolled to his side, eyes widening in pain. He found his knees and reached for the dropped bow. The clan murmured. A hundred yards distant, Waill stood perfectly still. Mourn pulled an arrow from the dirt, but barely began his draw before his string snarled into the arrow twitching from his ribs. Gingerly, he set his bow and arrow in the grass. A far-off look washed across his face. He grabbed the arrow in his chest with both hands and pulled.

It slurped free. Mourn staggered, blood dripping from his wound. Teeth bared, he picked up his bow and drew it back. His elbows quivered, jogging his aim; he breathed through his nose, jaw clenched, until his arms steadied. He fired.

He sat down before the arrow landed. The arrow slammed into Waill's chest, spinning her into the grass. She didn't move. Dante sprinted back to Mourn.

"Help her," Mourn waved.

Dante goggled. "Shut up and lie down!"

Mourn lurched halfway to his feet, bloody hand bunching in a fist. "My deal was with her. What happens if she dies?"

"Lyle's balls!" Dante charged across the slope. The one-eyed norren was already crouched beside Waill along with three other clansmen. The man turned to Dante, reaching for his sword. Dante held up his empty hands. "I'm a healer, gods damn it. Let me see her."

"You die if she does."

"Yes, yes. Get out of my way."

The man frowned, trying not to let hope get the better of him.

Dante knelt. The arrow stuck from the left side of Waill's chest. For a moment he feared it had hit her heart, but her chest was rising in shallow jerks. He reached for a knife and cut her clothes from the wound. The shaft had sunk deep between her ribs.

Dante wiped blood on his pants. "You'll have to push it out the other side."

The norren glanced between each other, silently conferring. The one-eyed man nodded and rolled Waill onto her side. Dante cleaned his knife on his sleeve and cut open his much-abused left forearm. Beside him, the one-eyed man grabbed the arrowshaft and bore down. Waill snarled, eyes clenched shut. The arrowhead broke through her skin. The one-eyed norren snapped off the fletching and drew the broken remainder from Waill's body. Her blood flowed thickly, pulsing with the cycle of her beating heart.

Nether roiled from Dante's hands into the hole through Waill's chest. Blood gushed unabated. Dante could feel the impatience of her clansmen, their fear and worry ready to morph into rage and pain. But he could feel the changes in Waill's body, too. Torn vessels sealing shut as nether smoothed rough edges together. Flesh meeting flesh and becoming one flesh. Within a minute, she stopped bleeding. Within two, both holes through her chest were covered in firm black scabs.

Dante popped to his feet and ran to Mourn. Blays bore down on the bandage he and Lira had wrapped around Mourn's chest, putting pressure to the wound. The cotton sopped with red. Dante delved inside, flooding the norren's veins with hungry nether. Mourn's eyes stayed closed as Dante stabilized the bleeding.

The one-eyed norren walked up, hands sticky with blood. "We'd like you to stay here until she wakes up."

Blays cocked his head. "So you can stab us if she doesn't?"

"She will. Will your friend?"

"I think so," Dante said.

He nodded. "Then she will want to speak to him when he does."

"I think you can trust him," Lira said as he returned to Waill. "He's protective, that's all."

"So are mother bears," Blays said. "And I wouldn't want to share a den with one after I shot one of her cubs."

"I'm going to clean up and move the horses." Lira stood and headed for the lake. "Yell if he betrays you."

By the time she returned, the one-eyed norren, whose name was Skall, had brought Dante and Blays into camp proper and served up pan-fried fish and bread.

Aroused, perhaps, by the smell, Mourn stirred, blinking through the pain. "Did I not die?"

"You'll be fine," Dante said. "As your physician, however, I insist you refrain from armed duels for the next three weeks. Ideally, for the rest of your life."

Gingerly, Mourn touched his bandages. "Has anyone ever told you getting shot by an arrow really, really hurts?"

"Blays. Repeatedly. And without shame."

Blays wiped fish-grease from his mouth. "Well, it *does*."

No member of the clan spoke to them except Skall, who came by to ask Mourn how he was doing and nod at his fast recovery. Dante woke at dawn, lightly sore. Birds peeped from the birches. Fish rose to suck insects from the surface. Skall came to him while he explored the far side of the lake. Waill was awake.

Her face was pale, haggard. "I hear you didn't let me die."

"I'm saintly like that," Dante said. "We needed to make sure you stuck to your promise."

"Skall would have kept it for me." She turned to Mourn. "You shoot too well."

"Like I had a choice," Mourn said. "I couldn't let *you* have a second shot."

"I couldn't believe it when you got back up. I knocked you on your ass!"

"I should have stayed there. It was much comfier."

Waill smiled, then coughed into her hand, which she then checked for blood. "The Clan of the Golden Field will stop our raids. And ensure no one else takes our place. Let the farmers know."

Mourn nodded. "Then our sollunat is fulfilled."

"Good." She gazed out on the quiet lake. "If the humans march on the Territories, you know where to find us."

Dante packed up his bedroll. They made their goodbyes and rode north from the lake. He was tempted to contact Cally via loon then and there, but wanted to confirm their deal with Brant first and then deliver all the news to the old man in one fell swoop. It would be more impressive that way. Really drive home to Cally why he trusted so much to two of the youngest figures in the Sealed Citadel.

Without the need to hunt for tracks or norren wildsign, they reached the road by nightfall and the town of Shan shortly thereafter. With Mourn looking worn out, Dante bought rooms in an inn and hired a rider to make all haste for Brant's with the message they would return tomorrow—accompanied by an announcement.

In the morning, Dante checked Mourn's wound, which was crusty and disgusting but showed no signs of excess redness or swelling, followed it up with a brief walk around town to restore his appetite, then returned to the inn for a breakfast of beef, bacon, bread, and green beans topped with crispy onions. After so many cold, hard meals on the trail, it made him never want to stray from the road again.

At Brant's three-winged manor, the brawny lord met them with an anxious smile. "What's the word?"

"Hello, for one," Dante said.

"Don't play coy. Spill your guts or I'll spill them across the pig troughs."

Blays yawned. "I hear beer's a peerless interrogation technique."

Brant's smile was as open as the fields. "Then prepare to be tortured within an inch of your life."

The kitchen was warm and smelled of rhubarb and cherries. Brant brought up a small barrel of hoppy beer and poured cups for everyone, including Fann, who'd come down from his chambers. Dante and Blays laid out the events of the last few days. Lira watched, sharp-eyed, interjecting any details they'd forgotten. Mourn gazed into his beer. Occasionally, he verged on a smile.

By the time the story finished, Brant gazed at Mourn with awed horror. "You just *stood* there? While she shot you?"

Mourn shrugged. "The risk to the challenger is why so few challenges get made. What would the world be like if you could kill your leader whenever you wanted? It would be a pretty bad world, I'd say."

"That sounds awful enough as it is!" Fann said.

Brant considered all this over a long drink. "Do you trust the clan to keep their word?"

"I do," Dante said. "The norren tend to be honest. On the rare times they're not, they're so devious you won't know you've been tricked until it's too late to matter."

"You lot are trouble," the farmer grinned. "I'm glad we're on the same side."

The other baronets filtered in through the evening. Once again, they didn't push for details until after a dinner of pork ribs with mustard seeds and pillowy yellow bread studded with dried cherries. Dante and Blays then told the story again, their words clumsied by beer.

At the end, the lords laughed, heads shaking. Even gaunt old Raye shook Mourn's hand. "You very stupid or very brave?"

Mourn shrugged for the hundredth time that day. "If I were very stupid, you couldn't trust my answer either way. So I suppose we must conclude it's bravery. Until the next time I run away."

Raye laughed gruffly. Brant poured beer. Dante paced himself as best he could under the festive circumstances; he still needed to speak to Cally. He didn't get the opportunity until several hours passed on the clock and several refills passed through his bladder. In the quiet of his upstairs room, Dante clicked his brooch to the old man's setting. Cally answered seconds later.

"How goes the hunt?"

"All hunted up," Dante said. "We've got the grain."

"Stupendous!" Cally said in his ear. "How'd you manage that? Did anyone die?"

Dante took a long breath, preparing to relate the story for the third time that day, then shook his head. "Too drunk. Just get a bunch of silver in a wagon and steer it this way. I'll tell you more tomorrow. Afternoon."

"This is nonsense. I fund your trip around the country, and you get so drunk you can't even tell me about it?"

Dante belched. "You can either hear it told crummy tonight or told well tomorrow."

"Worthless." Cally sighed. "It better be worth the wait."

In the morning, of course, Dante was little more articulate than the night before. Fortunately, any early morning updates to Cally were staved off by breakfast and packing and goodbyes to Brant and Jilla, and then, after the ride back to the main road, by concerns they were going the right way (Fann assured him they were) and then by the pressing need to keep both eyes open for bandits, poor footing, and the general lay of the western land. Thin clouds skidded across skies so bright they practically crackled. The wind no longer felt so cold. Snow rested on the southern peaks, but those were fifty miles away or more.

It felt, at last, like the first days of spring.

11

And over the next few days, spring acted like it had something to prove. Lukewarm gales battered the high grasses, followed by days-long rains that soaked their cloaks and left the horses steaming and gamey. Most nights they slept under tarps in the fields. Anywhere with an inn, however, Dante shelled out for a night under a roof and a morning next to a kitchen. If there was ever a time to keep spirits and energy high, it was now, when they might not taste success again for many weeks and many leagues.

Cally was unreservedly pleased to hear about the deal they'd swung in Tantonnen. A caravan had already been dispatched to bring the initial payment to the farmers and pick up whatever reserve grain they could part with before the first harvests. In the meantime, nothing major had emerged from Setteven. The king's men had dispatched a small force from Dollendun to put down riots on the eastern fringes of the Territories, but the matter was expected to resolve quickly, and without a fight. The norren lands had never been wholly peaceful—the clans were too numerous, grudgeful, and splintered to wholly resist the urge to raid and squabble—but they had always melted into the hills and forests at the first sign of Gaskan troops.

"Don't be afraid to push them on the pass," Cally had concluded, referring to Dante's strategy toward the merchants of Gallador Rift. "They talk quite sweetly about water's ability to overcome, but how long will it take to wear a new way through the mountains? Hmm? How much tea will rot on their shores when the Dunden Pass is shut to all those new markets in Mallon?"

"I'm not sure how convincing that will be," Dante said. "We

don't control the pass and never have."

"Yes, well, whatever comes of all this, we can all but guarantee a shakeup of the administration of the Norren Territories, can't we? And which city is the largest and closest and thus most likely to wind up with de facto control of the pass? What do you think I'm bending Duke Hullen's ear about right now?"

"Nothing, I'd hope, or he must be very confused about what his ear has done to deserve it."

"Oh, enough of your negativity. I'm beginning to think these things might be more curse than blessing." Cally shut down the loon.

The land sloped upward mile by mile, a rise as gentle as a fog. Blue mountains sat in proud deltas to the northwest. The road bent to meet them. They stopped at a simple town astride a swift and rocky stream. Dante settled them in at the inn, a two-story rectangle with flared eaves and a millwheel splashing in the turbid creek. The bartender's eyes were dark and bright and stayed locked to Dante's brooches, which he hadn't bothered to hide due to the semi-official nature of their trip. Anyway, it was good for the priests of Narashtovik to be seen outside the Citadel. Too many rumors flew about what they did behind their walls. See a man enjoying a beer, and it's much harder to believe he'll be speaking with demons later that night.

The bartender lingered after delivering Dante his second and final beer, gaze pinned to the ivory carving of The White Tree. "Are you from Narashtovik?"

Dante nodded, somewhat guarded. "For the last few years, anyway. Mallon-born."

"There's word you've had a hand in the norren troubles." The man glanced around the room, as if to reassure himself the walls sported no ears. "If the king's army comes to the Territories, do you think Narashtovik will be safe?"

"Unless the king has a thing for sacking innocent lands. Anyway, Narashtovik is the seat of Arawn. Why are you worried?"

"My sister lives in the city. I wonder if—" The door opened, welcoming in a cold wind and two sour-looking men. The bartender straightened and left to greet them. He glanced Dante's way more than once before Dante retired for the night, but didn't speak to him again until morning, and only then to say goodbye.

From the town on the stream, the deeply-rutted dirt road became a highway of travel-worn stones glued together with sandy cement. Here and there, a weed poked from the cracks, but otherwise the road looked younger than Dante himself. Traffic grew more frequent: two-mule farming wagons, peasants on foot, caravans with bright banners and the brighter spears of mercenaries.

They reached the road into the mountains eight days out from Tantonnen. Three great peaks stood from the mounded hills, their slopes green, their caps white. Shorter mountains ran along a line that extended some thirty miles northeast and southwest. The pass was an easy climb, cold but snowless, the stone road carrying them past grasslands squishy with meltwater. High-peaked homes and warehouses formed a township just below the crest of the pass. With the shadows of the mountains swallowing the road, Dante stopped for the night.

Dawn warmed the green lowlands, but hadn't yet reached the top of the pass by the time they crossed to the other side. Below, a great lake twinkled between the misty rims of the valley, miles in length and impenetrably blue, dwarfing the waters Mourn had dueled beside in the wilds of Tantonnen. In spots, the mountains descended in sheer cliffs, the road switchbacking along the face of the grass-tufted rock. Below the cliffs, the land was carved into terraces, giant green steps leading down to the lake. Thick green bushes grew in serpentine rows. Their leaves smelled spicy and sweet and rich. Tea bushes—the product of which was boiled, strained, and served across Gask, Mallon, and every other island, province, and territory the tradesmen of Gallador could reach.

Without breaking stride, Blays snapped off a tea branch, stripped its leaves, and tucked them into his satchel, scattering the twigs beside the road. Lira watched him steadily.

Blays rolled his eyes at her. "They won't stink like thievery once we boil them."

She shook her head. "Bad seeds makes for bitter brew."

"Oh, what do time-honored proverbs know? I've never met a pure seed in my life."

"Maybe you need to travel in different circles."

"Zigzags are more fun." Blays urged his horse forward. "They're more likely to take you places like this."

A vast city swamped the shore. Masts bristled the piers. Ferries splashed between the banks of the city of Wending and the islands smattering the water. Smoke lingered in the heavy valley air, mingling with the morning mists steaming off the massive lake.

"I hope you fellows like boats," Fann said. "Because our host lives on one of those islands."

"Boats." Blays glared at Dante. "You can bring a man back from the dead, but you can't make us fly? Not once?"

"I can't bring a man back to life," Dante said. "Cally says no one can. Not in this day."

"Huh. I thought you saw some guy resurrect a dog once."

"I thought I had, but I'm not sure it was dead to begin with. Or if it was, that what came back was alive."

"Oh, forget it."

Rather than the clapboard slums typical of city fringes, the upper slopes of Wending were dominated by green lawns and isolated villas. Crooked trees grew at deliberate intervals, their crabbed branches trimmed. Even in the early hour, men with pikes stood on the front stoops, backs straight, eyes watchful. The houses they guarded had been modeled after the farms on the hills: sprawling ground floors and terraced upper floors with stepped towers standing five and six stories high. The curved eaves gave the roofs a tentlike look. Next to every manor, a golden pole jutted fifty feet into the sky, isolated in a circle of gravel raked into alternating spokes of white and black.

"What the hell is that?" Blays said. "I mean, besides a big old pole?"

Fann shot him a distressed look. "A temple."

"It looks like a very sickly tree."

"These people come from ancient lines of traders. In olden days, they planted brass-capped poles at crossroads where the gleaming metal would attract the eye. Even the most ephemeral bazaars took on the air of sanctuary. Few use the poles in that way now, however. Across Gallador, they've become houses of worship."

"Not much of a temple if everyone's got one," Dante said.

Fann shook his head briskly. "Quite the contrary! These were nomads, remember. In modern times, services are held at a different swappole every week. Some of the larger orders may not meet at the same pole more than once a year. By the way, don't approach one without flipping a coin at its base."

"Why not?" Blays said.

"It's considered akin to shitting in the well."

"So should I not do that either?"

Fann sighed. The poles all but disappeared as they entered the city proper and its smells of manure, lake-mud, and the savory tea sold from carts and teahouses in every single plaza. The corners of roofs swooped and curved. Squat, short-legged horses trundled through the streets, carts strapped to their thick bodies. Men and women wore bright, skirtlike things slit to the knees.

It was like they'd crossed the mountains into another world. Yet at the same time, Wending was nothing more than another major city, with the same wood and stone and pressing flesh of all the others. Fann led them to the ferries, stabled the horses at the massive barn beside the docks, and hired a man with a rowboat and a sibilant accent. Two heavy-shouldered men paddled them across the cold, deep waters to Bolling Island, a sharp ridge of rock a few hundred feet long and less than a hundred across. Stairs climbed from its jetty. There, Fann hired a waiting porter to help with the luggage and escort them to the house of Lord Lolligan, where they were to stay.

A servant let them in to the foyer of the five-layered house, where they waited in a receiving-hall insulated against the lake's chill by lush carpets. Padded benches and paintings of sloops on misty lakes furnished the room. Lolligan emerged shortly, a thin, avian old man with a pointed white beard and light brown skin.

"You may as well sit," he said, eyes creasing with a smile. "Unless you plan to stand for the next three days."

"I don't take your meaning," Dante said.

"Because it was deliberately unclear. In less obscure language, the man you want to see is named Jocubs, and he won't see you for three days."

"We'll see about that," Blays said. "We've got places to be."

Lolligan tipped back his chin. "That's precisely the problem. So does everyone else."

Nevertheless, he let them down to his private pier, where two of his servants rowed Dante and Blays to another island a fraction of a mile further out on the lake. There, they called on a terraced house much like Lolligan's, if a little older and statelier, and were brought to a closed-off deck overhanging the lake. Jocubs was not in. They were met instead by Brilla, a woman who was unobtrusive in appearance but whose cool command made clear she was used to speaking for the household.

"I'm afraid Lord Jocubs is not available to see you," she said. "I am sure he'll be pleased to hear you came to announce your arrival in person."

Dante leaned forward on his padded green bench. "We're pressed for time. Our meeting with Lord Jocubs will only take a few minutes."

"A few minutes Lord Jocubs does not currently possess."

"What if we wait here?" Blays said.

"Then you will be waiting for three days, which I assure you would be more comfortably passed at Lord Lolligan's."

Dante rubbed his mouth. "Perhaps he can squeeze us in at the end of the day."

Brilla tented her hands. "Regrettably, the end of the day is already accounted for."

"Is every second of his time blocked out?"

"Of course not. That would be ridiculous."

"Is every *minute*?"

"All the important ones," she said.

Dante's brow lowered. "Then perhaps we can intrude on some of his unimportant minutes."

"Impossible." Her dark hair swung as she shook her head. "That would make them important minutes."

"And thus accounted for?"

"You can see the bind I'm in."

"So he can stay up late!" Blays thundered. "Taim's sagging ass! Our rider beat us here by a week at least to set this up in advance. We're here to stop a *war* and your lord is too busy counting tea leaves to spare us fifteen minutes?"

Brilla gave him a look that could have withered all Tantonnen. "I'm not stopping you from seeing him. I'm just explaining to you why you can't."

"Oh yeah? Then what would you do if I ran upstairs and kicked in his bedroom door?"

"Obviously I would stop you."

"You're lying like a rug that's very tired," Blays said. "Either that, or you honestly don't understand—"

Dante cut in. "There are issues at stake much closer to Lord Jocubs' interests than any conflict. Dunden Pass, for instance."

Brilla's gaze snapped away from Blays. "What about it?"

"Narashtovik continues to be concerned about reprisals from Mallon about the last war," Dante lied. "We believe the pass may need to be restricted. Possibly even shut down."

"You can't do that."

"Nevertheless, we may. We had hoped to kill two birds by bringing the matter to Lord Jocubs, but if we have to move on before he's free—"

Brilla held up her fine-fingered hands. "I'll let him know. That's the best I can do."

"I'm sure that's true," Blays said. "I'd hate to be anywhere near when you show off your worst."

Her lips compressed into a tight line, but she fared them well at the door. Lolligan's boatmen rowed them back to Bolling Island. Lolligan sat in his receiving-hall holding a lively conversation with Fann and Mourn. He looked up with a cheerful smile.

"How did it go?"

"I have no gods damn idea," Dante said.

"Well, you'll find out soon enough," the old man said. "Or not."

"What, are you related to Brilla?" Blays said. "You both equivocate like you were born into it. Like you had to convince your moms to have you in the first place."

Lolligan laughed, dry yet cheerful. "Do you know what Galladites are most often compared to?"

"Mossy stones," Fann said.

"And why is that?"

"Because your people live in close proximity to a great many rocks?" Mourn said.

Fann shook his head. "Because they're so slippery."

"Indeed," Lolligan smiled. "What good is a contract you can't wriggle out of? What good is it to want something if everyone knows about that want? That is how business survives when everything else perishes."

Dante narrowed his eyes. "You seem awfully upfront in your desire to help us."

"Oh, that's because I'm more gambler than businessman. And I see Narashtovik—more specifically, the man who runs it—as the sneakiest bet to hitch my wagon to."

A servant coughed from the doorway. It was time for dinner. The lake shimmered pinkly through the floor-to-ceiling windows. The meal was a bevy of trout found nowhere but the lake, seasoned with black and red peppers and a savory tea-based sauce. Lolligan made no rituals before it was served.

A letter arrived from Jocubs before dessert. The lord would see them tomorrow afternoon.

Jocubs received them on the same enclosed balcony where Brilla had given them the verbal run-around. Jocubs was elderly, stately, with winglike gray eyebrows that turned up at the ends. His bald head was as shiny as the lake and he moved with the slow confidence of a man who's always known a servant would catch him before he fell. For all that, Dante liked him: he smiled readily, and insisted they forget his title.

"I'm puzzled why Callimandicus would be worried about the pass at this juncture," Jocubs said. "It's been what, six years since your little squabble with Mallon? If it takes them that long to respond, surely they're not much of a threat, eh?"

"The thing is, Callimandicus is very old." Blays reached for his lake-chilled champagne. "It makes him prone to forget that everyone younger has better things to do than stew about the past."

"I'm sure I don't have to mention we find that pass very useful. It would be a shame to have to run a new road through the southern mountains. Which would run closer to Wending, of course, but why tip a rolling cart?"

Dante smiled. "I think we can talk him down. But we wanted to be certain you still had a use for the pass if Callimandicus does wind up its steward."

Jocubs' winged brows leapt. "Does he think that's likely, too? I must say I haven't heard one thing about this whole mess that doesn't smell like a buzzard's gut. I'm beginning to think we'll level out status quo."

"He disagrees, I'm afraid. I assume Wending has no interest in a war in the Territories?"

"Celeset, no. How do we ship tea to Mallon when there's a horde of damned soldiers clogging up the road?"

"Rolling carts and tipping hands, et cetera," Blays added.

The elderly man grinned. "You sound downright lakeborn."

"Narashtovik doesn't want war, either," Dante said. "We feel a certain paternal sympathy for the norren, for one. For another, I'm afraid Setteven may be misinterpreting the acts of a single clan for statewide unrest."

"It sounds like you need an audience with the Tradesman's Association."

"How do we make that happen?"

"Well, I could ask for one. I am the head of it." Jocubs chuckled, then leaned back on his bench and folded his hands across his modest belly. "I can schedule our meeting within, say, eight days."

"Eight days?" Dante said.

"Does time pass more slowly in Narashtovik?"

"It's just that we have other places to visit before we head home."

Jocubs lifted one thatchety brow. "And I've got to assemble a quorum of the Tradesman's Association of the Greater Valley of Gallador, some of the busiest men and women in the entire empire. Compared to that, putting the brakes on a war might be easier."

Dante laughed. "Fair enough. Please let us know when the time is confirmed."

He returned to Lolligan's home happy enough. Even with an eight-day wait, they'd remain slightly ahead of schedule. A schedule that was somewhat arbitrary to begin with. In truth, he and Cally had been expecting more movement out of Setteven by this point—aggression along the borders, tough talk, more levies. Instead, all fronts had been quiet. Perhaps King Moddegan felt no need to stomp out a few unruly bugs. Perhaps all their worries of war were just phantoms. Even if things were progressing behind the scenes, the movement was too slow and small to notice.

Lolligan agreed Jocubs' timeline sounded reasonable. "If anything, it's on the fast side. Everybody must have already dragged their fat asses back to town to cover them up before bad times hit."

"How do you think the negotiations will go?"

The old merchant snorted. "Heard anything about not rocking the boat yet? Tipping the cart?"

"What about shaking the baby?" Blays said.

"Surprised that one hasn't caught on yet." Lolligan gestured at the shimmering lake. "The men here, they like to keep things smooth. We have a fish here. The cadd. Pudgy things about the size of your thumb, with yellow spots and a mean little beak. By and large, cadd eat anything that's too small and too slow to get out of the way—snails, minnows, the bones of other fish. They won't look twice at something their own size. But once in a while, if something in the water's bleeding bad enough, or thrashing around just so? The entire lake flashes yellow with cadd swarming for a bite."

"So don't be a snail?" Blays said. "Words to live by."

"What I'm saying is they'll eat you alive if the opportunity looks tasty enough."

"I suspect that may be the chief rule of existence," Dante said.

"I think we're overlooking the crucial issue here," Blays said. "The chief concern, as far as I see it, is we have eight days ahead of us and zero things to fill them with."

Lolligan smiled, the sharp triangles of his mustache twitching. "I can occupy a few of those days. If you find it tragically boring, you can spend the rest of the week drinking away the memory."

"You should be a salesman!" Blays clapped his hands to his thighs and stood. "What are we going to see?"

"Nothing much. Just the most vital ingredient to a happy and healthy life."

A pink field stretched for a mile in all directions, flat and glittery as a pond, bowled on all sides by craggy brown hills. It was shockingly warm; Dante had already shed his cloak and was currently sweating through his doublet. A few yards away, women crouched and hacked at the field with short, sharp metal hoes, scuttling forward as soon as they loosened the soil. Boys dawdled after them, shoveling the crumbly pink dirt into wooden buckets. Lolligan grinned like a proud grandpa.

Blays sniffed. "Is this it?"

Lolligan whirled, gaping angrily. "Do you have any idea what you're looking at?"

"Dirt?"

"*Dirt*?"

"Pink dirt?"

Lolligan shut his eyes and forced the anger from his face. "That's salt. Just growing from the ground. Ripe for the plucking, if you have the right to pluck it. Which I do."

Dante knelt and touched the ground. Hard, solid, crystalline. Lightly gritty. "Can I taste it?"

"That depends on how much money's in your pocket." Lolligan smiled and gestured grandly. "Be my guest."

Dante touched his fingertips to his tongue and rolled the grains around his mouth, letting them dissolve. "It's different. Sharper. Almost a little sweet."

"Exactly. Sprinkle that on a steak, and you'll never again be able to pass a cow without taking a nibble off the flank."

The trip had taken the better part of three days. From Bolling Island, Lolligan had rigged up his flat-bottomed sailboat and cruised north across the lake to a gap carved straight through the hills. A shallow canal led them to another lake that was notably squatter than Gallador proper. From there, Lolligan docked at a busy little town, hired a pack of rugged, shorthaired horses with funny, pushed-in snouts, and led them beyond a craggy ridge. The land descended through a hellscape of sharp, broken rocks, steaming, sulfurous pits, and hot pools on top of bulbous yellow rock that looked like frozen snot. After another row of barren hills, they finally reached the salt flats, a pink sea even stranger than anything they passed along the way.

Lolligan passed the voyage telling them how he'd made his fortune. The first son of a wealthy tea merchant, he'd inherited enough wealth to last an era, then swiftly lost it through a series of bad investments and worse bets. After twelve years of living hand-to-mouth, including four years as a mate on a single-masted cog, he returned to Wending on Gallador, gambled all his savings on high-altitude plots the other tea-men had utterly failed to turn fruitful, and promptly sowed the soil with seeds picked up during his years at sea. The resulting tea leaves were scrawny, little larger than the last joint of your pinky. His friends feared he'd be ruined a second time.

But his tiny leaves made delicious tea. Since they were so small, supply was scarce. Demand soared—and prices with it. In the two decades since, others had moved in with small-leafed brews of their own; that elevated him to the fringes of respectability, but the politicking of the traditional tea-growers kept Lolligan excluded from the inner circles. Including the TAGVOG Jocubs ruled over. Lolligan seemed to regard this exclusion with equal parts "who needs 'em" humor and needling resentment.

"Not bad," Blays said there on the pink plain. He licked his fingers. "Salty."

"Where do you get your salt in Narashtovik?" Lolligan said.

"The sea?" Dante shrugged.

Blays wagged his head. "The salt fairy."

"The salt—?" Lolligan pressed his palms together, elbows splayed. "Look, why don't you take a box back with you? Narashtovik hasn't been much of a market for a long time, but I get the impression all that has changed."

He barked orders at a boy. The boy sprinted toward a wagon parked just past the flats, sandals flapping.

"Is this why you took us in?" Dante said. "To sell us salt?"

"It's *a* reason. I like to have more than one."

"I thought good traders didn't make their wants known."

"Except when they do. Such as when the product's quality speaks for itself." The boy returned with a small wooden box. Lolligan took it and gazed at the woman and children chipping and scooping the pink field. "Some people use norren, you know. They can sure haul their weight. Have a bad habit of dropping dead in the summer, though. I don't think they're built for this heat."

Blays blinked against the crystal-reflected sun. "We came all this way for *salt*?"

The trip back took just as long as the journey out. Dante wanted to be in top shape for the meeting with the TAGVOG, leaving a single night to peruse the city and take in a drink. At Lolligan's manor, Dante gathered up the team and took the boat into town. They passed one nondescript pub, then took up a bench in the second they found, a three-story watering hole with a tented roof. Its second floor rested on pilings above the lapping shore, open to the cool lakeside winds.

Blays demanded they try the local flavor, a murky white liquor called mullen that tasted nutty and earthy and mixed well with hot and sweetened tea. They drank from slender, square-bottomed glasses like fluted vases.

Fann turned his glass in a slow circle. "Talk, that immortal butterfly, made the rounds while you were out."

"Oh yeah?" Blays said. "What kind of flowers did it assault?"

"The rose of trade. I heard several proposals that Gallador's support in Setteven could be acquired through an exclusive deal or three with Narashtovik. As well as Cally's commitment to pave the main roads."

"Too good for dirt, are they?"

"That sounds promising," Dante said. "Mutually beneficial, even."

Fann tipped his head to one side. "I got the impression there was the expectation of heavy profit. There was talk of sheep."

"Cost us less than raising an army, won't it?" Blays said. "Or holding a funeral for every person in Narashtovik."

"Unless we got a mass grave," Dante said.

"You'd probably like that. All jammed up like that, you might be able to force a woman to touch you."

"I'll just have to pray the gravediggers finish their work before rigor mortis wears off."

"I think I'm off to bed," Fann smiled tightly. He rose. Mourn joined him on the brief walk to the piers. Lira stayed, scanning every patron as they came and went.

"I hope this isn't too boring," Blays said to her. He pointed to Dante. "I find it pretty dull myself, and he at least *pretends* like I have some influence around here."

Lira smiled at the steam rising from her tall glass. "You think I find your company disinteresting?"

"His? Definitely."

"In the last few weeks, we've attacked a nobleman, freed a passel of slaves, foiled an assassination attempt, and traveled halfway around the empire speaking to some of Gask's most powerful men." Lira sipped her mullen. "Before that, getting left for dead by pirates was the most exciting thing to happen to me in years."

Blays turned to Dante, laughing. "I think she actually likes this."

"Spent too much time around you, no doubt," Dante said.

"No such thing. That's like having too much summer."

"Summer's awful," Lira said. "If I have to sweat, I prefer to earn it in other ways."

"Like what?" Blays said, straight-faced. "Long runs and cold baths?"

Talk came easy, but a couple hours later, even Blays was ready to leave. They stood, buttoning cloaks, draining the last of their mullen.

Lira adjusted her collar. "I think we may be followed home."

"Oh yes?" Dante said. "Is that because you're crazy?"

"It's because we were followed here."

"What?"

"Man in the northwest corner. Blue cloak. Don't look."

Dante scowled. "I wasn't going to."

"Well," Blays murmured, "that raises an interesting question, doesn't it?"

Dante shot him a look. "Oh no. No, we don't know this city well enough for that."

"Is the big bad wizard afraid of one hired goon?"

"If he has a knife? Or friends in a dark alley? Yes. Yes I am."

Lira clunked down her glass. "What's being talked about like I'm not here?"

Dante patted his chest, ensuring his brooches were in place. "Whether to catch a boat straight home, or take a leisurely stroll through the city."

"I think we should walk," Blays said.

"We know what you think."

"Do I get a vote?" Lira said.

Dante glanced at the door. "Depends if it's a good one."

"If he means us harm, it's better to draw him out now than be attacked unaware."

"Damn it." Dante snugged his cloak around his neck. "Let's go for a walk."

The open-walled pub had been plenty chilly, so the transition to the outside air was minimal. The wooden steps rocked under Dante's feet. He hit the damp streets and headed up the slope toward the heart of the city. A minute later, wood creaked behind them.

Dante forced himself not to look. He tightened his cloak again and passed beyond a circle of lamplight—the lamps here were few, placed only at major squares and the tall brass swappoles. Faint haze diffused the shine of the stars and half-moon. Blays whistled "Reeling Rilla," as out of tune as usual. Lira spent a lot of time gazing into any glass windows they passed. It was a bit after ten and the streets were sparse with people—plodding drunks, hurrying pedestrians, women standing in tight wraps and knee-high skirts while men sat behind them, fiddling openly with knives or clubs. Dante made a left turn toward a well-lit square of short grass and broad, crablike trees that had just begun to grow new buds.

He strolled straight through the park, pausing often to admire the artfully trimmed trees, and stopped in the light of another pub to hold a false discussion about whether it looked like their kind of place. He and Lira "overruled" Blays. They moved on. Occupied with memorizing landmarks and routes and keeping their orientation straight, Dante could no longer tell if they were being followed. Instead he led them through a meandering semicircle that brought them back within a bowshot of the docks, where he stopped in front of an empty, gaping warehouse.

Lira risked a look behind them. "Nothing the last five minutes."

"Ready to head home?" Dante said.

Blays nodded. Dante crossed the slick stones to the docks. The skiff's oars stirred the black water. They spoke of nothing important until they were back within the warm walls of Lolligan's house.

"Must have just been scouting us," Blays said then. "That dawdle through the park was an engraved invitation to stab us."

"That's what I was going for." Dante turned to Lira. "What'd you see?"

Her eyes wandered to the ceiling. "Short. Thin. Male. Unobtrusive. Dark hair. Hitch in his step."

"A hitch? Like this?" Dante limped in a circle.

"That's a wobble. This was more of a hiccup." She demonstrated, jerking her spine straight with every other step. "Not that exaggerated, but you get the idea."

"Maybe it's Robert," Blays grinned. "After us for rum money."

"We could use him about now," Dante chuckled. He unclasped his cloak. "It's probably just one of Jocubs' men making sure we're on the up-and-up. But keep your eyes peeled."

"Well, I'm in for nightmares now," Blays said. "Have you ever thought about how gross that expression really is?"

The day before their meeting passed with blessedly little excitement. A letter arrived from Jocubs. The TAGVOG had its quorum. They would meet at his house at one o'clock the following day.

The morning of the event, Dante rode a skiff into the city and took a long walk in the early sunshine. He felt calm and ready. He returned to Lolligan's at noon and, accompanied by Blays and Fann, was rowed to Jocubs' island. A servant showed him to the carpeted dining hall. A dozen-odd merchants were already there, primarily old and male, but disrupted here and there by unwrinkled or female faces. Servants danced between the men of means, bearing gold trays of olives and figs and sweet port that tasted of chocolate and prunes. They brought fish, too. Dante lost count at ten different kinds—one type red as beef, two baked and headless, three fried whole in skins and heads and tails, one mashed up with soft cheese in a salty, savory paste which the merchants ate on thin slices of toast. More and more old men filtered into the vast room, accompanied by one to three servants and secretaries apiece, who drifted around their fat employers like pilot fish. Dante was introduced to face after face, forgetting the names attached to them as each new one shuffled up to greet him. The room was in constant, dizzying motion, a slow whirl of forty estate-holders and a hundred attendants.

Conversation shifted to his thoughts on the potential conflict and Narashtovik's stance to it, official and otherwise. Dante found himself in the middle of a sea of faces. Abruptly, he realized the meeting had already begun. He faltered, then laughed as if at a private joke: no place handled its business quite like anywhere else. How large and strange and wonderful the world was.

"It's a fundamentally simple position," he said to the school of curious merchants. "We don't want war. We've seen it too recently to believe any good can come of it. Furthermore, we know the norren too well to think they mean greater Gask real harm. We're concerned for our own lands, as well as our neighbors—even friendly armies tend to leave muddy tracks. There's no need and no want for one half of the country to march on the other.

"We know Gallador carries heavy weight with the king. Without the taxes your ships and wagons bring home, Moddegan would have no army to send forth in the first place. That's all we're here for. With your help, we can spare a lot of strife and a lot of lives."

A smattering of applause followed, though it wasn't particularly that sort of gathering. Dante expected to be assailed with a public back-and-forth afterwards, but instead the room dissolved into a dozen different knots of conversation. For a moment, he stood isolated and ignored. Then, one by one, they came for him.

The first was a man in his early thirties with a widow's peak and an arch smile. "I hope you're ready for this."

"This being?" Dante said.

"You've just made an offer. Now come the counters. You don't expect our aid will come for free, do you?"

"Narashtovik's not so different. We're ready to make any reasonable agreements."

"Well, I support you." The man swept back his hair. "I've scheduled my first caravan this spring. Fresh leaf bound for Bressel. Would hate to delay just because a few tribes of overgrown men would rather spend their time fighting than shaving."

The second to approach was a middle-aged woman whose skirt brushed the floor; when she walked, she appeared to glide over the plush carpet.

"Quick speech," she said. "That's good. Fewer details to offend the sensitive."

"I didn't even know I was giving one until halfway through."

She smiled with half her mouth. "Frankly, the clans have never shown much concern for the safety of their roads. Calm them down and you'll convince a lot of the people in this room."

He thanked her and she moved on. Most of those who spoke with him over the next hour were the newcomers, the fringe-dwellers, those who needed every leg up they could get. They queried him on trade pacts and the northern markets for tea and salt and fish. The elder men—the finest-dressed, the easiest with their laughter and pronouncements—stuck to their clusters, chuckling and snacking.

Eventually, one of these epic figures detached from his cohort and swayed over to Dante. His silk skirts rasped. His gray muttonchops swept into his bristling mustache, all of which was thick enough to impress any norren. His olive skin was as craggy and pocked as the sulfurous hills by the salt flats.

"I wonder if," he said, "at the end of the day, we have any influence at all on the movements of men and kingdoms?"

"You and me personally?" Dante cocked his head. "Because I imagine King Moddegan has rather a lot of influence on the movements of Gask."

The man waved a fleshy hand. "You're from Narashtovik. You believe Arawn has no influence over the actions of our earthly king?"

"I suppose he could. He tends not to intervene directly." Dante smiled wryly. "I think he laughs hardest when a man's folly is his own."

"To put it another way, would we be speaking now if Moddegan's ancestors hadn't annexed the Norren Territories three hundred years ago?"

"I don't know. I doubt it."

"So our king, it can be said, is playing out the story written for him by his ancestors."

"That would mean you and I are, too."

The man's muttonchops lifted in a smile. "We're all at the mercy of ghosts."

The merchant gave a slight bow of his head and turned to rejoin his compatriots. That was more or less the end of the dialogues. One other youngish man approached him with questions about Narashtovik and was interrupted by a servant, who informed Dante he should stay until after the quorum dissolved. This took the better part of three hours. That evening, Jocubs beckoned

Dante and Blays into the enclosed balcony, leaving the servants to fetch tea and sweep up the dining hall.

"Well." Jocubs eased himself onto a bench, glancing at the sunset on the lake. "I hope you had a good time."

Blays jerked his chin in the direction of the hall. "The fish were so good it's a wonder you don't live in the lake with them."

"I'm glad." He folded his hands on his stomach and gave Dante a sideways look. "I hope it wasn't too imposing?"

Dante shrugged lightly. "Not at all. Although I'm confused about what we accomplished."

"With exceptions, the Association sympathizes with you. We have a few peripheral details we'd like to work out with you—I don't think most of us knew how large Narashtovik had gotten—but I think you can count on a positive vote at the assembly two weeks from now."

"Is that a joke?" Blays said.

Jocubs blinked, lower lip outthrust. "If so, please tell me what struck you as funny. I've always wished myself wittier."

"Two *weeks*?"

"Yes, I think so."

Blays laughed, glancing at Dante in disbelief. "And *then* you'll reach a decision? Then what the hell was this party for?"

A frown gathered on the merchant's face. "To see if your proposal was worth pursuing. The next two weeks will be about working out the specifics. Some of the estates represented by the men you met are the size of small kingdoms."

Dante's head buzzed. "I don't suppose this can be hurried along."

"Not in any significant way." The man leaned forward and patted Dante's knee. "It will be fine in time. If it takes this long for Gallador to shift course, just think how long it would take the entire kingdom to come to grips with something weighty as a war!"

Dante expressed his thanks, turned down a final glass of port, and walked down to Jocubs' pier. "Well, so much for our schedule."

"So much for our youth," Blays said.

"Maybe we should just give up. Run off to be pirates."

"Wait, is that an option? Why didn't you tell me that years

ago?"

Dante nodded at the skiff tied along the dock. "There's our flagship. Let's go. Lake-pirates are a thing, right?"

"If not, we can make them a thing." Blays stepped over the side of the hull. Down the pier, two men dislodged from the boathouse and hurried down the planks. "We'll blaze watery new trails for highwaymen everywhere."

The boatman paddled them back to Lolligan's, where the old man asked Dante for a detailed recap of the quorum. While Dante spoke, Lolligan cocked his head, frowned at spots on the wall, and muttered to himself, petting his pointed mustache with a single finger.

"Choker," he said once Dante finished.

"What?"

"Lord Choker. The elderly man with the muttonchops who spoke about ghosts and strings? He's the only part I can't figure out."

"Well, that's good," Dante said. "Because I don't understand *any* part."

"It's straightforward enough."

"And so is an ant's nest—if you're an ant. If the TAGVOG already knows they want to send a delegation to the king on our behalf, why do they need another two weeks to finalize that decision?"

Lolligan waved a sun-browned hand. "This assembly wasn't about deciding whether they should try to talk down the warhawks. Other than those who dabble in arms and armsmen, none of the TAGVOG is keen on a fight. Today, they were judging *you*. How much Narashtovik wants their help, and how far you will bend to provide it. They've bought themselves two weeks to suss that out and maneuver to leverage you to the hilt."

"Excellent," Dante said. "While they're off counting coins, the king is counting troops. And unless his abacus is bent, he'll soon discover he has far more than the norren."

"When in doubt, look to the path of the crowd." Lolligan gestured across the water toward Jocubs' home. "If those old bastards thought time were running short, do you think they'd wait two more weeks? Remember, to these men, ignorance is the water between them and gold. Information is the boat they use to cross it."

Dante nodded, comforted. Most of these men had built their fortunes through shrewdness, caution, and prudence. Even the lure of squeezing Narashtovik for every ounce of its excess silver would only push them to tempt fate so far.

They were all wrong, of course. The king would hand down his proclamation the next day. It reached Gallador just two days after that. In the style of all great ultimatums, it brooked just two outcomes.

The norren would rebel, or never be able to again.

12

On hearing the king's proclamation, Blays had one of his own.

"Horseshit." He replaced his tea cup on its saucer. "A sixty-pound sack of horseshit."

Dante felt sick. "Horseshit isn't nearly offensive enough. This is...apeshit. At least."

He switched on his loon. On hearing the news, Cally was silent for a full ten seconds. "Well, that's no good."

"Not unless you're a mortician," Dante said. "Or a vendor of rebel banners."

"Unless you feel like defecting—and at this point I wouldn't blame you—there's no reason to stay in Wending when the king's decision has already been made. See what there is to see at the cove. Come back through the lakes on your way home and see if the merchants can talk Moddegan down, but don't waste a lot of time if they're waffling." Cally hmm'd. "Leave Fann behind to grease whatever wheels he can reach. He won't serve any use at Pocket Cove. Except as breakfast."

The orders cleared Dante's head. Fann accepted his charge with a silent nod; he was used to being dispatched to courtly settings as soon as the road turned rough. Blays clapped his hands. Mourn turned to gather his things. Lira smiled strangely and reached for her hip for a sword that wasn't there.

Lolligan was equal parts apologetic and eager for them to stay. "We don't know how the path may fork from here. Moddegan could be being deliberately outrageous in order to appear benevolent when he scales back his demands."

Dante gazed at the sparkling lake. "I won't bank on that."

"Then talk the TAGVOG into talking him down. There's still time."

"I don't understand how this city works, Lolligan, and I no longer have the time to learn. The king has made his decision. It's time for your friends to make theirs."

"They're not my friends," Lolligan muttered.

Dante wanted no more of it. For what little good it would do, he composed a brief letter to Jocubs, then took a rowboat into the city to pick up provisions while the stables prepped the horses. Waiting at the bakery, he realized he had no desire to go to Pocket Cove.

But it wasn't a choice. They were ready to move by late afternoon. The sun was already within a hand's height of the western peaks, but the roads in Gallador were the best Dante had ever seen (besides the sheer mastery of those in Cling, anyway). Riding by night would be no danger. He squeezed his knees against his horse's flanks, urging it forward.

As soon as the city shifted from rowhouses to farmland, he sped to a trot, swerving around an oxen team. This was no time to rest the horses. Everything would be moving faster now. By the king's order, the Territories were to be parceled out in four-mile squares. Each clan was to be registered with one of a score of new baronetcies and would remain restricted to their new territory by force of law. In addition, every four years each clan was required to provide one fit male slave in tribute; if no males fit the bill, a female would suffice. If a single clan denounced or defied these new conditions, King Moddegan claimed express authority to pass through any and all lands on his way to quell them; if the rebellious clan could not be found, its neighbors would be held accountable until it was located.

That last bit was the poison pill. Disinclined as they may be to accept the heavy hand of human rule, a majority of norren, particularly those in the cities, would rather accept it than face invasion. But there were at least two hundred clans. Probably several times that many. Dante couldn't believe the Nine Pines would accept this treaty. No doubt they'd be just one among dozens of rebel clans. War was no longer a question of *if*, but *when*.

Meanwhile, should the clans defy their nature and acquiesce—

either through threat of invasion or forced to by battle—Moddegan had set himself up to feast on the loyalty of all the powerful men vying for those new baronetcies and the lands, status, and titles that came with them. No doubt several of Gallador's tea growers and salt miners would not only jump ship from the TAGVOG's desire for peace, but would dig extra deep to help fund the war. It was a masterstroke, the overbearing play of a man fully confident he couldn't lose. And Moddegan was right. Soon, the norren would be forever quelled, penned and farmed like cattle, unable to trouble him ever again.

Unless.

And a dwindling "unless" at that. The ultimatum gave the tribes three weeks to register and two months to volunteer their first slaves. With so little time to spare, Dante couldn't see spending more than three days at Pocket Cove. It wouldn't be enough to win the favor of the People of the Pocket. His only hope for discovering the cove's secret—whatever had kept them from being conquered, ever—lay in the observations he drew for himself.

Observations which must run deeper than the land itself. The Pocket Cove was supposedly surrounded by sheer cliffs on all sides, but that would do nothing to prevent a naval invasion. Which Gask had attempted, many years ago. Their fleet had disappeared as if it had sailed off the edge of the earth. The king at the time announced victory anyway, adding the cove to the mounting list of imperial acquisitions, but the People had never, so far as Dante knew, paid taxes, tribute, or homage to Setteven, and to this day remained independent in all but name. If Dante could ferret out whatever secret saved their sovereignty, perhaps he could employ it to do the same for the Norren Territories.

The far side of the mountains took them through a thick forest of bamboo. They rode hard, switching horses and pace to keep their mounts fresh. Budding trees blanketed the hills. For three days they saw nothing but wind-washed grassland. Lightning streaked between mounded black clouds. Hailstones popped from the grass, salting the road and stinging Dante's hands. The towns were small things, a few dozen houses at the crossroads, the green fields speckled with white sheep, gray goats, and black crows.

For a morning and an afternoon, they passed nothing at all. Yellow grasses and graying stone. The road stopped as if erased. To the west, a black line lay along the horizon, thick and unbroken.

"What the hell is that?" Blays said. "Looks like Taim took a great big quill and tried to scratch out the end of the world."

"So the legends say," Dante said.

"Wait, he did?"

"Yeah. Right after he beat Gashen in a mountain-throwing contest and then baked a potato so hot even he couldn't eat it."

Blays scowled. "This is why no one takes priests seriously. The stories you make up as jokes aren't any crazier than the ones you worship in your books."

"They're cliffs," Lira said.

Dante turned in the saddle. "Cliffs?"

She nodded, looking him in the eye. "Tall, rocky slopes. Typically vertical."

"*What* are cliffs?"

"Tall, rocky slopes—"

"That!" Blays pointed at the thick black line. "We're here!"

"So can we finally know what brings us here?" Mourn said. "Besides our horses?"

Dante quickly explained Gask's history of failed invasions. "The People of the Pocket have been protected by more than cliffs. We're trying to figure out why no one can get in or out."

"They get out when they want," Lira said. "But few recognize the People when they see them."

"What makes you so sure?"

"They sail south sometimes. We saw them in the Carlon Islands every few years."

The black cliffs rose three hundred feet from the plain, perfectly sheer, unclimbable. A shallow scree of broken stones rested at their base. Dante halted to consult the maps copied from Cally's library. The originals were poorly scaled and very old, but they indicated a pass through the cliffs not far to the south. Some five miles later, dusk forced them to encamp. There had been no breaks in the rock nor any gentling of the slope. The vertical black stone was striated like gills, blocking off the heavens.

"Question," Blays said around their fire. "If no one can get in, why do we think there *is* a way in?"

"Because the maps say so," Dante said.

"Those things are older than Cally's balls."

"I'm pretty sure *those* aren't any older than Cally himself."

"Then thank Arawn you've never seen them."

Dante blinked. "When did you—?"

"Anyway," Blays went on, "if they came from the kind of books Cally reads, they're automatically suspect."

Dante unrolled one of his parchments and held it to the firelight. "Look, the road ended here. Just north." He tapped the map, then another spot below that. "One of the passages is supposed to be here, right before this Blackcairn place. That should be less than a day's ride."

"Sure, we've already wasted four. What's one more?"

"We're not *wasting* anything. We're not the only ones working on this, you know. Cally's got a squad of diplomats in Setteven. He and Olivander are probably working out how to levy an army for Narashtovik right now. Scores of different clans are plotting how to fight back on their own." Dante paused to accept a hot heel of bread from Mourn; the crust was lightly charred, the white steaming and fluffy, gooey with butter and speckled with fresh-picked lowleaf. "All those people are making the normal preparations for war. We're out here to bring back something *strange*."

They kept the fire lit that night. The light and smoke would carry far across the grassland, but they were at the edge of the world, a step beyond the map. There were dogs to keep at bay, too, wild things with howls like sobbing mothers. Despite their yips, Dante slept well, the fire's warmth easing the stiffness from his legs and back. In the morning, he brewed tea as the others woke. They rose easy, as if revitalized by more than the tea: but by the knowledge they were in a nowhere-place, a realm where nothing could help them but themselves. That knowledge was bracing, a kick to the heart that could last the whole day.

They rode out with the light, skimming the face of the cliff. Small black birds burst from the brush. The sun surged across the grass and died on the black rock wall. At noon, they stopped to eat dried beef and bread. Dante's border-world energy had left him. The cliffs were featureless, unchanging, as if the gods had hacked them into a rough idea in the early days of creation and forgotten to ever return and finish the fine details.

With the sun sliding down the sky, a black mound rose from the grass. Broken stones sat in a forty-foot mound. Time-tarnished bones poked between the rubble.

"Well, I see a black cairn," Blays said. "Now where's the way up?"

Lira frowned at the cliffs. "Maybe we haven't gone far enough."

Dante reached for his pack. "There's another map, too. It agrees with the first. The passage is north of Blackcairn."

"Perhaps they were once right and are now wrong."

"Then there should be *something*. A cave-in. A rockslide that buried the trail. I haven't seen anything but blank walls."

Mourn scratched his beard. "Maybe we don't know what to look for."

To mollify his doubts, Dante headed south past Blackcairn, riding with Lira at a distance of two hundred feet from the cliffs while Blays and Mourn rode right beside the looming stone. After two hours and ten miles, Dante turned around and headed north again, passing Blackcairn. Cally had advised him to expect missteps, to do what he could and move on without allowing the weight of failure to sap his resolve. Yet Dante couldn't help the bitterness he felt, the inward-pointing knives, the hard knowledge he might have done more, and better. The trip started with such promise. After their success in Tantonnen, every day since felt squandered, a drunken chase after things beyond his understanding. How large was the world that so much of it felt like a foreign place?

"Here's something," Mourn called from beside the rubble of loose rocks footing the cliffs. "I mean, here are a lot of things. But here is something new to us."

Dante drove his horse through the grass and jumped to the ground. Mourn knelt, pointing at a clear print in the dirt, its edges rising from the hardened mud as steeply as the cliffs.

"You're sure that's not us?" Dante said.

"Not unless one of us snuck out here while the rest of us were on the road. This track is at least three days old."

"Can you say where it leads?"

Mourn shrugged at the slumped stones skirting the sheer face.

"Not without lying to you."

Blays swung down from his horse. "Here's a question. We're what, twenty miles from the road? What kind of idiot would come that far for nothing?"

"A very clever one." Dante slid into the shadows of second sight. Nether gleamed on the underside of leaves, winked from the gaps in the splay of broken rocks. Slowly as a flower follows the sun, he scanned the cliffside, feeling its silent face. Southward toward Blackcairn, at the edge of his vision, a deeper blackness rippled from the slaty rock.

"What?" Blays said. "You've got that look."

"What look?"

"Like you just heard Lady Swellchest has been widowed."

Lira turned from the cliffs. "Lady Swellchest?"

Dante slung himself atop his horse and trotted south. The nether set into the cliff was rectangular, dark as moonshadow. The size of a doorway. He dismounted and walked up to the shadows. He let his focus fade. The rectangle of nether disappeared, replaced by solid stone. He reached for the cliff. His hand disappeared into the wall.

Lira gasped. Blays laughed. Dante peered at the nether set into the cliff. The rectangle of false rock hung like a tapestry from three strands of shadows. He snipped them—one, two, three—and the nether collapsed like a watery blanket, oozing into the clutter of real rocks below. Where it had hung, a narrow staircase gaped from the face of the cliff.

"I'll stay with the horses," Mourn said.

Blays snorted. "Bravely volunteered."

"I'm not going up those stairs. My shoulders will get stuck. Along with all the rest of me. Then you'll have to cut off my arms, and I won't be able to do anything with the horses at all, except watch sadly as they flee into the wild."

"You're staying with the horses," Blays said.

Dante didn't bother asking Lira what she wanted to do. From his horse, he grabbed his sword and shitsack—which was not at all what the word suggested, but rather a highly portable bag of dry rations, extra waterskin, flint and steel, bandages, and other small necessities, a bundle Blays had named based on the word you'd yell while grabbing it up and running away—and made sure Mourn still had his loon.

"Speak up if anything strange happens," Dante said to the norren. "We'll let you know when we're on our way back."

"And just how fast we're retreating," Blays said.

The stairs were so narrow Dante's heels stuck past their edges. On the second step, he threw out his hands, convinced he was falling, then leaned forward and started up. The staircase turned 90 degrees, leaving him encased in dazzling blackness. His breathing echoed from walls which sometimes brushed both of his shoulders at once. Tingly heat flowed from his stomach. It smelled musty, dusty. It was perversely warm and humid. He fumbled for his torchstone. White light spilled over the darkness. The stairs seemed to widen, to fall away from his shoulders. He could breathe.

"Lost already?" Blays said behind him. "I suggest trying 'up.'"

Dante grinned. His nausea faded. He continued up. The stairs switchbacked every thirty vertical feet, each flight identical to those before and after. Was he certain the shroud of nether had been nothing more than an illusion of rock? What if it housed a doorway into another world composed entirely of this stairway? What if he lifted his foot from the final step and found himself back on the first?

A draft tickled his nose, wet and salty. He cornered another switchback and blinked against the faint light. He rubbed his thumb across the torchstone, extinguishing it; Blays yelped, then emerged into the diffuse sunlight, swords in hands. Around another turn, Dante faced a rectangle of gray light. He edged forward, shielding his eyes with the blade of his hand. He emerged from a massive black boulder onto a high, misty plain. Streamers of fog coursed between irregular pillars of black stone. Moss and short green shoots clung to ledges and faults. Water trickled down the weathered pillars, pooling in algal puddles. A frog sprung from Dante's path.

"We didn't just die, did we?" Blays said. "This is how I always pictured the fields of Arawn."

Dante shook his head. "The fields of Arawn have no sun. Only starlight."

"Remind me to die in another country," Lira said.

Somewhere above the mist, the sun hung in the west, reorienting Dante after the twisting passage up the steps. He headed the direction of the murky sun, keeping the nether close. Water dripped ceaselessly. Thumb-sized black birds flitted through the mist-scoured boulders. As Dante passed beneath a lintel of shrubs strung between two pillars, a centipede as long as his arm unspooled from the waxy leaves. He dropped back with a strangled gasp. Blays whacked it in half, leaving one end metronoming from the high shrubs while the other half smacked the ground and wriggled sinuously.

Blays wiped off his sword. "Maybe it's never been conquered because nobody wants the damn place."

"Remind me to never close my eyes again," Dante said.

Lira stepped around the writhing carcass. "When I signed on to protect you, I didn't imagine it would lead me to realms like this."

"Turn back whenever you want," Dante shrugged.

With a thick crunch, she stepped on the centipede's head. "Did I say I was scared?"

The going was hampered by puddles and slick rock and sudden bogs of mud. After an hour's travel, they might have made three miles. The flat highlands slanted down into slick soil loosely bound by flatulent-smelling clumps of kelpish plants. Dante's boots pulled and squelched. Despite the chill, a thin, clammy sweat glued his shirt to his back. A hundred feet downhill, more boulders loomed in the mist.

The shadows flickered. Mud slurped beneath Dante's foot. He stopped dead. "Run!"

He charged downhill, muck yanking at his feet. Blays and Lira smacked along behind him. The ground quivered, rumbling; uphill, a shelf of mud dislodged like a god slurping a crater of pudding. At first it flowed slower than their heavy, slogging steps, but soon gathered speed, a semi-solid tumble of mud and vines and death.

Dante stumbled, pitching forward, clawing at the mud while his momentum carried him forward. Somehow, he found his feet. The slope flattened. Pillars poked through the muck, misty and mossy. He dodged through the first line. A thirty-foot-high blade of rock stuck from the ground. He leapt against its face, palms tearing as he pulled himself up the slippery stone, muddy boots kicking for purchase. Ten feet up, he rolled onto a broad ledge and reached down to pull Blays up. Together, they hauled Lira up behind them.

With a deafening gurgle, the wave of mud hit the flats. Sludge poured between the boulders. Dante forced himself higher, nails scraping through the cushy moss. A stench of cold, damp rot engulfed him. He reached the crest of the ridge and flopped on his side, panting, feet dangling from the other side. Blays and Lira followed, soaked and muddy.

Mud burbled among the boulders, swallowing some whole. Stones ground and groaned. Dante wiped his hands on a patch of fuzzy green lichen.

"Gashen's bursting hemorrhoids," Blays said. "Got out of there just in time, didn't we?"

"Too soon for the liking of some," Dante said.

"Like who? The centipedes?"

Dante stood, wincing at the pain in his elbows and knees. The spar of rock was nearly four feet wide, but in the breeze-blown mist, he felt like he could fall at any moment. He cupped his hands to his mouth. "I know you're there!"

His shout died in the silent gray world. Blays sighed. "What do you think a centipede's voice sounds like, anyway? I'm thinking a raccoon choking on a rattlesnake's tail."

"Come out!" Dante hollered. "Before I make you find out what's at the bottom of this mud!"

Water trickled down the stones. On a rise of rock forty feet away, a woman materialized in the mist.

"Holy shit!" Blays said.

She gazed at them, motionless, dark hair framing her face. She smiled, raised one hand, her wrist wrapped in red, and waved. "Goodbye."

Black, mothlike force gathered in her hands. Dante's eyes went wide. He drew on the shadows, too, feeding them with the blood welling from his scraped hands. The woman tipped back her head, pausing her work.

Beside him, Lira held out both hands, palm down, and rolled

them at the wrist until her palms faced the sky. "Worlds within worlds."

The nether flowed away from the woman's hands. "What are you doing here?"

"We came to—" Dante snapped his mouth shut. In a rush, he understood. "We came to discover why Pocket Cove has never been invaded. But I suppose we can leave now."

The woman's red wrap fluttered around her wrist. "Do you find our world hostile?"

"Yes. And I've just figured out how you keep it that way."

"Unfortunate," she said. "Now that you know, you cannot leave."

"That's downright uncivilized," Blays called across the gap. "I feel so unwelcome, I think I might just turn around and go home!"

"Please come with me. What happens next is not for me to decide."

Blays dropped his voice. "Alternately, we kill her and run away before her friends come out to find what happened."

Lira gave him a dark look. "The People don't kill as indiscriminately as you. We should go with her."

Dante stared through the mist. It would be easy enough to turn back; the woman's hold on the nether was strong, but not strong enough to save her from what he could command. Still, though he knew *how* they protected their land, it wasn't the type of knowledge that would allow him to use their methods himself. He needed to know more.

"We'll come with you as friends," he said. "The kind of friends who don't try to kill each other."

The woman nodded and climbed off the edge of her ridge. Dante followed suit. The descent was much trickier than his terror-aided climb up, and he nearly slipped three times, banging his knee hard enough to draw blood. At the bottom, he lowered himself to the thick layer of mud. His boots sunk to the ankles, but he could walk.

The woman introduced herself as Asher and squelched west across the mud. Dante followed absently, lost in his second-sight, keen for any telltale glimmers of nether around her hands. Hard stone once again thumped beneath his boots.

"When have you met our people?" Asher asked Lira some time later. "Who taught you that sign?"

Lira didn't take her eyes from the misty horizon. "I grew up in the Carlon Islands. When I was old enough, I began hiring on ships as a swordsman. This lasted a few years. My final assignment was with the *Shadow*. It did a lot of business with your people."

"I know of the *Shadow*," Asher said. "I saw it just last fall."

"Good to know it survives. My last voyage with it was three years ago. It was the summer. We were meeting one of your vessels at Harl Island to buy all the barnwhelks it could carry."

"Barnwhelks?" Blays said.

Lira nodded. "Snails."

"*Snails?*"

"When fresh, or properly dried, they can be used to treat the venom of most other creatures of the sea," Asher said. "In most parts of your country, a handful of barnwhelks will buy you a household."

"New idea," Blays said. "We forget all this slave business and become snail-hunters instead."

"This is enough about snails," Asher said. "You were saying?"

Lira stepped around a knee-high swell of slick black rock. "We were on the piers finishing the exchange when the pirates struck. The Eyeteeth Gang. We were outnumbered—grossly. Those of us with blades went to the docks to hold them off while the *Shadow* and the People of the Pocket shoved off. We managed to hold them off just long enough. Most of my fellows fell. I tried to fight to the death, but the Eyeteeth took me instead.

"They wanted to know where the *Shadow* had gone, as well as the vessel of the People of the Pocket. I didn't tell them."

Asher's expression darkened. "What did it cost you?"

Lira pulled back her lips and pointed at the gaps where her eyeteeth had been. Dante looked away. He'd assumed they'd been lost to simple rot.

"Those," she said, "as well as two of my toes, and all my toenails."

"But you didn't speak."

Lira shook her head. "I was sworn to protect the *Shadow*."

Asher cocked her head. "But not the people they did business with."

"Revealing the People of the Pocket's destination could have compromised the *Shadow*'s location. In any event, it would have compromised the *Shadow*'s interests, and would have been a violation of the spirit if not the letter of my vow. After a few days, the Eyeteeth knew my cause was lost. They readied to kill me.

"But a few days was all the time the People of the Pocket needed to return. The Eyeteeth had taken several of their crew as well. The People's nethermancers wiped them out. They would have killed me, too, for what I had seen, but a woman named Istvell had seen me keep my tongue throughout it all. She gave her name for me. I was saved."

Asher held her hands out palm-down and rolled her wrists until her palms pointed at the fog-matted skies. "And she showed you worlds within worlds."

"She showed me worlds within worlds," Lira nodded.

"That is why you're here with me and not back there beneath one hundred feet of mud."

"I don't think that's the only reason," Dante muttered.

Asher smiled as coldly as the mist. For the next two hours, they walked in silence through the sweating stones. The sun waned, its fog-blocked glare drifting toward the horizon. The mist thinned abruptly. They stood on black cliffs above light blue seas, rhythmic waves hissing over a beach of black sand. Asher crossed to a doorway carved into the side of a rocky mound. White light blossomed in her hand. She led them down another long, enclosed stairwell, emerging from the bottom into the pink rays of sunset.

Lira took a long breath of salty air through her nose. "Have outsiders ever seen this?"

"Sometimes." Asher walked south across the strand. "Then they are given the choice to stop being outsiders or stop being alive."

To the north, a spectral call of *oot oot oot* floated down the shore. Asher's feet whispered on the sand. Down the beach, a proper door opened into the cliffside. Asher opened it, revealing a high tunnel lit with the unblinking white glare of torchstones. Their feet echoed in the closed space. Laughter rang down the halls. Asher turned down two side passages, stopping in front of a door made from something papery and semi-translucent.

"Please don't leave this spot." She opened the door, revealing mounds of blankets and white light, then closed it with a whisper. Low voices seeped through the thin door. She returned a minute later and gestured them inside.

On the far side of the stone room, a woman sat on a pile of blankets, her black hair shot through with gray. She wore snug, featureless black clothes and a red scarf on her wrist, which fluttered as she gestured to the blanket across from her. Dante sat, trying not to gape. Nether rolled from her like heat from a stove. She did nothing with it—in fact, she didn't even appear to have summoned it—but he could feel it nonetheless, a dark ocean he'd never felt from anyone besides Cally himself.

"Please tell me what you know," she said. "Please don't try to lie."

Dante forced himself to meet her eyes. "All I have are guesses."

"Then kindly tell me what you guess."

"The cliffs keep most out. I don't know whether you shaped them or simply found them useful. When armies came, you buried the soldiers in mud or sand until they stopped coming at all. If even that doesn't work, you seal off your caves and leave the invaders to wonder where you've gone."

She gave him a look as sturdy as the walls. As stony, too. "Where are you from?"

"Narashtovik."

"Is Narashtovik still a possession of Gask?"

He risked a short laugh. "Not for long, though our independence might be as short-lived as a dayfly. The king will march on us soon. I came here to learn how you've resisted every army that's come your way—in the hopes we might do the same."

She nodded, gazing toward the ceiling. "I see. Every people should rule themselves, if ruling themselves is what they want to do."

Dante leaned forward. "Then you'll teach me how to move the earth?"

"Of course not," she laughed. "I'm afraid we don't give a shit. Why do you think we're behind these great black walls?"

Dante blinked. "But we have a common enemy. If you help us,

you help yourself."

Her brows lifted as slowly as a sunrise. "They're not my enemies. Enemies can only be enemies if they have the ability to hurt you."

"I'll swear on anything never to tell. Never to use it against you. Why are you the only ones with the right to defend yourselves?"

"We aren't. But we are the only ones with the right to our secrets, if you please." She leaned back, folding her hands in her lap so her fingers overlapped at a right angle.

Helpless fury rose in Dante's throat. He wanted to shake her until the knowledge popped right out her throat. What she knew could change the world. Could forge him into a weapon every bit as strong as the Quivering Bow. To deny him that felt not just heartless, but monstrous.

"This isn't just for my sake." He fought to control his voice. "This is for the entire norren people. King Moddegan will cross their lands before he gets to us. And he doesn't consider them human."

"I sympathize. That's why I'm letting you leave. Which I urge you to please do now." She shut her eyes.

Asher detached from the wall. "I will take you back to your land, please."

"It's time for us to go," Lira said softly.

Dante wanted to scream. Instead, he stood. Asher took a torchstone on her way out. It lit their way across the twilit beach, up the stairs, and across the miles of misty plateau. They crossed the last hour under full cover of night, their path through the rocks and mud lit only by an unseen moon and the lunarly glow of the torchstone. Dante stayed silent all the way to the staircase back down to the plains.

Asher halted there atop the carpet of broken rocks. "Please don't come back."

"But you've been so helpful," Dante said.

"Worlds within worlds," Lira waved.

Asher nodded. "Worlds within worlds."

She disappeared up the staircase. Mourn's fire flickered in the grass. Dante didn't speak on the way there. As Mourn rose to greet them, a crackling, banging rumble rolled from the cliffs.

Dante whirled. Rocks and dust sprayed from the black wall. The remains of the staircase crumbled to the plains in a pile of rough shards.

13

The plains rolled away, the same empty miles they'd crossed just days before. Dante let Blays and Lira fill Mourn in on what had happened in the Pocket. He pushed his horse until it sweated and heaved. The return to Wending and the lakes of Gallador was their last chance to stave off the coming strife. He resolved not to fail.

A day's ride from the western peaks of the rift, he pulsed Cally's loon. The old man answered at once. Dante related the details of their trip to the cove, expecting Cally to respond with derision and complaints, but he turned thoughtful instead.

"So they make the land do their dirty work for them," Cally mused. "Wish I'd thought of that one."

"Can you move the earth?"

"If I kick it hard enough."

Dante sighed. "Do you have any idea how it's done?"

"Oh, I have *ideas*," Cally said. "You could plant a rock beneath a stick holding up a giant vat of mud, and then use the nether to crack the rock. But it sounds like the People of the Pocket are a smidge more sophisticated than that."

"I get the feeling they could carve a statue of you without lifting a finger."

"Interesting that you put it in those terms. For the most part, we think of the nether as a brute force, a thing that roughly grabs or bludgeons. An extension of our arm, perhaps, if our arms were made of large hammers. Yet they seem to have precise command of the ground. Are they using finer tools? Or are they employing a different approach altogether? Maybe they're literally convincing the earth to move!"

"I know this much," Dante said. "They're skilled. Highly. I'd love to see a fight between their leader and you."

"I don't get in *fights*. I have far too much dignity for that." Cally coughed up something wet and substantial. "Speaking of squabbles, the norren haven't been quick to leap into one. None of the clans, towns, or individuals of interest have officially defied the treaty."

"Oh? And how many of them have officially fied it?"

"Few," he admitted. "Still, it's reason for hope, if hope is something you find useful."

It was, as much as Dante might like to deny it. The following morning, he took to the road with something like a smile. White caps rested on the green mountains. A light haze softened the world, muting the early morning light. His horse stepped lightly. They climbed into the pass where a forest of bamboo sliced the sunlight into a thousand yellow wedges. The snows had retreated to isolated patches of blue-white shade, leaving the ground sodden and soft. The haze burned away by the time they crested the pass. Below, the lake of Gallador glittered like the land's most precious gem.

A warm spring wind followed them into Wending. They stabled beside the docks and rowed to Lolligan's. The old man answered the door himself. He smiled, but it didn't reach his eyes.

"And how are the People of the Pocket?" he said. "Do their eyes really glow red? Is the lightning that shoots from their ass lethal, or just part of the show?"

"They're creepy," Blays said. "If the rest of the world dropped dead, their only complaint would be the stink."

"Wait, you actually *met* them?"

Dante rolled his eyes. "And gained nothing from it. What about here? Has anyone's mind budged an inch?"

Lolligan's tanned brow wrinkled. "Been a lot of talk. Even by the standards of people who do nothing but talk."

"Good talk?"

"Not by your standards." Lolligan glanced from his doorway, as if expecting to spot men in black masks lurking in the bushes. "I get the idea the Association isn't as unified as Jocubs wants you to think."

Dante locked eyes with the mustached man. "What gives you that idea?"

"The king's treaty proved that if they want to move against it, they need to do it now. Yet they haven't. I think there are some war-hawks in the TAGVOG, and their strategy is to do nothing but stall until there's nothing that can be done."

"Then we'll have to force the issue," Dante said. "Do you have any paper? I think it's time to send Jocubs a letter."

Blays gasped. "Are you sure you want to be that bold? What will people *say*?"

Inside, Dante penned a brief letter in his finest hand, blotted the ink, and sealed it with a dab of black wax. Lolligan's boatman rowed away to Jocubs' isle. He returned in less than an hour with a letter of his own. An invitation to another dinner two days later.

Dante sent out his clothes to be washed. Went into town for a haircut and shave. Had his boots resoled and relaced. He spent the remaining time hanging around tea houses in the fancier districts, trolling for gossip and insight. The former was torrential; the latter, a dribble. One rumor stated that Jocubs would marry his first daughter and the fortune that came with her to Moddegan's second son if only the king revoked the treaty in favor of peace. Simultaneously, another claimed Jocubs would raise the army himself if Moddegan *didn't* lead his country to battle. Others claimed Moddegan was coming to town in person to rally support for his cause. The one thing they all agreed on was that the future looked uncertain, and that uncertainty was bad for anyone currently doing well.

The night and morning before the dinner, Dante sequestered himself in his room at Lolligan's, drafting speeches to hit this point home. By definition, every one of the merchants at the event would be a successful man or woman. A few of them might secretly hope to benefit from the upheaval. Most, however, would suffer. A few might lose it all. Wars were costly things. If Moddegan's silver started to dwindle, no one knew who he might turn to for aid—and what threats he'd make to ensure he got it.

Dante finished with hours to spare. He spent them bathing away the salt and grime of the trail. At the pier, he was surprised to see Blays had done the same. Their boat pushed off, Jocubs-bound. At the chairman's island, rowboats and sailboats clustered around the docks, which creaked with men and women in bright skirts and fur coats. They milled into the banquet hall, where servants stood ready with platters and crystal glasses.

Jocubs' avuncular laughter rolled across the room. Dante could barely see him behind the swarm of men and women vying for his word. Dante slid along the picture windows, maneuvering closer, accepting a servant's offer of wine and a pastry smeared with farmer's cheese and baked trout. He recognized many of the men and women from the prior event, and he smiled and chatted with them while he waited for a break in Jocubs' admirers. The room smelled of tea and woodsmoke and charred pepper-pike.

Dante caught his break an hour later. Beside Jocubs, a merchant's young wife tipped back her head, laughing without reserve, her cleavage soaring. Heads turned. Dante wedged himself next to Jocubs, whose winglike eyebrows were raised in amusement. Seeing Dante, he smiled warmly.

"I'm glad to see you made it back from the west with no loss of limbs or sanity."

Dante smiled back. "There was nothing there but grass and cliffs. The only risk was being winded to death."

"Ah, is it windy there? It's been unseasonably warm here. Good seasons ahead, I think." Jocubs scuffed his feet left, right, left, smiling apologetically at his own superstition.

"And how did the time treat Gallador? Does this dinner mean you've reached a decision?"

Jocubs turned to the window, smiling at some distant peak. "After we eat, good man. We wouldn't want to put anyone off their meal."

Dante found himself subtly replaced by a whip-thin man with a triangular mustache and a hungry eye. He let himself be pried away, and was soon engaged by a man he'd met at the last quorum, the youngish one with the widow's peak and knowing smile, who reintroduced himself as Ewell.

"Ever figure out the cost?" Ewell said.

Dante cocked his head. "The cost?"

"Of striking this bargain."

"Besides precious days of my life?" Dante gazed at the burbling crowd. "I think they're still figuring the price out for themselves."

"How strange," Ewell said. "You don't tease a hungry fish. You just drop your hook."

"Have you heard—?" Dante's breath left him in a groaning whoosh as Blays drove his elbow into his side. In the same instant, the crowd went silent as a fog. Several glanced Dante's way with looks as if he'd farted in their soup.

"We're ruined," Blays hissed. "They've played us from the start."

Dante rubbed his ribs. "What are you yammering about?"

"Stand up on those delicate little toes of yours and look."

All the room's attention had turned to a door in the far wall. Dante craned his neck, but couldn't see past the well-fed wall of traders. He shuffled to one side until he found a gap in the quiet crowd. Across the room, a young man with a striking jaw and severely cropped blond hair strolled up to a smiling Jocubs. As if sensing Dante's gaze, Cassinder turned, met his eyes, and smiled.

Fear and fury fought for Dante's heart. Jocubs cleared his throat in a way that was somehow humble yet piercing. The mounting murmur stopped cold.

"Today, we are graced by a man whose name speaks itself," Jocubs said. "We are happy to have him. Honored, too. I introduce Lord Cassinder of Beckonridge."

Cassinder smiled thinly at the floor. "I'm happy to be here. It means good things to know I am welcome. I thought that might not be so." He paused, still smiling. Someone coughed. A glass clinked. Cassinder went on as if there'd been no stop at all. "Turmoil is frightening. I wouldn't have blamed you for questioning the king. But wealth depends on labor. Labor depends on loyalty. You prune an unruly hedge for its own health. This takes work. Sweat. Blood, if there are thorns. But when you are done, the hedge grows back. It takes the shape you have imposed on it." He looked up, smile stretched to the breaking point. "I am glad to garden together."

Light applause accompanied the nodding heads of the crowd. Dante bulled his way forward, shouldering tea-lords and their stately wives until he stood face to face with Jocubs. The merchant buried his smile and nodded discreetly to the door. Dante followed him out to his enclosed deck. Sunlight bounced from the lake, shimmering on the walls. The room was warm and smelled of drying mussels.

"I'm sorry," Jocubs said simply. "Things happened very fast."

"'Things'?" Dante said. "Is that how you pronounce 'betrayal' in Wending?"

Jocubs gazed down on Dante from beneath the lintels of his brows. "This isn't personal. This is a matter of pragmatism."

"It's going to be pretty gods damned personal to all the norren who die!"

"Do you think we gave that no thought? We gleaned the palace intended to enforce the king's will through any means necessary. We used what leverage we could to convince them to take the targeted approach. A barber's knife instead of a farmer's scythe."

Dante closed his eyes. His head hummed. "Everything could have been different."

Jocubs laid a warm hand on his shoulder. "I'm truly sorry. We're all doing what we can."

Dante pulled away and headed through the muffled hallway to get Blays. The banquet hall was a screeching riot of laughter and wheedling and clawing hands. He struggled through the hot crush of people and found Blays watching the room from one of the walls.

He grabbed Blays' sleeve. "We're leaving."

"Sure you don't want to leave our noble friend with a tap to the jaw? You never know. He might like it."

"Only if we follow it up with a stab to the neck."

"Hello," Cassinder said behind them. Dante spun. The lord smiled his thin smile. "You've changed shape since I saw you. Weren't you a Mallish merchant before?"

"We upgraded," Blays said. "How's the home?"

"Rebuilding quickly. Norren backs are strong. Untiring."

Dante jerked his chin to the milling merchants. "How long have you been involved in this?"

Cassinder gave him a glassy look. "Since always. Money makes men forget themselves. My place is to remind them of theirs."

Dante leaned in until their faces were inches apart. Cassinder's breath smelled of mint and wine. "Funny. I sometimes remind people it is everyone's place to die."

The man laughed softly. "I could have you arrested right now."

"Go for it," Blays said. "If I'm going to the irons, I might as well kill you now and get my money's worth."

"Not while there's better to come," Cassinder said. "I believe in choice. I believe you will choose foolishly. I will laugh when you're hanged."

Dante turned away before his clenching hands found the man's throat. As he knifed through the throng, he found a note in his hand, as if it had always been there. He glanced from side to side. Men laughed in each other's faces. Blays shoved his back, propelling him forward. Dante clutched the note and stuffed his hand into his pocket. Blays didn't stop pushing him until they dropped down the front steps on their way to the docks.

Dante scowled against the afternoon sunlight. "Will you quit shoving already?"

"You had that *other* look," Blays explained. "The one where happy people are about to become sad little cinders."

Dante had too much to say, so he unfolded the note instead. It was short as an oracle, composed of blocky capitals: "COHBEN INN. ROOFTOP. MIDNIGHT."

He handed it to Blays, who a few short years ago couldn't even read his native Mallish, but had picked up the Gaskan script as soon as he bothered to try.

"Someone gave me this on the way out," Dante said.

Blays smoothed the paper against his palm. "Well, we're doing this."

"What if it's a trap?"

"Then we reprimand whoever's trying to trap us."

Dante glanced at the boatmen patrolling the dock with buckets and mops. "It's just like Lolligan said. They were stringing us along while playing the capital on the other end."

"Very rude. Rudeness that should be punished."

"We'll see what our mysterious messenger has to say tonight. Beyond that, it may be time to head home."

Blays grinned ruefully. "This trip didn't go too well, did it?"

"We got the norren some food. No one can speak ill of food."

"Unless it's pickled."

They returned to Lolligan's. Dante gave a brief account to the others. Mourn's face darkened behind his beard. Lira nodded stoically.

Fann looked crestfallen. "These men speak too much, don't they? I am beginning to believe a man only talks at length when he doesn't want you to know what he really thinks."

"I had a bad feeling the last few days," Lolligan said. "I'm sorry it came to this."

Dante's anger had left him too hollowed out for anything to do anything besides take a nap. Blays left to scout out the Cohben Inn. Dante woke in darkness, as refreshed as if he'd had a good long cry. The servants had saved him some supper, whitefish and bamboo shoots in a thick gravy of mashed onions and chilies. The spice drove the last of his sleepiness away.

"Pretty typical inn," Blays reported. "Places to drink and places to sleep."

"How far?"

"Thirty minute walk from the landing. Figured we'd put Mourn and a bow on a roof across the street, Lira in the alley below. You know how I like to be able to run if things turn nasty."

Dante nodded, wiping his spice-dripping nose. "How's the neighborhood?"

"Horrible? Would that be the word? I wouldn't be surprised if the mattresses were stuffed with corpses."

"That's not very practical. You'd have to change them out every month at least."

Blays brushed crumbs from the table. "I think you're overestimating the quality of the service in this inn."

They borrowed plain dark clothing from Lolligan's servants and left a minute after eleven. The city docks were quiet, gentle waves lapping over the pebbles. Blays led them uphill through whitewashed rowhouses and tidily clipped parks. Soon the walls turned unpainted, weather-chapped; the green lawns disappeared in favor of raked stone and individual trees. A three-quarter moon lit snaking alleys and haphazard homes attached to and built on top of much older stone structures. The few windows that weren't shuttered were glassless holes opening on dim rooms. On the corners, men sat on chairs, exposed to the wind, swigging from leather flasks. A whole crew of sailors reeled past, singing a rhythmic song that was either about oars or penises. Torches fluttered from the more ambitious inns and pubs. Otherwise, the streets were dark as a closet.

The Cohben Inn's only identification was two sticks of bamboo crossed above its crooked doorway. Like everything in the neighborhood, it was wedged between two other unornamented structures, but it stood a floor taller than anything within several blocks.

"Not sure how much use Mourn's going to be as a sniper when he can't cover the roof," Dante said.

Blays shrugged. "We'll stand on our tiptoes. See if we can't convince whoever we're meeting to do the same."

He led them across the street into the kinking alley behind the buildings that faced the Cohben. Washlines webbed the space between the upper floors. Ramshackle decks jutted below shuttered windows. Pots clogged these platforms, sporting yellow sticks of withered plants. The walls were winter-warped wood, poorly chinked.

"Think you can make it up?" Dante said.

Mourn tipped back his shaggy head. "There's a chance I do and a chance I don't."

Blays stared at him. "Is there even a point to saying things like that?"

"You don't think it's important to remember that everything's uncertain?"

"When I'm climbing a roof, I want to be convinced there's *zero* chance my brains wind up slopped all over the street."

"Well, to each his own," Mourn said. "I will do my best. If I don't make it, I'll yell. Involuntarily, I suspect."

This was good enough for Dante. He watched the rooftops as they moved to the alleys behind the Cohben, which were more or less the same as the backstreet they'd left Mourn in, except they smelled somewhat worse of urine. Recessed doorways stood in the faces of nearly every building, as if the passage had been specifically designed to hide armed lookouts. Lira chose one halfway down the alley and disappeared into its shadows.

"I can't imitate a bird call to save my life," she said. "Or your life, for that matter. So if there's trouble, I'll yell, too."

"Works for me." Blays stepped toward the inn's back door, then glanced back over his shoulder. "And thanks."

Her teeth flashed in the darkness. Blays tried the door, which opened with a squeak and a shudder. The public room was smoky, the product of a chimney that hadn't been swabbed in ages. A group of men rattled dice at a table. The walls were scrawled with carved initials and symbols, mostly animals and body parts. Dante rented the last available room on the top floor and clumped up the stairs.

His room was tight-walled and all too redolent of the alley's stink. He locked the door behind them and swung open the shutters. Blays poked his head out the glassless window and gaped upwards. "These are the stupidest roofs I've ever seen."

Dante leaned out the window. Above, the eaves flared away from the roof's edge. "Maybe they were built to discourage people from walking on roofs. No one has ever walked on a roof for a socially acceptable reason."

"We're not committing a crime here."

"Yes, but if we're meeting at midnight on a roof in the shitty part of town, chances are we'll be conspiring to do so."

"Right now I'm more interested in conspiring not to break my leg." Blays pulled inside and knelt to paw through his pack, emerging with a steel hook and a line of rope as thin as his finger. He lobbed the hook up at the roof, hanging onto the rope's loose end. The hook screeched over the clay and fell down, banging against the shutters below them. Blays swore, then repeated this exact sequence a half dozen times while Dante gritted his teeth and listened for the angry thump of the innkeeper's boots on the stairs. Finally, the hook secured with a clink. Blays yanked to make sure it was secure, then knotted the loose end around the shutter's lower hinges. As casually as if he were hopping off a step, he swung into the open air and scrambled up the rope. Dante gaped up after him.

"Come on, you sissy," Blays stage-whispered from the roof. "What's the worst that could happen?"

"Dying?"

"Only if you have overcooked-noodle arms."

Dante reached for the rope. "I wonder what's killed more men over the years. Wild animals? Or masculine taunts?"

It looked worse than it was. Though he lacked Blays' natural athleticism, years of travel and sporadic sword-practice had left him honed and lean. He pulled himself up hand over hand. When his elbow cleared the eave's lip, Blays grabbed his sleeve and hauled him in. There, the upturned edges of the roof proved beneficial, giving them something to bang into and grab hold of if they were to slip on the dew-slick tiles.

Blays leaned forward and headed up the steep roof on all fours. On the other side of its peak, the roof plateaued in a shelf some three feet wide. Blays slid down to it and Dante followed, seating himself. The flat stone street waited sixty feet below. The midnight bells tolled while he caught his breath. He squinted at the roofs across the street, but it was too dark to see if Mourn had made it to the top.

The bells rang a final time, were overtaken by silence. Blocks away, a man cackled and whooped, his voice bouncing down the streets.

"Think Cassinder's pranking us?" Blays said.

"I don't think he has the imagination."

"Right?" Blays laughed. "He talks like a dead person trying to remember how it felt to be alive."

A voice murmured behind them. "He's more dangerous than you think."

Dante whirled, tipping. He flung out a palm and caught at the roof. A figure crouched just behind the roof's peak, dressed from head to toes in midnight blue. Eyes peeked from two diamond-shaped cuts.

"My gods," Blays said. "Have we been ambushed by a towel?"

The fabric over the figure's mouth puffed with a single laugh. The laugh was a woman's. "This is no ambush."

"That's good, because we've prepared an elaborate counter-ambush that would wreak terrible harm on any real ambushers."

She shook her head. "This is a proposal."

"But we just met."

Dante almost shoved Blays off the roof. "Propose away."

The woman slipped over the peak of the roof, joining them on the narrow shelf. "Do you know what happened at Jocubs' today?"

"Sure," Blays said. "We got royally screwed."

"Jocubs represented the view of a slender minority," the woman said.

"Then what does the fat majority say?" Dante said.

Behind her cloth mask, the woman's look was unreadable. "That he struck a deal. One that will benefit him and those with him at the top. Everyone below will have to scramble to avoid the coming flood."

Dante shifted his weight across the wet tiles. "Then what are you willing to risk to divert the flood altogether?"

"That depends on what you're willing to risk to help us."

"Easy answer. We've already risked everything."

"Support for the capital hinges entirely on Jocubs' ability to whip the others in line." Her eyes were as gray as a winter sea and steady as the streets sixty feet below. "But no one likes the lash. Jocubs doesn't look out for our interests any more than he manages yours—he used you, leveraged your presence to get Setteven's financiers to give him everything he asked. I'm sure the terms were fat, too. But he favors his friends. When a road charges a new toll, he doesn't pay. The taxes on whatever blend of leaves he happens to be growing never rise. Whatever deal he's struck with Moddegan and Cassinder, most of us will never see it. Our words and our votes don't matter. As long as he's in charge, they never will."

"Is this going where I think it's going?" Blays said.

"What's the solution?" Dante said.

"Very simple," the woman said. "If you want the merchants' backing, all you have to do is kill Jocubs dead."

14

A cold wind flowed over the roof. Dante rubbed his mouth. "Why don't you kill him yourselves?"

The woman's mask shifted in a smile. "So you'll be blamed."

Blays laughed. "Well, that's honest."

"Who do you work for?" Dante said.

"Change," she said. "That's all you need to know."

Blays sniffled against the cold. "Generally, I prefer to do a little thinking before committing to an assassination. How can we reach you?"

"Hang a flag from Lolligan's roof. White for no, black for yes. Our offer expires at this time tomorrow."

"We'll let you know," Dante said.

She nodded and vaulted over the roof's peak, disappearing with a single clink of tiles. Dante climbed up the roof, slid down to where their hook still clung to the eaves, and shimmied down to the open window. Half an hour had passed since they'd taken their room. On their way out into the alley, the innkeeper gave them a funny look.

Lira's silhouette emerged from a doorway. "Someone vaulted across the rooftops a few minutes after you climbed up. They left the same way less than five minutes later."

"Sounds right," Dante said. He cut across the main street and back into the alley where they'd left Mourn.

"So what happened?" Lira said.

"Bad things," Blays said.

"But you look fine."

"Oh, not for us."

"All this coyness is getting old." There was a sharpness to her voice Dante hadn't heard before. "The less you let me know, the less I can help you take your goals."

"You'll hear it when we explain to Mourn and Lolligan." Dante cupped his hands and hissed up at the dark walls of the alley. "Mourn!"

"I exist," Mourn replied faintly. A foot scuffed high above their heads. Mourn lowered himself from a high balcony, stretching his toes to meet the deck a story below, clinging to a clothesline for support. He reached the ground, nodded to himself, and joined them without a single question. Dante headed toward the docks, staring down every man who glanced his way, looking over his shoulder at every scrape of foreign feet.

At the island manor, Lolligan opened the front door himself, too bright-eyed to have slept. He sent a servant for tea and bread and fish spread.

"The later the meeting, the more interesting it tends to be, eh?" The tradesman smiled, beard ruffling. "Now spill it before I drop dead of anticipation."

For a moment, Dante considered lying, or claiming it was too sensitive a matter to discuss—he'd only met Lolligan a couple weeks ago, and there had always been an eagerness to the old man that suggested he was pursuing submerged angles of his own—but right now, he had no choice. He needed Lolligan's knowledge. He had to trust him.

The story didn't take long to tell. By the end, a strange smile had worked its way across Lolligan's face.

"This is funny to you?" Dante finished.

Lolligan's eyebrows jumped. "In a way that's wry and sad. Over the years, there's been more than one attempt to dislodge Jocubs from his perch atop the swappole. Nothing ever changed. It's like corking up a tea kettle—and now the pot has burst."

"So this is real? They actually want Jocubs dead?"

"I'm positive all kinds of people want that old son of a bitch dead. I wouldn't be at all surprised if someone were finally willing to do something drastic. I'll ask around tomorrow."

Lira's mouth had been half open all the while. She glanced around the padded benches where they sat. "Are you seriously considering this? *Murdering* him?"

"I don't think we have another option," Dante said.

"Yes you do. The option to not murder him."

"I'm going to choose to not choose that," Blays said.

She set down her tea and stared at Blays. "You, too?"

"Don't look at me like that. I won't *enjoy* it. Unless we make him slip in a puddle or something."

"You can't just kill a man for disagreeing with you."

"Really?" Blays said. "Isn't that what all killing is about? Who's going to stop us?"

Her lips contracted to a tight line. "*You* should. You should know better. Warriors don't stab each other in their beds. The same is true if you're fighting in the field or in a council hall."

"This is simple calculus," Dante said. "If we kill him, one man dies. If we leave him be, thousands of norren will be killed and enslaved."

"You don't know that." She stood from her bench, pacing the snug room. "None of us knows the future. The only certainty is death. That's why we must always act in life in a way that will make us proud in death."

Blays slurped the last of his tea. "I'd be pretty proud if we cut this fight off at the roots."

"This has worked for us before," Dante said. He gazed at his hands. "It isn't pretty. But sometimes it's necessary."

"Decisions like these are what define you." Lira crossed her arms and turned to the door. "I don't think I want to be part of this."

"Then it's time for you to make a choice," Dante said. "This is who we are. When we need to, this is what we do. If that's not you, you can leave at any time. Nothing's keeping you here."

"Except my honor." With her back to them, she turned her head over one shoulder. "But I suppose you'd only laugh at that."

"Of course not," Blays said. "Not while you're standing right there."

Mourn cleared his throat with a thunderous rumble. "I don't think anyone will judge you for going your own way."

The room was silent. Lira nodded twice, as if to herself, and retook her seat. "I may yet. But if Jocubs has in fact betrayed us, then it is our right to take revenge."

Dante lifted his eyebrows reached for his loon. "Guess I'd better raise Cally."

"Why in the world would you do that?" Blays said.

"Because he's in charge of this whole thing?"

"Do you think we're making the right decision?"

"Not really, no, but I figure we haven't destabilized a region's governing body recently, so we better go ahead with it anyway."

Blays rolled his eyes. "Well, what's Cally going to say? Either 'Yes, go ahead and do that thing you were already planning to do,' or 'No, that's so dumb that if it were a person it would forget what food is for—and if you do it after I've told you not to, I'll wear your skin for socks.' Would that actually stop us? What's the point?"

"When you put it like that? I guess there isn't one." Dante turned to Lolligan. "Find out if this is real, then. And ready the black flag."

Dante's attempts to sleep through the morning were thwarted by a steady clamor of boatsmen hollering their approach, knocks on the front door, and storms of laughter drifting from the rooms below. It sounded as if half the merchants of greater Gallador had spontaneously decided to pay Lolligan a visit. Dante didn't need to be told the truth: that they'd been invited over so Lolligan could determine whether they were serious about wanting to murder the leader of their order.

This being the case, Dante spent most of the day in his room, venturing out only to visit the kitchen or one of the bathrooms that emptied into the lake. Instead, he read passages from Lolligan's copy of *The Cycle of Arawn*, which was a more recent translation than the one they favored in Narashtovik, and a firsthand account of the Rafting Wars, an 800-year-old conflict fought between the long-ago tribes of Gallador's lakes. Contrary to the title, these back-and-forth raids had primarily featured canoes and outrigger sailboats—the few bamboo rafts employed by increasingly desperate warriors had proven difficult to control and easy to destroy. Yet rather than accepting repeated offers of peace, the three tribes who'd used the quick-to-build rafts had pushed on until the very end, provoking their rivals into a final counterstrike that had left every man, woman, and child of the three tribes dead. Dante finished just after sunset and wandered his room, contemplating another trip to the kitchen even though he wasn't hungry. As he considered whether there was any meaning to the extinct tribes' steadfast refusal to quit fighting, Lolligan knocked on the other side.

"I couldn't exactly ask them outright," the merchant said. "For the same reasons, they couldn't answer outright either. But the offer is legit."

"How do you know?" Dante said.

"Their anger. It felt genuine. Real enough to hold on to."

"Got anything more concrete than that?"

"Possibly." Lolligan touched the points of his mustache, swaying absently from foot to foot. "I saw my friend Ulwen today. She's a good woman. Harvests bamboo from the mountains. There's a lot you can do with bamboo. Chairs. Chicken coops. Interior doors, if you're not too picky. You can even eat it, if you cut off the right parts and boil it long enough. No one else bothers with it on a large scale, because they think bamboo is just for those too poor to afford stone or hardwood, but that's exactly what makes it worth Ulwen's while. Two decades of bamboo has earned her a small fortune. Her vision is just what the TAGVOG needs. But because her fortune's small, and her product isn't one they use or favor, the TAGVOG will never make Ulwen more than a peripheral member."

"Everyone's frustrated with their position sometimes," Dante said. "Their solution usually isn't murder. Unless they're in the Assassins' Guild."

"That isn't what tipped me off. That's the context behind the story she told me. A story everyone in Gallador already knows." Lolligan pointed to the history book on Dante's table. "Did you read that?"

"It was fascinating. It's hard to imagine a time so long ago."

"After that war, the tribes held a few more, and then discovered everyone else in the world seemed to want our tea, too. So instead of raiding each other's villages, we came together to raid the world's coffers. The city of Wending began to take shape. To keep order, it was decided to elect a tyrant every three years. One man who had to be obeyed no matter what your tribal or familial loyalties. This system had its snags, but it worked smoothly for several generations. Until the election of a man named Kayman.

"Kayman was a teaman. Self-made. Worked for years as a sailor and bodyguard, then started his own farm, wound up one of the wealthiest men on the lake. Everyone loves a man like that. When he ran for tyrant, he was elected easily. At that time, the lakes and their cities all flew different flags. They all had their own tolls and taxes and regulations about what could come in and what could go out. To Kayman, this was terribly inefficient. Just as easily as he'd bought out the farms that made his fortune, he spent the next three years conquering, absorbing, and allying with every town, tribe, and county on the lakes. For the first time, Gallador was united.

"He went unopposed in the next election. Not too surprising. Nor all that surprising when he announced his plans to annex the eastern plains. Some people thought it would be easy—just nomads thataways, they'll run right off—but others weren't so sure. Regardless, Kayman sent a legion over the mountains. Presumably, it was a disaster."

"Presumably?"

Lolligan nodded. "Gallador never heard from them again, but who knows. Maybe the soldiers all deserted and married five wives apiece and lived very happy lives. Again, regardless, Kayman assembled an even larger force. This time, his doubters outnumbered his supporters, but what could they do? He'd been elected. Still, the lakes had been weakened in the wars of unification. So far as they knew, the first legion had been massacred to the last man, and Kayman's second wave was only three times as large. A few of the nobles feared another loss would leave us helpless against a counterattack. They held a meeting to decide whether to assassinate Kayman. After the meeting, they held a vote. Do you know what happened then?"

Dante hunched his shoulders. "They killed the hell out of him?"

"They left him be. They let him march into the east. His army was destroyed. The nomads, having enough, sent back a force of their own late in the summer. Gallador was theirs by winter. A hundred years later, Narashtovik conquered the nomads and Gallador too, and another hundred years after *that*, some upstart barbarians from the western woods destroyed Narashtovik and took Gallador for themselves. We've been owned by outsiders ever since." Lolligan rubbed his throat. "That's the story my friend Ulwen told me. The story every citizen of Gallador knows."

"I suppose that's convincing enough," Dante said.

"Also, after that, she told me she and some others had been setting aside a fund for years, and were ready to hire three hundred mercenaries from around the lakes as soon as the black flag flies."

Dante didn't know whether to laugh or strangle him. "They've got a private army in the works? You left that until the end because why?"

Lolligan smiled sharply, spreading his fingers wide. "Because that is how a salesman closes the deal. Are you buying?"

"All the way," Dante said. "Run up the flag."

The flying of the flag wasn't half as dramatic as Blays would have liked. To conceal it from all eyes but the only pair that mattered, Lolligan waited until nightfall, then sent a servant to the roof, flag in hand. Dante and the others remained inside. Somewhat resentfully, the same servant returned to the roof fifteen minutes after midnight to take the flag back down.

In the morning, Lolligan found a scrap of black fabric pinned to the front door. Following breakfast, most of the household squeezed into Lolligan's boat and headed for the city. Lolligan was off to hire a half dozen new servants—men whose arms would bulge under their sleeves. Fann headed toward the hills to make the rounds among his wealthy friends and gather any gossip concerning Jocubs, Cassinder, and whatever else was worth knowing. Blays and Mourn holed up in a dockside pub to watch the traffic from the lake for Jocubs or anyone close to him with the intent of following them into the city. And accompanied by Lira, Dante headed for the city's main library.

His purpose was twofold. First, to brush up on any local poisons that might be surreptitiously introduced to Jocubs' food or water. And second, to find out whether the merchant-king had been foolish enough to register a copy of his manor's floorplan with the city archives. It wasn't out of the question. Though the notion was rarely spoken aloud, a rich man's manor was often thought of as a monument to himself, and gifting archives with records of that monument—its meaning, its history, its architecture, even its cost—was a way to gild its legacy in local lore.

Not that it would be wise to ask about poisons in one breath and then the design for Jocubs' home in the next. Dante would see what he could do to find these things on his own before enlisting any help.

He had expected the library to be a monastery or converted wing of a cathedral, but it was a thing all its own, a four-floor square that occupied its own block. A swooping roof shaded elegant stone pillars. Two massive statues of pike flanked the front walk, resting on their tails, long bodies curved into an S. The high doors stood wide open. Dante headed inside, frowning, ready to be ushered away by a blustering monk or officious servant. Instead, a black rope barred his passage. A man in a clean white uniform stepped forward, hands clasped behind his back.

"Day's entry will be two-and-three, please."

Dante stopped short. "Two silds and three pennies? Just to go inside?"

"For the day, yes."

"It would cost less than that to *buy* the book I need."

The man tipped back his head, eyes downcast. "Yes, but the Library at Moor contains many thousands of books. In those terms, it is surely a bargain."

Dante set his jaw and reached for his purse, counting out two silver and three iron. The steward glanced quickly at Lira.

"That will be per person, sir."

He sighed, paid, and walked from the foyer into a vast hall of shelved books. Old men milled through the stacks, taking down titles and thumbing cautiously through the yellow pages. A woman in white approached and offered her help finding Dante's title in exchange for three pennies more. Despite the prick to his sensibilities, he paid up. Under the pretense of having fallen in love with Jocubs' home, he asked for any and all materials related to its planning, construction, or history. In one sense, the woman in white earned her keep—she searched with him for three straight hours— but that did little to mitigate Dante's frustration when she turned up nothing. After so much talk of Jocubs, he could hardly ask about poisons now, and even after three hours navigating the dry and dusty shelves, he had no hope of finding anything about them on his own.

He left angry. The afternoon was warm and muggy. His clothes rasped against his skin. Beside him, Lira was placid and silent as ever.

He gave her a sidelong glance. "Don't you have anything better to do?"

She stepped over a greasy puddle. "I'm here to keep you safe."

"From the high danger of a library. I could be papercut at any moment."

"Belittle all you like, but you walked out in perfect health."

Back at Lolligan's, the group compared notes. Blays and Mourn hadn't seen anything all day, but they seemed highly unconcerned about their lack of progress, probably because they were both half drunk on beer. Fann confirmed their lack of results—from what he'd gathered, Jocubs and Cassinder had practically fortified themselves on Jocubs' island, and weren't expected at any dinners, parties, quorums, or appearances for weeks. Lolligan at least had something to show for his efforts. He'd hired seven swordsmen, three of whom were already quartered in the servants' wing. He hadn't been the only one bringing on new arms. To hear him tell it, there had been more merchants and bureaucrats prowling the steelyards than mercenaries.

Dante went to his room to stew. He was still stewing late that night when Lolligan came to his door, a clever smile matching his clever mustache. The woman in the blue mask had arrived.

She didn't want to come inside. Instead, they gathered in the grass beneath a manicured tree, moonlight sifting between its spiky, gnarled branches. The scent of the lake was all around them. The woman was dressed in her midnight bodysuit, her eyes white behind its slits.

"Your decision makes us happy," she said softly. "Now we decide how to proceed."

"I assume kicking in the front door is out?" Blays said.

She shook her head. "That strategy would not be effective."

"Really? Because I think he'd wind up pretty dead. Pretty really dead."

"This is the problem."

"Oh, I see. You only want him *half* dead."

She chopped both hands downward. "We want his death certain but its cause unclear. We want his followers to be confused, not suspicious. Obvious assassination provokes too much sympathy. It would provoke too much of the TAGVOG into crossing over to the king's side."

"Poison his household's food," Dante said. "It'll look like they ate bad fish."

"There must be thirty people in his household," Lira said. "Servants. His family. You'd kill them all, too?"

Dante scowled over the water. On the city pier, a buoy tolled in the darkness, far off and forlorn. "It was just a suggestion."

"A needlessly ruthless one."

"You guys act like you've never thought about how to kill someone before," Blays said. "Set fire to his house and shoot anyone who runs outside. Pour a jug of poison down his ear as he sleeps. Hire a family of snakes to slither in through his window and give him a big fat kiss."

"I like the poison one," the woman said. "It is simple and deniable. Also it does not require us to know the language of snakes."

"We need to find a way to sneak into his house, then." Dante gestured across the calm waves to the dark blot of Jocubs' island. "It doesn't sound like he's leaving it any time soon."

"So we need to go kick in his front door?" Blays said.

Lolligan cracked his knobby knuckles. "Men like him always have other ways in and out of their castles. It makes them feel clever. I've got a few back doors myself."

"I failed to find his floor plan today," Dante said. "Maybe we can ask him to draw us a map."

Blays nodded. "Or save us a whole bundle of trouble and poison himself."

"His weakness is vanity," said the woman in blue. "Attack his weakness."

"Send over a stranger who'd like a tour of his island palace," Blays said. "A stranger with blood as blue as a drowned sapphire."

The woman snapped her fingers. "We have someone we can

use."

"That's it, then." Dante knocked on the rough trunk of the tree. "Find us a way in, and we'll do the rest."

It was a good plan. Simple, swift, and unsuspicious. And it failed before it began.

The woman in blue came back the next night. She had sent a boat to Jocubs' island with a letter of introduction for a wealthy young traveler who yearned to see the house he'd heard so much about. The boatman hadn't been allowed to step foot on Jocubs' docks. One of the four guards standing watch explained that Jocubs and Cassinder were deeply engaged in critical plans, and please understand they could not be interrupted, no matter who came calling.

Back beneath the tree and the moonlight, Dante sighed hard enough to rattle the branches. "Guess it's right through the front door after all."

"We could do that," Blays said. "Or we could use my perfect idea."

"Which is?"

"We send a letter to Cassinder asking for an audience. While you grovel and apologize for Narashtovik's insubordination, I take a look around and see if there's a way in. Or a way to take care of Jocubs then and there that isn't too obvious."

"That sounds awful. What's so perfect about it?"

"Two things," Blays said. "First, it attacks Cassinder's arrogance. There's no way he'll turn down the chance to watch you prostrate yourself."

"I think I know the second thing," Dante said.

"Second, you'll hate every moment of it."

"I knew the second thing." Dante glanced between the others. "Anyone have a better idea? Please have a better idea."

If they did, they kept it to themselves. Dante stayed up late composing the most polite and beseeching letter he could stomach, then dispatched it to Cassinder at Jocubs' home first thing in the morning. While he waited for the boat to come back with a response, he raised Cally on the loon. They hadn't spoken in days, and it took Dante several minutes to bring him up to speed. A carefully explicated speed—Dante told him nothing of their plans regarding Jocubs.

"Unfortunate," Cally said. "No doubt the king offered the damn lake-traders a better deal than we could ever swing. You ought to just burn down the whole valley and be done with it."

"That would show them," Dante said. "Have you heard anything new from the world? The norren?"

"No. And if the clans are hoping that ignoring the ultimatum will slow Moddegan down, they'll have to hope harder. He's raising troops across the north."

"What are we going to do, Cally?"

"Don't worry, son." The old man laughed. "If they come for Narashtovik, we'll build a boat and sail to the north star. Or die heroically! We're never forced to face a single fate."

Dante knew "son" was just a phrase, but Cally had never used it towards him before. He opened his mouth, ready to tell Cally the rest of the plan to overthrow Jocubs and sway the lakelands back to their side, but the loon went silent.

Cassinder replied in the afternoon. He was happy to hear from Dante, and would welcome his visit two days hence. Dante was glad the invitation wasn't for that same day. The cold glee in Cassinder's response had Dante ready to blast a hole through the wall. Or through Cassinder. Or, to kill two birds with one stone, to blast Cassinder through the wall instead.

Lolligan produced a vial of clear, odorless poison. Before crossing the waters to Jocubs', Blays sealed it with wax and concealed it in his underclothes. This turned out to be uncannily wise — when they stepped off on Jocubs' docks, the guards searched them top to bottom, taking Blays' two knives. Dante smiled internally. Two small blades were nothing compared to the poison in Blays' underpants, the nether in his own veins.

The stately terraces of Jocubs' home were strangely quiet. Dante was led to a small den heavy with carpets and wall-hangings that helped insulate it despite the lack of a fireplace. On the pretense Dante wanted to speak to Cassinder alone, Blays waited outside.

Cassinder took thirty minutes to arrive. He entered as quietly as a knife, closing the door without a click, not bothering with the formal one-step retreat of greeting under such circumstances. His smile didn't warm his eyes. "This can't be easy for you."

Dante stood. "How's that?"

"To admit to a man's face that you wronged him. That's why you're here?"

"Among other things."

"Good. If it weren't, this conversation would end now." Cassinder sat on a backless chair, his spine straight. "Then let me hear it."

"The raid on your household was a mistake," Dante said, managing not to clench his teeth. "The norren we were with deceived us. We deceived ourselves, too. I let things get out of hand."

"Are you sorry?"

"That's what I just said."

"You didn't. You danced around the words like a three-legged dog. I wonder if you mean them."

Dante stared past Cassinder's shoulder. "I'm sorry."

The man touched two fingers to the blond stubble on his head. "And there it is. What now?"

"I would hope my mistake hasn't endangered the long relationship between Narashtovik and Setteven. We support the norren in many ways, but it feels like Gask is two steps from civil war. How has it come this far?"

"Because we let it," Cassinder said. "We indulged. We did not make our expectations clear. Our subjects in the southern hills did what helps themselves rather than what builds the empire as a whole. It is now our responsibility to correct them."

Dante's eyes narrowed. He forced his face to go blank. "What is your proposal?"

"Before the Settives took hold of this country, we followed a different set of laws. When a man killed, we didn't kill him. We made him a servant to the family whose son he had taken. When he went, his older brother went with him. If he had no older brother, it would be his younger. If he had no brothers at all, it would be his best friend. The killer became a simple servant, but the older brother had a higher responsibility. If the killer didn't rise on time, his brother would beat him. If the killer misfed the family's cows, and one of the cows died, his brother would whip him. And if the killer grew frustrated, and killed another member of his new family, then his brother would kill him."

Cassinder held his gaze, perfectly still. "The norren have

sinned. Can Narashtovik be their older brother?"

The nether stirred in Dante, licking along his veins. "If that is our responsibility."

The young lord stood, adjusting the hem of his doublet. "That is how we keep the peace."

"My lord..." Dante said, hoping to stall him, to give Blays as much time as possible to continue his rounds of the house, but Cassinder didn't turn. He closed the door behind him, as if Dante weren't there at all. His feet whispered down the carpeted hall. A servant arrived moments later.

"I am afraid the house must be vacated," the man said. "We'll find your friend and bring him to you on the docks."

As he was led from the house, Dante examined every doorway, nook, and staircase in sight, but there were no obvious weaknesses, no flap-doors or person-sized cracks large enough to wiggle through with no sign of entry. Guards stood by the outer doors, some wearing Jocubs' colors, others wearing the pine green of Cassinder. By the time Dante reached the pier, he was ready to fling himself into the water and let it take him where it may. Ten minutes passed before Blays appeared on the path to the docks, escorted by two guards and looking as relaxed as a three-hour nap. The pair rode back to Lolligan's in silence.

Inside the house, Blays grinned hugely. "If your face is any indication, your meeting went just as poorly as expected. Also, you're ugly."

"Oh dear. How will I ever convince you to marry me?"

"Maybe you can get rich?"

Dante flopped down in a chair. "It would be much easier than trying to do good. How did your search go?"

"Pretty great!" Blays said. "I took a highly illuminating shit."

"Did your brains go with it? You were supposed to be searching for a way in!"

"It's funny. There I was, perched on this wooden bench, when I discovered a strong draft doing strange things to my nethers. Once I finished up my first priority, I braved my health and sanity and stuck my head down the same hole my ass had just occupied."

"Really? And how did the family reunion go?"

Blays stretched his arms wide. "The crapper was as wide as a chimney! Dark as one, too, but I could still smell. You know what I smelled?"

"The inside of a toilet?"

"Yeah, but a surprisingly not-awful one. Then I started listening. And you know what I heard?"

Dante pressed his palms against his forehead. "My endless screams?"

"Splashing. Soft, gentle splashing."

Dante lifted his head. "How wide did you say it was?"

"At least four feet by three," Blays grinned. "As far down as I could see. Did I mention the bathroom was on the same floor as Jocubs' bedroom?"

"I think it's time to find Lolligan."

According to his majordomo, the salt merchant was on business in town. When he returned, Blays explained his suspicion that the toilet opened straight into the lake. Lolligan's mouth fell open with laughter.

"I have no doubt it does. Why didn't I think of this to begin with?"

"Because it's disgusting," Blays said. "We're going to need some more clothes. Preferably something you won't mind having covered in shit and then dropped in the lake as we swim home."

"How soon can we make this happen?" Dante said. "Ulwen, has she hired her troops? Will she be ready to move if Jocubs' supporters smell a rat?"

Lolligan nodded, smiling sharply. "There's hardly an idle mercenary in town. Everyone's been hiring new help and it hasn't raised an eyebrow. Unrest is coming, you know."

"You don't say." Blays bent at the waist to touch his toes, grunting as he stretched. "Guess we'd better practice climbing up a toilet."

One of the five-story terraces that made up Lolligan's home had been disused since the previous summer. Including its chimney. The next two days, while they weren't coordinating with Ulwen and the woman in blue, Dante, Blays, and Lira spent their time clambering up and down the wing's largest chimney, a square vault roughly three feet to a side and some thirty feet high. As it turned out, the enclosed space was just tight enough to make climbing easy. By bracing two or three limbs against the sooty bricks at any one time, Dante could push himself up the flue without the use of a rope or tool. Blays and Lira were more agile yet, scaling the vertical rise in less than two minutes.

That left two wildcards: finding the lakeside entry to the toilet, and widening the hole through the boards at its upper end enough to climb through. After discussion, Dante decided not to try to advance-scout the entry's location—either they would find it on the night of the attack or they wouldn't. As for the boards up top, through experimentation in the chimney, Blays discovered he could brace himself securely enough with two feet and one hand to use his remaining hand to pry loose or saw through a wooden plank with minimal noise or time. It was even easier if he could secure a rope to the seat and dangle from that while he worked. All told, Dante estimated they could swim in, climb up, break through, deliver the poison to Jocubs, and climb back out in no more than fifteen minutes.

"I want to kill Cassinder, too," he said once he made that calculation.

Blays lifted his brows. "Do you think that's a good idea?"

"Extremely."

"Let me put this another way. Do you think that's more or less likely to get us exposed or killed in the middle of this ridiculous mission?"

"Cassinder's a duke, something like ninth in line for the kingship—with no concern or sympathy for the norren. If he winds up the general in charge of a legion, he'll massacre them. I'm sure of it."

Blays gritted his teeth. "If one fat old man dies, well, that's what fat old men do. If a fit young duke dies on the same night? That'll stink worse than the route we're taking to get there."

"You're right." Dante let the idea slip away like a pleasant dream. "But if the chance pops up, I'm taking it."

That was all the more preparation they needed. They let Lolligan know they were ready; Lolligan let Ulwen know they would move that night.

Dante napped through the day, waking for dinner. He dressed in a black cap and shirt and skirt and socks. The bells of midnight rolled over the inky waters. For another two hours, they gazed through the windows at Jocubs' island, where a pair of torches continued to burn with a strange white flame. A crescent moon barely outshined the stars.

Lolligan went with them to the dock. After Dante, Blays, and Lira settled into a small rowboat Lolligan had stripped of any decorations, the old merchant untied the rope and knelt on the planks of the dock. His wrinkled face was taut, as if he were finally realizing the significance of the hour to come.

"I hope we're doing the right thing," he whispered. "Good luck."

He threw them the rope; Blays caught it and coiled it in the prow, then shoved off and grabbed an oar. Lira took up the other. Dante knelt up front, watching the black water. They rowed slowly, the splashes of their paddles no louder than the ripples and gentle waves. As slowly as a mounting storm, Jocubs' island grew in size, a black mound lit at its lakeward-facing point by those two white lights. The rowboat swung wide around the dark side of the island and angled in to where the five-layered house sat flush against the water.

Miles across the lake, a white light bloomed in the darkness, riding many feet above the surface. Dante hunched forward and squinted until he was certain the light was moving against the steady backdrop of the far shore.

"There's another ship out there."

Blays pulled his paddle from the water. "What kind?"

"It looks big. Too far away to tell."

"Then we'll keep moving."

The boat crept forward. Dante split his attention between the distant vessel and the approaching island. He could make out the manor's curling eaves now, the glint of its windows. Once, a man paced along a balcony, and Dante coiled the nether in his hands, ready to strike the man dead if he called out a warning. The figure disappeared inside.

Blays steered the boat to within a few yards of the short, rocky cliffs supporting the house, where a guard would practically have to lean off a deck's railing to spot them. An outlying face of the house ran straight down into the water. Somewhere below it, a hole would open into the flue of the toilet.

Dante glanced back across the lake. The vessel had cut the distance between them in half. He still couldn't make out its hull. Just that strange white lantern hanging from its prow.

A light that matched the ones on the northern tip of Jocubs' island.

"That's what Jocubs and Cassinder have been waiting for," he whispered over the wash of the waves. "That boat is coming here. It'll land within an hour."

15

Blays shrugged off his cloak, grinning grimly at the distant ship. "Then I suppose we'll have to hurry."

Dante twisted to face him. "You still want to go through with this?"

"Do you think the contents of that boat will make this any easier tomorrow?"

Above, the house was silent, dark. "No. This is our best chance."

"So quit arguing and let me go climb up that toilet."

Blays shucked off his cloak and shoes and slipped over the side of the rowboat. He paddled along the flat rock of the house, then bobbed up, filled his lungs, and disappeared beneath the black water. Two bubbles popped to the surface.

Water soughed against the land. Toward the city, the buoy clanged to itself, as far away and irrelevant as childhood. Dante loosened the small leather bag around his neck, fished out his loon, and turned the brooch to Mourn's setting. He pulsed it once. Two seconds later, he tried again.

"Yes?" Mourn answered softly.

"There's a ship coming this way," Dante whispered. "I don't like the looks of it."

"What should we do about it?"

"Get ready."

"That's unhelpfully unspecific," Mourn said.

"Tell Lolligan and our masked friend," Dante said. "I'm sure they'll come up with something."

He cut the connection. The talk had distracted him from the fact Blays still hadn't returned; the water was open, silent. Dante's gaze leapt to every splash and ripple. How long had Blays been gone? Well over a minute. Closer to two. What if he'd gotten caught underwater? Stuck in a pipe or a grate? Dante leaned over the lip of the boat, rocking it. Stars shimmered on the water. Should he dive in? He returned his loon to his pouch, where it clicked against the wax-sealed vial and cloth-wrapped lock picks. He stripped off his cloak and took three long breaths, flooding his body with air. He filled his lungs a fourth time and threw one leg over the side. Below him, a pale face broke the water. Dante tipped back into the boat, banging his ribs on the bench.

Blays grabbed the edge of the boat and peeped over the edge. "Found it."

Dante righted himself, glancing at the house's balconies. "How do you know?"

"Because it smelled like shit and I wanted to die. Pass me the bag and I'll get the rope up."

Dante handed him the bag with the rope and pry bar. Blays tucked it under his arm, saluted, and disappeared under the water. Lira paddled to keep them away from the rocks while Dante watched the white light across the lake. The boat it was attached to was a dark blot on the moonlit waves. It had advanced fractionally by the time Blays returned and gestured them into the lake.

The cold water gripped Dante like an unrelenting hand. He fought not to gasp as his head slipped below the water. Beneath the surface, Blays' kicking feet churned a trail of bubbles. Dante followed them like a lifeline. A broad shadow loomed ahead; Blays dived deeper, disappearing beneath it. Dante's ears popped. His heels banged and scraped against something hard and scratchy. The ceiling pressed above him, an unbroken plane of rough-cut stone. Air bubbled from his mouth. He flattened himself against the stone, struggling, as if he believed he could swim through rock as easily as the black water. The last of his air burst from his nose. He rolled over to hammer at the stone. A hand grabbed his wrist and yanked him forward. He rose into a tight square, brushing between two warm bodies and bursting from the water with a gasp. The stink hit him a moment later, a choking scent of feces in all stages of aging.

Blays and Lira crowded beside him, breathing through their

mouths. Something brushed Dante's face. He pawed it away, felt the wet rope. He could barely see his own hand. High above, the sliver of moon trickled through a skylight above the square hole of the seating platform. Small things bobbed around his arms and chest. He was glad for the darkness.

Blays maneuvered around him and grabbed the rope. A foot bonked Dante's face. The rope swayed in the water, stirring the trapped sewage. Dante craned his neck to keep his face clear. Above, Blays scrabbled against the slick walls. Something plopped into the water. The rope jiggled. Blays gave a soft whistle. Dante grabbed the rope and climbed up, the spatter of water echoing up the flue. The rope swayed, banging him into the tight walls, dislodging sludge and coating him in foul stink. He breathed shallowly but could still taste it on the back of his throat. He paused halfway up to gag.

"Do not do whatever you're doing," Lira whispered from below.

He continued up. The square of moonlight expanded. Blays had pried away enough boards to crawl into the bathroom without squeezing his shoulders. After the ascent through the toilet-flue, the tight room felt palatial. Water splashed below, signaling Lira's climb. Blays stood on the bathroom rug stripped to his underpants.

"What are you doing?" Dante whispered.

"I don't want to walk around covered in shit. I don't care if it is the fashion." Blays nodded at the rugs. "Don't want to leave tracks, either."

Dante peeled off his shirt, skirt, socks, and gloves until he was down to his smallclothes, the pouch at his neck, and a long knife tied to his thigh. Lira emerged from the toilet, hopped to the floor, and stared.

"Like it's nothing you haven't seen before?" Blays said.

She smirked and stepped out of her outer clothes. Dante wadded the soiled linen into a ball, dropped it down the chute with a splash, and wiped his hands on the carpet. They drew their knives. Blays padded to the door and eased it open.

Silence spilled into the bathroom, the kind that leaves your ears ringing with its purity. Blays slipped into the hallway. Light lined the cracks around a door down the hall, but it was otherwise as dark as the night. Blays crouched forward. A cough sputtered from elsewhere in the house, muffled by doors and space. Blays shrank against the wall, but the coughing stopped, consumed once more by that perfect silence. The hallway terminated at a wide wooden door. Blays nodded significantly and reached for the handle.

It opened, sparing Dante the trouble of fumbling with the picks in his pouch. Inside, moonlight coursed through unshuttered windows, painting the room in silver-blue shadows. Jocubs snored thickly from amidst a canopy bed with the same tented peaks as his roof. Blays eased the door shut. Dante took the vial from his pouch and clamped it under his armpit to warm it. Blays cocked his head, gesturing toward the bed. Dante held up his palms and shook his head: the closer to body temperature the poison was, the less likely Jocubs would wake before the fluid ensured he never would.

Dante waited half a minute for the vial to warm, then crept to the bed. Silk sheets rumpled around Jocubs' middle. White hairs curled on his slack chest. His snores smelled like sour beer. Dante ran his thumbnail around the vial's tiny neck, breaking the wax. He pulled the glass stopper and leaned over the sleeping man, but was struck by a moment of moral vertigo. He was about to kill this man; did this man deserve it? Why had Jocubs crossed to Cassinder's camp? For personal gain, promises of riches and titles? Or to avert the king's wrath from his homeland of Gallador? If the latter, how could Dante fault him for placing the safety of his friends, family, and countrymen over a horde of strange giants living far to the east?

But if those were the rules, nor could Dante be faulted for placing Narshtovik and norren above the people of Gallador. Whether Jocubs had signed his treaty to join the ranks of royalty, to preserve his people, or both, he must have felt very secure as he shook Cassinder's hand: he was tucked away in the lakeland rifts, a week's hard travel from the flashpoints at the borders. He must have smiled. He must have thought himself very wise.

But every choice carried consequences. And the reach of war knows no boundaries.

Dante dripped the clear liquid into the old man's ear. Jocubs stirred, sluggish, pawing at the side of his head. He didn't open his eyes. Dante waited for him to settle back into the covers, then poured another dose. Jocubs' gray hair grew slick and damp. The thin fluid seeped into the folds of his neck. He let out a long, ragged breath. His chest slumped in thin and shallow breaths. He seemed to wither, to retract into his own flesh.

Bright parchment rested on his bedside table, enscribed with fancy script and fresh ink. Dante folded the papers into his pouch. He gestured toward the door.

Jocubs shot up in bed, shrieking. Dante moaned. Jocubs shook his hoary head like a dog, clawing at his ear. He screamed again. A shudder wracked his body, jiggling his hairy stomach. He hunched forward, bearish, and dribbled foam from his lips.

His wild eyes fixed on Dante. "Who are you? Help me! Bring me water!"

Blays leapt forward and socked Jocubs in the temple, thumping him into the sheets. He gurgled. His chest shuddered and went still.

"That was gross," Blays muttered. "I think it's time to—"

The door barged open, spilling light and an armed guard into the room. Lira's knife caught him in the neck. He stumbled to the floor, blood fanning onto the thick carpet. Blays scooped up his sword and blew out the candle he'd dropped. Shouts rose from down the hall. Dante cut the back of his left arm, smiling against the pain. Nether swelled in him like an incoming tide. He rushed out the door.

Blays jogged after him. "Where are you going?"

"To find Cassinder."

"Is that secret code for 'get the hell out of here'? Because right now—"

Feet thumped down the dark hallway. Swords glinted. Dante lashed out with a blade of raw nether. Just before it reached the guards, it burst in a shower of white sparks, sizzling away. The pale glow lit Cassinder's face, ghostlike, smiling.

"Oh shit," Dante said.

Cassinder stepped forward, flanked by guards. "Most men of quality teach their sons to swing a sword. But what's a blade compared to this?"

He thrust a spear of white ether at Dante's heart. Dante shouted in horror.

There were few nethermances he truly feared. It was possible the king had a pet sorcerer or three with the power to beat Dante seven times out of ten. But Dante's power was unearthly, particularly for his age. In fact, throughout all of Gask, the list of netherslingers who could stand toe to toe with him and expect to walk away alive might start and end with Cally.

This was not true of the ether. Every single ethermancer, no matter how raw and untrained, posed a mortal threat to Dante. He knew too little of the ether to fight it with any efficiency. He could oppose it with brute force, sure, slinging gobs and walls of shadows at the incoming light. In most cases, his talent with the nether was strong enough to overcome his disadvantage nonetheless. He could tire his opponent out, and then strike, or simply overwhelm them, striking with a tide of nether too fast and cold for any but the strongest to resist.

If he and his ether-slinging enemy were anywhere closely matched, however, victory was far from a given. In that case, the enemy could wear *him* down, forcing him to expend clumsy amounts of nether to avoid dying on deliberately spare thrusts of ether. Dante could be overwhelmed, too. Even losing his focus for a fraction of a second could mean the ether would be on him before he knew what was happening.

He'd trained to overcome this weakness. But it was a weakness that could only be patched over so far—and Cassinder appeared to be uncommonly strong.

Dante met Cassinder's attack with a wild charge of nether. The two energies flared into a puff of light. Dante fell back, keeping the shadows close at hand. He'd tried to study the ether a dozen times throughout the years, but each time he found he could no more manipulate its solid, steady presence than he could give birth. He would rather face a mother bear in her den than a trained and able ethermancer.

A knife whipped through the air, burying itself in Cassinder's shoulder. The man dropped to his knee with a sigh.

"I like blades, personally." Blays shifted his stolen sword to his empty right hand. "They don't care who they cut."

He grabbed Dante by his bare shoulder and yanked him down the hall. Glass shattered from Jocubs' room; Lira stood in front of a gaping hole in the window, gesturing with her knife. Blays slung his sword at Jocubs' motionless body and dived headlong out the window. Dante followed, yanking his pouch from his neck and holding it above his head. He plunged into the cold lake, water smashing around his head. Lira burst into the water beside him.

"Where's the rowboat?" he said.

"Off on a journey of its own." Blays spun in the water, orienting himself toward Lolligan's. "It's time to see whether we've absorbed anything from all these fish we've been eating."

He leaned into a crawlstroke. Dante turned on his side, paddling with one hand while he held the pouch aloft with the other. They weren't a hundred yards from the island before the first arrows whooshed across the darkness. Their points were bright with fire, illuminating the foam of Dante's kicks. The first few arrows missed handily. The next volley slashed into the waters mere feet away, fizzling and popping. Dante sensed a cool power gathering on the deck of the house. He turned to face it, kicking in place. A bolt of white ether streaked through the night. Dante punched his free hand from the water. Shadows streamed forward. As they met the ether, the sizzle drowned out the hissing arrows.

Dante continued swimming. Cassinder didn't attempt another attack. Dante and the others swam from bow range, arrows plunking into the water behind them. The island fell away into the night. Across the lake, the secret ship and its white lantern advanced toward the dead merchant's home.

Lanterns lined Lolligan's shores. Dante hauled himself onto the rocks, chest heaving, shivering so hard he thought his arms would shake loose from his torso. Someone swaddled him in blankets; hands guided the three of them to a roaring fire in Lolligan's private quarters. A servant pulled away Dante's sodden underwear and replaced them with a full set of dry clothes. Under a mound of blankets to his left, Blays' teeth chattered aloud. To Dante's right, Lira stumbled while stepping into her skirt, her limbs too stiff to function. She dropped below the blanket a servant had hoisted for privacy, landing hard on her knees and palms, breasts swinging between her bent elbows. The servant rushed to cover her. Dante had barely pulled on his pants when the doors opened. Lolligan, Ulwen, and the woman in midnight blue rushed into the room.

"Is it complete?" the woman said behind her mask.

"In the sense that Jocubs is dead, yes," Dante said. A shudder tore through his muscles.

"Is there another sense?"

"Sight, hearing, smell, and touch," Blays said. "I know we engaged at least that many. The guys on their side probably tasted some blood, too."

Dante breathed out slowly. His shudders ceased except for a twitch in his calf. "It's not over. Cassinder saw us. We fought him. The house is thick with soldiers. Thirty or more."

Lolligan folded his arms, elbows tucked tight to his sides. "I'm afraid we'll need to revise those numbers upwards."

"How so? His loyalists in the city can't have heard yet."

"The ship Mourn told us about?" Lolligan said. "It landed at Jocubs' while you were still in the water. It launched just a minute ago. It'll be here any moment."

Crouched among his blankets, Blays laughed in disbelief. "How many men do you have here?"

Lolligan glanced between Ulwen and the masked woman. "Mercenaries? Just twenty. We sent messengers into the city as soon as Mourn mentioned trouble, but it could be an hour before reinforcements arrive—if they arrive at all."

Blays stood, shedding his blankets. "Bring me my swords."

Lolligan drew back his head. "You're not serious. You just swam across a freezing lake!"

"And after a feat of heroism like that, I'd be especially upset about getting stabbed to death. Swords. Now."

Lira rose. "I'll need mine as well."

"Mine, too." Dante didn't bother to stand. "For whatever good it will do me."

Servants brought their arms along with an assortment of armor from Lolligan's stores, most of it antique. Blays wrapped iron-banded bracers around his forearms. Lira tried on a chainmail shirt, hurrying through her forms to test its flexibility. Dante lifted a tall shield—the enemy would be bringing archers—but it pulled on his arm with untenable weight. Across the lake at Jocubs', the newly-arrived ship rowed from the pier, lanterns off, and hove toward Lolligan's island. Lolligan's men swarmed to the northern beach, a flat stretch of rocks that stood just about the waterline.

"Pile that beach up with junk," Blays gestured. "Anything we can hide behind." Soldiers and servants hesitated. Blays turned to Lolligan. "I'm going to start grabbing furniture. All right?"

Lolligan grimaced, twisting the end of his pointed mustache. "Just leave the chairs with the blue felt. They were my grandfather's."

He ordered the back doors propped open. Blays jogged inside and came out with a wooden chair over his shoulder. Seeing that, Lolligan's men streamed into the house. The old salt merchant shut his eyes to the ransacking. His mercenaries came out with chairs and tables. Groaning pairs of men hoisted couches and mattresses. A team of four lurched under the weight of a dresser. Wood cracked inside the house. Two servants hustled outside, grinning madly, a door held between them. They piled it all in front of the rocky beach.

The ship loomed nearer, oars churning from both its decks. Blays ordered Lolligan, Fann, and the servants inside.

Fann fiddled with his hat. "That will be away from the fighting, yes?"

"Unless things go bad!" Blays said.

"Excellent." Fann and the others scurried inside.

Mourn joined the soldiers on the beach, as did the woman in blue. They both carried bows and thick sheafs of arrows. They were barely in place before the first arrows flew from the ship. These splashed in the water and plinked from the beach, testing range. A shout went up. The ship's oars backbeat against the lake. It slowed to a halt within easy bow range. The arrows ceased.

Cassinder's soft voice boomed unnaturally. "Three people have to die: those who killed Bil Jocubs. If you prefer, all of you can die as well."

Blays vaulted onto an overturned couch. "If you prefer, you can kiss my ass! And you know where it's just been!"

He ducked as an arrow whisked over his head. He leapt back behind the makeshift walls of furniture. Cries rang out from the ship. Chains clanked and creaked, lowering longboats from each side of the galley. Volleys of arrows covered the soldiers' descent on the rope ladders. Dante counted roughly twenty men per longboat. Another twenty archers in the prow. An unknown number of soldiers in reserve. Lolligan's troops were outnumbered at least twofold; if the galley's decks were full, as many as a hundred soldiers might stand against them. Dante took out his knife and carved a red line across his arm.

"Can you at least not smile when you do that?" Blays said.

"Was I?"

"Always. It's like your forearm killed your mom and you're giving it the death of a thousand cuts. It's got so many scars it's no wonder you didn't bother with a shield."

Mourn sniped at the archers on the deck, knocking two into the water. An arrow threaded through the barricade and pinned one of Lolligan's men to the ground. The mercenary writhed, screaming. Dante ignored him. He needed all his energy.

The longboats shoved off from the galley, shielded at their bows by thick hides. Dante lobbed a spike of nether at one of the archers on the galley. The man staggered, gagging blood. Dante smiled: Cassinder hadn't tried to stop him.

He closed his eyes and let the nether come. Shadows coated his hands to the elbows. The longboats stroked forward. When they were halfway between the galley and the beach, Dante stood, oblivious to the arrows hailing down around him, and flung out his hand.

The side of the rightward longboat exploded in a hail of splinters. Men hollered, shielding their faces from the shrapnel. Water gushed through the yawning hole. Soldiers leapt up to bail it out with buckets and bare hands. Mourn and the woman in blue popped up to pick them off. Soldiers flung themselves over the broken longboat's edge, paddling for shore in heavy armor. Most sunk beneath the placid waves.

The second longboat beat on. Flaming arrows whapped into the barricade, driving the mercenaries into cover. Fire licked over feather mattresses. Other arrows arced far overhead, clinking on the clay roof of the house and clacking into the wooden walls. Two servants dashed from the house, one carrying rags and a jug, the other with a flaming brand. An arrow knocked the man with the torch to the ground. The man with the jug raced on, skidding into cover beside Mourn, who poured oil on a rag, knotted it around an arrow, and glanced at the empty killing fields between the barricade and the house. He poked his arrow into the flames of a smoldering table, lighting the oily rag, then fired into the front of the galley.

The hulled longboat slogged on, barely above water. The other ship groaned to a halt on the shore. With high cries of battle, men piled over its side. Blays thrust up his sword and dashed through the burning furniture. Dante's body buzzed. He leapt to his feet and charged after Blays, Lira right beside. Lolligan's soldiers cheered and joined the charge.

The galley's arrows felled two men before they met the invaders. As Blays closed on the enemy, a spear thrust at his body. He met it with his lefthand sword, intercepting it near the tip and letting it slide past his chest as he closed. He drove his other sword into the spearman's exposed gut. A man in the red and white of Moddegan's soldiers chopped diagonally toward Lira's neck. Forearms crossed, she knocked aside his blade with hers, then grabbed his sword hand with her empty one, pivoted, and slung him over her hip. He cracked into the rocks. His helmet jarred away. With a backhand swipe, Lira cleaved in the side of his skull.

Behind her, a man cocked his sword and drove it toward her spine. Dante splayed his hand. A black blade severed the man's hand at the wrist. It fell to the rocks, still clutching his sword. His stump continued its forward thrust; his grin fossilized as his eyes tried to process the bloody absence where a hand and its weapon should be. He swayed and collapsed into the rocks, kicking.

Blays pivoted away from an overhand strike and spiked his blade into his attacker's extended neck. The man sank to the hilt, gargling blood over Blays' hand; Blays pivoted again, turning the man's body into an incoming spear. Its point pierced deep into the dying man's back. Blays slid his sword free and shoved the man to the ground, yanking the embedded spear away from its wielder. The disarmed man backpedaled, tripping. One of Lolligan's soldiers dropped to one knee beside him, stabbing the man through the chest.

An arrow streaked toward Blays. He sidestepped and struck it down midflight. A man in red charged Dante, a rectangular shield covering him from chin to shins. Dante held his ground and fired a bolt of shadows through the man's eye. The body tumbled forward onto the shield, skidding over the rocks.

Firelight lit the rocky shore. Every man in red lay among the wet stones, writhing or silenced, dying or dead. A burning arrow lanced from the barricade into the hide shield on the banked longboat's prow. Blays hollered and swung his sword in a circle, waving Lolligan's men back to the safety of their makeshift wall. Arrows volleyed from the galley's deck and ricocheted from the abandoned rocks.

Rhythmic cries erupted from the galley. Oars thrashed at the water, rotating the ship sidelong to the island. The galley began a slow advance. In moments, the archers on its forward deck would have clear fire on the barricade's flank.

Shouts filled the air to the south. A dozen men rushed through the dark yards of the house, bows in hand. They swarmed up the stairs to a third-floor balcony which was level with the firing platform on the galley. Two men pulled down the balcony's canvas roofing and draped it over the railing, providing some measure of cover for the others, who immediately rained fire on the archers in the galley.

"Fall back!" Blays yelled.

Covered by the men on the deck, the soldiers pinned behind the fiery barricade raced toward the safety of the house, ducking low, shields held above their heads. Dante ran with them. Sporadic arrows whisked between them. One man fell, an arrow buried in his leg. Lira ran back and helped him to his feet.

Another band of reinforcements sprinted up from the pier. With the house between them and the galley, Dante took stock of the wounded. Four of Lolligan's men had died down on the shore. Another six had been shot or badly stabbed in the scrum. While those still fit to fight thumped across the house to get to the decks and fire on the galley, Dante called out the servants, who helped him bear the wounded into the dining hall. Dents in the rugs showed where chairs and tables had once stood. Now it was perfectly empty, the ideal place to stretch out the bleeding men and see to their wounds. Dante patched up the two unconscious men with the blood-hungry nether, then left the others to be bandaged by the maids and footmen.

He ran outside onto the balcony. Men erupted in cheers. He grinned, but the noise wasn't for him: past the dark shore, the galley had turned, thrashing northward across the lake. On the many decks of Lolligan's home, sixty-odd mercenaries hollered, ringing their swords against their shields.

Dante ran from deck to deck until he found Lolligan, Ulwen, and the woman in blue, whose clothes clung to her body, sodden with sweat and water and blood. They smiled from the balcony, watching the galley retreat.

"What are you standing there for?" Dante said. "Let's get on a boat and finish them off."

Lolligan smiled, but his eyes were creased with worry. "I think we've done all we can tonight."

"What are you talking about? Their men are decimated. Their sorcerer is wounded and weak. We can take them."

"He speaks to the future," agreed the woman in blue. "They attacked us first, in the concealing shadows of darkness. Who would say we don't have the right to fight back?"

Lolligan nodded. "To hound them across the lake, however? To hunt them down and kill them? How do we argue *that* was a mistake? That it was forced upon us?"

Anger flashed over Dante, as much for this sudden split in solidarity as for the fact Cassinder was escaping over the black waves. "That man is one of the prime reasons the palace is pushing for war. Erasing him from the equation brings us one step closer to peace."

"Then there is tomorrow." The woman in blue gestured at the dark blot of the galley. "What if we spend our men tonight, and the dawn brings a fleet of the king's ships?"

"Not to mention potential pushback from Jocubs' supporters in the TAGVOG," Lolligan said. "If you want us to be able to stand with you and the norren, we'll need the manpower to stand firm against our enemies here."

Exhaustion dropped on Dante like a fog. His muscles felt trembly, weakened by the climb up Jocubs' water closet, the swim through cold waters, the battle on the shore. Sapped by the demands of the nether, his mind felt like the longboat he'd hulled: sluggish, sinking beneath the surface of a cold abyss.

"It compromises us all, doesn't it? This struggle." Dante shivered. On the north shore, fires hissed as servants doused the mounded furniture with buckets of water. Bitter smoke boiled across the island. "We'd better leave tonight, then. It will be much easier for you to pass off whatever story you please when Jocubs' killers aren't around to be questioned."

Lolligan tipped back his head, eyes glinting in the moonlight. "That might be for the best. Do you still have my salt? On the road, a small luxury can make all the difference."

Dante smiled. "I still have your salt."

"All I ask is you save a pinch for whoever runs your kitchens." He frowned at the city. "You should leave for your own safety, too. Mennok knows what new horrors tomorrow will bring."

"Blays would advise you to tell as many different stories as you can and let confusion win the battle for you."

Lolligan chuckled, shaking his head. "Thanks for all your help. Let's meet again in safer days."

Dante went downstairs to round up the others. The house smelled of blood and smoke. Lira had a gash on her upper arm, and a fist-sized bruise on Blays' chest was already magenta and swollen, but none of their group bore wounds that would slow them down. Hurriedly, they cleaned their swords and packed their clothes. A rowboat awaited them at the dock. At the stables, the boy rubbed his puffy eyes and slogged off to fetch their horses.

Dante settled their accounts and rode east. Everyone was as tired as the stablehand, too exhausted to even ask where they were headed. Then again, maybe it was obvious: they were going home.

Dawn spilled over the western mountains when they were halfway up the pass. They stopped for breakfast, or the world's latest supper. Green mountains ringed the long blue lake. Pillars of smoke rose from hundreds of different chimneys. Birds peeped from the branches, pecking at fresh buds and hard green seeds.

"Pretty, isn't it?" Blays said. "I hope Moddegan doesn't decide to burn the whole valley down."

"At least that would slow down his march on the Territories," Dante said.

Lira glanced up. "Was that what this was about?"

Dante gave her a brief glare. "This was about letting a people choose their own leaders."

"Specifically, leaders who want the same things we do."

"I'm fine with what we did." Dante swung up into the saddle. His head thudded. It would be hours before they reached the next town and the beds it would offer. Lira's accusation followed him all the way.

16

Ants scrambled in and out from the mouth of their sandy hill, unaware of their impending destruction. And what could they do if they knew? Run? Escape to the safety of their deepest tunnels? They certainly couldn't *stop* it. Their fear, their anger, the frantic waving of their antennae, none of it would make the slightest difference to the coming disaster.

Kneeling in the dirt, Dante shaped a finger of nether and pushed it into the top of the hill.

He meant to dislodge a single grain. Instead, the rod of shadows shoved over the hill's entire top into a crumbling caldera. Ants wriggled in the sand, forcing their way into daylight and air. Dante stripped the shadows away until they were as nimble as a pin, then brushed sand up the half-ruined hill. Grains slid back into a lazy pile.

If he wanted, he could push a boulder. He could crack the side of a cliff, shearing rubble into a lethal rain of falling rocks. He could pound the anthill into a hard-packed hole, killing everything inside it. But all that was physical brawn, nothing more. The People of the Pocket hadn't been moving the earth by brute force. They had reshaped it. Made it grow like the body and branches of a tree. And however much Dante fiddled around in the dirt, he couldn't begin to replicate that.

Still, he practiced during every stop they made along the eastward road. The mountains of Gallador faded into the spring haze. Grass bent in the wind and danced in the rain. They saw no sign of pursuit from the lakelands. Still, they rode swiftly, trotting and walking until their horses grew tired, then swapping them out for their spares.

He looned Cally two days out from Wending to let him known they may have led a revolution.

"*May*?" Cally said. "What part is uncertain? The torches and pitchforks, or your participation in waving them?"

"We don't know how it turned out," Dante said. "The king's soldiers might have come back and put it down."

"The king's soldiers?"

"The ones we fought." Dante sucked in his breath. "Unintentionally."

"Were they in disguise?"

"Uniforms."

"Were you?"

"Disguises wouldn't have helped. Cassinder was leading them."

"So you fought—with swords and the like—against the king's own troops." Cally's fingernails clicked against something hard. "Well, this ought to help the norren quite a bit."

"You think so?" Dante said.

"Certainly. Now Moddegan will ignore them altogether and come straight for us instead."

"Cally, at this point do you really think there's any hope we can stop this?"

"Sure. So long as every last norren agrees to a treaty they'll never, ever agree to."

"That's what I thought. Wending's merchants were ready to enlist themselves at the king's side. We just turned them into rebels."

Cally sighed. "I suppose you've done me a favor. Now when I tell the Council this is all your fault, I won't have to lie."

Pedestrians and horse-teams trickled west, outnumbering the eastern traffic ten to one. After two days of this, curiosity got the best of Blays, and he planted himself straight in the path of a man, his wife, and their three children, all on foot. The man stopped, stiff, fist clenched near his belt.

"Don't worry," Blays said. "We're not bandits. Anymore. Why are you headed west?"

The man glanced at the odd assortment of Dante, Lira, Mourn, and Fann. "To get out before the soldiers get in."

"Think it'll come to that?"

"Norren won't budge." The man gazed at Mourn. "Guess we have to instead."

Mourn stared at the road. "We're not the ones making threats."

The man tightened his fist. Blays raised his eyebrow. The man hunched his back and continued down the road.

Dante made no detours until the wheatfields of Tantonnen. At the town of Shan, he broke north to Brant's estate. Again, Brant opened the door himself, greeting them with a grin, his thick arms crossed over his gut.

"Heard you've been sowing troubled seeds."

"Doesn't sound like us," Blays said. "Must have been some other Blays."

"Funny. I heard two young men from Narashtovik fell in love with the daughter of some mucky-muck teamonger. When they tried to abscond with the lady, the merchant objected, so they dumped a sack of tree-cobras in his room while he slept."

"Definitely not us," Blays said. "Me, I'm promised to my one and only. And as for him," he said, jerking a thumb at Dante, "I don't think he even knows what a woman is."

"Nonsense," Dante said. "They're the ones with the dresses and nice smells, aren't they?"

Brant beckoned them inside. "Whatever the case, the whole deal wound up in some ripping nighttime brawl. Last I heard, King Moddegan sent a half dozen galleys upriver to put down the fighting."

Over dinner, Dante gave the farmer a more accurate if censored version of events, and was happy to hear that not only had the Clan of the Golden Field ceased their banditry, but were suspected of having slain a crew of human highwaymen who'd begun attacking wagons themselves. Narashtovik's first payments had already arrived, too. In response, the farmers had dispatched their first load of grain to the Territories not two days ago.

"Nice to know one thing in the world's going well," Dante said.

"It's the best things have looked for us in years," Brant said. "If you could just get Moddegan and the norren to let go of each other's throats, we'd have to build you a statue."

They rode on. Smoke hung on the western plains. At a bridge over a swift and noisy stream, Blays stopped to stock up on water and feed the horses. Dante picked through the reeds on the muddy banks and called to the nether hiding under the algae-slick stones. Shaping it into a black stylus, he folded his hands in his lap and traced his name into the muck. Nether lurked in the mud, too, as well as in the water that welled up in the letters of his name, pinpricks of darkness that he pooled in his palm. How could he speak to the soil? Make it move in tune with the nether it contained? Shadows rushed to his hands. He pounded the nether into the mud, splattering himself and the stream, obliterating his name.

A hundred miles from Narashtovik, the black woods swallowed them up. Cally raised Dante on the loon and told him to hurry home. He wouldn't explain why. Dante resumed at a gallop. They reached the city in two days. Cold spring rains battered the rooftops, swirling the streets into a slurry of horse dung and mud. Men ran from doorways with their hoods pulled tight over their heads. Atop the Pridegate, guards watched Dante pass; they were as still as the rooftop gargoyles, rain ticking on their metal helmets. Compared to the ebullience of Thaws, the streets were desolate, tense, a place to be fled rather than enjoyed.

At the gates of the Sealed Citadel, Dante pulled back his hood and called out his name. A guard leaned over the battlements and disappeared inside the gatetower. The portcullis cranked into the walls with a cacophony of clunks and shrieks. A footman splashed across the courtyard. Cally was waiting.

Inside the keep, Dante shed his sopping cloak and jogged up the stairs, Blays behind him. Cally sat behind his desk, tapping the blunt end of a quill into a blob of ink spilled on the surface of the dark wood. He nodded at them without looking up. His eyes were sunken, ringed with wine-dark circles. His white hair lay flat against his head. Blue veins traced his unusually pale face, as if he'd already joined Arawn in the other world where sunlight was a stranger, left to wander endless fields under the silver of the stars.

"You got here quick." His voice was as flat as his hair. "That's good."

Blays rested his hand on the hilt of his sword. "Either something's wrong or you're starting to show your age. Since you haven't crumbled into a pile of dust, I'm guessing the former."

Cally smiled wryly at the spilled ink. "Is it that easy to tell?"

"Oh, no. Only if you've got eyes."

Cally dropped the quill and steepled his fingers against his chin. "There was another riot in Dollendun. Moddegan's troops marched across the river to put it down. They did. They burned down half the norren quarter, too."

"Are you kidding me?" Dante said.

"The clans have gone berserk. At last count, 23 had rejected the treaty. The chieftain of the Clan of Twinstreams actually shoved his copy up his own ass just so he could shit it back out."

Dante pushed his fist to his forehead. "I'm guessing Moddegan didn't lay down his crown and do the apology dance."

Cally gazed at the congealing ink. "I haven't received the official announcement yet. But rumor, as always, outraces the sun. The clans have been outlawed. Any norren who resists the commands of Gaskan soldiers, lords, or officials elected or appointed is to be seized as property of the crown. Or killed without penalty." Cally looked up, impossibly old. "It's been decided. He's going to war."

"Well shit," Blays said.

"You're the one who's been saying this could happen all along," Dante said. "Or was I getting you mixed up with some other 120-year-old head of the Council of the Sealed Citadel of Narashtovik?"

The stormheads of Cally's brows collided. "Yes, but among the manifold risks and rewards of supporting the norren, early war was literally the worst outcome. It's hardly fair."

"Fair?" Dane laughed. "Even if this was our worst nightmare, I assume you planned for it."

"That doesn't mean I have *good* plans. When the most powerful man in the known world decides to come stamp you into paste, there's not a whole lot *planning* can do for you."

"You always have options," Dante said. "You can always fight back."

Cally rolled his eyes, mustache twitching. "You can leap off a cliff, too, but it won't get you any closer to the moon."

"Let's assume we've only got a few months left to our tragically brief lives," Blays said. "What's going to be the most fun for us to do in the meantime?"

A smile fought through the thicket of the old man's beard. "Okay. Fighting back."

Blays thrust up his fist. "So let's take a cue from the norren, stuff that treaty right up our ass, and shit it back out!"

"We're not doing that."

"Then at least let us go drive those red-shirted sons of bitches out of the Norren Territories."

"The Council's going to hate this," Cally smiled. "Brace yourselves for shouting."

He scheduled the meeting for four days later. In the meantime, he dispatched riders to recall Olivander from the villages of the eastern foothills, where he was running headcounts on men of fighting age, and to fetch Kav from his estate on the northwest shores. The rains continued, tumbling from the tight ceiling of clouds. Sometimes it poured down in great seaside squalls, solid sheets of water that flushed down the hills and flooded the basement of the barracks. At other times, the rain descended in a dewy mist, glomming Dante's eyelashes and slicking the cobbles. It was in such a rain that Cally insisted on taking Dante to the graveyard.

Most of the graves on the northern hill were centuries old. A scant handful were adorned with the pine boughs marking the anniversary of their occupant's passage. Moss clung to stone markers. Some of the tomb-pillars had toppled, lying cracked in the weeds. Cally passed Larrimore's marker, clean and white. Damp grass soaked the legs of Dante's pants. His cloak hung heavy and damp from his shoulders. His hands were as frigid as the dead.

"Are we scouting your future resting place?" Dante slicked rain from his eyes. "Or have you decided you'd rather die by a cold than a sword?"

Cally glanced over his shoulder, his beard as disheveled as a dog after it crawls from a lake and gives its first shake. "This is for your benefit. You seem incapable of learning in civilized settings, so I thought I'd return our classroom to the site of your greatest success."

"This is another lesson? I hope it's more useful than your last one."

"If a sponge fails to absorb a puddle, you don't blame the puddle."

"That's assuming the puddle is made of something that can be absorbed rather than something thick and intransigent and altogether muddy."

"Odd you should say that." Cally stopped in front of a rain-churned flat of dirt and grass. "Mud is precisely what we're about to dive into."

Dante frowned at the grave-studded field. "I hope you're still speaking metaphorically."

"Honestly, I'm not sure." With some difficulty, the old man knelt in the grass, splaying his hand into the muck. "Let's see if we can get this to move."

"I was trying that the whole trip back here. Nothing came of it except a few dead ants."

"That's because you are stubborn, and occasionally stupid." Cally squinted at the sloppy ground. "My theory is that mud, being muddy, will be easier to move than rock, what with its rockiness. Yet we should think of both when we think of how to move either. The commonalities will allow us to stab neatly at the heart instead of flailing in the dark."

Dante knelt beside him, rain soaking into the knees of his pants. "They're both nonliving substances."

"But do we know they're pure of life? What if these fine grains include bits of bone? What if the water that made this dirt mud once passed through a bear's bladder or a goat's veins?"

Dante paused with his hand halfway to the mud. "Then this is a very disgusting world we live in."

"Few things have ever been only themselves. This is part of what I meant to impart to you about cycles. In a way, all the world is Arawn's mill, grinding old into new in a ceaseless turn."

"If it's all the same substance, does that mean the rock is the nether and the nether is the rock?"

Cally cocked his rain-sodden head, staring into the brown sludge as if Dante had just swept it aside to reveal a cache of rubies. He shook his head sharply. "No. We'd feel it. But that's good thinking. What else?"

Absently, Dante picked up a twig and began drawing a bunny in the mud. He stopped with the second ear half-sketched. "What if there is no stick?"

"You're beginning to talk like me. I don't like it."

"To draw a rabbit, I have to use this stick." He held it up, mud clumped around its tip. "If I want to knock down one of those grave-pillars, I have to call the nether to me, shape it, and send it slamming into the rock. What if I found a way to throw out the stick?"

Cally's eyes slitted. He snatched away the stick and poked at the wet soil. "Now that is an idea."

Dante burrowed his focus into the mud, plumbing it for drops and trickles of shadows. He grabbed these up and tried to shake them like a dog shakes a squirrel. Cally smacked him in the side of the head just hard enough to dislodge his hold on them.

"What the hell was that for?" Dante said, rubbing his head through his hood.

"Don't just trample in like a puppy that's caught its first whiff of cheese. That's your whole problem. *Look*."

Cally's eyelids drooped. His eyes became as cloudy as the rain pooling in the dirt. Dante looked, too. Shadows webbed the mud, infesting it, inhabiting it, embedded within and containing it, diffusing it like cream stirred in tea, yet as separate from it as the planks of a wracked ship are from the swirl of a maelstrom. He didn't touch the nether, except to trace it with his mental fingers. He simply watched, looked, and listened.

After a full hour, Cally unfolded his legs with a grunt. He stood and stretched and flapped his rain-soaked cloak. "Well, I suppose that's enough of that. Try to work this out though, won't you? You could stroll across the Territories founding new forts with a snap of your fingers."

"Why don't you figure it out?" Dante shivered. "You're supposed to be the master."

"Yes, and the main perk of being the master is making your apprentices do your work for you."

The old man strode down the hill, stiff from the cold. The upcoming meeting of the Council was entirely Cally's business, leaving Dante with no immediate responsibilities for the first time since Thaws. He spent most of the following days watching the dirt. Twice, he tried to move it, but with the nether embedded in solid soil rather than collected and shaped in his hands, it was like trying to push a wall. Perhaps it was even more like trying to push a mountain.

The rains came and went. So did the riders, passing through the Citadel gates with news from the outlands and heartlands. Several clans had begun organized raids on the human border towns. Casualties had so far been light: a few soldiers and guards, a couple norren warriors. The first of Moddegan's conscripts—four hundred men from the Happark lowlands—were said to be inbound as an emergency stopgap against the clans.

At the pub, Blays nodded at the news. "That'll keep the local taverns in business. Zero of those men are going to step outside whatever town they're parked in."

"Think so?" Dante said.

"For certain," Lira said. "It'll be weeks before they have the strength to start striking out in force. It could be months."

Dante frowned. "Well, that's not how I would do it. The clans rarely number more than fifty people. If I were commanding the border troops, I would split them into three forces—150 to guard whatever city's at greatest risk, 150 ranging far afield to keep the clans scrambling, and the remaining hundred troops on regular sweeps between their base in town and the neighboring regions. This third force could reinforce the rangers when called for, too."

"Fiendishly strategic," Blays said. "Unless the norren decide one clan plus one clan equals all your men are dead."

"So you'd just sit in town and twiddle your thumbs?"

"Do I look like a coward?"

"I can't tell with your back turned like that."

Blays snorted. "Moddegan doesn't need any bold stratagems and derring-do. Do you know how huge his empire is? He can just advance town by town, county by county, hill by hill. The same way Mourn plays Nulladoon. The same way time decays us all to empty dirt."

"That's a bit dark," Dante said.

Blays took a long pull of his palebrown, a spring blend of spiced rum and citrusy wheat beer. "You've spent enough time with the clans, Mourn. Do you really think a few scattered tribes can do anything to stop an army of 20,000 men?"

Mourn rolled his mug between his hairy hands. "That question is dishonest. If all you do is compare a small number to a big number, the small number will never be the favorite."

"But that's all it is," Blays said. "A numbers game. They've got them, we don't."

Dante set down his mug, arranging it so the handle faced him perfectly. "What about what you told Cally the other day? That we had to fight back?"

"Of course we'll fight back. But that won't mean we'll *win*."

The table went silent. The smell of roasted lamb hung in the air, greasy and savory, undershot by boiled carrots and garlic and onions. Men murmured, mugs clunking. Their grim tones and slow words echoed Blays' mood.

"Are you all right?" Dante said.

Blays gazed out the smeary window to the street, which was nearly pitch black other than the rain gleaming in deep pools. "I just wonder if we've done the right thing. We do these things, and at the time they look right, but you come home and you put them together and somehow they've added up to this bullshit war. If that's the result of all those good decisions, maybe they weren't so good in the first place."

"But they would look different if Moddegan had responded different," Mourn said. "If he only responds with badness, our decisions will look like wrongness no matter what we do."

"That's the truth right there." Lira gripped Blays' wrist. "You have to do what your heart and head tell you is best. No matter how the world might lash back. If you don't do what you know is right, how can right ever happen?"

Dante kept his peace. That wasn't quite how he saw it—if getting eaten by a bear struck you as unfair, then perhaps you should keep your hands off a mother's cubs—but the discussion had already moved into the saferoom of platitudes. Blays drained his cup, plunked it down, and walked to the bar without a word. Dante scuffed his boots across the gritty floor, then ran his mind across the dirt there, seeking out the pricks of shadows contained within the grains.

Mourn nodded at the bar. "I think he is in trouble."

"He'll be fine," Dante said absently. "Everyone has moments of shadow."

"And Blays' are about to manifest in the punching of that man."

Dante twisted in his chair. At the bar, Blays faced down a man whose fists and mouth were bunched in anger. The man stepped forward, shoulders rolling beneath his deer-fur coat, throwing Blays into his shadow. His shoulders were those of a smith or a woodcutter: a man who spent all day swinging something heavy and metal.

Blays smiled, swaying. "Is this how you met your wife? Who can say no after they've been beaten into sleep?"

The man cocked his fist and threw a looping right hook. Blays stepped inside it, flicking his left wrist along the man's incoming arm to take control of the punch. In the same motion, he turned his hips and straightened up on his bent knees, driving a hard uppercut straight into the man's advancing chin. His teeth clicked so hard Dante winced.

The man reeled backwards like gravity had just turned sidelong. He banged into the chairs behind him, knocking another man to the ground with a yelp. A mug shattered. The man hung there from the chairs, muttering to himself, eyes fluttering. Blays grabbed the downed man's drink and gulped it down. Two men broke through the pressing onlookers. Like their half-conscious friend, they too had the hard-hewn arms of woodcutters.

Blays flipped the empty mug at their feet. "Back the fuck off or join him on the floor."

Mourn plowed up to the bar, Lira and Dante behind him. The taller of the woodcutters leaned toward Blays.

"Apologize. Do it good enough, and I won't take your jaw away."

"None of that is going to happen," Mourn said, dropping his voice even lower than its typical rumble of falling rocks.

The two men turned. They tipped back their heads to meet Mourn's eyes. The fight fled from their faces.

"What's this?" the man said. "Start up trouble, then send in your slave to bail you out?"

"Slaves aren't allowed to strike citizens." Mourn advanced, broad-bowed as a war galley. "I am not a slave."

Dante wedged his way between them, dwarfed on all sides. "It's time to stop doing dumb things."

"Then start by getting out of my way," the woodcutter said. Dante pulled back his cloak to expose the silver and sapphire brooch of the White Tree. The woodcutter lowered his hands, expression turning pensive. "We didn't come for trouble, sir. But I just saw my friend get punched by this whining mosquito here."

"Then maybe you should see if he's all right." Dante tipped his head at Blays. "That one happens to be my friend. We'll see he gets safely home."

"I'm not going anywhere." Blays pointed at the man he'd punched, who had lowered himself to the floor, head held between his hands. "He bumped into *me*."

Dante bulged his eyes. "There's plenty to drink at the Citadel."

Blays rolled his eyes. "Fine. I think I'll go vomit on your bed."

"I'll go with him," Mourn said.

"I don't need a nursemaid," Blays said. "Unless she's a damn sight less hairy than you."

"And I don't like the way I'm being stared at." Mourn rested his hand on Blays' shoulder. "Come on."

They left, followed by the steady gaze of the crowd. The woodcutters helped their friend to his feet. Dante returned to their table and pulled out a chair for Lira. She swept off her cloak, face flushed with battle-spirit, and let out a long breath. A hunched and wizened beerboy had followed them to the table, rightly guessing they'd be in the mood for a drink. Lira ordered two more palebrowns.

"I hope he's all right," she said after the drinks had arrived.

"He put that man down without getting touched," Dante said. "That woodcutter will be wearing Blays' knuckle-prints for a beard for the next week."

She glanced at the door as if Blays might have snuck back in, then leaned across the table, breasts pressing against her doublet. Involuntarily, Dante remembered how she'd fallen beneath the servants' towel as they dried themselves at Gallador, those flashes of pink and white.

"I mean what he was talking about before. He sounded defeated."

"It gets to him sometimes." Dante shifted in his chair. "This isn't baking pies. Our business requires making people unhappy. Sometimes we have to make them dead."

She held there, half-stretched across the table, eyes steady. "It doesn't get to you?"

"Only when I can afford to let it."

"And what do you do then?"

"Read. Research. Learn the nether."

Lira leaned back and sipped her drink. "Just like I stretch or run or practice my forms. I suppose that's best. The only person you can always count on is yourself."

He drank, too, buying himself a moment. The room felt suddenly warm. Thick, too. Lira's words felt like a letter written long ago, thick with references long lost to time, impenetrable. He took another drink.

"I've found a few people I can count on," he said. "But you have to hold them close. It's so easy to get lost in the wind."

She met his eyes and nodded. They finished their mugs and another round after that. The crowd thinned.

"There's something I don't understand," Dante said.

Lira glanced away from the window. "Just the one thing?"

"Among the universe of things I don't understand, there is one thing I would like you to help me understand right now," he amended. "How can you be so...inflexible?"

"I'm guessing you're not talking about my joint-locks."

Dante shook his head. "Not unless your ethics have joints. And if they do, they're bad ones, because I'm pretty sure there's a lot of stuff you'd never bend on."

"Like what?"

"Like, if it came down to you or me, your silly vow would convince you to sacrifice yourself."

She raised a brow. "You wouldn't do the same for these norren of yours?"

He sloshed his mug. "Not a chance."

"What are you talking about? I've seen you put your life at risk for them a dozen times."

"That's different. I don't *know* I'm going to die. In general, I'm foolishly certain I won't. But if I were ever in a situation where I knew with perfect certainty it would be my life or their freedom?"

He shrugged. "You would be left staring at the cloud of dust in the spot I had just vacated with all haste."

Lira smiled at the corner of the ceiling. "I suppose you think you're being a clear-eyed, pragmatic realist."

"Are you scoffing at me? You're scoffing. Well, if the king and all his men strolled up to you with their swords and said, 'Listen, declare the norren should be slaves or I'll run you through,' I don't see what's so noble about telling the truth and being skewered like a truth-telling pig. What good does that do anyone?"

"Because—" She leaned back, waving her hand over the table. "No. I've had too much rum. I'll say no more."

"What?"

"It's stupid."

Dante waggled his empty mug. "Well, I've had too much, too, and will surely forget whatever is stupid by morning. So out with it."

She rubbed her forehead with the back of her hand. "If the king were in front of me, I'd tell him the truth: the norren should be freed."

"But you'd be stabbed. To death."

"It doesn't matter." Lira laughed at herself and shot him a quick glance before looking back to the cup in her hand. "I believe that if I impose my will on the world, the world will bend."

Dante blinked. "Wait, like sorcery? Why didn't you tell me?"

"No, not like that at all. I believe that when you stand up for what's right despite the consequences—*because* of the consequences—people take notice. Your will changes their minds. And maybe there is a mystical component, too. Like if the gods see right action, it reminds them to change the world for the better." She glanced up. "Is that stupid?"

"No." He set his mug on the table so gently it made no sound. "No. It's beautiful."

For a fleeting instant, her smile was happy, light. Then it became ironic once more. "But you disagree."

"I don't know. I don't think you can count on men or gods to remember what's right. To pick up the torch of your cause after kings and demons have struck it from your hands. If you want to change the world for the good, you have to be willing to put on the mask of the villain."

"Even if it means lying. Killing. Betraying all other values you hold dear."

"If that's what it takes."

"If it takes wrong to do good, then how do you know you're doing good at all?" She drained her cup and clunked it down. "Well, I've embarrassed myself enough. Shall we leave?"

They rose together, smiling and unsteady. In the streets, rain misted from black skies, hissing on the corner torches that burned with the smell of whale fat. Lira said something about the rain and sins; he laughed, his own voice racketing down the empty street. As they approached the Ingate, the clouds tore wide open, battering them with sheets of icy water. Dante grabbed her hand and ran for the gate. Beneath its stone cover, they laughed again, breath curling from their mouths.

Lira flung her hand at the pounding rain. "What d'you say happens first? That stops, or Moddegan sticks our heads on pikes?"

"Who cares?" Dante said. He grabbed her belt and pulled her to him. Her lips were rain-cooled. Her mouth tasted like hops and sliced orange. For a moment as sharp as shattered glass, she was there with him, alive and bright beneath the gates, together in a pocket of safety from the rain and the cold and the darkness. She drew back, stiff. He cocked his head. She shook hers briskly.

He stepped away. She turned to the rain still tumbling from the sky. "It's just rain, isn't it? What are we afraid of?"

She walked into the night. Rain beat Dante's hood. In the Citadel courtyard, he said goodnight. He took a fat bottle of beer with him to bed. Candles blown out, he listened to the rain against the window.

"On the whole, we've failed," Cally said. "We've failed so thoroughly you'd think it was our express mission." Several members of the Council voiced objections. Cally just laughed from behind his chair at the table, hands clasped at his back. "Don't cry out against me. Look at the facts. Moddegan came down with demands that couldn't possibly be met. The norren have been pushed from sullen discontent into outright rebellion. The western counties have already sent their first musters to Setteven, whose standing troops have already been dispatched to the borders. All the while, we've stood back, hands washed, faces innocent."

"Not that innocent," Kav said.

"Yes, well, shit happens. At the very least, we didn't push as hard as we could. We made no counter-threats against Moddegan. No alternate treaties suggesting that Narashtovik be made steward of the Territories, for instance, or that the capital abolish slavery in exchange for the official registration and restriction of the clans. Instead, we operated through half-measures—and now we're left with a complete disaster."

Wint wrinkled his sharp nose. "Is this going where I think it's going?"

"I would hope so," Cally said. "Unless you're not half as clever as you or I believe."

"Can we move ahead already?" Tarkon said, hunching his bony shoulders. "At this rate, Dante's going to miss the birth of his own grandchildren."

A few of the Council laughed. A few more frowned or glanced away as if they'd just caught a whiff of an unexpected latrine.

"Then I'll cave to public opinion and keep this brief." Cally placed his palms on the table, long white hair spilling past his ears. "It's time we go to war, too."

"I knew it," Wint said, head wagging.

"Cally," Kav said in his modulate tones. "With all due honor to yourself and your office, I wonder if your motives aren't unfortunately confused."

Cally laughed, high and reedy. "Is that a very roundabout way to ask about Gabe?"

"If you'd rather put it that way."

"For those of you who haven't pried into my personal history, here's the short of it. When I was exiled by Samarand, I left for Mallon; in Mallon, I befriended a monk named Gabe. A norren. Thoughtful fellow, even by the standards of monks. We kept in contact through letters and the like. It was through his help that I was eventually able to reclaim my place here. In exchange, I promised I'd see what I could do for his people."

"*That's* what this is about?" Wint said. "Paying off your old debts to one forgotten friend?"

Cally impaled Wint on his green-eyed gaze. "My conscience isn't deep nor demanding. I could have bought it off with a sack of silver to a needy clan. But I looked, and I thought, and I tested. It turned out I liked the norren. I like the value they place on thought and craftsmanship and craftsmanship of thought. They are worth preserving. They are worth fighting for. There is no reason—no matter what the king has to say about debts of bondage and that the norren's ability to carry so much weight is proof of their place as our two-legged donkeys—for them to be enslaved and subjugated by the whim of the king."

"Except that he can make them," Somburr said, eyes darting around the table.

"There's no *good* reason. None that fits Arawn's scheme of justice."

"Now that's a curious evocation," Wint said. "I think one could rightly argue Arawn is all but unconcerned with Earthly justice."

"What are you talking about?" Dante said. "The parable of Arawn's mill isn't just the story of how a disturbance in the heavens made him grind nether instead of ether. It's an express metaphor for justice. Just as the heavens are flawed, so too is the earth. But while the nether may be flawed and unstable compared to the purity of ether, it's ours to shape—and so is our fate."

"And 'fate' will be the operative word," Kav said. "If we actively resist, Moddegan's second tour will take him to Narashtovik. The norren won't provide enough resistance to do more than slow him down. It's just a short march from their hills to our coast. We'd be lucky to make it through the winter."

Cally laughed humorlessly. "I see."

"Is this a joke to you?"

"Oh, I'm laughing at myself. It seems I've failed again." Cally replaced his hands on the table and leaned forward, spine crackling. "This time, I've failed to make myself clear. We're not here for a discussion and this isn't a vote."

Kav's brow crinkled. "Then just what is this about?"

"To tell you where we're going next: to war."

17

The ensuing discussion followed a predictable cycle of outraged revolt, exasperated skepticism, and bitter resignation. Dante sat back, allowing the combatants to exhaust themselves. Cally didn't need his support. Cally was the high priest of Arawn, the ultimate authority of both the Sealed Citadel and all Narashtovik. Barring violent revolt then and there in the Council's chambers, his word was law: Narashtovik would fight alongside the norren.

Not just yet, of course. Neither group had a proper fighting force, for one. For another, there remained the chance, however vanishing, that nothing would come of this at all, and that Moddegan and some norren high chieftain would glare at each other from across the field, fling down their swords, and rush to embrace each other, all misdeeds forgotten. Better to delay the formal announcement that Narashtovik was ready to make hate until after the other participants had committed themselves.

In the meantime, they would set the stage. Olivander would return east to muster the townships, then head to the mountains beyond to see if any of the free peoples cared to war against Gask in return for ongoing recognition of their independence from Narashtovik (which, if the norren prevailed, would declare independence of its own, creating a buffer state between Gask and the free tribes). Kav could harness his deep reservations toward their involvement by traveling to Setteven to petition the king and any other nobles who'd listen to cool down and seek a peaceful solution. Several council men and women would tour cathedrals and temples on both sides of the border, pressuring local priests to petition their own mayors and baronets to provide political opposition. Somburr still had links to a de facto spy network he'd belonged to earlier in life, and would leverage those for whatever they were worth. Most of the elderly members would remain in Narashtovik with Cally to maintain home rule.

And Dante, naturally enough, would travel to the Territories to conduct forward operations.

"Specifically, you're going to organize the tribes," Cally told him once the Council had hammered the major details flat (a process that wound up spilling over into the next day) and the last of the other members finally vacated the chambers. "Inasmuch as such a thing is possible, anyway. I recognize that bringing those squabbling bands together is like trying to fill a bucket with water scooped by hand when the bucket is also made out of water. But whatever hope we have at this point rests on uniting them, however temporarily."

Dante smiled. "Why do I always get the jobs that can't be done?"

"Because it's funny to watch you try. Furthermore, you not only have extensive experience with the clans, but with the method I plan to help unite them with."

"Loons?"

Cally looked up. "Precisely. I put together several more while you were gallivanting around the country. Not enough for all the clans, but it should be enough to spark a confederation."

"You're just going to hand them out."

"No," Cally said. "You are."

Dante twisted his sideburn between his fingers. "How are we going to keep them from falling into enemy hands? Right now they're about the only advantage we've got."

"Since I am so very clever, I have already solved that plan. For one thing, I have made them to resemble norren earrings. The sort of thing any Gaskan blueblood will dismiss as tribal bric-a-brac. Secondly, I'm only sending you with one of each pair. The others will stay with me. Even if one of the loons winds up in the hands of a sorcerer who recognizes artificery when he sees it, and even if he is then able to threaten, trick, or torture a norren chief into confessing what the loon is used for, he'll be navigating with half a map."

"I see."

"You're not convinced?"

"We figured out how to make them easily enough, didn't we? The court has nethermancers of its own."

"Only the ones who couldn't hack it on the Council," Cally scoffed. "Anyway, if this is our lone advantage, logic demands we leverage it to the hilt. Start in the borderlands. Once the clans there are working in tandem, then you can see about hitching the inland clans to the team."

It was already mid-afternoon, but there was no time left to waste. Dante dispatched servants to ready horses and provisions. Blays received the news of their latest trip with a broad grin.

"Another ride into the wild, huh? Can't wait."

"What are you so happy about?" Dante said.

"We'll be out of the rain and killing Settevite bastards. What's *not* to be happy for?"

Dante alerted Lira and Mourn, then returned to Cally's to update his maps with the latest news of riots, raids, and skirmishes. There had been more fighting on the outskirts of Dollendun. He planned to head there, rendezvous with the clans who'd been making forays into the burning city, hand out some loons and offer whatever personal aid they could provide, and then continue south all the way to the fringes of Tantonnen, where they could enlist Waill and the Clan of the Golden Field to act as the centerpiece of the region.

That was the plan, anyway. If Moddegan gathered his troops slowly enough, they might even see it through.

Cally brought out a sack filled with carved bone earrings. Groomsmen brought around the horses. Mourn considered his thick-legged mount with his usual pensiveness. "I think I've traveled more in the last two months than I did in any year with the Nine Pines."

They rode out an hour before sunset. The city soon faded into the haze of rain. The rain took two more days to disappear, chased away by a blustery wind that blew itself out overnight, leading to a clear morning just this side of warm. They each had a spare horse and switched them out every few hours. At their pace, they would reach Dollendun in a couple more days.

They never made it.

That afternoon, smoke bloomed to the southwest. By the time they reached the town, the fires had burnt themselves out, but the film of smoke remained, seething up from the scorched shells of houses. Dante checked his map, but it made no mention of the town; by his reckoning, they were some ten or twenty miles from the border into human lands. Towering figures flung buckets of water on the smoldering coals. Cave-homes stared down from the hills. Dante and the other two humans drew dark looks on their way to the relatively untouched north end of town, but they were saved, perhaps, by the presence of Mourn—unbranded, unshackled, even armed with a sword and bow of his own.

Foot- and hoofprints dried in the muck of the streets. Sobs filtered through broken shutters. Arrows poked from the ground and the walls of unburnt homes. Blood crusted the stones of the main road. The first undamaged inn they passed was closed, but the second had its doors wide. Inside, a handful of norren sat in tired silence, soot griming their nails and ringing their eyes. Behind the bar, a dour woman watched them with open hostility. Her hair was drawn back in a bun so large and round it resembled a second head.

"What happened here?" Dante said.

She gave him one look. "Jainn must have left the stove on again."

"Oh yeah?" Blays said. "Cooking king's-soldiers-surprise again?"

The woman almost smiled. "It has a way of flaming up."

"Who resisted?" Dante said. "Townsfolk?"

"Wandering do-gooders."

"A clan? Which one?"

"Of them."

It took Dante a moment to realize that wasn't a foreign norren word. His temper flared. "It's critical we speak to the clan. We're here to help them fight back."

The woman glanced between the four of them. "Quite a host you've brought, too. The king will be running scared in no time."

Dante crossed his arms. While he composed himself, Mourn gave the woman a small smile and a smaller nod. "We'd like to speak to the chief. If that can be arranged, we'll be here in town for the next few days."

"No we won't," Dante said. "We can't waste time here when Dollendun's being overrun by—"

"Yes, we will." Mourn turned to him and bent down until their eyes were level. "We came here to answer need. Look at this town: is there any question that it is in need? If we leave without helping, haven't we declared there are some who aren't worth saving?"

Dante nodded jerkily. The woman watched them go, motionless as a grave-pillar. Mourn marched them back to the burnt-out rows of houses on the south side of town. The gazes of the locals were as cold as the sunset. Wails carried down a hoof-churned side street. Mourn led them to another inn where the tables had been piled along one wall. On the floor, norren lay head to toe, groaning and bleeding, some unconscious, tended to by silent men and women bearing bandages and rags. As Mourn stepped inside, the tallest norren Dante had ever seen arose from the wounded, detoured to the wall to pick up a chair, and stopped a few feet from the door, chair cocked back in one hand as easily as Dante would brandish a torch.

Mourn nodded at Dante. "This man is a healer."

"Step outside." The norren's voice was as low as a bear's. "Continue stepping until all you can see are the empty hills."

Mourn advanced a single step. "Take my head if he harms one soul."

The man drew back his head. A drop of blood slid from his hand and spattered the floor. "Kneel, then. Your face to the wall. And speak to Josun Joh if one word's been a lie."

Mourn turned and knelt along the wooden wall, eyes closed, hands folded behind his back. The towering norren grabbed Dante's neck with his free hand and half-carried him across the room to a norren whose brown hair was matted to her head by blood and sweat. Her face was ashen, twitching. The man crouched down and unwrapped a blood-soaked rag from around her middle. A rope of gray-pink intestines oozed from a gash in her stomach.

Dante inhaled with a hiss. The man's hand ground into the muscles of his neck. Dante reached for his knife; the hand clasped his throat, crushing it closed.

"I can help," Dante gasped. "Please."

The strangling pressure eased. Dante coughed, massaging his throat. Once his coughing had settled, he cut a quick line on his left arm. Shadows flocked to the gleaming blood. He balled them in his hands and lowered his palms to the woman's blood-slick belly.

"Water," Dante muttered.

Footsteps plodded between the moaning wounded. Dante pushed the loop of intestine back inside the woman's feverish body and held it in place with a firm hand. The nether flowed from him to her, seeking torn flesh, spurting veins. Dante took long breaths to fight the dizziness that still seized him when faced with the worst of wounds — particularly those of the gut and their hot, sour stink that threatened to close his throat as firmly as the norren man's grip. The woman barked in pain, head contorting to one side. Boots clumped across the floor. Dante's dizziness evaporated. Nether rushed alongside her rent belly, mending it like a pink zipper.

A jug thrust into Dante's view. He took it with one hand, other still clamped to the woman's stomach, and splashed water over her wound, rinsing loose scraps of flesh and pink water to the floor. He removed his hand from her body. The cleansing water revealed clean and unmarked skin.

The norren man sank to his knees and leaned forward to press his forehead against the woman's. He spoke her name, but she slept. He rose with tears dripping into his beard. "She's my wife."

Dante poured water over his grimy hands. "And she will be for years."

He nodded to the ranks of wounded. "Can you help the others?"

"A few. There are limits."

"I humbly ask you to exhaust them."

Dante nodded, stood, and shuffled to the next victim, a man so young his beard was still patchy. His right arm ended just above the elbow. A belt knotted it off in a tourniquet. A far easier fix: all Dante had to do was stop the bleeding.

He beckoned to the shadows. Mind half-submerged in his

work, he heard the tall man approach Mourn at the wall and bid him to rise. Dante ran his fingers along the severed arm, snagging bone. Scabs followed wherever he touched.

"We'll leave you here," Mourn said from beside him. "There is work elsewhere, too."

"Thank you," Dante said.

Mourn paused mid-step, as if puzzled, then thumped away. The door closed. Sunlight shrank from the windows. The unwounded norren lit candles, brought Dante water and stitches and cotton, which he turned to with increasing frequency as the nether grew stubborn and his head grew sluggish. Still, this work came easier than it ever had, as if the fickle shadows had decided, this once, that his work was their work as well. He helped heal a dozen villagers before he reached for the nether and found it wasn't there.

The tall man—his name was Soll—insisted Dante stay at his house, where he was fed seared beef and smoked salmon to "repay his body for its labors." He ate until he had to be helped to bed.

At breakfast, Mourn joined him. Soll had found the others last night fresh off digging a survivor out from beneath a collapsed barn. Today, they planned to continue to clean up wreckage and to patrol the outlying fields against any return of Gaskan soldiers. Dante accepted this without complaint. As much as he wanted to continue to Dollendun, he wanted to finish his work here first.

He spent the day at the makeshift hospital, tending to the lesser wounds he hadn't had the strength to mend the day before. Norren came and went to watch him work, moving on in silence. He napped through noon and woke halfway refreshed. At suppertime, he rose with Soll's help to move to the next patient and found none remained.

"Come," Soll said. "Farren wants to see you."

"That's nice," Dante said.

"The woman at the Inn of Three Fingers."

"The one who talks like her words cost a penny apiece?"

"That's her," Soll smiled. He walked Dante across town. Norren swung massive hammers into charred walls, bashing them to the ground. Others shoveled wreckage into wheelbarrows. At the Inn of Three Fingers, Farren offered Dante a single nod.

"The Clan of the Broken Heron is camped outside town."

"They're the ones who fought the king's men?"

"Chief's named Hopp. If you can keep your eyelids apart, he'll see you tonight."

Dante knew he couldn't, so he returned to Soll's to nap again. He woke after dark sore but relaxed. The others were just getting in.

"No time for dinner," Dante said. "We have a meeting with the clan."

"The clan can wait," Blays said. "My stomach can't."

Lira socked him on the arm. "Eat while you ride. Or are you one of those people who has to hang on to the saddle with both hands?"

"Just one. I need the other to cover my eyes."

Soll put together a sack of bread and sausage and showed them the way, leaving his brother to tend to his still-mending wife. A three-quarter moon drenched the grass in silver. Four miles east from the town, he crossed a stream threaded between two hills, then followed it north for a few hundred yards until Mourn pointed out a trio of fallen sticks.

"Wildsign."

He'd no sooner spoken the word than five norren warriors emerged from the trees lining the streambed. They peered at Soll, nodded, and led the group further through the trees.

The Clan of the Broken Heron had no fires or children. They slept and sat beneath the trees, trimming twigs from arrow shafts, sewing ash-rubbed bone and dull bits of metal into cured leather hides. In a moonlit clearing, a man of late middle age laid clean lines of black paint onto a circular canvas tied to a wooden stand by leather thongs. He was beardless, the first shaven man Dante had seen since Dollendun. On his stubbled right cheek, a circled R was branded into his skin.

He didn't look up from his paint. "I'm told you're a friend to the norren in Plow?"

"We're a friend to all norren," Dante said. "Are you Hopp?"

"How can you be friend to all norren? Are you my friend? Are you friend to my enemy clans, too?"

"Yes, in fact. It's my intent to ensure that you and all your enemies survive to keep killing each other for generations to come."

Hopp glanced up, mouth half-open as he considered Dante. "You're from Narashtovik?"

"And we're here to make both our homelands free."

"You think we can't keep ourselves free?"

Dante took a step forward, holding the bag of loons. "I don't know. I do know we'll have a better chance if we all stand the same line."

"I see." The branded norren laid another stroke of paint on his canvas and chuckled in satisfaction. "We'll be fine on our own."

Dante quashed a surge of anger. "Do you know what loons are?"

"Do you?"

"As well as how to build them." He held up the bag of earrings. "We want to give one to each of the clans. We can coordinate movements. Attacks. Bring all the norren to bear against the king's armies."

A woman laughed from the darkness. Dante startled. She sat against the trunk of a nearby tree, her remaining teeth white in the moonlight. Hopp smiled over his painting.

"Okay," he said.

"You'll take it?"

"Who wouldn't want to fight together in perfect harmony?" He held out his hand. Dante fished a loon from the bag and set it in his palm. It was bone and bluish silver, the color of moonlight.

"A drop of blood on the bone will link it to you," Dante said. "Let us know whenever you see Gaskan troops. With enough warning, we can prevent what happened in Plow from befalling any more towns."

"That would be nice, wouldn't it?" Hopp said. "Good night."

The contingent of warriors saw them back across the river. Soll led them back towards town.

"Chalk this up to cultural differences," Blays said, "but I didn't get the idea he took that very seriously."

"It's hard to say," Mourn said. "Not hard in the sense that I find the words physically difficult. They are no harder than other words. But in the sense that norren can be guarded even between clans. Trying to read their responses to humans is like reading the face of a fish."

At Soll's, Dante tried to raise Cally to tell him the news, but the old man didn't answer. Dante paced, contemplating a second attempt, then realized it was somewhere after 2 AM. He went to bed and tried again in the morning.

Cally answered within seconds, his tone somewhere between annoyance and amusement. "I take it you made contact with your first clan."

"Did Hopp reach you?" Dante said. "What did he say?"

"I will recount the entire conversation. First, there was a fart. Followed by 'Goodbye.' Then came a splash. Our chat concluded with an hour of what sounded like rushing water until the loon went dead."

"A...fart?"

"Yes," Cally said. "That's what I choose to believe, anyway, as the alternative would be far worse to contemplate."

Dante rubbed sleep from his eyes. "Maybe a child got ahold of it."

"The timbre was notably adult. Of the voice, that is."

"Okay. I'll go speak to him and find out what happened."

"Do that. Where are you, anyway?"

"A town called Plow," Dante said. "Few miles from the border. Yesterday, Moddegan's men burned half of it to the ground."

"Plow," Cally said, distant. Paper ruffled in the background. "Somburr's been in Righmark the last three days. That's due west on the borders. Two days ago, he reported a troop heading east. Another left yesterday."

"A second wave?" Dante glanced at the sunlight through the window. It was at least nine o'clock, approaching ten. "I'll ride out this minute. If Hopp's got any doubts about us, this should put them to the grave."

Mourn was already awake. Lira answered at a knock. Blays didn't; Dante had to barge into his small room and rip the sheets away from his bed. As they readied, Dante found Soll pulling planks from a charred home down the street. He nodded at Dante's request to act as their guide and led them back into the wild.

The Clan of the Broken Heron hadn't moved. Soll was intercepted by a man and a woman a bowshot from the camp. After a brief and somewhat tense discussion, they took Dante alone to Hopp, who knelt by the stream, shirtless, washing black paint from his hands, as if he'd kept painting all night. His back was crossed with switch-thin scars.

"What happened?" Dante said.

Hopp smiled at the water. "I was inspired."

"To drop your loon in the water?"

"Are you sure that's what happened?"

"No. You might have thrown it instead."

Hopp took his hands from the water and dried them with a cloth finger by finger. "I dropped it. I couldn't find it. Have you come to give me another?"

"If you're sure you won't drop it." Dante reached in his pocket. "I've got another gift, too. More troops are inbound from the west. They could reach Plow today."

Hopp squinted through the sunlight bouncing from the stream. "Someone ought to do something about that."

"We'll help if you'd let us. We're stronger than we look. I'm one of the strongest nethermancers in the land."

"Why are you so keen to help?"

Dante splayed his palms. "Why is every norren in the world so suspicious of that?"

A woman laughed the same laugh from the night before. Again, she leaned against a tree, concealed by the grass and the tree's low boughs.

Dante gasped involuntarily. "Are you scaring me on purpose?"

"An old woman can't rest her back?"

"It wouldn't be an issue if she rested more loudly."

She laughed dryly. "This reminds me of a story. It's a story from very long ago. No one who was there is alive to remember it. Instead, we remember for them. Do you want to hear my story?"

Dante glanced through the trees in the direction of the others. "Of course."

"Everyone should listen as well as you." She hunched forward, speaking to the space between them. "And so. Long ago, foxes lived in trees. Why did they live in trees? To hunt what was there, and to go unseen by the creatures of the ground. Foxes never fell.

When they did fall, they waved their tails and landed softly. This is how one fox was spotted by a passing votte.

"The votte thought about pouncing, but the fox was already back among the limbs. It sat on its haunches and said, 'There is a fire. Why don't you come down?' The fox flicked its tail and said nothing. The votte sniffed the air. 'Can't you smell the smoke? Get down from that tree, or the smoke you smell will be your own bones.' The fox sniffed, nodded, and said nothing.

"The votte began to pace in the dirt around the trunk. 'This is unreasonable,' it said. 'I can see the fire there on that hill. What do you think you're going to do?' The fox squinted between the leaves, saw the fire, and said nothing. 'The flames are here,' the votte said. 'I can feel them like a smothering hand. Its smoke is maggots in my nostrils. And you're in the tree! Come down, and run with me!'

"But the fox was gone. The votte ran. The flames pursued." The old woman lowered her hand, bladelike, to her lap. "Much later, when the world changed, the fox changed with it, and moved to the ground. This is the end."

"What's a votte?" Dante said.

"I don't know. I've never seen one. They're gone."

"Did they all die in the fire?"

"Why would you think that? Do you think the fire burnt the whole world?"

"Give me another loon," Hopp said. "We've got plenty of scouts. We'll tell you if they come to take the town."

Dante smiled and handed him another earring. "Give us the word and we'll be there."

The old woman watched keenly as he returned across the stream. Blays spat out a blade of grass he'd been chewing. "How'd it go? Did the conversation actually take place via mouths this time?"

"No. Now if you'll excuse me, I need a moment with the creek."

"I'll be upstream. Far, far upstream."

"He took the loon," Dante said. "He'll tell us if they see the soldiers. Be ready for a fight."

They returned to Soll's, keeping the horses saddled and their weapons handy. Compared to the racket of industry of the last couple days, the streets were as silent as the wilds: while they'd been out, Soll's brother had spread word another troop might be approaching. The locals had taken to their homes with swords and hammers and spears and axes and hoes.

Hours dragged on. They ate a light lunch of cheese melted on flatbread with greens and herbs plucked from Soll's back garden. Dante killed a few minutes by checking on Soll's wife. She was pale and had lost weight. Her arms were perversely thin for a norren; when she sat up in bed, they hung from her shoulders like broken flowers. She spoke and gestured freely, however, and her stomach was pale and cool, free from infection.

The loon pulsed a couple hours before sunset. Dante's heart pulsed with it.

"I heard from your chief," Cally said in his ear. "They've located the soldiers. Hopp wants you to meet the clan at Farrow Hill at once."

"Where's that?"

"You know, I'm not quite sure. As it turns out, I'm more than a hundred miles away. If you'd like to wait two or three days, perhaps I can ride out and find it for you."

"Did he say anything else?"

"He did not."

"Then I need to go," Dante said. "If you never hear from me again, build me some statues." He broke the connection. The others stared at him, eyebrows raised. He turned to Soll. "Where's Farrow Hill?"

"Farrow Hill," he said slowly. "South and southwest. Eight or ten miles."

"Can you take us?"

"On my back if I have to." He gestured to his wife's room. "I still owe you the world."

They mounted up and rode south along a dirt path through the grass. Mice darted away from the clop of hooves. Borbirds squawked from the sparse and thorny trees. Dante rode fast over the rising path. The ground rolled for several miles, then began a steady climb. Every stir of the grass made Dante's eyes dart and his heart skip. The hill leveled off. Ahead, the stark ruins of a stone tower waited in the wind. Behind, the land spread like a full-color map, a sprawl of green grass and the haphazard squares of rich brown farms. Dante could just make out the ribbon of the road. Around it, Plow was a tiny cluster of dark mounds.

Blays gazed at the collapsed tower. One wall stood twenty feet high, orange lichen encrusted to the dark stone. Most of it lay in an uneven mound, half-buried. Grass and spring's first blue wildflowers sprouted between the cracked stone.

"So where is everybody?" Blays said.

Dante reached for his loon and made sure it was aligned to Cally. "You there?"

"Yes," Cally said a moment later.

"Well, they're not. Have you spoken to Hopp again?"

"I would have let you know if I had."

"Can you raise him? I just want to make sure we're in the right place." He switched off.

"That's Farrow Tower," Soll pointed. "There is only the one, and it is on Farrow Hill."

Dante stared over the distant plain. "This feels wrong."

"They probably figured we could win the battle by ourselves," Blays said. "Honestly, I can't blame them."

"I'm sure Hopp farting into the loon was just a sign of respect."

"I don't know why we're even wasting time out here. We should march straight to Setteven, storm the palace, carve a tunnel through everyone who gets in our way, and slap the king with a wet glove until he makes Mourn king."

"I don't want to be king," Mourn said.

"That's all right." Blays wiped wind-blown grit from his eyes. "You can cede the crown to me."

Wind rustled. Birds chirped. Three minutes later, Dante's loon pulsed. "What'd he say?"

"He's not responding," Cally said. "Do you think something's wrong?"

"I don't know. There's at least forty warriors in their clan. Unless they all fell down the same well, I'd expect one of them to have made it out here."

"I'll inform you the moment I hear a thing. I know how you get when things are uncertain."

The link blanked out. Dante stared down the hill, straining his ears so hard they rang with strange tones. He began to sweat under his doublet. Blays trotted around the crest of the hill and found nothing but open grass. As the sun dropped, the wind grew steady and cold. Dante felt sick, tingly, his head overrun by questions and doubts.

"What exactly did Hopp say to you this morning?" Mourn said.

"Nothing. That he'd take the loon and scout for the soldiers."

"That's all?"

"That's all." He blew into his hands to warm them. "There was an old woman with him. She told me the story of the fox and the votte."

A frown unfolded beneath Mourn's beard. "How does that story go?"

"I don't really feel like swapping campfire tales just now."

"Just tell me how it went. Please."

Dante gave him a look. His eyes were anxious, guarded. Dante sighed and repeated the story of the querulous votte and the silent fox.

At the end, Mourn winced like he'd just taken a big bite of soup and chomped down on an unexpected bit of bone. "We should go back to town."

"What is it?"

"That story wasn't a story. Well, it was. It told about a thing that happened. But it was also a test."

"Of his patience?" Blays said. "It didn't even have an ending."

Mourn shook his shaggy head. "Because there is no ending. The fox can't trust the votte and it doesn't need to because this isn't the first fire it's seen. It already knows the signs of fire and what to do when it comes. And long after the vottes have died or gone away, foxes live on, because they know when to change."

"Oh," Dante said.

"You see?"

"Right."

"All I see is two cryptic assholes," Blays said.

"The norren are like the fox," Dante said. "I don't know if the votte is Narashtovik, or Gask, or humans in general. Either way, they can't trust us and don't need us."

"So Hopp sent us on a votte hunt," Blays said. "Just for a laugh?

Or to get us away from something?"

"Lyle's balls," Dante said. The sun neared the horizon, piercing and red. "We'd better get back to town."

Twilight slowed their return. It was full dark by the time they rode into Plow. Men jogged down the streets armed with bows and spears and pitchforks, whooping and laughing. Soll pulled aside one of his neighbors to get the news. The Clan of the Broken Heron had ambushed a detachment of the king's men miles north of town. Not a single redshirted soldier had survived the skirmish.

"Is it always going to be like this?" Dante said. "We come with aid, and they send us off in the wrong direction and laugh behind their hands? What will they do when an army of ten thousand sweeps through the hills?"

"You must understand," Mourn said. "Who are you to a clan? Do you look any different from the king?"

"Then let's move on. Try a different group. They can't all feel this way."

"We *could* waste our time," Blays said. "Or we can try something that'll work."

"You've got a better idea?"

"It's very simple. We stop being human and start being norren."

"I'll see what I can do." Dante splayed his hand, grabbed up a fistful of nether, and flicked it at Blays. "Kablam!" The shadows flashed in a shower of sparks. "Oh dear, it didn't work. Should I try again?"

"If you're having fun," Blays said. "But my plan's a little simpler." He grinned at Mourn. "I think we should join a clan."

18

Dante shook his head. "That is among the dumbest things you've ever said. And I once heard you ask what a female rooster was called."

Blays quirked his mouth skeptically. "I would rather not know that than have to grow up in the kind of place where it's common knowledge."

"Like where? The world?"

"Like your hometown. Not that you can call two cottages facing each other a town. Anyway, it's not like you can tell what sex they are by looking at them."

"It's a chicken!"

"Anyway, what do you know?" Blays waved his hand for peace. "Mourn, is this dumb? Or is it in fact brilliantly smart?"

Mourn's eyes shifted. "If you could join a clan, you would be taken much more seriously by many other clans."

"Can we join a clan?" Dante said.

"To my knowledge, which is not exhaustive, and is in fact quite limited, when you consider the small fraction of norren I've known personally, or heard reliable information about, during my as-yet brief life on this—"

"Will you get on with it?"

Mourn folded his arms. "No human ever has."

Dante turned to Blays. "You see? Dumb. Dumb in the way of a rooster with its head cut off."

"Oh, that doesn't mean anything," Blays said. "Look then, how does a norren join another clan? You guys must marry outsiders now and then."

"I'm not marrying a norren," Dante said.

"Is it the hair?" Mourn said. "Norren women aren't any hairier than human women. Not so far as I've been able to tell, anyway."

"It's not a species thing. I'm not marrying *anyone*."

"Women everywhere will be happy to hear it," Blays said. "Now will you answer the question, Mourn?"

"Well," he said. "There is marriage. There is also a debt system wherein if you can't repay what you owe to a member of another clan, and you're not well-liked enough within your own clan to be worth starting a feud over, then you may be offered to the other clan as a temporary slave, with the right to join that new clan once your period of slavery has concluded."

"How long does that take?" Dante said.

"Two or three years, typically."

"We'll just ask Moddegan to hold off the invasion until then. He seems reasonable."

"That's it?" Blays said. "What if you just like some other clan more?"

"Well, you could simply ask to join," Mourn said. "A clan can do whatever it likes with itself, can't it?"

Blays threw up his hands. "Why didn't you start with that?"

"Why don't we skip all this?" Dante said. "Why don't we just go to the Clan of the Nine Pines and get their backing to distribute the loons?"

"I'd rather not," Mourn said.

"Why not?"

"Because they might kill me."

"Well, that seems a bit reactionary," Blays said.

"I abandoned the clan in time of war. It would be their right."

"The Clan of the Broken Heron is right here," Lira spoke up. "What can it hurt to ask them?"

"This could work," Mourn said. "Right now, no one takes you seriously. If you were adopted by a clan, many others would suddenly discover that what you have to say is worth listening to."

"Fine," Dante said. Down the street, torches whirled. Norren laughed in their booming voices. Four men heaved around a corner, leaning forward as if into a gale, lifting their knees high as if wading through water. Taut ropes stretched behind them. Torchlight splashed over the bodies of four red-shirted soldiers bouncing through the muddy streets. "But if Hopp says no, we move on. Without argument."

Dante told Soll to go home to his wife and led the others through the hills to the stream. Even in darkness, he found it and the campsite readily enough, but the clan was nowhere in sight—they'd left nothing behind but fish bones and latrines. Dante rode along the stream half a mile in both directions and found nothing but grass and trees and moonlight. Shortly before midnight, he returned to Soll's, where the looming norren opened the door and promised to help them find the Broken Herons in the morning.

He came through. Following the slaughter of the king's soldiers, the clan had relocated several miles south to recuperate and hunt fresh fields. Warriors snored in the morning sunlight. Those who were awake came to stop Dante's band with spears and swords, but on the word of Mourn and Soll, they were allowed once more to see Hopp, who sat on a broad rock by the stream, flicking a lightweight hook above the surface of the water.

The chieftain didn't turn. He sighed through his beard. "Why don't you save us all the trouble and throw that sack of yours straight in the stream?"

"We're not here about the loons," Dante said.

"Then are you here to congratulate me?"

"Yeah, hell of a victory," Blays said. "It was so impressive it's inspired us to join your clan."

Hopp laughed, his thick middle bulging under his deerskins. "I don't think you're tall enough. Maybe we could hang you from your ankles for a month?"

Mourn shuffled his feet and gazed at the bed of grass beside the streambank. "They are regrettably serious."

Hopp gazed between their somber faces. "You are, aren't you? What do you even know of the Clan of the Broken Heron?"

"That you destroyed a troop of the king's soldiers with minor losses," Dante said. He glanced at the old woman who sat motionless beside a tree. "That even though I couldn't hear it, you were kind enough to tell me how to be a better friend."

The woman laughed softly. Hopp smiled slowly. "And what makes you worthy of the clan?"

"That's not for me to decide."

"Are we finally getting somewhere?" the old woman said.

Hopp touched the R branded on his cheek. "No. I see no claim to our clan. No right to even ask it."

"We were there when the Clan of the Nine Pines freed the Green Lake from Lord Cassinder," Dante said. "We brought peace between the Clan of the Golden Field and the farmers of Tantonnen, securing bread for your people against the upcoming war."

"Damn, that sounds outright heroic," Blays said. "Not to mention the four years we've spent bringing the Territories food, silver, and weapons. Put it like that, and you could say we're already a de facto clan of our own."

"Or that you are the cause of this conflict in the first place," Hopp said.

Dante tipped back his chin. "Would you rather go on as slaves to the king?"

Hopp smiled tightly, distorting the R branded on his cheek. He nodded downstream. The creek ran straight for hundreds of feet, gushing around boulders beneath the canopy of willows. Hopp pointed to a rue tree just before the stream bent and disappeared behind the willows.

"See that rue? Swim to it, and you can join the clan."

Blays began to unbutton his doublet. "Is that it?"

"Without taking a single breath of air." The beardless norren raised his shrubby brows. "Think your devotion to the clan will support you after your air runs out?"

"Well, that's just obstinate." Blays shrugged out of his doublet and set to work on his belt.

"What are you doing?" Lira said.

"Going for a dip. With my head underwater, I won't have to hear any more of this nonsense."

"That must be three hundred yards! No one can swim that in one breath."

"We'll see about that." He finished with his belt and plonked down in the grass to unlace his boots. Dried mud crusted the fraying laces. "Anyway, what's there to lose? If I can't do it, I pop up for a few deep breaths, we all share a good cry, and then we move on."

Lira turned to Hopp with a look that could slice a falling feather. "Your test is absurd. What will it prove?"

Hopp stretched his arms behind his back, shoulders bustling. "Whether he's got gills?"

Blays flung his boots at Dante and stood to shed his pants. "Keep those dry. There's nothing worse than walking around with squelchy boots." He glanced at Hopp. "Well, going to watch me? If this is on my honor, why don't you turn your back and I'll holler when I'm there?"

Hopp grinned, wolfish, and stood, knees popping. He gestured palm-up at the stream. "You've got spirit, don't you? I'm suddenly wishing I'd gone with a task that was remotely possible."

"Your loss. Or mine, if I bang my head on one of those rocks." Reduced to his underwear, Blays waded into the stream, grimacing as the hill-fed cataract washed over his calves. Another step plunged him to his thighs. He took three long breaths, swelling his muscled chest and bulging his belly. He sighed down at the swirling currents. "The balls are always the worst, aren't they?"

Before anyone could answer, he lunged forward, diving into the stream. Lira swore. Hopp strode along the banks. In confusion, Dante jogged after him, scanning the foaming water for a hint of Blays. For some seconds he saw nothing but the constant rush of water, opaqued by turbulence, rippling over half-hidden stones. Splashing pulled his gaze downstream. Thirty yards away, far past where Dante had been tracking, Blays burst from the surface, keeping his face below the water as his arms and legs churned. The current pulled him along, doubling his natural speed. Dante sped to a light run to keep pace. Hopp, Lira, and Mourn thumped beside him. Three warriors who had been listening from a distance sprinted to catch up.

A boulder cleaved the stream dead ahead. Somehow Blays spotted it through the roiling chaos of bubbles and water, cutting along its left flank. A quarter of the way to the rue's Y-shaped trunk, the stream narrowed and deepened, submerging any rocks. Blays cruised onward. Dante tore through the grass, splashing in the reeds. Halfway to the tree, Blays slowed, legs faltering; as if remembering where he was, he pushed ahead, thrashing at the hurtling water. Dante realized he'd been holding his own breath.

He let it go in a whoosh, tasting sweet spring air.

The stream curved gently. Blays drifted toward the right bank, his bare back a splash of white atop the dark water. Fifty yards from the rue, he stopped moving.

"Arawn's mercy!" Lira shouted. She charged forward, angling toward the bank, stripping off her doublet. Blays floated on, borne on the current. Dante rushed after Lira and grabbed her arm.

"Stop! He's almost there!"

She whirled, mouth agape, and punched him in the jaw. He staggered into the damp grass. She rushed on, hopping as she yanked at her boots. Dizzy and nauseous, Dante lumbered to his feet and ran after her, overtaken by Mourn, Hopp, and the three warriors. Just before the rue, Lira slogged into the water, fully clothed except her bare feet. She dived into the stream and thrashed towards Blays. Beside him, she threw her arm over his chest and pulled his head from the torrent.

They banged into a rock, spinning crazily, disappearing under a white flush of water. Dante yelled. Their heads popped back up. Lira sputtered. Blays hung limp. She paddled for shore, sweeping downstream. A few feet from the bank, she found her footing and hauled Blays toward the thicket of reeds. Dante splashed into the stream. Her face was white, sopping, furious. She tensed as if to punch Dante again, then pivoted her hip to sling Blays' loose body forward. Dante ducked his shoulder under Blays' arm and dragged him onto dry land.

Lira flopped Blays on his back. His arms slapped into the grass. She bore down on his pale chest, pumping it repeatedly, hard enough to crack a rib.

"What the hell are you doing?" Dante said.

"What we do when men drowned in the islands." She pumped again, then sat back, heaving, hair straggled down her face. "Come on!"

Blays lay cold and still and white. In a panic, Dante called the nether from beneath the leaves and stones, but he had nowhere to send it: no wounds to knit, no blood to stanch. His ears roared. Two minutes ago, Blays had been joking, grinning. Lira gave his chest another series of compressions. His head rolled, mouth half-open, tongue pale as a cave fish. Lira yelled, a rising cry that could split the world. She hammered her fist against Blays' chest.

Water gouted from his mouth. He coughed, chest wracking, limbs flapping. Lira laughed through shocked tears. Dante's lip throbbed where she'd punched him.

Blays sat up and blinked at the rue tree upstream. "So do we get new names? I don't know why you'd join a new tribe if you don't get epic new names."

"Like the Man Who Thought He Was a Fish?" Dante said.

"I was thinking more along the lines of Warrior Whose Balls Were So Big They Scared Away the Sun."

"You cheated!" Hopp said. "You just floated the last bit."

"Bullshit. I didn't take a single breath of air." Blays tried to stand and staggered. Lira reached for one arm, Dante the other. His skin was as cold as shadow. He coughed again, spitting stream-water. "See?"

"I don't remember saying if it could be air *or* water."

Blays snorted, shivering, and turned to the three warriors who'd joined the chase. "Which was it?"

Two gazed away into the trees. The third glared at them, letting the silence draw out, then turned to Blays. "Just air."

"Roast your eyes," Hopp cursed. He clapped his hands and faced Dante. "Who's next to prove their devotion to the clan?"

Nether leapt to Dante's hands. "Do you listen to your own words? *One* of us had to swim for all the rest to join."

"You're right." Hopp grinned wolfishly, stretching his scar. "Can you blame me for wanting to drown a couple of you and save me the trouble?" He extended his hand, palm down in the norren way. "Welcome to the clan."

Cally was less than impressed with their triumph. "How do you know this isn't another of their games? Have you actually done anything clannish yet?"

"We just joined this morning," Dante said into his loon.

"It seems to me this is a perfect example of that particularly norren sense of humor where they're more than content to go on making fun of you for as long as it takes you to figure out that you're being made fun of."

"What?"

"They're playing you for a fool. They'll keep you safely tucked away in their camp while you delude yourself that once you earn their trust, they'll allow you into the inner circle of clan chiefs. What proof do you have this is worth a moment of your time?"

"None," Dante said. "But if we don't try it, we'll never reach these clans at all."

Cally grunted dubiously. "And what about the dozens of others who would gladly accept our loons right now if only you bothered to visit them?"

"If they'll take loons from any old idiot out of Narashtovik, then send any old idiot out of Narashtovik."

"That could make a certain amount of sense."

"Give it a try. Please. If it turns out you need us to distribute them after all, we can leave this place. But unless we give this a shot, half the clans will never give us the time of day."

"All right," Cally allowed. "But only because I don't think I've ever heard you say 'please' before."

Hopp had been circulating through the milling members of the clan for a couple hours, presumably to explain why their numbers had been suddenly bolstered by four new members, three of whom were humans. He returned as the sun peaked, beckoning his new charges in with a swirl of his hand.

"It's time to discover what you can do for your new family," he said. "You're all warriors, whatever that means to you?"

Dante nodded. "I can command the nether. Blays and Lira, they're handy with a—"

"Fine," Hopp said. "What nulla do you possess?"

"Fletching," Mourn said.

"That right? Bone, stone, or metal?"

"Bone and stone." Mourn gazed at the grass. "I'm waiting to work with metal until I perfect the fundamentals."

Hopp nodded without any sense of approval. "How about the rest of you?"

"Healing," Dante said.

"I don't have one besides fighting," Blays said. "Unless looking good counts."

"Then I have an idea for you." Hopp smiled, eyeteeth white in the late morning sun. "Perhaps it's catching fish?"

"I don't think so. My appeal transcends most species, but I think fish are too dumb."

"Let me put it this way: go catch your clan some fish. In fact, perhaps *all* your nulla is to catch fish."

"Are you sure this is how we can best be put to use?" Dante said.

Hopp drew back his head, affronted. "Do you want your clan to starve? What could be more important than keeping them fed and ready to swing their swords? In Narashtovik, does food simply drift in through the windows every night?"

"No, but it is delivered to the kitchen every morning, because we buy it. Why don't we just go into town and lay down some silver?"

"Because." Hopp closed on Dante, leaning down until their eyes were nearly level. Dante flinched; it was like standing in the path of a toppling tree. He smelled fresh sweat and crushed grass. Hopp tapped him on the side of the head. "What do you do when there are no towns? Where do you buy your fish from then? If you fling your coins in the stream, do you think it will belch forth trout?"

Dante sighed and stuck out his hand. "Then give us our poles and let's be done with this."

"Poles?" The norren chief cocked his head. "You will use spears. Bad news: we are out of spears."

"What are you talking about?" Blays gestured at two warriors sparring down the stream. Long staffs spun and clacked, metal tips glinting in the sun. "I suppose those are just very long pole-mounted knives?"

"Those are fighting spears. You do not use fighting spears for fishing. Would you use your father's battle-sword to gut a hog?"

"Depends. Is the hog armed?"

Mourn grabbed Blays' shoulder, bunching the doublet's fabric in his fist. "We'll make our own spears. I'll show you if you don't know how."

"It's easy enough, isn't it?" Blays said. "We just have to find a spear-tree."

Hopp smiled to himself as they tramped downstream in search of suitably straight branches among the willows and walnuts.

Dante trampled after Blays through the thigh-high grass. "This whittling will surely help us win the war."

Blays grinned. "You never know. What if Moddegan attacks with a deadly force of twig-men? We'll pare him to ribbons."

"I assume this is one of their tests. We're going to have to fish our hearts out. Fish like we're at war with the fish."

"If trout don't want to be slaughtered in their streambeds, they shouldn't be so delicious when buttered and fried in a pan."

Blays jumped to catch hold of a walnut's lowest branches. He scrabbled into the tree, showering Dante with bark. Dante glanced upstream. Mourn and Lira were dozens of yards away. A branch cracked, but any other noises they made were drowned out by the babble of the stream and the mindless drone of insects whirring through the slumping willows.

"When did you and Lira become a pair?" Dante said.

"What?" Blays glanced down, hands gripping a long branch half as thin as his wrist. "What did she say to you?"

"It was more of a nonverbal cue. In the form of a punch to the face."

"When did that happen?" Blays laughed. "Did you make a pass at her?"

"Earlier this morning when I tried to let you continue drowning for the good of the land." Dante touched his swollen lip. "Haven't you noticed the bruising?"

"I try not to look directly at your face." Blays tensed, pulling the branch down with a sharp crack. Bark and leaves showered Dante's upturned face. Blays tossed the limb to the ground. "You're not mad, are you?"

Dante set to the fallen branch with a knife, trimming twigs and skinning bark to shape it into a spear. "Why would I be mad?"

"Because you always are? I don't know. Sometimes people get mad."

"Well, I'm not."

"Good. Guess I thought you might think it would distract us from our duty or something."

Dante grinned up into the branches. "How dare you two be making moon-eyes at each other? The fate of norren freedom depends on us stabbing these fish!"

Blays pulled down a few more branches, then climbed down to help carve them into killing points. Lira and Mourn caught up with them, spears in hand. They splashed along the cold stream until it widened to a gentle flow among the rocks. Sunlight cleaved through the clear water. Current-drawn weeds pointed downstream, dragonfly nymphs clinging to their stems. Flies circled, buzzing in Dante's ears. He waded into a sluggish eddy beside the bank. Dark missiles of trout lurked in the willow-dappled shadows.

His first thrust missed. So did his second and his fifth and his twentieth. Mourn jabbed, smiled, and cleared his spear from the water, a fish struggling on its tip. After an hour, the norren had landed four. Lira and Blays managed one apiece. Dante had none. His breeches were soaked to the thighs, his patience strained to its peak. Mourn frowned, stepped down from a flat rock, and slogged through the water toward Dante.

"The water lies to you," he said, bulk hunched over the water as he peered at a trout lurking beneath a wall of reeds. "Well, not really. In fact, it's just kind of flowing there not saying anything at all. But the fish isn't where it shows you. It's lower." He struck at the trout with a splash, withdrawing an empty spear. "Well, you get the idea."

Dante did, but his arms and eyes didn't. He didn't land his first fish until mid-afternoon, after they followed the stream to a naturally dammed pond. In those languid waters, Dante acquitted himself with two fish by dusk. Lira and Blays had five and four respectively; Mourn shamed them all with 17. They headed home for camp, each step squeezing water from the rivets of their boots.

Under twilight, Mourn knelt beside Hopp and unrolled the tarp that held their cleaned fish, heads still attached.

"28 fish." Hopp gazed among the men and women seated around the banks of the stream. "39 warriors. This does not add up."

"Got bread?" Lira said.

"Sure."

"That's enough for me."

Hopp gave her an unreadable look and rolled up the tarp. "It had better be. The ground sees no seeds until waiting mouths are full."

Dante ate his bread without complaint. He got up before sunrise to reach the pond by dawn and catch the fish while they were first stirring. He caught a trout and a sunfish before the others splashed into sight.

Ever since Dante had literally been punched into awareness, it was like a spell had been broken between Blays and Lira. They pushed each other in the water, splashing, laughing, teasing. At times, they disappeared around a bend for twenty minutes or more, returning flushed and grinning. During their disappearances, they rarely brought back fish. Dante waded the waters next to Mourn, talking about the norren, about Narashtovik and Mallon, about responsibility and risk and life. Mourn was a slow thinker, as plodding and deliberate in thought as he was with his footsteps or his Nulladoon play, but he was thoughtful, deep, capable of questioning his own assumptions in ways most men would never think to. Hours flowed as quickly as the stream.

Days spun by. When spearfishing grew too frustrating, Dante gathered walnuts, walnut-sized snails, and the tender roots of cattails. He plucked breadgrass and mushrooms and wild carrots. On their fifth day, they returned with enough fish to feed themselves as well as the rest of the clan.

Much like when Dante and Blays had traveled with the Clan of the Nine Pines, the warriors of the Broken Heron paid them little mind. One morning, a woman stopped Dante before he could depart to the stream to show him how to fashion strong hooks from the bones of fish. Another evening, two men came by to swap stories of Dante and Blays' travels throughout the Territories. One challenged Mourn to a friendly wrestling match which Mourn lost after a long struggle.

These interactions were the exceptions to their isolation. The rest of the clan sparred, rested, painted, hunted, scouted, mended weapons and armor and clothes. So often left alone, Dante spoke to the earth. It didn't answer back. He let his mind sink like water through its surface, past the turf and the damp confusion of roots and worms and last year's leaves. Somewhere below imagination, in the silent beds of dirt and stone, the nether rested, untouched, a deeper shadow than the darkness of the underground. Dante let it stay there, watching it, nothing more.

After a week, the Clan of the Broken Heron picked up and walked downstream to the northwest, covering some 15 miles before bedding down. In the morning, Hopp came to them with fishing poles and hooks and cunningly tied lures of feather, fur, and shiny metal.

"Turns out we had these all along," he said. "Go ahead and use them if you want."

At first, Dante returned to the rod with relish, but standing on the bank and waiting for a fish to strike was far less fun than creeping into the water and impaling it with a single thrust of a spear. He fixed a bit of wood near the end of the line and wedged the butt of the pole between rocks. He left it there to catch what it may, rushing back to it, spear in hand, whenever it bent under the weight of a strike.

That evening, they returned to find the clan in bloody disarray. Men limped to the stream to wash their grimy hands and faces and put cold water on their cuts and scrapes and burns. A handful of warriors were gone entirely. Dante found Hopp by the creek, shirtless, wincing. Blood dripped from his hand into the water and swirled downstream.

"That's why we moved," Dante said. "You got word of a battle."

Hopp chuckled. "With such sharp eyes, it's no wonder you catch so many fish."

Dante watched him bleed, seething. "We can stab more than trout, you know."

"Keeping us fed is vital. It leaves the rest of us to fight. Why does anyone ever want to be chieftain when all you get to do is rebuke foolish questions?" Hopp pressed a cloth to his wounded hand, breath hissing between his bared teeth.

"Let me see."

"I'm fine. No one ever died of a cut finger."

"Yes they have. By the thousands. Because a finger and any cuts it carries is the most likely thing to touch dirt, feces, stagnant water, and all the other spoiled things that spoil the body too." Dante came around Hopp's side and grabbed the man's thick wrist. "Now let me see."

Hopp glared at him like an angry cat, then extended his bloody left hand. The tip of his index finger was nearly severed, hanging by a flap of skin. Blood pattered the grass. Dante sealed it back together with a cord of black nether.

Hopp wiggled his finger. He licked his thumb, wiped away the blood, and gave Dante a shrewd look. "I thought they exaggerated what you did in Plow."

"For all I know they did. Now bring me anyone you want to stop bleeding."

A line of wounded cycled between Dante and three men who waited to dress the minor cuts and scrapes with needles, stitches, cloths, liquor, and water. Dante chatted with those he treated, piecing together the day's battle. The clan had rendezvoused with three others just after dawn, rushing down a hill to enswarm a legion of some 120 Gaskan troops in the thick shrubbery between ridges. They broke the surprised redshirt soldiers quickly, pushing them to the very bottom of the valley, but as the norren mounted to rush down the fold and overwhelm them, a cavalry troop burst over the hills and flushed the norren into the brush. From there, they fought a running back-and-forth among the brambles and walnut trees until the chiefs, concerned about the possibility of more reinforcements on the way, beat a slow retreat under cover of the trees. The kingsmen tried to pursue, but after a ferocious norren counter killed eight men in moments, the redshirts backed off to bow range, peppering the clans until the norren slipped away into the hills.

Their adopted clan had lost five warriors in the battle, with another nine suffering modest-to-serious wounds Dante healed as best he could.

At dawn, the clan left the stream and cut north at an easy pace. Three hours and six miles later, they settled back down beside a pond. Mourn strung his bow and shot three mallards, two on the water and another from the sky. Dante saw to those who still needed seeing, then took his rod and spears and caught fish in the yellow haze of a waning afternoon that smelled of budding plants and the gentle rot of still water.

This pattern continued for several more days. The clan recovered. Blays and Lira popped off into the tall grass. Dante fished and tended and gathered. Warriors began to invite Mourn to sit with them during meals. Sometimes he accepted; others, he declined, eating with Dante instead.

Hopp called a meeting. It wasn't a meeting like the Council of Narashtovik, where members were brought together to reach a consensus, but a meeting where a newly-established ruling would be handed down from on high. Previously, the clan had sent out four or six scouts at a time. But Hopp had heard more soldiers were on their way. Henceforth, a full quarter of the clan would be sent out to range at any given time. They would scout in shifts. The shifts would begin that night. There would be no exceptions, including Hopp and the old norren woman who spent most of her days sitting beneath the trees. The humans would scout, too.

Dante was assigned to that first night along with nine other warriors. He'd been up since dawn and didn't trust himself to stay alert through the night. He was paired with a woman named Yola who rarely spoke except to tell him he was too loud. She slipped up the hills as if she'd been walking them her whole life (which as far as he knew she had), bow in hand, undisturbed by the rising cackles of nocturnal birds and the whisper of rodents in the grass. A cold half-moon touched the hills with silver. Before cresting each ridge, Yola dropped to a crouch and crossed the peak, then knelt in the grass and waited, watching the horizons for silhouettes.

After the warmth of the mid-spring days, the frigid night felt like another world, a place where the cold and dark might last forever. But Dante walked that world as if he'd been born to it. Birds hooted. Crickets chirred. His steps stirred the scent of wet dew on broken grass. When the dawn came, chasing that world away in a bloom of ethereal gray-blue, he was more excited for the next night than he was to get to bed.

He asked for and received ongoing nighttime shifts. Blays and Lira asked to scout together and were denied, which Blays complained about until Dante told him he was scaring away the fish.

One afternoon, a scout returned to tell the clan he'd seen a trio of armed men a few miles west headed their way. Hopp arranged a picket and roving sweeps, but the men weren't seen again. Three times they saw scouts from other clans. Once a full clan passed two miles to the south, and every warrior of the Broken Herons readied arms until the wanderers were identified as the Clan of the Lonely Hill, a distant cousin-clan that was generally but not always on good terms with the Broken Herons. Hopp walked out to see them and returned unscathed.

Dante reached Cally via loon and learned the old man had sent Somburr and Hart, the old norren councilman, down to the Territories to try their hand with the tamer clans. They'd already distributed a handful of loons. More surprisingly, most of the chiefs who'd accepted the artifacts appeared to be using them as intended. Cally had already helped organize a successful raid on the outskirts of Dollendun; three clans acting in concert freed sixty prisoners from the farms they'd been taken to after the first riots. Cally was trying to put together a series of attacks on the road to cripple the king's supply line into the city, but rumors from Setteven claimed the first major force would be arriving within weeks—a thousand men or more.

Dante passed that on to Hopp. Hopp nodded. "Thank you. Now go fish."

Mid-spring became late spring. Warm breezes smelled of pollen and green. The Broken Herons moved camp twice more. Two of their scouts killed one of the enemy and brought his body back to be buried out of sight. A visitor from a friendly clan told them about a skirmish on the fringes of Tantonnen. She didn't know which clan was involved. Dante wondered whether it was the Golden Fields, and whether Waill and her people were all right.

He was eating a lump of pan-cooked flatbread and watching the dragonflies skim the stream when his loon pulsed. He assumed it was Cally, but the signal was coming from Blays.

"Hello," Dante said. "I wasn't aware you knew how to use these."

"Sure I do. Me and Lira talk dirty through them all the time. Where are you?"

"On the sudden verge of vomiting."

"Well, finish that up and get over here. I think we've found a scout."

Dante chawed off a chunk of bread. "So kill him," he said, spitting crumbs.

"I don't like what I'm seeing." Blays described the lay of the land, a double-crowned hill not a mile west of the camp at the stream. Dante grabbed his sword and ran west up the ridge, sweating in the buttery sunlight. He headed down a slope thinly wooded with birches. At the bottom, marshy grass sprayed water from his thumping boots.

"Yeah, I see you," Blays said. "You run funny. Arms out like a drunken bird. Keep heading straight up the hill. Okay, go right a bit. A little more. Can you see me yet?"

Dante smacked away a branch before it hit his face. Below the hilltop, a figure emerged from a stand of trees and waved its hands above its head.

"Arawn's liver!" Dante said. "A hideous monster just leapt out from the woods."

As he approached, Blays closed down the connection and put a finger to his lips. "Follow me."

Blays hunkered down as they reached the ridge, weaving behind thick bushes with sweet-smelling purple flowers. On the other side, two of the clan's warriors lay prone behind a screen of shrubs. They didn't look up as Blays and Dante slid in beside them.

A small valley bowled out below them, flanked on all sides by hills. A couple hundred yards away in the valley's swampy bottom, a man in plain brown dress moved across the flooded ground, stepping between tiny islands of turf. He stopped regularly, bending down to examine the weeds and muck. Each time, he glanced at the horizons, stood, and walked on to the next island.

"He's tracking you," Dante whispered. "Don't you think you'd better move?"

"We've got a while yet," Blays said. "Question is, who's he tracking us *for*?"

"You want to follow him back?"

"And if he starts to get too close, I figured you could kill him as quietly as killings get."

Dante nodded. A fly landed on his sweaty neck. He shrugged it away. Down in the bog, the tracker plodded along, checking for bootprints, scanning the ridges, and repeating. After several minutes he turned and hurried for the far hill.

Blays frowned. "Does this seem off to you?"

"What's his rush?" Dante said.

"There's no way he saw us through this brush. He didn't even look this way before running off."

The man retreated between the birches, topping the hill and dropping over the far side. One of the warriors turned to Blays. "If we're following, let's follow."

Blays stood. Dante dug his fingers into the soil and pushed himself off the ground. His fingertips thrummed. He paused there, as if frozen in the middle of a pushup, honing in on the faint vibration.

"Wait," he said.

The thrumming flickered away. Had he imagined it? Had his hands fallen asleep? He lowered his mind through his fingers to the dirt. He could feel movement there—not with his fingers, not in the way you feel the kernels on a corncob or the grain of wood on a chair, but in the way you feel an intruder moving through a pitch-black room.

"We're going to lose him," the warrior said.

"Wait!"

The thrumming wavered, threatening to fall away completely. Dante delved deeper, tracking the vibration through the solid earth until it burst around him like a heavy rain, pattering and irregular. He followed it further until he could feel it physically, a light tapping on his ribs and shoulders, a dozen or more blows per second.

"What are you doing down there, hiding an erection?" Blays said. "Just get up and walk it off. I promise not to make fun of you until we're back in public."

Dante shook his head sharply. "I think...the earth is talking to me."

"I am too, and I've known you for longer. Let's go."

The taps tapped on, harder than they'd been mere moments before. There was a pattern to them, too, far too complex for him to break it down, but just prominent enough to recognize it was there.

"In five minutes, you can laugh at me all you want," Dante said. "Until then, get down and be quiet."

Blays gave him a long look, then crouched back down behind

the brush. The warriors murmured to each other. For a second, Dante thought the whole farce of him being a fellow clansman was about to break down, then they too hid themselves behind the budding branches. Dante's arms quivered. He pushed himself upright and knelt. He brushed his hands off on his pants and touched them back against the dirt. The feeling was gone.

It didn't come back. He sat perfectly still, watching the silent valley with a thunderous heart. One of the warriors sniffed. Dante scowled at the ground, willing the thrumming to come back.

"Holy shit," Blays breathed.

Dante snapped up his head. Back the way the scout had retreated, men in red spilled over the hilltop. Horses along the flanks, lances shining in the sun. Dante reached for his loon and turned the brooch to Mourn's setting.

"Okay?" Mourn said after some moments. "Is this working?"

"Tell Hopp to move the clan," Dante said.

"All of it?"

"Yes."

"To where?"

"Anywhere the army I'm watching isn't."

"Oh," Mourn said. "And where is that? Just out of curiosity. And my desire to be of any help to Hopp at all."

"Two hills to the west. About a mile and a half away and shrinking fast."

"Oh. I'm just going to tell him that it may be time to run, then."

"Let me know once the clan's on the move," Dante said. "If you guys take too long, we'll come up with something to distract them."

"Like running away screaming?" Blays said.

Dante shut off the loon. "That works for me."

Over the next few minutes, he discovered he was wrong about the army. Specifically, it wasn't an army—more of a legion, some two hundred footmen and 21 riders. At the bog, the soldiers stopped to rest their horses and themselves, stoking fires to boil the stagnant water. Mourn reported in. The clan was heading north. Dante and the scouts backed up the hill and over the ridgeline. On the other side, they ran to the northern hill and waited behind a screen of leaves for the legion to reappear and continue its march to the west.

When they rejoined the clan to be spelled by fresh scouts, Hopp nodded at Blays first, then Dante. When they ate dinner, a warrior named Rone invited them to eat with him and his friends beside the banks of the stream.

The walls came down. Warriors greeted Dante in the morning. Blays and Lira joked with the other couples. Mourn was invited to another wrestling match, which he won. When Dante expressed wonder at how quickly the clan's reception of them had thawed, Mourn just shrugged.

"'Thaw' is the perfect word for group decisions among norren. The ice looks stable for weeks, then you wake up one morning to find it's cracked and swirled away."

However the thaw had happened, Dante was glad to see the ice depart. He'd been feeling displaced. Not lonely, exactly. As much time as Blays spent with Lira, he was still around, as was Mourn. He spoke to Cally every two or three days, too. But each had concerns of their own. Between that and being surrounded by nearly forty warriors who had treated him like an ill-dressed stranger at a fancy party, their new nods, chuckles, and hellos felt as warm as the midday sun.

Four days after he, Blays, and the two scouts had narrowly averted a most unwelcome battle, Hopp shook him awake before dawn and then moved on to roust Blays from his tangle of blankets and Lira.

"Up for a trip?" Hopp asked once Dante had been to the latrine and had a cup of wintrel tea boiled from fresh leaves.

"I don't know. Wouldn't you rather I go catch breakfast?"

"There will be time for that later." The chieftain brought three more warriors with him, leaving the old woman in charge of the clan, and led the trek south. Dante followed without question through the chilly dawn and dewy morning. Miles and hours later, Hopp trudged up a hill. Dante startled. At its top, a dozen norren sat on a circle of lichen-encrusted stones. Several greeted Hopp by name. Several more stared unabashed at Dante and Blays.

Hopp wandered to the middle of the circle of stones. A general silence followed him. He smiled at Dante. "I thought it was time for you two to be introduced." He swept his hand around the circle at the seated norren. "These are the chiefs of your clan-cousins. My chiefs?" He gestured back at Dante and Blays. "These are the two newest brothers of the Clan of the Broken Heron."

19

The chirrup of insects swelled in the silence. Dante laughed softly. He didn't know what he'd been expecting: to be upgraded to hunting deer, perhaps, or taken on a historical tour of the places where the Herons' most famous philosopher-warriors had died. He'd stopped actively pursuing Hopp's trust about three days into his fishing career. He'd expected Cally to call him off long before he had the chance to convince Hopp into taking the loons.

"I'm not sure if you've noticed this, Hopp," a white-bearded man said at last. "But those appear to be humans."

"The Broken Herons must have one shocked father," said a red-haired woman.

Several chiefs laughed. Hopp smiled back wryly. "Do you trust me?"

"Up to about here." The white-bearded man placed his hand halfway between navel and heart. "Sometimes more about here." He grabbed his crotch.

"I made the decision to bring them into the clan. I then decided they were worthy of it. If you trust me, trust my decisions."

"Even the sun's too hot some days," said a man missing the first two fingers of his left hand.

"And when the sun is too hot, do you send it away?" Hopp said. "Or do you bear it and walk on, knowing it will be tolerable again tomorrow?"

The red-haired woman blew her bangs from her eyes. "When the sun chooses to scorch us, it can't be replaced. You can."

"You must not trust me very far at all if you think I'm choosing to burn you."

"Trust who you will." She folded her arms across her chest. "We'll do the same."

Hopp tipped back his beardless face to stare at the sky, as if he couldn't take what was down on earth any longer. "Do you think I think this is a joke? A whim? Since joining our clan, these humans have fed us. Healed us. Delivered us from danger. Before joining our clan, they helped the Nine Pines liberate the Green Lakes. Josun Joh's rainbow beard, I hear they almost killed Cassinder of Beckonridge. Have any of *you* done half as much?"

There were a couple murmurs. The white-bearded man peered between Dante and Blays. "Did you really nearly kill him?"

"Twice," Blays said. "Does that make it better or worse?"

"If the third time succeeds, it will be better, because he is an arrogant man, and will assume his previous escapes weren't flukes but his natural blessings. When death comes, then, his surprise will be outmatched only by his terror."

"That's a hell of a thing to be smiling about," Blays said.

The white-bearded man's eyes glittered. "Cassinder was behind the proposal to siphon slaves from the clans every three years. Mark my words."

"What's his problem with you guys, anyway? Did one of you slap him around as a kid?"

The red-haired woman shrugged. "He wants us for our work in mines and fields and homes."

"Interesting, isn't it?" Hopp said. "By inference, he must think the product of labor is divorced from the spirit of that same labor. Otherwise, he'd be afraid his tomatoes, ore, and freshly washed clothes would sprout legs and strangle him in his sleep."

A few of the chiefs chuckled. The three-fingered man waited for it to stop. "Tell us the plan so we can say no and be on our way."

"Do you know about loons?" Hopp said.

Dante watched their expressions closely. Three nodded casually and immediately. Four more nodded hesitantly, as if they'd heard of such things, but weren't certain whether they existed. The remainder were more guarded yet.

"These two brought a set from Narashtovik," Hopp said. "Enough for every chief to have one. No more fire-signals or horns. This is a chance for all of us to strike on the same cue, to switch strategies on the fly, to adapt our tactics before the redshirts have even caught on to our last move."

"I know my own clan," said the redhaired woman. "I'm not going to be bossed around by the gnarled warlocks of Narashtovik."

Throughout the talk, Dante had hung back outside the circle of fallen stones. He walked forward until he was a couple paces behind Hopp. "We won't tell you what to do. All we'll do is provide you the means to draw your plans together."

She shook her head. "Still, I know my own clan."

"That shit doesn't matter anymore!" Hopp hollered. The chiefs sat straight in shock. Hopp stalked among them, spit flying. "Do you think this thing with Setteven is nothing more than a clan-feud? Do you think isolated clans scattered across hundreds of miles will even slow their armies down? Is a bear turned back by a single sting? It takes a hive, Kella."

Kella swept her red hair from her face. "We've always survived."

An old man looked up from his seat on one of the fallen stones. The skin of his face and arms was tanned and sun-slackened. "Applying old ways to new challenges is a guaranteed grave."

"Try this with me." Hopp produced Dante's bag of loons with a flurry of clicking bone and metal. "If it fails, curse my name on Josun Joh's front steps. Kill me in my sleep and piss on my bones. I've seen the human soldiers trampling our grass. The Clan of the Broken Herons can't drive them out. Nor can the Nine Pines or the Snarling Cougar. The clan-of-clans? They might have a chance."

The white-bearded chief rose from his seat, hand extended. "I will take one."

"Then I will, too," said the three-fingered man. "If only to argue down all your dumb ideas."

One by one, all the others stood and received their loons. Through it all, Kella stood with arms folded, face sliding into a deep scowl. When all the others were busy glancing between their new loons and her, she flung up her hands.

"I should take your lands when you die," she said. "But if you're bound for Josun Joh's starry hills, I'm coming too, if only to have eternity through which to mock you."

Hopp smiled and handed her a loon. Dante explained how to

bind it with themselves with a drop of their own blood, which two chiefs balked at, fearing dark sorcery, until Dante convinced the white-bearded chieftain to try it. The man sealed the loon and concentrated on the link. A few seconds later, he jumped back a step.

"There's a voice in my ear!"

"Does it sound 12,000 years old?" Dante said.

The man's gaze dulled. "He says insulting your elders is a good way to ensure you'll never have the chance to become one."

"That would be Callimandicus, high priest of Narashtovik. All your messages will be routed through him."

"Or his assistants, he says," the white-bearded man said. "He can't be up for all hours of the day."

This display broke any remaining resistance from the chiefs. Once their loons were all operational, they ran down the hill like children, dispersing among the rocks and grass until line of sight was broken. There, they passed riddles and jokes and insults through the loons. Sudden bursts of laughter racketed over the whisper of wind in the grass. Once they'd all tried them out and Dante had warned them not to leave the connection open for more than an hour per day, the chiefs said their goodbyes and went their separate ways.

"Thank you for defending me," Dante said as they headed north down the hill.

Hopp glanced at him sidelong. "You expected different?"

"I thought you thought I was a backfired practical joke who would be cut loose as soon as I failed to bring back a fish."

"That would be a funny thing for a chief to think of one of his clan-sons." Hopp handed over the bag of loons. It was notably lighter. "Keep these safe. I have the feeling we'll need more soon."

With the loons distributed across the local clans, they quickly located the 200-man legion that had nearly caught the Herons unaware. Too large for any of the clans to have opposed on their own, the legion had advanced unmolested twenty miles east to Borrull, a norren village that had grown inside a former fort. According to a refugee, the residents had been caught unawares, forced to surrender and leave their homes with whatever they could carry. Borrull was positioned on a butte, protected on three sides by sheer cliffs and on the fourth by a thick stone wall. The dozen nearby clans could muster five hundred fighters between them. Hopp doubted it would be enough to retake the fort.

"What does it matter?" Dante said, poking at his bowl of too-hot fish stew with a wooden spoon. "They're cut off. Miles behind our lines."

"And what part of the body are people most afraid of being stabbed in?" Blays said.

Dante frowned. "The balls?"

"The back, you idiot. If we turn ours toward the frontlines, it could wind up sheathing two hundred Gaskan knives."

"So post a scout with a loon near the fort. If they try to move out, he alerts the clans."

"That's how you'd treat this blister?" Hopp said.

The wind shifted, blowing sweet, dry woodsmoke into Dante's eyes and nose. He picked up and moved around the fire. "Is the fort actually impregnable?"

"Have you ever known one that was?"

"Pocket Cove might be. Aside from that? Unbreakable fortresses are as mythical as wish-granting fish."

"You've caught enough to know, haven't you?" Hopp picked his teeth with a fish bone. "So what do you suggest?"

"We go see this place for ourselves."

"Anything else?"

Dante gave him a look. "Do you always speak in questions?"

"What form of speech is better than a question? A statement is certain. A question is fluid. To make progress, isn't it better to flow than to sit?"

"I've got one for you then," Blays said. "What's stopping us from going and taking a look?"

Hopp got out his loon and spread word to Cally they were looking for any information about Borrull, particularly routes inside. In the morning, Hopp decamped the clan and struck east through the low hills, covering most of the distance to the fort before settling down in a grass-lush draw, where he sent scouts to stand guard and search for water. Dante napped as soon as they made camp. It could be a long night.

At twilight, Blays splashed water on his face, startling him from his blanket. Dante swiped water from his eyes. "That is not an acceptable way to wake a person."

"Yeah, but it seemed like it would be fun."

"My thudding heart disagrees."

"Tell it to shut up. We're on the move."

Dante stretched, ate a few strips of dried venison, and joined the small team, which consisted of the three humans, Mourn, Hopp, and Erl, a relatively short norren with a long bow and the steady, quiet focus of those who know how to use them. A second contingent of warriors had already advanced to a high hill halfway between camp and Borrull. At its top, they'd gathered wood for a bonfire to light in case the king's soldiers sallied from the fort; ideally, the redshirts would be misled by the signal fire while Hopp's advance party rallied with the reserve contingent to the north. Dante suspected these preparations would wind up completely unnecessary, yet he admired their cunning nonetheless, the easy coordination between clansmen. No wonder the tribes still thrived hundreds of years after the Gaskan empire had swallowed their lands.

Hopp led them through the early night's darkness in a brisk walk. They moved in silence, pausing whenever an unseen animal crackled through the dead leaves. With the hill looming ahead, hooves thumped across the grass not thirty yards away. Dante jerked down instinctively. There was nearly a second of silence between each bound—not the churning thumps of a charging horse, but the soaring strides of a deer. Hopp flashed him a grin, teeth white in the moonlight.

The land rose in a wedge to Borrull, plateauing some three hundred feet above the surrounding ground. A couple small fires flickered atop the butte. Hopp circled around the sheer cliffs that surrounded three sides of the fort. He had expressed some optimism they'd find a hidden stairway, an old shepherd's trail or the like, but the cliffs were every bit as impassable as those surrounding Pocket Cove, with screes of loose rock slumped against their feet. After a few hours, their group returned to the front of the wedge convinced its slope was the only way up. The rise was half a mile long and a few hundred yards across, a blank stretch of open grass. Any trees had been lumbered long ago. It was a killing field, coverless and exposed.

A road reeled straight up the slope's middle. Hopp paralleled it at a distance of fifty yards, grass brushing his thighs. It swallowed Dante to the waist. Mice hopped in the darkness. Near the top of the plateau, a wall of black stone stretched from one edge of the cliffs to the other, hiding the town behind it. A quarter mile from the fort, Hopp stopped and knelt in the grass.

"What do you think?" he murmured. "Probably about as close as we get, huh?"

Erl shook his head. Blays clucked his tongue. "I don't know how much more there'd be to see, anyway. It wouldn't be much of a wall if they'd left any man-sized holes in it."

A mouse paused in the dirt eight feet to Dante's right. "Hold on a minute."

He lashed out with the nether. The mouse fell in half, bisected through its ribs, twitching. Dante muttered. Another mouse hopped through the grass a few seconds later. This time, Dante shaped a pin of shadows and poked it through the mouse's skull. It fell down without a sound.

He had it back on its feet a moment later. It waited in perfect stillness until he commanded it to run up the hill. It disappeared into the jungle of grass.

"What did I just witness?" Hopp said.

"Dante's love of animals in action," Blays said.

The mouse hurtled through the high stalks, dew clinging to its fur. Dante withdrew his vision. "Spying. And if they can pick off that mouse, we may as well pack up and go home right now."

Sprinting all-out, the undead mouse reached the walls within minutes. Hints of smoke reached its nose. Two turrets flanked the iron-banded doors of the gate. Dante sent the mouse squirming underneath the doors. It entered a short, fat hall with a second set of doors waiting at its end. Black arrow slits were cut into the walls. If the norren were able to break through the first doors, the defenders would choke the hall with their dead before they could pound through the second.

But there was no grille. He wouldn't have known what to do about a grille.

He brought the mouse back outside the doors and ran it along the walls just to see what it could see. Another turret stood near both ends of the wall, commanding the plains. Besides that and the rounded merlons along its upper edge, the wall was all but featureless, solid granite several feet thick and some fifteen feet high.

Dante dropped his sight from the mouse. "There are gates."

"What, for getting in and out?" Blays said. "I would have thought they'd just jump off the cliffs. Much faster."

"I can bring down gates."

Hopp peered at him in the moonlight. "By yourself? Are you hiding a battering ram on your person?"

"And it makes walking quite a chore," Dante said. "Listen. Doors are built to keep men out. They're not much good at stopping the nether."

Hopp grinned, foxlike. "Do you suppose it's time for another meeting?"

As valuable as the loons had already proven to be, conducting a full-fledged discussion between a dozen chieftains was well beyond Cally's capabilities as the hub of their web. Instead, Hopp reached Cally, who in turn spoke to the chiefs about an in-person battle-council. Two days later, Hopp took Dante and Blays to reconvene at the hilltop with the circle of stones. All the chiefs from the previous gathering were there: red-haired Kella; sunweathered old Wult; three-fingered Stann. There were also two more chiefs Dante didn't recognize and one he did, a middle-aged man whose left cheek was nearly beardless from crosshatched scars—Orlen of the Nine Pines.

"You're quite a ways from your homeland," Dante said.

"My homeland moves as I do." Orlen gave Dante a blank look. "Has Mourn died yet?"

"Would that make you happy?"

"I won't know until I hear it."

"He's fine," Dante said. "He's found a new home with the Clan of the Broken Heron. As have I."

Orlen laughed. "I had heard that. I didn't know whether to believe that."

"Where's Vee?"

His smile became a small thing. "In the valley of Josun Joh. Or dead in the woods on a hill beneath the sun and shade. Whichever you prefer."

Dante drew back his head, searching for words of condolence that wouldn't be as trite as all the rest, but the moment passed. Hopp stood and called the group to order, a process that involved naming all those present whose names he knew and asking the names of any he didn't. Once that was accomplished, he ran his hand down his stubbled face and gave the chiefs his sly grin.

"What would you say if I said we could retake Borrull?"

Kella glanced up. "Since you like humans and their ways so much, I would ask what you want carved on your grave. "

"I would like it to say 'Why Do You Care Who Is Buried Here?' Moving on, I have the following to say: we can retake Borrull."

"Is that something we need to do?" Kella said.

"We don't *need* to do anything," Orlen said. "But I would *like* to kill any soldier who steps foot on our lands."

"I haven't written any books on the art of war, but Borrull is a fort. Unless you like dying, you don't attack forts."

"You do if you hate the people there."

Kella cocked her head. "The Nine Pines is smaller than I last saw it. How did that happen?"

Orlen's nostrils flared. His former impassivity seemed to have been replaced by something feral and reckless. For a moment, Dante feared he would stand, cross the circle of stones, and drive his clenched fists into Kella's face, ending the meeting then and there, but Orlen smiled abruptly.

"And if that's what it takes to drive the redshirts out, the Nine Clans will shrink to none."

"I would rather take my clan to new hills than bury them on Borrull."

Stann scratched his beard with his three-fingered hand. "What's the strategy, Hopp? Tell me it's better than marching up and knocking down the gates."

"You don't think that would work?" Hopp said.

"I think we'd be better off fortifying the base of the hill and starving them out." Stann raised his eyes at Dante. "Humans eat, don't you?"

"Whenever we're not too busy killing our neighbors," Dante said.

"Well, then that would be my vote."

"I'm not talking about chopping down the doors." Hopp pointed at Dante. "He's a nethermancer. How long would it take you to knock them down?"

Dante tipped his head to the side. "If I'm not interrupted? A matter of seconds."

"The gate is all they have," Hopp said. "If they retreat to the houses, then we burn the houses."

Wult pushed his white hair away from his sun-lined forehead. "My clan will go if others go."

"Why not try the siege?" Stann said. "They may do something dumb. Enough pressure cracks a stone."

Kella waved her hand. "My clan lives on the wind. I don't care about a few hundred fools cowering behind a wall."

Assault them, besiege them, ignore them—with no central authority to make the decision, the chiefs debated these options for more than an hour. Hopp pressed them opportunistically, darting in to ask pointed questions or interrogate unfounded assumptions about the dangers of a frontal assault after the fortifications had been essentially nullified, swaying two more chieftains to pledge support to an aggressive attack, but that was the best he could do.

"They can't hurt us from behind their wall," Kella summarized. "If they come out to try, then they're no longer behind a wall. That's when we strike."

Hopp stood. "Then the Broken Herons will watch the fort to make sure the redshirts do no harm while we wait. You know how to speak to me if you change your minds."

As if the chiefs had been waiting for a moment like this, they stood as one, breaking into groups of two or three or wandering away from the circle of stones. Hopp set off without a word.

"I never thought the clans would let an enemy stay in their lands," Dante said. "We could do this!"

"Don't you think I know that?" Hopp said over his shoulder.

"Then what now?"

"Like I said. We watch the hill."

Back at the camp, Dante found Mourn to tell him he'd seen

Orlen. "He seemed wrathful. Vee died. It sounds like the Nine Pines have seen battle."

"It's what they do," Mourn said. "Along with all the other things they do."

"You're not...upset?"

"Of course I am. It wasn't the clan's fault I left. Except for the portion of the clan that is Orlen and Vee. But I don't want them to die for that. Not when they were fighting for their cousins' lives."

Dante nodded, falling silent. Perhaps Mourn was right. Orlen had manipulated them without shame, but it had been an impersonal act, collateral damage in pursuit of a noble goal. Still, if Dante had been in Mourn's place, he would have felt betrayed. Furious. Righteous. He might even have accepted news of Vee's death with something like a happy sense of justice served.

Hopp relocated the clan to a pond a few miles from Borrull, rotating scouts in and out of the nearby hills. Dante took his turns with neither joy nor complaint. He checked in with Cally twice over the following week, but the old man had no major news. A few more border-skirmishes. The further enlistment of troops in the far west. After some hard words towards and from Gallador, both the merchant league and the king had reached a detente; according to Cally's sources, the lakelands had no intention of providing support to the king's armies, but showed no inclination to resist in any way, either. Cally congratulated Dante on that point before cutting off the loon to field a message from a norren chief.

Eight days after the meeting, a low horn blasted across the pond. Dante pulled in his fishing line and sprinted towards the sound. Other Herons rushed down from the hills. The horn sounded again, rippling through the warm springtime air. At camp, the warriors strung bows, belted on swords, and strapped on leather breastplates and bracers.

"What's happening?" Dante said.

A woman named Gwenne tied her loose hair back into a tight bun. "The Clan of Laughing Foxes surprised a troop of redshirts. Redshirts fought them off long enough to make a run. They're headed for the fort."

The clan was ready within minutes. Leaving behind their tents, blankets, spare shoes, and everything else except weapons and the small pouch of food, water, salt, and other essentials each warrior carried at all times, they jogged east for the butte of Borrull. Four scouts sprinted ahead, bows in hand. Lira jogged between Dante and Blays. Her face was as calm as the pond they'd left behind.

The scouts returned in minutes. The king's men were just beyond the next ridge, on the verge of reaching the slopes up to Borrull. Hopp gritted his teeth and shouted his clan on. Forty-odd warriors raced up the hill and spilled down the other side. In the shallow valley, a troop of some fifty men in red shirts marched up the base of the butte. The clan gained quickly until the enemy soldiers spotted them in the open grass. Faint shouts lofted from below as the redshirts broke into a jog, hampered by exhaustion and their wounded. The clan reached the bottom of the valley while the enemy was just a third of the way up to the safety of the wall.

A high trumpet blared down from the fortress. Hopp swore. Riders spilled from the open gates, followed by dozens of foot soldiers.

"We're too late," Hopp yelled. "Get back up the hill. Fast as you can!"

Dante turned and retreated with his fellow warriors, several of whom snarled, frustrated by the lack of battle. He glanced over his shoulder, gathering up the nether in preparation for a fight, but the soldiers from the fort met those running up the hill and stopped to help them up to the cover of Borrull. When the clan reached the ridge, Hopp paused to let them catch their breath and assess the enemy. A mile away, the swarm of redshirts clustered outside the wall and funneled through the gates.

They jogged back to their lakeside camp. Hopp dispatched scouts and spent several minutes exchanging loon-messages with the other chiefs. Blays went to the shore to towel off his sweat. He'd been bathing with some frequency lately. Shaving, too.

"Well, that was fun," he said when he returned, damp-haired. "I suppose it beats maybe dying."

Dante leaned over at the waist to stretch his back and legs. "But now they've got 250 men instead of 200, I'd say our overall chances of maybe-dying have shot right up."

"Let me ask you something: do you care?"

"Do I care if I might die soon?"

"Yeah."

"A bit," Dante said. "In the sense that yes, completely, I care. What are you, insane?" He paused, mouth twisting between a grin and a grimace. "Wait, you're not in love, are you?"

Blays flapped his hand. "That's not what I'm talking about. Does this feel real to you? Does it feel like a war? The kind of thing bards sing songs about?"

"Sure. I'm working on a song myself."

"Really?"

"I call it 'The Ballad of History's Greatest Sorcerer, and His Homely Sidekick Whose Name Was Unfortunately Lost to Time.'"

"Come on."

"Too long?"

Blays shook his head at the pond. It wasn't long until sunset and yellow light poured in through the branches of the trees. Flies floated down to the water and disappeared in swift ripples of rising fish. Someone had lit a fire. Smoke and pan-fried fish drifted on the cool air.

"Maybe it'll sink in soon," Blays said. "But right now we're standing by this pond. We're about to eat some fish. There'll be salt and white pepper and whatever those spriggy little herbs are. We'll get up with the sun and we'll fish and walk through the hills and come back and sleep."

"And we just got back from chasing a gang of Gaskan soldiers until more mounted soldiers chased *us* off."

"But now we're here. By this pond."

"And it doesn't feel like five miles between us and those soldiers," Dante said. "It feels more like five thousand."

"Exactly!" Blays nodded.

"Nope," he said. "Feels like war to me."

Blays made an exasperated noise and wandered off to find Lira. In truth, there were moments where it did feel like an idyllic dream, like one long voyage between streams and hills and mountains with no pressing destination in sight, but those moments were few, compressed between endless thoughts of days to come, of fishing to feed the tribe so it could fight, of practicing intricate tricks with the nether to keep himself sharp, of probing the earth to learn its language and raise walls to keep the enemy out. He tried to notice the light on the pond, but soon found himself thinking of the clans instead, and what he would do when it came time to knock the doors of Borrull right off their hinges.

He was right to think that way. The next day, Cally contacted him to pass along the latest rumor. An army had departed from the borders not thirty miles to the west, hundreds strong. Dante told him to tell the other chiefs. Minutes later, Cally spoke to Hopp instead: the chieftains had requested another meet.

"Think they're ready now?" Hopp grinned.

Dante shook his head. "The more I learn about norren, the less I know. At this point it wouldn't surprise me if they suggested leaving the hills to the king and building a ladder to the moon."

Hopp sent a quarter of the clan as pickets to the west. At the hill crowned by the seats of stones, the faces of the chiefs were hard and sober. Hopp didn't say a word. He planted himself on one of the long stones, smiling like a fox with a gosling hanging from its mouth.

"So as far as I can tell," Stann said in a clear voice that quickly silenced the pockets of conversation, "we're seeing their strategy emerge. It goes something like this. Capture the strongest point in the region. Which they've done. Move in a force strong enough to hold it against any nearby clans, which they're doing right now. Once that's established, they hole up in their fortress to prevent counterattack while remaining able to deploy hundreds of troops at once to smash any clans in sight, pinning down the region and whittling our disorganized little bands into splinters. This lets them control a big old chunk of the border and keep their own lands safe until their real armies take the field."

"Smart," Wult said, weathered face crinkling in annoyance. "Why can't Moddegan be dumb about it instead? Would make our job a hell of a lot easier."

Orlen stood and gazed straight up at the clouds that had mounted over the last few hours. "If we don't want them to do this, we should stop them from doing so. If we don't stop them from doing so, we admit we want them to do this."

Kella scowled. "It's not as as simple as that."

"I think it is." Stann didn't so much as glance around the circle. None of the other chieftains moved, either, but Dante could feel

THE GREAT RIFT

their assent nonetheless—the norren had reached one of their mysterious unspoken agreements. Stann turned to Dante. "How close do you have to be to bring down the doors? Within bowshot?"

"Thereabouts," Dante said. "It's subtler work than just smashing them down. Call it two hundred yards."

"I assume you work best when you are not being punctured with arrows."

"Unless I'm specifically working at bleeding, yes."

"Then we attack under cover of night. And under the cover of a big wooden shield." Stann took a look around the circle. "We must move today. Prepare as we march. If this new army reaches Borrull before we do, we'll lose the whole region."

Several chiefs stood immediately and jogged away from the hilltop. Hopp grinned and smacked Dante's back hard enough to stumble him.

"You're sure you can do this?"

"Fortunately for our chances, hinges don't fight back." Dante tugged the hem of his doublet to straighten it after his near-fall. "If you can give me a minute, I'll give you the fort."

Hopp smiled proudly, glancing at the other chieftains on his way down the hill. The norren was proud of *him*, Dante realized, as well as being proud of his own canniness—taking three humans into his clan must have been a terrible risk on some level, a gamble of whatever prestige he held with all the other clans. Blays had fulfilled Hopp's "test" by managing to only half-drown himself in the stream, yes, but there was no higher law holding Hopp to his end of the bargain. Taim, Josun Joh, Arawn, none of them had formed in the clouds to scowl down at the chieftain until he relented and took the three humans into his tribe. Hopp was a man for whom pragmatism came before honor. He'd break his word without hesitation if he thought it would make for a better tomorrow. He'd seen something in the humans, then. Some use or potential that convinced him to roll the dice. Not only was that gamble about to pay off, it was about to do so in front of fifteen other clans.

The Broken Herons moved east, covering half the distance to Borrull before nightfall. Dante gazed at the stars from under his blankets. He'd been in enough fights, scrapes, skirmishes, and battles to forget more than one, but he'd never been part of a siege of this size, let alone served as its cornerstone. As terrifying as that thought was, it was thrilling, too. A breath of cool air. The wind between an albatross' feathers. The night-dewed grass beneath a tiger's paws. Feared and fearless.

Away through the brush, Lira moaned. Dante struck out with the nether, neatly slicing a twig from the tree above his bed.

He woke sluggish and thickheaded. He wished for tea. The Broken Herons tramped east. They halted regularly to forage, rest, and wait for word from the scouts, but moved fast enough to encamp by mid-afternoon in a stream-fed valley some two miles southwest of Borrull. Several clans and some three hundred warriors were already there, mending shields, sharpening blades, fishing, wrestling in a foreign, upright style where victory was achieved by flinging the opponent to the ground. After each throw, sweep, or trip, the downed warrior bounced to his feet, laughing or wryly determined. More than once, he asked his partner to walk him through the technique that had just introduced him to the ground. If any old rivalries lurked among the divergent clans, Dante didn't see them that day.

Stann summoned Dante over at dusk to inspect the shield they'd rigged for him. It was more of a mobile wall than a shield: seven feet tall and ten feet wide, gently convex, with three horizontal slits at his eye-level. Leather handles had been nailed behind either flank, allowing for two warriors to carry it while Dante hid behind it. It smelled of fresh-cut wood, but had clearly been built by a craftsman whose nulla was woodwork—the planks sanded smooth and splinter-free, the viewing slits straight and perfectly parallel. Dante's doubts about the plan backed swiftly away.

Scouts came and went as night settled on the hills. The last of the clans arrived under starlight, swelling their numbers past seven hundred, outnumbering the men behind the wall three-to-one. In a straightforward siege, the odds would be far from overwhelming. In one where the front door would be knocked to the ground within two minutes of first contact—one where the attacking size was larger not only in numbers, but in the tree-trunk-like mass of their individual warriors, too—it would not be an easy night for the redshirts.

A ripple spread through the camp. It was time to march.

Seven hundred pairs of feet flattened the grass of the hill. Scattered clouds dimmed the moonlight. Spears swayed over the high heads of the norren. Nether danced between pebbles and twigs. They reached the rim and spilled into the waiting valley. The butte of Borrull rose from the darkness. The clans carried no banners. They sounded no horns. Hunching along in loose formation through the breeze-ruffled grass, the warriors were nearly halfway up to the fort before the first trumpets sounded from above.

Torches pricked up along the wall. Shouts tumbled down the slope. Blays grinned. "Think they've seen us?"

"Either that or they've spotted an alarmingly large rat in the kitchen," Dante said.

"Let's see how they feel about the one that's about to chew through their doors."

"If it turns out I can't, and they shoot me, don't tell Cally I was trying to plink off a hinge. Tell him I was trying to lift the whole wall over my head."

"You think that will make you sound *smarter*?"

Flaming arrows launched from along the wall, falling through a long arc before burying themselves in the ground. Their shafts burnt on, denoting range. The norren halted a few yards from the nearest. Atop the wall, arrowheads glittered in the torchlight. Silhouettes moved between the rounded merlons.

"Turn back or be slain!" a commander bellowed from up the hill.

Orlen strode up to the nearest arrow, yanked it from the ground, and broke it in his massive hands. "Within an hour, every redshirt behind that wall will be dead. To avoid that fate, I advise leaping from the cliffs, and taking your chances with the ground."

Norren hollered from up and down the lines. The twang of twenty bows hummed through the night. Orlen turned his back and walked away. Seconds later, a forest of shafts planted itself in the ground where he'd stood.

Hopp loomed beside Dante. "Ready for the big surprise?"

"I hope you've picked some strong men to hold that shield."

"I can vouch for Coe," said the chief. "We'll see how I do."

He beckoned Dante along the ranks to the giant wooden shield-wall. A gigantic norren waited at one of the handles. He nodded at Dante. Hopp grabbed hold of the other side and counted down. The pair hoisted it inches off the ground and shuffled forward.

Dante's heart pulsed. He walked with them, his breath echoing from the close wooden wall. Through the three slits, his vision swayed with the pace of the two norren. Despite the claustrophobia of it all, at least he could still run if it came down to it. In a siege of the eastern kingdoms several hundred years ago, a sorcerer named Federick had had the brilliant idea of enclosing himself inside a wheeled platform of pure iron to protect him as he set to the time-intensive work of blasting a large hole through the massive enemy walls. Once he got into position, an ethermancer among the enemy forces had let Federick work for long enough to drill through four feet of stone, and then, with Federick's strength depleted and his attention diverted, the ethermancer knocked off one of Federick's wheels, trapping him in place, and then turned the ether to the heating of the iron enclosure. Within moments, Federick halted his attack. Within minutes, the entire battlefield smelled like sweet pork.

Dante could at least be certain he wouldn't be cooked. Still, when the first flaming arrow rapped into the wall, he jerked back with a snarl.

"Did you think they wouldn't shoot?" Hopp chuckled.

"Shut up and carry."

"Are those the last words you'd speak to your chief?" Hopp said, mock-aghast.

Another arrow smacked into the wall, several more right behind it. Dante cut his arm. Nether swirled from the grass as if hungry for the tide of blood that would soon sweep from the wall. "This should be close enough."

The two warriors set down the shield with an earthy thump. Dante leaned close to the slits. The doors stood within two hundred yards. Closer yet would have been even better — the nether got clumsier the further away you sent it, and required proportionally more energy to manipulate — but he didn't want to open himself to sidelong fire from the turrets at either end of the wall.

Arrows whacked into the shield and whumped into the earth. Dante shaped the nether between his hands and winged it towards the far-off doors. The gates were inward-swinging, hinges hidden behind the doors themselves, unreachable. Unreachable to anything except a paper-thin blade of nether. It sluiced through the crack between door and wall and cleaved through the thick iron. From his investigation with the mouse, he knew each door had four hinges; four doors in all. One hinge down, fifteen to go. Dante smiled.

Something slammed into his back, pitching him into the shield. His left lower back felt hot and numb. He swore dully.

"Where did that come from?" Hopp shouted at Coe. Coe shook his head quickly, moving to put Dante between himself and the shield.

"Where are you going?" Dante said. He turned. Wood clacked into the wood of the shield, jarring him. He craned his neck. When he saw it, his knees sagged, his vision swarming over with foamy white spots.

An arrow stuck from just below his lower ribs. While he faced the fortress, he'd been shot in the back.

20

He fell to his knees, head hot and fuzzy. A huge hand clamped his forearm, stopping him before he hit the ground. Hopp shouted something Dante couldn't make out. As if he were rising from a pool of warm water, the fuzziness fell away, draining the spots from his eyes as it went. Downhill, two slim figures burst from the ranks of norren. Lira and Blays. They sprinted to their left, headed for the edge of the cliffs.

Hopp leaned into the straps, lifting the shield a couple inches from the ground. He began to move it backwards.

"What the hell are you doing?" Dante said.

"Getting you out of here!"

"Set down that shield. I have a job to do."

Hopp leaned down to meet him eye to eye, as if examining him for signs of sudden insanity. "You've been shot."

Dante gestured toward the edge of the butte. "And my best friend just ran off to slice the one who did it into little red ribbons. Right now I fear more for the shooter's safety than for my own. Now are you going to break off this shaft, or am I going to knock down these gates with an arrow wobbling from my back?"

Hopp shook his head in disbelief. "Is your brain in your back, too? What are you thinking?"

Hopp grabbed hold of the arrow and broke it effortlessly. The pain finally hit, returning the swam of white spots to Dante's sight. He half-collapsed again. Nether surged to the blood dappling the damp grass. He brought a thread of shadows to his wound, just enough to tamp down the pain. He couldn't risk healing himself wholly. Not before he had the gates down.

He willed himself to his feet. The spots faded. Hopp kept the shield upright while Coe maneuvered tight behind Dante to serve as a norren shield. The pain was a dull burn in his back. It seemed to fuel the nether as potently as his blood. He slung another paper-thin blade through the hinges of the door. A third. A fourth. He leaned against the slits. The door held firm. Had he missed a hinge? Left one half-severed? He wasn't thinking straight. His mind was clouded by the denial of the wounded. As he'd sent the blades through the hinges, he could feel the shadows biting cleanly through the iron, but seconds later, he couldn't be certain. He summoned another handful of shadows.

At the front of the wall, the door tilted, exposing torchlight behind it, and fell to the ground with a bang.

Heartened by the rumbling cheers of seven hundred norren, Dante struck at the next door. Not the one next to the one he'd cut down. That doorway was already open. He could faint at any minute. He might not have time for all four doors.

Instead, he hurled the next blade at the door directly behind the first. He felt it shear through the iron like a knife through stiff paper. A single scream echoed from the hallway between the gates.

He cut the next hinges in a haze of pain and exhaustion. He threw the final knife of nether, guiding it to the last hinge, and found the door had already fallen.

Norren roared. Warriors surged up the slope, shields held above their heads. Arrows conked into the wood and slashed into flesh. Dante sagged. Hopp grabbed him with one hand and held onto the giant shield with the other. Warriors poured around them. By the time Hopp set Dante down in the trampled grass back out of arrow range, the entire army of clansmen had run past. Uphill, metal clanged on metal. Men screamed and swore and laughed awful laughs. Dante's ears buzzed. He twisted around for a look at the arrow.

"What do you think?" Hopp said. His fists were wet with blood.

"That it's very dark." Somehow, Dante found the torchstone in his pouch and blew it into life. He raised it to Coe, who watched in silence, accepting the gleaming stone. In the white light, the blood slipping around Dante's wound was as bright as coral. The snapped shaft jutted a hand's-width from his back. Fighting off the urge to faint, he met Hopp's eyes. "Well, what are you waiting for? Pull it out."

"Of your back?"

"Why? Do I have another one in my ass?"

"You will bleed. You might bleed until you've bled to death."

"I'm my own best shot. If I pass out now, I might not wake up. Now get this out of me and we'll see which one of us is the fool."

Hopp smiled tightly. "How long do you think you can keep giving your chieftain orders?"

"I won't know that until you make me stop."

Hopp yanked. Dante screamed and doubled over, writhing. The white spots turned gray, then black. Hopp was slapping him, shouting, his branded face so comically alarmed Dante chuckled, wincing at the lance of pain that followed. Were the shadows in his vision the waiting nether, or an oncoming and lasting sleep? He groped for them and they shivered like wind-struck leaves. Nether, cool and fluid, mocking and distant and hungry and indifferent. He brought it to his wound, but it was like shaping dry sand.

Hopp wiped the blood with a wet cloth. This fresh pain was icy, not fuzzy, and it jolted Dante halfway from his fog, centering him. He sat in the grass down the hill from a panic of screams and clangs. He smelled smoke, dry and spicy. A great white column rose from behind the wall.

His hand was warm. It was pressed to his wound, which was bleeding quite a lot. His other hand was cold.

Clumsily, ploddingly, he balmed the nether to his wound. The heartbeat of pain eased to a stinging itch. Two figures ran in from the cliffs to his left. Dante tried to stand and fell to his knees. Hopp drew his sword with a whisper of leather.

"Is he all right?" Blays' voice was strained. "You're sitting up!"

"More like falling sat," Dante said.

Lira glanced upslope at the sound of a horn. "We found the shooter."

"You did? What did he say?"

"Well, if I remember right," Blays said, "it was something like 'Aaaahhh!'"

Lira jerked her chin toward the cliffs. "He leapt off."

"He leapt?" Dante said. "Did he make it down?"

"Bits of him sure did!" Blays knelt down across from Dante. He glanced across the trampled fields, as if enemy legions might be hidden in the bent grass. "You know what this means, don't you?"

"Blays, I was just shot." He twisted to see his wound in the darkness. Blood glimmered, but the flow had ceased. "I'm not sure I'm not still passed out and dreaming."

"It means you were betrayed."

"What are you talking about?"

"Set up. Sold out. Hung out to dry. Betreasoned. Turned-coat-against." Blays pointed to the left and downslope. "How else would they know to deploy a lone sniper? To specifically target you? We found his little camp over there, hidden in the grass."

Hopp drew back his head. "Who knew about this but the chiefs and our clans? Which of them would possibly sabotage the entire battle?"

"That's what I'm about to find out. Also, I should probably go help with that war thing up there."

"I'm staying with him until he's safe," Lira said, standing beside Dante. "I still owe him."

Blays hiked up his belt. "Leave me to fight a legion of redshirts by myself. Very loving."

"If you need a hand, just ask one of the hundreds of norren warriors."

Blays grinned and dashed uphill. Lira touched Dante's shoulder. "Are you all right?"

"Better than a minute ago." Throughout the talk, he'd been weaving himself back together, stopping up squirting veins, bringing flesh back to flesh. It was more than muscle, skin, and fat—something else had been punctured, too. He feared it was his kidney. He didn't allow himself to look too closely at what the nether mended. He simply guided it from afar, bridging his torn matter back together, restoring what had been ruined to its natural form. "You should go up with the others."

She just laughed. "I'm not interested in having this conversation again."

"Hopp's here."

Hopp smiled his fox's smile. "And now that he's made sure his newest brother won't be the battle's first loss, he should join the fight before his other siblings start to wonder where he is."

The norren unfolded from his crouch and handed over the torchstone. He reached back to touch the greatsword on his back and lumbered uphill. Fighting had broken out atop the wall, swords flashing in the torchlight. A body plunged off the side and didn't rise. The norren had flung open the remaining two doors in the half-wrecked gates and the passage was clear of battle.

"Looks like they're kicking ass," Dante said.

"Forts only work as long as the gates are closed." She peered at him in the light of the torchstone. "You could kill me right now, couldn't you? After breaking down a wall and saving yourself from a mortal wound. You could still kill me with a gesture."

He saw no point in lying. "Yes."

She gave him a strange smile, an ethereal thing better meant for a fairy-circle in a pitch black wood. "It's a wonder all your type hasn't been burnt alive."

"In Mallon, we're kept as the attack dogs of the nobility. You can be killed for flashing the wrong talent at the wrong time." He shifted, testing his wound. It pulled, but the pain was a faraway ache, more the memory of pain than something real. "Cassinder isn't the type to brook threats to his power. If the Norren Territories fall and Narashtovik follows, I expect we'll be forced to serve in Setteven or be hanged from the highest branches."

"He's a ways from the throne yet."

"He'll move closer if he acquits himself in the field. Anyway, Moddegan hasn't exactly displayed a Mennok-like patience and wisdom towards threats himself. Would be easy enough for an ambitious man to plant him in a grave." Dante leaned forward onto his knees and found he was able to stand. "Shall we join them?"

"Are you insane?" Lira rushed to grab his arm. "Ten minutes ago you had an arrow through your back. Sit back down before you keel over and I have to explain to Blays why I'm holding another man in my arms."

Dante shrugged free. "If we never fight except when we're in perfect health of mind and body, we'll never fight at all."

He didn't test himself yet by running. He could walk fine, if stiffly, but there was an alien weakness to his legs that was neither the exhaustion of overexertion nor the soreness of the day after. Bodies lay scattered in front of the gates, mostly human. Arrows jutted from the grass. A bow twanged and Dante jerked down his head so fast his teeth clacked. He could smell metallic blood and the hot, fetid belch of punctured guts. Cries and orders barked through the streets beyond the wall. He and Lira drew their swords with the hiss of steel on leather. Blood tacked the floor of the hallway through the gates. Dante touched one of the severed hinges as he passed. Its edge was as sharp as scissors.

Dozen of bodies lay beyond the second set of doors, human and norren alike. Most of the norren showed arrows in their chests and necks. Most of the humans had been gashed open by giant swords and axes. More than one had been beheaded or outright struck in half. Suddenly fearful he'd see Mourn among the dead, Dante tried to catch a look at each face, but the numbers were too many, the darkness too deep.

Past the wall, a few dozen homes scattered the plateau. They were a mix of human and norren styles—some stone, some wood, some earthen; some boxy and squared, some round, others set flush into the sides of short rises. All had high-peaked roofs to keep off the snow. Several of the wooden ones crackled with flame. Corpses sprawled in gardens. Down the street, a gang of goats trotted past, bawling in confusion.

Off to the left, clan warriors shouted to some twenty of the king's men, demanding they lay down their arms. Dead ahead, a host of norren surrounded a large wooden structure that may have been a church—though Dante doubted that; even city-bound norren worshipped with little organization, heading instead to the forests and hills for their rare rituals and official celebrations—and were busy hacking at the door with heavy axes. Others knelt, bows in hand, to exchange fire with redshirted soldiers sniping from the upper floors.

Dante broke into a jog. An arrow whisked past his head. He raised a bloody hand and knocked a hole through the archer's forehead. The man flew back from the window in a mist of blood. With a creak and a boom, the doors gave way. Norren surged inside. Steel rang against steel. Dante hit the edge of the crowd and tried to force his way through. Hillocky shoulders bounced him back. He opened his mouth, then let it close without a word. Demanding passage based on his name or title wouldn't budge them an inch. These were norren clan-warriors. They had no more use for the prestige of Narashtovik than they would for lace slippers.

He pulled the nether to his fists and used it to shove men and women aside until he reached the door. Behind him, Lira laughed in a way that might have been disapproving. Inside, norren and men battled between rows of benches. Shouting carried from a stairwell to Dante's right. The voice was Orlen's.

Dante pounded upstairs. The third floor opened to an A-frame room with bare rafters propping up the steeply pitched roof. Ten soldiers in red cloaks stood across the room with their hands up, swords at their feet. A step in front, a man with a tidy salt-and-pepper beard and several silver medals on his doublet faced Orlen, who held his gleaming sword high above his shoulder. Close to twenty norren crowded behind him. Dante recognized several members of the Nine Pines. With a lightening of his heart, he saw Mourn was there, too.

Orlen's sword twitched toward the commander. "Stay completely still or I will make sure you are no longer capable of movement besides whatever parts of you the worms and ants carry away."

"What kind of man are you?" The commander's face was a mixture of anger and fear. "What kind of man strikes a—"

"Your tongue counts as you!" Orlen shouted. Dante couldn't remember hearing the chief raise his voice before. "Kneel!"

One of the Nine Pines leaned forward. "Orlen—"

Orlen whirled, his scarred face contorted like a wolf driven mad by its own wounds. "Why would you think I want you to speak, either? Does it look like I want anyone else to speak?"

The commander held his clenched fist out toward Orlen. "If this is how you honor your—"

Orlen pivoted on his heels. His sword wheeled. Its blade passed through the commander's neck without slowing down. The man's head tumbled across the floorboards. His body stayed upright, his arm lowering as slowly as a man falling asleep in a chair by the fire. Then he fell, a cut puppet.

His men shouted in protest and fear. Dante wedged through the throng of norren. "What the hell are you doing? He was surrendering!"

"He moved," Orlen said.

"And if you look closely you'll see he doesn't have a fucking sword!"

Orlen smiled sickly. "Who do you think set fire to those houses outside? It wasn't us. What do you think they're hoping to burn?"

Mourn moved past Orlen to crouch beside the body of the dead commander. The redshirted soldiers watched with stark expressions. Dante stood square on Orlen. Boots scuffed behind him.

"There's no excuse for war crimes." Dante gestured to the unarmed soldiers. "These men are prisoners."

"Of their consciences, for now," Orlen said. "Soon, of hell."

Mourn unfolded the fist of the dead man. He blinked, then plucked something hidden in the man's hand.

"I will tell you what Orlen is doing," Mourn said. "He is destroying the evidence of his crime." He unfolded his hand. In his palm rested an earring, part silver, part bone. A tooth dangled from a silver chain. "Why did this human have this?"

Orlen went still. Dante's heart went dark. "It was you."

"He was supposed to wait." Orlen didn't turn.

"What is happening in this room?" Mourn said softly.

Dante tried to force Orlen to meet his eyes. "Do I tell him or do you?"

"I told them how to kill him." Orlen swiveled his chin toward Dante. "They were supposed to wait for my signal. They must have deduced you were bringing down the gate."

Mourn sat back on his haunches, the loon forgotten in his hand. "Why would you want Dante dead? He is the one who should want *you* dead. Unless *that* is why you want him dead."

Orlen laughed. "He's the reason Vee's dead, you traitorous coward. He's the one who touched the fire of war to the brush of our hills."

Mourn's face flooded with horror. "You're the one who lured him into an attack on Gaskan royalty."

"And you helped too."

Mourn vaulted to his feet and grabbed Orlen in a clinch. Orlen gasped, face white. One of the Nine Pine warriors shouted. Three others advanced, swords in hand. Orlen staggered back and then lowered himself to sit crosslegged on the floor. The bone handle of a knife projected from his heart, twitching with each beat.

"I only regret I didn't get to see both sides burn," Orlen said. He frowned down at his hands, then slumped to the side.

A terrible silence descended on the room. Dante backed up a step to stand beside Mourn. Lira followed.

The clansman who'd shouted out swiveled his face at Mourn, his loose black hair swinging below his chin. His words were barely audible over the patter of blood. "Why did you do that?"

Mourn lowered his hands to his sides. "He tried to kill my brother after blaming him for his own faults. He risked the lives of every norren here to settle a delusional score. And he'd already betrayed Dante—an ally—once before! Why do you think I left the clan in the first place?"

The long-haired man exchanged glances with the other warriors of the Nine Pines. Dante reached for the nether. Lira's hand drifted toward her sword. The clansman lowered himself to his knees.

"I will follow you across the hills."

The other eight warriors of the clan in the room followed suit in both gesture and word. Dante gaped. "You're not going to...kill him?"

The long-haired warrior gave him a sly smile. "What would possess a clansman to kill his own chieftain?"

"Oh no," Mourn said. "No!"

"You are loyal. Thoughtful. But fearless to act on your conscience when it is stung. We all speculated why you had left the clan. If you did so out of honor to a man you barely knew, what kind of honor will you bring to the Nine Pines?"

Mourn bared his teeth. "Tragically, I can't accept. That is, I *could*, but at the same time, I can't. I have since joined the Clan of the Broken Heron."

The warrior stood and clapped Mourn on the shoulder. "Then we will see what your new chief has to say. Perhaps it is time for the Broken Herons to come to the Pines to roost."

Dante shook his head in disbelief. Behind him, a man coughed.

The soldiers. He tapped Mourn's arm. "Let's get these men outside. I mean, if that is in accordance with your wishes, my liege."

Mourn groaned through his beard. To the Nine Pines warriors, he said, "Please see they are unarmed."

The warriors removed the few weapons the soldiers still had and marched them downstairs, where a few more redshirts had decided to surrender rather than join the corpses draped over broken benches and splayed across the floor. Outside, the streets smelled like charred flesh. Lira quickly found Blays. The fighting was over. Hopp had survived, too. Kella hadn't. Stann had taken a spear in the gut and might not make it through the night. All told, three-quarters of the redshirts had died or were expected to, leaving sixty-odd prisoners. Norren casualties amounted to just over seventy, a tenth of their force. While a team of warriors set to work digging a mass grave, others reeled up pails from the wells to put out the fires still raging in four of the wooden houses.

The king's soldiers watched this with sullen despair. Dante soon learned why.

Once the first fire was out, two warriors went in to check for survivors. Their howls pierced the night. Inside, a dozen norren women lay dead. Some were burnt beyond recognition, but others showed staved-in skulls, the blood not yet clotted. All had splints on their broken shins.

Dante didn't try to stop the norren. The warriors ordered the prisoners out of the great hall where they'd been temporarily quartered and marched them to the edge of the butte. Pairs of norren warriors grabbed the redshirts and, one by one, flung them over the side of the cliff.

Only one of the soldiers tried to run. He was cut down midstride. The others went without speeches or anger. Once it was finished, no one went down to check whether any of the men had survived.

Dante went to Stann to treat the strategist's spear wound. Midway through the process, Dante passed out cold.

He slept for two days, or so he was told when Blays woke him up. He sat up hard, the wound in his back twingeing. "Two days? What about that incoming army?"

Blays shook his head. "Camped about ten miles west, say our scouts. Meanwhile, we just killed two of theirs a few minutes ago. Best guess is they'll arrive in force tomorrow afternoon."

"What are we going to do? Are the gates still down?"

"Sorta."

"So we're only sorta exposed to the swords of a thousand soldiers?"

Blays rolled his eyes. "You do remember what happened, don't you? That thing where you sliced the hinges straight in half, rendering them totally useless as hinges? One of the norren smiths is working on some new ones, but with as little time as we've got, they're not going to be half as strong."

Dante swung his legs out of bed. A bed in a room he didn't recognize. His legs were shaky, but his bladder demanded he put them to use. Blays pointed out the privy and hung around outside while Dante made its acquaintance.

"So did Mourn really stab Orlen in the heart?" Blays said through the door.

"Assuming Orlen had one."

"Hopp released him from the Broken Herons, you know. He's in charge of the whole Nine Pines. Is that clan very wise or very dumb?"

"I think norren spend a lot of time thinking," Dante said. "If they've already worked out exactly what they want from a leader, they can choose a new one in a snap."

"Mourn actually begged Hopp not to let him go. Hopp just smiled that dog's smile of his. I think he might be evil."

"Considering we're still members of his clan, I hope he uses that evil for good." Dante finished up and stepped back into the hall.

"Are you all right?" Blays said. "Judging by the smell, you've died and I'm talking to a ghost."

Dante brushed past him. "Are you just now learning what toilets are for?"

"If I had any lingering doubts, being forced to climb up one cleared those right up."

"Well, let Lira and Mourn know I'm up and around, if they care. I'm going to get ahold of Cally."

Blays headed outside. Dante returned to his room, found his

loon, and clicked it over to Cally. Instead of Cally's ragged voice, he heard the pregnant nothing that told him Cally was already speaking to someone else. Five minutes later, he heard that same eerie non-sound. Ten minutes after that, there was no noise at all. Cally's loon was dead or shut down.

Dante dressed, ate, wandered outside. Mid-afternoon sun painted the plateau in warm yellow light tempered by a winding breeze that still smelled lightly of ash and charred fat. Hammers rang on wood and metal. Norren were thick in the streets, pulling down wooden houses and hauling the planks to a fresh palisade in the throes of construction behind the main wall. Dante recognized several members of the Herons, Nine Pines, and the other clans he'd recently fought beside, but he found himself wandering away from their labor to the east end of the butte. It was just a couple hundred yards from the center of the village, but it felt as isolated as his last two days of dreams.

He stopped at the cliffs where the king's soldiers had been chucked to their deaths. He'd been drawn here. Called by a voice too deep to hear. The smell was as faraway as the cries of the hawks. Not too bad just yet—that tolerable lull between the knifing stink of fresh guts and the lung-clogging reek of rotting ones. Far below, blackbirds hopped among the bodies, pecking eyes and tongues. Shadows flitted between broken fingers and teased the cracks in skulls. An unseen pressure pulled on Dante's collar, drawing him closer to the stark edge.

He backed away, crossed the village to the disabled gates, and walked down the slope to where it met the valley floor. Within an hour, he stood before the scree of stones at the foot of the cliffs, corpses broken among the rocks like fat and fleshy eggs.

Flies buzzed in schools. Birds squawked and hopped from dinner to dinner. But there was more than birds and flies among the swollen dead. There was nether, too. Lurking in half-seen pools that dissolved as soon as he looked at them straight on. Sweating from the men's pores and crow-pecked sockets. But it wasn't only escaping from the bodies to the ground. It was rising from the ground to the bodies, too, as if the violence of their landing had cracked a vein in the earth. As if the dirt had been waiting to reclaim the flesh that had been born from it.

In an instant, his understanding shifted as roughly as thunder and as radically as a landslide. Moving the earth wasn't about speaking to the earth. It was about finding the death in the earth. Finding the death and making it move. Move the death, move the earth.

Blood lay maroon and drying on the rocks and broken limbs. It wasn't hard to follow into the soil. He simply followed the nether, the unstable streams of shadows waiting below the surface. He grabbed hold of them and yanked.

Stones scraped and groaned. A chasm veed apart, four feet long and two feet wide. Crows shrieked and took flight. A shattered body tumbled into the short abyss, landing with a wet crunch. Its feet jutted above the parted rocks. Dante skipped back a step, then laughed at his own skittishness. Dust sifted onto the corpses and stones.

He repeated this on a smaller scale, parting the dirt into furrows fit for planting potatoes. Moving the nether and the earth with it taxed his strength at a fraction of what it would cost to muscle aside the earth itself. Were Arawn's shadows acting as a lever? A net knit through the tumble of earth and rock that, when tugged, exerted its power over everything within its weave? The weakness in his legs and the faint pain in his back stopped him from running all the way back to Borrull. It was late afternoon. After confirming with Hopp the Gaskan army was still encamped ten miles to the west, Dante set himself to the earthen ramparts the norren were piling behind the stone wall. At his command, dirt flowed uphill, forming loose mounds the warriors tamped down with shovels and their own feet. In the scheme of things, his efforts weren't much. By the time his strength gave out, he'd added some ten feet to the left wing of the rampart, raising that stretch just above his head. But it helped. And he was there as much for the practice at earthmoving as for the aid he could give to the fortification. As with all things, skill could only come through effort.

The effort and its immediate results left him flushed with wonder and hope. Cally's loon remained blank, however. Ravenous, he paused for dinner, then went to find Blays and explain what he could do.

Blays nodded slowly. "So you can move dirt from one place to another, can you?"

Dante snapped his fingers. "Like that."

"That's going to come in very handy if we're attacked by a wild pack of sand castles."

"Look, this is just a start. In time, I may be able to form whole ramparts overnight."

Blays jerked his thumb at the norren toiling on the earth wall despite the twilight. "Looks like they've tapped into the same magic."

Instead of speaking, Dante sought the ground-up bones and powdered skin embedded in the dirt beneath Blays' feet, then yanked it six inches to the left. Blays fell straight on his ass.

"Make more sense now?" Dante said.

Blays hopped up, smacking dirt from his pants. "All that proves is I'm drunk."

"Are you?"

"What, you *aren't*? We're going to be attacked tomorrow!"

"You're right. I have the sudden urge to start drinking until I can't stand up. Think they'll kill a man with a hangover?"

Blays waved a hand through the darkening air. "Quit bitching and start thinking. You may have forgotten this, what with your fancy loons that let you talk to someone hundreds of miles away, but that army doesn't know a thing about what happened here. As far as they know, this fort is still manned by two hundred of the king's finest."

Dante folded his arms and considered the ground. "There's a chance, however small, they'll reappraise the situation when they see the walls are manned by a horde of bearded giants."

"So don't let them see that."

"Sorry, I still don't know how to stop the sun from rising. I'll see if I can work that one out before bedtime."

"It's a lot simpler than that, dummy. We've got three humans here—and we can stick a lot more on the walls."

Dante gaped. "Those bodies down there look like overcooked stew. We can't just prop them on the merlons and expect the enemy to wave hello."

"Lyle's balls, do I have to do everything?" Blays said. "Conjure up some of those visions of yours. A score of red-shirted soldiers watching impassively from the battlements. Lure a bunch of the king's men into town, then seal up the gates with a big plug of dirt to cut the rest of them off. The norren behind the walls get to go all choppy on the troops inside while the warriors on the wall go all shooty on the redshirts trapped outside."

"That," Dante said, "is not a bad idea."

"Of course it's not. It's a great idea. If I were paid by the idea, I could retire off that one, that's how great that idea is."

"I'm going to talk to the chiefs." Dante glanced across the grounds. "Meanwhile, I've got a much more important mission for you."

Blays straightened. "What's that?"

"Fetch us the celebratory rum."

Blays nodded solemnly and ran away. Dante found Hopp speaking with Mourn inside the foyer of one of the round earthen homes. He laid out the plan. Hopp chuckled, grinning his foxy grin, and raised his brown brows at Mourn. "What do you think?"

Mourn stiffened. "I'm not a strategist. Unless speaking unlearnedly about strategy makes me one. But I have no formal training in strategy."

"You think I do? Strategy's about guts and intuition. You're a chieftain now. Don't you want to act like one?"

"I would argue that chieftaincy is not defined by the role itself, but rather by the individuals who fill that role." Mourn gave Dante a dubious look. "But it sounds like a pretty good plan."

"We could just post the real-life norren along the wall," Dante said. "Convince the redshirts this isn't the hill they want to die on."

Hopp shook his head sharply. "We're going to have to kill an awful lot of them before we can convince the rest to go home. Don't you think we're better off behind these walls than meeting them in the field?"

Dante had no rebuttal for that. In the streets, norren worked by torchlight to carve arrowshafts and fletch them with the feathers of the village's geese and turkeys and chickens. Dante returned to the house he'd been quartered in. The clank of the smiths' hammers woke him more than once. In the morning, the gates were back up and ready to be closed, though a soft-spoken smith whose nulla was clearly ironwork assured him the new hinges were ill-fitting and brittle, prone to breakage under any serious assault. Too starved to think straight, Dante thanked him and headed out for a breakfast of chicken and bread.

The scouts returned while he was still belching. Gask's army was on the move. At rough count, it bore a thousand footmen and some eighty cavalry. Half again what the depleted clans could muster. Good odds regardless, if one were behind strong gates and not battle-worn from a previous engagement. Less so when the day's plan involved letting scores of the enemy walk straight through the gates.

Dante climbed the turret on the left side of the mended doors to watch the green valley and the opposite ridge. Behind him, warriors scooped away the rampart immediately behind the gates to hide it from the enemy until the redshirts had already passed into the killing zone. Norren lugged sheafs of arrows up to the walls and distributed them at intervals.

Just before noon, ten riders crested the far hill. Dante hurried to put on a uniform claimed from one of the dead bodies. It had been scrubbed and restitched, but it still smelled like blood and worse. The gates closed with a boom. A stern call silenced the work of hammers and axes and chisels and shovels. Blays and Lira, the other two real humans participating in the farce, ran up to the battlements, kissed, and spread out along the wall.

Dante waited for the riders to start up the base of the wedge to Borrull, then summoned the images of several more guards. At first these were nothing more than fuzzy silhouettes, shadow-figures that took none of his strength to maintain but looked perfectly real from a half mile away; as the riders grew near, he filled the figures in with increasing layers of detail until you'd have to be standing right next to them to see they weren't breathing.

The riders pulled up ten yards from the gate. A lean-muscled man with a thick black beard shucked off his helmet and squinted up at Dante. "Hail and such."

"To you too," Dante said, doing his best to neutralize his Mallish-Narashtovik accent.

The rider gazed across the battle-churned field and boot-stomped sod. "All's well?"

"Had an attack a couple nights back. One of the tribes—a big one. Put them down easily enough."

"Typical," the man laughed humorlessly. "Well, the rest of us are just thataway. Be seeing you in a couple hours."

Dante nodded, heart bumping. The rider turned his horse and headed down the dirt path. The others followed. As the men hit the valley, Dante prayed to Arawn they wouldn't circle around the butte and find the pile of bodies bloating between the rocks, but the mounted scouts continued straight back the way they came. Dante dispelled the shadow-figures. The men crossed beyond the hill.

He signaled to Stann. Stann tipped back his head and let out a long, upward-lilting note. The norren burst from the houses, jogging to positions along the wall. Others continued to make last-minute additions to the wooden palisade and the earthworks supporting them. Men carried up water and food to those on the walls. The sun inched along the sky.

Less than two hours later, the far hill turned black with men. Scores of horsemen, hundreds of footmen, a flock of ox-driven wagons that slowed their progress to a casual walk. Dante sweated in his false clothes. He returned his silhouettes to the battlements and probed at the dirt in the tunnel beneath the gates. It too was freshly blood-soaked, thick with death and nether. Ready to respond.

Warriors flattened themselves behind the merlons. Dante sharpened the lines of his illusory guards. The army rumbled down the hill and started up the butte. Dante's nerves thrummed. Impossibly, the king's men continued on, oblivious to the counter army lurking among the fortifications. The human soldiers carried unstrung bows and sheathed swords, shoving each other, joking, faces grimy with the sweat and dirt of a long march through hostile lands. And then they stood before the gates, a blanket of troops smothering the grasses. Horses snorted. The smell of their sweat climbed the walls. Dante straightened atop his tower, raising a hand to the rider who pranced forth, his lightweight red cape snapping behind him.

"General Varrimorde, Earl of Junland," he called in the crisp and regal accent of his homeland, a rich farming county bordering Setteven itself. "I request entry for the king's army of the Varton

Forest and surrounding lands."

Dante saluted and barked a command down to the gates. Wood and hinges creaked. The Earl of Junland faced his troops and hollered them forward with the elegant nonsense of martial commands shouted loudly enough for an army to hear. Dante fought down a giggle and the urge to vomit. Were they really letting an enemy army stroll through their front door? The first troops emerged on the far side of the wall, a mixture of cavalry and their aides. Infantry with spears and swords and studded armor followed them through.

Varrimorde frowned at the empty grounds, the fresh ramparts, the burnt and disassembled husks of houses. "What has happened here?"

Hopp screamed like it was the end of the world. Scores of norren popped up from behind walls of wood and stone, unleashing a punishing volley of arrows. Men screamed among the twang of bows. Varrimorde whipped out his sword.

"To arms! Treachery! To arms!"

Confusion rippled through the men outside the gates. They reached for bows and swords. Inside, the surviving soldiers fumbled out swords and spears and charged the palisaded archers. With a great cry, the men outside the walls surged into the tunnel.

Time to cut them off. To plug the gates and slaughter those trapped inside. Dante dispersed his shadow-figures with a wave and plunged his focus into the dirt beneath the redshirts' trampling feet. The nether waited. He grabbed hold and yanked—but the dirt held firm.

21

Dante froze. Soldiers rushed through the open gates and into the storm of arrows and blades raging around the ramparts. Varrimorde jolted from his mount, an arrow sticking from his hip. His cavalry screamed in anger and galloped behind the palisades, swords glinting in the sun.

Again Dante grasped the nether in the soil between the gates. Had he pulled too hard the first time, like whipping a tablecloth out from under a set of dishes without spilling a one? Or had his entire control of the earth been a fluke, only to falter when his failure might mean the death of everyone here? He pulled again. Again, the nether moved, but the dirt between its shadowy strands stayed put.

His head went dizzy. He forced himself to slow his breathing to a steady tide. He saw at once. Knifelike, he had honed in on the nether itself. He needed to relax. To move not just the nether but all it was bound to. Like that, he could feel the weight of the dirt, the solid strength of the pebbles and stones. He yanked on the dark net a third time. A great rumble boomed from below. Men shouted in alarm. Dante sucked in the dirt like an outgoing wave and mounded it to the top of the tunnel. A half dozen soldiers were swept up in the rush, instantly crushed beneath a tide of dirt. The flow of men into the village stopped cold. On the other side of the plug, swords whacked into the earthen wall, as if the locked-out soldiers could simply chop their way through.

The norren on the walls poured fire into the shattered ranks trapped inside the fort. At the base of the steps, Blays and Lira fought side by side, falling back under a throng of redshirts hoping to push up the steps and carve into the archers crouched behind the walls. Dante ran forward, slinging a bolt of nether through the neck of the foremost soldier. He fell in a red spray. The man behind him stumbled. Blays jabbed forward, impaling the man on his own momentum. The man's dying weight forced him back, unbalancing him against the steps and exposing his lead leg to an incoming sword. Lira knocked it aside with a backhand sweep and grabbed the attacker's wrist with her bare hand. The man pulled back on his arm. Lira flowed after him, keeping clamped on his wrist while her elbow bent and slammed into his face. His sword clanged on the steps. She buried her sword in his belly.

Dante struck out again, aiming for another neck, but his hold on the nether was wobbly, weakening. The lance of shadows clipped the man's collarbone. He shrieked, flailing at an enemy who wasn't there. Blays stabbed him in his turned back and kicked him down the stairs.

The crowd at the steps had been reduced to a couple. Something similar had happened along the ramparts, where the cavalry had cut their way through the norren lines before succumbing to spears and arrows. Horses thrashed in the dirt, trying to rise and flopping to their bellies. Scattered redshirts fought on, falling swiftly beneath the hammerblows of the norren's outsized weapons. A group of four of the king's men cut down a pair of warriors from a clan Dante didn't recognize. A band of norren rushed them, howling, and the four soldiers bolted toward the stone houses across the field.

Cut off from the rest of their troop, with all their officers dying or dead, the few survivors flung down their weapons and raised their hands. The norren on the wall swiveled to the opposite side and fired down on the men still trying to dig through the dammed gate. In less than a minute, the survivors outside broke, fleeing downhill in a mad run, arrows whisking between them, felling them into the hot grass. They abandoned the wagons and the wounded. A knot of men remained trapped under the gates, unwilling to risk a run. Instead, the archers climbed down inside the walls to set up behind the arrow slits. The redshirts' screams filtered up to the wall where Dante sat to catch his breath.

Like that, it was over. All that was left was to tend to the wounded—death, for the king's men, who were cut down and dragged to the cliff's edge. Their own warriors were carried on shoulders and stretchers to the great hall above which Orlen had killed the commander and Mourn had killed Orlen, where the benches had been emptied out to build the palisade. Warriors set to work digging out the gates. A handful leapt down from the walls into the grass to chase down the oxen and bring the wagons up to the village. When Dante called, the nether hesitated, sapped by his struggles with the earth, but he left to the hall to do what little he could for the wounded.

Inside the hall, he could hear the screams from the cliffs. This wasn't war with all the niceties between squabbling kings. It had passed beyond that; in mere days, it had become something twisted and vicious; the norren fought the way a wounded lion fought, half-mad and pitiless. Any humans who came to the Norren Territories to hurt the norren would never go home again.

Dante washed his hands of blood and returned to the hard yellow sunlight. Warriors milled everywhere, washing up, hauling the barrels and sacks from the captured wagons into a pair of the houses built into the ground. Others dug a mass grave for their own dead. Their apparent lack of regard for the departed was curious, almost disturbing. There was nothing organized about it. Some cried while others dug. When the hole was deep enough, they filled it with bodies, then walked away. There were no public words. No tombstones or eulogies. Within minutes, the fallen returned to the hills that had birthed them. Was this, too, the product of their nomadic lives? Why leave a gravestone when you might never return? Was it one more sign of their stoicism? And why did it bother him? It somehow seemed more final, as if the dead were already long gone and soon forgotten. He hadn't been with them long enough to understand.

Hopp again came through without a scratch. He grinned at the torn-up ramparts, but his eyes were pained. "Cut it a little closer there with the gates, didn't you?"

"Considering I just learned how to do that yesterday, I'd say I did pretty good."

"We are alive. It could have been worse."

Dante nodded at the blood-soaked wall of raw dirt. "How many losses?"

"Fifty. Sixty." Hopp's grin soured. "Do they always have so many horses?"

"The rich ones do. Fortunately for us there are always more poor."

"Well, I don't like them. The horses. Or the men who ride them. What can we do about them?"

"Spears help," Dante said. "If you can figure out something more effective than that, we'll never lose another battle."

Dante had felt oddly detached from the victory. Moody, unenthused. The talk with Hopp helped a little. So did the contents of one of the wagons: casks of beer and rum, which the norren quickly distributed throughout the yurts and houses of the village. Others hauled broken chunks of the palisades and piled them into crackling bonfires—not because there was any need for warmth, but because lighting huge fires was simply what one did after a big victory. Some sang songs, minor-keyed and angrily joyous. A pair of Broken Herons slung Dante up on their bumping shoulders and hauled him to a spot beside the fire. A mug was sloshed into his hands. The undiluted rum brought tears to his eyes. The wet wood threw thick white smoke into the sky. Strangers joined the circle around the fire to ask his name and give theirs. He found himself laughing. When they urged him to tell them what he'd done to make the earth rise, he told them of his first two failures and how he thought they might all die because he'd promised the impossible, and they laughed, too.

He was far from sober when Blays found him. Blays' grin was crooked and devilish, and at first Dante assumed he'd been off in a bedroom with Lira somewhere. And maybe he had, but he also bore something far more interesting: General Varrimorde's marching orders.

Dante stood, open-mouthed, and extricated himself from the celebrants at the fire. Inside the stone house where he was quartered, he sat down in the lamplight with the leather-wrapped bundle of papers.

The orders were more or less as Stann had surmised. Varrimorde had been charged with taking command of the fort at Borrull and operating as the backbone of Gaskan military operations in the region—checkmating any major threats, should they appear, while smaller divisions were dispatched to the front to take the towns beyond the border one by one. There were no contingency orders for what to do if the fort was lost. It simply hadn't been planned for. Furthermore, no legions larger than a couple hundred men were expected to arrive in the Territories within the next four weeks. Everything had hinged on Varrimorde's campaign at the fort.

Dante sat back and rubbed his hand over his mouth. "It'll be days before the survivors make it back across the border. Days after *that* until they get word to anyone who can make a decision about what to do next. Even if they push up their schedule, we have two weeks or more before they can mount another threat against the Territories."

"I'm sensing something fiendish," Blays said.

"Well shouldn't we?"

"Of course. We're can't let the norren in the border towns sit there in chains when we could be stomping redshirt ass so hard the king tries to outlaw boots."

Dante rolled his lip between his teeth. "Would still be risky. If we get knocked out trying to retake the towns, the Territories will be back to defending themselves with scattered clans."

"We can't not take that risk." Blays stood up to prowl around the table. "All the mucking around we've done down here, that boils down to a pledge to the norren to protect them. To keep them *out* of trouble. If we've got norren cities occupied by Gaskan troops, we're honor-bound to liberate them."

Dante set down the papers and peered at Blays. "Honor-bound? You've been spending too much time with Lira."

"Well, it's true, isn't it? We made a bond to better their lives. If we don't keep that bond, we've betrayed them."

"Maybe the best way to better their lives is to consolidate what we've got before we go dashing about with banners in hand."

"What's this? *You* were the one who brought up striking back."

"And then your reasons for agreeing were so dumb I reversed my mind."

Blays snorted. "It's a smart play either way you look at it. Our whole philosophy is to press every advantage we get, isn't it? Well, we've got an army of angry giants. I'd say that trumps their nothing of nothing."

"I'm going to get ahold of Cally," Dante said. "Then we'll see what Hopp and the chieftains have to say."

To Dante's mild surprise, Cally answered in an instant. "I hear a certain someone convinced a certain substance to flow in ways that substance never should."

"It turns out you don't move the earth," Dante said. "You move the nether, and the earth moves with it."

"That doesn't make any sense. You *always* move the nether. If what you say is true, I'd be knocking down walls and tearing down ceilings every time I summoned it."

"You have to kind of relax when you do it. Go slow but strong. Like pushing a bookshelf across the room. If you push too fast, the whole thing topples over."

"I see," Cally said. "My suggestion to you: never try teaching."

"If I could show you it would make a lot more sense."

"Next time you're back in Narashtovik, then."

"In the meantime, we've got a conundrum," Dante said. "As far as we can tell, we just smashed the enemy's only major force in the region."

"So counterattack."

Cheers thundered from outside. Dante glanced out the window. "What, just like that?"

"Is there a better time to counterattack than when the enemy has nothing to counter-counterattack with?"

"Sure. When he's got nothing *and* he's drunk in bed."

"Moddegan and his viziers thought conquering the norren would be like plucking bearded, cave-dwelling flowers," Cally said. "You just broke their advance legion. What if you can kick them out of the Territories entirely? Would they sign a peace treaty then?"

"You think so?"

"Arawn's bowels, no," the old man chuckled. "But you never know."

Dante clicked off and wandered outside. Drums beat steadily, as low and monotonous as a heartbeat. Norren moved about the fires in what some might call a dance. To Dante, it looked more like sparring: warriors crouched low, lashing out with straight kicks their partners intercepted with kicks of their own. In unpredictable rhythms, they pivoted on their heels, lurching in to deliver slaps to their partners' faces and chests. The snapping fires cast long, swift shadows over the battle-torn grass. Dante found Hopp smiling wickedly on the perimeter.

"Didn't get enough fighting during the day?" Dante said.

"You've never seen our dance of conquering before?"

"Why would I have? I've only been warring alongside your people for months now. You're normally so open with outsiders."

"You wouldn't have had the chance," Hopp said. "You don't see this before any old skirmish. This dance is reserved for the big invasion of enemy lands."

Dante tried to read Hopp's face, but his head was clouded by the headache of departing liquor. "Invasion?"

"We've decided we don't like seeing any of our cousins in chains." The fire washed Hopp's branded face in white and red. "We're going to take our lands back."

It didn't wind up as much of a fight.

Two more clans came to Borrull the next day. The chiefs left a token force to hold the fort while the main army headed south at a jog. They hit the river three days later. The first village they reached was defended by fewer than twenty redshirts crowded into a single house. The norren shot them down as they fled out the back door, arrows sprouting from the redshirts' backs like sudden weeds. It was over in minutes. After, norren wandered from their hillside houses, gazing on the dead soldiers with secret smiles before rushing to embrace the sweating clansmen who'd set them free.

A handful of villagers joined them as they camped outside town. Another clan met them in the fields the next day. They captured a second village that morning and a third by afternoon. The Gaskan troops in both were token forces that might not have been able to withstand a single clan. If General Varrimorde's army had been in place at Borrull, with roving legions sweeping away any clans that poked up their heads, the village garrisons may have been able to keep their norren charges in check. Before the combined army of the clans, they were snuffed out like embers that had strayed too far from the fire.

At Cling, the garrison of sixty human soldiers had dug a hasty trench across the switchback path up the cliffs, fortified on the trench's downhill side by a fence of sharpened sticks. From their perch, they fired down on the plaza, arrows peppering the clan-warriors and plinking off the mosaic of the salmon. A frontal attack would be as bloody as a birth. Instead, Hopp pulled Dante aside, then embedded the bulk of the troops in the shops around the plaza. As they took shelter, Hopp led Dante and two clans' worth of warriors up into the hills west of town. Two hours later, they emerged on the upper end of the cliffside roads.

Below them on the switchback, the redshirts shifted their ranks to point their spears uphill. Just four men shoulder to shoulder could block the road completely; with fifteen ranks of the king's men, clearing them out could cost dearly. Instead, Dante sat on his heels and followed the death into the ground beneath them. He found it and pulled.

It was a clumsy job, less powerful by half than what he intended. An eight-foot section of cliffside road—that seamless road laid down by a norren master, a road that would have stood for a thousand years—cracked away from the slope, crumbling downhill in a deadly rain that swept a dozen men down with it. The others leapt away from the avalanche with panicked shouts. Hopp hollered and the norren pincered the human defenders from above and below. Bodies splashed into the plaza below. It was over in minutes.

A chunk of the docks and riverside houses had been burnt to the foundations. Most of the remaining houses were empty of norren and humans alike. The few residents they found told them both peoples had been taken inland, deeper into Gask. The humans, presumably, as refugees; the norren as slaves.

Not all had been taken. A few remained as servants to the soldiers. Others were prisoners, locked into a cave carved into the base of the cliffs. That was where they found Banning, the lanky graybearded mayor, chained in total darkness to a rough stone wall.

Dante's torchstone lit the way. Banning raised his shaggy head. One of his eyes had been put out, the socket crusty with blood and pus. His lean face had become skeletal, stretched over his broad cheekbones until his nose stood out like a lonely mountain. The fingers of his right hand were crushed, mangled. The room smelled like urine and sickness.

Recognition gleamed in Banning's remaining eye. "You again."

"Quit talking." Dante knelt next to him. He could feel the old man's heat before he touched his pale skin. Infection raged in his veins. His gums were white. He grabbed Dante's arm, chains clanking, but his norren strength had become childlike.

"My painting."

Dante called forth the nether. "Now's not the time for that."

"Now's the only time!" His shout broke into a hoarse croak. "Get me my painting, you baby-legged son of a bitch!"

"What's the matter with you?" Blays said. "We're here to help."

"My painting. The girl by the river. The paints, too. Remember where my workshop is?"

"Yeah, off in the woods with—"

"Good. Then quit gaping at me and go get my gods damned painting." Banning slumped against the cool wall and closed his eye.

Blays pressed his lips together, ready to object, then ran out of the cavern. Dante stayed with Banning, but the nether couldn't bring back the old mayor's eye or untwist his fingers. For all Dante's efforts, it couldn't fight off the fever, either. Banning's chest fell in shallow jerks. Sometimes he drifted off, head snapping upright whenever his chin fell too far. As Dante soothed his pain, two warriors braced Banning's chains, set a metal wedge against them, and struck them off with blows from a sledge. The iron bracelets dangled from the man's wrists. He let his hands rest on the grimy rock floor and closed his eye.

Feet pounded down the dim hall. Banning's eye whipped open. Blays hustled inside with a canvas on an easel and a rattling kit. Banning tried to lean forward and slumped back against the wall.

As the old man swore, Blays set down the kit and cracked it open. Bottles of paint sat in jostled racks, stoppers crusted with reds and blues and greens. He placed the easel in front of Banning and stepped back.

"All better?" Blays said. "Or should I go fetch your smock, too?"

Banning grinned up at him. "Don't think I won't stand up and slug you."

Dante helped him lean forward. Banning's skin burned. He had the sour, uric smell of something that hasn't moved in too long. His unbroken left hand trembled as he reached for his brushes and paints. To Dante, the canvas looked nearly complete: a portrait of a young norren woman beside a gray river, her smile as light as the waters were dark. Spidery trees hung over the banks, threatening to snag the girl's hair and shoulders, but a glowing halo held them at bay from her head. The image was so vivid Dante could almost hear her laugh.

Banning dabbed the brush into a pot of gray. His hand shook, flicking tiny driblets of paint. Sweat slimed his brow. Teeth gritted, he steadied first his breathing, then his hand. He touched the brush to the canvas.

That first touch was like the touch of a torch to dried hay. Banning's remaining strength coalesced into his hand, swooping and dabbing and flicking across the canvas. He croaked commands without looking from his work. Dante handed him rags and paint and brushes and a jar of cleaning-water. Ten minutes later, he signed his name in black on the corner of the canvas and wilted against the wall. His sweat had dried long ago. With a plunging stomach, Dante realized the aged mayor had simply run out of sweat: he was out of water, out of strength.

"Granddaughter in Dollendun," Banning whispered. "Corra." He nodded at the pretty young girl in the painting, then leaned his head back against the wall, eye squeezed tight. "That's her. Can you give her this?"

"Of course," Dante said. He blinked at the painting of the bright young girl warded from the darkness of the world.

He never knew if Banning heard. When he turned, the old man's face had gone slack and smooth, his pain forgotten. Dante pushed the man's shackle up his wrist. He felt no pulse.

One of the warriors had to turn away. Blays rubbed his mouth with the back of his hand. "I'll stay here until the painting dries. Her name was Corra?"

Dante nodded. He helped the warriors bring the body up from the cave. It was shockingly light, as limp as worn-out clothes. While they buried the town's dead norren together atop the cliffs, other warriors dragged the dead redshirts to the piers and pitched them into the river to feed the fish.

They stayed in Climb for three days, waiting on wagons of grain from Tantonnen. Warriors foraged and scouted the woods. One new clan joined them each day, swelling their army to more than a thousand. Once the wagons arrived, Hopp led them northwest along the river that marked the border between the Norren Territories and Old Gask. Blays took the painting with him. The next three villages were emptied of redshirts. Word had spread. At the fourth, the heavy corpses of norren lay in the streets. The only sounds and motion were the buzzing of flies, the guilty trot of dogs fleeing the gnawed bodies. At the next bridge, Mourn split the Nine Pines away from the army to hunt down the killers, taking his loon with him.

"Promise you won't fight unless you can win," Dante told him.

Mourn watched the wind blow the trees. "No."

"What do you mean, no? How is you dying going to help us?"

"The Nine Pines will die when we choose to die."

Dante frowned. "Taking to your new role after all."

"I may not want it. In fact, there is no 'may.' I *don't* want it. I would rather be asleep in a field somewhere, or alive in another time. But this is what my clan wants of me."

"I just meant it was fast. If you won't promise that, at least promise me you'll choose your last words in advance. Otherwise when the moment comes you might say something stupid, and we'll have to pretend we never knew you."

Mourn grinned sheepishly, the old Mourn again, if only for a moment. "I promise. Unless I drop dead before tonight. I think best at night."

They clasped hands. Mourn joined his warriors. The Nine Pines strode across the bridge with their bows and swords.

As soon as the body of the army made camp, Dante's loon pulsed. Across the long miles, Cally giggled.

"Got a surprise for you tomorrow."

"A good surprise?" Dante said. "Or a Cally-surprise?"

"I said it was a surprise. By definition, if I were to tell you what it was, it would not be a surprise, contradicting my original statement with a paradox we might never unravel. Best to leave the universe intact, then, and leave it a surprise."

"Whatever it is, it appears to have driven you insane."

"Only time will tell, my boy. Now get some sleep! You never know what the morrow brings. Best to be well-rested for it."

After that, Dante had no idea what to expect. Cally in the flesh, perhaps. A cask of flounders fresh from Narashtovik's north bay. A fine set of ponies. The next afternoon, two scouts came back at a run to speak to Hopp and Stann. As the army marched on, the river bent left. Around a rocky spur, the land flattened, revealing a great host of men.

The warriors laughed, jogging through the flat plain to meet their far-flung cousins. Hart and Somburr were there, too, dressed in the black and silver of Narashtovik, the silver brooch of Barden clasping their cloaks around their necks. Hart looked younger than Dante'd ever seen the wizened norren councilman.

"We brought you something," Hart said.

"Looks like more like a thousand somethings," Blays said.

"About 1200, last count. I think we picked up a few more along the way."

Dante gazed in shock at the mingling warriors. "From the eastern reaches?"

"Mostly the northern grasslands." Hart smoothed his robe over his paunch. "We'd heard you were doing well enough for yourselves here in the west."

"Better than I feared," Dante said. "It's good to see you. I think I need to speak to my chief now."

Blays fell in step as Dante tried to spy Hopp among the towering crowds of norren. "This is an awful lot of warriors."

Dante shook his head. "I'd say it's leapt from an awful lot to a hell of a lot."

"You know what hells are good for? Unleashing."

"But who is sinful enough to deserve such unleashment?"

"First off, let's exclude ourselves from consideration. With that out of the way, King Moddegan would top my list, but like all good kings, he's whacking off in a tower while his soldiers get gutted. Next I would suggest Cassinder on grounds of general bastardliness, but I have no clue where he is." Blays took a breath. "At this point, I'm out of ideas and I'm getting frustrated, so I'm going to suggest we just go burn the shit out of Dollendun and see what happens next."

"That's what I was thinking." Dante jerked his chin at the mountains due west, behind which lurked the northernmost lake of Gallador. "If we take Dollendun, the lakelands are the only major route into the Territories. Even if the merchants let the king's men through, they'll be delayed by days."

"Sure, it makes strategical sense, too. I was more interested in just really pissing them off."

Hopp was keeping his usual remove from the boisterous union of men and women, many of whom were distant relations of one sort or another. He gave Dante and Blays a nod. "Quite a troop, don't you think?"

"On a completely unrelated note," Blays said, "how far is Dollendun from here?"

Hopp's mouth bent in a wry smile. "Think we'd have enough?"

"Only one way to find out."

"We'll send the scouts tonight." Hopp rubbed his thick forearm. "Still a lot of norren on the eastern shore of the city, I hear. Wonder if they're happy about the king's troops keeping them locked in their homes?"

He conferred with the other chiefs while the two wings of warriors continued to integrate, passing news from their homelands and tracing family lines until they found common relatives. It didn't take long for the chieftains to reach a consensus. They'd bivouac behind the bend in the river while the scouts snuck into Dollendun. Equipped with loons, they'd report their findings, at which point the army would make its next move. Blays asked Hopp to tell the scouts to be on the lookout for a young girl named Corra.

The night was one of songs and drinks and fires. Dante couldn't have slept if he'd wanted to. The cheers and group holler-alongs didn't die down until two in the morning. They resumed, if somewhat less vigorously, by eight in the morning, propelled by the standard group sleeping dynamic: at night, no one gets to sleep before everyone's ready to sleep; in the morning, everyone's woken as soon as the first two people get up and start talking. While the warriors were more than friendly, and several of the new arrivals plumbed Dante for stories about the battles at Cassinder's manor and more recently those at Borrull, he found himself feeling isolated, pensive and restless. At a lull in the early afternoon, he excused himself to the latrine and wandered into the woods. For the rest of the daylight, he practiced moving the earth. Nothing major. The equivalent of a shovel-load at a time. Any more and his control tended to slip, the nether slicing through the rich brown dirt as quickly as if the soil weren't there at all. When it came to a handful of soil, however, he could move that as reliably and precisely as his own foot. He set his dogged mind to understanding each step of the process before allowing himself to move on.

He couldn't say how much progress he'd made by the time Mourn loomed him two days later to tell him the Nine Pines had killed the killers and were on their way back to norren lands. Dante told him to hurry, which turned out to be wise. The scouts reported in that same day. Dollendun was manned by several hundred redshirts. Hard to say how many, given that they were distributed among five or six different barracks, towers, and walls, but at least eight hundred, perhaps twice that many. The norren outnumbered them, in other words, but not great odds when it came to the capture of a city.

Hopp invited Dante to the war council as his advisor of human affairs. Stann recounted the details with his typically slavish attention to numbers.

"Risky," he concluded. "A lot of troops in a city full of human citizens who could readily become troops. Cities aren't good things to attack."

A chieftain named Tenner shook her head, braids brushing her shoulders. "Everything is a good thing to attack if it is attacked in the way that is right to that thing."

Stann gave her a peevish look. "If you know of the right way to attack a city, I have two ears for you."

"I don't agree that Dollendun is a city."

"No?" Hopp smiled. "Then is it a very coincidental proximity of houses?"

"I think it is two cities," Tenner said. "One norren, one human. Only one of these is hostile to us."

"That's the spooked hare, isn't it," Stann said. "Don't know which way it will break."

Hopp lifted his brows. "Let me ask you this. Will we ever have a better chance of taking it?"

Stann exhaled noisily. "Not unless we find a way to become potato-people who can bud new warriors as we please. The question is whether we *need* to take it."

The council went silent in that particular norren way that meant everything relevant had already been said. Hopp clapped his hands.

"Next question, then. Do we attack by day? Or by night?"

Dante's grin was as wild as the hills. Reluctantly, Stann helped bash out the strategy: get the scouts to alert the norren still in Dollendun to prepare; march to within ten miles, sleep through the first half of the night, and resume movement at midnight to catch the city at dawn; meet up with the Dollendun norren rebels, who would act as guides and auxiliary support as the army branched out to strike as many of the redshirts' fortifications as possible before the king's garrison could retreat to a single defense. After that, the clans would reconvene and launch an assault on whatever was left.

It sounded good. It sounded better than waiting for the king to muster an army the norren could never match.

The army stirred in the afternoon and marched north along the river. "March" wasn't quite the word; there were no formations or drummers to the gathered clans. Just a steady, long-legged stride, the product of long generations crossing the hills and plains on their own two feet. At times Dante had to jog to keep up. At sundown, they stopped in the woods to eat and sleep. Whistles woke him while the sky was black and studded with stars. The march resumed within minutes. Dante's heart beat steadily and quickly, bringing him swiftly to alertness.

The clans poured from the forest into the bare lands surrounding Dollendun. The dark and sleeping city gave no sign it knew what was to come.

22

Something was wrong. Smoke rose from the middle of the river. Orange flames reflected from the black waters.

"Oh look," Blays said. "The river's on fire again."

Dante gazed across the water to the western shore, but it was too dark to make out any movement. "Some might consider that a sign."

"Of Arawn's favor?" Lira's eyes flicked to his brooch. "Or his disdain?"

Dante shook his head. "Of people who don't want us to cross the bridge."

Blays grinned at her. "I think you take his faith more seriously than he does."

"It just looks that way because Arawn doesn't care." Damp grass squelched under Dante's feet. The night was cool, but far warmer than the last time they'd been this far upriver. Despite the retreat of the cold, the city was quieter, too. "Men are the ones who keep trying to drag the gods down to earth. The gods don't give a damn what we do to ourselves."

"That's not how I was raised," Lira said.

"That's because you're not from here."

"Neither are you!" Blays said.

"Well, I learned better."

The advance troops jogged away from the thudding mass of marching warriors. Some paused at the tents and yurts flanking the city. Silhouettes of norren pointed to a three-story tower of fresh blond pine standing at the edge of the tents. The lead warriors sprinted up to it, ducking to avoid any fire, and found the door was unlocked. They disappeared inside. A bird's whistle sounded, halting the army mid-stride. Moments later, the warriors emerged from the tower, their postures upright and casual. They waved the army forth.

Norren citizens popped from the tents to watch them pass. Blays beckoned a woman over to ask what was going on.

"The same thing I told the others."

"Let's pretend I haven't heard because I'm not the others," Blays said.

"Then I would tell you, in a tone of increased annoyance, that the redshirts fled their posts three hours ago. They retreated across the river. An hour after that, the bridges went up in flames."

"Their scouts must have seen us," Dante said. "Either that or those bridges insulted them for the last time."

"How strange," Blays said. "For a moment I imagined we just drove the king's armies from one of the largest cities in his empire."

"Sounds like a tactical retreat." Lira touched the handle of her sword. "What do they care if we take the norren shore?"

Dante suspected she was right and the next few hours bore that out. Among all the round-windowed wooden cottages, the courthouses, pubs, and guard stations, they found no living humans and few dead ones. Most of the bodies lay in the burnt places, bones and twisted limbs poking from entire blocks of blackened timbers. The norren they spoke to repeated the recalcitrant woman's story: the soldiers had pulled out just hours before the army's arrival, torching the bridges behind them. There had been neither explanation nor violence. Just a swift and total withdrawal.

The chiefs encamped at the road along the piers. Scores of scouts roamed the streets. Others struck north to find the nearest bridge. Despite the lack of any official announcement, a brief meeting of chiefs assembled in the public room of one of the pierside taverns.

"Did anyone anticipate this?" Hopp said.

Old Wult shrugged his bony soldiers. "Never figured the redshirts would run from a city just to get away from a bunch of—what do they call us? Grass-munchers?"

"Too dumb to build homes," said the braided woman.

"Shaggies," volunteered a man who wasn't much older than Mourn, reminding Dante he hadn't heard anything from Mourn since the prior night. He touched his loon.

"Duckies," Hopp said. "Since you're ducking the question of where we go next."

"Would have to find a bridge if we wanted to press the attack," Stann said.

"If?" Dante said.

"That was one of the words I said."

"The biggest of them, I'd say. Why back down now?"

Stann tapped the stumps of his fingers against the table. "Bloodthirsty, aren't you?"

"Not especially." Dante jerked his head westward toward the river. "I'm just not looking forward to waiting around to learn what's to come from the heartland."

"Crossing a river to attack a fortified city is a bad idea. Unless the idea is to spend the next decades of your life watching your bones be slowly flushed down the river."

That was the end of discussion. Everyone was too tired from the two marches and the anticlimactic fizzling of their battle-nerves. In the morning, Blays and Lira were nowhere to be found. Dante reached Mourn through the loon and learned the Nine Pines had been delayed and wouldn't reach Dollendun till the following day. There was a listlessness to the troops in the tents. Dante felt it, too. He went down to the docks to think amidst the smell of clams and the sound of gentle waves against the rocks. A mile across the river, the western shores waited.

He was still trying to plot out their next move when Blays thunked down the dock in a dead run and pulled up beside him, panting. "Come on. Need your help in the north end of the city."

"Did you just run all that way?"

"I was going to fly, but I must have left my wings in my other pants."

Dante tapped his brooch. "You do know you could have used your loon?"

"Yes, but then I wouldn't have been able to throw you in a sack and drag you along behind me if you said no."

Dante stood, knees cracking. "What's up, anyway?"

Blays ran his hand down his mouth. "I found where Corra lives."

"Who?"

"Corra. Banning's granddaughter. From the painting, you heartless, shriveled-up tuber."

"Oh." He jogged after Blays, who'd already started back up the boards. "Is she all right?"

"I said I found her house, not her. Up all night searching." Blays looked it, too: his blond hair flat and greasy, his eyes red and puffy, filled with the haunted glaze of the sleepless. "One of her neighbors recognized her from the painting."

Dante frowned over the quiet streets. Dollendun was in better shape than Cling, at least. For all the early riots, there was little sign of war. Two square blocks of rowhouses were torched. Shattered windows here and there. Anti-human graffiti on the sides of the Chattelry Office. The corners of homes showed strange sigils Dante assumed were the urban equivalent of wildsign.

There were living norren, too, mostly female and young. They walked the streets uneasily, double-taking as they saw the two humans running down the cobbles. Most relaxed when they saw the colors of Narashtovik. Others fled down alleys and slammed doors.

Blays stopped in front of a shack on the north fringe of town. Lira waited inside a room furnished with a cot and a chair and a table with a scattering of pencils. Drawings covered the walls, clearly childish, with shaky lines and distorted proportions of faces and dogs. Yet parts showed a clear sophistication, too, with swoops and fine details that suggested the girl had already found her nulla.

"What now?" Dante said, sure he was missing something.

Blays pointed at the floor. "Do your thing."

"My thing?"

"With the blood."

"You'll have to be more specific."

Blays sighed in frustration and knelt, tapping the ground beside crusty red spots that blended into the dirt floor. "The thing where you follow the blood to the person. The neighbor said she was dragged off by soldiers. We have to help her."

Dante crouched down beside the dried droplets. "How do you know it's hers?"

"Who else would it belong to?"

"Her brother? One of the soldiers? Her very unlucky cat?"

"What does it matter if it's a soldier's? Then we'll find him and break his arms until he tells us where she is."

Dante nodded absently, drawing the nether from the corners of the room. It came readily, smelling blood. "What if she's across the river? There must be hundreds of captives over there."

Blays' brow crinkled. "And if I'd made a promise to their hundreds of granddads, I'd be tracking them down, too. I made a pledge to Banning. If we don't keep our pledges, what separates us from the skunks?"

Dante let the nether flow to the dried blood and asked it where it could find more of that blood. A dull pressure sprouted in his head. It pointed west, of course. "Why are you so ready to risk your life to rescue her from the terrible fate of scrubbing the floors of some barracks?"

"She's a 13-year-old girl!" Blays exploded. He hooked his fingers into Dante's hair, clawlike, and rattled his head back and forth. "That's why they took her! She's not scrubbing any fucking floors!"

Dante waited for Blays to release his hair. He sat down and calmed his breathing. "She's alive. Across the river."

"Just point me in the right direction." He glanced at Lira. "You coming?"

She nodded once. "If it's important to you, it's important to me."

Dante cocked his head at her. "What about your pledge to protect *me*?"

"You've got two thousand norren clansmen camped out in town. If they can't protect you, I don't know what good I'd be."

He smiled with half his mouth and pointed in the direction of the pressure in his head. Blays strode out the door, Lira behind him. Dante followed into the warm afternoon sun. "How exactly are you going to cross the river?"

"What do you care?" Blays said over his shoulder.

"Are you taking a boat?"

"I thought I'd just run myself at the water real hard and try to skip myself across."

"Then either go at night or go far downstream first. They'll be watching the river like hawks. Hawks who hate people who try to cross the river in boats."

Blays tipped his head back at the sky. "It's hours till nightfall. Tell me if she changes location before we go."

"Of course," Dante said. "I'll be there at the oars with you."

"Oh."

"You thought I was staying here?"

"I must have been tricked by your resistance to every single aspect of my plan."

"Well, I do think it's moronic," Dante said. "But in my experience, that's when we do our best work."

Blays grinned. As they waited for the sun to slide behind the trees, Dante checked on Corra's direction several times, but if her location changed, it was too minor to make out. They took the rowboat shortly after nightfall. Scattered torches flickered across the western half of the city. After rowing hard to the river's middle, they slowed to lessen the splashing, pulled a foot downstream by the current for every foot they pulled themselves closer to land. Two hundred yards from shore, Dante cast a cloak of shadows over the boat, just thin enough to see through. The hull ground against the smooth pebbles of the bank. While Dante watched the dark houses, Blays and Lira hauled the boat halfway from the water. The grinding wood sounded loud enough to shake Dante's teeth loose.

The current had dragged them more than a mile north of the girl. They'd dressed in dark clothes, non-uniformed, and slipped down the streets at a light jog. Oval shutters hid whatever was behind them. Candlelight slipped through the cracks of a few, but most were dark, abandoned as the redshirts retreated and the norren army arrived just across the waters.

Bootsteps scraped in rhythm around the corner. Dante ducked into the lee of a high-steepled church encrusted with Narashtovik-style gargoyles. Lira and Blays pressed in beside him. Three soldiers scuffed down the street, clubs in hands, swords at their belts. Their voices carried on the calm, cool air.

When the soldiers' footsteps faded, Dante cut through a neighborhood of slanted shacks and hungry-eyed dogs that barked for blocks after they'd departed. He skirted a plaza where a single inn remained open, low talk filtering from its shuttered windows. Three stalls had actually been abandoned. Scraps of cabbage and bread lay sopping on the cobblestones. The pressure in Dante's head grew each minute, drawing them closer to whoever's blood had been spilled upon the shack's dirt floor. If they were lucky, and Corra too, it would be hers.

The pressure spiked to the point of pain. Dante stopped in the shadow of a rowhouse and turned in a slow circle until that almost-pain was aligned like a third eye in the center of his forehead. He pointed across the street to another rowhouse on the corner of a wide and empty intersection.

"If she's here, she's in there."

Blays showed his teeth in something that wasn't a grin. "Let's go."

"Hang on," Dante said. "See anything small and dead?"

Lira pointed to a lantern on the side of the rowhouse. A moth fluttered above the dim light. "How about small and living?"

Dante knocked it down with a flick of nether and delved into its eyes. His stomach lurched. Its flight was slower yet more erratic than a fly's, dropping suddenly before boosting itself back to its prior height. He directed it towards a crack in the shutters. It banged into the wall four times before slipping through, leaving Dante with an instant headache that could have been the result of the nethereal link or simply out of sympathy.

Inside, diffuse lamplight showed a man in a chair with a blackly gleaming bottle tucked into the crook of his elbow. The man swung his head to stare straight into Dante's eyes. A note of panic rose in Dante's gut—but he was watching the moth, nothing more. Dante spun the moth into a cramped kitchen and then up the stairs into a dingy room lit by candles and whatever moonlight fell through the open windows. Two men in red cloaks murmured to each other across a table. Another slept fitfully on a bed of blankets and clothes. Up the next set of stairs, a tight hallway showed four doors, all closed.

Dante let the moth fall into death and waited for his head to start spinning. "One soldier on the ground floor. Three more on the second. I don't know what's on the third."

"Corra?" Blays said.

"Whoever's blood we're following is on the third floor. I couldn't squeeze my moth under the doors."

"Whatever that means, it sounds disgusting. So, what—bust down the door, stab everything in sight?"

Dante shook his head. "I've got something subtler. Watch my back."

He opened a cut on his arm and sneaked across the street to press his eye to the crack in the shutters. The man with the bottle slipped his hand in his pocket, fumbled with his crotch, and glanced upstairs. Unwilling to risk a lesser wound that might give the man time to cry out, Dante called forth the nether, shaped it into a wicked blade, and slung it through the man's neck.

His head tumbled to the ground. The bottle stayed tucked in his elbow. Blood jetted from his neck. On the floor, the head blinked, jaw tensing. Dante tried the door and found it bolted.

"What's the holdup?" Blays whispered. "Forget where your foot goes? The answer is through the door."

"Wait." Dante recalled the nether to his hands and sent it flowing into the headless body. Its limbs shivered. It reached for the bottle, quivering, and set it on the floor with a soft thunk. It stood and stumbled to the door to claw at the lock. Blays whipped out his swords. Dante held up his palm. "It's all right."

The body grabbed the bolt, snicked it open, and stepped back. Dante swung open the door. The headless automaton stood perfectly still besides the blood coursing down its neatly bisected neck.

Blays choked, swallowing down a scream. "What's the *matter* with you?"

"I don't like getting slaughtered by hordes of soldiers?" Dante jerked his chin at the stairs at the back of the room. "The others are up there."

Blays shuddered. His feet creaked on the floorboards. He eased up the stairway like a stalking ghost. Dante followed, Lira right behind. At the landing, a tight corner concealed them from the room beyond. Blays paused there, blades pointed down, and charged.

The two men at the table bolted upright, shouting. Dante knocked one back down with a spike of nether straight through the heart. Blays hacked down the raised arm of the second man and stabbed him through the throat. The sleeping man woke without a word and leapt from his pile of clothes. He backpedaled toward the window. With her free hand, Lira grabbed his flapping cloak and swept out his legs with a crescent-shaped kick. She drove her sword into him as he fell, pinning him to the floor.

Three of the upstairs rooms were empty. They found her in the fourth lying on a scratchy straw mattress. She wore nothing but bruises.

"Corra?" Blays said. She blinked at him, blanket pulled to her chin, eyes as bright as stars. The norren girl was shorter than Dante, but the lankiness of her limbs belied the fact that wouldn't last. Blays beckoned her forward. "We're friends of your granddad's. You need to come with us."

She glanced at the floor as if she could see through it, then uncurled and stood, blanket pulled tight around her bony shoulders. Lira's gaze dropped to her bare and black-soled feet.

"Go down and watch the door, Blays," Dante said. "I'm going to get her some boots."

He descended to the second floor while Blays continued downstairs. He wrenched the boots off one of the bodies and brought them back up to the girl, who sat and mechanically laced them up. Her white shins stuck from the tops of the boots like broken wishbones. She looked up at Dante with eyes like forgotten silver.

Blays led the way back to the boat. They heard no horns or bells or cries. The city was dark, silent, as if holding its breath. Dante climbed into the boat and offered Corra his hand. Blays waded into the river to push them off, then rolled over the side of the boat. Their paddles stirred the black waters.

They reached the eastern shore without incident. At the outskirts of the army's camp, Blays found an empty home and led the girl inside. He and Dante filled a basin with water from the well and brought it to Lira, then closed the front door and walked into the street.

Blays booted a pebble down the cobbles. "Thanks."

"Of course."

"They deserved to die."

Dante nodded absently. "She looks okay. Just quiet."

"I'll show her the painting tomorrow," Blays said. "You should be there too."

Dante didn't think he'd be able to sleep, but he was wrong. Sleep always found a way.

Mourn and the Nine Pines arrived in Dollendun at noon. The clan had hunted down the soldiers who'd massacred the village and slaughtered the redshirts in the night. Mourn relayed this news with no joy. His voice held an implacable justice, as if the vengeance meted out on the soldiers hadn't been caused by him, but through the unstoppable clockwork of the cosmos. Dante had thought it more than strange the Nine Pines had been so swift to appoint him as their new chieftain, but their decision couldn't have been better.

Blays found Dante in the square and brought him back to the abandoned home. By daylight, Corra looked less pale and bedraggled. Lira had combed the tangles from the girl's dark hair. As Dante and Blays came into the house, she didn't say a word, merely followed Dante with her star-bright eyes. Blays untucked the painting from under his arm and presented it to her. Corra leaned forward like a leery terrier approaching a stranger.

"Grampa," she said.

"That's right," Blays said. "He asked us to give this to you. He said—"

Corra picked up the stretched canvas, carried it into her room, and quietly closed her door. Blays smiled in frustration. "Well, that's one way to respond to your dying granddad's last gesture."

Lira stared him down. "It's the first word she's said."

"I'm not complaining. I'm commenting. That that was weird. Because it was."

"Given what she's been through?"

Blays held out his palms. "I'm not complaining!"

Dante escaped to let them work through their disagreement for themselves. Five days after the norren occupied Dollendun, their scouts came back from the north. Downstream, the next two bridges had been burnt, too. The nearest intact crossing was some 150 miles down the river. More than halfway to Setteven itself.

At the war council, Stann laid out his case. Continue to occupy the eastern shore. Send a peace treaty to Setteven requesting the return of all slaves and the immediate cessation of hostilities. Offer to remain a part of greater Gask, with all the requisite taxes and tributes that involved, in exchange for the revocation of the king's ultimatum and for the total dissolution of norren slavery. If King Moddegan refused, let him come try to take the Territories for himself. The army of clans wouldn't leave until the treaty was signed.

A part of Dante knew Stann's plan was the wise course. What more could they do? March on Setteven, and plague the capital with norren dead? Leave the Territories undefended to rush out and terrorize Old Gask? The empire's heartland wasn't like the sparsely-peopled Norren Territories or the yawning woods around Narashtovik. Even with Dollendun and Gallador taken out of the equation, any of the cities of Setteven, Yallen, Voss, or Fonneven could raise five thousand fighting men in an instant if they felt genuinely threatened. So long as the norren stayed put on their side of the river, the king's war effort would be hobbled by the usual politicking, apathy, resentment, and costs. No peasant wanted to die fighting a race of towering giants who just wanted to be left alone. Anyway, if there was to be a clash of armies, let it come here, on their home ground, behind their own defenses.

Yet another part of him thought it was a mistake. The liberation of the Norren Territories must have been a shock to the king. But no step of their campaign had yet touched *human* lands. To talk Moddegan into peace, they would first have to cast the shadow of fear on his heart. They should take the western shore. Torch the palace. Carve Moddegan's name in hundred-foot letters on a hill above Setteven, and then carve an equally large dagger above it.

Instead, they were settling in to be sieged.

The chieftains found a warrior whose nulla was calligraphy and began drafting their peace proposal. Dante wandered off to a deserted house and pulsed Cally through his loon.

"We need more sorcerers," he said once the old man answered.

"Why would you need more of *those*? They're such trouble. Always turning things into other things. Knocking down walls when walls are sorely needed."

"Because right now our mighty troop numbers all of me. I've heard of one or two among the norren here, but they sound like minor talents. I don't know where Hart and Somburr got to—either they went off to rally more clans, or they're here and I've lost track of them."

Cally hmm'd. "Are you admitting you're insufficient?"

Dante rolled his eyes at the dirty wall of the silent house. "Aren't we supposed to be famed for our priests who can shape the nether like Arawn himself? How will it look when the ethermancers of Setteven smear us across the streets?"

"Bloody?"

"Gutty, too."

"I'll see if any of the Council would like to volunteer," Cally said. "Then I will pull rank on the monks, because that is what rank is for. Do you think you'll be able to survive two more weeks without them?"

"If I don't, we'll know who to blame," Dante said. "You."

The chieftains sent their messenger downstream to the king. Dante spent a day walking around the city. If a fight came, he didn't like the look of the north end of town. The south and east were far from impregnable, but there were some hills there to aid the defense, and a tightness to the streets that would squeeze enemy troops into vulnerable narrows. By contrast, the north of Dollendun was set on a flat plain. The houses were scattered and rural, the streets perversely wide. It would be no task for the redshirts to overrun them with sheer numbers, then use the structures for cover as they advanced on the heart of the city.

So just past the last of the northern houses, he started raising ramparts of dirt. He didn't use a shovel. He used the nether, taking hold of its earth-embedded weave to drag the ground up with it. Slow work. He'd only lifted a mound six feet high and twenty feet long before he had to lie down in the shady grass for a nap. Still, it wasn't his intention to build a wall around the city all by himself. He just wanted to see if such a thing could possibly be done.

Judging by his first day of work amongst the grass and flowers and beetles and bees, the answer was no. After putting together a stretch of rampart fifty feet long but just waist-high, his touch passed through the nether like water through river-weeds; it stirred, swayed, and stayed put. The following day, three norren emerged from the houses and stared at him for ten minutes. He figured they were just gawkers, killing time watching the man who could move dirt by waving his hands, but an hour later they returned with shovels and picks and ten more men. Wordless, they set in beside him, hollowing broad ditches on the exterior of the fortifications and pitching soil up the growing slopes. Dante squinted at the river and smiled.

The next morning, the norren at the ditches doubled in number. By the end of a week, hundreds of men and women toiled with shovels throughout every minute of daylight, putting their restless nomad energy to work protecting the city that had become their present home. Citizens trickled in, too. Some dug. Others brought food and water for the workers. A handful sang or danced or told stories while the warriors rested in the shade. Blays showed up of his own accord for a few hours every day before returning to Lira and Corra. Whenever Dante walked back to the house, Corra watched him with those sparkling silver eyes.

Blays was there in the fields when a hunched young norren approached Dante with his hands tucked into his sleeves. Dante straightened, letting the nether slip away, and wiped his arm across his brow. The days had turned warm.

"Excuse me," the norren said. His beard was patchy enough he might have been a teenager. Instead of meeting Dante's eyes, the youth gazed past his shoulder.

"Yes?" Dante said.

"Is the idea here to keep the enemy out?"

"That's the general theory of fortification, yeah."

"And you're doing this with earth?"

"Sure enough." Dante gestured at the river flowing bluely to his left. "If we can, we might flood the ditches with water, too."

The young man nodded and frowned at the ground as if asked a particularly fiendish arithmetic problem. "What are your feelings on explosions?"

"I prefer not to be near them."

"Oh." The norren turned to walk back to the city.

Dante jogged after him. "You can't ask a question like that and then just trot off. What brought you out here?"

"Well." He folded his hands back into his sleeves and furrowed his brow, staring past Dante's shoulder again. "Explosives. I can make them."

"And you think an incoming army might not appreciate being blown up."

"Wait, won't they?"

Dante hid his smile. "What's your name?"

The boy straightened. Freed from his hunch, he was a good four inches taller than Dante. "Willers."

"How do you set off your explosives, Willers?"

"Fire works good. Yeah, you touch the fire to the explosives and then the explosives explode."

"I'll take all you can give me."

The kid was so shocked he looked Dante straight in the eye. "Really? It won't be *too* much. I have to mix a few things and two of the things are hard to find even when you know where to look."

"Whatever you can get." Dante gestured at the half mile-long line of raised dirt and the scores of norren working to make it even longer. It was a quarter of the way to a small hill. If they could reach it, the north face of the city would be sealed by the rampart. "We've got a lot of ground to cover."

Willers nodded quickly and scurried back the way he'd come, leaning forward so far into his strides it looked like he'd topple right over.

"I didn't know we'd get to blow things up," Blays said. "If I had, I would have conquered a city much sooner in life."

"Well, we all have regrets," Dante said.

"At least we're here now and have the prospect of blowing things up in the future. I feel like that's what's truly important."

Around them, warriors dug on. Messages came and went from Cally and the scouts, but from the only one that mattered—the message to the king—there was no word. Day to day, Dante's movement of the earth felt no different from the one before, but after a week, he could pile up dirt or sweep it down without conscious thought. He was stronger, too, able to add a hundred yards to the ditches and ramparts each day before the nether grew fluttery and weak.

Two weeks to the day, the messenger returned. Most of him,

anyway. All his possessions had been confiscated; he'd been forced to walk naked for miles from Setteven before a farmer, finding he had no clothes that would come close to fitting, offered the norren a long cloak. His right hand had been confiscated, too—the hand that had delivered the treaty.

He had another message, too. The armies of Gask had finally mustered. They would begin their march to Dollendun in days.

23

"Well, that's a relief," Blays said, wandering away from the plaza where the announcement had been made.

Dante goggled. "It's a relief that we're days from being attacked by thousands of people with bows and swords and devices that can crush us with rocks?"

"It beats digging ditches all day."

"Yes, and now we can use those ditches for our own graves."

Blays gave him a skeptical look. "It's a relief to know that whatever's happening, it's probably not going to continue happening for much longer. Either we'll use the streets to bleed to death in or to dance down with funny little hats on our heads. I'm tired of waiting to see what they'll do next. Well, pretty quick I won't have to."

"That is sort of comforting," Dante said. "In a very horrifying way."

"See, it's all about perspective. You'd be lost without me."

Within hours, norren citizens began filing into the camps to enlist in the makeshift army. It became quickly apparent there wouldn't be enough proper weapons to go around. Smiths took to forges and banged on metal. Fletchers sent their clansmen out to gather wood and feathers while they carved fresh shafts. Others found flaky stones and sat in circles, swapping stories while they chipped the rocks into points for arrows and spears. The Clan of Dreaming Bears proposed a raid on one of the barracks across the river. They planned to send scouts that night to find where the redshirts' arms might be cached.

Dante returned to the rampart on the north end of town. It was nearly complete, its line extending from the river to within a bowshot of the small hill that would help command their flank. He'd been hoping to curve the line of dirt south around the hinge of the hill and cut off the eastern approach to the city as well. He doubted he'd have time. He'd have to string up whatever ramparts he could between other hills and buildings, doing his best to funnel the invaders down a couple of streets where the bulk of the norren could stand firm.

Willers came to him that afternoon with a cotton bag the size of Dante's fist. It was unnaturally heavy and shifted like sand. It smelled sulfurous, hellish, like something dredged up from a lake inside a steaming cave.

"What's it made of?" Dante said.

Willers blinked past his shoulder. "Materials."

"That only you know about?"

"No, lots of people know about them. It's how they're put together they don't know."

Dante hefted the lumpy bag. "How big a burst will this produce?"

"If you are within five feet of it, it will quickly spread you across many more feet. If you are within twenty, you might fall down, or be upset with your ears for refusing to stop ringing."

Dante walked across the grass to a stop some forty feet away, set down the bag on top of a small mound of dirt, and walked back to Willers, who was staring at the bag with horrified anticipation, as if it were a puppy about to piddle on his neighbor's rug. Dante sent the nether to it in a flash of heat. A white flash seared his eyes; as the heat touched his skin, thunder rolled across the plain and smacked him deep in his chest. He blinked away the stars. A claw of black smoke rose from the scorched dirt.

"How did you make it burst without touching it with fire?" Willers said.

"I've got tricks, too." Dante rubbed his ear. He could smell the smoke now, ashy and acrid. "It won't stop them altogether. But it may give them something to cry about."

"If they're sad, will they go home?"

"Who knows?"

He looned Cally to ask for all the soldiers Narashtovik could put together. Cally said he'd see what he could do. He did not sound optimistic.

Neither was Dante. For all their tricks and troops, it would still be a numbers game. And the numbers favored the king. What happened if the norren were defeated here? There were still many clans scattered throughout the Territories, but not all that many. Too few to resist if the redshirts broke through. Once they were quelled, he had the sick feeling the king would turn his armies to the north. To Narashtovik. Cassinder would see to that. Their meddling would not go unpunished.

His expression must have been dark enough to chill the dead. As he sat in a chair in the front room of the abandoned house, Corra wandered from her room and fixed him with her shining eyes.

"What's wrong?" she said.

He glanced up sharply, so shocked to hear her speak he nearly forgot what he'd been brooding on. "It's nothing."

"This is nothing." She swiped her hand through the air, fingers trailing, then pointed at his head. "That is something."

"Do you really want to talk about the war?"

"Why are you afraid? I saw the soldiers in that house."

Dante managed to smile and frown at the same time. "Four soldiers is one thing. But there's an army on its way. No man can reverse the tide by himself."

She folded her hands at her waist. "So why don't you run away?"

"I can't. This is my fault. And the fault of hundreds of others dating back to the day the first human took a norren for a slave. So maybe I'm blameless. Reacting to the mistakes of long-dead men. Trying to set right what was set wrong." He leaned forward, elbows on his knees, and stared at the dirty wooden floor. "But I don't think there would have been a war right now if we hadn't been tempting one. For that, I do share blame. I wonder if it would have been better to leave the norren alone to suffer the lesser burden of bondage. Soon enough, win or lose, thousands of them will die."

"But what if the lives of their children are better for years and years and years?"

"I doubt I'll be alive to see that."

Corra clutched her arms to her ribs. "Why wouldn't you leave to live upon a mountain? Where no one can hurt you and you will never know about everything that's wrong?"

He glanced up. Her eyes were their brightest yet, burning from the hollows of her cheeks. He took a breath. "You know that painting your grandpa made you? He had to finish it with his left hand."

She cocked her head. "Why would he do that? He always painted with his right."

"Because someone destroyed his right hand. For fighting back. But he finished the painting. It was the last thing he did before he died."

"He painted me?"

Dante nodded. "You're his granddaughter. You've got his blood. Even if they ruin your hand, you can finish your painting."

She blinked several times, face pinched together by an invisible hand of emotion. "Thank you for telling me that. About Grampa."

Dante nodded. That, too, might have been a mistake, telling her. At times it would haunt her, knowing her grandpa's dying moments were spent slumped over her picture. But she needed it. A knowledge of defiance. That until the day you met Arawn in that starry field, no matter what arose against you, you could stand and stare it in the eye.

Perhaps he'd needed to hear that, too.

He continued his work with the norren on the ramparts. The Clan of Dreaming Bears sailed across the river and sacked a lightly-guarded barracks, bringing home barrels of swords and spears. The citizens drilled in the squares. Steel flashed in sunlight. Stone points clacked against the cobbles. Arrows thrummed, smacking into bales of hay. Men and women hauled water from wells and the river. Through the loons, the scattered scouts let them know the king's army had left Setteven, eight thousand strong at the least. More would join as the army crossed the miles between the capital and Dollendun.

A contingent arrived from Narashtovik two days later. Three of the Council's priests—quiet Varla, brusque and vulgar Ulev, and dark-haired, cunning young Wint—along with ten monks of lesser talents, including Nak. Dante met them with a smile, even Wint. It was good to see old faces. They would help greatly, too. The least of the monks was worth any ten soldiers. Together with Dante and the two norren adepts, it would make for a troublesome force.

"How did you get reined into this?" he asked Nak.

Nak puffed his cheeks in embarrassment. "I volunteered."

"Why the hell would you do that?"

"So that when you triumph, I can boast to the ladies I taught you everything you know."

"You're not much of a monk, are you?"

Nak's plump cheeks bulged in a frown. "If a monk can end lives in the name of his god, he ought to be able to create lives, too."

Dante showed them around. Introduced them to Mourn and Hopp and a few of the other chiefs. When Dante explained he'd joined Hopp's clan, the priests gave him curious looks, but raised no questions about what that meant for his loyalties to Narashtovik.

The incoming army was covering nearly twenty miles per day. By the time it ranged within a hundred miles, norren scouts estimated it had gathered another thousand men. On the evening it camped some forty miles from Dollendun, the boats arrived. The oars of fifteen war galleys lashed the water, plying upstream to dock on the west bank. Blays watched with Dante from their own piers.

"I don't think they're bringing more troops," Blays said. "I think they're here to ferry the redshirts in Dollendun over to our side of the river."

Dante peered through the twilight. "What makes you think that?"

"You know how bad those boats stink. But have we seen a single soldier hop off since they've docked?"

"Makes sense. Use their fleet to divert us to the shores while their main army marches in from the north."

"Those things move like ducks on the water," Blays grumbled in grudging admiration. "Big, stupid ducks filled with hundreds of people who want us dead."

"That isn't a very duck-like want," Dante said.

"Then why are they always honking at people? Does that sound like something that wants to be friends?"

"I once spent several days thinking about ducks."

"What would possibly possess you to do that?" Blays said.

"Cally."

"Oh."

"Yeah."

"Wait," Blays said. "Hey. Wait. Then you must know the thing it is that ducks do best."

"Quack?"

"Sit." A grin spread over Blays' face, unstoppable as a blush. "They sit there. Like feathery, bug-eating idiots."

Dante drew back his chin. "You've got an idea."

"I've got an idea."

It was foolish and wonderful and perfectly Blays. Best of all, it would work. As night fell, Dante burst into laughter, his giggles rippling over the waters. He told Blays to tell Hopp to get to work on fortifying the shore, then ran north to get to work himself, the torchstone lighting his way.

The next day passed with terrifying swiftness. He obsessed about hours. Each hour meant a mile. One mile closer for the king's army to approach. Of course it didn't quite work like that. Some hours the army would be stopped to rest. Other hours they would march and march, covering two or three miles every sixty minutes. But in the aggregate, for each hour the army existed, it would cover the better part of a mile. It had been forty miles away whenever it set out that morning. It could cross that distance in two days. 48 hours. He had 48 hours left. Not that he was certain he would die in the fighting. But in the normal course of life, you wake in the morning with the expectation you will continue to live for years or even decades. For tens of thousands of hours. Hours too many to mark or measure or care; in fact, there was no conscious expectation of decades of life at all. Just an unconscious assumption running so deep you never thought of it at all.

Dante could count 48 hours. After that, he might have no more hours, or a single one, spent in battle, or 40,000 until he died in bed with a smile embedded in his long white beard. He didn't know. He didn't know and he couldn't know, and so his heart beat as if it were trying to work a lifetime of beats into the few hours he had left.

The norren finished connecting the rampart to the northern hill. A couple inches of groundwater had seeped up through the ditch below the earthworks' outward slopes. Dante strode to the river, where a small dam of land held the waters from the ditch, and took hold of the nether lurking beneath the dark soil. He slid the damming earth up onto the rampart. Cold brown water sluiced into the ditch, flooding it to a depth of three feet.

They sent away those unable or unwilling to fight—the children, the elderly, the crippled, those whose beliefs forbade the shedding of blood. Most of the women stayed to fight. They sent Corra away, too, her painting in one hand, one of Blays' knives in the other. She didn't wave. Just watched Dante from over her shoulder as she walked down the road southward from the city.

24 hours. Twenty miles. Both went by in a blink. The scouts confirmed the redshirts' movement. In all likelihood, they would cross the remaining few miles in the day, camp nearby for the night, and attack with the dawn.

Clan warriors drilled civilians in advances and retreats. Others helped erect barriers of wooden spikes across the main roads and dumped debris across others. The chiefs finalized their strategy. Assuming the main body of the king's forces would come down through the north on their side of the river, while the troops quartered on the western shores landed via boat to attack from the flank or rear, the norren forces would be divided similarly—most deployed to the northern edge of the city to man the ramparts or shadow the army south if it tried to swing around on them, while a smaller force would be left near the shore to fend off the amphibious assault. In true norren fashion, several clans would be dispatched to roam the streets, killing any scouts, delaying expeditionary forces, and keeping watch for any major flanking movements.

Dante and Blays would be posted on the shore to oversee Blays' plan. Six hundred norren would be with them, including their clan and the Nine Pines. They might be outnumbered twofold or more. Then again, so would their main troop.

He didn't touch the nether that day. Typically, a few hours of sleep would refresh him, but he wasn't certain he would sleep at all that night.

As twilight fell, the smoke of scores of fires rose from the forest north of town. Dante watched from the docks. The last gray light flickered on the water. Blays and Lira were a ways up the shore; Blays stood behind her, arms around her waist. They didn't appear to be talking. Just watching the smoke bloom and the light fade.

As the night took hold, firelight shined through the black pines. Waves sloshed against the docks. Dante's loon pulsed, startling him.

"How does it look?" Cally said.

"Like we're in line for morning introductions."

"How do you think you'll do?"

"Oh, I expect I'll kill at least twenty people, personally. We'll see where it goes from there."

"I meant as a whole, you dolt," Cally said.

"Well, we're outnumbered. By a lot. Then again, I would bet on a norren clan-warrior over a redshirt grunt ten times out of ten. Then again again, the norren aren't used to fighting in groups this size, and many of them have never fought before."

"Well, I sent five hundred men your way earlier in the week. I'm sorry I couldn't get them to you sooner, but if you can hold out for a few days, they may arrive in time to help."

"Good." Dante shook his head. "You know what? I have no idea how it will go tomorrow. Put me in a room with four men with swords, and unless I trip and break my head, I can tell you what's going to happen. Fifteen thousand armed men shaking their spears at each other across one of the biggest cities in Gask? River-borne invasions? Sorcerers on both sides? I don't have a clue, Cally. Not the skinniest, most malnourished, runtiest little clue. This time tomorrow, I could be recounting you our great victory, or I could be telling you nothing at all, because I am at the bottom of a mountain of bodies. What if this is the last time we ever speak?"

"I think you should calm down."

"Should I? How often have you stared across the night at a thousand enemy campfires?"

"Just once," Cally said.

"When?" Dante scoffed.

"During the Third Scour."

Dante was about to declare him a liar; the Third Scour had taken place over a century ago. He remembered, with the usual jolt, Cally was well older than that. "What happened?"

"As it turns out, I lived."

"In the battle."

"It was in the Collen Basin. Just after we took the palace." Cally cleared his throat. "If you're any student of history, then, which I know you're not—"

"I know about the battle for Collen Basin."

"Then why am I telling you this? We had the palace for two weeks before the baron's reinforcements returned. A true rabble. Disgusting. But they had fine steel while we had pitchforks and dysentery. What kind of a universe is this where a case of diarrhea is in charge of deciding who's right and wrong? The gods are laughing, I say.

"Regardless of our gastrointestinal distress, we dug in while they advanced. I remember thinking we had better than half a chance; that the enemy were primarily conscripts out of Larkwood who didn't give a damn about the Basin. That and mercenaries, also from Larkwood, who'd been mere bandits until their silver started flowing from the baron rather than from whoever they could rob. Meanwhile, I was right around your age, however old you are now, except significantly more advanced."

Dante snorted. "I highly doubt it."

"My attitude exactly! So you can understand why I was less worried than I perhaps ought to have been. They simply had too many men, you see. That's what it came down to. That and the dysentery. We stuffed the buildings around the palace plaza with archers, and gummed up all the doorways in with tables and garbage and the like, but the enemy lit fires. What do you know! Archers don't like breathing smoke and flame any more than the rest of us. They pushed us back inside the palace, then smashed out those great red windows—have you seen them? No, of course not, they were smashed—and poured inside. We fought in the halls until you could hardly stand from the blood.

"Things got so desperate a group of us decided to lock ourselves in the old-fashioned dungeon cells and shoot anybody who got near the bars. Which doesn't make a lot of sense, in hindsight, but as I said, desperate."

"What happened then?" Dante said.

"Oh, we couldn't find the keys. So we ran away instead."

"If I've got this right, then, what you're saying is just when things look their darkest, I should run away as fast as I can."

"What I'm saying is I was certain I would die, but then I lived for another hundred years. Most of them happy." Cally stopped; through the loon, Dante heard him swallow some water or tea. "Look, right now you don't know how the next day will turn out. Yet you fear the worst even though you can't possibly know it will come! How can these things coexist? You *don't* know what tomorrow will bring. You might win. You might lose. You might win and die or lose and live. In the end, a single thing among all these possibilities will be the one thing that happens—and you won't know what it will be until it does. Probably not even then! Discovering these unknowns, these possibilities, that should be a joy. Whatever happens, you'll get the gift of knowing *what!*"

It sounded like nonsense, yet Dante found himself comforted. He wanted to tell Cally as much, but something held him back, an emotion oddly like resentment. Instead, he gazed at the black water, the campfires burning through the forest.

"Thanks, I think."

"Well, if it gets that bad, you *can* always run."

He closed the connection. Dante wandered up the shore, smelling mud and fish that had been dead for so long they barely stunk. If he had thoughts, he didn't remember them afterwards. Just the memory of the cool evening and the wash of waves upon the shore. It calmed him. He wanted it to be this way forever.

Blays found him there a couple hours later. The blond man grinned. "Figured you'd be here. When it comes to water, you're like something that loves it."

"Where's Lira?"

"Bed. In no condition to walk."

"Don't say anything more, or this night will come to blows."

"Oh, it already—"

Dante pushed his tented palms against his nose. "Forget it. I'm just going to go challenge the entire enemy myself."

Blays laughed. "Listen, whatever happens tomorrow, the first bit's going to be fun."

THE GREAT RIFT

"I'm sure it will provide fond memories as I'm gargling my own blood."

"I think we're doing the right thing, you know."

"Do you?"

"I haven't taken a census, but I'm going to go out on a limb and predict that 100% of the norren slaves would prefer to be not-slaves."

"The issue," Dante said, "is whether they would prefer to be living slaves or dead not-slaves. And whether it's any of our business to intervene."

"Well, we did. Oops."

Dante laughed through his nose. Then it overtook him, rib-hitching laughter that had him shaking his head at the river. "Oops!"

"We should probably put that on our tombstones."

"That or 'It seemed like a good idea at the time.'"

Blays grinned. "I'm going to put an arrow on mine pointing to yours, and then make mine say 'All his fault.'"

"Oops."

They laughed until silence took them, the hush of night, the whisper of waves.

"Anyway," Blays said at last. "If I only have one more night of sleep ahead of me, I'd like it to be a good one."

"See you on the frontlines," Dante said.

Dante waited just a little longer before going back to the house. One last look at the moon. The stars. The silvery heavens and their cycle of perfection. He should have looked sooner, looked longer. There was no more time left.

He slept. He meant to see the sunrise, too, but he woke to the full light of early morning and the blare of war-horns. It was time.

24

Blays burst through the door before the horns faded. "Well, come on! You wouldn't want to miss the big war, would you?"

Part of his mind leapt to awareness, as if it had been waiting all night for this moment. His body was still clumsy with sleep; as he tugged on his pants, he toppled back into his mattress. He had little armor to don. Iron bracelets for both wrists, with a slightly larger pair clasped above each elbow. A leather vest composed of boiled patches sewn into supple deerskin, keeping him flexible across the hips and abdomen, along with a collar of similar construction. That was it. The rest was sheer decoration, the armor of the psyche: his black cloak, silver-trimmed. The brooch of Barden clasping it together. And his doublet, velvety black, the thick silver ring of Arawn's millstone sewn into the center of the chest.

He was ready.

The morning was already warm, thick with the moisture of the river and the forest. The barricades around the main plaza were manned by a skeletal defense. The footprints of thousands of norren soldiers led north to the ramparts. Dante jogged west to the shore where hundreds of clan warriors and Dollendun citizens sorted through arrows, wiped down swords, and stretched their limbs, working up a light sweat. Hot tea awaited Dante on the docks. One of the perks of rank.

"They started loading up around dawn." Blays nodded across the river. On the far bank, the galleys waited beside the deepwater docks.

Dante sipped his tea. "And how's our fleet doing, Admiral?"

"See for yourself!" Blays swept his hand upstream. There, some twenty rowboats bobbed beside the pier, occupied by two-man teams of norren. Three little candles burned in the bow of each boat. As he watched, the first boat cast off its line and pushed into the river.

"Excellent."

Wint appeared beside him. The young Council priest's dark brows were pinched in a skeptical line. "Do you really expect this to work?"

"Define 'work,'" Dante said.

"Provide any positive impact whatsoever on our chances of success. Are you hoping their captains will laugh themselves over the railings?"

Beside Blays, Lira stared Wint down. "These two have made a living out of appearing so foolish that no one takes them seriously until it's too late."

Wint shrugged, his expression taking a humorous edge. "Forgive me for being concerned about my fate when that fate rests on the outcome of a smattering of rowboats versus a fleet of fully-staffed war galleys."

"Yes, well, you're forgetting something," Blays said.

"Enlighten me."

"Those aren't rowboats. They're little wooden dragons."

Wint's head jerked once, as if he were in pain. Or suppressing a shake of his head. Dante poured himself more tea, not that his nerves needed it.

Brassy horns trumpeted from the woods to the north, jolting him, spilling steamy tea over his hand. Distant figures moved through the trees. Swarms of them. Masses. A living, breathing army. Pierced by sunlight, the river gleamed richly blue. The rowboats were a quarter of the way across it when the galleys shoved off and hoved toward the eastern banks.

The galleys' oars centipeded through the water. Dante watched, along with hundreds of warriors, as the rowboats closed on the galleys in the middle of the river. From a tight formation, the rowboats split apart, a pair moving to intercept each enemy vessel. Sporadic arrows flew from the topdeck of two of the galleys, stopping one of the rowboats cold. The rest were ignored.

Unchecked, they slipped alongside the surging galleys like the pilot fish sailors see in the slipstreams of cruising sharks. One rowboat drew too close. The galley's prow rammed it head-on. The smaller craft disappeared beneath the blue. Across the rest of the rowboats, one norren in each stayed seated and paddling while his or her partner stood and latched fast to the galleys with spikes and ropes. With their boats secured to their huge hosts, the standing norren produced small packages and affixed them a couple feet above the waterline of the galleys' curved hulls.

The norren reached for their candles. Not that Dante could see the flames across half a mile of glinting waves and sunlight. But he had watched the norren practicing the day before. Those whose candles had gone out went for flint and steel. Sparks sprayed from the shadows of the galleys, which plowed on across the river, foam curling from their fronts. A cry went up from one of the vessels. Too late, men appeared on the railings to fire in earnest on the norren below. The norren cut their ropes and rowed furiously away from the warships.

One rowboat lagged behind, its two-man crew struggling with the package they'd attached to the galley hull. Dante's breath caught. The norren and the rowboat they stood in disappeared in a flash of white.

The bang of the explosion rolled across the shore just as the second one flashed further down the line of ships. Wood and water splintered through the air. A string of flashes lit up the galleys. Shattered wood tumbled in smoldering arcs. Great booms thundered over the water, followed by panicked screams and hasty orders. Atop the bows, shaken archers regained their footing and pelted the paddling norren.

Not all of Willers' bomb-bags went off. Not all opened more than a perfunctory hole in the galleys' sides. But half the boats trailed smoke from lethal holes punched through their sides, cold blue river water gushing into the void, quelling the fires with clouds of white smoke. Up and down the shore, norren cheered. The galleys redoubled their strokes to reach land before sinking.

"Shoot," Willers said from Dante's elbow, startling him. "That didn't work at all."

"What are you talking about?" Dante said. "Those two on the left are going to be housing fish within minutes. Five or six more will have to push in straight to shore if they don't want to sink. We'll slaughter them the second they land."

"Yeah, but they *all* should be doing that. I used everything I had in those bags."

Blays waved a hand around. "You're expecting too much out of life, kid. If you can sometimes blow up just half the things you want blown up, consider that a screaming success."

"Pitiless Arawn," Wint said, flipping his black councilman's cloak off one shoulder to expose his narrow sword. "This may yet work."

The undamaged vessels slowed to match the wallowing ships that were taking on water. The two doomed galleys launched longboats and filled them with men. A few redshirts plunged straight over the railings in panicky confusion. To the north, a monstrous group cry echoed through the streets.

The battle had begun in earnest.

Strange, then, to be on its less exciting flank. As clanging metal and the screams of the dying filtered from the main scrum a couple miles away, the scene by the river was quiet, punctuated by the sough of oars and the occasional order barked from the ships' captains. Orders which played out exactly as Dante hoped. Forced to rush their landing, the galleys could no longer sail up or downriver to form a beachhead away from the norren defenders. Instead, the fleet rushed straight in, carried just a few hundred yards downriver by the currents. Two foundered well before bow range. As the remaining ten slogged on, the norren jogged down the shore, set up wooden planks above their heads to act as shields, and readied their bows.

The exchange of arrows was thin at first, both sides probing range. As the galleys closed, thick swarms flew back and forth, thunking into the wood of the shields and hulls alike. Dante hung back out of range. He wasn't much with bows. Besides, he had better plans for the day than dying of an arrow through the throat.

Men and norren fell and screamed. Dante helped establish a triage center, attending to the wounded warriors with the perfectly mundane methods of bandages, stitches, and liquor. The norren archers forced the redshirts belowdecks until the galleys ground into the shore. As rope ladders tumbled over the boats' sides, the archers reemerged, covering debarking soldiers with a punishing hail of arrows.

Norren arrows slaughtered the first wave of redshirts, leaving corpses bobbing in the shallows. Scores of living soldiers leapt into the water and splashed for dry land. Norren warriors rose, bellowed from the depths of their lungs, and charged. Blays flashed Dante a tense grin and ran to join them.

Dante followed, reaching for his sword with one hand and the nether with the other. The two sides collided in a burst of blood and steel. Blades slashed through the sunlight. Blays ducked an arrow, swearing. Norren swords hammered the human soldiers into the waves. The redshirts' advance halted just below the waterline. As a norren fell, gut-stabbed, Blays darted in to stab the attacker's neck while his sword was still engaged. Lira flowed into the gap created by the falling man, flicking her sword into the ribs of another who hadn't yet responded to the sudden collapse of his flank.

Dante splashed in to support Blays' left. His heart beat like an ancient dance. He was all right with a sword. Skilled enough to hold his own. He didn't want to burn through all his nether just yet, though, which left him playing a risky game: hesitate with it, and he could wind up wounded or worse; spend too freely, and he might have nothing left when the battle needed it most.

A redshirted soldier stumbled through the knee-deep water. Dante thrust out his sword, piercing the man's chest. An arrow whisked past his ear. He flinched, putting him in range of a probing spear. He bashed down its point, flung out his hand, and sent a needle of nether winging through the spearman's eye.

Red flowed through the foam. Coppery blood and sour guts mingled with the scent of mud and freshwater. Dante stabbed at a turned back. A black bolt of nether sped past his shoulder, slamming an incoming soldier into the water.

Dante whirled to find the source of the shadows. Wint splashed up beside him with a smirk and a wink.

"Morning," the other councilman said. "I won't pretend it's a good one."

Ahead, the norren pushed the redshirts back to the sides of the boat and cut them down. To Dante's right, Blays crossed his swords against a thrust, rolled his right arm to flick the trapped sword away, then jabbed his lefthand sword through the opening in the man's defenses.

The remaining redshirts surrendered within minutes. Not that there were many left. Many had died in the initial explosions. A few had drowned with their ships. Hundreds had died on the shore, feathered by arrows and hacked by swords, bobbing between the motionless boats. Far fewer of the giants floated down the river. Dante doubted the norren had lost a hundred men.

He left the warriors to round up the prisoners and haul them off the boats. He pulsed Mourn through his loon and got no response. Neither Blays nor Lira had taken more than scratches and bruises during the lopsided battle. Wint looked no worse for wear, either.

"We should do that more often." Blays slicked blood and water from his blades. "Why use these when we can let explosions do the fighting for us?"

"Yes, it's all peaches and cream over here. Now let's just go take care of the remaining ten thousand men and we'll call it a day."

"Give me a minute to catch my breath. Anyway, maybe we should wait to venture toward those ten thousand men until our troops here are ready to go with us."

The wait was torture. Clamor sifted through the deserted streets, a background of blurry chaos interrupted by dagger-sharp screams. Dante pulsed Mourn again, got nothing. He wasn't too worried; Mourn's arm was likely too busy hacking at the king's soldiers to fiddle with his loon. Along the shore, warriors caught their breath, sat down to drink tea and beer and water. Some gnawed on flatbread and dried venison. The wounded washed up and waited for others to bind their cuts. After ten minutes of resting, with Dante preparing to rush off by himself, Mourn looned him back.

"Come northeast up Farron Street with all you've got," Mourn said. "We're going to need it."

"How's it going?" Dante said.

"Bloody. Deathy. Very bad on both sides. They're attacking like there's no tomorrow, which I suppose is true for many of us, but I think we can hold on. Hurry."

Mourn dropped the connection. Dante grabbed Blays by the elbow. "Lace up your boots. We've got to go."

He spread word to the chieftains, who moved to rally their clans. Within a minute, five hundred men and women jogged behind Dante up Farron Street. A major boulevard, it was one of the few they'd left unobstructed. Dante's gaze darted between rooftops and doorways with every flutter of pigeons and rats and crows. For a better part of a mile the street was completely empty of people. The roar of battle grew by increments. It was a paralyzing sound, a terror-laced blend of clangs and screams and thumps, enough to root Dante's feet in place. Instead, he ran toward it.

"Where are you?" Mourn looned him a minute later.

"A ways up Farron," he said. "That church with the two-pointed spire is just up ahead."

"Keep going," Mourn said. "There's an incoming cavalry charge. Slow them down or find us first, or we'll be trapped between the enemy and a canal."

"Got it," Dante said. He turned around and jogged backwards to face the division of norren following him. They filled the street for two blocks. "Cavalry incoming! We've got to link up with our flank and help them withdraw before—"

Down the street, a crackling bang slammed into his ears. Several of the warriors flinched. Others gaped, eyes as bright and round as the full moon. Dante whirled. Not a block away, the sky-scraping spires of the church tumbled into the street with an earth-shattering thunder.

The clamor of the collapse hit them first, followed by a rushing cloud of dust. Dante knelt and shielded his face.

"Did you feel that?" he shouted to Wint.

Wint coughed, dust clinging to his black brows. "Ether. A vast spike of it. Immediately preceding the collapse."

Dante nodded. He felt like vomiting. The road ahead was blocked by dust-choked rubble as high as a man's head. As he watched, the front of the stone church sloughed right off, piling into the debris with another smothering gray cloud.

"What the fuck is happening?" Blays said.

"They've blocked us off," Dante said. He batted at the dust, squinting at a stone tower on the other side of the church. "Enemy sorcerer. It's Cassinder."

"Forget that idiot! We have to get to Mourn!"

More thunder rumbled down the street. Dante braced himself, but this wasn't the avalanche-like clatter of a collapse. It was rhythmic. Drumming. His stomach squeezed into a fist. "It's too late."

"Like hell!" Blays said. "We just passed that big old street a minute ago. We'll take it instead, loop around—"

"That's them," Dante pointed. "The cavalry."

"Then that's a pretty convincing argument to stop standing around!"

He'd felt the spike of ether that prompted the second collapse, too. Seen it winging from that stone tower. And sensed in his bones who had done it. "Lead the norren around to Mourn. I'm going after Cassinder."

"I'm coming with you," Lira said.

"No you're not!" Dante burst. "Do you have any idea how dangerous he is? Did you somehow miss that gods damn church he just knocked down? Do you think your spine is stronger than that spire?"

"No. I do think you can keep me safe from Cassinder while I keep you safe from everyone else."

Behind them, the norren flowed back down the street, seeking an alternate route. The trample of cavalry faded beyond the blockage of rubble. Frustrated anger surged through Dante's veins.

"I don't have time for this. You want to get blasted into caseless sausage, go right ahead."

Down the way, the norren flowed into a cramped side street, hoping to cut northwest around the blockage. Dante backtracked at a dead run. Blays, Lira, and Wint followed, boots slapping cobbles. The high rowhouses on the left side of the street formed a solid block, but an alley opened between them a short ways down, overhung with wash lines and dangling vines. Inside, it jogged right, then left; Dante fought to keep oriented. He dashed into the narrow street beyond, taking a left to parallel Farron Street. The tower loomed ahead, fifty feet high and capped with a high cone roof.

"What kind of a power can he command if he's capable of

knocking down a church?" Wint said, his constant smirk long since disappeared.

"I've fought him before," Dante said. "He's not that strong. He's either exhausted himself or he had help."

"How are you so sure it's him? The king commands any number of ethermancers."

"He has a signature. He wields ether the same way you'd stab someone with an icicle."

With the tower nearing, Dante slowed, moving close to the safety of the rowhouses. The noise of the maneuvering horsemen and norren had grown distant, their feet a faraway rumble. Dante found himself in a pocket of silence. It had been a couple minutes since the collapse of the church. More than enough time for the culprit to dash down the tower steps and disappear into the streets. Dante felt suddenly foolish, a puppet of his own anger. He shouldn't be chasing phantoms through the streets. He should be with the norren, fighting off the charge designed to smash them.

"Oh no! You're here." Cassinder's cold voice dripped from above. He stood on a stone balcony on the top floor of the tower. He smiled like a dead man. "I wanted to kill you in Narashtovik. After you've seen everyone you know die."

Dante's anger condensed to a needle of clarity. "Why are you doing this? You're practically a prince. Why do you need norren to work your lands for nothing?"

"Because they should."

"Funny," Blays said, "because I think most would rather barndance on your brains."

Cassinder's laugh was as dry as August chaff. "The gods don't care for their wants. Neither do I. Does that mean I'm doing the gods' work?"

"You'll have the chance to ask them in a moment," Dante said.

"They are norren," Cassinder said. "Not human. *In*human. They don't think and feel as humans think and feel. They live under the skies. Homeless. What else is homeless? Dogs. Even birds build nests. Dogs are ours to train. To be forged into the tools of our will. A dog that can't be trained is a dog that must be killed."

"I've lived with them," Dante said. "Fought and eaten and slept beside them. Been betrayed and hated by them, too. Enough to know they're human in everything but name."

"Thank you for the conversation. It may have saved my life." From his perch in the tower, Cassinder nodded down the street, his dead man's smile still fixed on his face. Dante glanced behind him. Sixty soldiers ran straight their way, red capes flapping.

"Hit him!" Dante hissed at Wint.

Wint grimaced. "There's no time—"

"*Do it!*"

Wint scowled, summoned the nether, and hurled it at Cassinder's high head. Cassinder chuckled and knocked it aside with a burst of ether. Silvery sparks exploded from the meeting of forces, falling harmlessly and winking away.

Dante delved into the nether embedded in the stone of the balcony, took hold, and yanked the entire platform six inches forward.

Cassinder gasped. The balcony, cut away as neatly as a halved apple, plummeted toward the ground. Dante sprinted past the tower laughing like a fool. The boots of the others pounded behind him. Less than a block away, sixty soldiers pursued.

The balcony smashed into the street. Dante risked a look back. Shattered pebbles pinged across the cobbles. A motionless leg lay draped over a broken stone. The body it was attached to was hidden from sight by the ruins.

Dante took a left at the intersection beyond the tower, following the route the cavalry had taken a few minutes earlier. The cobbles showed fresh scrapes of horseshoes.

"If we're running *away* from those guys," Blays said, pointing at the soldiers behind them, "is it smart to run *toward* the much larger and nastier brigade?"

"I'm hoping it will take us to our troops, too," Dante said. "Anyway, did you see that?"

"What, the part where you dropped Cassinder off an invisible cliff?"

"Yeah!"

"No, must have missed it." Blays burst into laughter. "Did you see his face? He couldn't look more surprised if the king demoted him to Chief Shit-Taster."

The scuffs of the horses were easy to follow even over the bare stone. After a right turn through more rowhouses, the street continued for a couple blocks before terminating against a canal. Those two blocks were littered with scores of dead norren. Horses writhed and brayed among the dead, legs broken, spears and arrows jutting from their forequarters. A handful of redshirts glanced up from the wounded comrades they'd been tending to.

"Oh shit," Blays said.

Dozens more norren bobbed lifelessly in the canal. Easily three hundred dead on their side alone, possibly more. The scent of blood baked in the warm sun. Dante could taste it, too. He'd bitten his cheek.

Behind them, the pursuing soldiers rushed around the corner, pinning them against the canal just as the cavalry had pinned the norren. Dante whirled and ran straight for them. Nether streamed to his hands, fed by the blood in his mouth. He sent it slashing toward the front line in an indiscriminate blade. It scythed through the front rank. Torsos fell from legs. The second rank screamed, skidding on their heels. Before they could decide to press on, Wint lashed out with precise bolts of his own, spraying blood over the third rank. With ten men dead in the span of seconds, the others turned to run back the way they'd come.

"Showoff," Blays said.

"We need to get out of here before they come back to test whether I dislike swords as much as everyone else." Dante jerked his chin south in the direction of their main camp. "Let's get back to the plaza. See where the battle's gone."

"To hell, I'd say."

"That was just one skirmish." Dante didn't look back at the dead. "It doesn't mean the day is lost."

The words were sunnier than he felt. There was no time to search for Mourn among the dead. As they jogged back toward the plaza near the piers, taking back alleys and shortcuts wherever they could, Dante's stomach felt increasingly hollow. Mourn wasn't replying to his loon. Cally's produced that soundless sound that meant it was already in use. Bodies scattered the streets. As many norren as human. That wasn't good. Not when they'd started the day down two to one.

They returned to the barricaded plaza without incident. Hundreds of clan warriors waited behind palisades and debris. As they threaded between smashed furniture, Hopp stood from behind an overturned table, a tired smile touching his branded face.

"Has your day been any better than ours?"

"Started off pretty good," Dante said. "Since then, it's been thoroughly not-good."

"I've got a question for *you*, Chief," Blays said. "What the hell happened to holding the ramparts?"

Hopp's smile faded. "What can you do against so many? Their archers fired on the ramparts while the foot soldiers swept around to hit us from behind. They paid for that, but we had to withdraw to the city. One of our divisions got separated. Cavalry hit them. Cut them into strips of grass."

"Mourn was with them. Do you know if he got out?"

Hopp shook his head. "I haven't heard."

"So what's the plan from here?" Dante said.

"We've both lost a lot of people. I think the Gaskans are regrouping somewhere in the eastern part of town. The chiefs know to rally here. I think we'll have enough to make a second stand."

They took up place beside him on the barricade. Battered clans and individual warriors flowed in over the course of the next hour. Dante saw no sign of Mourn. He recognized one member of the Nine Pines, but the woman had been separated earlier in the day and knew nothing of the fate of her clan. He was deeply heartened, at least, to see the return of Nak and Ulev, along with most of the monks.

"What about Varla?" Dante said, picturing the graying councilwoman silently slinging nether from atop the rampart.

Ulev shook his head. "Some towheaded, blue-blooded son of a bitch struck her down with a smile. Varla was whippin' 'em into black pudding right up till then."

Dante nodded. He hadn't known the woman too well. She'd been so quiet he wondered whether anyone had truly gotten to know her. But with that silence had come a stolid rationality the Council would miss dearly. He thought about trying to reach Cally again, but the black news of her death could wait. He couldn't risk running Cally's loon dry before the day was done.

There were too many norren to guess their exact number. Fewer than the start of the day, that much was clear. By at least a quarter. Maybe as much as half. Dante hoped most of the missing were still making their way through the city. On their way to the hills, even. Better to run away than to be left dead in the streets of a foreign town.

The survivors dug in behind the blockades. Archers arranged themselves for clear firing lanes on the two roads into the north side of the plaza—the remaining streets had been choked with rubble and garbage. Scouts were sent out in pairs to catch any probes or sudden attacks.

It was an unnecessary gesture. For whatever fancy maneuvers the king's army had pulled off earlier in the day, their strategy now appeared to be one of blunt force. They marched down both northern streets at once. Just before bow range, they charged.

Norren arrows flew as thickly as locusts. Nether streaked between volleys, picking off the survivors. Five ranks flopped dead in the street, piling to the knees of the soldiers pouring in behind them. Ether crackled down the street in a bolt of white lightning, blasting apart the foremost barricade in a hurricane of splinters and blood. As if a dam had been broken, the red-garbed soldiers flooded through the gap.

The clan warriors roared and rushed to meet them. After years of fighting beside Blays, Dante found himself falling into a rhythm of battle that required no conscious thought. They fought like two arms of the same body. Except Lira was there, too, weaving in among the redshirts like a perfectly complementary third arm, stabbing in snake-fast thrusts, using her empty hand to disarm and grapple, sweeping soldier after soldier to the ground and Blays' waiting blades.

The norren themselves fought like angry spirits. Between the combined reach of their arms and their swords, they could strike a human soldier down before the enemy could touch them. Their swings fell with brutal strength, battering aside blocks as if the enemy swords weren't there at all. Chainmail was no defense; their blows simply broke the bones beneath. Two or more redshirts fell for every clansman.

But they were still too many. They must have picked up more conscripts on the final march to Dollendun. They poured through the streets, overrunning the plaza's barricades one by one. Gaskan ethermancers blew holes through the lines before the priests of Narashtovik engaged them with the nether. Pale sparks bloomed over the battlefield. Both sides exhausted themselves quickly, however, and the battle was soon reduced to swords and sweat and bloody fury.

Step by step, the norren were forced back. Dante caught a nick to his left arm. Blays took a slash across his thigh that bled freely but was too shallow to slow him down. Lira snagged the pinky of her free hand in a man's belt mid-throw; as he fell, her finger snapped audibly. She paled, retreating behind Blays as sweat washed down her face, but she lunged in moments later when a redshirt closed on Blays' flank.

The redshirts pushed halfway through the plaza. The norren's right flank fell back across the lines. As if there were ropes tied among the warriors' waists, the center and the left followed. So did Dante. Without being ordered, they found themselves in wholesale retreat from the plaza, running south along the shore of the river as the redshirts trampled behind them.

"That was nuts," Blays panted, swords in hand. "How is anyone alive right now? Like, in the world?"

Dante shook his head. How many had died over the last few minutes? Five hundred on their side alone? A thousand? Whatever the figure, two or three times as many redshirts had fallen in the square. By the time they'd retreated, blood streamed along the cracks in the cobbles. It had stunk like hot metal and fresh guts.

"I don't know," he said. His arms hung loose, muscles burning. He couldn't find his breath. "I don't know."

The forest of pines swallowed them whole. Behind them, the diffusing Gaskan lines halted and turned around for the city. The chiefs called a halt a mile later. Warriors collapsed in the carpet of pine needles, chests heaving.

Blays thumped down beside a fir. "It's not happening. We can't wade back into that. Not with what little we've got left."

Dante nodded, numb. He glanced up sharply. "Cally sent more men. It's not much, but if we can meet up with them, maybe we can draw the redshirts out. They suffered worse than us."

He pulsed his loon. Cally responded at once. "You're alive! Unless you are a looting killer. In which case, be forewarned: I am a vengeful spirit! Woe to whomever takes this relic from its rightful owner!"

"Of course it's me," Dante said. "This loon's tied to my blood."

"Yes, but there's nothing to prevent a cunning usurper from using your freshly spilled blood to forge a new link. Anyway, this is beside the point: you're alive!"

"And lucky to be so. We lost. We're sitting in a forest two miles from the city and there's no way we can take it back."

Cally's sigh crackled across the loon. "I'm sorry. This must break your heart. But remember: you just fought off the heart of the Gaskan empire's power—and you lived. This war isn't over."

Dante wiped sweat from his forehead. Salt flaked from his hair. "How far off are those troops you sent? Can Olivander muster any more?"

"I'm sure he can scare up a couple hundred by tomorrow, but will that be enough? Perhaps we should fall back to lick our wounds, rest up, and return from hibernation with an army even larger than before."

"All right, but in the interests of not dying in the meantime, where are the men you already sent?"

"Hang on, I just updated the maps this morning. Where did I..." Papers shuffled. Cally cursed softly. A door creaked. Cally's voice became distant; he'd turned away from the loon. "Closed and private doors should be knocked upon first. Who are you?"

Three quick steps thumped across the floor. Cally shouted, a single note of alarm. Boots scuffled over the floor. Cally cried out again. Something heavy struck the floor. Footsteps hurried away. The door creaked and clicked shut.

"Dark hair," Cally gurgled. "Skunk." Liquid drummed the wooden floor.

"Cally?" Dante said.

"Listen! Skunk! Short. Quiet—a whisper."

Muffled chokes filtered through the loon. A long and liquid breath. And then a surge of nether so strong Dante somehow felt its darkness through the line of the loon. It engulfed him, cool, pacific, as yawning as the night sky—just as terrifying, just as welcoming.

The nether withdrew as swiftly as a wave. Dante heard no words, no more gasping. Just the drumming of fluid against the floor.

"Cally?" he said. "*Cally?*"

25

He listened, helpless. Liquid tapped upon the floor. If he closed his eyes, he could see it, bright red droplets gleaming on the hardwood as Cally's eyes took on the shine of glass. Nether buzzing like flies around the puddle and the wound in the old man's neck that had spilled it. Nether rejoining the planks of the floor, the air, the world it had long ago left to become a part of Cally's body. The cycle of Arawn cranking through one more turn.

"Cally's dead."

Blays glanced up. "Huh?"

"I said Cally's dead."

"Did you take a whack to the skull back there? Cally wasn't at the battle."

"In his room in Narashtovik," Dante said. "Someone attacked him. I heard it through the loon. I think they cut his—"

He doubled over, retching. Blays jumped away, then moved back in, reaching for Dante's shoulder. "Are you all right? What's going on?"

"They killed him." Dante hocked and spat, wiping his mouth with his sleeve. "He's dead. We have to get back."

"How do you know that?"

"Because I heard him get attacked and bleed to death! He tried to heal himself, but he just..." Tears stung his eyes. He wiped them away, careless who saw. "We have to go. In five seconds I'm going to start running and I won't stop until I'm in Narashtovik."

Blays glanced at the warriors slumped throughout the glen. "What about that whole war thing?"

"They don't need us now. Cally does."

"He does? Not to be cruel, but just what do you think—?"

Dante shoved him in the chest, staggering him through the fallen needles. "We honor his life and finish what he started! There's no clear mechanism for who takes over now. If Kav grabs the reins, maybe he starts whispering to his noble buddies back in Setteven and next thing you know we're back where we started—the norren as slaves, Narashtovik as the king's property. We have to stop that." He took a swift and shuddering breath. "And find and kill whoever did this."

Blays nodded, somber. "I'll gather up my stuff. Oh wait, I don't have anything."

Lira frowned faintly. "We should ask Hopp. We're a part of his clan, too."

"We'll ask," Dante said. "But I'll only hear one answer."

Hopp rested beneath a tree a short ways off, chewing leaves plucked from the shrub beside him. He gave Dante a rueful smile. "That didn't go as we'd hoped, did it?"

"Callimandicus has been killed," Dante said. "My chieftain in Narashtovik."

Hopp raised an eyebrow. "Are you patronizing me? I know who Cally is and his place on your Council."

"Then you know I have to return."

"What would you do if I forbade you?"

"Leave in the night. And if you tied me down, I would break the bonds and then your legs."

"Would you show the same ferocity for my sake if someone came for me?"

"No," Dante said. "But I'd bare one fang, at least. Maybe two."

Hopp laughed. "Should I have made you renounce your kinship to Narashtovik before accepting you as one of my own? I won't stop you from leaving, but I won't release you from your responsibility to your clan, either."

"We're all part of the same clan now. I won't forget this." Dante glanced northeast toward Narashtovik. "Cally's loon is still open. If it runs out of nether before someone shuts it off, it'll quit working, along with all the loons linked through it."

"So I won't be hearing from you for a while?"

Dante shook his head. "Or from the other chiefs, either. You'll be back to the old ways."

"What will you guys do?" Blays said.

"What we always do," Hopp shrugged. "Return to the hills."

A frown crept over Blays' face. "They'll keep coming."

"Then they'll discover that fighting the clans in their own hills and woods is not the same as fighting them in nice open streets with all the room in the world for their horses to run."

Dante smiled grimly. "We'll be back as soon as we can."

"See to it," Hopp said. "Otherwise, when someone asks me where my humans went, I'll tell them you're a disgrace to your species and your former family of the Broken Herons."

For all his other concerns, that still meant something to Dante. As they headed out of the makeshift camp in the vague direction of Narashtovik—without pausing to gather up Wint and Ulev and the monks; they would only slow him down—he vowed silently to return and do honor to his adopted clan. He knew, too, the chances that might never happen. He could be killed yet. Be driven from all Gask by the conquering redshirts. Become so enmeshed in the scrambling of the beheaded Council that his three months of fighting and fishing and sleeping alongside the Herons could retreat like last week's dreams. Life moved too quickly. Too cruelly. Isolated from all other matters, he could have spent happy years wandering the Territories alongside his clan brothers and sisters. A few months with them wasn't enough. Probably, that would be all the time he ever got.

He ran as much as he could. Neither Blays nor Lira complained. The road from Dollendun would take them to Narashtovik, but he wanted to avoid that for several miles beyond the city. There would be scouts. Even if they dressed as refugees, dozens of men had witnessed them killing Cassinder. Someone would want them dead for that.

At a farmhouse where winter wheat stirred in the summer breeze, heavy-headed and golden, Dante gave the farmer everything in his pockets for three workhorses. It was a fair price. Even so, the farmer didn't want to make the deal, but Dante didn't give him a choice.

The workhorses weren't bred for distance running. Dante didn't care. He took to the road and spurred home toward the Dead City, sweating atop the galloping beast. Four days later, it died within sight of Narashtovik. He left it in the woods by the road and ran the rest of the way.

The city was little changed from their last visit. Hotter. Sticky with the humidity curling off the bay. He arrived at the Citadel gates filthy and exhausted and half-starved. They'd eaten what little they could find along the way: boiled roots, dandelions and greens, a couple of fish. It didn't matter. His physical hunger was less than his hunger for answers and revenge.

He parted ways with Blays and Lira and jogged up the stairs to his room. The windows were closed; it was stifling, cobwebbed, smelling of dust and evaporated water. He ordered up a bath and peeled off his clothes. The water was cool, relaxing, but he found himself shaking in the basin, stirring the water into ripples and blurps.

The same servant who'd brought up the basin and his water returned as he dressed. Kav had requested Dante's presence.

"No," Dante said.

"I may have taken the truth for a dance." The servant's eyes darted. "It wasn't so much a request as a demand."

Dante gazed at the young man, who looked away. "Has Kav taken charge since Callimandicus died?"

"More or less."

"Which one? More? Or less?"

"More," the young man said. "You've got Olivander rustling up men to the east, Hart and Somburr off gods know where, you and Ulev and whoever else fighting redshirts—well, Kav took a step forward, and everyone here nodded along."

"What happened to Cally?"

"Don't you know?"

"I want to hear from you," Dante said.

"Well, he was...killed. In his room, what, five days back."

"How?"

The man lowered his face. "Somebody slashed his throat."

"Who did it?"

"Well, nobody knows. Except the fellow that did it, I suppose." The young man met Dante's eyes. "Will you see Kav now, sir?"

"Tell him I'll be there shortly."

When the servant left, Dante buckled on his sword, rolled up his left sleeve, and cut a small line on the back of his arm, just deep enough to draw blood should he need the nether. He pulled his sleeve over the wound and went to see Kav.

Kav waited at the head of the table in the council hall. He sat comfortably in Cally's former seat, his carved, elegant features composed into a picture of concern. He gestured to an empty chair.

"Sit, please."

Dante stared at him for two seconds before slinging himself into a chair. "What do you want?"

"To see for myself that you'd come back," Kav smiled. It didn't last, resolving quickly to his stony concern. "I assume you've heard."

"That our leader died? You could have fooled me. Someone's sitting in his chair right now."

Kav didn't glance down at his seat. "Someone has to take the reins while we go through the appropriate channels to appoint a successor. Things are too precarious to allow the stallion of Narashtovik to bolt in the meantime."

"I suppose you're right." Dante leaned back. "Who found the body?"

"Georg. The monk who'd been helping him run those loons of yours. Which I understand have since been broken. How did you hear so fast? Weren't you in Dollendun?"

"Word of something like that travels fast. When I heard, I traveled faster."

"I see," Kav said. "And will you be staying with us for the foreseeable future?"

"Until I find the one who killed Cally."

"We are, of course, already working on that. I believe we may be quite close."

Dante leaned over the vast desk. "What have you found?"

Kav eyed him, waving the fingers of his right hand a fraction of an inch. "I can't disclose that just yet. Obviously I will let you know as soon as it's plausible."

Dante nodded. He flexed his hands to keep from strangling the aging blueblood. "Are we through here? I've got work to do."

The creases at the corners of Kav's mouth deepened. "Then I wish you luck."

He went straight to Blays' room. He barely had the presence of mind to knock before barging in.

Blays was alone inside. "What's up?"

Dante closed the door, bolting it. "Someone had Cally killed."

"I thought we already knew that."

"Nobody knows who it was. Not even Cally. If it was no one he knew, the killer must have been hired. So who would want Cally dead?"

"Everyone in Gask?" Blays shrugged.

"It's called the Sealed Citadel for a reason," Dante said. "The gates are manned at all times. Whoever got in would have to have been helped — by someone in the Citadel."

"We broke our way in, once upon a time."

"Yes. Sure. *Anyone* could have done it. A badger could have crawled up the storm drain with a knife in its teeth. But it's far more likely the killer was let inside." He jerked his chin in the direction of the meeting hall. "I just spoke to Kav. He's already taken Cally's place. He's being very tightlipped about his search for the culprit."

Blays smiled. "Is someone jealous?"

"He's got time and motive. It's no secret he's always wanted Cally's seat in the Council. He still talks with his old friends the lords of Gask all the time. He can clear our work from the board with the sweep of his arm — he curries favor with King Moddegan by killing Cally, steps in to take the old man's place while half the Council's scattered across the country, and immediately sues for peace."

"I suppose you want me to break into his room, then."

"Would you?"

Blays grinned. "Well yeah. I liked Cally too, you know."

Dante's own smile felt creaky. He wasn't sure he'd made one since Dollendun. "I'll try to snoop out his schedule. If he isn't planning to be away from the Citadel any time soon, we may have to manufacture a way to get him out of here."

He went straight to the servants. He couldn't flat-out ask for Kav's appointments and time-tables, because servants talked as much as anyone else, and any whiff of his plans could cause Kav to change everything. But he could make inquiries. About when he could see Kav, for instance. Dante himself was too busy today, he explained, but what about tomorrow? Evening? It turned out that wouldn't do: Kav was scheduled to deliver Cally's weekly sermon at the Cathedral of Ivars. Too bad; what about the day after?

Dante left with an appointment he had no intention of keeping and went to inform Blays of their window. The following evening, as half the Citadel's residents crossed the street to the cathedral, Dante locked himself in his room, feigning illness. When the horn blew to announce the mass, he slipped into the hall with Blays.

Kav's door was just down the hall. Dante drew forth the nether and guided it into the lock. Blays was faster; with a flick of his picks, the door tumbled open.

"That was awfully quick," Dante said.

"They're all the same here."

"That doesn't explain why you know how to pick them."

Blays shut Kav's door behind them. "Because I'm regularly called on by you to break into people's rooms?"

The room was lavish with rugs. Tapestries insulated the stone walls. Candles and books coated the windowsill and two desks. The bed was canopied in burgundy velvet. It was still the room of a priest, however, and thus was small. Quick to search. Dante rifled through drawers. Blays pawed through racks of finery. The third drawer of the desk was suspiciously shallow. Dante's knock was hollow. He pried away the false bottom of the drawer, revealing a cache of letters.

He spread one in front of Blays. "What language is this?"

"Gibberish," Blays said. "The native tongue of the Empire of Gibber."

Foreign symbols covered the pages. It was not a script Dante had ever seen. He saw no names or dates, either. The paper looked relatively fresh—unyellowed, no scent of must on it. Of the thirty-odd letters, Dante stuffed three into his pocket, hoping Kav wouldn't notice so few had been taken.

"It's some sort of code. What's he hiding?"

"That mean we're done here?"

"Let's go," Dante said. Blays spat on the floor. Dante gawked.

"What did you do that for?"

"Because spitting on people's floors when they don't know about it is fun." He eased the door open and snuck into the hall. As Dante stood watch, Blays tricked the lock back into place. Dante fought the urge to run back to his room. There, he spread the three letters on his desk and began to copy each one out onto a fresh sheet of paper.

Blays stood before he'd finished the first paragraph. "I think I'm going to leave you to this."

"But we're doing something sneaky!"

"And it's fascinating stuff, the copying of nonsense from one sheet of paper to another sheet of paper. But I bet if I go see Lira right now, she will take off her clothes and throw me around."

"Have it your way."

The door clicked shut. Back in Kav's room, Dante had lost himself in the break-in, but with Blays gone, the raven of Cally's death returned to his shoulder. Dante kept copying, hoping to drive its impossible weight away through sheer tedium, the numbness of repetition. It helped. Darkness fell. A seaborne breeze stirred the curtains, flushing away the moist air stagnating inside his room. He began comparing the letters. Making a list of all the symbols, as well as how many times each was used, and examining where certain pairs occurred—particularly of the same symbol. He examined three-letter words in an attempt to nose out Kav's name, silently wishing Kav's parents had named him in the more traditional polysyllabic Gaskan style that would have made his name stand out like a midnight candle. Dante went to bed just before dawn, sleeping naked atop the sheets.

It hardly helped; he woke up midmorning sweaty and flushed. On his balcony, he strung up a sheet to shield himself from the sun and got to work. The heat was tolerable so long as he didn't move. Four hours later, he'd made no headway on the code. The symbols blurred together, meaningless, aloof. He'd been interested enough in codes as a teenager to comb the library texts about substitutions and the like, but that interest had evaporated along with his fascination with snails and dead frogs. After dozens of false leads and dead ends, zero progress, and the mounting dread he was failing his mentor and friend, Dante folded up his notes and went to the scene of the crime.

Cally's door was unlocked. The inside of the room felt cool and as prehistoric as the rings of stones where the norren chiefs met. A desk rested beside the door to the balcony. Next to it, a wine-dark stain dominated the wooden floor.

Dante knelt beside it. The nether still clung to it sluggishly. This stain had been inside Cally just days ago. The nether, too. The floor was otherwise spotless. As hard as the servants had scrubbed, there was no erasing this marker of the man's death. If Dante closed his eyes, he could still picture him: his piercing eyes, typically full of mocking good humor, but capable of filling with insight or wrath in a moment's notice; his absurd white beard, dense as a thicket and twice as wild; his bony shoulders that bore the gnarled strength of a desert tree.

All that reduced to a red-brown stain.

Dante's sorrow hardened into hot-forged anger. On hands and knees, he scoured the room for stray drops of blood. If there were any here besides Cally's, it could be the killer's. A single drop would be enough to trace it through the nether back to the assassin. But he found nothing. He thought, for a moment, of searching for stray hairs or fingernail scraps instead, but the room had been swept, scrubbed, and scrubbed again. Anything left behind would be from the servants.

He sat in the middle of the floor and gazed across the silent space. There was nothing he could do here. There was nothing to find. No one to question. He was the closest thing there had been to a witness. Unless the killer made a mistake—returned to the room, boasted drunkenly in a tavern—all he could do was work on the codes and hope they contained proof of what Kav had done. On the off chance the killer *did* return, Dante went to the pantry, slaughtered a mouse, and brought it to Cally's room, and brought it to unlife to act as his sentry. That done, he returned to the heat of his chambers and sat down with Kav's letters.

Hours of scribbling and comparing got him nowhere. He went down to the courtyard and entered the monastery, combing the stacks for works on cryptography. Two hours later, he had two books. One was a history written three centuries ago, an account of the codes used during the Farraway Wars that took place some six hundred years earlier. The book looked to have few specifics, but the Farraway Wars had been a bizarre hotbed of espionage, secrecy, double agents and double-crosses between some eight mountain cities that no longer existed, and the conflict had been notable for their secret codes and symbols as well. The second book was a general theory of cryptography, or at least as the field had stood 140 years ago when it had been written. He began with that.

Two days later, he was ready to burn his books, Kav's letters, and the whole stupid city. As he strolled through the courtyard to clear his head, he saw something that lifted his heart: Somburr passing through the gates.

He looked haggard, even twitchier than normal. Dante went to him at once, but a servant beat him there. Kav must have been waiting for him. Hart was with him, but the servant paid the elderly norren no mind.

Dante greeted Hart with a smile. "I'm glad to see you back."

"Beats the alternative, doesn't it?" Hart scratched his white beard. His forehead was shiny with sweat. "I wish we'd brought back better news."

"Oh?"

"The king's army struck out from Dollendun two days after we lost the city. Somburr knows better than I do, but my impression is they mean to race across the Norren Territories, then turn north and come for us."

Dante gritted his teeth. "So fast?"

Hart sighed into his meaty fist. "I think the idea is that there are two brushfires threatening the kingdom: the norren army, and Narashtovik. If the king's men can douse the main blazes, they can use the rest of the year to stamp out the sparks of rebellious clans."

"Bold," Dante said. "Maybe dumb. Why not spend a year or two to wrap up the norren? We're not going to be any stronger two years from now."

"Again, I think there are two things at play," Hart said. "First, without Gallador's silver to back their armies, I think the lords of Gask are already feeling the pinch to their purses." He smiled wryly." Second, I think they are very, very mad at us."

That brought a smile to Dante's face. "Then it's all been worth it."

He propped open his door to coax the ocean breeze through his room and to defray suspicion as he sat in his doorway, one eye on his book, the other watching the hallway for Somburr. This tactic proved to be wholly useless. After an hour of a closed-door session between Somburr and Kav, Kav called a general assembly of the Council.

The council chambers looked barren. Cally was gone. Varla, too. Wint and Ulev were still in the norren wilds. Olivander remained in the eastern foothills gathering troops. That left seven councilmen out of twelve. Dante hadn't seen their ranks so depleted since the battle at the White Tree more than five years ago.

"Somburr's spies have paid off yet again," Kav said once everyone was settled. "If you would, Somburr?"

Somburr's gaze flicked between the other priests. He squirmed in his chair. "I have some insight into the enemy's strategy. My source says it's straightforward. They'll knock out any major resistance left in the Norren Territories, then march on Narashtovik without delay."

He fiddled with his collar, finished already. The priests exchanged glances.

"Well shit," Tarkon said.

"How long are we talking until they're here?" Dante said.

Somburr pinched the bridge of his nose with his brown fingers. "We'll all be dead in three weeks."

Tarkon repeated himself. Merria leaned forward, a sneer creasing her lined face. "I'm sorry, did you say three *weeks*?"

"Here is how my source expects it to play out," Somburr said. "The Gaskan army will make one more effort to confront the combined clans. My source anticipates this will result in the dispersal or outright destruction of the clans. Either way, a small portion of the army will be split off to control the Territories and destroy any holdouts, but it is further anticipated the Territories will surrender at this point. A few clans will still defy the king, but when haven't they?"

Somburr paused, chin twitching. "Once that is accomplished, they will march straight here. That march is anticipated to take seven to ten days. Leaving a full timeframe of three to four weeks before the Gaskan generals are sitting in this room congratulating each other on their victory."

"That is one potential outcome," Kav intoned. "And one somewhat less than sunny. Yet there is another option."

Dante could see straight through the nobleman's thinking. "Oh no there isn't."

Kav ignored him, meeting the eyes of the others instead. "We could surrender."

"Bullshit," Merria said. "Olivander would never stand for that. You try to pull that off and Cally will burst from his grave and strangle you himself."

Kav frowned delicately. "There is a point when the honor of resistance becomes the folly of futility. I fear we have reached that point."

"Fear away," Dante said. "That doesn't change the fact you're not the master of this council and it's not your decision to make."

"I never claimed I was," Kav said peevishly. "And yet I will not follow a path that ensures Cally is the last to ever rule the Council. We cannot disgrace him and this institution by committing strategic suicide in lieu of facing the facts."

Most of the Council looked pained, resigned. Merria was the only one who appeared outright defiant. Somburr looked disturbed, blinking repeatedly, his mouth tightly pursed.

"In any event," Kav continued, "it is not my intent to enforce a decision here and now. Only to broach the option and give us ample time to prepare in case events unfold as Somburr's source foresees."

Dante clamped down his anger. They would not surrender. Not if he had to kill Kav himself and lead the troops from the very front. With no intention of tipping his hand, he left as soon as the meeting dissolved and returned to his room. He frowned. Had he left his chair pulled away from his desk? He'd hidden Kav's letters in his copy of *The Cycle of Arawn*. He pocketed them and headed to Somburr's room. After he knocked, Somburr cracked the door an inch, eye gleaming whitely from the dimness of his room.

"Yes, Dante?"

"Can we speak?"

"We are speaking as we speak."

"Inside," Dante said. "Alone."

Somburr's mouth turned down at the corners. "Are you going to knife me?"

"I'm not going to knife you."

"Good. Just be aware I will know before you try and will have no qualms about knifing you first."

Dante agreed. Somburr let him inside. Three sets of heavy drapes blocked the windows, reducing the sunlight to nothing and leaving the room as hot as summer cobbles. Two candles shed a little yellow light around the spartan room.

"Who do you think killed Cally?" Dante said.

Somburr cocked his head. "A professional. Hired."

"By who?"

"The list is heavy enough to break your foot, isn't it?"

Dante examined Somburr's middle-aged face. He didn't know whether he could trust the former spy, but he ultimately had no choice: he couldn't prove the identity of the killer on his own. "I think Kav may have had something to do with this."

"He exploited the situation very quickly," Somburr said. "Highly suspicious."

"You've thought about this?"

"Who hasn't?"

"Anyone who's inclined to not accuse their leader of treason?" Dante said.

"Contemplating whether someone could be guilty isn't the same as accusing them of being guilty." Somburr narrowed his eyes at Dante. "You, for instance, are highly ambitious. Perhaps you were tired of waiting for Cally to die. Also, you have been prosecuting this war with great ferocity, haven't you? Maybe Cally agreed with Kav and wanted to end it. Maybe you couldn't let that happen."

"You think *I* did it?"

"I doubt it," Somburr said. "But unless a thing is impossible, I don't like to rule it out."

"I think it was Kav," Dante said. "He stepped in like he'd been expecting it. I found these, too." He took out the three letters he'd taken from Kav and handed them to Somburr, whose face took on the eager gleam of a child in the bakery. "Why would he write them in code?"

Somburr clawed the letters from Dante's hand so smoothly he hardly felt them go. "He's been sending an extraordinary amount of letters ever since you burned down Cassinder's house. They've *all* been in code."

Dante's blood went cold. "I need you to tell me everything you know about Kav."

"Born in 867 P.C., the second son of Ronnimore and Allyria, Baron and Baroness of Landry. Showed first signs of nethereal talent at 13 and took to the priesthood at 17. His older brother died in mysterious circumstances two years later, leaving Kav with a clear path to the barony, which he took only to leave in the hands of a steward in 897, when he returned to the priesthood with a clear path to the Council of Narashtovik. To the best of our knowledge, the family barrister had wrangled a way for him to retain ownership of his lands and title even though priestly bylaws require—"

Dante cut him off. "You know all this off the top of your head?"

"Of course," Somburr said. "Would you like to know what I know about you?"

"Are his ties to the capital still as strong as they look?"

"One of Kav's first cousins is 16 steps from the throne. 15? No, it's 16, forgot the Duchess of Derriden. Kav's younger sister is married to the third son of the Earl of Prater. The other blood ties are more complicated unless you understand Nollen Theory. Do you? No? No matter. Moving on, Kav visits his homestead west of Dollendun one to three times each year. He's spoken with Moddegan in person more than once. To summarize, he has many long-standing connections to the king, the capital in Setteven, and any number of noblemen across Gask."

"Do you think you can decode those letters?" Dante said.

"I have before. I haven't tried to break his latest codes. He changes them yearly, not that it helps. What he ought to do is hire me to create his codes for him, but if I were to suggest that, he'd know I'd broken his old ones, wouldn't he?"

"We have to act fast," Dante said. "Try to decipher the letters. I can get more if you crack the code. I'm going to have a look at Cally's body and see if Kav's assassin left any clues on it." He touched Somburr's elbow. Somburr flinched. "Can I trust you,

Somburr? This isn't just about the Council. All Narashtovik depends on this."

Somburr grinned like a ferret. "Why wouldn't you trust me?"

"Because for all I know, *you* did it."

The other man giggled. "That makes me wish I had. It would mean I've done a wonderful job misleading you to Kav."

Dante smiled and left him with the letters. He walked out of Somburr's room and into a forest of armed guards. Several monks were there, too. Competent nether-users. Shadows roiled in their hands. They were backed by two members of the Council on top of that: silent old Joseff, and Kav.

"Dante Galand," Kav said. "I will keep this simple. You are hereby charged with the murder of Callimandicus, High Priest of Arawn, Viceroy of Narashtovik, and one of my oldest friends."

26

Laughter burst from Dante's throat. "On what grounds? That you're completely insane?"

Kav held out a knife, brown with dried blood. "This was found in your room while we were at council."

"For one thing, that's not mine. For another, *all* my knives have blood on them. Have you seen my arms? I cut myself more often than most men have breakfast."

"This was the just the gust that cracked the limb," Kav said. "I feared this was your work from the very start."

"Cally was my first teacher," Dante said. "I wouldn't be alive without him. I would never have come to Narashtovik. He was my *friend*. Lyle's bruised balls, why would I kill him?"

"Because he was going to ask for a ceasefire."

"No he wasn't!"

"I spoke with him myself," Kav glowered.

"Sounds like he was making a joke you didn't get," Dante said.

"He was extremely uneasy about the prospects of a direct war with the king. He was ready to begin negotiations." Kav laid the heavy knife along his palm. "Besides, I tasted this blood with the nether. It's Cally's."

Dante's world went red. "Someone put that in my room. Or you've had it all along and are using it to get me out of the way. I was three hundred miles away when he was killed!"

"As if you couldn't have paid someone to do it?" Kav favored him with a tight and furious smile. "In fact, isn't that exactly what you endeavor to do in this letter?"

He produced a piece of bleached parchment. Dante didn't bother to look at it. "I didn't write that."

"I wished to deny it myself, but when we compared it to the other letters in your room, the writing matched." The nobleman's face grew pained. "My denial starved, withered, died."

Dante snatched the paper from his hand. His head filled with stars. The handwriting was his—the same tilt to the f's and t's, the e's drawn in a single outward-spiraling loop—but the words weren't anything he had ever put to paper. And the words spelled out death.

"This isn't mine," he said.

Kav bared his teeth. "Is that not your writing?"

"It's a forgery. A fake. I didn't order Cally's death! Are you doing this, Kav? Are you implicating me to sweep away your tracks?"

"Enough!" Kav thundered in the tones of a patrician who's spent decades in the pulpit. "I've told no lies and done no wrongs. We found what we have found. You will have time enough to rehearse your defense from the cells beneath the Citadel."

Nether condensed around Dante's whole body, fog-like. The guards drew back, swords wavering. Dante forced the shadows to dissolve away. The act was as hard as drinking boiling water.

"I'll find your lies," he said. "And then I'll kill you."

Kav snorted and gestured at the guards. "Bind his hands."

They locked him in chains and marched him to the disused dungeons beneath the keep. It smelled of must and old urine. As far as the scant torchlight showed, he was the only one there. The guards brought him to a room walled with stone and closed the iron door with a clang.

"You will be allowed to speak on your own behalf at the appropriate time," Kav said through the grille. "Despite your treachery, you are still one of Arawn's children."

"Then let me speak to Blays," Dante said.

"This reminds me. If you make any attempt to escape, your friends will be killed."

Dante pressed his face against the metal bars slitting the window. "Don't."

"Then don't do anything stupid," Kav said.

"Send Blays."

Kav disappeared from sight. A torch in the hallway shed the barest light into his cell. He wondered if it was the same one Larrimore had locked him in long ago when he'd bluffed his way into the Citadel with the intent of assassinating the woman who'd ruled it. He walked the corners of the room, fingers trailing the cool stone walls. There was nether in them. Faint, but present. Was there anything in the world beyond the shadows' touch?

He allowed himself to be angry for a while. He needed to let it boil away, leaving him with a clear head capable of establishing Kav's guilt and exonerating himself. Somburr's decryption of the letters might accomplish that, but he couldn't depend on it. His life—Narashtovik, norren freedom, everything—hung on proving Kav was the one who belonged in this cell.

So he sat, reached out for the nether, breathed. Soon, he calmed. There could be something that would help him on the knife. There could be something on Cally's body. What about Cally's last words? Skunks and whispers—had he been attacked by someone who smelled foul? A fishmonger? A dung-shoveler? Unlikely to help just now, that. Yet if he could find the killer, he was certain he could make the man talk. If he could make the man talk, he could out Kav's treachery to the world.

At least it was cool in the dungeons. He lay on the stones, hands clasped behind his head. He must have slept; footsteps woke him some time later. Blays' face appeared in the grille.

"Man, what have you done now?"

"Oh, nothing much," Dante said. "Just murdered Cally."

"Very talented of you," Blays said. "Weren't we two hundred miles away at the time?"

"You know how these things go. I must have hired an assassin in my sleep and forgotten all about it in the morning."

"Oh, I assassinated five people that way just last year."

Dante laughed lightly. "So."

"How long you got before they post your head on the city gates?"

"Three weeks at most. They may want to save me as a gift to the Gaskans. Executing me in front of the generals would send a strong message that Kav's ready to bring Narashtovik back in line."

Blays nodded in the gloom. "And just to be clear, you'd rather *not* be drawn and quartered in front of the cathedral?"

"Ideally, no." Dante explained Somburr's involvement with the letters, and his own thoughts about where to go next. "I could be one clue away from exoneration. But I can't do much from inside these walls."

"If I can get you out, we'll have to find the evidence in a hurry," Blays said. "If Kav sees you strolling around the streets, he's not going to wave hello. Unless it's with a butcher knife."

Dante smacked the stone wall. "Don't worry about breaking me out. Worry about finding something to tie Kav to Cally's death."

"Got it." Blays pressed his eye up to the bars in the window. "You're taking this pretty well."

"A prison is only a prison if you let it imprison you."

"Nevermind. I see the madness has already set in." Blays disappeared.

Dante faced the wall and sat and thought. He had no way to gauge the time. Trays of food were brought in. A bucket was brought out. Three days passed. Or was it four? Blays dropped by to let him know he hadn't been able to find where Cally's body was being kept, but that Wint and Ulev had made it back safely to Narashtovik. There had been another clash between the Gaskan army and the union of the clans. Both sides had been bloodied, but the norren had fallen back once more. The clans had splintered, dispersing into the woods beyond Dollendun.

When Dante wasn't sleeping, he worked with the nether, letting his thoughts come as they may. The food came twice more. The bucket went away twice more. Blays returned.

"I think I found something," he said.

Dante rose. "Oh?"

"You. It turns out you're in prison!"

"Very good. Now please tell me you found a reason for me to leave."

"Well." Blays paced beyond the iron door. "I can't find the body. But I did find someone who knows where it is."

Dante ran to the door. "Who?"

"I don't know, some servant who heard I was looking for it. Sounds none too happy with the way Kav's handling things. Guy's name is Amwell. Know him?"

"No, but there must be three hundred employees of some kind or another inside the Citadel's walls. And in case you've forgotten, we've spent most of the last three years crapping in the woods. I don't recognize half the faces here anymore."

Blays clapped. "All right. So here's the plan. Tonight, I come down and pick the lock. They've only got three or four guards up top, so it should be no problem for you to put them to sleep or kill them if we have to. I could try to drug them, too, if you know something I can get ahold of by tonight. Meanwhile, me and Lira will have a little wagon parked up top. I put you in a sack, I carry you outside in the sack, sling you in the wagon, and roll you out the front gates. Once we're past the walls, we'll meet up with Amwell and head off to see the body. If anything goes wrong, we'll have a grappling hook with a team of horses—"

"Sounds complicated," Dante said. "How about I just walk out through the tunnel I dug?"

"What?"

"I dug a tunnel."

"Let me see your hands," Blays said. Dante stuck them through the window grille and Blays turned them this way and that. "Funny, your fingernails still seem to exst."

"I used the nether," Dante said. "I moved the earth until I was past the outer walls, then plugged it on either side so no one would see the holes. I can open it back up in seconds."

"Well fine, if you want to be boring about it. How's 1 AM sound, then?"

"When is that? I don't have any idea what time it is down here."

Blays tapped his teeth. He smacked the wall between himself and Dante. "Can you open this up, too?"

"Sure."

"Then I'll come down at one, you let me inside the cell, and we'll both walk out the tunnel."

"You want me to break you *in* to prison?" Dante said.

"Just for a few minutes! It's perfectly sane in this context."

"See you at one," Dante grinned.

He napped immediately afterward—in the timeless darkness, sleep came whenever he wanted. When he woke, he felt the contours of the wall, the nether waiting there. Blays jogged down the steps a couple hours later.

"Guards didn't want to let me down again," he said. "But since you're their master and all, I feel I should warn you they're susceptible to bribes."

"Sounds like I owe them a promotion." Dante pushed his palms together, then spread them apart. The wall between them curled inward, stone flowing like cool syrup.

"That was disturbingly vaginal," Blays said.

"If that's what you think, Lira may need to see a physician," Dante said. "Come on."

He parted the thin layer of rock papering the hole at the back of his cell, revealing a smooth-walled tunnel just wide enough to walk down without turning his shoulders. He lit a white light on his fingertip and strode down the passage.

"So there's basically nothing that can keep you imprisoned anymore, is there?" Blays said.

"They could make the walls out of wood or metal," Dante said.

"Which you could then smash through."

"Well, it depends how thick it is."

Blays tapped the side of the wall. "Or they could stick you in a big glass box and put the box underwater so if you broke the box you'd drown."

"For the sake of global sanity, I'm glad you're not a fan of torture."

Over the span of a few steps, the tunnel changed from stone to dirt, sloping up beneath them. After another hundred yards, a set of hard-packed dirt steps appeared, terminating in a blank wall and ceiling.

Dante waved Blays away from the steps. "This probably won't collapse all over me, but you might want to back off."

"I'm just going to head back to your cell. Better yet, back to my room."

Dante took hold of the nether webbed through the dirt atop the staircase and pushed. A black hole opened above his head, spilling dirt and warm, moist air into the tunnel. Stars dotted the gap through the ground. Dante jogged up into the grass just outside the walls ringing the Citadel.

Blays glanced up at the walls and gestured him forward. A slight and black-haired man waited for them in an alley two blocks from the Citadel. Blays nodded. "Dante, meet Amwell."

Dante shook hands. "Thank you for meeting us."

Amwell bobbed his head. "Thank you for meeting *me*. I never met Callimandicus—I've only served the Citadel a few months—but I admired him for years. I don't believe for a second that you killed him."

"Well, we may be about to find out who did. Lead on."

"He's in the carneterium." Amwell started down the street toward the hilltop cemetery.

"Oh goody," Blays said. "Think we'll have to fight any wights?"

"Do you know where, exactly?" Dante said. "That place is huge."

Amwell nodded. "I work there, sir. And it's the most curious thing—since Kav brought his body to us, no one else has seen it. We've actually been ordered to keep the room sealed."

Blays snorted. "Well, that is the standard procedure for investigating a murder, isn't it? Lock up all the evidence, then accuse someone at random?"

"There's only one reason Kav wouldn't look at the body," Dante said. "And that's if he were already perfectly aware who killed him."

"How will the body help, anyway?" Blays said. "You're not going to...do anything funny, are you?"

"What do you mean?"

"You know. Make him sit up and tell you what happened."

"Are you crazy?" Dante said. "Why make him sit up when I can make him dance? Just wait till you hear what I've got in store for *your* corpse."

"Oh no. No, that's not happening. If I'm ever about to die, I'm going to kill you first."

"Then I'll have to preempt your preemptive strike." Dante wiped sweat from his hairline. After the stagnant must of the dungeons, the air tasted salty and fresh. It was still blood-warm even in the dead of night, however, humid and horrible. They strode through the grassy field surrounding the hill. "Just so you know, I'm totally out of ideas if this doesn't work."

Blays nodded sagely. "Well, there's always suicide."

Amwell led them to the hole in the base of the hill. Above the entrance, a stone plaque showed Arawn's millstone, the North Star perched upon the tip of its pole. Amwell unlocked the door and lit a lantern in the foyer.

"Please follow me, lords." He turned and smiled. The lamplight gave his black hair a brown halo. The man led them through the mazelike catacombs. Within minutes, Dante was hopelessly lost; if Amwell were to drop dead, Dante would stand a better chance of tunneling back out than of finding his way back to the entrance. The passages smelled of death old and new. It was managable stench, however; the carneterium workers used balms and the nether to slow the decay, dousing the tunnels and rooms with perfumes. In spots, the scent of wildflowers drove the smell of rot away completely.

At last, Amwell stopped in front of a closed door no different from the two score they'd already passed. He slipped the key into the lock and turned to Dante. "He is inside, my lord."

Inside, a stained shroud covered the body on the stone platform in the middle of the room. A withered foot projected from the shroud's edge. Dante found a lantern on the wall and lit it with a thought. A hooked chain hung above the table. Dante affixed the lantern to it, ran his hands through his hair, and peeled the shroud from the body.

It was easy to pretend it was just another corpse. He'd seen hundreds in his young life. When he'd helped establish the carneterium, he examined dozens just like this. The neck wound on his current subject appeared to have been the lethal strike. It stretched across the man's throat, black with crusted blood. It was a wonder Cally'd been able to talk at all. The skin on the man's left hip, knee, and shoulder was white, marbled with reddish lines, but the areas around the blanched skin were brown-black and bruised.

"Was he found resting on his left side?" Dante said.

Amwell tipped back his head and considered the ceiling. "I believe so. How can you tell?"

"That bruising there. Seen it on a lot of bodies. It looks identical to a beating, but I believe it's just where the blood comes to rest inside them once they die—it always shows up around the parts of the body that have rested on the ground." Dante made his way down the corpse. There were no other obvious wounds. That fit with what he'd heard through the loon. He went to Cally's fingernails, hoping the old man had fought back and scraped the man; if he found any foreign blood, he could follow it to the killer. But Cally's hands had been scrubbed and cleaned. Fingernails, too. Except a crease of blood along the thumbnail. Dante's heart leapt. He touched the nether within it, but there was no accompanying pressure to point him toward the man who'd done it. It was Cally's, remnants of his futile efforts to quench the gash cut into his throat.

"Was anything removed from the room?"

Amwell gazed at the ceiling again. "A small rug. Soiled. His clothes, of course." He frowned. "Oh. And this." He went to a desk at the side of the room and returned with a white handkerchief spotted with blood. "This was fresh when we found it. Strange, isn't it? If Lord Callimandicus had used this to stanch the bleeding, you would expect it to be drenched, wouldn't you? But there are just these little spots."

Dante snatched it up and reached for the nether in the dried brown spots. Pressure bloomed near the middle of his forehead. "Which way am I facing right now?"

"South. South-southwest, I think. Isn't that about the direction of the Citadel?"

"It is."

The man's mouth parted halfway. He stepped under the lamplight, gazing down at Cally. "Does that mean the man who did this..?"

Dante stared at him. Beneath the light of the lamp, Amwell's hair had that same two-toned appearance Dante had noticed when they entered the carneterium. While most of it was black, a few patches were a rich brown, including a solid stripe that ran back from the left side of his head.

"Do you dye your hair?" Dante said.

Amwell didn't look up. Instead, he went still. Too still. "Can't say that I do. Why do you ask such an odd question?"

Dante caught Blays' eye, then nodded at Amwell, making a small gesture they'd worked out years ago for times such as these. Blays darted in behind the man, locking his arms behind his back.

"What are you *doing*?" Amwell shouted.

Dante closed on him, running his fingers through the hair on the man's scalp. His black hair was indeed black from root to tip, but his brown hair showed three shades: deep brown with a tinge of gray at the tips, where it was exposed to the sunlight; then black down to just above the roots. There, in a layer as thin as a cotton undershirt, the hair was stark white.

Dante's skin prickled. "You skunk."

"Let me go!" Amwell twisted to his left, trying to free his arms, but Blays bore down, cranking his wrist to the edge of breakage. Amwell gasped and went slack.

"That's what Cally said as he was dying," Dante said. "'Skunk.' I thought he meant the killer was foul-smelling. But he was talking about hair. The stripe on your head that's white like a skunk's."

"This is madness! I am a tender to the dead, not an *assassin*!"

"You were too eager to lead me along. How long have you been spying on me? To learn what would set me at Kav's throat?" Dante waved the blood-spotted handkerchief. "This is Kav's blood, isn't it? Where did you get this? Did he toss it out after shaving?"

"I don't know what you're talking about!"

"He's not the only one," Blays said. "Why am I on the verge of breaking this guy's arms over here?"

"Tell him," Dante said. Amwell wriggled again. Blays bent his wrist. Amwell went white as bleached parchment. Dante beckoned the nether to him, cupping it in his hands, spending some of its own strength to make it blackly visible to common eyes. Theatrically, he grabbed it in both hands and bent it into a wicked crescent. He extended his right hand, palm-up. As smoothly as a patrolling pike, the blade honed in on Amwell's throat. Dante smiled without humor. "Talk before this sorcerous sword bites through your throat."

Behind Amwell, Blays grinned at Dante's show. Amwell jerked away from the nethereal blade. Blays shifted his hips to take the man's weight and rotated his arm. Something popped in Amwell's wrist.

"Stop!" he shrieked. "I was sent by Cassinder of Beckonridge. I've been working with Wint for months."

"Wint? From-the-Council Wint?" Dante goggled. "To do what?"

"I don't know," Amwell said. Dante touched the nether to his neck and let him feel the chill. Amwell gasped out half a curse. "I think we were meant to undermine the Council. I just did as I was told. That's all I know!"

"Undermind it by cutting off its head?" Dante said. Amwell shuddered, ashen. Dante fought down the fury surging through his blood. "Now you're going to repeat this to the rest of the Council."

"What happens then?"

"That's not for me to decide."

The man's face twisted into a fearful sneer. "I want your assurance I won't be killed. My confession must be worth something."

Dante returned his gaze. "I'll do all I can."

Dante took down the lantern from the chain. Amwell led on. Blays relaxed his grip on Amwell's wrists. The circle of lantern light receded from the room. The body of Cally fell into darkness.

They emerged into the humid night. Amwell made no effort to resist or escape. The front gates to the Citadel would be closed, as they always were, so Dante guided them back to his tunnel to the dungeons, continued through his cell, and took the steps up to the ground floor, where he encountered three very surprised guards.

"I need the Council assembled at once," Dante said. "Don't try to stop me. If I am in the wrong, let my fellow priests destroy me."

Two of the guards wavered. The third, an older man who'd often seen to Cally personally whenever the old man had business in the city, nodded deeply. "Where shall we tell the Council to meet?"

"In our chambers," Dante said. "Wait to bring Wint until the end if you can. If you care for your own life, for Arawn's sake don't tell him why we're meeting."

The three men followed him into the Citadel proper. The entry was scantly lit by slow-burning candles. One of the guards plucked one up to take into the unlit stairwell. Once they reached the upper floors, the guards peeled away to roust the councilmen from sleep. Dante headed straight to the main chambers, where he instructed Amwell to sit in a chair in the corner on the right side of the doorway, out of sight until one had stepped inside the room.

"What happens if Wint goes batty?" Blays said. "Putting him in an armlock won't stop him from killing everyone with magic flying shadow-daggers."

"I thought you had strategies to fight people like us," Dante said.

"Yeah, and I bet a lot of them end with me dying horribly."

"I can handle him," Dante said. "He won't attack anyone. It would only prove his own guilt."

"Fine," Blays said. "Guess I'll just sit back and enjoy the drama."

Tarkon was the first to arrive. The old man gave Dante an amused smile. "Is my memory that bad? When did we move the prisons all the way up here?"

Dante grinned back. His cheer was short-lived. Somburr came next, examining the scene with the quiet intensity of a bird of prey. He perched near the back of the room, watching. Joseff came next. He was as silent as always, but his long-faced stare spoke volumes of wary suspicion.

Then came Kav. His eyes glimmered with anger above his aquiline nose. "What are you doing out of your cell?"

Dante made sure the nether was close. "I decided lying alone in the dark was less productive than figuring out who really killed Cally."

"You killed your former leader and now you defy your new one?" Kav summoned the nether to his hands in a black blur. "If you won't abide by the process of law, then it's time to enforce an older form of justice."

"Stop it!" Dante said. "Tricking us into tearing out each other's throats is all part of their plan!"

Shadows tumbled around Kav's hands like mad moths. "What are these vagaries of yours? Is it *your* plan to confuse us until we no longer know true from false?"

"Just wait until Wint is here." Dante held up his empty hands, letting the nether dissolve away. "If you're not satisfied by what I tell you then, I won't fight back."

Kav hesitated, lips pressed together so tight they went bloodless.

Tarkon cleared his throat. "Let him talk, Kav. Whatever he's got to say, you know it's going to be a hell of a lot of fun to hear."

"I don't consider that a sound basis for letting a known assassin walk free." Kav's frown turned thoughtful. "How did you get out of the dungeon in the first place?"

"I walked through the wall," Dante said.

A few of the priests chuckled. Kav's frown found its former depths. "You're not helping your case any."

"I'll show you the hole once I've acquitted myself."

"Is there no boundary to your arrogance? Your—"

Kav broke off, distracted by the arrival of Wint. Wint kept his smart, sharp features carefully composed, but when he saw Amwell sitting in the corner, he flinched. It was just a hint of movement, a flickering retraction of his neck, and Wint composed himself an instant later, but Dante had been watching him as unblinkingly as the full moon. With that flinch, the last of his doubts dissolved on the wind.

"Hi, Wint," Dante said. "Want to tell them how you had Cally killed?"

Wint laughed in disbelief. "Was this your scheme to be released from prison? To shift the blame from yourself by casting it on others as carelessly as you'd throw a sheet over an old chair?"

"I was speaking with Cally on my loon as he was dying. He identified this man." Dante pointed to Amwell, who gave Wint a sickly stare. "Please tell them what you told me, Amwell."

Amwell dropped his gaze and spoke in a swift monotone. "I was sent by Lord Cassinder to work in conjunction with Wint. Our express purpose was the neutralization of this council."

"Stars of Arawn," Tarkon whispered.

Kav's nostrils flared. "Including the assassination of Callimandicus?"

Amwell's lips curled from his teeth. "Including that."

"This entire conversation is a disgrace to this room," Wint said, casting about for support. "There's no evidence here. Just the fabulous claims of the real killer and some drunk he hired from the street."

"And that assassin who tried to kill me when I returned during Thaws?" Dante said. "Did I hire him too?"

"I can't keep track of all your enemies for you."

Dante pulled the handkerchief from his pocket and handed it to Kav. "This is your blood. They planted it to make me come for you. Just like they must have planted the knife in my room."

Kav turned his head to Wint as levelly as if it were on a swivel. "Is this true, Wint?"

"This is nonsense," Wint said. "Absurdity. Maniacal slander. Nothing this child has said would last two seconds at formal trial, yet—"

"That's my blood on that rag!" Kav said. Even his snarls had a regal tone. "Don't disgrace this room with any more lies!"

Wint's righteous smile tightened until Dante feared it might break. Nether flickered throughout the room. Wint gazed out the black windows overlooking the bay on the far side of a room.

"I have a story for you," he said. "Once upon a time, there was a young man born to a poor family. The son of a fisherman and his wife. The boy studied diligently—perhaps obsessively—discovering a facility with the nether and a knack for theology. Despite the fetters of his lowly station, he was allowed to enter the priesthood. As a monk, his station no longer mattered. These people didn't care *who* he was born to. All that mattered was what he was born to do."

Wint circled around the long table, still watching the windows. The priests and guards tracked each one of his movements. He ran his hand over his mouth. "This order was so egalitarian, in fact, that when opportunities opened in the highest order of its ranks, the boy (who had, in truth, since become a man, though not that long ago) was allowed to apply and test for one of those positions. Miracle of Arawn! He was accepted.

"Yet short years after the ascendance of this son of a fish-gutter to the highest ranks of the land's holiest order, stormclouds appeared on the horizon of that order's future." He opened the windowed doors to the balcony, revealing low, black clouds that hugged the night's humidity close to the city. "What would be the right metaphor for the decision this group had reached? It was as if a bear cub, on seeing its mother feasting on a stream full of salmon, suddenly decided it had more in common with the fish, and decided to scheme with the salmon against its own mother. Madness. Hubris. A decision that could only result in the destruction of the cub by the very jaws and claws that had raised and fed it.

"Let us back away from poetry. This priest, then, on seeing that the body to which he belonged had opted to betray its mother, decided he would do whatever he could to save his institution's life. No matter the cost. No matter if it meant being branded a traitor himself—exiled, hated, scorned and besmirched centuries after his name should have faded into history's great haze. So he spoke to those his institution would betray. They suggested a solution.

"The solution was extreme. Vile. Even worse than this son of a fisherman had imagined. Yet bitter as it was, it wasn't half so bitter as the poison pill of witnessing the destruction of the order that had allowed this son of no one to taste the fullness of the world. So he accepted. Knowing it would likely mean his own death, too—of his physical body, as well as no more and no less than his soul—he took up the dagger, for all its weight."

Wint stepped onto the balcony. He turned to face the priests. Nether whipped around his face and hands. "I was instructed to kill Dante. Dante, the one pushing us to betray the motherland that would surely maul us. When that didn't work, I killed Cally, who was no less enthusiastic, and attempted to destroy Dante again by blaming him for Cally's death. On learning Dante was on the verge of escape, I sought to reensnare him, and in the process lead him to kill Kav, whose will was too weak to trust he would sue for peace after all. All for the sake of my city, Narashtovik, and its Council I love so well."

Beneath the black clouds, Wint tipped back his head. "I can't see Arawn nor his mill. The skies are too dark. Will they ever clear?"

He took a step back, hit the balcony railing, and flung himself over its edge. He disappeared without a sound.

Kav cried out. Dante rushed to the railings. So did the others. Cloth flapped in the wind. Far below, something heavy and wet met the ground with a spatter.

"Arawn's sweet wheat," Kav whispered. Dante turned to ask him what next. Amwell rose from his seat in the corner and wandered to the door, glancing about to see if anyone was watching. Dante reached out, clawlike, for the nether in Amwell's heart. He squeezed.

Amwell's face went white. He gasped, eyes frogging, and pawed at his chest. He fell and was still.

"What did you just do?" Blays asked softly. "You said you'd let him live if he helped you."

Dante frowned. "He killed Cally."

"But you made him a promise."

"The man who killed Cally doesn't deserve promises. He deserves death."

Blays flung out his hands. "Then tell him that from the start! Don't lie to him. Don't promise him life when you mean to give him death. This isn't a game."

"I know that," Dante said. "Games have rules. We can't afford to."

"Well, maybe we should. Maybe if we did, I wouldn't lie awake thinking about that guy's face."

"Rules are a luxury for those with the power to play by them. I'll start worrying about what's fair as soon as King Moddegan stops forcing me to scramble for my life."

Blays shook his head. "You know, nobody makes you do anything. You always have a choice."

The rest of the room watched in silence. Dante turned away from Blays and met Kav's eye. "I'm sorry I thought it was you. Things are moving so fast. I moved too fast as well."

"I can't damn you without damning myself for the same sin." The hard planes and regal curves of Kav's face aligned into a single pained look. "We can't seek peace with the people who killed Cally. Do we have any chance of winning this war?"

"Hell if I know," Dante said. "But if we don't, at least we'll all die together. Should we get started?"

27

From atop the city's outer Pridegate, Dante let out a yell and scrambled down the stairs. Five hundred men shouted and pursued him up the boulevard. Sunlight struck the cobbles as hard as his own boots. He risked a glance over his shoulder. Faces snarled. Swords and spears glinted. Dante pushed harder uphill, sweating in the stagnant summer swelter. Footsteps rang closer and closer. He had nothing more to give. The first troops caught him, falling in beside him with taunts and jokes.

He grinned back. The citizen conscripts had been learning fast. Not that it took any great discipline to retreat from a hypothetically breached Pridegate to the next line of defenses at the Ingate. But it wasn't the most straightforward activity in the world, either. The sprinters had to lead the way and ensure the route ahead was clear while the main body of conscripts had to stay cohesive enough to reform if they were overtaken by cavalry. Then came the issue of what to do once they reached the Ingate—learning to make their way through it in a reasonably orderly fashion, to rush up the stairs to take fresh positions, to call out when they were ready to close the gates behind them.

Which the conscripts quickly did, with a minimum of fumbling or confusion. Pretty good, considering the Citadel guards had just rounded them up this morning.

"Well done!" Dante called from the tower flanking the main passage through the Ingate. "Soon enough we'll be the finest retreaters in all the land. See your sergeants for your next instructions."

He continued uphill to the Citadel. He had an appointment

with Kav. Nothing major. Just to decide how they'd spend the few days they had left.

Dante detoured to his room for long enough to towel off the worst of his sweat before continuing to Kav's. There, Kav glanced up from a desk laden with messages, marching orders, and maps.

"I've recalled Olivander," he said. "The messenger should reach him within two days. Assume he'll require an equal amount of time to finalize his recruitment and three more days to return with whomever he's been able to muster."

"A week," Dante said. "Should beat the king's armies here, at least. Any word what they're up to?"

"Conquering. At an alarming rate. And northward-bound, to boot. They could beat Olivander here if they wished, but it appears they're content to spend no more than half of each day marching and the rest quashing all norren in reach."

"Sounds like we'll owe the norren a monument before this is done."

"If we have any stone left after our graveyard is finished." Kav brushed dust from his doublet. "So where are your brilliant, beyond-the-bend-in-the-river strategies for overcoming the inevitable?"

"Should I have some of those?"

"I have been led to believe it is your stock in trade."

"I don't know anything about defending a city from an army the size of another city. Quite frankly, I'd be looking to Olivander's lead on that front." Dante rubbed his eyes. "Anyway, absurd and half-assed schemes are Blays' specialty. If I can pry him away from Lira, I'll see what he has to offer."

Kav nodded, then pursed his mouth in a way that showed the tips of his teeth. "I am not sure of the most graceful way to broach this. But I want you to know that, for whatever role I might be currently occupying within this madness, I intend for it to be temporary. If the Citadel's still standing once this is over, its next leader will be decided through the standard channels."

"By murdering the current leader and snatching up his mantle?"

Kav chuckled. "Preferably something a hair more civilized than Cally's methods."

Dante went to the dungeons to seal up the tunnel he'd bored

between the Citadel and the outside, then made a circuit of all three of the city's main walls—Sealed Citadel, Ingate, and Pridegate—to ensure they were intact and sound. He finished his rounds just before nightfall. Somburr came to his room minutes later. Inside, the man fished into his pocket and produced the letters Dante had copied from Kav, along with an additional set of papers: translations.

"I'd forgotten all about those," Dante said. "What do they say?"

Somburr gave him a sharp look. "Can't you read? Do you spend all that time propped up over books just to trick anyone watching into thinking you're literate?"

"I can read. I just figured you can, too, and had already applied that heroic skill to the contents of these letters."

"Okay. They're love letters."

"Love letters? Why would he bother to encrypt those? I've never seen anything about celibacy in the *Cycle*."

Somburr tapped the folded papers. "They're from a man."

"Oh."

"Yes. Do you want to blackmail him?"

"What?" Dante reached for the letters. "My plan from here is to put them back and never mention them again."

"I can take care of that." The letters disappeared in Somburr's pocket. "Are you sure you don't want to blackmail him?"

"Double sure."

"Well, have it your way. Maybe another time."

Somburr departed. Day by day, the city grew more quiet and more loud. Quieter because those citizens unwilling to defend it began to leave it, dispersing to the far eastern hills or by boat to Yallen or even driving their wagons into the hinterlands of the Norren Territories. Louder because as the daily clamor diminished, what few sounds remained rang all the harsher: the constant clank of blacksmith's hammers, the shouts of sergeants drilling volunteers, the occasional thunder of a rider bearing some new message from the lands beyond the walls.

With the institutions of the Council and city guard kicking in to oversee the bulk of the logistics, Dante found himself with an unfamiliar abundance of free time. Working with the commander of the guard, he helped raise a few new earthworks to shore up the city's most vulnerable points, such as down on the bay where there were no walls against a seaborne invasion, but he could only work for so long before the nether gave out. Then he was just one more man with a shovel. Instead, he selfishly left the digs to spend his time as he pleased.

Some he spent walking. Enjoying the warmth and the sunlight. Twice, he went to the ocean to watch the fish from the docks and to wash off the suffocating humidity in the cold northern waters. He went to visit the marker on Cally's grave at the top of the hill. If they had a future, a stone monument would be erected in its place, but for now it was nothing more than a wooden pole. When Blays and Lira weren't busy in their rooms, he spent time with them. Lira insisted on teaching them some of her most desperate grappling techniques. Dante appreciated it, and went through her drills and sparring with as much energy as he could muster, but a thick fatalism had settled over his shoulders. Two or three weeks from now, it would all be over. What could he learn in two or three weeks that would make any difference? At this phase, what could it possibly matter?

Rather than depressing him, this feeling liberated him. He began to see the small things. The sharpness of the leaves backlit by sunlight. The skitter of sand crabs dislodged by the break of the waves. The shine of sweat on a woman's neck as she lifted her arms to clip clothes to a line. At times the sharpness of the world stole his breath. These sights were everywhere. Thousands of them in a single day. There weren't enough eyes to see them all. Perhaps that was the worst of what was to come: soon enough those eyes, already too few, would be lessened by another few thousand, leaving that many fewer witnesses to the world's golden wonder.

And sometimes life felt no different at all. The specter of war shuttered businesses across the city, but had no appreciable effect on Narashtovik's public houses. If anything, they grew more boisterous than ever, with laughing drunks spilling out the front doors by noon and by night. It was just such a place Dante and Blays found themselves on one of those summer nights when the sun threatens to never set at all—it was past nine o'clock, by the cathedral bells, yet the sun still hovered above the western forests, splashing the tavern with yellows and reds. To combat the too-snug humidity, Blays ordered mugs of summer ales, light and sweet and basement-cooled. They drank within the shade of the wall, fanned by the breeze through the open windows.

"We could tell the redshirts we surrendered last month." Blays wiped foam from his upper lip. "Just tell them to turn around and go home. Maybe by the time they got all the way to Setteven they'd be too tired and sweaty to bother coming back."

"Sure," Dante said. "Hoist a few of the king's banners over the Citadel, smile a bit, offer them our nicest teas."

"I'm not giving them any tea."

"Our third-finest, then. Those barbarians will never notice the difference."

"Consider it added to the list." Blays appeared to be taking actual notes. He squinted over his parchment, lips moving soundlessly. He dotted the sheet with his quill. "Now then. Alternately, we burn the city to the ground ourselves—quite safely, of course—then spread the rumor Arawn's already taken his vengeance on his treacherous servants."

Dante sipped his beer. "No good. That would just entice them to march in and piss on the ashes. Which I assume we'd be hiding in."

"You can't hide in ashes. One wrong sneeze and the jig is up."

"Fine. We'll hide in smoke instead. Very difficult to piss effectively on smoke."

Blays' quill scribbled. "Piss...on...smoke."

"It's called the Dead City, right? Maybe we can convince them it's full of deadly, deadly ghosts."

"Why don't you build a few tunnels beneath the city for us to move around through?"

"Could be useful," Dante said.

Blays snapped his fingers. "Got it. Build big old pits and camouflage them so the redshirts just march right into them. Like giant tiger traps."

"That could work on the front ranks. But after they've fallen, that will be the end of it. Anyone who's too stupid to not wander into a giant hole would have already stabbed themselves to death trying to eat dinner."

"So pair it with a giant distraction. A two-hundred-foot naked lady blazed across the sky! They'll be too busy goggling at the heavens to see the hole right in front of them."

Dante took a long drink. "This is not getting us any closer to not being murdered."

"You've gotten pretty good at digging ditches without a shovel, aren't you? Why don't you bury their whole army under an avalanche?"

"I don't have that kind of power. Anyway, we'd have to lure them under a giant cliff or something, and Narashtovik is sadly lacking in giant cliffs." Dante rubbed his eyes. "What did we learn at Dollendun?"

Blays narrowed his eyes. "That explosions are fun and hordes of armed men on horseback aren't."

"Cavalry will still be a problem. The city's too big to block all the streets. What can we do about that?"

Blays drove his finger down into the table. "*That's* when you spring the tiger trap."

"That might work. What else?"

"Man, I don't know. How many tiger trap-related ideas can one man come up with?"

"It pains me to say this, but will you forget the tiger traps? So we don't have any bombs. We don't have any loons. What do we have that they don't?"

Blays shrugged. "Two giant sets of balls."

Dante rolled his eyes. "Unless we plan to roll them down the hill at the redshirts, I don't see how that's useful."

"*And* one giant penis."

"Is that all we've got? Tiger traps and courage?"

Blays drank contemplatively. "Seems to me the real lesson in Dollendun is when they've got ten thousand men, tricks can only take you so far."

"Narashtovik's only got a standing army of about two thousand," Dante said. "And half of those troops were more of a sitting-army as recently as last year. Their training's not going to match Setteven's soldiers. I don't know how many men Olivander will bring back—a few hundred? At least they'll know which end of a sword is which. That's more than can be said for some of the citizens we've conscripted."

"Oh well," Blays said.

"Oh well?"

"As in 'Oh well, not much we can do about it now but have a drink.'" Blays did just that, then laughed. "Sorry. Is that obnoxious? For some reason I just can't convince myself to care."

Dante grinned. "Same here. It's like this is happening to another person."

"Another person who I also don't care about."

"Have we seen too much? Become jaded to even the worst horrors?"

"I don't think that's it." Blays stood, mug in hand. "I mean, if I find out the keg is empty, I'm still going to scream pretty damn loud."

That was the last they spoke of the invasion that night. Dante spent the next few days wandering around the city looking for opportune places to sink tunnels and tiger traps. Hammers rapped constantly as men boarded up their houses. Grocers began to shutter their empty shops, too; the remaining citizens had begun to hoard, buying up all foodstuffs in sight. Kav assigned the monks to update the decades-old system of rationing Narashtovik's granary. Dante began a tunnel to link the Citadel's basements to the far-off catacombs of the carneterium. An escape hatch, should worse come to worst.

Olivander rode into the city, the banners of Barden flying from his troop of 120 horsemen and another six hundred foot soldiers gathered from the east. He'd heard the gist of the recent infighting—Wint's betrayal, the attempt to set the Council against itself, Dante's proof and Wint's subsequent suicide—yet was still shocked to hear the story in whole.

"It sounds like the king's already half ruined Narashtovik," he said in his steady baritone. "Now he sends his army to finish the job."

"Think they'll have enough to do it?" Dante said.

From the steps to the Citadel's front door, Olivander gazed over the men being shuffled across the courtyard for the barracks and stables. There were clearly too many; some would have to be quartered in the abandoned houses beyond the gates.

"I got fewer men than I'd like," Olivander said. "But we may have enough. If the walls hold. If the people fight back. If the Council, depleted as it is, holds strong." The goateed man glanced down at Dante. "What do *you* think?"

"I have no idea. Something this big is beyond my capacity to predict."

Olivander grinned. "*You* admit not knowing something? Are we sure Wint didn't kill you and replace you with an impostor before he died?"

"Perhaps I'm getting older," Dante scowled. "But I suppose you'd know better than me."

Olivander snorted, but he was pleased to see Dante and the guards' progress drilling the conscripts. He took over from there to march the fresh soldiers around Narashtovik's boulevards, leaving Dante with even less to do. Men toiled in the streets from sunup to sundown, dragging rubble across the thoroughfares, erecting wooden walls with spiked prongs at key junctures.

Dante finished up his tunnel and, after consultation with Olivander, set to work on a tiger trap just before the intersection of a deliberately unblocked street halfway between the Pridegate and the Ingate. There, he convinced the stones to roll away, the dirt to part and hold. By the next day, it was twenty feet deep, ten across, and a full forty feet wide. Men sawed thin planks and laid them over the gap. It would hardly divert the enemy, but with a little luck, it might cripple a cavalry charge at a key moment.

The latest scouts returned. The king's army was marching north. If they didn't slow down, they'd be on Narashtovik within three days.

The buzz of activity became an ear-drilling whine. Dante went to the outskirts of the city to ruin the roads, littering them with ditches and holes. The day before the redshirts were expected to arrive, a man ran in from the outlying houses, screaming and waving his staff above his head.

"They're coming! The enemy is here! The king's army is upon us!"

The nether leapt unbidden to Dante's hands. His heart leapt unbidden to his throat. A quarter mile of low houses blocked the view between himself and the southbound road. He jogged to the road and headed out among the deserted homes, many of which had been abandoned decades and decades ago during the repeated sackings of Narashtovik. Some were no more than empty lots, weeds growing among the teeth-like foundation stones. He peeled off his shirt, a light doublet emblazoned with the sigil of Narashtovik. The redshirts might ignore a shirtless commoner. An official of Narashtovik would face a much more critical reception.

He passed a row of pine trees, their scent thick on the sun-baked air. Three hundred yards down the road, a legion of men marched into the hinterlands of the city, hundreds strong.

He turned to dash back to the walls and raise the alarm, then stopped dead in his tracks. The men weren't wearing uniforms. There was something wrong with their builds, too. Their heads were too high, their shoulders too bulky. Dante turned to meet them. He carried the nether, too, but as he grew closer, he let it fizzle away. When he saw the man at their front, he broke into a grin.

"Mourn!" he cried. "I thought you were dead!"

"Surprise." Mourn's beard was thicker. Beneath smears of soot and dirt, his bare arms showed fresh scars and half-healed cuts.

"Are you all right? How have you been?"

"If the period of my life before the last few weeks can be considered good, the last few weeks should be classified as not-good."

"Same here. I was imprisoned for murder, but it turned out I didn't do it." Dante smacked his thigh, smiling so hard his cheeks hurt. "What's happening in the Territories?"

Mourn tipped his head. "A lot of losses. A lot of deaths. For the redshirts, too, but those creatures multiply like they are not actually humans, but flies in crafty human disguises."

"I know what you mean. They're supposed to be here tomorrow."

"Supposed? Did you invite them? Because it would be strange to invite someone in to burn down your city and forcibly impregnate your women."

"It was an accidental invitation," Dante said. "I believe it was left on His Lordship Cassinder's doorstep during some ridiculous hunt for a make-believe bow?"

Mourn smiled for the first time since his arrival. "The world is very odd, isn't it?"

He had some four hundred norren with him. The Nine Pines

and Dreaming Bears, along with the remnants of five other clans and a hodgepodge of survivors separated from their warrior-families during the skirmishes ongoing across the Territories. Mourn's troop would be no small addition to the city's numbers.

Blays clapped when he saw Mourn. Lira gave him her small polite smile. Many of the guards stared; norren freemen weren't uncommon in Narashtovik, but few lived in the city on a permanent basis. They probably hadn't strolled into the city in such numbers in generations.

Dante offered to put them up in the rowhouses just beyond the Citadel walls, but Mourn refused, electing to encamp in a park down by the bay instead. That night, the four of them went to a public house as they had so often months before, but something had changed. Silence stalked their halting conversation. Even Blays was hunted by it, smiling vaguely and nodding distantly when addressed. As soon as they finished swapping news of the days since Dollendun, they paid more attention to their beers than to each other.

Scouts came and went throughout the morning. Dante stayed close to the Citadel and the news the riders brought there. In the morning, the redshirts were ten miles away. By noon, they'd cut that to five. Guard-commanders shouted orders across the courtyard, directing their troops to the walls. The three sets of doors to the Pridegate were sealed. Horns squawked from across the city. Young men hauled arrows and swords and bows and spears to the walls. Olivander saddled the cavalry and ran sweeps of the outskirts in search of enemy scouts and sneak attacks.

Mid-afternoon, Narashtovik's scouts reported the king's army had encamped in the pine forests a mile from the city. The smoke of scores of campfires rose from the black woods. As the army showed no signs of coming any further that day, Olivander pulled most of the men from the Pridegate but doubled the scouts beyond it.

In the neverending dusk, Dante went to his balcony to read and soothe his nerves. Instead, in the warmth of the setting sun, he fell asleep. He woke in total darkness and bolted to his feet. Not because of any horns or fires or signs of war. But because he'd meant to see his friends before whatever came with the morning. Now it was too late.

He paced his room, angry with himself. A few minutes later, a door clicked in the hallway. He poked out his head, hoping to see Blays, but Lira strode down the hall instead, wearing shorts, a thin shirt, and a knife.

"Is Blays awake?" he said.

She shook her head. "Wore him out."

"I'm sure he's as happy about that as I am unhappy to hear about it."

She laughed. She didn't do that often. "What did you need to talk to him about?"

Dante shrugged. "Nothing much. Impending death. The end of the world. That sort of thing."

"Are you nervous about tomorrow?"

"Does feeling the urge to barf up your skeleton count as nervous?"

"That depends. Have you done anything to provoke your skeleton?"

Dante laughed. "I need to ask you something."

She raised an eyebrow. "If you really need to ask, you wouldn't ask whether you could."

"Do you two love each other?"

"Does that matter?"

"It probably does to Blays."

She answered without hesitation. "Yes."

"Good," Dante said. "Then you don't owe me any longer."

"Says who?"

"You owe him—and he owes you."

Lira tipped back her chin. "I can have more than one duty or loyalty. He knows who I am. I won't change for him."

Dante scowled in the darkness of the hallway. "What if I told you I value his life above mine? So the highest service you can pay me is to keep him safe tomorrow?"

"Then I'd call you a liar."

"Don't you dare."

She'd been flirting with a smile, but quickly cast it aside. "Are you serious?"

"It's probably safer to pretend that I am."

"Lyle's balls, you're intense sometimes." Lira stared him down. "You saved my life. That kind if debt isn't penciled onto a ledger. It's chiseled on stone. Unerasable."

His jaw tightened. "This war probably would have come eventually. The norren would never stand to be enslaved forever. It's a war I still believe in. But I share too much of the blame for why it's happening here and now. If that caused any harm to come to him..."

"Then what?"

"I don't know."

"I don't either." She nodded once. "I'll keep him safe."

She drew her knife and cut her right palm. Her eyelid twitched. She handed him the knife. He followed suit, but had taken a blade to his own skin too often to flinch.

"What's this?" he said.

"It's how we seal agreements in the islands."

They shook. Her hand was wet and warm. When their hands dropped, he sealed both wounds with a balm of nether. She flicked her hand, glancing down sharply.

He smiled. "No sense going to war with a cut on your sword hand."

"I wouldn't have noticed." She smiled back. "I'll see you in the morning."

She walked toward the stairwell and headed down. On a whim, Dante decided to roam the city himself. He descended to the basement and took his tunnel to the carneterium. There, he emerged into the sweaty night and climbed the cemetery to the hill. Cally was there. So was Larrimore. Samarand and the Council members who'd died beneath the White Tree were there, too, although he'd forgotten where their tombs stood.

He nodded in whatever direction they may be in and continued up the grassy slope. He wasn't here for them anyway. It smelled like fresh leaves and a warm sea. Bugs of all kinds chirped and whirred. Beneath the ground, they silently ate. He touched the nether in the soil, felt the blank spaces of the coffins embedded within it.

Fires twinkled in the forest to the south. At the crown of the hill, Dante tipped back his head. The stars twinkled just as brightly. Jorus, too. The polestar. The crux of Arawn's mill. Some people prayed to Arawn—god of death, god of cycles—but Dante didn't. He knew the ancient god would pay him no mind.

So he hoped instead.

When he finished, he returned to his room and slept dreamlessly. He was up with dawn's first deathly blue hints. He dressed, put on his metal armbands and his sword, and went to the walls of the Pridegate without stopping for a breakfast he might not be able to keep down. The city was as silent as a snowfall. In the gray of the mounting dawn, Olivander was already atop the Pridegate, watching the city as if preparing to grab it by the throat.

"You didn't have walls in Dollendun, did you?" the middle-aged man said.

Dante shook his head. "We built a rampart, but that just encouraged them to come in through the side instead."

"I think we'll hold," Olivander said, as if convincing himself. "I think we'll spill too much blood for them to push through. They'll siege. Cally's been stocking up provisions for years. Will it be enough? Will the norren who still survive in the Territories push back hard enough to force the king to leave us in peace? That, I think, is how we do this."

"A siege? You mean I'll finally get to stay in Narashtovik for longer than two weeks?"

Olivander's trim beard quirked with a smile. "Don't get ahead of yourself. Someone will have to head the daring runs through enemy territory."

"Here I thought there would be a silver lining to Cally's passing—that I would no longer be called upon every time we need to do something ridiculous."

"I thought you and Blays did these things because you liked them."

"Maybe," Dante admitted. "But even the wicked can use a vacation."

As the sun rose, proper light scared away the ghostly land of predawn. It was already hot enough to have Dante sweating. Mourn brought the norren to the walls. They stuck together, saying little. A scout pounded up the road to the gates. The redshirts had broken camp a quarter hour ago.

Olivander sounded the horns. Soldiers jogged from the inner ring of the city to take up positions on the outer walls. Several members of the Council joined Dante and Olivander; the others were spread out along the miles-long sweep of the Pridegate, ready to react to any enemy sorcerers.

"What's going on?" Blays said when he appeared on the wall a few minutes later. "Boy, it looks like you guys are gearing up for a fight or something."

"Nothing of the sort," Dante said. "We were just going to sit down with the redshirts and discuss Allandon's *Transubstantiated Ethics and the Deceit of Carvahal*. A war's only broken out over that twice."

"I'm not even going to pretend to pay attention to that."

Atop the Pridegate's twenty foot walls, which in turn stood halfway up the rising slope of the city, Dante's line of sight ran to the edge of Narashtovik with few obstructions. It was from this clear vantage that he watched the king's army enter the city.

At first they flowed blackly from the forest, a dark, sluggish, molasses-like mass. That flow broke into separate streams as thousands of men diverted into four columns, each of which took a different one of the four main north-south roads to this flank of the Pridegate. Once this mass drew within a mile, its individual features grew more distinct. Red banners flapped above ranks of swordsmen wearing hauberks and spearmen clad in the oaky hues of boiled leather. A line of warhorses strode at the head of the main column, riders masked in plates of solid metal that glinted in the summer morning sun.

The stomp of their steps rolled through the sticky air. Rhythmic. Maddening. A planned avalanche. Dollendun had been different. Dante had only seen the boats, not the army's main body. The gathering of so many men intent on murdering them was eerie and awesome and terrifying.

"Is it too late to tell them the city's full of deadly ghosts?" Blays said.

"We may get a chance to find out," Dante said. "I think I'm about to start moaning."

Narashtovik's commanders hollered last-minute orders. To Dante's left, walltop defenders shuffled nearer the gates to meet the attackers. The king's army continued on, step by step, eating up what little distance remained between them and the walls. Close enough now to make out individual faces, to smell their miasma of travel and sweat. The front lines stepped within easy bowshot and stopped cold. The waves of men behind them rippled to a halt.

A lone rider emerged from the front lines, his warhorse stepping as lightly as the summer rains. Some ten yards in front of his troops, he halted and turned sidelong. Instead of the king's red, he wore pine green.

"I will now deliver the king's terms," he said. His voice was soft, almost soothing, yet it carried on the air like the streamers of morning mist that blew in from the bay and threaded through the city streets.

It was a cold voice, but that wasn't what gave Dante goosebumps. "Son of a gods damned bitch!"

"What?" Blays said.

Dante pointed below. "That."

Before the Pridegate, the man in green tilted back his head to regard the black-clad troops lining the walls. "Surrender. Lay down your arms. Swear fealty to King Moddegan of Gask. Disband the Council of the Sealed Citadel. Hand over all norren within Narashtovik to the custody of the king and his appointed executors. Turn over control of the city to me, Cassinder of Beckonridge."

"What the hell?" Blays said. "We killed that guy!"

"Apparently he got better," Dante said.

"You've met Cassinder, yes?" Kav said from beside them.

"Sure," Dante said. "In the sense we've spent the last few months trying repeatedly to kill each other."

Kav smiled ruefully. "Then perhaps you'd like to deliver our response."

Down in the street, Cassinder pulled off his steel helmet. One of his eyes drooped. A mass of pale scars surrounded the socket.

Dante straightened and advanced to the edge of the wall. "I am afraid to inform you that we are unable to accept your terms on the grounds that the only man in Narashtovik with the authority to accept them has been killed. As you ordered. As the king authorized." Dante did his best to look pained. "It is with great sorrow, then, that I am left with a single response: fuck you and the horse you rode in on!"

Cassinder bobbed his head. "Very well."

He wheeled his horse. As he returned to the ranks, he flung both hands above his head, open-palmed. Ether streaked from six points within the redshirts' ranks, glaring, as hot and white and angry as liquid steel. Dante didn't have time to shout. The ether crashed into the walls. The doors of the Pridegate came tumbling down.

28

Stone roared and groaned and crackled and burst. When Dante moved soil and stone, it was smooth, silent, graceful. The ethermancers' attack was not. Instead, it was a hammer-blow of pure force, the combined power of Setteven's strongest sorcerers blasting the gates and the surrounding stonework straight to the ground.

Dante fell with them.

Men shrieked. Nether whipped from Narashtovik's priests, too late to stop the attack, but perhaps in time to punish those who had made it. The floor disappeared beneath Dante. He tumbled through the open air, dust and pebbles pinging his face. As soon as he understood what was happening, he hit the ground.

His spine jarred. His elbow cracked. His head whiplashed into the cobblestones. Fist-sized stones rained down around him, bouncing from the street. It was very quiet. The shouts, the screams, were they coming from another world? It was so gauzy, too. The dust. The dust was part of it. He could taste it, gritty and slightly bitter. But the gauze was more than the dust. Things were fuzzy. Soft and smeary at the edges. He tried to rise and flopped back down. His elbow hurt. Dimly, foggily, but it hurt. So did his head. So did his back.

"Mourn!" he heard Blays call. "Take the norren and hold the gap! We have to hold them off while our men retreat!"

Olivander's baritone barked across the screams. Black-clad soldiers ran uphill deeper into the city. To the Ingate? Already? Why would they fall back so fast? Dante gritted his teeth and swung himself to a sitting position. Towering norren thundered past him, swords and shields in hand. Bellowing. Finally, Dante saw the hole in the wall. The very large hole where there had once been gates. And the tide of redshirts swirling in through it.

The norren met them head-on. Steel clashed. The screams changed pitch. Became shriller. Pained. Men died, cut down by the norren's pounding blades. Blood slicked the still-settling dust.

"Come on." Someone hooked a hand into his armpit. Blays grimaced down at him, face coated with dust and sweat. Someone else took his other arm. Lira. Together, they hauled him to his feet, which were perplexingly reticent to follow his demands. Narashtovik's soldiers continued the retreat to the safety of the Ingate. Supported on both sides, Dante stumbled along behind them.

The sounds of battle faded, replaced by the thump of scores of boots and the heavy breathing of men in full stride. The retreat was orderly enough. As orderly, at any rate, as could be hoped for in a movement involving thousands of men with swords running away from thousands of enemy men with swords. It was good they'd practiced the maneuver. Otherwise the battle might already be over.

They maintained their orderliness at the Ingate, where soldiers waited to pass through its narrow gates. Heads popped up along the walls. Men took up bows, nocking arrows. Pain throbbed in Dante's elbow and head. That was good. He was stepping out of the fog.

"I think I can walk on my own now," he said. Blays and Lira exchanged a look, then gradually lessened their hold on him until they were certain his feet were ready to fend for themselves. The three of them joined the crowd of soldiers in the wide plaza waiting to pass through the gates. Dante glanced downhill. "Do what I think just happened really just happen?"

"You mean the part where they blew down the wall like an angry god?" Blays said. "I thought it was you priesty boys' job to stop the enemy wizards from ruining our day."

"They were too fast. Normally these battles have a lot of preliminary pageantry. Speeches and the waving of flags and whatnot. They hit us the same way we hit the fort at Borrull."

"Those assholes!"

"Are you sure you're all right?" Lira said. "Heads shouldn't bleed. Yours is."

Dante touched the throbbing at the back of his skull. His fingers probed warm, matted hair. He twiddled them in front of his face. "Well, I don't see any brains."

"Not a surprise," Blays said.

Lira nodded to the Ingate and the black-clad soldiers passing through it. "Why won't they just blow up this wall, too?"

"They'll try," Dante said. "But they've already spent a lot of their power. And if you're alert, it's easy enough to stop. We'll have to post our people around the wall. Be vigilant."

Within two minutes, the last of the troops were filing through to the other side. The three of them milled at the rear. Back in the direction of the Pridegate, the norren ran into view, long legs carrying them ahead of whatever pursued them.

"Looks like our cue to get inside," Blays said.

They crossed beneath the shadow of the gates. Dante lingered, scanning the approaching norren for Mourn. The warriors reached the plaza. Hoofbeats thundered to Dante's left.

"Oh shit."

"What?" Blays said.

Dante rushed into the square. Cavalry galloped down the cross street toward the plaza. They'd be on the norren in seconds. Mourn and his men would be slaughtered.

Dante sprinted straight for the horsemen. He dropped to his knees, skidding across the cobblestones, and slapped his hand against the ground.

The earth shook. A trench leapt apart just feet in front of the cavalry. With no time to react, the first line of riders fell headlong into the narrow pit. Horses' eyes went white and wild. The second row of riders tried to jump or turn but fell instead, ensnaring those behind them in a tangle of reins and legs. Dante raced back toward the gates. The norren beat him there, funneling through. Horses screamed. Men, too. Down the road, redshirt infantry jogged into view, bound for the Ingate.

The gates creaked, shuddering as they began to close. Dante hurried through. The portcullis clanked down behind him. The norren stood inside, hands on knees as they caught their breath. Dante found Mourn among them. A bright gash trickled blood down his left arm.

Mourn jerked his head in the direction of the felled horses. "That was nice of you."

"You're too useful to lose this early in the day." Dante glanced among the clan warriors. "Lose many?"

"How many is 'many'? A clan's-worth. Most days, that is many. Today, I think it will be a blade of grass on the plain."

"That's a poetic way to put it." Up on the walls, bows twanged. Enemy arrows sailed overhead and clattered in the square inside the Ingate. Dante pointed to a tent across the square where men in robes came and went. "Take your wounded to the monks. And thank you, Mourn."

Mourn nodded and grunted at his troops. They headed for the tent, some leaning on the shoulders of their clan-brothers and sisters. In the shadow of the wall, Blays and Lira hugged briefly. Dante climbed the stairs to the top, keeping his head low, and hunkered behind the safety of a merlon. Around him, men stood, fired, ducked, and repeated.

Dante risked a look through a crenel. Redshirts busily pushed broad wooden barriers into firing range, setting up beachheads for their archers while the bulk of their troops stayed clear of the no man's land in front of the gates. Dante stilled his mind, wary for the first flicker of ether, but none came. Either the enemy sorcerers were biding their time, or they'd snuck off to find an unmanned section of the wall to attack next. Did the city have enough priests, monks, and minor talents to protect the Ingate against attack? How could they possibly keep watch over every foot of the wall?

The warmth of morning became the heat of day. Dante drank a full flask of water and wiped his mouth, gasping. The king's men continued to build their makeshift barricades and exchange arrows with the defenders. Their assault was not particularly effective. It struck Dante as more of an effort to keep Narashtovik's soldiers occupied than to pose any serious threat.

Dante healed the split on the back of his scalp, stopping as soon as he stopped the bleeding—this day, he'd need every scrap of nether he could command. Two cassocked monks tromped up the steps. He assigned them to keep both eyes on the battlefield below, then jogged along the westward curve of the wall in a low crouch.

After traveling just a couple hundred yards, he could almost forget a battle for the city was raging behind him. Down one street, the bodies of a dozen un-uniformed civilians lay among a handful of dead redshirts. Further along, men jogged down the street at a cant, buckets of well water sploshing their knees as they hurried to a house smoldering down the block. Dante stretched his mind as far as it would go, letting his other senses fade. Away from the arrows of the enemy, he straighted to his full height and strolled past scattered soldiers on watch for sudden attacks.

Something glimmered as briefly as a wisp of sunlight reflected from a rippling stream. Dante got down on hands and knees and crawled along behind the merlons. The glimmer repeated in his mind with the ethereal glow of the shifting spots he saw whenever he closed his eyes. He stalked on. The lights in his head increased in frequency and intensity. He peeked past the wall. Not fifty feet away, a woman hunkered against the base of the Ingate's wall. She was dressed plainly. No red, no uniform of any kind. But a steady stream of ether pulsed from her to the wall. Pebbles clattered against the ground.

Dante drew on the nether waiting in his drying blood and fired it toward the center of her head. Engaged in her sabotage, she didn't notice until the last second. Ether flashed wildly. Enough to knock his strike off course. Not enough to make it fizzle away. Instead of piercing her skull, the nether slashed into the side of her ribs.

She dropped hard to the ground. Blood poured into the cracks between cobbles. She clamped her hands to the wound. Ether glittered. Dante snuffed it out with a wave of his hand. She gasped for breath, blinking back frustrated tears. He watched her die, then waited there another ten minutes, mind open to any sparks of ether. None came.

A boom rolled across the city from the gates he'd left nearly an hour before. Dante backtracked at a jog. The plaza swung into view. A watermelon-sized stone hung in the air high above the no man's land; an instant later, it smashed into the walls. Stone splintered, vomiting shards across fleeing soldiers.

"Oh, there you are." Blays pushed away from the merlon he'd been cowering behind, brushing dust from his doublet. "Go off to take a nap?"

"The usual. Just off saving all our lives."

"Well, in case you haven't noticed, they have trebuchets."

"So?" Dante said.

"So trebuchets are to walls what wild dogs are to unattended children."

Dante shook his head and edged past a protective merlon. An arrow whisked past his head. He tried again. Far up the street feeding into the square, three trebuchets stood in various postures of readiness. At one, soldiers strained against the long lever holding the sling, raising the counterweight back into position. Dante reached out with the nether and snapped one of the struts connecting the counterweight to the lever. Wood groaned and cracked. The counterweight gave way, booming against the ground. With the weight removed from the other end of the lever, the team of straining men sat down hard.

Blays laughed through his nose. "You're really not fair, you know that?"

"I'm going to find some monks to take care of the others," Dante said. "Don't want to wear myself out too soon."

The two monks he'd seen earlier were just past the hole the trebuchet had smashed through the wall's deck. Dante edge along the wreckage and directed the monks to focus on the two remaining siege engines' most vulnerable parts. Nether winged across the plaza—only to disperse in a sizzle of black and white sparks.

"I didn't do that," one of the monks said.

The other rolled his eyes. "They stopped it, you dolt. Haven't you ever fought another sorcerer before?"

"Have *you*?"

"No, but Tobin has, and he told me—"

"Quiet down and try again," Dante said. "Every spark of ether they use to nullify you is one less spark they have to throw against the walls."

The monks turned back to the plaza, chagrined. Across the way, a man pulled the pin from a loaded trebuchet. Its firing lever whipped through the air, driven by the massive counterweight, slinging another head-sized rock through the air. The monks destroyed the device's lever while it was still vibrating. The rock landed short, whacking into the cobblestones twenty feet in front of the walls and ricocheting straight into their base with a sickly thwack.

The monks' next attack on the siege engines was stymied by a sorcerer hidden somewhere in the buildings at the opposite end of the square. So was the one that followed. The remaining trebuchet got off one more shot before the monks knocked it into splinters.

This back-and-forth continued through the next hour, resulting in little more than a few chunks taken out of the walls, several piles of kindling where trebuchets had once sat, and seven exhausted monks. Archers fired back and forth. Shouts rang out across the city. The bells tolled two o'clock. Dante and a large fraction of the soldiers on the wall switched places with the reserves below. Along with Lira and Blays, he went to one of the square's public houses coopted by the defenders. It felt good to be out of the sun. He sat, sore in his back and his elbow, and sipped an assortment of water, beer, and tea.

Blays toweled sweat from his moisture-flattened blond hair. "Does it count as a battle if my sword hasn't got any blood on it yet?"

Lira patted his hand, making a face at its dampness. "Patience, sweetness."

"They haven't had to fight rival sorcerers in generations," Dante said. "They'll adapt soon enough."

He'd no sooner said the words than a messenger burst into the pub, chest heaving. Someone handed him a beer, which he chugged in seconds, sleeving foam from his mouth. To Dante's incredulity, he explained the enemy had killed the few scouts manning an eastern section of the wall, then used the ether to carve a crude set of stairs into the side of the Ingate. Hundreds of redshirts had swamped the wall, overwhelming the light resistance until Olivander rode in with his cavalry, dismounted, and retook it foot by foot. Once the king's men had been beaten back, Olivander blasted out the lowest steps in the makeshift stairs, thwarting them.

Blays got his own taste of blood not long after. Cries rang out from the west. They rushed to the walls. A half mile from the gates, the attackers had brought in ladders and swarmed up the walls. Three hundred of the enemy had climbed up before Dante and the others joined a charging brigade of defenders. The fighting was close, vicious, angry. Boots splashed on bloody stones. Men fell from both sides of the walls, moaning in the streets, arms and legs and spines shattered. Lira left the fight with a deep slash to her left wrist. Dante retreated with her, sending the nether to mend her parted flesh. They lost nearly as many men as the redshirts before they pushed them back and smashed the ladders.

Yet they held. Their archers picked off enemy soldiers one by one, slaughtering the group that tried to wheel a battering ram up to the gates. Fires rose around the city. The plaza behind the Ingate smelled of blood and smoke and sweat. Dante heard Kav's lung had been pierced in a duel with another sorcerer. Ulev was tending him personally, but even if he lived, he'd be useless for the rest of the day, perhaps longer.

The afternoon crawled on. The sun baked the blood to the stones. Soldiers began collapsing without wounds. They were brought to the tents for shade and beer and water. Beyond the gates, the redshirts extended a line of wooden walls toward the Ingate. Narashtovik's archers set their arrows alight and let fly. As if the king's army had run out of ideas, they hung on the fringes of bow range. Their numbers dwindled.

As the sun's heat finally began to wane, bitter horns piped from the northeast side of the city. Dante's heart sank.

Blays's mouth hung half open. "That's the signal, isn't it? They're through the walls."

"It's time to fall back to the Citadel." Dante clutched his sweaty temples. "Why isn't anyone sounding the retreat?"

"Aren't you the highest-ranking person here?"

Dante scanned the walls. Archers fired sporadically. A trio of monks in their lightest robes kept an eye on the battlefield. A ways down the wall, Somburr's thin, twitchy form was unmistakable, but there was no sign of Olivander. Kav had been wounded, removed from action. The only others with seniority over him — Hart and Tarkon — were old men who hadn't held up well in the scalding afternoon. They'd been brought to the Citadel to act as reserves. Cally, of course, was long gone.

He called for the retreat.

They'd practiced this, too. The subtle spread of orders through simple hand signals. While a skeleton crew remained at the walls to support the illusion nothing had changed, the rest jogged down into the square and gathered into formation. Dante passed word to the Citadel guards commanding the mixed forces of soldiers and citizens. He and a small team would scout the route ahead. The main body of their forces—some 1500 men or more, with more yet having shifted to the battle to the northeast—would follow them to the Sealed Citadel three minutes later, with the crew on the walls descending to follow another three minutes after that. Ideally, they would all be safely behind the Citadel's walls before the redshirts managed to break through the abandoned gate.

Dante grabbed a monk and two guardsmen dressed in Narashtovik's black. With Blays and Lira, they headed north up the gentle slope towards the colossal spire of the Cathedral of Ivars and the Citadel behind it. The shouts from the plaza at the Ingate faded, replaced by the dull roar of men and arms from somewhere to the north. The streets were otherwise silent. Pale faces stared from third-floor windows. A few thousand citizens remained, unarmed, isolated. What would happen to them as the king's men marched on Narashtovik's last defense?

The tall rowhouses draped them in soothing shadows. The five o'clock sun came in at yellow angles, dazzling the glass windows of the finer shops. Up the street, a handful of redshirts sprinted across the pavement. Dante flattened against a rowhouse, waiting for their footfalls to fade. He continued on, the pandemonium of battle echoing through the abandoned streets. He crested a small rise. The boulevard was a straight shot into the square between the Cathedral of Ivars and the Sealed Citadel. There, a mass of redshirted men clamored around the still-open front gates, swords flashing against those of Narashtovik's soldiers.

"We're too late," Dante said.

Blays flung out his hands. "Why are the gates still open? What are they thinking?"

"They're waiting for us."

"If they wait much longer they'll be waiting on Arawn's doorstep instead." Blays pointed at the sky. "They'll never hear us from here and if we get any closer we'll be chopped into breakfast.

Do that thing where you make stuff appear in the sky and tell them to close the damn gates!"

"We'll be trapped out here!"

"So what, dummy? Did you dig that tunnel for fun?"

More redshirts surged into the square every second. Dante exhaled in a frustrated sigh. He sucked the nether from the shadows of the buildings and sent it straight for the sky above the Citadel. In fifty foot letters, purple and twinkling, "CLOSE THE DAMN GATES—LOVE, DANTE" appeared in the air.

"I dunno," Blays said. "Might be too subtle."

Dante turned to the monk and two soldiers who'd come with them. "Go back to the others. Tell them *not* to go to the Citadel. They're to meet us at the carneterium instead."

"My lord," the monk bowed. The men ran back down the hill.

Blays gestured in the direction of the other hill on the north end of the city. "Lead on, exalted one."

"*I* didn't establish the rules of propriety," Dante grumbled. At the Citadel, the gates squeaked with a mighty grind of metal. The fighting below redoubled. Dante smiled. "I hope you didn't just get us all killed."

"That depends a lot on the effectiveness of your tunnel, doesn't it?"

Lira gestured forward. "If you two don't quit jabbering, we're dead either way."

"Sorry, love." Blays ran down a side street, then cut north to skirt the Citadel from a distance. A cheer went up. Either they'd just lost, or the defenders had finished sealing the doors.

The hill that bore the cemetery and carneterium swelled above the Ingate. The northern door through the walls was open, deserted. A couple hundred corpses scattered the plaza on both sides. Clearly this hadn't been the site of the main battle. The roads beyond were just as desolate. The houses stopped. Dante slowed as he jogged into the grassy field leading to the carneterium. Something stirred within the tall yellow grass.

"Get down!" Blays shouted.

Dante peered ahead, frowning. Blays plowed into his back and tackled him to the ground. Two arrows whooshed overhead. Lira rolled onto the dirt beside Blays. A lone oak stood twenty feet to

Dante's left. He crawled for it, hidden beneath the grass. An arrow fired blindly through the stems. Dante flung himself behind the tree trunk. Across the field, three men in nondescript green waited with bows bent in their hands. They loosed their arrows as soon as they saw the whites of Dante's eyes.

Arrows rapped into the trunk. Blays burst from the grass, zigzagging toward the archers. Dante gaped in horror and called out to the nether. It slithered to him from leaves and grass and dirt. One archer took a shot at Blays, firing wide. Lira ran pell-mell behind him, eyes locked on the archers' hands. Dante slung a spike of shadows toward a man taking hurried aim at Blays. The archer fell with a cry.

Another took a quick shot at Blays. As the man released, Blays dived forward, landing on his shoulder and rolling through the grass. He popped up within sword range and lunged forward. Both his blades plunged into the archer's stomach. Blays pivoted, using his swords as levers to put the dying man's body between himself and the final scout. The man's arrow thunked wetly into the corpse's back. Lira closed on him. He took a whack at her with his bow. She intercepted it with her wheeling left arm, rolling her forearm to absorb the blow, then grabbed the bow and yanked it forward. The man leaned with it. Her sword found his throat.

"What were you thinking?" Dante called as he ran to them. "They had bows! The long things that fire other long things across long distances!"

"The tunnel's right around here, isn't it?" Blays said. One of the men groaned. Blays stabbed him without looking down. "What if they'd found it and were running off to tell Cassinder?"

"Then I'd seal it up."

"Yeah, after a thousand men boiled out of the basements and clued you in. Come on. Let's make sure this place is clear."

A cooling sea breeze ruffled the grass. Nothing else stirred the field or the hill. Inside the carneterium, the entry to the tunnel was just as empty. The first of their troops arrived minutes later, led by the two guards and the monk.

"Get them inside as fast as you can," Dante said. "It's a straight shot from here to the Citadel basements."

Dante lit one of the torches kept in the entry to the carneterium and dropped into the tunnel. It was cool, moist. His boots echoed with every scrape. He alternated walking and jogging, preserving his sun- and battle-flagged strength.

Blays frowned in the snapping torchlight. "If this is what it's like down here, remind me to be buried aboveground."

"What does that mean?" Lira said. "Like, in the air?"

"Sure. Just put me in a coffin and hang the coffin from a branch. Little kids can use me as a swing."

A draft puffed down the tunnel. Dante emerged into the gloom of the basements. Rats skittered among spilled grain and casks of wine. As he climbed the staircase to the ground floor of the keep, the sounds of battle met his ears.

The courtyard was a sea of blood. Around the sealed gates, soldiers of Gask and Narashtovik lay dead in equal measure. The defenders had already hauled an unknown quantity of the slain to a ghastly pile beneath one of the walls, but hundreds remained. From the thirty-foot walls, archers plunked away at the redshirts on the other side, who returned fire, lobbing arrows into the courtyard on high arcs.

Across the way, Olivander spotted him and trudged over. His goatee and hair were in disarray, clumped with blood and sweat. His face was just as haggard.

"Reinforcements will be here any minute," Dante said. "They're coming through the tunnels."

"There's some welcome news. Their sorcerers broke through on us. Tried to do the same here, but Hart and Tarkon held them off."

"How's it looking now?"

Olivander shrugged wearily. "We've worn them down, but paid in turn. They still have the numbers. If they break through again, we can finally rest."

"Sounds like you could use me on the walls." Dante headed up the stairs. The walls around the Citadel were even higher than the Ingate. Dizzying. Exposed to the still-warm sun. The scene beyond was much as it had been at the Ingate: a clear field across most of the plaza, scattered pockets of archers hidden behind planks to keep the defenders honest. Thousands of men were spread out in the monstrous shadow of the cathedral, others spilling into the streets forking from the plaza.

These conditions held for another hour. Smoke trickled through the cooling air. Dante did little more than watch, conserving his strength. It was a smart choice. An hour later, with the sun continuing its slow descent to the west, chaos exploded across the battle.

It began on the cathedral. Along its roof—taller than the Citadel walls, half as high as the keep itself—men appeared by the dozens, setting up makeshift shields and firing down on the defenders along the wall. The city's soldiers hunkered behind their merlons, sniping back as best they could. As Dante ran nearer, Somburr's slim form popped up from behind the battlements. Nether whisked from his hands, slashing into the enemy ranks, knocking them from the roof. They screamed as they tumbled and thumped to the plaza.

More replaced them. As Dante brought the nether to his palms, cries went out along the wall to his right. The tops of ladders materialized above the stonework. Black-clad soldiers rushed to meet the attackers scrambling up the ladders. Blays and Lira ran toward them in a dead run. Dante swore and followed.

It wasn't just ladders. There were two mobile staircases, too, wheeled up while the defenders' attention diverted to the archers on the cathedral. Men poured from the stairs, laying into the massed defenders. Blays threaded through the lines, Lira matching him step for step. Dante drew his sword.

Blays ducked a looping swing and buried his blade in the ribs of a redshirt. Lira blocked the sword of another, grabbing his wrist and holding both their swords in place. She kicked out his knee. He shrieked, fell, died under the spear-thrust of a guardsman behind her. Blays blocked a downward cut with an outwards flick of his wrist. With his second sword, he stabbed through the hole opened in the man's guard.

Dante lunged opportunistically, hanging back, jabbing at any exposed flanks or overextended limbs, picking up the scraps of Blays and Lira's carnage. Blays fought as if he were literally two men, his twin blades blocking and probing and slashing independent of each other. Whenever he brought them to bear on a single redshirt, the target fell in seconds. Lira's unorthodox style threw every man she faced off guard. When they advanced, she fell back. When they regrouped, she advanced. She flowed away and after them like a malevolent sea. Every time they slipped, every time they hesitated, or their sword swung too far, she pounced upon their weakness, dropping them to the stone floor.

Over the next five minutes, they advanced by inches. Bodies piled along the raised stone defenses. Dante's sword arm grew heavy, sluggish. Blays and Lira showed no signs of slowing down. Dante refreshed himself with a small burst of nether. Blood spattered Blays' face, Lira's empty hand. The redshirts began to give them a wide berth, clustering to engage the Citadel guardsmen instead.

A spear jabbed into the neck of the guardsman next to Blays. The defender fell, gurgling, collapsing into Blays' knee. Blays toppled. A blade followed him down, diving into his gut. He screamed. Before his attacker could withdraw, Lira hacked off the man's arm at the elbow. Blood fountained from the stump. Dante punched out his fist. Shadows slammed into the man's head, bursting it in a hot red shower of blood and stinging shards of bone.

"Get him out of here!" Dante yelled. "To the monks in the Citadel!"

Blood masked Lira's face. Dante moved past Blays, wreathing his hand in visible shadows. It discharged none of his strength, but was enough to drive back the line of attackers for a crucial second. Lira hoisted Blays on her hip and retreated through the ranks of defenders. Blays' hand was clamped to his gut, dark blood oozing between his fingers.

Someone shouted. A sword flashed for Dante's throat. He knocked it back with an awkward swipe and stumbled against a guardsman, who brought down his attacker. Another two minutes of fighting and Dante's arm was too heavy to lift. He withdrew, letting fresh troops cycle in for the fight to reach the staircases.

Wheels squeaked from the square. Below, a covered ram rolled forward, a pitched roof protecting the men pushing it along. The archers on the walls, still harried by those perched on the cathedral roof, concentrated fire. Arrows thwacked into the wooden cover. One of the men at the ram fell away, clutching at an arrow stuck straight through his leg. Two more dropped dead, leaving a trail of corpses behind the rolling ram. By the time it disappeared

THE GREAT RIFT

into the entry to the gates, it was reduced to a crawl. The remaining men wouldn't have the strength to lift it, let alone to batter down the doors.

Laughter echoed from within the gates.

The doors exploded inward in a roaring flash of ether. As splintered wood and warped metal spun into the courtyard, Cassinder dashed away from the ram toward the safety of the redshirts' lines. He'd been hiding somewhere inside the ram. Sneaking in until he was too close to stop. And now the gates were open. It was over.

Dante hurtled a lance of shadows at Cassinder's back. An instant before it would tear out his heart, it sprayed into sparks, deflected by a sorcerer somewhere in the enemy crowds. A thunderous cry rippled across the king's ranks. As one, thousands of men charged the fallen gates.

Dante stared, dazed. How many men massed outside the gates, stopped, however briefly, by the guardsmen plugging the gap? Five thousand? What now? Surrender? Flee? Fight to the last? They could attempt to retreat through the tunnels. Regroup in the Norren Territories with whatever clans were still alive to fight. Conduct a guerrilla resistance until their spirits or their lives at last gave out. But what would happen to the citizens who stayed in Narashtovik? And after all the blood spilled in the last few months, how could they hope to resist the next wave of the king's men?

His mind split, paralyzing him. Fight and die. Leave and lose hope. Two halves. Two worlds. Neither acceptable.

He screamed so loud the redshirts tipped back their sweat-streaked faces. He screamed until his sight turned red. As the scream faded from his ears and the red fell from his eyes, he knew what to do.

He ran down the steps, joggling the soreness in his back. Men snarled and slashed and bled for control of the gates. The redshirts had already pushed their way inside, an expanding bubble of men that would soon burst across the courtyard and flush away any remaining defenders. Along the walls, archers poured fire into the men still beyond the gates. Soldiers in black shirts ran down the steps as fast as they could.

"Get back!" Dante said. "Get to the keep! Get away from the

gates!"

Some paused, confused to see a Council priest ordering them away from the battle. Others went on as if they hadn't noticed, pressing toward the gates in a last effort to repel the invaders. Dante wanted to scream again.

Olivander ran down the Citadel steps, sword in hand, his expression as hard and flat as his shield. Dante threw himself in the man's way.

"Pull back as many troops from the gates as you can!"

"They'd be on us in seconds!" Olivander said.

Dante met the older man's eyes. "That's what I'm counting on."

Olivander's gaze was weary, but there was still steel in it. "What do you have planned?"

"Leave just enough of our men to slow them down. Then get back and stay back."

Olivander's jaw worked, as if he were ready to spit out fresh arguments, but he laughed instead. "Good enough. If we're to die today, let it end with one last act of your madness."

He strode across the courtyard toward the crush of men. Dante turned and walked toward the keep. Olivander hollered orders in a ragged bass. Three-quarters of the way to the keep's steps, Dante knelt and faced the battle.

Olivander gave a final shout. Narashtovik's soldiers scattered from the fight, leaving a handful behind. Dante called out to the nether. He sang to it. He cursed at it. He pleaded with it and commanded it. Rivers of shadows flowed from the dead mounded around the gates. It pooled from the ground and came to him in huge gobs. It condensed from the air, clinging to his skin.

At the gates, knots of redshirts broke from the scrum to chase down the fleeing soldiers. Most raced straight ahead. Toward the keep. Toward Dante. Dante shaped the nether, reaching down into the stone floor, the dirt beneath it, the bedrock beneath the dirt. How old was it? As old as Arawn? Shadows circled him like a plague, so dense he could hardly see the army closing on him. He took the nether in his fist and drew it to the ground.

Ethereal white flashed from the coming crowd. Cassinder ran ahead of the soldiers, face locked in a fish's grin. So focused on the nether, Dante caught the bolt at the last second, knocking it away in a spray of twinkling sparks. The excess energy slammed into his ribs, flattening him into the cobbles.

"You were right to kneel!" Cassinder shouted. "You'll *all* kneel! Until you've forgotten how it felt to stand!"

Silver winked in the air. A knife slapped into Cassinder's chest, staggering him. Lira sprinted past Dante, sword in hand.

"No!" Dante screamed. "Lira, stop!"

The enemy soldiers hurtled forward. Cassinder raised a hand. Lira threw another knife. Another second, and the soldiers would be on him. In horror, Dante brought the nether back to him in an angry stormcloud, a swirling mass that blotted out the sky.

He touched his finger to the ground.

29

Beneath his finger, the stone was dusty. Still warm from a long day spent beneath the ceaseless sun. Beneath his finger, the stone cracked.

A black line raced toward the charging army. With a deafening roar, the soil wrenched apart, cobbles and dust spilling into the expanding crevice. A great rift opened in the earth, growing wider and wider as it tracked away from his finger, thundering ahead; nether surged through his body, far more than he'd ever channeled at once, perhaps more than he'd commanded across the course of his entire life, a searing, crackling, ice-cold force that yanked the bedrock apart at the seams.

The soldiers froze. Cassinder's face contorted in terror. Fear flashed across Lira's face. Then she met his eyes and smiled gently.

The rift swallowed them all.

In an instant, a thousand men tumbled away with a single scream. The crack hurtled outward. Huge slabs of stone creaked and fell into the bottomless depths. As it reached the gates, the devouring hole swallowed the king's men and Narashtovik's soldiers alike. It gobbled the ground beneath the gates. The wall splintered, crumbling, raining rubble into the gap. The rift swept past into the plaza. Thousands of soldiers in red shirts wailed and disappeared into nothing.

Dante collapsed. Cheers of disbelief surged from the norren and black-clad soldiers who'd fled the gates in time. Dante tried to rise, but his arms and legs lay still. He tried to blink against the dust sifting into his eyes, but his eyelids wouldn't twitch.

Swords rang on swords. Through the haze of dust and pain and nether, he watched, paralyzed, as the soldiers of Narashtovik closed on the few of the king's men who'd escaped plunging into the abyss. Steel clashed. Men in red ran for the gates, but found them obliterated, the way out demolished by a pit with no bottom. Some dropped their swords and threw up their hands. Others ran along the walls in confusion, searching for doors that weren't there. Others yet fought and died.

Crushing hands grasped Dante's shoulders. Mourn's face swam into view. One of his eyes was swollen shut, blood crusting his split eyebrow. He picked Dante up and set him gently on the steps of the Citadel.

"Are you all right?" Mourn said. "Dante?"

Dante's throat wouldn't work. Voiceless, he gazed back at Mourn. Mourn rose, knees cracking.

"I'm going for help. Stay here. And please don't die as you are staying."

The norren swung from sight. Dante knew that time was passing—people were moving in the courtyard, and people only moved over time—but had no sense of how much. After some more time, Olivander appeared with Somburr. They spoke his name. They tried to reach him with the nether, to soothe his wounds, but there were no wounds to soothe, and when the nether touched him it slid right off, hissing angrily, dispersing back to the cracks within the stones. Mourn stood a short ways off, watching. Blays staggered outside, holding a bloody bandage at his side. He grinned in naked disbelief at the hole punched through the world. When he saw Dante, he swallowed his grin as quickly as the earth had gulped down the soldiers.

"Dante?" he said. "You all right in there? Just stunned at your own magnificence, are you?" He slapped Dante's cheek lightly. "Hey. You all right? Where's Lira?"

Mourn moved in and pulled Blays aside. They spoke in low tones on the fringe of Dante's dotty vision. Mourn pointed to the rift. Blays' chin jerked. He shook his head like a wolf with a rabbit, like a dog that's been stung. Mourn reached for his shoulder.

"No!" Blays yanked himself away. He ran to Dante, leaning close to his face. "Where did she go? Dante, what did you do to her?"

Dante struggled to move. To blink. to speak.

"Did you take her?" Blays' voice went soft. "No one matters to you, do they? Not when they get in the way of something you want. Is that what happened? You saw your chance, so you took it, no matter the cost?" He turned to the rift. Lying on his back, Dante couldn't see it. Blays' eyes went bright. He swung back to Dante, face contorted. "What did you do to her? Did you kill her? *Answer me!*"

But he couldn't. He could barely think. Blays cocked his fist and swung. Dante's head snapped back, giving him an upside-down view of the keep's steep walls. He didn't feel a thing. His head lolled forward. Blays struck his face again.

"Did you kill her? Did you drop her down that hole? Did you even hesitate before you did it?" Tears streaked Blays' face. Sunset flashed from the blade in his hand. It angled toward Dante's neck, a silvery road to oblivion. Mourn loomed behind Blays' shoulder, eyes bulging above the thicket of his beard. The sword wavered.

Dante's throat clicked. "She—"

The world went black.

He saw stars.

Silver on black. Points against a field. A forever of stars. The most beautiful sight in the world. Some danced, some twitched, some swam in slow and mysterious circles. But there was a pattern to all of it, a cycle, and if you watched those swirls close enough and long enough, maybe you could understand...

Someone coughed.

He couldn't open his eyes. At first he thought he was still paralyzed, but his lids were gummed shut, crusty and dry. He picked at them with his right hand. His fingers were chilly. He pried the seal from his right eye. Light sliced his vision.

"You're awake!" a familiar voice said from beside his bed.

Dante's throat was too dry to reply. He swabbed awkwardly at his left eye. Sunlight glared from everything, dazzling him. He slitted his eyes. A plump, robed man stood over him.

"Nak," Dante said. "Do you have any water?"

"Let me check my pockets." The monk grinned, as much at seeing Dante conscious as at his own joke. He turned to a dresser where a pitcher of water stood ready. The water was as lukewarm as the room, but Dante drank it down without stopping. He belched, eyes trying and failing to water.

"Where am I?"

"The monastery. We've been tending to you since you fell unconscious."

"Fell unconscious?" Dante sat up dizzily. His bladder ached. He gestured toward his waist. "I need—"

Nak nodded, went for a pot, and turned his back. Dante shrieked. Nak rushed back to the bed. "What is it?"

"My hand!" Dante held up his right hand. The first two fingers, the tip of his thumb, and half his palm were as black as the space between the stars. "Was I burnt?"

"Sort of."

"What do you mean, sort of'? How can I be *sort* of burnt?"

"It's nethereal in nature. We think. We don't think it's harmful, but it may be permanent."

"Permanent?" Dante waved his hand around. "It looks like I've been eating coal with my bare hands!"

"With the amount of nether you channeled, you're lucky your whole body doesn't look that way." Nak pursed his lips. "You're lucky you *have* a body."

Dante turned his hand front to back and back to front. The stained skin was matte and abrupt, with no transition between the blackness and the normal skin around it. It felt slightly cool, like a rock left in the shade, but it otherwise felt normal to the touch. Still, he reached under the covers with his left hand. Nak turned his back. By the time Dante finished with the chamber pot, his memory had clarified. The battle. The rift. Something more.

"What happened, Nak?"

"Well, that was it!" The balding monk grinned. "A few hundred redshirts escaped the city alive and uncaptured. They headed west at humorously high speed. We're already hearing that the norren have driven the occupiers from the eastern half of the Territories."

"They have?" Dante sat up. He managed to stay up. "How long has it been?"

"A week? Make it six days. The first day just felt like two."

"I meant since I fell asleep."

Nak gave him a sidelong look. "It's been six days."

"That's not possible."

"I suppose it is possible that it has only been one day, and the sun has ambitiously decided to cross the sky six times instead of once. But I've been sitting here myself every day."

Dante gazed blankly. Six days. Then again, what did it matter? The Citadel stood intact. Narashtovik stood free until the king's next move. What else could—?

He whipped to face Nak. "Where's Blays?"

Nak frowned down at his hands, twisting them in his lap. "We don't know."

"Is he off getting drunk somewhere? Is he all right?"

"He left in the night," Nak said softly. "The same day you fell asleep. We haven't seen him since."

"What? Where did he go?" Dante struggled to swing his feet off the bed. His limbs moved as clumsily as if he were trying to drag a door through water, broad side first.

"He didn't say a word." Nak scowled, pushing Dante back into the covers. "Stop that, you fool. You haven't eaten in days."

"I have to find him."

"You *have* to do as I say. Eat something. Then we'll see about Blays."

Dante didn't have the strength to protest. He'd need Nak's help just to get out of bed. The monk padded off for several minutes, returning with a plate of oven-blackened toast and cold, boiled chicken. Dante gulped it down, spilling crumbs over the sheets.

"Okay," he said. "Help me up."

"I don't think that's a good idea," Nak said. "Why don't you eat and drink a bit more and then we'll see."

"You just said that. Now help me out of this bed before I drag myself over there and strangle you."

"Food first. Your nonsense can come later."

Nak took the plate and left again. Dante scowled at his useless legs. Well, he knew how to bring them back to order. He beckoned to the nether. It hesitated, flicking along the base of the walls, then rushed to his hands. He sent it coursing through his veins.

He seized. The nether's touch was icy, stinging, hungry. Dante shrieked. Nak rushed through the doorway, robes flapping, eyes wide. The world collapsed to a silver pinhole, then went dark.

When he awoke, the sun was brighter. Nak was gone. Dante propped himself on an elbow and reached for a glass of water waiting on the bedside table. It tasted dusty. The plate of bread and salami beside it tasted good enough. Nak crept through the door, saw he was awake, and gave him a frowning smile.

"Well, look who isn't dead after all."

"The nether stung me," Dante said, picking a bit of anise-flavored salami from between his teeth. "Like a hive of liquid bees."

Nak nodded. "Shadow sickness."

"What, you have a word for it?"

"We've been studying these things for centuries, you know. The condition's not unheard-of. It should fade within another few days." Nak glowered down at him as sternly as the pudgy monk could manage. "In the meantime, would you leave the gods damned nether alone already?"

"Where was Blays treated for his wound? During the battle?"

"Why in the world would you want to know that?"

"Because if I can find his blood, I can find him."

Nak slitted his eyes. "By using the nether. Which I have specifically forbidden you from touching."

Dante slung one leg out of bed and set to work on the other. "Then you can do it for me. And if you won't, I will. Who knows what'll happen then? I could explode. You'll be scrubbing Dante-pancreas from the walls for weeks. Is that what you want, Nak?"

The monk slapped his hands to his cheeks. "On the condition that you leave the shadows where they are." He pointed to the shadow of a candelabra painted on the floor by the thick sunlight. "You see that? Don't touch it."

"Agreed."

Nak went back out the door, giving him a worried look. Dante eased from bed. Standing made him dizzy. He waited for the rush of spots to fade. Still, he was stronger than the first time he'd woken up, able to walk with minimal support from the chairs and tables around the room.

Nak came back ten minutes later. "The barber recalls Blays being treated in the Winter Hall. I don't know how much good that will do us. Practically half the city was treated there."

He moved to lend Dante his shoulder. Together, they shuffled out of the monastery. Heat shimmered from the sun-stoked paving stones. Nak led him into the keep and the Winter Hall, a sprawling, high-ceilinged feast-hall whose southern-facing windows caught whatever sunlight was to be had during the winter's shortest days. The tables and chairs had already been replaced. The rugs, too. Beneath them, the floor was black granite, polished smooth. Any stains had been scrubbed away.

Dante's heart foundered. His stomach soured. "What about the rags?"

"What rags?" Nak said.

"The ones they used to clean this room."

"Seeing as they were full of blood, they got thrown away."

"Where?"

"In the graves with all the bodies, I think."

Dante turned for the door. "Take me to them."

"Oh no." Nak grabbed Dante's arm. "You aren't seriously considering rooting around in mass graves for a bloody old rag."

"I'm not considering that at all."

"Thank heavens."

"I've already decided to do it."

"I won't allow it," Nak said. "The men in those graves have been dead for a week. You'll catch the bad air for certain."

Dante pulled himself loose from Nak's fleshy fingers. "I have to find him, Nak! I have to tell him what happened! If Lira hadn't stopped Cassinder, we'd all be dead."

"You aren't going to find him by pawing around at a bunch of dead bodies."

"Then I'll ask a servant!"

"Fine." Nak circled in front of him before he reached the door. "Do you want to see the bodies? Do you want to see what there is to find amongst the rot and ruin? Then I'll take you to the dead."

"Good." Dante let himself be led to the foyer, where Nak ordered for a carriage. As it clopped up outside, Dante frowned at the hole in the ground where the gates had been. A passage had been cleared out of the rubbled stone to one side of the rift. The carriage was shaded but stifling. It bounced across the courtyard, slowing to a crawl as it eased through the gap between the walls and the chasm. Past the screened windows, the broken ground fell away into darkness.

The streets smelled of death. Not thickly, not of fresh decay, but with a faint insistence Dante soon grew used to. Pedestrians and riders strolled along the streets. Still fewer than before the army had made its march on Narashtovik, but moreso than in the ghostly days leading up to the battle. Hammers squeaked on boards, prying them free from sealed-up windows and doors. Brown blood and twinkling glass lay here and there, but there was shocking little notice that ten thousand hostile soldiers had entered the city just over a week before.

The carriage rolled under the intact Ingate and through the shattered Pridegate into the low shacks and decades-old ruins of crumbling houses. He could do it. It would be messy, but any rag bearing the blood of a dead person would produce no pressure in Dante's mind at all. Those who were still within the city would pulse strongly. All he had to do was find those that produced a faint pressure and follow them out of town.

He smelled the grave before he saw it. Thick, rancid, strong enough to purge the salami from his stomach. The carriage swung off the road over sun-hardened soil and yellow grass. Ahead, the ground was bare and deep brown, recently overturned. The carriage rocked to a stop. The horses snorted in dismay as Nak hopped down into the noonday sun and offered Dante a hand.

Past the filled graves, a giant, shallow gash lay open to the sun. Beside it, men toiled with leather gloves and thick smocks, slinging the dead into the last stretch of the mass grave. The bodies were impossibly fat, the skin greasy, black and green. Flies whirled in greedy torrents. The smell was monstrous. Evil. The workmen wore bandanas over their mouths, the cloth stuffed with crushed mint. Dante swallowed down bile and lowered himself over the edge of the grave.

Moist soil spilled over his ankles. Bodies lay on top of bodies, limbs akimbo, skin sloughing. Yellowish fluid seeped into the dirt and muddied the bottom of the pit. A brown cloth lay under a man whose face was so swollen his skin had split around his eyes. Dante touched the rag with the lightest tickle of nether. He felt no sting. No pressure, either. He took a long, high step over the bloated man. His foot squished down into something that gave beneath him. He toppled, thudding down onto the swollen body. His splayed hand plunged straight through the man's stomach into hot, wet goo. Tears flowed down Dante's face.

"Good gods!" Nak called from the lip of the grave. "Are you all right?"

Dante nodded numbly at the field of bodies. It was hopeless. Blays was gone.

He asked every soldier, cook, porter, priest, and maid at the Citadel, but none had seen Blays leave. Blays' room had been emptied, swept, and scrubbed. Not by the servants. By Blays. To ensure he'd left nothing behind for Dante to follow.

Dante sat in his room amidst the heat. His thoughts were as useless as the dogs lying in the shade beneath the trees in the city below. When the world was so large, how could you find someone who meant to get lost?

Whenever he closed his eyes, he saw Lira's smile as she fell into the void. He thought he'd have trouble sleeping, but instead that's how he spent most of his time, napping fitfully throughout the summer heat, waking to half-remembered dreams of guts hanging from bellies and arms that ended at red elbows. Everything took on a bitter taste. From the balcony, he thought he could smell the stink of fish dying on the beach. The days were so hot they left him gasping. His stomach churned at all times; he was hungry but had no appetite, and when he forced himself to eat more than a few bites of fresh bread, he felt as swollen as the men in the graves. He read, but couldn't remember the pages he'd just turned.

In the evenings, parties flowed into the streets. Bonfires roared in the squares. Their laughter was the cackling of demons. Their fires were the mouths of damnation. Dante drank himself to sleep.

Olivander summoned him three days after he'd woken up for good. The man's quarters were trim and quaint. The corners of his bed were tucked. Wooden carvings of stags and bears battled on the mantel.

"Glad to see you up and running." Olivander smiled, well-rested, no longer battle-gaunt. "We could use your help. Again."

"We?" Dante said. "Where's Kav?"

Olivander shook his head. "I'm what passes for leadership for the moment."

"Oh dear," Dante said, finding a brief spark of energy. "Sounds like I ought to defect."

The man chuckled before turning sober. "That's the thing. The threat isn't over. The king has more men yet. What if they arrive while we have no front gate?"

"I suppose we'll be killed."

"And we can't build a new gate so long as that bottomless crevasse is in the way."

"So you want me to reverse it."

"Can you?"

"Not as quickly," Dante said. "But I'll see what I can do."

The project did not enthuse him. Stand under the sun and will a hole to become a not-hole. He went to the courtyard and knelt beside the rift. A cool breeze wafted from its depths, stirring the stench of decay. At least it wasn't bottomless, then. He hadn't touched the nether in days, and he reached for it with the hesitancy of a man testing his leg after it's been freed from a splint. The shadows came readily, winging up from the mass of bodies lying at the bottom of the hole. Dante let the darkness soak into the walls of rock and dirt. Starting at the narrow crack where the touch of his finger had opened the world, he began to bring it back together.

Two hundred feet below him, rock flowed like mud, oozing into a seamless whole. Some parts responded to his every touch, as if waiting to be reunited; other sections were bullish, stubborn, forcing him to coax them from their slumber with deft jabs and caresses of nether. He soon forgot about Lira, about Blays, about the dying faces he saw in his sleep. The work absorbed him. Focused on his breathing, the sweat trickling down his hair, and the intricacies of creation, he forgot, for a while, to hurt.

Too soon, he lost his grip on the shadows. They wavered, refusing to weave through the cool stone. A warning tingle spread through his limbs. He sat back, waiting for it to fade, then returned to his room and went to bed.

At dawn, he stepped outside and found the air was nearly

chilly. He thought about going back for a coat, but knelt beside the hole, letting his mind get lost in the labyrinth of nether. He buried the dead beneath a flood of limestone. After half an hour with the earth, his power was spent. He went to the monastery's archives and requested the most frivolous novels the monks could find, picaroon epics of pirates and bandits and rebels. He found himself chuckling over their dashing gambits and ludicrous escapes. He often woke with his face pressed against the pages, a dot of drool between the elegant penmanship of long-dead scribes.

On his third day with the rift, a wind sucked in a fog from the sea. Streamers of mist furled around the spire of the Cathedral of Ivars. The air cooled. When Dante was done for the day, he took a blanket to the balcony and read beneath the overcast skies.

On the sixth day, the day he was certain he would fill the last of the shallowing hole, he crouched in the space between the wall and the rift, lifting stone up from the depths. Hooves clattered across the square. As they neared, he glanced up. A rider galloped straight for him. The man's face was smudged with sweat and dirt. His horse was lathered and gasping. He gave no sign of slowing down. Dante leapt to his feet and ran from the narrow passage into the courtyard.

"Hey, you idiot!" he cursed as the man thundered past close enough to stir the air. His horse smelled of fresh, meaty sweat. "What's your problem?"

The man didn't glance back. Dante swore some, anger blossoming from the field of his sorrow. He had barely brought himself to return to the crack when he heard the rider's news.

The lakelands of Gallador had rebelled. King Moddegan had sent Narashtovik a treaty. He offered the end of the war—and the end of norren slavery across Gask. As a gleeful servant summoned him to chambers for an impromptu meeting, Dante fumed.

Olivander's grin was as broad as the bay. It threatened to fill the depopulated council chambers—without Cally, Kav, Varla, and Wint, the room felt cavernous and empty.

"It's finished," Olivander said. He slapped parchment onto the table. Its capital letters were as finely illuminated as the monastery's gilded copy of *The Cycle of Arawn*. "As you sign this treaty, feel free to sigh in relief."

"Fuck that," Dante said.

Olivander stiffened. "What?"

"Moddegan's making us *grants*. Concessions. You only make concessions from a position of power—something he no longer has." Dante's hands shook. His anger surged up his throat and over his head, as searing and potent as if he were sinking into a cauldron of boiling oil. "I want independence. For us and for the norren. That's what we've died for. Cally. Lira. All the rest. If Moddegan wants these lands to remain a part of Gask, he can try and fucking take them."

"Would you really risk another battle?"

"In a beat of my heart."

Olivander rubbed his goatee. His gaze traveled between the rest of the Council. "Does this sound like suicide to anyone else?"

Tarkon shrugged his bony shoulders. "To hell with the king. If we want to govern ourselves, we'll never own a better chance."

"Gallador won't be simple to reensnare," Somburr said, speaking around his thumbnail as he chewed it. "I'm hearing they intend to fight. There are only a handful of passes through the mountains. Fall's coming soon. Will Moddegan want to fight through the winter?"

Hart combed his thick norren fingers through his white beard. "I've got two minds on this one. Emancipation's more than I dreamed. If we snub that, we could lose everything. But we could also gain the world."

"If we demand independence, our work's far from done," Olivander said. "We'll have to maintain our army. Replenish our arms and food. Train monks to become priests and young talents to become monks."

"I'll go to the clans," Dante said. "Let them know that, if and when the time comes, Narashtovik will stand with them again."

"Is this our will?" As the Council nodded, Olivander smiled in disbelief. "Very well. Let the madness live on."

He sent the king a message of their own. It required no response. Declarations need no signatures from the kings they leave behind.

Dante returned to the crack in the courtyard. The bottom was just twenty feet deep now, sandy white limestone peppered with brown and black and green. His anger remained, but it had diminished to a safe simmer. He used it as fuel. The ground rumbled, shimmering like a wind-tousled lake. Limestone lifted like a long, deep breath. When it rose to a few feet below the surrounding surface, Dante filled it in with a wave of dirt, tamping it down with a flourish of dust.

Cheers rang throughout the misty courtyard. He turned. All the Citadel had turned out to watch him right what he had broken. He smiled.

The feeling didn't last. Without work to steal his focus, Lira's face crept back into his waking dreams. Blays', too. The anguish that had shattered his face as he stood over a paralyzed Dante and first understood she was forever gone.

To fill the void, he found Cally's notes and set to work constructing new loons. If they were to coordinate with the clans against whatever else rose against them, they'd need a way to speak to each other again. He finished his first pair by the end of the night. He built them to be pendants, setting a hooked fang of the badger-like kapper into a piece of unshaped black iron. When the first pair was done, he rose with a grin, but it was after midnight, and he had no one to test them with.

He went to a tavern instead. The first drink tasted like relief. The third, numbness. The eighth, peace. He was sicker than ever when he woke. On the verge of vomiting. His skin as hot as sun-baked cobbles. As he worked on another pair of loons, he drank a beer to soothe his nerves. He caught Somburr in the hallway and got him to help try out the first set. They worked like a dream.

He stopped work around six o'clock. The sun was still many degrees from the horizon, but it was late enough to return to the public houses. He went in plain clothes. If anyone recognized him, they said nothing.

That became his routine. While laborers dug the foundations for a new set of gates, Dante sat in the windows of pubs, watching the streets. He never saw Blays. Once, he got in a fight; the other man started it, something about the looks Dante was giving his woman. Dante knocked him to the ground with a blunt wallop of nether, locked the man in place with shadowy chains, and laughed as he poured his beer over the man's paralyzed head.

A servant found him in the pub the next day. Olivander wished to see him at once.

Dante didn't stand. "What for?"

"He didn't say, my lord."

"I'm not going to apologize. When I'm here, I don't represent the Council. Anyway, he started it."

"All he told me is he wants to see you."

"I don't know. It's pretty comfy here."

The man clasped his hands together. "My lord, if I go back without you..."

Dante rolled his eyes. "Fine. Once I'm done with my drink, we'll go see what Captain Noble wants from me now."

He took his time. The messenger sat awkwardly, watching the other patrons. After the last sip of spiced rum, Dante slammed down his mug, stood, and wiped his mouth with his sleeve.

"Well?"

The man nodded and opened the door for him. Sunset dwindled behind the blankets of fog. The air was a neutral non-temperature. Breathing felt good. Dante strolled along behind the messenger, letting his anger ferment to match the contents of his stomach. What did Olivander care if he'd knocked around some fool? Who gave a shit? Weeks ago, Dante had killed five thousand men in a single stroke. Nobody had complained about *that*. They'd thrown a feast in his honor while he slept, and a second when he woke. The messenger glanced over his shoulder as Dante laughed.

The first layer of stone had been set into the foundation of the gates. Twenty soldiers stood to block the open space. They let Dante through without a word. In the Council's chambers, Olivander was surprised to see not just Olivander, but the other six surviving priests as well: sprightly old Tarkon, stolid Hart, silent Joseff, foul-tongued Merria, bitter Ulev, owlish Somburr. Dante nodded their way and took his seat.

"For the last few weeks, I've acted as steward to the city," Olivander said in his baritone. "But I wasn't appointed. I accepted the mantle through default. But now it's time to do things right."

"Well, why not you?" Dante said. "You've been on the Council for years. You know how to order an army around. Sounds good to me."

"Because we've already made our decision."

Dante pushed his knees against the table, rocking his chair back. "Glad to hear it. Congratulations."

Olivander chuckled richly. "You're congratulating yourself."

Dante's knee slipped. He nearly fell from his chair. "What?"

"Will you accept the position of high priest of this council?"

"Are you all insane? I'm only 22! Do you know how drunk I am right now?"

"Sounds to me like you were just celebrating early," Tarkon said.

"Why not *you*?" Dante said to him. "You've been here for an eternity."

"That's exactly why it shouldn't be me," Tarkon cackled. "Put me in charge, and I might wander into the cathedral after forgetting to put on pants. How about you, Joseff? Can you even chew your own food?"

Joseff laughed hoarsely. "No. That's why I eat with a fork and a hammer."

Dante shook his head. "You'd be perfect for this, Olivander. You're so...reasonable."

"That's why I make a very fine advisor," Olivander said. "And I *advise* you to take the position."

"No. I can't. I don't know anything about running this city. This order."

Olivander snorted. "Like this isn't what you've dreamed of since the moment you first set foot in this room. Your ambition is hardly a secret, Dante. You wear it like some men wear a new cape."

"Maybe that's exactly why this is a bad idea."

"Then I have a compromise for you. If there are no objections, I'll continue as steward." Olivander raised his eyebrows at the other councilmen and was met with nods and shrugs. "In the meantime, you're my shadow. My sponge. Absorbing everything that goes into the administration of Narashtovik and the Citadel. When you're ready, the mantle will pass on to you."

Dante held up his palms. "*Why?*"

"You have ideas no one else does. You dream big, and just

when it looks like that dream is about to crash, you do something else no one else can do—and save it. Callimandicus chose well when he took you under his wing. You are his heir."

Dante blinked at sudden tears. "I'm nothing next to Cally."

"Yeah, well, you should have seen that fool at your age," Tarkon said. "Take the position. There's more than one of us on this council for a reason. You do anything too dumb, you can be sure we'll let you know."

"You'll all help me?" Dante said. The Council of Narashtovik nodded. He blinked again. "I accept."

It was a nice ceremony. The Cathedral of Ivars was packed with familiar faces and strangers who might one day become friends. There were speeches. Rituals. Rich dishes of duck and fish and fruits. Beer and wine and spirits. At the end, after they pinned him with Cally's old brooch—the tree of Barden, carved from bone supposedly harvested from the White Tree itself—they literally carried him across the street back to the Citadel.

He returned to his room fat, drunk, and happy. Yet he still felt the void. The abyss. The hole that couldn't be filled.

Working with Olivander helped. There was so much to do. On Dante's insistence, Nak was promoted to the Council, an honor he attempted twice to decline before Dante told him it wasn't a choice. They opened nominations of other monks. Dante drafted messages to Brant in Tantonnen to bargain for more grain to bolster Narashtovik's supplies in the event of a second siege. Others went to the scattered clans. Meanwhile, they awaited word from Gallador and their former king. Dante hired three trackers, gave them a two-word message, and sent them into the wilds in search of Blays. Day by day, the stonework around the missing gates climbed to its former heights.

The sun came and went, but the worst of the summer had passed. As fall neared, King Moddegan gave his reply. In exchange for their neutrality in the ongoing conflict in Gallador, as well as ongoing considerations for rights of passage and the ongoing continuation of all existent agreements in trade, Narashtovik and the Norren Territories would be freed.

As the city whooped and drank and cheered and kissed, Dante

drafted a letter to Gabe, the norren monk of Mennok who had, in a way, caused this all.

Somehow, Dante found time to continue forging new loons. When he had eighteen pairs, he arranged for a trip into the newly independent Territories. It was a small delegation. He insisted Nak come with him. Olivander made him take another monk, a handful of servants, and a dozen of the guard's finest. Under the warmth of morning, they left the Citadel and headed south.

In the norren lands, whole towns had been burnt to the ground, abandoned to the sun and the wind. Crows circled the hilltops, pecking at fresh bones. Whole fields lay scorched and black. At other towns, hammers and saws rapped and soughed. Clans moved over the plains. Dante spoke to chieftains, swapping stories, news, and congratulations. After three weeks of travel, he tracked down Mourn and the Nine Pines in the hills east of Tantonnen.

"You?" Mourn laughed. "In charge of Narashtovik?"

Dante laughed back. "I told them they were making a mistake."

"Are they? Then perhaps it is a good one."

"And how about you? How are you finding the perks of command?"

"To be more demanding than perky." Mourn frowned and waved a hand at the men and women sitting in the shade of low, gnarled trees. "Do you have any idea what it's like trying to get thirty warriors to walk in the same direction? It's worse than when Orlen had me shepherding you and Blays."

Dante's smile froze. He struggled for more to say. "It's so funny. All this time, we fought a war against a man we've never met."

"Incorrect."

"When have *you* seen him?"

Mourn shook his head and smiled. "We *won* a war against a man we've never met."

He stayed with Mourn two more days, then moved on through the grassy plains. Hawks soared on the warm air. At last, among the patchy pines below Dollendun, he found the last clan he'd come to see.

"High priest of Narashtovik?" Hopp grinned. "You do understand that among the Clan of the Broken Herons, you're still nothing more than a lowly cub?"

"The lowliest," Dante said. "Have any pants that need scrubbing?"

"Yes, but I'll have to save a few for Blays to do. He must remember his place as well. Where is he?"

"On a trip of his own."

"Is it an interesting one?"

"I can't say."

"Ah." Hopp narrowed his eyes. "Is everything good?"

"Fine," Dante said. "How are you? How are my clan-brothers and sisters?"

Hopp waited another moment before explaining they'd lost many warriors, but in the weeks since the king had renounced his claim to their lands, the men and women of the Herons had set about replacing those losses with impressive vigor. Dante nodded when he should nod, laughed when he should laugh.

But Hopp watched him too closely. "I ask again: is everything good?"

"It is," Dante said. "I'm just tired. This is the first time I've been able to slow down in months."

A warm breeze carried the smell of pollen and pines. The sun was sinking, its gauzy rays piercing the shield of needles. Crickets chirped and whirred.

"Well, it's too early for sleep," Hopp declared. "How about we pass the time with a story?"

"All right."

"Good. This is the story of Davran. Do you know the story of Davran? Good. Davran was a norren who lived long ago. Hundreds of years. He lived in a small town on one of the small rivulets that led into the great river. When he was young, he was kindly. Adults adored him. Many young women did, too. But the only woman he could see was a girl named Yoren.

"Yoren was beautiful. Have you seen the glaciers in the mountains? The water they feed to the lakes? Yoren's eyes were as green and vivid as the water of the glaciers. She could fight, too, with sword and bow. Her nulla was in the weaving of rope and the tying of knots. Unusual, but so was she. Do you know how much you can do with a good knot? Even a bad one can hold something fast for the present, or confuse the most cunning of men. And Yoren tied Davran into knots, too.

"With his tongue so knotted, he couldn't speak to her. Every time he saw her, and couldn't speak, that pulled the knot in his heart that much tighter. Davran's nulla was wooden carvings. Small ones. Itty bitty models of people and animals and places. To say to Yoren what his knotted tongue couldn't, Davran set to carving. He carved tiny pines and tiny deer. He gouged a streambed out of a plank, and when he smeared the stream's tiny banks with bear fat, it could even carry water. From bits of wood as small as a pea, he carved birds, and perched them in the pines. He carved himself, happy and hale and adoring. And lastly he carved her. On the final piece, he spent weeks of patient labor, shaving away the splinters with a razor until he captured each curve of her cheek and muscle of her arms. The carving was beautiful. Stunning. So real that when Davran looked at it he fell in love with it just as he had with Yoren.

"All this time, Davran had lived in retreat in a shack in the woods. When his little world was finished, he returned to the larger world. And discovered Yoren had married.

"He went back to the shack. He smashed the world he'd spent months creating. He lit a fire and smiled as the statue of Yoren burned."

Hopp paused to smile and drink from a wineskin, which Dante gratefully accepted. It tasted like pears and was strong enough to sting his eyes.

"Once his little Yoren had burnt down to cinders, Davran raged and wept and pounded the trees with his fists. He carried his anger for years. Longer than he'd even known Yoren. In time, he cooled, just like all fires do. He began to create again. Carving little trees. Little birds. Little people. He carved and carved and carved. Locked away in his shack, he built whole worlds to keep him company. Then again, he had all the time in the world, because in the depths of his anguish, he'd vowed never to see another person again, believing they were good for nothing but pain. And he stuck to that vow. And he carved and carved and carved. He built new shacks to host his world. If you'd seen it, you would have clapped and cried. Yes, even you. They were that wonderful. If you looked at them from the corner of your eye, you'd swear the little wooden birds were chirping, the young girls were laughing.

"As we all do, one day Davran died."

Hopp stopped. Dante looked up. "Then what?"

"Then nothing. Because he didn't know anyone. He died. And because there was no one to see them, his little worlds died with him."

Dante frowned. "Then how do *you* know about it?"

"Because Josun Joh saw. How do you think?"

"What I think is that this is one of those stories with a moral. Are you trying to teach me something?"

"If I were, do you think I'm stupid enough to think you'd listen?"

"I don't know. We can all be pretty dumb sometimes."

They were silent for a time. Shadows dappled their arms as they drank from the wineskin. Hopp pointed to the dragonflies wheeling above the cattails at the edge of the pond the clan had camped beside.

"See the dragonflies? The way the light glistens on their wings? Aren't they beautiful?"

Dante looked. They weren't. They were as scaly as dead lizards. Their eyes bulged. Their mouths clutched at lesser flies, shredding, grinding, casting away their prey's wings and sticklike legs. They were hideous. Monsters of nightmares.

"Blays is gone," he blurted.

Hopp's face fell. "Dead?"

Dante shook his head. His eyes blurred. "I killed Lira. I didn't want to, but I had to. They would have married some day. I killed my brother's wife, and now my brother is gone."

Dragonflies gleamed and soared. Fish broke the surface of the pond and disappeared without a trace. The sun sank lower every minute, flagging, drawn helplessly to the parted jaws of two hazy mountain peaks. Its failing light did nothing to drive away the ghosts. He knew they would always be with him.

ABOUT THE AUTHOR

Along with *The Cycle of Arawn*, Ed is the author of the post-apocalyptic *Breakers* series. Born in the deserts of Eastern Washington, he's since lived in New York, Idaho, and most recently Los Angeles, all of which have been thoroughly destroyed in one of his books.

He lives with his fiancée and spends most of his time writing on the couch and overseeing the uneasy truce between two dogs and two cats.

He blogs at http://www.edwardwrobertson.com

Printed in Great Britain
by Amazon